By Susan Howatch

CASHELMARA
PENMARRIC

CASHE

LMARA

by Susan Howatch

SIMON AND SCHUSTER   NEW YORK

Published by Simon and Schuster
Rockefeller Center, 630 Fifth Avenue
New York, New York 10020

SBN 671-21736-4
Library of Congress Catalog Card Number: 73-22333
Designed by Jack Jaget
Manufactured in the United States of America
Printed by The Murray Printing Company, Forge Village, Mass.
Bound by The Book Press, Brattleboro, Vt.

2   3   4   5   6   7   8   9   10

Contents

Part One

EDWARD
Duty   *1859–1860*

Tall beyond the common lot of men and powerfully built. . . . Even illness seemed to pass him by and his last years found him as vigorous and upright as a palm tree with eyes and brain undimmed and the teeth still firm in his jaws . . .

Edward I
—L. F. SALZMAN

Chapter One

There were two subjects I never discussed: my dead wife and Cashel-mara. So when I first met a woman with whom I could discuss both subjects with ease, it was hardly surprising that I should once again flirt with the idea of marriage.

I had been a widower for eight years by the time I visited America in the spring of 1859. My friends had long since convinced themselves that I was wedded to my wife's memory, but none of my friends ever seemed to consider that even the most cherished memory does have certain shortcomings. One cannot conduct a stimulating conversation with a memory; one cannot take it to the theater or to the country or to bed. The void in the bedchamber is the least of one's problems, since a man in my position can always find a mistress; but the void elsewhere is less easy to fill, and I had begun to despair of ever finding a woman who would do more than spend my money, flaunt my title and bore me to death.

Naturally I had no wish to fall in love. At my time of life a man makes himself a laughingstock if he succumbs to some ludicrous infatuation, and, besides, I had too much pride and good sense to behave like a young swell half my age. I merely wanted a certain kind of companionship, preferably provided by a mature, good-looking, sympathetic woman intelligent enough to meet the demands of my public life and agreeable enough to respond to the requirements of my private inclinations, but unfortunately, as I soon discovered, such admirable women always seemed to be married to someone else.

"It surprises me that you show no interest in younger women," said my brother David to me once. On the third anniversary of my wife's death I had rashly confided in him that I might consider remarriage if I could only find a woman who suited me. "If you could meet a girl like—"

"My God," I said, exasperated, "am I to hear yet another paean in praise of Blanche Marriott?"

Blanche Marriott was at that time David's favorite topic of conversation. He had met her that summer when diplomatic business had taken him to the United States, and in between his negotiations with the Americans on the touchy subject of the British searching of slave ships he had somehow contrived to escape from Washington, visit New York and call on my wife's cousins, the Marriotts. I too had visited New York once and called upon the Marriotts, but that had been years ago when Francis, the present head of the household, had been a boy of fourteen and his two sisters, Blanche and Marguerite, were still unborn. However, on the strength of my brief past acquaintance with Francis I had given David a letter of introduction to him, and when David had eventually returned to England I had been obliged to listen to his lyrical descriptions of the fifteen-year-old Blanche.

"Fifteen!" I exclaimed, scandalized. "David, your tastes are becoming positively pagan!"

"I think of her purely as a daughter," he answered happily. Men who make remarks like that are always men who have never had daughters. "My admiration for her is wholly innocent."

"I hope your wife believes you."

When David was harboring one of his romantic notions he became incredibly naïve, and I was not in the least surprised when he told me he wanted to invite Blanche to England so that his wife could present her at court.

I never heard his wife's comment on this ingenuous scheme, but presently when David confessed to me with a sigh that he had abandoned his aspirations I wasted no time feeling sorry for him. Half the fun David derived from his romantic notions came when he was forced to abandon them; he liked to yearn moodily for a week or two like some pastoral swain in a popular painting. Indeed, as far as I knew no romantic notion of his had ever been consummated, for

12

consummation would have been a great anticlimax, and his wife, by whom he was secretly intimidated, would have been much too severe to make such reckless behavior worthwhile.

I was very fond of David. When he died three years after his encounter with Blanche I felt the loss profoundly, for he had been my last link with the remote past, the only person who had shared my early memories of Cashelmara. I was still adjusting myself painfully to his death when I received a long and eloquent letter of sympathy from America.

Blanche Marriott had seen David's obituary in the *Times* and had written to say that she mourned with me in my bereavement.

I was surprised and touched. I wrote back, not expecting to hear from her again, but presently she sent a second letter, and soon, almost before I was aware of what was happening, we were conducting a regular correspondence.

"I seem to have taken your uncle David's place in your cousin Blanche's affections," I said, amused, to my daughter Nell. "I can't quite think why, but I admit it's very pleasant. She writes the most charming letters."

"It's good of you to take the trouble to write to her when you're so busy, Papa," said Nell. "Poor girl—orphaned so young! No doubt she has a great need for a mature male relative whom she can regard as a father."

I found this remark extraordinarily irritating, and after that I no longer spoke to Nell about her cousin.

Blanche was eighteen by this time and evidently most accomplished. I learned that she played the piano, took lessons on the harp, spoke French and Italian and read all those women's novels which have given the decade the name of the Feminine Fifties. She did not seem to care about the political issues of the day (to my relief; I heard quite enough about those at Westminster), but she told me about the current events in New York—the enlargement of the Astor Library, the establishment of the Cooper Institute, the Staten Island riots and the great fire that destroyed the Crystal Palace in Bryant Park. Her descriptions of the fire were so graphic that I told her she should try her hand at a novel, and she said yes, she would like to write a novel just like *John Halifax, Gentleman,* which she was rereading for the ninth time.

I was entertained. I saw no harm in such an agreeable correspondence, and, besides, I liked the idea that somewhere in the world there was a charming young woman who not only wrote regularly to me but ended each letter by expressing the hope that one day she might make my acquaintance in person.

Shortly after her twentieth birthday she sent me a sketch of herself drawn by an artistic friend.

"Very fetching," said my daughter Nell when I was unable to resist showing the picture to someone. "But, Papa, why should she send you such a thing?"

"Why shouldn't she?" I began to feel irritated, and this was unusual, for Nell was my favorite daughter. "I see nothing odd about it."

"Supposing when I was her age I had sent a sketch of myself to your friend Lord Duneden!"

"It's not the same thing at all," I said, more annoyed than ever. "You're not related to Duneden, and I'm related by marriage to Blanche."

"I see," said Nell and tactfully changed the subject. I never had the chance to discuss Blanche with her again, for shortly after that conversation in the March of 1859 Nell died in childbirth, and once again I was left with a gaping void in the fabric of my life and an almost unendurable sense of loss.

This time, however, I was so angry that there was barely room for grief. I was angry with everyone—with Nell's stupid oaf of a husband, who had taken her to his Dorset manor for the confinement instead of letting her stay in London where she could have had the best possible care; with the poor dead infant who had deprived his mother of life; with the foolish people who wrote to me afterward to say how grateful I must feel that I still had three surviving daughters to console me in my bereavement. Everyone knew that I was estranged from Annabel and Madeleine and separated by over a thousand miles from Katherine. I received no consolation from them and I expected none.

Finally I felt so full of anger that I lost my temper with my closest friend when he called to offer his sympathy.

"What use is sympathy to me?" I shouted at Duneden in a paroxysm of bitterness and rage. "What do I care about sympathy? Everyone I've loved best is dead. No, don't dare remind me of all I have left. I'm well aware of all that remains to me—old age, loneliness and death. God Almighty, what a prospect!" And I proceeded to rant against death with such a fervor that Duneden insisted in alarm that I immediately drink a double measure of brandy and soda water.

When I stopped shouting long enough to drink the brandy he tried to soothe me by suggesting I go away for a while. "A sojourn on the Continent, perhaps," he murmured, "or a quiet sea voyage—above all a change of scenery."

"There's nowhere I want to go," I said morosely, "and no one I want to see."

Less than a month later I was boarding the Cunard steamship *Persia* at Liverpool on my way to America to meet Blanche Marriott.

II

Naturally I did not decide to go to America solely to meet Blanche. I was not my brother; I did not harbor foolish notions about a young woman of twenty whom I had never met, but since I had decided to travel to take the edge from my bereavement and since I was interested in recent American developments in agriculture, there seemed no logical reason why I should not call upon the Marriotts in New York.

On the twelfth of May, 1859, after a quiet eight days at sea, I steeled myself to withstand the blast of American civilization.

Was there ever a city like New York? Perhaps London might once have resembled it, a medieval London, its shining palaces of unimaginable riches rammed cheek to jowl against squalid hovels of unimaginable poverty, the raucous cries of the beggars drowning the strident bargaining of the merchants and above everything, beyond the clamor and noise and smell, the splendid skyline of church spires glinting in the sun. It had been many years since I had set foot in New York, but as the ship edged closer to Manhattan Island I remembered the reek of the rivers and could almost hear the endless cacophony in the mean smoky alleys north of the Battery. My memories sharpened. I could recall the stevedores shouting to one another in a dozen languages, the pigs rooting in the rubbish on every street corner, the bright lights blazing each night from the brash new buildings on Broadway. New York was a primitive town, its better neighborhoods groping to imitate the architecture of Georgian London; but although in my opinion it was hopelessly plain, I defy any visitor not to be hypnotized by its vitality. Even from my position on deck, still separated from land by the waters of the harbor, I found myself already stupefied by the pulse of the city's frenetic daily life.

Francis Marriott met me at the pier allotted to the Cunard steamship line. I recognized him without difficulty, although age had enhanced his marked good looks and given him the poise he had lacked as a boy. He had unusual eyes, brown but light, white even teeth and a peculiarly brilliant smile.

"Welcome, my lord!" he exclaimed. "What a privilege! What a delight! What a rare pleasure!"

Such effusion did not surprise me, for Americans are notoriously effusive. I have always regarded it as part of their un-English charm. Smiling, I thanked him, shook his hand and said how pleased I was to return to America after such a long interval.

The formality of customs inspection had already been completed on the boat, and fortunately a man in my position need not trouble himself with the regulations which hinder the progress of visitors entering a foreign country. When I had instructed my manservant and secretary to attend to my possessions, I paused only to accept a dinner invitation from the British Consul, who had also come to the docks to welcome me, before I battled my way through the riffraff to the Marriott carriage.

It was abominably hot. Sweat prickled my neck, dust tickled my nose, and above in the hazy sky the alien sun was blazing on those rutted teeming streets.

"What—no pigs?" I said, peering out of the window as the coachman cracked his whip at beggars and horses alike.

"Pigs! Land's sakes, they've all been banished to the piggery uptown! I can tell it's been a long time since you were last here, my lord."

"No doubt I shall see many changes."

"You will indeed. Wait till you see the new buildings! We have a beautiful park now, you know, and the finest Catholic cathedral in the Western Hemisphere is being constructed on Fifth Avenue."

"I suppose you have the Irish immigrants to thank for that."

"Well, we'd best not talk about immigrants," said Francis, still smiling, "since it's a subject that makes a lot of people here ill-humored."

"Still?" I said, remembering how America had finally managed to slam the door in the face of the hordes of Irish who had crossed the Atlantic to escape the famine ten years before.

"My lord, the increase in population, the difficulties it creates . . ." And he embarked with gusto upon a description of New York's problems while I listened politely. At last I managed to deflect him by murmuring with a smile, "In England we're more interested in President Buchanan's attitude toward secession."

16

"Ah, Buchanan knows what he's doing," said Francis confidently. "There'll be no war. No one wants war—so bad for trade and the stock market suffers." Both Francis and his father had made fortunes on Wall Street. "Even talking of war is a crime in my opinion. Gold has already gone into hiding, and as for commercial credit . . . Things have never really recovered since the panic of '57, when Ohio Life failed and the Bowery Bank collapsed." And he talked for a minute longer on financial matters before we drifted into a discussion of my voyage, the welfare of my family and the welcome that was awaiting me at the Marriott mansion north of Washington Square.

I would not have thought it possible that the mansion could appear more gross than I remembered it to be, but before he died Francis' father had ordered that the gutters and gargoyles be painted gold, and the innovation had enabled the house to achieve a new and unbelievable pitch of vulgarity. I am incapable of further description; all I can add is that Greek ideas had married Gothic affectations in the architectural plans, and the marriage had not been a happy one.

The carriage turned off Fifth Avenue, rolled through a pair of gates (also gilded, I regret to say) and swayed to a halt in the wide courtyard. As the footman helped me down I saw that a red carpet had been patted over the porch steps, and in the hall beyond another carpet of an identical shade of red rolled endlessly into the distance beneath a constellation of chandeliers.

"My family are all most eager to make your acquaintance, my lord," said Francis with his peculiarly brilliant smile. "My sister Blanche in particular has been counting the days till your arrival."

"I'm looking forward to meeting both your sisters," I said politely. Since Blanche could hardly have conducted her correspondence with me without his permission, I knew he must assume that her interest in me was reciprocated, but I had no wish for him to assume too much.

His family were waiting in the hall.

I saw Blanche at once. She was smaller than I had imagined, but her figure was exquisite. She had a pale, unblemished skin, high cheekbones and a long lovely neck. Having constantly told myself that I was certain to be disappointed when I met her face to face, I was now so stunned to discover that for once in his life David had not exaggerated a woman's attractions that I almost lost my composure altogether, and it was only with a considerable effort that I

17

maintained a neutral expression on my face while Francis was introducing me to his wife, Amelia.

Amelia was a large woman, her skin prematurely lined by the New York climate, her brown eyes bearing a perpetually worried expression. Perhaps she worried about her husband's infidelities, which, I felt sure as soon as I saw her, were numerous and varied. Her two children resembled Francis in looks. The girl, Sarah, was a pretty child with a spoiled mouth, and the boy, Charles, though shyer, had a bright, alert look about him.

"And now permit me," said Francis at last with a sweep of his arm, "to present my sister Blanche. Blanche, my dear, may I introduce . . ."

He was so enrapt at the opportunity of introducing Blanche to me that he quite forgot his other sister. However, fortunately by that time I had my wits about me again, and after greeting Blanche with the appropriate amount of courteous enthusiasm I turned to the small sandy-haired miss of seventeen who stood sulking in the background.

Francis brushed aside his absent-mindedness with a fine display of winning charm. "Ah yes! I see I'm so excited that I shall soon forget my own name! My lord, this is my sister Marguerite."

I felt sorry for the girl being so plain, particularly when I saw how jealous she was of her delightful older sister, so I took care to greet her with almost as much enthusiasm as I had greeted Blanche. This surprised everyone, I noticed, especially Blanche, and I realized then that I had deceived myself in thinking that no one could attach any importance to our correspondence with each other. However, even though I had been uncharacteristically naïve, I was still far from being a romantic fool. Resolving firmly that my attitude toward both girls was going to be wholly paternal, I decided I must take care never to favor one sister to the exclusion of the other during my short stay in New York.

But there was no denying that Blanche was extraordinarily beautiful.

III

"I shall miss you considerably when you go to Washington tomorrow, Cousin Edward," said Blanche to me three weeks later. "Isn't it possible for you to postpone your visit for a week or two?"

We were in the garden. An elm tree shaded us from the hot afternoon sun as we sat on a wrought-iron bench, and in front of us the lawn had a sickly brownish tinge which reminded me how far I was from home. To our left was a summer house, to our right a waterless fountain, and far away beyond the high wall we could hear the rattle of carriage wheels and the clatter of the horse carts as the traffic plunged up and down Fifth Avenue.

"We have so enjoyed having you in New York," said Blanche, sighing.

"I've enjoyed myself also," I said. That was much too true, unfortunately. Francis had wined and dined me with a zest that bordered on the feverish, and Blanche had always contrived to be at my elbow just when I was thinking how pleasant it would be to have her company. I admit that I was flattered by such attention, but on reflection I was not altogether surprised. Americans are susceptible to English titles, and, besides, my public career has not been undistinguished. If New York society wished to treat me as a celebrity, I was certainly not about to protest that they made too much fuss over too little.

"I shall come back here after my travels to Washington, Wisconsin and Ohio," I promised Blanche.

"I can understand you wishing to visit Washington," said Blanche, pouting very prettily, "because everyone says the state buildings are so fine. And besides, Lord Palmerston wishes you to convey his respects to the President, and of course men are always so interested in politics and diplomacy and that sort of thing. But why, oh, why must you visit Ohio? And Wisconsin! I can't see why anyone would want to go to Wisconsin."

"A farmer there has just invented a machine that might revolutionize reaping," I said, watching the way her rich dark hair lay coiled on the nape of her neck. "And in Ohio they have developed a mutant strain of Indian corn that might be suitable for cultivation in Ireland."

"I didn't think anything ever grew in Ireland except potatoes," said Blanche.

I did not answer. I never discussed Cashelmara.

"Did Cousin Eleanor share your interest in agriculture when she was alive?"

My watch was in my hand although I was unaware of removing it from my pocket. "Dear me," I said, surprised. "Look at the time! Aren't you going to be late for your harp lesson?"

"Oh, that horrid harp!" She smiled at me from beneath her lashes, and I noticed the fullness of her wide, mobile mouth. The air in the garden was stifling. I could not imagine how Blanche appeared so cool, and suddenly I longed to press my hot fingers against her pale skin until all the heat in my body had spent itself.

Without stopping to think I said abruptly, "When can I expect Francis to bring you to England to visit me?"

"Why, when you invite us, of course!" she said, laughing, and the next moment she had slipped her arms around my neck and was kissing me lightly on the cheek.

"Blanche . . ." But she was gone. She was moving swiftly across the lawn, and it was only when she reached the house that she turned, smiled and raised a white-gloved hand in farewell.

I was so shocked, both by her behavior and by the violence of my reaction, that I remained where I was for some minutes after she had disappeared into the house, but at last when I could think coherently again my first thought was to reassure myself. To be shocked by her behavior was foolish. American girls were notoriously forward, and it would be wrong to judge Blanche by the standards I would have set for my own daughters. And my own feelings? But they were known only to myself. I had done nothing foolish and still had every intention of behaving sensibly.

I was beginning to be confused, however, about what constituted sensible behavior. I had never been prejudiced against Americans, but did one marry them? Almost certainly not. The Marriotts were, in their own way, aristocracy, but by English standards they would be considered vulgar as well as foreign. But was I the kind of man who would be cowed by society's conventions, as if I were a newly arrived member of the middle classes with no confidence in my social position?

"I'll do as I damned well please," I said to the listless birds on the sundial, "whatever that may be."

It was curious that I worried more about Blanche's nationality than her age, but girls of twenty often married older men; there was nothing unusual about that. Of course she shared none of my deeper interests, but did I really want a woman whose sole virtue lay in her intellectual companionship? I thought not.

I sat thinking for a long time about what I did want, and then at last I returned to the house. It was quiet inside. Amelia had taken the children out, Marguerite had as usual hidden herself away somewhere—I had hardly seen her since my arrival—and Francis to my knowledge had not yet returned from his chambers in Wall Street. Upstairs I heard the soft, halting chords of Blanche's harp, and I decided to listen to her in the little drawing room next to the music room where she was taking her lesson. The two rooms were joined by a communicating door, which as usual stood ajar. Taking care to make no noise that might disturb her, I sat down, picked up a magazine in which I had no interest and listened with amusement as Blanche complained to her music master what a difficult instrument the harp was to play.

I thought she played remarkably well.

I had just settled down to enjoy a pleasant half hour when there was an interruption. Sharp footsteps rang outside, the door of the music room opened from the corridor and Francis' voice said curtly, "Blanche, I want to talk to you alone."

"For heaven's sake, Francis, I'm in the middle of my lesson!"

"I wouldn't care if you were in the middle of your prayers. Good day to you, Mr. Parker."

"Good day, sir," stammered the little music master. "If you wish me to wait downstairs . . ."

"I don't. You can get out. Now, Blanche," said my host when they were alone in the music room after this gross display of rudeness and ill-breeding, "what the devil do you think you're doing?"

"Francis! How dare you use such dreadful language to me!"

"And how dare you behave like a whore in a concert saloon! I saw you just now in the garden!"

"Well, you told me to be pleasant to him!"

"I didn't tell you to behave like a trollop! My God, what sort of an upbringing will the old fool think I've given you? You've probably ruined us both in his eyes!"

"Well, if I have it's all your fault! I never wanted to have anything to do with Cousin Edward. It was you, huffing and puffing at me ever since that beastly financial crash two years ago—write to Cousin Edward, keep Cousin Edward sweet, flatter Cousin Edward to pieces—"

"If you knew as much as I know about bankruptcy you'd see how important it is to keep on good terms with rich relatives!"

"Yes—an English relative! You, who despise Europe and everything European! What a hypocrite you are, Francis! It sickens me to listen to you sometimes."

"Be quiet!" shouted Francis. "Don't you dare have the impertinence to speak to me like that!"

"Impertinence! Who talks of impertinence? It was pretty considerable impertinent of you, don't you think, to tell me to go simpering after an old man!"

I left the room.

The corridor was shadowed and cool. Leaning against the wall, I pressed my forehead against the dark wallpaper, but when I realized I could still hear the voices raised in argument, I moved, groping my way along the corridor as if I were blind.

My fingers found a recess in the wall. I had reached a door I had never noticed before, and wanting nothing except to find some corner where I could be alone, I fumbled with the handle and blundered into the room beyond.

When the door was shut I closed my eyes and leaned back against the panels. There was a long moment of absolute silence, and then, just before I heard the small polite cough, my instinct told me that I was not alone in the room.

I remembered to straighten my back before I opened my eyes.

Marguerite was watching me from a chair by the window, and as I looked at her mutely I remembered that when I had first arrived at the house I had greeted her with almost as much enthusiasm as I had greeted Blanche.

I tried to speak, but to my horror I found that speech was beyond me, and it was instead Marguerite who rescued the situation. She said in a sympathetic but practical voice, "Can I help you, Cousin Edward?" And as she spoke I realized with a painful surge of gratitude that she had not forgotten my earlier kindness to her.

IV

Marguerite had been sitting at a table crowded with chessmen, but now she stood up. She was small, no more than five feet tall, and her wiry, sandy hair was dragged back reluctantly into the fashionable chignon at the back of her neck. She had a sharp, pointed little face, with a long thin nose and an angular chin, and her blue eyes were narrow, as if she regarded the world with acute suspicion. I learned later that she was shortsighted. When she stood up from the chess table I saw the pince-nez dangling from a black ribbon around her neck, but it did not occur to me that her suspicious expression sprang merely from her efforts to perceive her surroundings.

"You don't look at all well," she said. "Please, won't you sit down?"

She was looking at me in concern. I managed to say, "Thank you. I'm not used to the heat. In England . . ." But I could say no more at that moment. I sat down in the chair that faced hers across the chess table and stared at the array of ivory figures on the familiar black and white squares.

"Do you play chess?" said Marguerite. She was examining a white pawn with scrupulous care. "This particular game is from a book that Francis gave me years ago. Francis used to be very good at chess, but he never plays nowadays because he's too busy making money, so I play on my own. Amelia says girls aren't supposed to play chess, but I've always thought that's a very silly rule."

I had recovered myself enough to say in a normal voice, "How strange! That's exactly what my wife always said."

"Your wife? Did she? How splendid! Did she play chess herself?"

"Yes. She too had an older brother who taught her."

"And was she good at it?"

"She sometimes let me win, yes."

Marguerite laughed, and it was only then that I remembered that I never spoke of Eleanor.

"Will you finish this game with me?" she asked.

"If you like. Yes, with pleasure." All memory died, drowned in the fascinating abstractions of the chessboard. I turned to the familiar figures as if they were long-lost friends and groped yearningly for the moves that had once lain at the tip of my mental reflexes.

"You're much too good for me!" exclaimed Marguerite in admiration after the last move had been played.

"On the contrary, you play very well, and I'm slow through lack of practice."

"When was the last time you played?"

"Oh, that was fourteen years ago," I said. "At Cashelmara."

"Ah yes. Your Irish estate." She began to rearrange the chessmen on the board. "Fourteen years is a very long time. Why is it that you remember so clearly when you last played chess?"

I opened my mouth to make some brief evasive answer, but instead my voice said, "Because I was in Ireland on the eve of the famine. Because my wife had been desperately ill after the birth of our last child, and the journey to Ireland was the first she had undertaken in months. Because we brought our son Louis to Ireland despite the fact that we always kept the children in England for fear of disease. Because the day after Eleanor and I played chess for the last time Louis fell ill with typhus and within a week he was dead."

She was staring at me. I noticed there were freckles across the bridge of her nose.

"He was eleven years old," I said.

"Did your wife herself die soon after that?"

The question took me aback. I had been expecting some meaningless platitude intended to express her sympathy.

"No," I said after a pause. "My wife lived for another six years."

"Yet you never played chess again. Why was that? Was she angry with you? Did she blame you for your son's death?"

Startled by her sharpness, I said unevenly, "It was my fault in part. I shouldn't have insisted on taking them both to Ireland with me, but I thought the change would benefit Eleanor, and Louis was growing up, anxious to see the estate which would one day be his."

"Then why did she blame you?"

"She was already suffering from ill-health, and the shock of his death . . . disturbed her. When we returned from Ireland to Warwickshire she refused to see anyone and seldom ventured from the house."

"She went into seclusion, you mean?"

"Yes. There was a complete nervous collapse—other reasons for our estrangement too, of course, but . . ." I began to wonder if I had taken leave of my senses. I had never spoken of the estrangement before. Perhaps the combination of heat and shock had affected me more seriously than I had supposed.

"How long was it before you went back to Cashelmara?"

I was struck again by the absence of sympathetic platitudes. "Four years." I looked around the room. There was a Chinese screen along one wall and a Ming vase on a lacquered table. "Four years," I repeated, my voice disbelieving, as if I still could not accept the enormity of what I had done. "The famine years. I turned my back for four years on Cashelmara, and when I returned my lands were ruined, my surviving tenants were living like animals and the whole valley was little better than a mass grave."

She said nothing, but I was no longer aware of her. I could see the corpses by the wayside and the uncultivated fields and the stench of death clinging to the ruined cabins of Clonareen. I could remember going into the church in search of the priest and finding that all the candles had gone out.

"I behaved no better than the worst of the absentee landlords," I said. "Hundreds of people who should have been in my care died of famine and pestilence."

"But surely—"

"Oh, of course I've tried to make amends since then! I've reorga-

24

nized my estate, I've resettled my tenants, I've poured money into my lands, I've interested myself in all the latest agricultural developments . . ." I stopped. At last I said in surprise, "I felt so guilty. That's why I never talked about Cashelmara. And I never talked about Eleanor because I felt guilty about her too. It wasn't simply Louis's death. It was all those children and the last nearly killing her."

I was by the window, though I could not remember having risen to my feet. Outside the brown lawn swam in a blur of brilliant light which heightened the pain behind my eyes. "I was devoted to Eleanor," I said after a long time. "Our marriage shouldn't have ended in estrangement. We didn't deserve it. It was unjust."

A small hot hand touched my wrist. A small clear voice said with passion, "Life's quite horrid sometimes, isn't it? And so unfair! I know just how you feel." And suddenly I realized that *this* was what I had wanted to hear ever since my daughter Nell had died—not the endless hushed sympathy, not the religious platitudes, not the unctuous reminders that I should count my blessings, but someone telling me that, yes, life was often brutal and fate was often unjust and I was entitled to grieve and be angry.

"I know just how you feel," said Marguerite, and I knew that by some miracle she did indeed know and that in her knowledge lay the release from loneliness that I had sought so fruitlessly for so long.

I looked down at her. I no longer felt angry then. I no longer wanted to curse the injustice of death because I was simply grateful that I was still alive. And as I looked at Marguerite across all those years that separated us, I knew not only that I wanted her but that nothing on earth was going to stand in my way.

Chapter Two

I

I had no chance to pursue my interest in Marguerite immediately, for the next day I left New York for Washington to begin two months of travel in the interior of the United States. However, my departure seemed well timed. The thought of remaining a day longer beneath Francis' roof was at that moment intolerable to me, and although I was anxious to see more of Marguerite, I knew I should take time to reconsider my feelings toward her. As so often happens after an outspoken conversation, I had already begun to regret my frankness, and although I was convinced that Marguerite would be discreet, I wanted her to prove to me by her silence that I could trust her.

It is not my purpose to recount in detail every step of my journey around America. If anyone should ever wish to write my biography I would refer him to the papers I later wrote for the Royal Agicultural Society, "Mutant Strains of Indian Corn in the State of Ohio" and "Mr. John F. Appleby's Knotter—an Invention to Facilitate Reaping." My letter to Lord Palmerston on the state of the Union may be preserved somewhere, although from my experience of Palmerston it is far more likely that he tore up the letter and jumped on it. For I advocated a policy of strict noninterference with the internal affairs of the United States, and advocating noninterference to Palmerston was worse than waving a red rag at a bull. However, I had my reasons. On American soil I saw clearly that Americans were touchy about their relationship with England, much as a grown child is often touchy about his relationship with his parents. The Americans believed—with some justification, perhaps—that their country was much misunderstood in England, and although the majority of Americans I met were friendly to me, I was conscious of a large well of anti-British sentiment.

"Imagine the disaster for Anglo-American relations," I wrote to Palmerston, "if, in the event of a militant dissension here, England found she had backed the losing side. Better to back no side at all and wait to see which way the wind blows."

That shaft was aimed at Gladstone and Lord John Russell, who insisted on believing naïvely that the Southern plantation owners were just a bunch of British gentlemen with American accents who should be allowed to go their own way.

I was not totally unsympathetic to the South. I thought a strong case could be made for a state's right to secede, but despite that I did not believe the shame of slavery could ever be sloughed off by impassioned references to constitutional rights. I was continually assured by everyone that the division of opinion in America at that time arose from a purely constitutional issue, but it was clear to me, as an outsider, that while the burning issue of the day was supposed to be secession, people talked of little else except slavery.

"The talk here is all of Vicksburg," I wrote to Palmerston, "where a commercial convention has recently urged the reopening of the African slave trade and the repeal of all laws restricting slavery. Meanwhile, everyone is looking to Kansas, which is due to decide soon whether or not slavery will have a place in its constitution. The dissent in the country is deepening all the time, and after my audience with President Buchanan this morning I was convinced that he has no idea how either he or any other man can hope to resolve the problems which face America today and the crisis which threatens her tomorrow. It is hard to say how the presidential election may fare next year. It seems the Democrats will be divided, the Southerners for slavery, the Northerners for noninterference. The Constitutional Unionists too will compromise with slavery, but they have no leader of note. The new Republican party, which did so well in the last election, may have a notable leader, but he is an idealist and a fanatic, and if by his eloquence he should be elected, there will without doubt be civil war."

It was in Washington that I first heard Lincoln's name. It seems strange now in retrospect that as late as 1859 he was not well known in the East, but it was not until the following February that he seized the attention of New York with his address at Cooper Union.

It was a relief to leave Washington. It was not that I disliked the place. On the contrary, the grand concept of the new city impressed me, but American politicians are a rough crowd compared with their English counterparts, and the political climate of the day was so fraught with crisis that the atmosphere in the capital was as exhausting as it was abrasive.

The cornfields of Ohio proved the perfect antidote. I stayed on a large farm near Cincinnati by arrangement of the Government, there is no federal department that deals exclusively with agriculture, but the Patent Office, which has charge of agricultural matters, was most obliging in its introductions, and my host in Ohio received me very warmly. American hospitality can be second to none, and I enjoyed my stay all the more after my encounters elsewhere with anti-British sentiment. However, the mutant strain of corn proved disappointing. I could only conclude gloomily that it was unsuitable for cultivation in Ireland, and after dictating some notes to this effect I withdrew to Wisconsin to inspect Mr. Appleby's knotter.

Ohio had been uncomfortably hot but Wisconsin was cooler, and while I stayed at a small hotel in a simple country town, I congratulated myself that I was experiencing frontier life amidst the vast wilderness that was the true America. There was a Scandinavian flavor to the lakes and pine woods in the neighborhood, and I thought how much Eleanor would have enjoyed the scenery. We had traveled together widely at one time, but on our one expedition to America we had never visited anywhere so remote as Wisconsin.

Mr. Appleby's knotter was, like most inventions, brilliant but impractical, and I suspected that it would be many years before it could be marketed cheaply on a large scale. However, I admired the boy's achievement (he was only eighteen) and promised to send him a copy of my report to the Royal Agricultural Society. After that, my business completed, I set out by steamship eastward across the Great Lakes, and following a short but tedious land journey, I boarded another steamship, which took me down the Hudson River to New York.

To my dismay I found Manhattan as hot as a furnace. In the mansion on Fifth Avenue Francis' wife Amelia was making preparations to remove the family to their country mansion in the Hudson Valley, but although I was invited to join them there I had no desire to prolong my stay in the household. Excusing myself as civilly as possible, I told my secretary to book a passage to England on a ship

28

that sailed within the week, and once my departure had been arranged I felt free at last to turn my attentions to Marguerite.

She had been discreet. Neither Blanche nor Francis gave me any indication that she had betrayed the slightest detail of my confidences, and as soon as I realized this my mind was made up. I found it difficult to see her alone, for her brother and sister were continually fawning at my elbow, but one day when Francis was at Wall Street and Blanche was suffering yet another harp lesson I met Marguerite by arrangement in the little Chinese room where she played her solitary games of chess.

"I'm so glad you've given me another opportunity to play chess with you," she said, smiling at me. "I thought you'd be too busy to play again before you left."

"I wanted to talk to you." As I sat down opposite her I hoped my nervousness had not made me sound too abrupt. "We can play chess later, of course, but first there's something I want to say."

She looked astonished and then alarmed. "I hope I've done nothing to displease you."

"On the contrary you please me so much that I would like you to visit me in England next spring."

"England!" she gasped. "Me?" She looked as if she could hardly believe her ears.

"If you would prefer to postpone such a visit until you are older—"

"Oh no!" she said. "I'd truly love to come. It's just that . . ."

"Yes?"

"Francis will never let me go!" she said desperately. "Contrary to what you may think, he's dreadfully anti-British."

"Are you fond of Francis?"

"Yes, very," she said without hesitation. "I used to be his favorite when I was little, though now he cares only for Blanche, and since Blanche and I don't get along at all . . ."

"I see."

"And Amelia's horrid to me, worse than a stepmother. I do wish Francis had never married her!"

"So you're not perhaps as happy as you might be here in New York."

"I wouldn't waste away with homesickness if I visited Europe, if that's what you mean. In fact I'm sure I should fall in love with England at once and never want to leave."

"In that case you could stay as long as you wished."

"With you? Indefinitely? As a sort of adopted daughter?" She was sitting on the edge of her chair and regarding me as if I were a magician engaged in performing some staggering sleight of hand. "Oh, I should like that so much!"

"Well," I said, taking great care to speak lightly so that she could treat my words as a joke if she wished, "I have no need of any more daughters, but for some time now I've been in great need of a wife. However, if you prefer to regard me as a father . . ."

Her face changed. I stopped, made a careless gesture with my hands, laughed and leaned forward over the chessboard. "I hope my high opinion of you won't make you think harshly of me," I said rapidly, watching my fingers arrange the pawns into a square, "and I hope you won't think my proposal too gauche, but I haven't proposed to anyone since I was twenty-two, and I fear I'm sadly out of practice. Of course I'm far too old for you—"

"Old?" said Marguerite. "What do I care how old you are? I don't care if you're a hundred."

I looked up. Her small pointed face had a white, set expression. At first I thought she was angry, and then I realized with a shock that she was sick with excitement. My composure deserted me. I tried to speak, but she did not allow me to finish.

"I shall be quite old myself when I arrive in England next spring," she was saying in a rush. "I shall be eighteen by then. I shall be very grown up and very wise and you won't even remember how young I am now. I quite understand that my youth would be a dreadful disadvantage to you in your position, but I'd make amends to you in other ways, truly I would. I'm sure you wouldn't regret marrying me."

"My dearest child—"

"Of course I'd much rather be your wife than your adopted daughter, but adopted daughter seemed the most I could hope for. I mean, quite apart from the fact that I'm so horribly young, my hair is such a nasty color and I have freckles and you're so clever and distinguished and so . . . so . . ."

Despite my stupefaction I was unable to resist a smile. "Yes?"

"So very tall and handsome," cried Marguerite, bursting into tears.

I am uncertain exactly what happened next. All I know is that within a second I was on my feet; she was standing up and I was taking her in my arms. It never occurred to me to ask myself if this was prudent, and no doubt it never occurred to Marguerite either.

30

She had flung her arms around my neck and was weeping un-ashamedly against my starched shirt front. I pressed her closer to me. Her dress was closely fitted in the front, despite the inevitable surge of the crinoline at the back, and I was aware for the first time that, although she was slight, she was not so lacking in flesh as I had always supposed.

"Will you marry me next year in England?"

"I would marry you tomorrow—in the darkest corner of Africa if necessary!"

I laughed. "No, we must wait a few months in case you should change your mind." Her uptilted face was so close that I could have counted the freckles on the bridge of her nose, but it seemed infinitely more sensible to kiss her instead. Not wishing to alarm her, I did no more than kiss her cheek, but while I was still savoring the delicate freshness of her skin she turned her head impulsively and my mouth grazed her own.

She acted on instinct, for she was hardly experienced enough to act otherwise, but her instincts were extraordinarily sensuous. So astounded was I that for a moment I made no response, and she, thinking she had committed some appalling *faux pas,* blushed scarlet, withdrew from me and began to stammer apologies.

But I put an end to all conversation. Again I did not stop to think. I merely pulled her back into my arms and kissed her until we were both breathless, and then at last, after a long time, I said wryly, "If your brother could see us now he would be quite justified in asking me to leave his house immediately."

"Francis!" She was horror-stricken. "Heavens above, I'd forgotten all about him! Oh, Cousin Edward, he'll never let you marry me, never!"

I smiled. I took great pleasure in smiling, and my pleasure was immensely sweet to me.

"My dearest child," I said fondly, "Francis is going to be very, very pleased."

II

"Cousin Edward!" exclaimed Francis sociably. "How nice! I was about to come in search of you."

"Yes," I said. "Now that my departure is only two days away I suspected you might wish to speak to me about certain matters. May I sit down?"

"Of course!" He scrambled with alacrity to offer me the best chair.

We were in the smoking room on the ground floor of the house. It was a small masculine chamber furnished with comfortable rounded lounging chairs, and on the walls were hung pictures of handsome race horses. The windows, like those of the Chinese room upstairs, faced the garden, and as I glanced outside I saw Francis' two children, Charles and Sarah, playing tag around the fountain.

"We shall be so sorry to lose your company at last, Cousin Edward," Francis was saying in his fine, flexible actor's voice. "Blanche in particular will be entirely devastated."

"Blanche?" I had endured his tomfoolery for some days, and I did not feel inclined to tolerate it a second longer. "Surely you mean Marguerite."

He stared at me, and I noticed again what odd eyes he had. They were such a light brown that they were almost yellow, and his cheekbones, set high in his fleshy face, gave his eyes a faintly Oriental cast.

"Marguerite?" he said at last in confusion.

"Marguerite." I was speaking in a blunt, casual voice that I had never used with him before. "You've realized, of course, that she's in love with me."

He was stunned. We were sitting facing each other in our armchairs, but presently he stood up. He moved very slowly and clasped his clenched fists behind his back.

"Cousin Edward," he said, "I think you must be mistaken."

"I think not." I leaned back in my chair, stretched out my long legs and crossed them neatly at the ankles. "She has given me every indication that she wishes one day to be my wife."

There was an utter silence. I watched the color drain from his face and noticed what an enormous effort he was making to control his temper. He was thinking hard. I could almost hear his brain shifting from thought to thought as he tried to decide how much he dared say to me.

"Since you're her guardian," I said after a pause, "I naturally felt I should broach the subject with you before I left. I am anxious to marry Marguerite. I believe she would make me an excellent wife. With your consent I would like her to come to England to visit me next May, and then after she has seen something of the country and if she still wishes to proceed with the wedding I would like to marry her during the course of that summer. I'm well aware, of course, that our present acquaintance is brief, but I think the coming separation will serve to test our feelings and ensure that neither she nor I act rashly."

He said nothing, and when I saw he still did not trust himself to speak I added for good measure, "I realize this must come as a shock to you, my dear Francis, since you were apparently unaware of Marguerite's feelings for me, but as you have always treated me with such warmth I can only trust that the prospect of us becoming brothers-in-law will be pleasing to you."

He managed to say with difficulty, "Cousin Edward, she's very young."

"Come, Francis, girls marry at eighteen every day!"

"She's a little girl," he persisted stubbornly, and I realized that despite his recent neglect he was still fond of her. "She has had no experience of the world. She imagines herself in love with you because you have been kind enough to spend a little time with her. But she doesn't—can't—love you."

"You are, of course, entitled to your opinion."

"Cousin, I know Marguerite better than you do. For the last year or two she has been unhappy at home and, I regret to say, difficult to manage. Amelia and I have both tried hard to make life agreeable for her, but—"

"My dear Francis," I said, "I'm not in the least interested in listening to you apologize for Marguerite's real or imaginary defects. I'm interested in marrying her. We may both wish she were a little older, but I'm prepared to accept her as she is even if you are not. I must ask you again for your consent, if you please."

For the last time I saw him summon all his histrionic gifts. "Cousin Edward, forgive me," he said humbly, assuming a troubled, regretful expression, "but in all conscience I don't see how I can grant my consent."

"And in all conscience, Francis," I said, "I don't see how you can refuse it."

He looked blank. From that day to this I have never seen any man look half so blank as Francis Marriott when he first realized I was going to beat him to his knees.

"I've no idea what you mean by that," he said rapidly. "No idea at all."

Now it was my turn to stand up. I uncrossed my ankles, rose to my feet and slipped my hands into my pockets. I said nothing. I simply waited.

He tried to be casual, but he was unnerved. "You're very misguided if you think you can threaten me," he said with a debonair confidence and then saw that he had given himself away.

"Who spoke of threats?" I said. "I've no wish to threaten you, Francis. I merely wish to commiserate with you on your sad financial position. You lost a lot of money, didn't you, in the panic of '57, and ever since then you've been trying to recoup your losses so that you can continue to live in the style to which you have always been accustomed. And a very expensive style it is, isn't it, Francis, from your mansion on Fifth Avenue to the house off Madison Square that your mistress insisted you buy to accommodate her."

"How the devil did you—"

"I was curious about you, Francis. Before I left New York my secretary hired a private detective to make a few inquiries, and when I returned this week from Wisconsin I was appalled by the report I found waiting for me. You should never have tried to recoup your losses by gambling, Francis. I hear faro is a very dangerous game."

He stared at me. He still could not believe his ears. There was a white pinched look about his mouth.

"You're within an ace of bankruptcy," I said. "You're trying to borrow money, but no one wants to help you. This is a bad town for bankrupts, isn't it, Francis? To be bankrupt in New York is to cease to exist. What a terrible prospect you face, Francis! But how fortunate it is that you have a rich relative who might possibly be willing to come to your rescue!"

His self-control snapped at last. His whole body blazed with rage. "You . . . goddamned . . ."

"Spare me your curses and save your breath. You'll need it to give your consent to your sister's marriage."

"I'll never consent!" he yelled. All clarity of thought was at that moment far beyond him. "Never!"

"You've no choice."

At this he abandoned all attempt at civilized behavior and tried to strike me, but I had no trouble in avoiding the blow.

"Come, Francis," I said abruptly. "Hitting me won't save you from bankruptcy. Consenting to your sister's marriage will. Now hurry up and give your consent, if you please, because I'm becoming a little tired of being kept waiting."

He was trembling in every limb by this time. "You repulsive old man," he said when he could speak. "What do you do for entertainment in England? Molest ten-year-old scullery girls?"

34

I turned to the door. "I wish you joy of bankruptcy, Francis. Good day."

He let me reach the hall before he bowed to the inevitable and came groveling after me.

"Cousin Edward . . . wait . . . please . . . must apologize . . . under considerable strain, you understand . . . not myself at all . . ."

He was the one who was repulsive. He disgusted me. I looked at his fleshy face, at his dissolute, thick-lipped mouth babbling humiliating platitudes, and I was ashamed for him.

"Be quiet," I said, unable to stand the sight of him a moment longer. "Before I leave New York we shall see an attorney and sign a contract. I shall pay you the money on consideration that you consent to my marriage to Marguerite. Should you lift a finger to prevent the marriage I shall sue for the return of the money and return in person to America to see you adjudged bankrupt. Is that understood?"

"Yes," he said, still babbling. "Yes, of course. Whatever you wish."

"Marguerite is not to know of our quarrel. I've no wish for her to be obliged to listen to you abusing me for the next nine months."

"No. Of course not. I understand."

"She's to come to England with the finest wardrobe any young girl in her position could wish for, and your wife will accompany her as her chaperone. Your children may come too, if she wishes, but not your sister Blanche. And as for you yourself, don't ever venture to show your face in any of my houses."

"No, my lord. Very well, my lord. As you wish."

It was over. I had what I wanted. Nothing else mattered but that, and, feeling tired but satisfied, I strolled upstairs to the Chinese room and told Marguerite how delighted Francis had been to receive our good news.

Chapter Three

I

On my return to London I had intended to stay for a week at my house in St. James's Square while I wrote the first draft of my thesis on Indian corn. The city would be moribund by that time, for Parliament had long since risen, and I would have the opportunity to work without distraction before I retired to the country. I usually spent the autumn months at my estate in Warwickshire before journeying to Ireland for Christmas.

However, on arriving at St. James's Square after my train journey from Liverpool, I found awaiting me in the library not only a large pile of letters but also my son Patrick's latest tutor.

Of Patrick himself there was no sign.

"Where's my son?" I said sharply to young Mr. Maynard. "Is he unwell?"

Mr. Maynard was distressed. He shifted his weight from one foot to the other and looked at me with a most unhappy expression. "My lord, he . . . he . . ."

I cursed myself for hiring a tutor too young to manage the unmanageable and cursed Patrick for ignoring my kindness in engaging a congenial young man to supervise his activities.

"When did he leave?"

"Three days ago, my lord. He left a note . . ."

"Where is it?"

"Here, my lord."

The note was written on my notepaper in elaborate Gothic script, and Patrick had decorated the borders with watercolors of flowers. The resemblance of the note to an illuminated manuscript was striking.

"Dear Mr. Maynard," Patrick had written, "please do not take offense, but I am deuced bored with London and I think I shall go to Ireland to see my friend Roderick Stranahan. I will give you a good reference to my father. Assuring you of my best wishes for the future, I remain your affectionate pupil, PATRICK EDWARD DE SALIS. P.S. Thank you for all the lessons."

"My lord," Mr. Maynard was stammering, "I did not know whether or not to follow him, but as you were returning so soon I felt I should stay here until you arrived so that I could explain—"

"Quite," I said. "You may have a month's wages and an appropriate testimonial. Please leave my house at the earliest convenient opportunity. Good day to you, Mr. Maynard."

After he had stumbled from the room I summoned my secretary, and he came hurrying into the room with his writing case wedged tightly beneath his arm.

"Fielding, I've changed my plans and will leave for Cashelmara tomorrow. You may stay here until all my correspondence has been attended to and then you may go directly to Woodhammer Hall, where I shall join you shortly. Make a note to pay Mr. Maynard a month's wages and draw up the usual testimonial which I must sign before I leave. Now, if we can attend to as much of this correspondence as possible . . ."

We worked until half past eight that evening, and then I dismissed him, ate a mutton chop and told the link boy to call a hansom to the door.

I was glad to be in London again. In the cab I savored the cool night air, and as I watched the squares, houses and streets drift past I felt more than a world away from the suffocating heat of New York. I hoped Marguerite would love London as much as I did. I thought the house in St. James's Square would please her, although no doubt she would want to try her hand at redecorating some of the rooms. Women enjoy rearranging houses. I could remember Eleanor fingering her way busily through samples of wallpaper and swatches of upholstery material.

At last the cab edged into narrower streets, and I found myself again among the prim respectable villas of Maida Vale, their front gardens little bigger than postage stamps, their privacy protected by the plane trees that lined the road. When the cab halted by one of the houses I jumped down before the driver could offer me assistance and walked quickly up the path to the front door.

My key grated in the lock. Stepping into the hall, I called her name.

"Coming!" She hurried out of the sitting room, a candlestick in her hand, and said she had been expecting me every night for the past week because she remembered I was due to arrive back at the end of August. She said that she hoped I was well and that I had not been working too hard and what a wonderful doctor I had sent her to in Harley Street; her health was quite recovered and she felt a new woman. She was sorry her health had inconvenienced us both before I left. Would I care to come into the parlor for a few minutes, or . . .

"Yes," I said. "Thank you."

In the parlor she offered me refreshment, but I declined and sat down on the sofa. The room was small but crammed with little tables, bric-a-brac, trivial pictures and overstuffed chairs.

"How did you find America?" she asked politely. "I do hope the weather wasn't as warm as you feared it might be."

"It was very hot." I let her ask several more polite questions, but when at last she realized I had some important matter to discuss with her she fell silent and sat looking at me, her hands clasped tightly together in her lap.

I knew she was frightened, and I felt sorry for her. She was no longer young. Forty-five is a harsh age at which to begin again in the world, and she depended on me for every penny of her income. I had no idea how well she liked me. She was a widow who had once been Eleanor's dressmaker, a childless woman, pleasant, undemanding and accommodating. I had wanted no more than that, and she had wanted no more than a little home of her own and a modest income that enabled her to dress tastefully, employ a servant girl and donate a suitable little sum to charity each Sunday at church. Our relationship had existed for some years, and I supposed it had suited her as well as it had always suited me.

She listened calmly while I told her that I intended to marry Eleanor's distant cousin. When I had finished she said with care, "I suppose she's quite young."

"Yes."

"You're a lucky man. Not that you don't deserve it. Why

38

shouldn't you marry someone young? You look no older than a man of forty-five, and if you ask me the luck's not all on your side either. She ought to consider herself lucky too. Well, we can't all be so lucky, I suppose, although heaven knows I've considered myself fortunate enough during these last few years."

"I've no wish to destroy any good fortune I may have brought you," I said. "That would be a poor token of gratitude on my part. You must keep the house, of course, and I'll arrange for you to have an annuity."

Her relief was almost palpable. She gave me a quick warm smile and leaned further back against the sofa's plump upholstery. "That's very good of you," she said sincerely. "More than good, in fact. It's hard to make two words like 'thank you' seem grateful enough." She leaned forward again. "I wonder . . . in the circumstances . . . might I be bold enough to offer you some advice?"

I smiled. "You've been very sparing in offering me advice in the past. If you want to offer advice now the least I can do is listen."

"It's rather personal." She hesitated. "You mustn't take offense, but I've noticed with gentlemen who seem younger than their years . . . What I mean to say is, I think you keep so young because you've always led an . . . active life. But once a man of your age leads a less active life, even for a little while . . . well, for the sake of the young lady to whom you are affianced . . . I mean, you don't want to find on your honeymoon next spring . . ." She stopped. Fallen women are popularly supposed to be shameless, but by this time she was pink with embarrassment. "I wouldn't ever have dared say all that to you," she said in a rush, "if I weren't so grateful to you for your kindness and so anxious for you to be happy with your new wife next year."

"I understand," I said wryly. "Thank you."

"If I've made you angry . . ."

"No."

"Oh." She sighed with relief.

There was a pause.

"May I make you some tea?" she said hesitantly at last.

"Afterward."

She nodded. I was again conscious of her relief. Since there seemed little to say after that, we rose to our feet and, without speaking yet comfortable in the familiarity of our silence, moved from the parlor to her room upstairs.

It takes at least three days to reach Cashelmara from London, although communications are improving and Irish roads, owing to the proliferation of relief work during the famine years, are surprisingly respectable. There is a fast train from London to Holyhead, where one takes the steamer to Kingstown, and from Dublin one can take another train across the country to Galway. Either an "outside car" or a hired carriage will take the traveler north toward Leenane, where the well-known coaching inn stands on the shores of Killary Harbour, and eight miles short of Leenane lies a wild road which twists through the mountains to Lough Nafooey and the front door of my house.

CASHEL-MARA, the stone tower by the sea—a descriptive name, no doubt, but since I am writing of Ireland, no one should be surprised to learn that the house is miles from the coast and boasts no stone tower of any description. However, the original Cashelmara was indeed a stone tower by the sea. My ancestor, a Norman knight called Roger de Salis who fought with de Burgh in the conquest of Connaught, began to carve out a small kingdom for himself in the country north of Galway by building a fort at the mouth of Killary Harbour. Predictably the Irish did not approve of this ambitious stranger in their midst, and when the fort was sacked its lord only narrowly missed being mutilated by long knives. After this discouraging incident the land lay unclaimed for a time, but the de Salis heirs never forgot their shadowy inheritance in Ireland, and later when a de Salis found favor with Queen Elizabeth he obtained a royal grant of the Cashelmara lands along with his barony and spent one horrified year in Ireland before retiring to Warwickshire to build Woodhammer Hall.

For several centuries no de Salis was either sufficiently bold or intrigued to set foot on Irish soil. It took a man such as my father, a naïve and childlike eccentric, to journey to Ireland as a young man, fall hopelessly in love with Ireland and all things Irish and resolve to build a new family mansion for himself and his bride in the most beautiful part of all those thousands of acres he owned in the wilderness of County Galway.

My father was a man of great charm, little brain and no ambition whatsoever. Building the new family mansion was the most ambitious project he ever attempted, and I doubt that the project would have been completed if my mother had not kept his nose remorselessly to the grindstone. My mother did not like her mother-in-law, who was then residing at Woodhammer Hall (my father being, of course, much too softhearted to tell his mother she must move from the hall to the dower house). She saw Cashelmara as a means of escape, a place where she could be her own mistress at last. My mother was a practical woman, full of energy and determination. Her one unfortunate trait, the inability to see anyone's point of view but her own, often created difficulties, however, and later when this trait manifested itself in the form of religious fanaticism she spent her old age enjoying herself hugely by trying to convert the Irish to her narrow interpretation of the Anglican faith.

No one ever understood how my parents managed to produce a son of my tastes and inclinations, but my father was very pleased and spent much time with me when I was young. I can still remember riding on his back across the nursery floor. As for my mother, she regarded me as nothing less than a reward from God after she had been forced to endure a tiresome mother-in-law, my father's rapturous love affair with Ireland and three childless years of marriage. I grew up basking in the warmth of their love and admiration and thought myself a very fine fellow indeed.

It was not until I was eight that I was taken by my father on a visit to his younger brother, who resided at Woodhammer Hall.

"Zounds!" cried my uncle Richard, who was a typical Regency gentleman and a great rip in his day. "What a spoiled young pup! Trust you, Henry, to bring up a boy who thinks himself the devil of a macaroni just because he can stick a pin down the gullet of some defenseless fish!" And he set to work to teach me to ride to hounds and shoot straight and put up a fight when my cousins, both pugilistic young toughs, decided to use me as a punch bag for their games of fisticuffs.

I realized later when I was growing up that I was much more like my uncle than I was like my father. My uncle, of course, had realized this as soon as he had set eyes on me, and once his sons were dead (the elder was killed at Waterloo and the other died later in some Indian skirmish) he wasted no time in naming me his heir.

My mother thought this was unfair; my brother David, landless and penniless, needed Woodhammer Hall far more than I did. In vain David told her he did not want Woodhammer Hall. Once my mother had formed an opinion, nothing except a command from the Almighty Himself could ever have changed her mind. Besides, her opposition to my uncle's decision was also her way of disapproving of my uncle's influence on my life. She told me I had become boisterous, rowdy "and immoral too, I shouldn't be surprised," she said darkly, and added to my poor father, "Henry, you should speak to the boy."

My father had no idea what he was supposed to say to me, but he never argued with my mother. We spent a pleasant half hour drinking port together while he told me what a wonderful wife my mother was and how happy he had always been with her.

"Speaking for myself," he concluded with his peculiarly childlike sincerity, "I can't recommend matrimony too highly, but make sure you marry the right girl, Patrick, because I should imagine it's devilish inconvenient if you marry the wrong one."

Both my parents had called me Patrick. My father had chosen the name in celebration of his love of Ireland, and I was never called by my second name until I went to Woodhammer Hall.

"Patrick!" cried my uncle Richard. "God's teeth, Henry, only you could think it an advantage to label a boy an Irishman in that fashion!" And to me he simply said, "Did they give you a second name at the christening?"

So in England I was always called Edward, and as I grew up the two names seemed to symbolize my conflict as I struggled to decide where I belonged. As a child I thought of myself as Irish. When one is born and bred in a place it is hard to understand when one's fellow natives—and even one's parents—say one belongs elsewhere. England seemed very strange to me, but because, like other children, I hated to be an outcast I was willing to belong there if I could. But my English cousins called me Irish, and during the gloomier moments of my childhood I thought in despair that I would be accepted by neither country, unable to call any place my home.

Yet by the time I was a man I found myself equally at home in both countries and even fancied during one of my more arrogant phases that I had the power of choice in deciding where my roots lay. Having become well educated and cynical, I saw all too clearly that there was no advantage to me in yearning to belong to the most backward country in Europe when I could belong instead to the mightiest nation in the world, and for a while I neglected Ireland and pretended there was no reason why I should ever live there again.

But Ireland drew me back. My father died, and I went home to Cashelmara, matchless Cashelmara, and all the memories of my childhood came out to welcome me as I rode down from the hills along the road to Clonareen.

I knew then where my roots lay.

Cashelmara. Not a stone tower by the sea any more but a white house built by James Wyatt, surely the greatest of all those late eighteenth-century architects, who took the genius of Robert Adam and refined it with his classic simplicity and grace. It was a grand house, but it was not pretentious. A flight of eight steps led up to the plain front door, which was set squarely in the middle of the south wall of the house. On a level with the front door four windows stretched away to the left and four stretched away to the right. Above them on the upper floor were matching windows, all spaced with the same geometric precision, all decorated only with simple architraves, all long, slim and graceful. The basement windows, half above and half below ground, followed this same precise pattern, and far above them the pattern was echoed yet again by the windows of the attics. A pediment, stark and classical, balanced the vertical lines of the front door and the columns of the porch. There was no gross decoration, no fluting or curling or fussiness of stonework, and so nothing distracted the eye from those smooth clean lines arranged with unsurpassable taste and skill.

Matchless Cashelmara, incomparable Cashelmara—but no adjective could ever capture the peace and pleasure and satisfaction that overwhelmed me whenever I returned there after an absence in England. It would be insufficient to explain this extraordinary sense of well-being merely by saying that the house was beautiful. Of course it was beautiful, the most beautiful house I had ever seen. But it was more than that. It was my father's life work, my parents' happy marriage, my own idyllic boyhood spent far from dirty cities and the corruption of modern life. It was the past, the uncomplicated past seen far away at the end of the golden corridor of nostalgia, the rural simple world of yesterday untouched by the clamor of a thousand industrial machines, the roar of international revolution and the steady ruthless progress of science. I trust I am modern in my outlook. Indeed I have no patience with men who cannot move with the times, but after months spent in London immersed in the teeming confusion of modern life I always found it a comfort to retreat to the peace and seclusion of Cashelmara.

I found myself on the brink of that peace and seclusion on the evening of the third day after my departure from St. James's Square. I had hired a carriage that morning in Galway to take me the last forty miles of my journey, and when the coachman, who was young and inexperienced, looked alarmed at the prospect of driving along the rim of Connemara into the wilderness of the Joyce Country we had been obliged to waste time while I explained to him that I was not one of those landlords who were afraid to ride unarmed on their own estates. My tenants might waste their energies in barbaric faction fights, but no one wasted their time feuding with me because they knew if they wished to complain I would listen and if they wanted justice I would mete it out to them without fuss. I have never had any sympathy with the landlord who treats his tenants as animals and then moans in bewilderment when they regard him as the devil incarnate.

It was sunset when the carriage creaked through the pass between Bunnacunneen and Knocknafaughy and I was able to look down upon my inheritance. The lough, long and slender, lay limpidly below me, and far away at the other end of the valley I could see the road winding past the cabins of Clonareen toward Letterturk. The mountains ringed the valley. I knew all their names and had climbed each one of them in my youth. The carriage was easing its way painfully around a sharp bend, and as the wheels began to grind downhill at last I looked north across the valley, across the western tip of the lough, across the river and the bog and the walled potato patches to the studied stone elegance of my home.

Around the house lay several acres of woods framed by a high stone wall. The trees had been planted to protect the house from the winds which scudded up the valley, but from the front of the house, where a gravel sweep allowed a carriage to turn with ease, the drive zigzagged downhill so rapidly that the top branches of the trees by the gates swayed far below the basement windows. The chapel, my mother's pride and joy, stood above the house on the eastern perimeter of the grounds. Its small stone tower was visible above the trees as one approached the house.

It was still light when the carriage reached the gates. The sun takes a long time to set at Cashelmara on summer nights, and never in all my travels have I seen a sight to equal the finest of the Irish sunsets. The lough was now a pool of dark gold in reflection of the afterglow, and the mountains, black in shadow, glowed a dull crimson beneath the slashed and dreamy sky.

Everyone at the house was stupefied by my arrival, although they had no reason to be. I made a habit of descending upon them without warning at least once a year in order to prevent slothful habits developing during my absence, and my stern response if all was not as it should have been was legendary throughout the household.

"Is it really yourself, my lord?" said Hayes, the butler whom I had brought to Cashelmara ten years ago from Dublin. It was hopeless to expect any of the local men to learn about buttling without becoming drunkards, and although Hayes had his shortcomings he had improved, like port, with age.

"Well, who do you think it is, Hayes?" I said irritably as I stepped into the hall. Despite my irritation I paused just as I always did to admire this magnificent entrance to my home. The hall was circular, surrounded by a gallery on the upper floor, and far above the massive Waterford chandelier, the design of the ceiling reflected the design of the marble floor. To the right was the door that led into the saloon and a chain of reception rooms, to the left was the library and on the other side of the hall beyond the stairs were the corridors that led to the servants' quarters and the lesser rooms.

I sighed, savoring the familiar pleasure of my return, and then allowed myself to recall my irritation. "Arrange for a meal to be served in half an hour, please, Hayes," I said abruptly, "and tell the maid to air my bed properly this time. One warming pan is not enough. Where's my son?"

"I'm thinking he rode to Clonareen, my lord, with young Derry Stranahan."

"I want to see him as soon as he returns. Bring some brandy and water to me in the library, if you please."

The library was a square room that faced across the valley. The principal item of furniture was a huge desk that my father, in typical eccentric fashion, had designed himself, and, following my usual habit, I sat down behind it and glanced at Eleanor's portrait, which hung over the white marble fireplace. Closer to me on the desk stood the miniature of my dead son Louis. He was smiling. It was a good likeness, and not for the first time I wondered how he would have looked if he had lived. He would have been twenty-five by this time. He would have taken his degree at Oxford and traveled abroad in the required manner; perhaps he would have married. Without doubt he would have gone into politics, won a seat in the Commons, joined the Carlton Club . . . Eleanor would have been so proud.

"Here's your brandy and water, my lord," said Hayes from a long way away. "And, my lord, your son and Derry Stranahan are this moment riding up the drive."

I went to the window, the glass in my hand, and looked out at the son who had survived. Then before he and his friend could disappear around the house to the stables I set down my glass, left the library and opened the front door.

They were laughing together. They both looked drunk, but Roderick Stranahan, the boy I had fed and clothed and educated since his family had died in the famine, looked less drunk than Patrick. At seventeen one is more capable of holding one's liquor than when one is fourteen.

I waited. They saw me. The laughter stopped.

It was Derry Stranahan who recovered first from the shock. He slipped from his horse and ran across the drive to greet me.

"Welcome home, Lord de Salis!" he exclaimed, very bright-eyed and bobbish, and held out his hand for me to shake.

Young rogue, I thought, but it was hard to be angry with him for long. Meanwhile Patrick had dismounted. I was astonished to see how much he had grown, and I noticed too that his new height had accentuated his marked physical resemblance to me. I could see nothing of Eleanor in him at all.

"Papa!" he cried and rushed so unsteadily toward me that he tripped and fell flat on his face.

"I'm sorry to see," I said as Derry helped him to his feet, "that you're in no fit state to receive me in a proper manner. Go to your room at once, if you please, before all the servants see you in such a disgraceful condition."

"Yes, Papa," he said humbly and still, despite what I had said, delayed his departure by attempting to embrace me.

"That will do," I said, for I thought it unmanly for a boy of his age to indulge in such lavish demonstrations of affection, and besides I wanted him to know that I was angry with him. "Go to your room at once." And after he had gone I said sharply to Derry Stranahan, "Long before I left for America I strictly forbade Patrick to drink more than one glass of wine a day, and I strictly forbade either you or Patrick to drink poteen. Since you're the elder I hold you entirely responsible for this incident."

"Why, yes, my lord," said Derry, long-faced and mournful-eyed, "to be sure you do. But we were visiting my kin among the Joyces, and in Joyce country it's considered a mortal insult if you refuse your host's little token of good will."

"I'm well aware of the customs of the country," I said dryly. "This is not to happen again, do you understand? If it does, I shall be very angry. Take the horses to the stables and go to your room. I don't wish to see you again today."

"Very well, my lord. I apologize from the bottom of my heart, upon my honor I do. Might I have a little bite to eat before I go upstairs?"

46

"You may not," I said, privately cursing him for his charm, which made it so hard to treat him as severely as he deserved. "Good night, Roderick."

"Good night, Lord de Salis," he said sadly and ran with great grace across the drive to the straying horses.

Returning to the library, I finished my brandy and moved to the dining room, where I ate the bacon and potatoes which had been hastily prepared for me. It was only after I had dined that I could summon the energy to extract my cane from the cloakroom cupboard and toil wearily upstairs to do my parental duty.

Patrick had lighted both lamps in his room. As I entered I found him dusting the table by the window, but although I suspected he had been carving I saw no trace of the telltale sawdust, and only the watercolors, pinned to the canopy of the bed, remained to betray how he had amused himself since running away from his tutor. Among this collection I noted a fine painting of his favorite Irish wolfhound, two bad pictures of birds, an interesting sketch of Hayes's small daughter and a gaudy portrait of a long-haired gentleman whom I could only presume to be Jesus Christ.

I said nothing. He knew I did not approve of his pastimes, but he knew too that I tolerated the painting since it was preferable to any of his other pursuits. I had once caught him digging a ditch at Woodhammer Hall. He had solemnly explained to me that he was redesigning the grounds in eighteenth-century style and that the ditch was a ha-ha. Another time—again at Woodhammer—I had found him helping a thatcher repair the roof of a tenant's cottage. At least he could paint in private without causing undue comment, but his artisan inclinations, displayed so carelessly for all my tenants to see, had proved an embarrassment to me and I had been angry that he should have been so ready to make a laughingstock of himself. Recognizing that his interest in horticulture might be directed into acceptable channels, I had tried to teach him various agricultural theories, but Patrick had refused to be interested. He did not care a fig for cultivating a field of turnips, he had told me; it was much more fun to weed a flower bed and plant a row of marigolds.

"But, my dear Patrick," I had said in despair, "you cannot go through life weeding flower beds like a common gardener."

"Why not?" Patrick had asked, assuming that puzzled expression which always infuriated me, and I had been obliged to give him one of those tedious lectures about his station in life, the obligations which would one day be imposed upon him and the necessity that he should interest himself in estate administration and, out of duty, politics.

"Grandpapa didn't bother about that sort of thing," Patrick had objected. "He merely lived quietly at Cashelmara and did as he pleased."

"What possible relevance does that have to the conversation? Your grandfather lived in another age when people of our class did not consider themselves responsible for the social and moral welfare of the masses. The world has progressed since your grandfather's day, and even if it had not I fail to see why you should feel bound to follow in your grandfather's footsteps. You're my son, not his."

But in fact I often glimpsed my father in Patrick and thought it an ironic jest of heredity that I, who bore no resemblance to my father, had somehow managed to transmit that missing resemblance to my son.

Glancing again at the pictures hanging from the canopy, I made a great effort to be patient and fair.

"I should like an explanation," I began levelly, "of why you ran away from your tutor despite the fact that before I went to America I warned you what would happen if you ran away from a tutor again."

He made a small hopeless gesture with his hands and hung his head in shame.

"My dear Patrick, surely you must have something to say for yourself!"

"No, Papa."

"But why did you do it?"

"I don't know."

I was so exasperated that it cost me a great effort not to strike him, but I was determined to give him a fair hearing.

"Was your tutor unkind to you?"

"No, Papa."

"Did you dislike him?"

"No, Papa."

"Were you unhappy in London?"

"No, Papa. But I was a little lonely, so when I realized Derry would be home from school—"

"You knew quite well that I would never have approved of you staying at Cashelmara with Roderick without adequate supervision. Roderick's a fine young fellow, but he's at a mischievous age. Look at the trouble he led you into this evening! I blame him entirely for

48

your drunkenness, but I blame you for putting yourself under his influence in this fashion."

"Yes, Papa."

"Do you have anything else to say to explain your disobedience?"

"No, Papa," he said.

I looked at him helplessly. I did not want to beat him, but I had committed myself earlier to punishing him if he continued to run away from his tutors, and I did not see how I could avoid a beating without causing him to lose respect for me. Yet although like any other responsible parent I believed in the maxim "Spare the rod and spoil the child," I had begun to think Patrick had developed an immunity that made sparing the rod a matter of indifference to him. I realized, of course, that this must be an illusion, but, illusion or not, I now had my doubts about how far a beating would deter him from further wrongdoing.

"Then if you have nothing further to say," I said to him, "you leave me no choice but to punish you as you deserve."

"Yes, Papa," he said and took his beating without another word.

Such passive acceptance disturbed me, but I was very tired by that time, much too tired to consider an alternative form of punishment for the future, and after I had left Patrick I retired with relief to my private apartments.

The next morning I still did not feel inclined to grapple with Patrick's problems, so after breakfast I sent a note to my agent asking him to call on me and settled down to write at last to Marguerite. This raised my spirits considerably. I had just finished describing the voyage and was in the middle of a long sentence saying how much I wished she were with me when there was a tap on the library door and Hayes announced the arrival of my eldest surviving daughter, Annabel.

III

Eleanor and I had had many children, but the majority of them had died in infancy. In an age when more parents could expect to see all their offspring reach maturity we had been unlucky. No doctor could provide an explanation of our misfortune. Eleanor and I had both been healthy, and Woodhammer Hall, where our children had been brought up, had provided a robust rural environment. But five of our daughters had not survived the first year of infancy, and neither of our two eldest sons had reached his fifth birthday. For eight years

49

our daughter Nell, the first born, had been our only child to escape death, and in retrospect I feel this was one of the reasons why she became our favorite daughter; her survival had made her doubly precious to us. However, after a period in which we lost two daughters and two sons Annabel entered the world and was followed at regular intervals by Louis, Madeleine, Katherine, three more little girls who had died in infancy and finally Patrick. Madeleine, to my fury, had inherited my mother's religious fanaticism and become a nun, Katherine had married a diplomat and was now residing in St. Petersburg, and Annabel, after a checkered and scandalous matrimonial career, was at present living at Clonagh Court, the dower house which I had built for my mother at the other end of the valley.

"Good morning, Papa," she said briskly, sweeping into the library with her customary *élan* before I could tell Hayes that I would receive her in the morning room. "My servants informed me this morning that you had been seen arriving in the valley last night, so I thought I would call upon you at once, as there is something I must discuss with you. Dear me, how tired you look! I really think that at your time of life you should be content to lead a less peripatetic existence. You're not so young as you used to be, you know."

It would be impossible, in any description of Annabel, to exaggerate her tactlessness. It was beyond belief. She had inherited Eleanor's spirited approach to life, but for some reason the inheritance manifested itself in an unfeminine aggressiveness I thought profoundly unattractive. However, Annabel was handsome, and there is a type of man, I am always amazed to discover, who likes such Amazonian women with a will of their own and a tongue to match.

When Annabel, at eighteen, had been married to a political acquaintance of mine some twenty years her senior, Eleanor and I had heaved a sigh of relief. Much better for her, we reasoned, to be married to an older man who would provide a steadying influence. But never were we more mistaken. Eleanor died before the marriage was three months old, but I saw my son-in-law so worn out by his wife's escapades that after six exhausting years of marriage he sank to an early grave. There were two daughters in whom Annabel professed little interest, and presently she left them with their paternal grandparents in Northumberland and returned to London. In dread of what Annabel might achieve now that she had a widow's freedom and all London in which to display it, I quickly cast around among my friends and found yet another misguided man who found such women irresistible. I was about to coax him to propose when Annabel dumfounded me—and all the delighted society gossips—by running off with the chief jockey of the racing stables her husband had owned at Epsom.

I was so enraged that I did not trust myself to speak to anyone for three days, and when I eventually emerged from my seclusion I sent for my attorney, cut Annabel from my will and wrote a letter to her parents-in-law to say that on no account was she to be allowed to see her children. The horrified grandparents wrote back to say they entirely agreed with me, and we all waited to see what would happen next.

What happened, in fact, was that Annabel had a splendid time. Possessing a comfortable income from her husband's estate, she rented a delightful house on Epsom Downs and, by riding each day with her new husband, indulged her lifelong passion for horses. Society declared her irrevocably ruined, but it was obvious that no one could have enjoyed ruin more.

A year passed. I might have remained estranged from Annabel for longer if I had not had an invitation to attend the Derby that summer; and although my interest in horses is limited to their performance in the hunt, I decided I was curious to see Annabel's husband at work. However, the race was a disaster for him. He fell, and since I was humane enough to inquire after his injuries, I was soon face to face with his wife. I am not sure to this day how we patched up our quarrel, but Annabel can be very charming when she chooses. When I heard from her later that her husband's racing career had been terminated by his injuries and that they wanted to move far from all tantalizing glimpses of the Epsom racing world, I told her she could take him to the dower house at Cashelmara.

None of my friends could believe I had forgiven her, and no doubt all of them thought I was foolish; but I am a practical man, and I saw no point in refusing to recognize a marriage which, for better or worse, was *fait accompli.* Her husband was, of course, vulgar and ill-bred, but he was also civil to me and affectionate to Annabel. Was this really such a disaster? I thought not. There are worse fates for a woman than possessing an affectionate husband, and, besides, although I found Annabel exasperating, infuriating and often utterly monstrous, I was at the bottom of my heart not unfond of her.

"I trust you enjoyed your visit to America," she was saying as she offered her cheek for a kiss. "But it's just as well you've returned to Cashelmara. Papa, I want to talk to you about Patrick. I've been most perturbed about him."

"Because he ran away from his tutor in his customary fashion?" I gestured to her to sit down. "Yes, that was most unfortunate, but I spoke to him directly after I arrived last night and the incident is now closed. How is your husband?"

"Exceedingly well, thank you. Papa, I think you should separate Patrick as much as possible from Derry Stranahan. If I were in your shoes—"

"You are not," I said, "and are never likely to be in my shoes." There was nothing that irritated me more than receiving uncalled-for advice from aggressive, opinionated females, and, besides, I thought it ill-mannered for a woman to try to instruct her father in that fashion.

The snub was quite lost on Annabel. "Papa, you may not be aware of it, but Derry's becoming very wild. After I heard that Patrick was at Cashelmara I called to see him and found him in circumstances that would undoubtedly have reduced you to an apoplectic fit. He was in the dining room with Derry. The entire room was awash with poteen, and a girl—one of the O'Malleys; I think her name's Bridget—was dancing a jig with Derry on the table. This, if you please, was at five o'clock in the afternoon when I was expecting a sedate reception followed by tea! Of course I scolded them both and sent the girl away and I doubt if much harm was done, but the thought of Patrick being here alone without supervision was hardly pleasing to me. I asked him to stay with us at Clonagh Court, but he wouldn't, and if I hadn't known you were on the point of returning from America I would have been very worried indeed."

"Quite. Well . . ."

"Papa, I'm telling you all this not because I feel you should punish Patrick, who's hardly old enough to know better, but because I feel strongly that you should censure Derry. I've heard certain rumors too, you know, and after the incident I began to wonder what might have happened if I hadn't intervened. Supposing there had been some . . . some difficulty afterward about the O'Malley girl. You know the O'Malleys are always fighting with Derry's relatives among the Joyces. If your son and heir somehow became involved in a full-scale quarrel between the two families, it would put you in the most embarrassing position."

"I dare say," I said abruptly. "I'll look into the matter." She was annoying me so much that I had to make renewed efforts not to lose my temper, and the fact that her information was unpleasant only made me the more determined not to discuss it. "May I offer you refreshment, Annabel?"

"Thank you, but no. I'm sorry you should pay so little attention to what I've had to say. I should have thought—"

"I've said I'll look into the matter. Annabel . . ." I cast around for a new topic of conversation, and in my fury I chose the wrong one. "I would like to talk to you about the Marriotts," I said rashly before I could stop myself.

"Oh, yes?" said Annabel, cross that I should have decided to change the subject and began to tap her foot impatiently on the floor.

I suddenly discovered that I had no idea what I should say next. Should I tell her or not? I had intended to say nothing until the following spring when Marguerite could tell me in person to make our private understanding public, but I was overcome with an irresistible urge to talk about her and failed to see how I could do so without disclosing the understanding that existed between us.

"Well, pray continue, Papa. What is it you wish to say about the Marriotts?"

At the very moment I made up my mind to say nothing I heard myself remark casually, "Francis Marriott's younger sister Marguerite is coming to London next spring with Francis' wife, Amelia."

"Really?" said Annabel. "How nice. However, I never go to London nowadays, as you know, so I hardly think it likely that I shall meet them unless you invite them to Cashelmara."

"Marguerite is to be married in London next summer," I said in a tone of voice suitable for discussing the weather. By this time I was asking myself crossly why I should avoid discussing such a matter with my own daughter. To shy away from the issue could only suggest that Annabel intimidated me, and that of course was nonsense. "I was hoping you would attend the wedding," I added with a note of defiance.

"Oh, I don't think so," said Annabel, stifling a yawn. "I can't bear society weddings, and I've never met Marguerite anyway. Why on earth is she getting married in London instead of New York?"

"It's more convenient and she has no objection," I replied, crossing the Rubicon with a self-possession that by this time bordered on the reckless. "Her husband has estates in England and Ireland."

"Ireland!" I had her attention at last, and as she sat bolt upright I realized with appalled fascination that I had made a monumental mistake. "Cousin Marguerite will be coming to Ireland? Where does her future husband live?"

"At Cashelmara."

There was a silence. For the first time in my life I saw Annabel at a loss for words. We sat facing each other, she on the couch, I on the edge of my armchair, and far away on the chimney piece the elephant clock began to chime the hour.

"You," said Annabel slowly at last, "are marrying Cousin Marguerite Marriott?"

There was nothing to do but go through the motions of redeeming a situation that was already beyond redemption, so although I was furious with my blunder I managed to say in an equable voice, "Yes, she's the most delightful girl, and I hope you'll find it easy to be friends with her."

"Can my memory conceivably be serving me incorrectly or is she really only a child of seventeen?"

"She will be eighteen when we marry, and someone who is eighteen is no longer a child. Annabel, I realize that this news must necessarily come as a shock to you, but—"

"A shock!" She stood up abruptly and began to tug on her gloves. "Yes, it's a shock. Your hypocrisy always shocks me. And to think how virtuously you accused *me* of ill-bred vulgarity when I married Alfred!"

"You should be careful not to say things you'll regret later. When you meet Marguerite—"

"I've no wish to meet her. It's disgusting." She was already heading for the door, and her movements were oddly uneven. "Absolutely disgusting. You'll be the laughingstock of London. Everyone will say you're in your dotage. Really, Papa, how dare you think of making such an exhibition of yourself with a young girl! I declare I've never been quite so revolted in all my life!"

My fury, which had until then been directed against myself, now streamed toward her in a thick ungovernable tide. I caught her by the shoulders. I did not speak. I merely spun her round and shook her until I realized she was crying, and then I stopped, for her tears shocked me far more than any of her abuse. I had not seen her cry since her childhood long ago. She was the very last woman to indulge in noisy floods of weeping, and even now as I watched she dashed the tears from her eyes and reached for the door handle.

54

"Annabel . . ." I was already bitterly regretting my loss of temper, but I was too late.

"I refuse to receive Cousin Marguerite as your wife," she was saying abruptly. "You will, of course, wish Alfred and me to leave Clonagh Court and live elsewhere."

My spirits had sunk to such a low ebb that I barely had the strength to reply. "Why should your husband be penalized for your foolishness?" I said wearily. "No, stay at Clonagh Court and perhaps one day you'll overcome your stupidity. Meanwhile, pray don't return to Cashelmara unless you wish to apologize for the intolerable rudeness you've displayed to me this morning."

She did not answer. She walked quickly away, her shoes tapping a sharp rhythm on the marble floor of the hall, and presently I returned to my desk to resume my letter to Marguerite. But I could no longer write. I merely sat at the desk and looked around the room, but there was no solace for me there, only the clock ticking somnolently on the chimney piece and, close at hand by the inkwell, my son Louis smiling at me joyously from his small, exquisite gold frame.

Chapter Four

After the disastrous scene with Annabel I asked myself over and over again why I had been so misguided as to confide in her. To have confided in my mistress had been justifiable, since she deserved to know the arrangements I was making for her future, but where Annabel was concerned I had no such excuse for not holding my tongue until the engagement was formally announced. Perhaps I had been unwittingly trying to place Annabel in the role of confidante which had always suited Nell so well, or perhaps the truth was simply that Annabel had annoyed me so much that I had become quite unreasonable in my attempts to annoy her in return. A third possibility—that I was beginning to resemble an infatuated young man who talked of his beloved at every conceivable opportunity—was of course so absurd that I refused to entertain it at all.

However, one fact at least was clear. Having confided in Annabel, I was now obliged to confide in Patrick before he heard the news from her. I spent a careful ten minutes planning what I should say, and then with great reluctance I summoned him to the library.

"There is a matter I wish to discuss with you," I began and immediately noticed his expression of alarm. Did I so seldom have anything pleasant to say to him? I was perturbed enough to abandon my set speech and put him at his ease as quickly as possible. "It has nothing to do with your past conduct," I said at once. "It concerns my visit to America and your mother's cousins, the Marriotts. In particular it concerns your cousin Marguerite, the younger of Francis Marriott's two sisters."

He gazed at me in silence and waited trustingly for me to continue.

"I was very taken with Marguerite when I met her," I said, "and I've invited her to visit England next spring."

There was another silence. His expression was blanker than ever. Taking a deep breath, I plowed on. "I've resolved that she should join our family, Patrick. Before I left I broached the subject with her, and she agreed to permit the existence of a private understanding that we would be married next summer in London."

He continued staring at me as if he were waiting for me to say something else. I was just wondering in great exasperation if he had listened to a single word of my monologue when he said in a rush, "Oh, that's very nice, Papa. Is it proper for me to congratulate you?"

"I can't think why the devil it shouldn't be."

"Oh. Yes. Well . . . congratulations, Papa. Papa . . ."

"Yes?"

"Papa, will she . . ." He stopped again and blushed.

"Will she what?"

"Will she have children?"

"My dear Patrick!"

"I shouldn't mind if she did," he said, the words tumbling from his mouth. "I like babies. But, Papa, there's no need for you to do this, you know. I'm sure it must be very boring for you at your time of life to have to marry anyone, so if you feel obliged to remarry because you want another son, please don't put yourself to such great inconvenience, because I'm going to turn over a new leaf, I swear it. I'm going to work so hard at my lessons that you'll never be disappointed in me again."

"Patrick," I said. "Patrick."

He stopped. His face was flushed with earnestness, his eyes brimming with tears.

"My dear child," I said, disturbed, "you're entirely mistaken about my motives."

"I know you've always held it against me that I ruined Mama's health. Nell told me how you wouldn't even choose a name for me and that I was called after you only because no one knew what else to call me."

"If Nell told you that I hope she also told you that I thought your mother was dying and I was completely distraught. Do you suppose I would have behaved in such a way if I'd been in my right mind? And as for your accusation that I blame you for your mother's ill health, nothing could be further from the truth."

"But then why are you always so strict with me? If you really bore me no grudge you wouldn't beat me so often!"

"My dear Patrick," I said, relieved that we had at last reached the core of his misunderstanding, "you must realize that when a parent takes the time and trouble to correct a child he does so out of love for the child, not out of resentment or lack of interest. The very fact that I have never allowed your errors of behavior to go uncorrected should be proof to you that I cared very much for your welfare and was most concerned to give you the best possible upbringing. I'm only sorry you should have been so uncertain of my very deep affection for you. You're my heir. Nothing can alter that, nor would I wish it altered, though as we both know your conduct has certainly left something to be desired in recent months. However, that has nothing to do with my decision to remarry, and even if Marguerite does have sons you can be certain that my affection for you will remain unchanged. Now, please—no more such foolish talk, because it does no credit to either of us."

I had spoken as kindly as I could, but to my distress he began to cry. Hoarse sobs choked him, and he buried his face in his hands in a clumsy effort to smother his tears.

"Patrick, please," I said, upset, not wishing to be unkind but knowing I should be firm. "Control yourself. The situation doesn't call for such grief, and, besides, tears are unmanly in a boy of your age."

He sobbed louder than ever. I was just wondering in exasperation what the devil I was going to do with him when there was a knock on the door.

"Yes?" I shouted in distraction.

"My lord," said Hayes, "it's Ian MacGowan who's here to see your lordship, if you please."

MacGowan was the agent at Cashelmara.

"Tell him to wait." I turned back to Patrick as soon as the door closed, and to my relief I saw that he had found a handkerchief and was mopping up his tears.

"I meant what I said about turning over a new leaf, Papa," he assured me earnestly. "I shall be a new person altogether, I promise."

58

I said I was delighted to hear it. At last, after I had dismissed him as gently as possible, I heaved a sigh of relief, sent word to the stables to saddle my horse and went upstairs to change my clothes. Half an hour later I was riding with MacGowan down the road to Clonareen.

I could not remember when I had last had such an exhausting morning.

II

MacGowan was a Scot whom I had engaged after the famine to help reconstruct my ravaged estate. In dealing with the Irish one has to recognize their limitations. It is no use choosing one of their number to collect rents and run an estate with thrift and efficiency. Mac-Gowan, a gloomy Presbyterian, not only had the knack of dispelling the mists of Irish whimsy which clung to the subject of rent payment but was intelligent enough to indulge in the occasional glum act of Christian charity, and this meant that although he was disliked he was by no means loathed by the tenants. He lived in a comfortable stone house two miles away, but I suspected the comfort was marred by his wife, who was one of those brawny Scots women with a perpetually threatening expression. Their one son, a boy of thirteen, was a solitary child; his Scots blood and his father's occupation made him an outcast among his Irish contemporaries, but occasionally he would venture to Cashelmara in the hope of fraternizing with Patrick and Derry.

"How is your son, MacGowan?" I inquired tactfully as we inspected the estate that morning.

"Very well, my lord, I thank you. I've a mind to send him to Scotland soon to be educated."

"Oh?" I said. "A boarding school?" I did not want MacGowan leaving my employ and seeking a position on some Scottish estate for the sake of his son's education.

"A grammar school in Glasgow, my lord. My wife has relatives there, and Hugh could stay with them while he studied."

"I see," I said, relieved that I was to be spared the thankless task of seeking another agent. "An excellent idea, MacGowan."

My lands seemed no worse and no better than usual, poor by English standards but prosperous in comparison to conditions elsewhere in Ireland. After the famine I had managed to merge many farms into larger holdings that could be run profitably on English lines, but there were still countless small potato patches that I had left untouched. I was not like my neighbor Lord Lucan, who had evicted tenants right and left after the famine in the desire to improve his lands. Indiscriminate and unmerited eviction was then and is now too often the equivalent of murder, and although Lucan might have been able to overlook this, I would have despised myself if I had followed his example.

At Clonareen I had a word with the priest, spoke to the patriarchs of the two leading families in the valley, the O'Malleys and the Joyces, and inspected the fields of wheat and oats, which all looked promising. However, the small forestry scheme I had initiated high up on the mountainside above the village showed signs of failure, and I was disappointed to see how many of the young trees had died in my absence.

"It's the soil, my lord," said MacGowan gloomily. "You'll not find anything flourishing on land that's no better than solid rock."

This was MacGowan's way of saying, "I told you so." He patiently suffered all my attempts to farm my estate imaginatively, but I knew his heart sank to his boots each time I announced a new experiment to him. His only attempts at either warning or criticism consisted of his saying in a sepulchral voice, "I'll beg to remind you, my lord, that we are not in England," or, as in my disastrous attempt to cultivate the yam, "There are some things that grow in America, my lord, which God did not intend to thrive on this side of the Atlantic Ocean."

"I'm certain I can succeed with a forestry plantation in this valley," I said stubbornly to him as we surveyed the withered saplings. "This is simply the wrong site, that's all. I shall try again somewhere else."

"If your lordship were to remove the O'Malleys from their potato patches on the upper slopes of Leynabricka—"

"Certainly not. They'd starve to death, and I'm tired of seeing my estate littered with corpses."

"You could assist them to America," said MacGowan mulishly. He always had trouble extracting rent from the poorest of the O'Malleys.

"To die like flies in a Boston cellar?"

"God helps those who helps themselves," muttered the Scot who found it hard not to believe that every Irish immigrant had a thousand opportunities to become rich the instant he set foot on American soil. "My lord, I would be failing you as your agent if I didn't point out that if the land can produce potatoes it's likely that it can produce trees, and since nothing else can be cultivated there due to the excessive steep gradient of the mountain—"

"Quite," I said. "But unfortunately the O'Malleys cannot eat trees, so we must cast around for another site. I'm determined to pursue this, MacGowan."

But as we rode down the hillside again to Clonareen I had to admit to myself that the future prospects for the forestry scheme were not encouraging.

In Clonareen, where MacGowan and I parted, I wondered whether I might ride to Letterturk, where my brother David's son was still living in the house David had built on Lough Mask, but in the end I rejected the idea and rode back to Cashelmara. I had seen quite enough of my family that day, and although George was a good-natured fellow, I had always found him irritatingly sycophantic. He would be my heir if anything happened to Patrick, and I could well imagine him seething with indignation when he heard of my plans to remarry.

Naturally I avoided Clonagh Court. Even the sight of the tall gray house near the southern shore of the lough was enough to make me wince at the thought of Annabel, and although I spent the entire journey home trying not to think of our quarrel, I could not help but remember what had been said. If only she had not annoyed me at the start by ordering me about in that unfeminine and unfilial fashion! Then I would have kept my temper and avoided making mistakes. Besides, on the subject of Derry I knew she had exaggerated. I was well aware that Derry was inclined to be rash, but I like a boy with a bit of spirit, and none of his escapades had yet led him into serious trouble. Moreover, I credited him with too much intelligence to make a fool of himself and fall into his benefactor's bad books. He had had a hard and desperate early life, mitigated only when I had decided to interest myself in his welfare, and he had told me often enough that he never wanted to experience destitution again.

Annabel had told me with her inexcusable arrogance that I should ignore Patrick's part in the escapade and attend to Derry, but it seemed to me, determined as I was by then not to take Annabel's advice, that Annabel had drawn quite the wrong conclusions. Derry could be left to fend for himself; it was Patrick who needed my attention. Since I had to agree with Annabel that he could not be held responsible for the incident, I resolved not to censure him, but I saw clearly that now was the time to remove him from Derry's influence and give him the opportunity to make other friends. It was high time his horizons were widened, high time he had the opportunity to see more of the world in which he might one day play a notable part. If I let matters continue as they were I would be guilty of neglecting my duty. I owed it to Patrick as well as myself to make other, more ambitious plans for his future.

With the curiosity of hindsight I often wonder what would have happened if I had instead followed Annabel's advice, but of course such speculation can only be unprofitable. I only tried to do what I believed was right.

But perhaps what I believed would have been quite different if Annabel had not been so ready to insult my relationship with Marguerite.

III

Out of a desire to treat all my children fairly I wrote that evening to my daughters Madeleine and Katherine to inform them of my understanding with Marguerite, and the next day I made arrangements to return with Patrick to Woodhammer Hall.

It was on the evening after our arrival that I decided to speak to him. When we had finished dinner I told him he might stay behind with me to drink half a glass of port, and once the cloth had been drawn I took a deep breath before embarking on my speech. Around us the paneled walls of the dining room gleamed darkly in the candlelight, and from his portrait on the wall the Tudor de Salis who had entranced Queen Elizabeth stared scornfully down at us above his starched ruff. Woodhammer was full of paneled rooms and portraits of scornful gentlemen in ruffs. I am fond of the house; it was, after all, the sole home of my family for some three hundred years, and it would be strange if I were to bear no sentimental attachment for the place; but nevertheless one cannot escape from the fact that it is ill designed, old-fashioned and, in comparison to Cashelmara, hopelessly plain. I also find it depressing. So much dark paneling gives the rooms a somber air, and for some reason—indifference, perhaps—I have never bothered to install gas lighting to dispel the gloom.

"I think it's time you had the chance to meet more boys of your own class," I said carefully to Patrick. "I know you have friends here at Woodhammer among the servants' children, while at Cashelmara you've been friendly with Hugh MacGowan and Derry, but on the whole I think these friendships leave much to be desired. I haven't forgotten either that you told me you were lonely in London when I

62

was in America and that this was the main reason why you ran away to Ireland to seek Derry's company. And you were bored too, weren't you? Yes, of course you were. I've no doubt I would have been bored and lonely too at your age if I hadn't had my brother David for company. Well, Patrick, I've thought a great deal about this and I've found a solution which I believe will have great appeal to you. I've decided to send you to school."

His eyes widened, but he was clearly too overwhelmed to speak. Pleased that he should be so excited, I continued with enthusiasm: "I'm convinced you would enjoy it, Patrick. I've never considered such an idea before because, as your academic work was of such a low standard, I felt you would profit best from individual tutelage, but none of your tutors has ever been very successful with you, and I think now I was mistaken and that you need the stimulation of competition. I've decided to send you to Rugby. It's a very famous school, and the name of its late headmaster Dr. Arnold is a by-word in educational reform. I intend to write this evening to the present headmaster and arrange for you to be admitted in the new year."

He was looking at me so unhappily that I stopped. "Have I displeased you again in some way, Papa?"

With a jolt I saw he was not excited but appalled. "Of course not!" I exclaimed, trying not to wonder in despair why it should be so hard for me to communicate my good intentions to my son.

"Then why must I be sent away?"

"But I have just explained . . ." I took another deep breath and tried again. "It's no disgrace, Patrick, to be sent to study at one of the finest schools in the country. It's a privilege! I'm anxious for you to be happier than you've been of late, and I'm sure school would provide you with an exciting opportunity to make a fresh start—meet new friends . . ."

"But I don't want any other friend except Derry," said Patrick infuriatingly and set his mouth in a stubborn line.

I kept my temper. "My dear Patrick, I should hope you will always remain on friendly terms with Derry, but you must realize that even though for various reasons I've seen fit to give him an education and a roof over his head, he's only the son of an Irish tenant farmer." And I saw again as clearly as if it were yesterday my return to Cashelmara after the famine, the emaciated child shivering in the kitchen as the cook tried to feed him some gruel. Only the cook and her husband had survived among the staff I had left to tend the house in my absence, and I could remember the terrible guilt gripping me once more when I was presented with this new evidence of the ravages of famine and pestilence. When the cook had told me the child's family had died of typhus I had said, "Keep him here." He would not have lived a year in one of the overcrowded orphanages. Children were still dying by the thousand, and I had already seen a dozen children's bodies that morning along the road from Galway.

I recalled myself with an effort. "You must realize that you and Derry have reached the parting of the ways," I said to Patrick. "Derry has been privileged, it's true, and if he does well at his law studies after he leaves school next summer there's no reason why he shouldn't in time become a respected member of the middle classes. But even so his life is certain to run on a very different track from your own. Now that you're growing up you should be able to understand this, and, by the way, Patrick, on the subject of your growing up . . ."

And I steeled myself to talk to him about certain matters pertinent to his future private life.

Many parents believe that there are some subjects which should never be mentioned to their children, and certainly in respect of one's daughters this opinion may well be correct. Everyone knows that females have a special sensitivity to the rougher truths of this life, and it is only kindness to protect them from those truths for as long as possible. But I believe any man who either refuses to speak to his son on such matters or else delays speaking to him until too late is failing in his parental duty. My father had never performed such a duty, it was true, but my father had been a naïve eccentric. However, my uncle Richard had performed the parental duty one summer at Woodhammer Hall, and in later years I had always looked back at that interview with gratitude.

"I've no doubt," I said to Patrick, "that you have by now been exposed to Derry's very natural interest in the opposite sex. You are, of course, aware of the meaning of the phrase 'carnal knowledge.' "

He blushed scarlet and managed to nod his head.

"Very well. Now, it's not my intention to give you a lecture on morals. I'm not a clergyman, and besides you're quite old enough to distinguish between right and wrong. I merely wish to speak to you on practical matters. For example, we both know that fornication is a sin which a man should avoid, but human nature being what it is there is often a gap between what a man ought to do and what he actually does. What I wish to advise you about now is how to

64

conduct yourself in a practical manner when you find yourself confronted with this gap. Do you understand what I'm saying so far?"

He nodded again, still scarlet, and stared down at his empty glass.

"As a good-looking wealthy young man you'll soon find yourself subject to great temptations," I continued, feeling more at ease now that the homily was in progress. "It would be inhuman and from a pragmatic point of view not even advisable for you to expect yourself to resist every one of these temptations, but should you find yourself unable to avoid temptation there are certain elementary precautions you must take to avoid either begetting a child or contracting some particularly distressing disease or, quite possibly, both."

He was still speechless with embarrassment, so I gave him the required practical information and allowed him some seconds in which to digest it. Finally I added, "Are there any questions you wish to ask?"

He shook his head.

"Very well. But while we are discussing carnal behavior perhaps I should just say an additional word to you on a subject which is never normally mentioned and which is probably, in view of your sheltered upbringing, quite unknown to you. There are in this world certain unfortunate creatures—one cannot call them men—who desire only carnal knowledge of their own sex. Such knowledge is, needless to say, a vice peculiarly repugnant to all men of decency and grossly offensive to any concept of morality. I mention the subject only because these creatures often lust in their disgusting fashion after boys of your age, and since you cannot always lead a sheltered life it's only right that you should be aware of the existence of such dangerous and perverted behavior."

Patrick's flush had faded. He looked sick.

"I'm afraid I've been somewhat outspoken," I said, "but I speak only with your welfare in mind. The world is often a distasteful place, and the darker side of human nature can be dark indeed. It would have been wrong of me to let you go off to school believing that the world is the safe, comfortable place it seems to be when viewed from the nursery window. You'll understand that later and be grateful to me for speaking frankly with you now."

Patrick asked my permission to leave the room.

"Yes, you may go if you wish," I said and wondered immediately if I should have waited till he was older before making such speeches to him. But then I remembered Annabel's story. If Patrick was old enough to drink too much poteen and watch Derry dance a jig with a peasant girl on the dining-room table, he was old enough to hear advice on sexual matters.

Yet somehow I was uncomfortably aware that the interview had not gone according to plan.

IV

I remained at Woodhammer until November, for the hunting is excellent in that part of Warwickshire and ever since my youth I've enjoyed riding to hounds. It was a sociable time of year in the country, but despite various dinners and balls I managed to complete my thesis on Indian corn, write my report on Mr. Appleby's knotter and somehow find the time to supervise Patrick's education. I was not inclined to engage another useless tutor for him before he went away to school in January, and, besides, since I had spent the entire summer in America I felt it my duty to devote time to him that winter.

Meanwhile, Marguerite was writing from New York. She wrote every week, but as so often happens between the continents, the post was irregular and sometimes I did not hear from her for a month. She said that *A Tale of Two Cities* had just been published and the streets of New York were awash with tears for Sidney Carton. She said the "Fall Colors" were wonderful this year, and they had made a special excursion up the Hudson again to Francis' "Summer Place" to see them. She said Francis had asked her to tell me how kind and generous he was being to her and she thought this was "very bumptious" of him, even though he had just bought her a beautiful sable-trimmed "Highland cloak" for the winter. Francis had said to her that she was to be sure to mention the sable-trimmed Highland cloak. "Although why he should be in such a gale to impress you I can't imagine," she added. "Is there some secret which nobody's dared tell me?"

I smiled but replied evasively. She was never going to hear me say a word against her brother.

I had told none of my acquaintances in Warwickshire about my understanding with Marguerite, but before I left Woodhammer I did confide in my closest friend, Lord Duneden, who was staying with me at the time. I had received two very displeasing letters from my daughters Madeleine and Katherine, and I hoped that Duneden, who was also a widower with grown daughters, would feel sympathetically toward me.

66

"Thank you," Madeleine had written with chilling brevity from her Dublin convent, "for your letter bearing the news of your intention to marry Cousin Marguerite Marriott. Naturally I wish for your happiness and will continue to pray for you every day. I remain your devoted sister-in-Christ . . ."

This disapproval cloaked in religious language and garnished with the promise of daily prayers was offensive enough to me, but Katherine's letter from St. Petersburg made me seethe with rage.

"Dearest Papa," she wrote in her neat handwriting. "Thank you for your letter. Andrew and I were, of course, much surprised to learn of your marital aspirations toward Cousin Marguerite Marriott. We both wish you happiness but cannot find it in our hearts to offer you our congratulations. Indeed, since I so earnestly desire your happiness, I would beg you to reconsider your decision if I did not realize that it is not my place to advise you on such an intimate and personal matter. However, I beg instead to remind you that Society looks askance at any grave disparity in age between the partners of a match, and although American females may, if appropriately connected, be accepted in the right circles they are seldom admired since their ways are rarely compatible with English modes of conduct. I should not wish Cousin Marguerite to be unhappy in Society as the result of deficiencies for which she cannot and should not be held responsible. Nor would I wish you, dearest Papa, who are so well respected by your fellow men, to suffer the censure of those who would find such a match as you propose singularly unfitting. With the assurance that Andrew and I wish only to express our deepest love and concern, I remain your devoted daughter, KATHERINE."

I was so infuriated by this nauseating expression of filial piety that I immediately took the letter to Duneden and told him the whole story.

"Good God!" he exclaimed after he had read the letter. "Imagine a young girl having the courage to say all this to you, de Salis—and a young girl like Katherine too! I always remember her being such a quiet, shy little mouse! Well, well, well!"

This was not exactly what I had wanted to hear.

"But for God's sake, Duneden, supposing one of your daughters had written to you in that fashion! You don't approve of the letter, do you?"

He assured me he did not. "But, de Salis, are you sure it was wise to tell your family about this private understanding with Miss Marriott so far in advance of the time when your engagement is to be made public? After all, a great deal may happen between now and next spring."

"Are you conceivably suggesting—"

"Young ladies of seventeen are notoriously changeable. De Salis, if you weren't such a very dear friend of mine I wouldn't say this to you, but—"

"You think I made a fool of myself in America."

"I did not say that. But after all you were far from home amidst an alien society. I'm not suggesting that a man's judgment may be impaired by such circumstances, but—"

"You think I was temporarily deranged when I proposed to her. Very well," I said coldly, "we won't discuss the subject further. I apologize for embarrassing you with my confidence."

"But, my dear fellow—"

"We will not speak of it again," I said strongly, and after that there was nothing more he dared say.

I was so upset by his attitude that I canceled my customary visit to Cashelmara for Christmas and went instead to London. I felt in no mood either for absorbing myself in estate affairs or for welcoming the hours of solitude that were an inevitable part of any visit to Cashelmara. Instead I spent time at my club discussing politics with others who had returned early to town, and in my library I prepared a lecture I had been invited to give in January at the Royal Agricultural College in Dublin. I also visited my mistress, since she was the only person who seemed to regard my engagement to Marguerite as both right and natural, but oddly enough the more I visited her the less interested I became in going to bed with her, and since we had nothing to talk about outside the bedroom there eventually seemed little point in making the tedious journey to Maida Vale.

"Great chunks of ice are already floating down the Hudson," Marguerite wrote in a December letter, "and all the beggars in the streets are blue with cold. This is a dreadful climate! I can't believe spring will ever come. However, I shall now stop moaning and tell you about Matters of Importance, since that is what I'm supposed to write about in accordance with all the books on letter writing! Well, John Brown was finally hanged. Isn't it dreadful? It just proves how barbaric they are Down There, and I don't see why they shouldn't secede—good riddance, I'd say. There! So much for Matters of Importance and the books on letter writing! Now I shall tell you all the interesting things such as how cleverly you described the circle of your Warwickshire acquaintances and how much I wish I could be dining with you at Woodhammer under the stern eye of the Man with the Ruff. Talking of ruffs, I'm at present pretending to read the new book on Philip the Second of Spain, but in secret I'm halfway through *The Hidden Hand,* which is quite delicious, although Francis thinks novels like that are very low."

And at the end of her letter she wrote again: "Do you ever feel sometimes as if spring will *never* come?"

I wrote back to say I did, although whenever I took up my pen to write to her the bleakness of winter faded until I no longer minded the rain and the fog beyond the library window. I was writing more frequently to her by this time, although in retrospect I wonder how I found the time to do so. I was very busy. In the new year I journeyed north with Patrick to Rugby, and after I had installed him at the school I hurried to Ireland to give my lecture at the Royal Agricultural College. I almost visited Cashelmara afterward but thought better of it, for the next session of Parliament was beginning and I was anxious as usual to take my seat in the Lords.

I found it increasingly important that I should keep myself occupied, and for a time I succeeded admirably. All through February I devoted myself to affairs at Westminster, and then early in March on the very day I received one of my precious letters from Marguerite the headmaster of Rugby sent a telegram to say that Patrick had run away from school.

Chapter Five

I

It was awkward for me to leave London at once, but I canceled all my engagements and took the first available train to the Midlands. I was so sure that Patrick would be at Woodhammer that I did not stop there first but went straight to Rugby to confront the head-master.

It was not a pleasant confrontation. I was told bluntly that Patrick had not settled down at school; he had made no effort at his lessons and had been indifferent to attempts to discipline him. Since he was clearly unable to take advantage of the opportunities the school offered him, it seemed advisable for his sake to remove him from Rugby and engage a private tutor to continue his education.

"You mean he is expelled," I said furiously.

"Not expelled, Lord de Salis. Advised to leave."

"Don't talk to me in euphemisms! You're expelling my son be-cause you're unable to teach him! You're making him take the blame for your own failure!"

"You are quite mistaken, I assure you, Lord de Salis." Unlike me he did not lose his temper. "Nothing could be easier for me than to say that the son of such an eminent man as yourself would still be welcome at Rugby despite his refusal to study and despite the fact that he has run away. But if I took this line of least resistance in order to ensure your good will and avoid this distressing interview, I would be failing in my duty as a headmaster to do what is best for his pupils. Naturally we both wish to do our best for Patrick, and believe me, Lord de Salis, there can be no benefit to Patrick if he should return to Rugby."

I left. I knew better than to persist in defending a lost cause, but I was still very angry, and by the time I reached Woodhammer I was angrier than ever.

"Tell my son I want to see him at once," I said curtly to the butler as I strode into the hall.

"Your son, my lord?" said Pomfret, astonished, and all my anger faded as I realized that Patrick was not at Woodhammer after all.

I went to the smoking room, where Pomfret brought me brandy and water, and stared out of the window across the Elizabethan garden. Patrick must be in Ireland. He would be waiting at Cashelmara for Derry to return from his small Catholic boarding school in Galway at the end of the Easter term. I might have known that, despite all I had said to him on the subject, he would still seek Derry's company at every available opportunity.

The next morning I left Woodhammer Hall for Holyhead on the first stage of my journey to Ireland.

II

I traveled as fast as I could, and when I found there was no private carriage available for hire in Galway I took the Bianconi car bound for Leenane. At the junction of the road which led to Cashelmara I borrowed a nag from one of my tenants to save myself a walk, but rain was falling from sodden skies by this time, and when I reached my home at last I felt chilled, tired and dispirited.

"Where's my son?" I said abruptly to Hayes before he had a chance to begin a wordy Irish welcome.

"Your son, my lord?" said Hayes, echoing Pomfret at Woodhammer Hall.

"For God's sake, Hayes, he's here, isn't he?"

"To be sure he was, my lord, but he and Derry Stranahan left in the middle of last night to visit your nephew Mr. George de Salis of Letterturk Grange."

"What!" I began to wonder if I were losing my sanity. "Hayes, what you've said makes no sense at all. Why the devil should my son and Derry Stranahan, who's supposed to be still at school in Galway, leave here in the middle of the night to call on my nephew?"

Hayes made a valiant effort to explain. "It's trouble there's been in the valley, my lord, so there has, and the two of them wanting to leave the valley as quietly as a pair of field mice with no living soul setting eyes on them."

"What kind of trouble?"

"Terrible trouble, my lord, may the Holy Mother of God protect us all."

I was so exasperated that I nearly seized him by the facings of his coat and hurled him against the wall. "Hayes . . ." I began and then gave up. It was useless expecting a coherent explanation from him, and anyway I disliked questioning a servant about common gossip, particularly when it seemed that my son and my protégé had somehow behaved themselves so discreditably that they had had to flee the valley under cover of night. They must have been desperate indeed. Patrick detested my nephew George, who was twenty years his senior, and in normal circumstances would have sought Annabel's company at Clonagh Court.

"I want a hot bath, Hayes, a meal and some brandy and water. After that I shall ride to Clonareen, so please see that my horse is ready for me by the time I wish to leave. Oh, and send the carriage, please, to the hotel at Leenane, where Pierce will be waiting with my bags, and ask one of the stable boys to take that hopeless mare outside back to Timothy Joyce on the Leenane road."

It was obvious that I would have to talk to the priest to learn the exact cause and extent of the trouble in the valley.

The rain had faded to a fine drizzle by the time I came within hailing distance of Clonareen. It was still afternoon, but nobody seemed to be either working in the fields or gossiping with their neighbors. The silence disturbed me; the deserted homes reminded me of my return to the valley after the famine, and hurrying my horse I rode more quickly down the road to the village.

Clonareen is not a village in the English sense of the word, for there are no shops or post office, no village green or tavern or hotel for commercial travelers. Most of the inhabitants live at subsistence level; goods are exchanged by private barter or else are bought from passing tinkers. There are no pretty little cottages flanked with pretty little gardens either, only the cabins straggling by the roadside, a motley collection of mud walls and thatched roofs, and mingling with the stench of open drains float the pungent smell of burning peat and the pervasive odor of pig. The church stands on its own beyond the cabins, and the burial ground, vast and mysterious, stretches eerily up the mountainside toward the heavens.

I heard the fight as soon as I reached the corner that hid the church from my eyes. The air was rent with Irish curses, tribal shouts and the sickening crunch of wooden staves.

The sight of a faction fight always infuriates me. After devoting many years of my life to arguing at Westminster that the Irish peasant deserves a life superior to that of a medieval English serf, it plunges me into despair to see those peasants wallowing in their primitive condition like savages.

I stood up in my stirrups and shouted at the top of my lungs in Irish, "What in the name of God Almighty and all His saints is going on here?"

It is surprisingly easy when speaking Irish to lapse into the papist patois.

The nearest men stopped fighting and swung around to face me, their mouths gaping in astonishment. Taking advantage of their surprise, I rode into their midst and bellowed at those still fighting. When everyone was still at last I counted three bodies in the road, about forty heavily breathing members of the O'Malley and Joyce families and God knows how many women and children peeping over walls and peering from doorways.

"You bloodthirsty, empty-headed Celtic fools!" I yelled at them, and seeing the black flap of a cassock, I shouted after the escaping priest, "Father Donal!"

The priest sidled back sheepishly. He was a young man, not more than thirty, and since he was usually capable of sensible behavior I suspected his furtiveness sprang from shame that I had witnessed his impotence to stop the fight.

"What are you doing running away from your flock?"

"I . . ."

"Don't make excuses to me! Get those injured men out of the road and see how badly wounded they are. Where's Sean Denis Joyce?"

"Here, my lord," said the patriarch of the Joyce family, the blood still running from a welt on his forehead.

"And where's Seamus O'Malley?"

There was a silence. They all stood there looking up at me, and beyond them as far as the eye could see nothing moved except the clouds shifting across the towering hulk of Devilsmother, the mountain at the far end of the lough. The drizzle had stopped. The air was cold and clear.

"Well, where is he?" I demanded. "Answer me, one of you!"

A young man stepped forward. His face was familiar to me, but at that moment I could not remember his name. He was very dark and very uncouth and looked every inch a troublemaker.

"Seamus O'Malley's dead, Lord de Salis," he said, and to my amazement he spoke in not only fluent but intelligible English. Most of the Irish can speak a little English if they want to nowadays and can certainly understand more than they speak, but to hear good English spoken in that remote section of Ireland, particularly when Irish would have sufficed, was extraordinary.

"What's your name?" I demanded, so intrigued that I momentarily forgot the faction fight.

"Maxwell Drummond, my lord."

That was a grandiose name for a peasant. I was just wondering if I could have heard correctly when the name Drummond struck a chord in my memory and I knew who he was. His father, one of my best tenants, had come from the north, and everyone knows the men of Ulster are a very different breed from the men of Connaught.

"Ah yes," I said. "Drummond. You've grown since I last saw you. No wonder I didn't remember who you were. What are you doing here?"

"My mother was an O'Malley, my lord."

"So she was. Of course." Mentally reproving myself for my second lapse of memory, I looked at the O'Malleys. They were silent, watching us.

"I want a spokesman from you," I told them in Irish. "Who will speak for the O'Malleys?"

"I'll speak for them, my lord," said young Drummond and added boldly to his kin, "If I'm talking in his own tongue himself will soon be on our side."

I allowed myself a cynical smile, but the O'Malleys, who were the poorest and humblest clan in the valley despite their superiority in numbers, were evidently dazzled by the boy's dash and saw nothing naïve in his suggestion.

"Father Donal?" I shouted to the priest.

"Yes, my lord?" The wounded were being carried into the nearest cabin, and he was about to disappear through the doorway after them.

"Is anyone dead?"

"No, my lord."

"Dying?"

"No, my lord."

"Very well, since no one requires you immediately you can take me

74

and Sean Denis Joyce and young Drummond here to your house so that the dispute can be resolved peacefully. As for the rest of you—" I assumed my sternest expression—"go back to your work at once. If anyone else strikes a blow this afternoon I'll see him brought before the bench and jailed."

They dispersed sulkily, cross that I should have spoiled their fun. I could hear them muttering to one another as I rode up to the door of the priest's cabin by the church.

Father Donal's home was very grand for that part of Ireland. It had not only windows but also two chimneys, one for the hearth and one for the room "below" the kitchen where the priest slept. There was even another room beyond the hearth wall, or "above" the kitchen, as the Irish would say, where his sister the housekeeper slept. The kitchen itself was a large room furnished with a table, several chairs, a large chest and even a dresser along one wall. Multitudes of pots and pans hung by the hearth, and a bucket of water was simmering gently from a crane suspended over the fire.

Father Donal's sister was flustered at the sight of me. I accepted her offer of tea and thankfully sat down in her best chair by the hearth.

"Very well, Maxwell Drummond," I said to the boy. "You can speak first—but speak in Irish, if you please, so that Sean Denis Joyce cannot afterward complain that he did not hear every word you were saying."

The boy gave me a thunderous look but pulled himself together and launched into a terse narrative. I had to admit he did speak well. Making a mental note to ask MacGowan how the boy had been managing his land since the death of the elder Drummond a year before, I began to listen intently to my first account of the disaster.

It was worse than I had feared. When he had finished I made no comment but merely accepted the tea from Father Donal's sister and turned to the patriarch of the Joyce family.

"Very well, Sean Denis Joyce," I said. "Now it's your turn to speak."

Joyce, who was at least three times young Drummond's age, made a muddled, impassioned speech about wayward women and how everyone knew that the Wages of Sin was Death.

"And isn't that the truth, Father?" he added indignantly to the priest at the end of his peroration.

"Indeed it is, Sean Denis Joyce," said the priest doubtfully and shot me a troubled look.

"I see," I said before Joyce could begin another speech. "What you're both saying is this: Roderick Stranahan, who happens to be not only your kinsman, Sean Denis Joyce, but also my protégé, seduced the wife of Seamus O'Malley—your kinsman, Maxwell Drummond. O'Malley, rightly or wrongly, believed Stranahan's reputation to be bad and suspected the worst when he saw his wife talking to Stranahan one day earlier this week. Yesterday he followed his wife to the ruins of the Stranahan cabin on the other side of the lough and found his wife and Stranahan in certain circumstances. Neither of you can agree on the exact nature of those circumstances, but whatever they were neither of you dispute that O'Malley became so inflamed that he tried to kill Stranahan with a knife. At this point my son Patrick rushed from some hiding place in the ruins and knocked down O'Malley to give Stranahan the chance to escape. O'Malley quickly recovered, but when he saw that Stranahan and my son were already some way off he was so distraught that he proceeded to stab first his wife and then himself. By some miracle his wife survived and was able to crawl to the nearest cabin for help." I paused. "Do both of you agree that this is a fair summary of your stories?"

They had to admit it was. Finishing my tea, I stood up. "I would like to speak to the widow," I said to Father Donal. "Take me to her, if you please."

Seamus O'Malley's cabin stood on the south shore of the lough within sight of Clonagh Court and the paddocks where Annabel's husband reared race horses. The memory of Annabel and her advice was at that moment intolerable to me. Turning my back on Clonagh Court, I dismounted from my horse again and followed Father Donal past the piles of peat and pig manure into the dark smoky interior of the cabin.

The woman lay in fever on a straw pallet. Since she still had all her teeth, I judged her to be in her early twenties. After Father Donal had explained gently that I wished to speak to her, I asked one or two questions and listened to her pathetic halting replies. I did not stay long. I soon heard all that I needed to hear, and, leaving Father Donal with the poor woman, I retreated to the bohereen where Drummond and Joyce were waiting with my horse.

I swung myself into the saddle again. "Before reaching a decision I must speak to my son and Roderick Stranahan," I told them abruptly. "But you can be certain that once I've heard all the evidence I shall see that justice is done."

"If you find Derry Stranahan's to blame, will you banish him from your house, my lord?" demanded Drummond in his uncannily good English. "Will you tell him never to darken your door again?"

"Hold your tongue, boy," I snapped at him. "I've given you a fair hearing and promised you justice. To demand more than that is the height of insolence. Good day to you both." And feeling sick at heart, my limbs aching with weariness, I began my ride to my nephew George's house at Letterturk.

III

My nephew George was a bachelor, a bluff, hearty, good-natured fellow devoted to shooting, fishing and striding around his small estate with a masterful expression on his face. Once a year he went to Dublin to present himself at the Castle, but otherwise his social habits consisted of visits to Cashelmara to see me and the occasional dinner with other squires who lived on the shores of Lough Mask. I had always thought it a pity that my brother David had fathered such a dull son, but such thoughts made me feel I was being uncharitable to George, who, whatever his shortcomings, was a very dutiful nephew.

"My dear uncle," he gasped, steaming to meet me as soon as I reined in my horse outside his front door. "Thank God you've come!"

"Is Patrick here?"

"Yes—and that insolent puppy Stranahan, by God! Uncle, if you hadn't arrived I swear I would have turned him out of the house. There's a limit after all to what a man can be expected to—"

"I'm damned tired, George. Is there a groom for this horse?"

"Yes—yes, of course, Uncle. Forgive me. Peter! Lord de Salis's horse! Come inside, Uncle, sit down, rest . . ."

I managed to extract a glass of brandy from him, and as soon as I felt better I told him I wanted to see Patrick alone. It was ten minutes before Patrick summoned the courage to creep into the room. He looked pale, and before I could even open my mouth to reprove him he had started to cry.

"For God's sake, Patrick, pull yourself together and stop behaving like a child in petticoats!" I spoke more sharply than I should have done, but nothing could have exasperated me more than this readiness to burst into tears. "We'll start at the beginning," I said, restraining myself with an effort and speaking in a calm voice. "Why did you run away from school?"

"I hated it," he sobbed, weeping harder than ever. "I tried to like it but I couldn't."

"Why not?"

"It was like a prison. I didn't see why I had to be shut up in a place like that. I've done nothing wrong."

I ignored this attempt to wallow in self-pity. "Did you have difficulty with your lessons?"

"I can't do Latin and Greek. I've tried and I can't." More sobs.

"Didn't you make any friends among the other boys?"

"None of them liked the sort of things I like."

Considering his artisan interests and his other unsuitable pastimes, I was hardly surprised. "I suppose some of them were unkind to you," I said, trying not to be unsympathetic. "But, Patrick, you must learn to defend yourself and stand on your own two feet! I dare say school is a rough place at first, but—"

"Yes, you can only guess!" he cried, obviously too distraught to care how rudely he interrupted me. "You've never been to school! You don't know what it's like!"

"The only reason why I didn't go to school was that when I was growing up the public schools had a poor reputation and were patronized exclusively by the middle classes. But the educational system has altered in the last thirty years, and since I believe in keeping abreast of the times—"

"I won't go back there! I won't!"

"No indeed," I said. "They won't have you." I tried not to despair, wished I felt less tired and wondered what on earth I was going to do with him. "Since it seems pointless to discuss your education further at present," I said steadily, pouring myself some more brandy, "let us return to the subject of your extracurricular activities. Whose idea was it that you should come to Ireland?"

"Derry wrote and said his school had closed early because of an outbreak of typhoid fever."

"Did he suggest you should run away and join him?"

"No." He shook his head vigorously. "He only said he wished I was with him at Cashelmara."

"So that you could applaud his latest exploits in adultery!"

"Papa, I didn't do anything wrong. I never touched any of the women. All I did was watch sometimes when he . . . he kissed them. The only thing I ever did was hit Seamus O'Malley on the head. But, Papa, I had to do that because otherwise he would have killed Derry. He had a knife and was running berserk."

"Quite," I said dryly. "I suppose I must be thankful that you are at least loyal to your friends. Very well, Patrick, leave me now, if you please, and tell Derry I want to see him at once."

"Yes, Papa. But . . . but, Papa, aren't I to be punished?"

It was almost as if he were disappointed. Hastily dismissing this impression as a bizarre illusion, I decided he was merely incredulous at the prospect of escaping scot-free.

"Certainly you're to be punished," I said at once. "You're to be sent to a new school at the earliest opportunity. Now do as I tell you and send Derry to me immediately."

He stumbled from the room. I was just wondering whether I should pour myself a third glass of brandy when the door opened again and I was face to face with Derry Stranahan.

He wore exactly the right expression; even the movements of his body seemed penitent. Pausing six feet from the armchair in which I was sitting, he stared humbly at his toes as he waited for the inevitable wrath to fall.

"Well, Roderick," I said evenly, determined not to demean myself by losing my temper and depriving him of a fair hearing, "I've listened to Sean Denis Joyce, I've listened to Maxwell Drummond, I've listened to Patrick and now I suppose I must listen to you. What do you have to say for yourself?"

"I'm innocent, my lord," he said at once, the words rolling off his tongue as readily as melted butter from a tilted dish. "I'm only sorry if in my innocence I've caused you embarrassment."

"I see," I said. "A man is dead, his wife may be dying, men have been maimed in a faction fight, my son has been obliged to resort to violence on your behalf, but *you* are innocent. Continue."

"My lord, there was no adultery—and the assignation was none of my doing! The woman begged me to meet her—"

"In the ruins of your old home?"

"Yes, my lord. You see . . ."

My patience snapped at last. "That's enough!" I shouted, rising to my feet so swiftly that he jumped. "Tell me the truth this instant, for I'll not listen to another word of your lies! You seduced that woman, didn't you?"

"No, my lord," he said, and then as he saw my expression: "Yes, my lord."

"This woman was in fact only the latest victim of your escapades with the opposite sex. Isn't that true?"

He began to look frightened. I saw his actor's mask slip. "I . . . I meant no harm."

"You meant no harm! You deprived a proud, possessive, violent man like Seamus O'Malley of his wife, you thoughtlessly set out on a course which was certain to wreck the wretched woman's life, and yet you meant no harm?"

All his glibness was gone. He was ashen.

"Listen to me, Roderick," I said, forcing myself to speak in a calmer tone of voice. "As I told Patrick recently, I'm not unsympathetic to young men who find the opposite sex irresistible. But I have no sympathy for a young man who thinks only of his own needs, who treats a woman—no matter what kind of woman—without humanity and decency and who doesn't give a damn how many lives are ruined so long as he may go his own selfish way. Seamus O'Malley died by his own hand. That at least is clear, but it's also clear to me that the O'Malleys are justified in holding you partly responsible for the tragedy. Think again, Roderick! Can you truthfully tell me with a clear conscience that you're innocent of all blame?"

He could not, of course. After a moment's struggle he said haltingly that he wished he could undo the harm he had done.

"No doubt you do," I said, "but what's done is done, as we both know. Well, there's only one solution to the situation as it stands at present. You can't stay in the valley or the O'Malleys would soon make your life intolerable. You'll have to leave Cashelmara."

Nothing I said could have frightened him more.

"Please, my lord," he stammered, hardly able to speak, "please don't turn me out into the world without a shilling."

"My dear Roderick," I said coldly, "foolishly or otherwise I've spent a great deal of time and money on your upbringing, and there's nothing I dislike more than wasting time and money. You've been very irresponsible and have certainly gone to great lengths to prove your immaturity to me, but you've done well at your school and there's no doubt that you do show promise. I still intend to send you to a university, but I also intend to remove you from Ireland for several years."

I could see him thinking that he was to be sent to Oxford and allowed to spend his vacations at Woodhammer Hall. He had never been to England. By keeping him at Cashelmara, where Hayes and his wife had looked after him in my absence, I had underlined to him that despite my charity he was not to regard himself as a member of my family.

"That's very generous of you, my lord." He was so overjoyed that his eyes shone with tears. "I know I have no right to expect you to send me to the university after this."

"Oh, you'll go to a university," I said. "You'll go to Germany and study at the University of Frankfurt. And what's more you'll stay there and not show your face either in England or in Ireland for three years. Is that clear?"

It was. He was appalled. "Frankfurt! But, my lord, I don't speak German!"

"Learn it," I said.

That silenced him. I watched him as he gradually realized I had handed out a judgment that would be acceptable to both the Joyces and the O'Malleys: banishment but not total disgrace. I had washed my hands of him while still continuing to promote his welfare.

"It'll be an interesting experience for you," I said after a while. "Make the most of it."

"But . . ." He looked very young suddenly. "I don't know a soul there." But he was recovering himself. I saw him slip behind his actor's mask again and assume a pathetic woebegone expression. "I'll be all alone."

"Better all alone in Frankfurt with my money in your pocket," I said, "than all alone in the world without a penny to your name. Very well, Roderick, the incident is closed, but remember that if you ever get into such trouble again you needn't look to me when you start wondering where your next penny is coming from."

He nodded, still shaken, and told me soberly that he would remember all I had said. But I wondered how far I could believe him, and before George returned to the drawing room to insist that I stay the night I wished I had never set eyes on that emaciated little orphan who had crawled long ago through the back door of Cashelmara to beg for a spoonful of gruel.

Chapter Six

I

"Sometimes I think spring will never come," wrote Marguerite, and suddenly that sentence, repeated by her throughout the winter, seemed mechanical and cold. I read the letter again and again, and each time I became more convinced that the careful lines masked some troubled state of mind that she dared not reveal to me. She had written the letter in February, six months after she had last seen me, and she wrote as if she could not quite remember who I was.

I was in London by this time. Before leaving Cashelmara I had dispatched Derry to stay with some of his more distant relatives and had told him to stay there until I had made the necessary arrangements for him to travel to Germany. As for Patrick, I had decided that he should go to Eton when the new term started. I had been told once that Eton was the school that favored boys of gentler inclinations, and I hoped Patrick would find it easier to settle down there than at Rugby. Meanwhile, I was again obliged to spend time supervising his activities, but although this curtailed some of my attendances at Westminster, I was relieved; domestic issues were beginning to revolve around Parliamentary Reform again, a subject far removed from my interest in agriculture, and foreign affairs seemed to consist of nothing but a romantic but impracticable sympathy for Italian unification coupled with a hysterical Francophobia. Marguerite had asked me in her letter what was being said in

England about the American crisis, but I could hardly tell her that despite last summer's armistice people in England were still so terrified of a militant France once more stalking Europe that they would hardly have noticed if America had been wiped from the face of the earth.

Even Marguerite's paragraph about politics seemed out of character. She wrote as if copying one of the letter-writing textbooks she had professed to despise, and the free, bright style of her first letters, in which she had skipped nimbly from subject to subject, had now disappeared beneath the leaden weight of formality.

In April, a week after I had received this disturbing letter, I had a birthday. Fortunately no one remembered. I spent the day trying to occupy myself as fully as possible, but that evening after Patrick had retired I drank so much port that for the first time in weeks I was able to sleep as soon as my head touched the pillow.

The next morning I felt ashamed of myself for my weakness, and after taking some salts for my headache I tried to reason myself into a sensible frame of mind. Even if Marguerite no longer wanted to marry me, there was no reason why I should not enjoy her company during her visit to England. Why should we not remain on friendly terms? I would treat her as a daughter, and, besides, had I not insisted on the long engagement and separation so that either of us might change our minds later if we wished? I had been worrying about Marguerite ending the engagement, but perhaps when I saw her again I too would have second thoughts about marriage. Why not? It was possible. Duneden might have been right when he had hinted that my American surroundings could have impaired my judgment, and although I had believed Marguerite was suitable for me, I might have been so anxious to find a new wife that I had attributed to her qualities she had never possessed.

But the more I reasoned to myself in this sensible vein the closer I felt to despair, and finally, unable to do anything but sit by the window of my room in numbing idleness, I noticed that outside in the square the leaves were in bud on the trees and the daffodils were beginning to bloom.

"Sometimes I think spring will never come," Marguerite had written time and again throughout that endless winter, but spring had come at last, just as it always did, and now in less than six weeks I would be face to face with her once more.

I was dreading it.

Of course I made no arrangements for the wedding. That would have been tempting fate. I could hardly even bring myself to speak of Marguerite for fear the mention of her name would somehow cast a shadow over the future, and when Duneden inquired politely when she was due to arrive I could do no more than tell him the date and quickly change the subject. Fortunately I had no such inquiries from my daughters. Annabel had not communicated with me since our quarrel, and although Katherine wrote dutifully every month from St. Petersburg, she never mentioned Marguerite's name. As for Madeleine, I was hardly surprised when I heard no further word from the convent where she had incarcerated herself. No doubt she was too busy remembering me in her daily prayers.

April ended; May began. Thinking it might be less awkward for Marguerite, particularly if she wished to end our understanding, if she and Amelia did not stay at my house, I reserved a suite for them at Mivart's Hotel in Brook Street. They would be traveling alone. Francis had decided that his children were too young to make the long journey across the Atlantic, and of course Blanche was remaining with him in New York.

On the day the ship was due to dock I took the train to Liverpool, where I had arranged for us all to spend the night. Patrick was at Eton by this time, and so except for my manservant I was quite alone when I arrived at the Adelphi Hotel on that cool, wet spring day.

The train arrived on time at Lime Street, and thinking I would have at least three hours to spare before welcoming my guests, I walked without hurrying up the flight of steps and between the magnificent pillars into the hotel's hall. I was astonished to find the hall crowded. There were piles of baggage everywhere, and as I stood staring at the milling throng I suddenly realized that, although the people nearest me were speaking English, they spoke with American accents.

My heart gave a great lurch. I pushed my way through the crowd to the clerk at the desk.

"Did the boat arrive early from New York?"

"Yes, sir, it docked two hours ago. A very smooth voyage, I believe." He suddenly remembered me from my previous visit to the hotel on my return from America. "Oh, Lord de Salis! Pardon me, my lord, for being so slow to recognize you! I—"

"Has anyone inquired for me?"

"Yes, my lord. Certainly, my lord. Yes, a Mrs. and Miss Marriott are waiting in the grand drawing room."

The throng hummed noisily around me. After a while I became aware of my manservant asking if he should take the bags immediately to my suite.

I nodded. I did not look at him. I was in such a panic that I could hardly put one foot in front of the other, and then at last as I stood on the brink of the rejection I had dreaded for so long I was able to tell myself calmly: Worse things have happened to me, and I dare say I shall recover soon enough.

Finding the misnamed drawing room at the far end of the hall, I walked through the huge doorway into the elaborate saloon beyond.

She saw me before I saw her. The room was full. The unknown faces spun in a blur before my eyes, but suddenly I became aware of movement, of someone hurrying past the people and paraphernalia to the doorway where I had paused to stand alone.

She wore a dark blue traveling habit and a little dark blue bonnet, and her dark blue eyes blazed in her pointed little face. She seemed changed, and because she was not as I remembered her to be I found it hard to believe her presence was real. For a second I wondered if I were the victim of a hallucination, but when I noticed she was white with fright the reality of her presence streamed through me in a blistering blast of pain.

I cared for nothing then except to keep the pain hidden. I knew I must be very kind and very understanding and assure her fervently that I wanted only her happiness.

"Edward . . ."

I could hear her voice. There was a suffocating tightness in my throat.

"Oh, Edward, Edward, I thought spring would *never* come!" she cried, and the words I had read so often in her letters were no longer dead but infused with the most passionate life. I stared at her, not daring to understand, and she, terrified by my paralyzed silence, gasped wildly, "Oh, please say you haven't changed your mind! Please, please say you haven't changed it!"

And as I blindly reached out toward her she ran headlong into my arms.

III

"Your letters changed!" It was she who spoke, not I. "They became so cool and told me so little about what you were doing. Oh, Edward,

85

I was so worried! I wanted to ask if anything was troubling you, but I didn't dare, and afterward I found it harder and harder to know what to say to you."

I had not intended to burden her with my worries, but before I realized it I was telling her all I had not mentioned in my letters. I told her about my quarrel with Annabel, about my trials with Patrick, about my troubles at Cashelmara, and all the time I was really talking not of my children nor of my home but of my loneliness, my isolation, the repulsion that filled me whenever I thought of facing the future alone.

"At least neither of us need be alone now," said Marguerite. "How soon can we be married?"

I suggested that she might like time to prepare at length for a large wedding, but she shook her head in horror.

"I don't care about the wedding!" she protested. "Why should we exhaust ourselves for weeks organizing a pageant that will achieve exactly the same result as a little ceremony before a clergyman and two witnesses? All I want is to be married to you, Edward, and as far as I'm concerned nothing else is of any consequence at all."

IV

We were married five weeks later on the twentieth of June at the Berkeley Chapel in Mayfair. It was a quiet ceremony. The thirty guests were selected from my closest circle of acquaintances, and the American Minister, whom Marguerite had met in New York, gave the bride away. Not one of my children was present. Naturally I had not expected Madeleine to leave her cloister or Katherine to return from St. Petersburg, but Annabel had refused to answer my invitation, and Patrick, by his own behavior, had excluded himself from the guest list.

At the end of May, two weeks after Marguerite's arrival, he ran away from Eton and hid himself at Woodhammer Hall. My butler's letter telling me of Patrick's arrival reached me the day after the telegram from the headmaster of Eton.

I did not stop to think. My patience was exhausted, and I had been keeping my anger toward him in check for too long. First I wrote to my nephew George to ask him to remove Patrick from Woodhammer and keep him at Letterturk Grange until I returned from my honeymoon, and then I took a fresh sheet of paper and told Patrick what I thought of him.

"My dear Patrick," I wrote, "I was grieved to hear of your latest failure to behave in a manner which I might find in any way commendable and wish you to understand that I am deeply ashamed of your indefensible conduct. My shame is all the deeper since I have been obliged to ask your cousin George to escort you to Ireland and look after you until such time as I am able to attend to you myself. Pray make no attempt to journey to London for my wedding; in the circumstances I would feel unable to welcome you as a father should welcome his only son on such an important occasion. I remain your affectionate but disappointed father, DE SALIS."

I received no reply from Patrick, but presently George wrote to say that he had followed my instructions and that he and Patrick were back in Ireland. I was able to relax at last. Patrick no doubt would have preferred to stay with Annabel, but he clearly needed a man's supervision, and since George was probably only too anxious to avoid my wedding, I suspected that his new role of guardian would suit him as well as it suited me.

After that, determined not to let my perpetual worry about my son mar my enjoyment of Marguerite's company, I put all thought of his disgrace from my mind. Patrick had failed me. I had done all I could for him and still he had failed me, but now that no longer mattered. Nothing mattered except Marguerite, and when I walked down the aisle with her at last on that hot June afternoon in 1860 I felt as if I were walking backward in time until I stood once more amidst the splendor of my youth of long ago.

V

We were married.

Marguerite wore a plain white dress and a plain white veil and carried a lush bunch of yellow roses. She looked small, neat and astonishingly self-possessed.

I remember very little about either the ceremony or the reception. Duneden made a good speech, not too long, and all the guests wished us well in the usual fashion over glasses of champagne. Amelia had arranged for the reception to be held at Mivart's, and after we left the hotel we went not to the station but to my house in St. James's Square. It was five o'clock by that time, and I had decided we would be more comfortable if we spent the night in London instead of rushing off to the Continent on the first available train.

Marguerite had changed into a green silk dress, the jacket opening in a V at the neck and the wide sweep of the skirt trailing behind her in the smallest of trains. On the back of her head she wore the merest wisp of a bonnet with floating azure ribbons to offset the brilliant green of the silk, and her small hands were encased in a pair of exquisitely tight-fitting kid gloves.

We dined at eight. It was a simple dinner. We ate some cold salmon and a quantity of buttered potatoes seasoned with parsley and the smallest, most flavorful peas to be found that morning in Covent Garden. Afterward there was syllabub, which Marguerite loved with a great passion, and presently without pausing to drink port I followed her to the drawing room.

By this time she was wearing a gown of yellow brocade that left her shoulders bare, and the yards of blond lace trimming were studded with lavish artificial flowers. I can remember the light from the chandelier shining on the diamonds I had given her and the train of her gown rustling stealthily as she walked upstairs to the drawing room.

We stayed in the drawing room for some time, but it was still light when we went to bed. The days are very long toward the end of June.

We almost missed the train to Dover the next morning. Since I always woke at seven I had seen no reason to tell my manservant to rouse me at eight, and Marguerite, of course, had instructed her maid to wait for a summons. In the circumstances nobody dared disturb us, and when I awoke at last I saw to my horror that it was nine o'clock. Fortunately my secretary hurried to the station to delay the train for us, but we rushed so feverishly to be ready that in the end we were no more than five minutes late. I remember that we collapsed laughing in our carriage as the train steamed out of the station, and afterward both of us declared we had never before spent such a frenzied morning.

Marguerite wore a light-brown mantle shaped to her waist in front and flowing loose behind and a large round hat in anticipation of the sea air, and beneath the hem of her skirt I glimpsed her small feet encased in the narrowest pair of Adelaide boots.

After a smooth voyage to Calais we spent a few days in Paris, but since Napoleon III's militant attitudes had remained unchanged, the atmosphere in France was not conducive to a long visit. I was anxious to press on to Switzerland and Bavaria, where we could forget the echoes of last summer's war. That part of Europe had long been a favorite of mine, and I longed to share the splendor of its scenery with Marguerite. I speak German with a tolerable fluency; indeed I feel more at home among the German-speaking peoples than among the French, and even by the time we had reached Basel all my domestic troubles seemed as remote as the interior of China.

Before we left Bern, where we had stayed several days, I could not resist saying to Marguerite, "Are you happy?"

"I don't see how I could ever be any happier!" she said, laughing. "Isn't that obvious?"

"I wanted to be certain."

"You surely couldn't have thought I was acting!"

I said that I knew that some women did feel obliged to act a part occasionally, out of kindness. "I wouldn't think any the worse of you for it," I said with care. "I know any pretense would be made because you loved me and wanted to be generous, but Marguerite, you must tell me if ever I ask too much of you, because I don't want you to be unhappy. You mustn't think I wouldn't understand."

"But how could you ask too much of me?" said Marguerite, genuinely puzzled, but when I tried to explain what I meant she looked more puzzled than ever.

"Edward," she said firmly, interrupting me, "one of us is being very stupid, and I have a terrible feeling it must be me. Since I haven't the faintest notion what you're talking about, do you think you could please be a little more explicit?"

So again I tried to explain, and again we both became confused until at last Marguerite exclaimed incredulously, "But it's heaven! Don't all women feel that way?" And then, appalled: "Oh, goodness, aren't women supposed to feel that way?"

And it was not until that moment that I clearly saw how much I had always lacked during my cherished first marriage to Eleanor.

VI

"I never understood why Eleanor changed," I said. "It would have been easier if I had understood."

We were at Interlaken, and beyond the heavy velvet curtains framing the windows of our baroque apartments the flower-strewn meadows shimmered hazily beneath the mountain slopes. But as I spoke I could no longer see the mountains. I was looking back into the past toward bleaker times, and when I spoke I could hardly believe that my most private thoughts were at last being voiced aloud.

"It was true there were difficulties on the honeymoon, but we were young and in love, and few difficulties last long in those circumstances. Even after the children began to come all was still well.

Childbirth was never an ordeal for Eleanor, and she was anxious to make as great a success of motherhood as she had of marriage. Eleanor always had this strong desire to succeed. If she had been a man she too might have entered politics, but since a woman's world is more limited than a man's, she turned all her energies toward promoting my career and bringing up our family. We knew exactly how many children we wanted: two boys and two girls. I can remember how amused we were when we did succeed in producing first a daughter, then two boys and finally another girl. Eleanor said we should be proud of such efficiency, and we both laughed. We were very happy."

I was no longer aware of Marguerite's presence in the room. I was aware only of Eleanor, beautiful and elegant, dark-haired, dark-eyed and dazzling.

"But the baby died." The memory of Eleanor blurred. "The little girl. She was called Beatrice. When Eleanor recovered from the shock all she wanted was another baby, but although we did have another daughter she lived only three months, and then our two boys, John and Henry, both showed signs of consumption. I can't describe to you the grief we suffered. At first it drew us closer together, but after the boys were dead I realized that Eleanor was gripped with a morbid sense of failure—as if she had failed by providing me with only one child who had survived. I admit I did want another son, since it was important for a man in my position to have an heir, but I could have waited. I wasn't filled with this feverish urgency to replace what had been lost. But Eleanor could think of nothing else. She lost interest in the world around her until finally, thank God, Annabel was born, and Louis, and at last we had three healthy children again. For me that was enough. I never wanted more children after that."

The sun was streaming through the window, and suddenly I was back in the nursery at Woodhammer and Nell was slipping her small hand into mine as we looked into Louis's cradle.

"Eleanor understood. It was she who suggested that we should go away together for a while. She said she felt guilty because she knew she had neglected me during our saddest times. 'But I want to make amends to you,' she said. 'I want to be a good wife to you again, Edward, the best wife you could possibly wish for.' She was always striving for perfection, you understand. She had such very high standards. My mother used to say to her, 'What are you going to do, Eleanor, if one day you find you can't live up to those high standards of yours?' But I think she only said that because she was secretly a little jealous, just as mothers are so often jealous of successful daughters-in-law.

"Anyway, I accepted Eleanor's suggestion that we should travel, and that was when we came to America. We had always wanted to visit the New World, and at last it seemed as if we had the ideal opportunity."

I was in Boston now. I was looking out of the hotel window across the Common, and far away in the distance I could see the lights of Beacon Hill.

"But something happened to us," I said. "Eleanor found our intimate life together repugnant. I don't know why. She said she suspected it was because anticonception made her feel guilty; she felt she was violating the Church's teaching. But I couldn't believe that. She wasn't deeply religious. We went to church regularly, of course, to set an example to the children, but in private we both veered toward skepticism. Eventually Eleanor said she was sure all would be well again if we made no effort to prevent other pregnancies, and in fact this proved to be true. All was well again, but . . ." I stopped. For a long moment I could not speak, but at last I managed to say, "No, all was never well again. I wanted to believe it was, but it wasn't."

For the first time I looked at Marguerite. She was so motionless she scarcely seemed to breathe. Her eyes were a calm clear blue.

"My friends believed all was well. They said to me occasionally, 'You're a lucky man to have such a devoted wife!' Their wives had stopped sleeping with them years before; their wives no longer became pregnant. And when I saw my friends groveling in search of mistresses I began to think that perhaps they were right and I was indeed lucky. Eleanor was still mine, and she was such a wonderful companion, enjoying my interests, promoting my career, doing all she could to be a perfect wife. After a while I told myself to count my blessings and never allow myself to feel angry whenever she conceived another child I didn't want."

I was silent for a time. It was quiet in the room. Presently I was able to say, "We went on for some years like that—until Patrick was born. That was when everything ended. The doctor said afterward that she should never have another child, and she never spent another night with me again."

I frowned, remembering the past, dwelling on it once more in a fruitless effort to understand. "The curious part was," I said, "that when Eleanor was finally confronted with the fact that she was unable to behave toward me as a model wife should, she lost all interest not only in being a good wife but in being a good mother. She withdrew from me and she withdrew from the children. Of course she was very unwell for a long time, especially after Louis's death when she had a nervous collapse, but even later she never regained her interest in the children. I could understand her being indifferent to Patrick, who had ruined her health, but it was strange how she became indifferent to the girls. It was as if she had lost all her fear of failure, as if she had given up some terrible struggle and wanted only to accept defeat. She changed so much.

"And I never really understood why. Why was she unable to share a room with me unless she thought that we might conceive a child? This was obviously the only way in which she felt able to live with me as my wife, but why? Was I at fault? What did I do? Was there anything I could have done? I loved her so much. Before our final estrangement I was always faithful to her, and that wasn't easy. The doctor always advised her against marital relations when she was pregnant, and so there were often months on end when she slept in a separate room. But I accepted that because I loved her and because I knew that despite all our difficulties she loved me."

I looked at Marguerite again. There was an element in her expression that hinted I was on the brink of some deep, painful understanding, but instinct told me it was safer not to understand. "Eleanor really did love me, you know," I said, uncertain why I repeated the words but knowing it was vital we should both believe them. "Good wives always love their husbands, don't they, and Eleanor was such a perfect wife."

VII

Marguerite had fallen in love with Switzerland. By the time we reached my favorite inn overlooking Lake Lucerne she had bought fifty prints of various views, three dozen slides for her magic lantern, untold yards of Swiss embroidery and three cuckoo clocks. The weather was warm, each day brilliant with long hours of sunshine, and from the balcony of our room we could look across the lake to the soaring heights of Mount Pilatus.

"So this is what it's like to be in one's dotage," I said, amused, to Marguerite one afternoon. "I have no idea what's happening in Parliament. The entire British Empire may be in a state of collapse and I neither know nor care. I have no desire to read a newspaper, no desire to read a book—although I might consider a frivolous novel— no desire to write a thesis and no desire to do anything except stay here with you. I had always thought contempt led people to condemn those in their dotage, but now I know it's not contempt at all. It's jealousy."

Marguerite, who was busy filling her journal with elaborate descriptions of our surroundings, looked up. "If you're in your dotage," she said severely, "my new name isn't Marguerite de Salis. Edward darling, I wish you wouldn't think so much about your age. I don't think about it, so why should you?"

"I don't think of it much, but I can't help wishing occasionally that I was a few years younger."

"What difference would that make? Age is a state of mind, like lying on a bed of nails," said Marguerite obscurely and added as if to dismiss the subject, "Anyway, you're so fit and strong you'll probably live until you're a hundred."

"But what a dreadful fate that would be for you!"

She laughed. "I shall love you forever and ever," she said in that confident way people have when they are very young. "Don't you believe that?"

"I . . . would very much like to believe it."

My cynicism, that razor edge of my sadness, must have shown despite my flippant tone of voice. Abandoning her journal, she jumped up, ran across the room and kissed me. "Then you must believe it!" she said earnestly, "because it's true. Dearest Edward, you've given me everything I could possibly want. Indeed, I feel as if I'm an entirely new person. Do you truly think I shall stop loving you just because you'll reach old age before I shall? What a poor opinion of me you must have!"

"You know very well what kind of opinion I have of you!" I said, smiling at her, and suddenly all sadness vanished and I was myself again. I looked at her, and to my eyes she was beautiful, so small and neat, so smartly dressed, so fresh and vivacious and gay. "I love you very much," I said, and suddenly age no longer mattered; we had slipped into an emotional dimension in which time did not exist, so that now she was simply Marguerite, who loved me and who would love me as long as I lived to love her in return.

VIII

When we reached Zurich I wrote to my nephew George to ask him to send Patrick to London shortly before Marguerite and I returned from the honeymoon. I thought at least one of my children should be at St. James's Square to welcome their stepmother to her new home.

To Patrick himself I wrote, "You will to a great extent redeem your unfortunate behavior if you can present yourself to Marguerite in the best possible manner. When we arrive I want to see you well dressed in your best suit with your hair properly cut and brushed. I shall expect you to be civil, welcoming and attentive. This will not, I trust, be too much to ask of you." When I had signed the letter I added as an afterthought, "P.S. If you have grown again, you may summon the tailor and have a new morning coat made for the occasion with trousers to match. You may also have a new waistcoat, but *on no account* is it to be made in one of those loud tartans or checks. Ask the tailor to advise you about a color that is both tasteful and subdued."

Knowing how young men of his age often had no idea how to dress sensibly, I thought it well to be specific on this point. I had no wish for him to present himself in some dreadful Tweedside lounging jacket gaping to reveal a rainbow-striped horror beneath.

At the beginning of September we left Switzerland, journeying north through Bavaria to Munich before bearing east through the Grand Duchy of Hesse to Frankfurt, Coblenz and Cologne. We traveled mostly by train, although for a time we journeyed by steamer up the Mosel past the vineyards which for mile after mile covered the slopes of the valley. I had decided it was preferable to avoid France entirely, and when we left the German states at last we proceeded to Ostend, where a channel steamer conveyed us to England. On the whole it was a very pleasant homeward journey, although Marguerite thought the Lowlands unimpressive after the Alps.

Late in the afternoon of September 19 my carriage drew up outside my house in St. James's Square.

"So much has happened since we were last here!" said Marguerite, already overcome by nostalgia for the honeymoon, and I smiled as I took her arm and led her up the steps to the front door.

Patrick was waiting to receive us in the hall. I was glad I had foreseen how much he had grown again. He was almost as tall as I was now, and his hair, fair as mine had been at his age, was parted and arranged immaculately. His height made him look older than fifteen, and I thought what a pity it was that his behavior was so much less mature than his appearance.

"Welcome home, Papa," he said dutifully, stepping forward to shake my hand. "I hope you had a good journey."

I smiled to show him how pleased I was with his manners. "The journey was very pleasant, thank you," I said cheerfully. "And now let me present you to your cousin Marguerite. My dear . . ."

And then as I turned to introduce her I looked upon her face and saw with a terrible clarity that she was dazzled by him.

Part Two

MARGUERITE
Fidelity   *1860–1868*

Queen Margaret was young enough to be his daughter, and was some-times, indeed, ally and spokeswoman of her stepchildren in their quarrels with their father.

Cambridge Medieval History, Volume VII
—HILDA JOHNSTONE

Chapter One

I

Edward was fifty-nine when I met him and sixty by the time we were married, but as I never thought of him as being any particular age it was useless for well-meaning people to say that he was too old to be my husband and that marriage in such circumstances would be foolish. The fact was I did not care a rap whether I was being foolish or not. I wanted to marry him, and that was that.

Of course everyone believes he or she marries for the purest possible motives and I was no exception, but now, looking back, I can see I wanted to marry him for all the wrong reasons—to escape from my home, from a society that considers a plain girl a failure, from the despised spinsterhood to which, I was already convinced, I was irrevocably doomed. Edward's proposal floated strawlike past me as I floundered in my sea of troubles, and since I was convinced I was drowning I made the traditional gesture of the drowning victim and grabbed the straw with both hands. The straw became a raft; I was saved, and in the first flush of relief and gratitude I decided I was passionately in love with my savior. That was an illusion, needless to say, but it sustained me all through that dreary winter before we were married, even though I lived in constant fear that he would change his mind and end my hopes for salvation.

But he did not change his mind, and when at last I saw him again a curious revelation took place in my feelings. I saw him as if for the first time. When we had met in New York I had been so preoccupied with my troubles that I had not bothered to acquaint myself properly with his character and had retained only the most fleeting impression of his looks, so when we met again months later in Liverpool it came as a considerable surprise to me to be reminded how handsome he was. He was very tall, at least two inches over six feet—why had I not remembered he was so tall?—and very well proportioned, without trace of any such unsightly disadvantage as a middle-aged paunch or a bald pate. His hair was not, if truth be told, as thick as it might have been, but it was still plentiful. It was a dark straight brown tinged with gray at the temples. He had blue eyes, set deep, a charming smile and a fine-drawn but unmistakably pugnacious jaw.

I once again decided that I was passionately in love with him, and once again it was in fact nothing more than a fond illusion, but after we were married I did indeed discover what passion meant and then at last my wishful thinking became reality. I know it is not considered seemly for a young girl to own to passions which in novels are reserved only for the most earthy peasant females or notorious adventuresses, but since I intend this to be a truthful memoir I must confess that I enjoyed every moment of my honeymoon and daily became more enrapt with the stranger who was my husband.

No race on earth is as clever at being strangers as the British. They wrap themselves in formality, they withdraw behind veil after veil of exquisite politeness, they hide cunningly behind a bewildering array of carefully chosen façades—and what is a poor American, accustomed to demonstrativeness, democracy and demagoguery, to make of it all? Is it surprising that Americans, when confronted with such enigmatic behavior, make such dreadful mistakes? At first my brother Francis thought Edward was effete and eccentric. I disagreed, thinking Edward quaint in a mild Old World fashion, but it never occurred to either of us that beneath his aristocratic manners Edward was as tough as any New Yorker who has just made his first million. Americans think a man can be tough only if he talks loudly, clenches his fists and puffs out his chest, but Englishmen think this very crude behavior and have long since learned the art of annihilation with a smile. Edward was kind and considerate to me, good-humored, gentle and patient, but there was a hard streak in his nature that I never saw before we were married, and he had a will of iron that ensured he always got his own way.

He was, in fact, as an older, wiser woman might have suspected long before I did, not an easy man to live with.

I am not sure why he wanted to marry me. He said of course that it was because he was desperately in love with me, and of course I believed him; but love is such a flexible word, and I often wonder if his motives for marriage were as clouded as mine were. He was lonely; he made no secret of that, and he was also, I soon noticed, bitterly resentful of his increasing age. He could not have fallen in love with my looks, for I was very plain when we first met, but I think he did fall in love with my youth. So many snide comments are made about middle-aged men harboring passions for young girls that the temptation is to deny the significance of my age in our relationship, but although his age never mattered to me I suspect my age was very important to him.

Yet after the honeymoon I knew he did truly love me, just as I truly loved him, and when we returned at last to his house in London neither of us foresaw that we would plunge immediately into our first fully fledged marital quarrel.

II

I was not accustomed to marital quarrels. My parents had died when I was very young, so I had no memory of their marriage, and although my brother Francis and his wife were far from being infatuated with each other they had reached an arrangement with the result that their relationship was at least outwardly agreeable. When I was growing up I enjoyed thinking of myself as a poor unloved orphan doomed to stagger through life beneath a multitude of misfortunes, but as usual my imagination far outpaced reality. I might have been orphaned at a tender age, but since I was a member of one of the wealthiest families in New York I could hardly complain of poverty, and since I had an indulgent brother and an affectionate sister I could hardly complain either that I was unloved. Francis was so much older than I that I could look upon him as a father, while Blanche was near enough to my own age to ensure that I was never at a loss for companionship.

There was a strong family resemblance between the three of us. Blanche and Francis resembled each other physically; both were very good-looking. But Francis and I resembled each other mentally; we liked to learn and enjoyed best of all the puzzles of mathematics. When I was small Francis even taught me some algebra, but when he married his wife disapproved of such an unfeminine pursuit and the lessons ceased. I never cared for Amelia after that. At about this time my father's partner died; Francis took full control of the family fortunes, and his time for me was necessarily reduced. I went on adoring him from afar, just as any girl will adore an older brother who is clever and good-looking, but his preoccupation with other matters hurt me, and as I grew older I sensed also that he was disappointed in my plainness and feared I would be a failure when the time came for me to make my debut.

This makes Francis sound unkind, but he never deliberately meant to be unkind to me. He simply wished me to be successful, and when it seemed clear I would be a failure he could not help but be mortified. Francis was obsessed by success. Our father had expected a great deal of him, and for many years he had been not merely the only son of the family but the only surviving child. The whole future of the family's prosperity rested on his shoulders. My grandfather had founded a prosperous mercantile house, but my father had preferred to double his money on Wall Street, and Francis, with his mathematical inclinations and his gambling streak, had been well content to follow in my father's footsteps. He worked hard, he married well, he maintained our place in the forefront of New York society, but somehow in the stress of achieving so much the better side of his nature became bruised and he changed. He was disappointed in his marriage, and no matter how much money he made it always seemed necessary to make more.

By the time he was thirty-five he was privately bitter, but still his passion for success would not let him rest. He had to come first; the family had to come first; New York and America had to come first. The craving for success turned mere patriotism into chauvinism, so that he had no alternative but to hate Edward on sight. It was not Edward himself that Francis disliked—although their characters were hardly compatible—but the civilization which Edward represented, the civilization which held America second-rate and New York little better than an overgrown market town. Edward was by no means offensive on the subject of America. Indeed he paid many compliments to my country, but as with most Englishmen it was his unstated belief that all people but the English were "foreigners," inferior citizens of the world to whom the English, as good Christians, were obliged to be charitable.

The very phrase "second-rate" was enough to send Francis into a frenzy, and since Edward could not help but arouse Francis' worst instincts it was hardly surprising that they failed to become friends.

However, I loved Francis despite all his faults and even despite his growing preference for my sister. Blanche and I had been happy together as children, but once childhood lay behind us our relationship rapidly deteriorated. As the years passed I became jealous of her looks, jealous of Francis' awakening pride in her, jealous of her social success and jealous of her rosy future.

Jealousy is not an attractive emotion. I regret to say I became unnecessarily unpleasant toward her—poor Blanche, it was hardly her fault she was so pretty!—and although she begged me tearfully not to be so unkind, I hardened my heart and drove away all her offers to remain friends. Presently she too hardened her heart; she no longer needed my friendship anyway, for after she came out she had dozens of new friends in addition to all her beaux. Blanche hardly suffered from my foolishness, but I suffered very much. The fact that I had only myself to blame merely made my loneliness the more intolerable to me.

By this time I was seventeen, skinny, freckled and frustrated. I had already been to two formal dances and knew the dreadful humiliation of being a wallflower. Hating everyone and wallowing in self-pity, I spent my days either playing chess by myself or else writing reams in my journal about how miserably fate had treated me. I contemplated entering a convent, becoming an actress and even, I blush to relate, applying at the new pleasure house on Madison Square to see if they had a vacancy for a courtesan. So naïve was I that I thought that all such women did was to hold hands with their gentlemen callers and exchange kisses, but I yearned passionately to be kissed by a gentleman caller, and I was certain that if I gave my earnings to charity God would forgive me for my evil ways.

It was at that moment that I first met Edward. No wonder I did not care how old he was. At first it did not occur to me to think of him as a gentleman caller, but when he proposed I was certainly not about to ape the heroine of a romantic novel and refuse him with the conventional sigh that "it could never be." My immediate reaction was: Well, why not? And if that sounds grasping, practical and not at all conduct befitting a heroine, I can only apologize and repeat that I want this to be a truthful memoir.

How Edward won Francis' consent to the match I shall never know. I asked Francis, but he went a most alarming shade of puce and refused to answer. On my honeymoon I again asked Edward to enlighten me (I had begged in vain for enlightenment before he had left New York), but Edward merely gave me his charming smile and said there was no reason why Francis should not have been delighted by my splendid match.

"No reason in the world," I said, laughing, "except that you hate each other." And when he looked shocked by this bluntness (Englishmen are too polite ever to admit to hating anyone) I added, "I'm sorry if I'm not supposed to know, but I would have had to be blind and deaf not to notice."

But Edward refused to be drawn into a discussion of Francis, and after a while I realized that the enmity between them ran deeper than I had ever guessed. Francis had told me frankly that I should not expect him to visit me in England, but I had attributed this to his anti-British prejudice and thought he would overcome it in time. Now I began to suspect that there was more afoot than his characteristic chauvinism, and the suspicion was distressing. I would have loved Francis to visit me. I was sure he would have been proud of how fetching I had become (it still amazes me how vastly a powerful incentive can improve even the plainest girl's appearance), and since I was no longer jealous and frustrated I thought he would once more have found me far more agreeable than Blanche.

But the die had been cast. I had chosen Edward, accepted exile and had no regrets—except for wishing that the severance from my family were less complete. It would have helped if I could have talked more to Edward about those I missed, but since he refused to discuss Blanche as well as Francis our conversations were limited to Amelia and the children. The roots of Edward's antagonism to Blanche were also a mystery to me. He had made a great fuss over her when he had first arrived in New York, and I could only suppose she had given him offense by some thoughtless word which she had never dreamt would cause him such deep injury. Blanche was often thoughtless but never malicious. I tried to tell Edward that, but when he merely smiled politely I thought in exasperation that his remorseless neutrality was just as tiresome as a raging torrent of abuse.

It was an unfortunate situation, and when I returned to London at the end of the honeymoon I might have felt very homesick at the prospect of settling so far from my family had I not been so much in love with Edward. But I was ecstatically happy. Indeed so much at ease did I feel in our relationship that I fancied I knew him as well as it was possible to know anyone, and this was a comforting thought to me as we arrived at his house in St. James's Square.

His son Patrick was waiting to receive us. I was exceedingly nervous of meeting Patrick, who was only three years my junior, for when Edward had told me his son was a difficult boy who gave him great trouble I had imagined myself being presented to a sulky lout who had no trace of any social graces. I was therefore all the more astonished when I found not the lout I had feared but the most friendly, delightful and courteous young man I had ever met. I could not believe it. I boggled at him, so surprised that I forgot even the most elementary good manners, and when at last I remembered myself sufficiently to say "How do you do," I was still baffled by the discrepancy between what I saw and what Edward had led me to believe.

I think it was then that I first suspected I did not know Edward quite as well as I thought I did.

"I'm delighted to meet you at last, Cousin Marguerite," said my stepson. "I was sorry to miss the wedding. Please forgive me for being unable to attend. I hear it was a very nice ceremony."

"Um," I said. "Yes. Delightful, thank you."

"May I address you as Cousin Marguerite?"

"Drop the 'cousin' if you wish," I said, smiling at him. Americans do tend to be informal.

"My dear," said Edward, speaking to me exactly as if I were a child of six, "I don't think at this point that such informality would be proper."

I was so astonished that he should censure me in such a fashion in front of his son that I could only stare at him speechlessly, but he had already moved away from us toward the staircase. Around us in the hall the footmen were bringing in our boxes from the carriage, and the butler was fluttering around hissing instructions.

Patrick stammered, "Shall I order tea, Papa?"

"No." He could not have been more abrupt. He added to me over his shoulder, "This way."

Patrick was looking so unhappy that I had to smile at him again and tell him I was looking forward to continuing our conversation later. Then I followed Edward upstairs to our apartments.

He did not speak to me. He ordered hot water peremptorily and made a great fuss when it was not brought at once. His valet tripped over a bag and was abused; my maid began to look nervous; the entire atmosphere became charged with uneasiness. Finally we separated, he retiring to the dressing room, and with my maid's help I washed off the worst of the journey's dust, redressed my hair and donned a fresh day dress. Afterward, dismissing her, I listened at the dressing room door. When I heard nothing I guessed he had already dismissed his valet, and presently, summoning my courage, I knocked on the door and walked in.

He was standing by the window, his hands resting lightly on the sill, his mouth set in a narrow line. As the door opened he swung around to face me.

"You might at least have waited until I gave you permission to enter," he said abruptly.

The cleverest move I could have made then would have been to burst into tears, but I have never been the sort of female who weeps easily, and even if I had been I think I might have been too horror-stricken at that moment to have summoned even the dryest of tears. No one I loved had ever spoken to me in such a way before. Such icy rage was quite beyond the bounds of my experience.

I panicked. "How dare you treat me as if I were a child in the nursery?" I shrieked, sheer fright making me appear furiously angry. "And why are you in such a sulk anyway?"

At that point he lost his temper. That was a nasty shock to me since I had no idea he possessed a temper to lose. He said it was a pity I had no inkling how to behave, and he had been a damned fool to marry a girl who was obviously much too sensuous to give him a moment's peace of mind. "You're just like your profligate of a brother," he added, making the fatal mistake of relaxing his iron neutrality on the subject of Francis and I screamed at him, "Don't you dare say such a thing about my brother! Don't you dare!" But unfortunately he did dare and made several more insulting remarks about Francis' moral character until I cried hysterically, "At least Francis loves me, even if you don't, and I'm going right back to America to live with him again!"

Then at last, thank God, I reached the state where there was nothing else to do but burst into tears and weep passionately all over his shirt front. I am uncertain when his shirt front suddenly presented itself to be wept upon, but it arrived without noticeable delay, and when I felt his arms around me I knew the crisis was past. I had survived our first marital quarrel, and, having found it a dreadful ordeal, I resolved then and there that it was to be our last. One of the most appalling aspects of the whole incident was that I still had no idea why he should have been so angry with me.

He was apologizing in a shaken voice that sounded quite unlike him. I heard him say, "I'm sorry. It's not like me to be so foolish, but I care so much that I can't help myself. I can't bear to think you might not care for me as much as I care for you."

"But you silly, silly man!" I said, bewildered, through my tears. "You know how much I love you! How could you possibly think—"

"It was seeing you with Patrick," he said, and suddenly I sensed what a terrible effort it was costing him to be honest with me, and I knew I should make an equal effort to be understanding in return. "The two of you looked so young together . . . and Patrick looks much as I used to look when I was his age."

There was a silence. I was still groping for the right words when he said, trying to shrug off his awkwardness and his private pain, "It was nothing. Just a passing foolishness. You needn't be afraid I shall lose my temper every time you smile at a man young enough to be my son. Forgive me, if you can, and let's not speak of it again."

I kissed him. When I answered I tried to speak simply, because I knew I was too inexperienced to do anything else. "I'm sorry you were upset," I said. "Being sixty must be horrid sometimes, rather like being a wallflower at a dance. I hated watching Blanche smile at her partners even though I knew she didn't care a nickel-cent-piece for any of them." Kissing him again, I asked him if we might go downstairs and have tea. "Oh, and by the way," I said some minutes later after he had returned my kisses in a way which left neither of us in any doubt of our feelings for each other, "Thomas is coming next year, in April, I think, but I must ask a doctor soon to make sure."

He was dumfounded. I had given him no previous hint about my condition, but when he asked me why I had been so secretive I said merely that I had wanted the news to be a surprise.

"It's certainly a surprise!" he said, laughing, and he seemed so genuinely pleased that I screwed up my courage to ask him if he was sure he did not mind becoming a father again.

"Why should I mind?" he said easily, and then, remembering certain details he had confided to me about his first marriage: "This is your child, my dearest, not Eleanor's. The circumstances are very different."

I asked no more questions. I always felt it best not to pry into his relationship with Eleanor, and the more he told me about it the less I understood. As far as I could gather, she had become pregnant as often as possible in order to avoid sleeping with him—a clever ruse, since it was the only way she could have a separate bedroom and still remain in theory a good wife—and had refused to permit Edward to practice anticonception. I had never heard of the word "anticonception" before, and after I had deduced its meaning I was greatly surprised to hear that one could do anything, short of total abstinence, to prevent children arriving in the world. However, after acknowledging regretfully to myself that it was probably only one of many subjects about which I was quite ignorant, I did make a conscientious effort to regard Eleanor with compassion. Edward treated her behavior as if it were some strange malaise—a possibility, I admit, since madness can take the most unlikely forms when a woman is in her forties—but no matter how much compassion I tried to dredge up I still could not rid myself of the opinion that her behavior was not mad but just plain contrary. Of course it was impossible for me to say so. Edward had been devoted to her despite their troubles, and I supposed grudgingly that if she had been able to keep his devotion while trying to behave like a nun she must have had certain remarkable qualities.

"You mustn't be jealous of Eleanor," Edward had said to me kindly on our honeymoon.

"Jealous? I? Of course not!" I had exclaimed with a little laugh, but of course I was passionately jealous and longed to outshine her in every possible way. Like Francis, I love to come first. Being second is not my style at all, and I was delighted when Edward told me I was a much better wife in the bedroom than that beautiful, witty, intelligent creature whom I felt sure I would have detested on sight.

"The baby's going to be a boy," I said later after an eminent doctor from Harley Street had confirmed my condition. "I'm positive it's going to be a boy."

Eleanor had usually succeeded in producing girls.

"Well, Thomas is a fine name," said Edward, remembering my first reference to the baby, "and I should certainly like to have another son."

He was so very far from satisfied with poor Patrick.

Patrick was quite the most handsome boy I had ever seen. He did have a great look of Edward, particularly around the eyes, but his expressions were so different from his father's that the resemblance seldom seemed striking. His hair was an opaque shade of gold. Edward's hair had been that color once, I learned, although when he was a year or two older than Patrick the gold had darkened to brown. Patrick was not yet as tall as Edward, but he was clearly going to be just as tall and just as splendidly proportioned before long. He was still no more than a boy, and during our early conversations I began to feel as if I were indeed old enough to be his mother, but I was far from immune to masculine good looks, and there was no denying he was exceptionally beautiful. Of course I did not say so to Edward, but in private I was pleased that Patrick was so agreeable and pleased too that I did at least know one person still in his teens.

Edward had an enormous circle of acquaintances, but not one of them was under forty. I had long since reconciled myself to the prospect of moving in elderly circles, but I admit that when I first began my life in London the prospect still seemed intimidating. His friends were all scrupulously polite to me, but the English have many different degrees of politeness, and I suspected they regarded this young American girl who had so uppishly attached herself to London society as very much the ugly little cuckoo in their gorgeously feathered nest.

Soon my social life resembled an obstacle race that seemed more and more arduous to its sole participant. When one is first married one is not normally overwhelmed with callers, for both Americans and British respect the custom of "summering and wintering the bride," but because of Edward's position I soon found myself receiving the wives of his closer friends and being obliged to call upon them in return. This quickly proved to be a dreadful bore, for what could I, a young American scarce out of the schoolroom, have to say to a dowager duchess who had never thought it necessary to travel out of England? I immersed myself frantically in a study of the newspapers in order that I might talk about current events and spent long hours poring over Burke's Peerage in an attempt to familiarize myself with the aristocracy.

But worse was to come. Edward's great interest was politics, and soon there were stately political dinner parties to attend and countless excruciating "evenings." I could have escaped them by pleading to be exhausted by pregnancy, but I was in excellent health and disliked the thought of dissimulating to Edward. Besides, I hate to give in. Accordingly I set to work again in an effort to master British politics, but I could not help thinking it was tiresome of the British not to have a written Constitution, and I became bored with the so-called issues of the day. Soon I was even thinking how pleasant it would be to read about secession instead of the interminable wranglings about parliamentary reform and whether or not Mr. Gladstone should abolish the tax on paper.

However, I struggled on. I read John Stuart Mill's *On Liberty* and even, digressing from political and social issues, Darwin's *Origin of Species* before Edward realized what I was doing and put a stop to it.

"For God's sake don't talk about socialism and evolution at any house I take you to!" he exclaimed, horrified. "Read Samuel Smiles's *Self Help* if you must interest yourself in the social welfare of the masses, and try some poetry if you wish to progress further than your usual light novels. Have you read *The Idylls of the King?*"

I had not. I loathed poetry, and anyway I thought Darwin's theories were much more fascinating than Tennyson's fantasies. I was just at an age to rebel against Amelia's ruthlessly correct religious upbringing, and while still believing passionately in God (Whom as a small child I had identified with my elderly father), I was excited to think of all the self-righteous clergymen being flung into a frenzy by these new scientific hypotheses. But in Edward's circles such talk was heresy, and nothing, I thought, separated the old from the young quite so completely as the mere mention of Darwin's name.

"I suppose we must seem very conservative to you," said Edward sympathetically once.

And antiquated, I thought as I remembered the baffling intricacies of the English class system, but I said nothing. Of course there is a class system and an enormous amount of snobbery in New York too. In fact I admit that in one of my more unattractive moments I myself have even looked down my nose at a girl whose father's income did not exceed twenty thousand a year, but nevertheless the class system is so different in America, so much more casual and fluid, so much more—well, the only word for it is "democratic."

"Ah yes," said Edward with irony after I had said as much to him. "We are all watching the American experiment in democracy with great interest."

I supposed the irony was because he was convinced the democracy would soon dissolve into civil war. But I did not believe there would be a war. Francis did not believe it because it would be so bad for trade, and he was prepared to vote against Lincoln in the coming presidential elections.

"How would you vote if you were entitled to do so?" said Edward after I had shown him Francis' letter.

At first I thought he was teasing me. "Oh, Edward, what a question! You know women are quite incapable when it comes to political decisions!"

"Yes, but only because the majority of women are uneducated. They're not incapable *per se*."

I never ceased to be surprised by the unexpectedness of some of

Edward's opinions. On subject after subject he would display an annoyingly conservative outlook and then suddenly, just when one had given up all hope of a more flexible attitude, he would casually drop a remark so radical that one wondered how he avoided outraging all his old-fashioned political colleagues. Nowadays, when the political field is dividing into two such distinct parts, one forgets the earlier age to which Edward belonged, the age of coalitions and blurred party lines and independent political thought.

"Eleanor possessed the most exceptional grasp of political matters," he explained. "She had a natural aptitude for politics, it was true, but she had also been educated by a first-class governess. I don't believe it's desirable for women to be educated in exactly the same way as men, but I do think there should be more opportunities for women to receive an education such as the one Eleanor received. However, before we educate the women of this country we must first of all educate the men." He had slipped into his energetic House of Lords voice. "Every man in this country is entitled to at least an elementary education, and it's nonsense to say, as many do, that the working classes are incapable of profiting from it."

It was then that he told me about his educational experiment. He had sent an Irish peasant's son, Roderick Stranahan, first to school in Galway and afterward to university in Germany. "And now I'm considering a second experiment," he added with enthusiasm. "I have an interesting young tenant called Drummond, and I suspect he might benefit from being sent to study at the Agricultural College. Oh, it would benefit me as well as him!" he explained quickly when I commended him on his altruism. "He would return a more enlightened farmer and spread his enlightenment among my other tenants, who are all hopelessly backward in agricultural matters."

Agriculture was Edward's chief interest after politics, but as it was not a subject that interested me it seldom provided us with a topic of conversation.

Meanwhile, I was growing no closer to penetrating the steel-plated politeness of Edward's acquaintances, and eventually I became so dismayed that I even summoned the courage to complain to him. But that was a waste of breath. He merely denied my difficulties existed and assured me that everyone constantly told him how delightful I was.

"I'm so glad," I said, trying to sound cheerful, but I was plunged into worse gloom than ever. I knew that after all my extensive research I could no longer attribute my failure to my ignorance of English life, so I was forced to assume that my great sin lay in being an eighteen-year-old foreigner. Nothing could alter my age, but I decided that perhaps I could be a little less foreign.

"I've made up my mind to be more English than the English," I said one morning to Patrick. Edward had already gone to the library to dictate letters to his secretary, but Patrick and I were still lingering in the dining room. "I'm going to learn to speak with an English accent."

"The English have no accent," said Patrick, astonished. "They speak English. It's foreigners who have the accent."

"Oh, bunkum!" I said, hardly knowing whether to laugh or cry, but when he giggled and said how amusing I was I realized tears would be out of place.

"Anyway," he added, "why do you want to change? The English don't like foreigners who try not to be foreign. It's not playing the game at all."

"But what am I to do?" I wailed, feeling utterly defeated by English insularity.

"Why do anything?" said Patrick. "I think you're awfully nice just as you are."

"No one else seems to think so," I said morosely. "I've been here a whole month now, and everyone still seems to think I'm no better than a creature at the zoo."

"A month is no time at all!" protested Patrick, but unable to reply, I fled from the room, rushed upstairs, drew the curtains around the fourposter bed and burrowed inside under the comforter. There I gave way to the most abject self-pity and wept until I was exhausted. Presently I felt better. Sitting upright in bed, I remembered how in New York people had either ignored me or else hissed behind my back that it was a pity I was so plain. At least now, thanks to Edward, I was never ignored, and I always took care to dress fetchingly. Drawing the curtains once more, I left the bed and inspected my shape in the looking glass. Nothing showed; it was too soon, but the thought of the baby was so cheering that I no longer minded the middle-aged English regarding me as a juvenile freak. In fact I was even able to concede that Patrick was right and I had been expecting too much too soon.

Later I felt proud that I had reasoned myself into such a philosophical frame of mind, but nevertheless when Edward mentioned that evening that it was time for us to go down to the country, I at once longed to exchange the stultified grandeur of London for the pastoral peace of Woodhammer Hall.

III

One of the most dispiriting aspects of my introduction to London society had been that I had found it an ordeal even though the majority of people were out of town following the parliamentary recess. If I had been intimidated by the minority, how would I survive next year's Season, when I would be obliged to cope with society *en masse?* However, I put such gloomy speculations behind me when we left London and began to look forward to my first glimpse of Warwickshire.

Edward's annual travels, like those of other members of his class, usually fell into a steady pattern. When Parliament was sitting he would remain in London, his stay broken only by occasional lightning visits to Woodhammer or Cashelmara, but when Parliament rose he would retire to Ireland for a couple of months. Returning to England in October, he would respond to invitations to visit his friends before he journeyed to Woodhammer Hall, where he in his turn would issue invitations, look over his estate and indulge his passion for hunting. At Christmas it was time for Ireland again, but he would be back in London by mid-January, when Parliament usually reconvened. However, I had thoroughly disrupted his habits that year, first by marrying him in June in the middle of the Season, then by taking him away for two months on our honeymoon and finally by becoming pregnant and making the long journey to Ireland impracticable. Since I felt so well I had been willing to go, but Edward had refused to entertain the idea.

"Cashelmara is much too remote for you at present," he said at once, "and if you had any kind of mishap God knows how long it would take to summon the nearest doctor. No, you must remain in England for the next few months."

He had even suggested I might prefer to stay in London until after the baby was born, but the thought of foregoing my escape to the country appalled me.

"The country air will be so bracing," I said winningly, "and besides, we shall be back in London by January, shan't we?"

So with my doctor's grudging consent we departed in November for Woodhammer, and I prepared myself for two months of bliss.

But I was not accustomed to country living. After a life spent in New York I found my pastoral peace frighteningly quiet and the leisured pace of life positively sepulchral.

"There's no need for you to pay or receive calls now that your condition is more advanced," said Edward firmly after our arrival. "You must take every opportunity to lead a quiet secluded life."

"Just like a nun!" I exclaimed, smiling to hide my despair. "Dearest, I would so like to meet more of your friends. Couldn't we give just a tiny dinner party or two?"

So there I was again, thrust among the elderly English, who exuded their familiar glacial politeness, but this time I had no one to blame but myself. Edward was insistent in keeping our social activities to a minimum, and while he was out all day hunting and Patrick was closeted with his new tutor, I occupied myself by writing long letters to America and trying not to feel too homesick for New York.

It was not that I disliked Woodhammer, which was a mellow, beautiful house with tall chimneys and a formal Elizabethan garden. It was not even that I disliked England. The countryside around Woodhammer was filled with the quaintest little homes and villages. The village cottages had thatched roofs, and the churches, built of gray stone, were all hundreds of years old. Warwick too was a striking town, with whole streets of half-timbered houses and a castle so exactly like an illustration in a book of fairytales that at first I could hardly believe it was real. The English countryside was certainly good to look at and easy to admire, but it was, just as everyone says, very misty and damp, and the English for some reason are quite unable to heat their houses properly. I spent most of my leisure hours at All the servants thought I was eccentric, but fortunately pregnant women can be excused all manner of extraordinary behavior. Woodhammer hunched over a fire beneath three thick woolen shawls.

Another aspect of life at Woodhammer that annoyed me was the food. There was no variety of vegetables, only a nauseatingly high incidence of suets, pastries and potatoes. Once I even saw suet pudding, pastry and jammed potatoes all together on the same plate—touching one another. But when I tried to explain my repulsion to the servants they looked totally baffled.

This was not the first time I had been aware of the fundamental difficulty in communicating with the English. Communication should have been so easy since we were all supposed to speak the same language, yet frequently I could not understand a word they said, and even more frequently they would listen to me with that polite glazed expression which meant they understood me no better than I understood them. Now after many years I have adjusted my vocabulary so that I use few American words, but when I first arrived in England I must have been constantly using phrases which had either never been used in England or else had fallen into disuse at least a hundred years before.

However, despite these trials I eventually began to feel the English were becoming familiar to me. I knew by this time, for instance, that Edward's friends would not talk about the same subjects as Francis' friends would talk about in New York. New Yorkers are always talking about Europe. It is Europe this, that and the other. European fashions are awaited with bated breath, European news is discussed with great solemnity, European art and drama are imported to become the talk of cultural circles. Nobody mentions the word "Europe" in England; England is not considered part of Europe, and the other European countries are referred to (pityingly) as "the Continent," a large and of course inferior land mass somewhere to the east of the White Cliffs of Dover. English people go to the Continent to travel, to observe and occasionally to fight the French. Lesser English people go there to trade, but that is all done very tastefully, and few people speak of it. The English on the whole do not talk of the Continent. They talk of empire, scientific progress and politics. Unlike America, where no one of any breeding meddles in the political arena, politics in England is regarded as an exquisitely civilized game for the upper classes, not quite as jolly as fox hunting but affording all the pleasures of a smart select club while also offering the opportunity to Do One's Duty to the Masses. The English regard themselves as very, very civilized, possibly the most civilized race that God has ever been sensible enough to put in charge of the rest of the world, and the sooner a foreigner agrees to acknowledge the truth of this the sooner he will be accepted by English society.

"How well you've settled down here!" said Edward to me kindly as we prepared for Christmas. "Don't think I've been unaware of all the difficulties you've encountered."

But despite his awareness we were nearing the brink of another crisis, and my difficulties were by no means at an end.

Christmas is an emotional time for an immigrant. On the whole I had managed to overcome my periodic bouts of homesickness with tolerable success, but as the December days slipped past I was consumed with a longing to see my old home resplendent in snow and icicles. I was still recovering from the English ignorance of Thanksgiving, our unofficial but widely celebrated family festival at the end of November, and when my family's presents and Christmas letters arrived it was almost more than I could bear.

Francis wrote me a long affectionate letter, and I shed so many tears over it that in the end I had smudged every line of his handsome handwriting. Blanche wrote to me, Amelia wrote to me (I never thought I would ever be touched to receive a letter from Amelia), my nephew Charles wrote to me and even my niece Sarah wrote to me. Sarah, ten years old and the apple of Francis' eye, did not care to write letters, but she wrote two whole pages about all the parties to which she had been invited and all the dresses she intended to wear, and I found myself weeping all over again. Fond as I was of Charles, I was fonder still of Sarah—but that was because she was so like her father.

Blanche told me who had married or separated, Amelia told me which families had gone bankrupt and Francis told me how much money he was making. It was all deliciously un-English, and I caught a cherished glimpse of the brash tapestry of New York so far removed from dull, demure, decorous Woodhammer Hall.

"Does Francis mention the political situation?" asked Edward, realizing that I was yearning to talk about my family, and I said in a great rush to keep the tears at bay, "No, not much, except that he's afraid Lincoln might win the election, and he's shuffling his investments around just in case the market slumps. He doesn't like to think what will happen if there's a war. Everyone's buying clothes in case the price of cotton goes sky-high, and everyone's giving parties in case the worst happens, and some neighbors of ours gave a fancy-dress ball where champagne ran from a solid-gold cupid fountain in the lobby."

"Dear me," said Edward, "I hope they contrived to chill the champagne."

No husband could have been kinder to me than Edward during those difficult days, and I was just thinking for the hundredth time that a happy marriage made even the worst variety of homesickness endurable, when two important items of news from abroad reached Woodhammer. The first was that Lincoln had won the presidential election, and the second (of far more importance to me in my present state) was that Edward's daughter Katherine, prostrated by the sudden death of her husband, had begged Edward to leave immediately for St. Petersburg to bring her home.

"You can't go!" I cried. "The baby—I couldn't travel with you . . . Christmas . . . you'd never be back in time . . ." To my shame I burst into floods of tears. I was beginning to suspect that pregnancy was more than partly responsible for my weepiness those days, for, as I have already mentioned, I am not usually the sort of female who needs only the slightest excuse to burst into tears.

"I'm behaving abominably," I said. "I know I am, but I can't help it. I'm sorry for Katherine, but I don't want you to go."

"I don't want to go either," he said. "Do you think I would spend Christmas away from you if I could possibly help it? But Katherine's my daughter. She's been bereaved; she's ill and asking for my help. I have a duty to her."

"What about your duty to me?" I burst out, and rushed from the room before he should mistake my panic for anger and lose his temper. In the bedroom I again hid behind the curtains of the four-poster and prepared to weep myself into a state of exhaustion, but before I could shed a tear I felt a small tremor in the farthest recesses of my body. I sat up in great excitement. Presently the baby fluttered again, and after that I became much less cowardly and even moderately brave. When Edward appeared a moment later to console me I rushed into his arms and once more tried to apologize.

"I shan't be so alone after all," I said, explaining what had happened, and so a quarrel was averted, and the next day he departed reluctantly for St. Petersburg. I think even then he might have changed his mind at the last moment, but I was so determined to make amends for my childish behavior that I almost pushed him out of the front door when the time came for us to say goodbye. But afterward as I stood on the porch steps and watched the carriage roll away down the drive I did feel very low in spirits and might have felt lower still if Patrick had not slipped his hand affectionately into mine.

"I shall look after you until Papa comes back," he said, giving my fingers a reassuring squeeze. "We'll have a lovely Christmas together, you'll see."

He really was the most delightful boy.

Chapter Two

1

Patrick's tutor, an elderly, desiccated little man called Mr. Bull, had agreed to forgo his Christmas holiday that year in order to supervise Patrick during Edward's absence. But Edward had barely been gone an hour before Patrick produced a drawing which showed Mr. Bull leering at an insouciant cow and hung the picture from the dining-room chandelier for all the servants to view.

"That was a very silly thing to do," I said sternly when he re-appeared some hours later after playing truant from his lessons. "Mr. Bull was furious, and he's going to complain to your father."

"Papa's used to my tutors complaining," said Patrick irrepressibly. He yawned. "I hate tutors. My friend Derry Stranahan says people become tutors only when they can't become anything else."

As a punishment Patrick was set a long translation from Caesar's *De Bello Civili,* but after a morning's labor he emerged only with six clever sketches of Julius Caesar fighting Gnaeus Pompey. Caesar was tall and fair-haired like Patrick, while Pompey bore a most unfortunate resemblance to Mr. Bull.

"Do you *want* to get into trouble with your father, Patrick?" I asked, puzzled.

"No, but I think Latin is such an awful waste of time. My friend Derry Stranahan says it's morbid to keep a dead language alive long after it should have been allowed to die a dignified natural death. Would you like to see some of my other drawings?"

He was certainly clever with a pencil. I did not think his watercolors were exceptional—Blanche painted a better watercolor than he did—but he did draw well. More remarkable than any picture, however, were the woodcarvings he showed me. He carved birds and animals. Sometimes they were single carvings and sometimes they were part of a motif on a panel of wood. He worked in a tiny room in the attics where the sawdust lay thick upon the floor, and although his early work was crude he had clearly improved with practice. There was a delightful study of a cat with kittens and another of a setter with a pheasant between his teeth.

"You're very clever," I said truthfully, trying to imagine what Edward thought of his son's artistic inclinations.

"It's easy to be clever at something you like to do," said Patrick. "I'm very stupid at things I don't like." He smiled at me shyly. "Do you really like my carvings?"

"Very much." Instinct made me refrain from asking him directly what his father thought of them. "Have you shown your carvings to anyone else?"

"No, because Papa disapproves. He thinks it's like carpentry, and carpentry is for artisans."

"Does he know about your room up here?"

"Oh yes, but he doesn't take any notice so long as no one else knows about it. As a matter of fact Papa never takes any notice of something that doesn't interest him. My friend Derry Stranahan says—"

"You talk a considerable lot about Mr. Derry Stranahan, don't you?" I said with a smile.

"Ain't a man entitled to talk about his best friend now and then? Here, Cousin Marguerite, have the cat and kittens as a Christmas present from me."

"I'd love to," I said, "but I really mustn't if Edward doesn't strictly approve of your woodcarving. It wouldn't be right."

He was disappointed, so to divert him I suggested we go for a walk to the village. After that we fell into the habit of taking a daily walk together, and presently he asked if I would go riding with him.

"Oh, I couldn't do that!" I said, surprised. "It wouldn't be at all advisable in my condition."

"What condition?" he said, naïve as a boy half his age, and then blushed to the roots of his hair.

"You mean Edward didn't tell you?" I asked, astonished.

Speechless, he shook his head, and his embarrassment was so infectious that I too found myself without a word to say. We were walking back from the village on one of those mild misty mornings so common in an English winter, and ahead of us across the park we could see the tall chimneys of the hall.

"Well," I said at last, obscurely aware that I should defend Edward, "I've no doubt it's not proper to talk of such things so far in advance, but since I've mentioned it the baby's coming in April and he's to be called Thomas. But please keep it a secret, because I shouldn't like your father to be offended by any impropriety."

"No," he said earnestly. "Of course not."

He was still so acutely embarrassed that I found it impossible to talk of something else.

"I do hope you don't mind having another brother," I said. "I realize it must be tiresome for you in some ways, but think how nice it will be for Thomas to have a brother so many years his senior. My brother Francis is eighteen years older than I am, so I can speak from experience."

"Oh yes," said Patrick. "Quite. Papa is very pleased, I dare say."

"Fairly pleased, I think," I said in the most casual voice I could muster and changed the subject as fast as a juggler throwing a new set of plates in the air. "Patrick, tell me about your friend Mr. Stranahan. He does sound so vastly entertaining. Is there really no hope of him visiting us during these three years he's spending at the University of Frankfurt?"

"None at all," said Patrick, instantly diverted. "He got into an awful scrape in Ireland, you know, and Papa sent him to Frankfurt more for a punishment than for an education."

"But what did he do? I've never quite liked to ask before."

But Patrick was more than willing to amend Edward's reticence on the subject. Apparently, I learned, Mr. Stranahan had been falsely accused of misconduct by a drunken Irish husband who had tried to kill both him and the poor innocent woman involved.

"How dreadful!" I cried, but I found the gossip fascinating. The more vulgar side of my nature has always savored any scandal resulting from what the novelists call "unbridled passions." "Poor Mr. Stranahan!"

"Yes, wasn't it a shame! And it wasn't his fault a bit, but Papa will never admit that now. Unless . . . I say, Cousin Marguerite, do you think you could say a word to Papa about it when he comes home? I've tried, but he won't listen to me."

"I doubt if he'd listen to me either."

"Oh yes he would! If you could just ask him if Derry could come home for a holiday—"

"Well, I might," I said, suddenly seeing an unexpected opportunity, "but I'll do it only if you behave with Mr. Bull, Patrick, and stop driving the poor man mad by drawing pictures of him falling in love with a cow."

Patrick shouted with laughter and leaped in the air with joy. "Agreed!" he cried. "Agreed, agreed, agreed!" And he danced ahead of me along the path like some gorgeous golden puppy who has just been promised the juiciest and most succulent of bones.

II

Christmas came. We went to church in the morning, and afterward I rested before we ate dinner at three. In the evening there was no time to grow mournful thinking of Edward far away in St. Petersburg. We played backgammon together and cribbage, and presently when Patrick dressed up for one-man charades we both laughed at his foolish antics until we were too weak to laugh any more. Finally we decided it was time for a musical interlude, so I attacked the piano (I am a terrible pianist) and Patrick launched into song, but since his singing was no better than my strumming we made the most appalling racket together.

"I used to be able to sing," said Patrick regretfully. "I was a soprano. But now that my voice has changed I'm not sure what I am any more."

"You'll have a nice baritone when your voice is completely broken."

"It *is* completely broken!" he said, affronted, and we started to giggle again like two children in the schoolroom. I had not been so amused for months, and after spending so long dreading Christmas it was an enormous relief to feel so lighthearted. After supper we went to the servants' hall to watch the festivities, and Patrick introduced me to the young men and woman who had been the companions of his childhood. One of them was a maid in the still-room, one was a groom, one was the knife boy and the last, the cook's daughter, had done so well that she was now a parlor maid. Everyone was very merry and civil, and when we left at last I said to Patrick with a sigh, "It's really very pleasant here at Woodhammer, I must declare, although I admit I missed city life dreadfully at first."

"I like Woodhammer far better than London," he said. "I was born and brought up here, so it's home."

"You like it better than Cashelmara?"

"Cashelmara!" He grimaced. "Cashelmara's the end of the world." He seized my hand, slipped an arm around my waist and whirled me in a silent waltz around the great hall to the staircase.

"Patrick! Not so fast!" I shrieked, but when he laughed I laughed too, and we spun on through the shadows together. "Stop!" I gasped at last. "I must sit down!" So we sat on the settle before the enormous hearth, and suddenly I had a great longing for Edward's arms around me, for his long strong body pressing against mine. I sat very still, staring at the embers of the fire while Patrick talked endlessly about why he loved Woodhammer, and when I could listen to him again I heard him telling me in a hushed dreamy voice that the oak staircase had been carved by Grinling Gibbons.

"Yes, it's beautiful, isn't it?" said my voice, and I could see Edward in him so clearly that I wanted to reach out and grasp the elusive likeness, but the next moment it was gone and he was saying with boyish naïveté, "May I kiss you under the mistletoe before you go up to bed?" And he looked so handsome, his hair that rich dull shade of gold and his eyes bluer than any eyes I had ever seen. I had never known any young man who looked quite as handsome to me as he looked then.

"Oh, I don't believe in kisses under the mistletoe," I said. "Such a heathen custom. Good night, Patrick. Thank you for a lovely Christmas."

I left, my feet carrying me without faltering all the way to my room, but when I slipped into bed later I lay awake in the darkness for a long time. I felt I must be very gross and corrupt. Pregnant women were not supposed to yearn for passion during their months of waiting, but that night I longed for Edward as passionately as I had longed for him on our honeymoon, and deep within me was a core of anger that he should have left me alone for so long.

III

He came back two weeks later. He looked very tall—I always forgot how tall he was—and very handsome, and I loved him better than anyone in the world. All I wanted then was to take him to our room and tell him how much I had missed him, but of course this had to be postponed, for with Edward, swathed in black crepe, her pale, exquisite face hidden by the most hideous of veils, was his bereaved daughter Katherine.

"How do you do, Cousin Katherine," I said, determined to behave well despite the fact that she had never answered the friendly letter I had written to her after my marriage. "I was truly sorry to hear of your bereavement. Pray accept my deepest sympathies."

"Thank you, Cousin Marguerite." She was very formal and as cold as a winter wind from Canada. After she had thanked me there was an awkward pause before Edward suggested she might like to retire to her room before tea, and when she consented I was obliged to escort her upstairs.

"I'm glad you were well enough to travel," I said tentatively. "No doubt your health will greatly improve now that you're home again."

"Yes," said Katherine.

"I hope your journey wasn't too difficult."

"No."

"You must have been so relieved when your father arrived."

"Yes."

I was amazed not only by her monosyllabic woodenness but by her complete lack of gratitude. I wondered if it had ever occurred to her how much I had minded being deprived of Edward's company and how gravely he himself had been inconvenienced. Deciding I could dislike her all too easily, I tried to make allowances for her by reminding myself of her bereavement.

In her room she took off her veil, and I saw that she was indeed lovely. She was dark. Her eyes were fringed with long black curling lashes, and her skin seemed translucent in contrast. She looked younger too without the veil, and I remembered she was only two years older than I was.

A maid arrived with hot water. Katherine's own maid was already beginning to unpack.

"Is there anything else I can provide?" I inquired politely, and when she shook her head I hurried to rejoin Edward for our long-awaited private reunion.

We spent much time telling each other what a lonely, miserable Christmas it had been (I was very careful to understate how much I had enjoyed Patrick's company), and later after he had asked about Thomas he talked of his long journey across Europe to the icy splendor of St. Petersburg. He had visited Russia years before with Eleanor, and one or two of his innumerable acquaintances were still attached to the embassy there. Patiently I listened to his comparison of the Russia of yesterday with the Russia of today; eagerly I drank in his conclusions that not only had nothing changed but that nothing ever would change there, and all the time I was thinking hungrily how handsome he looked and how peculiarly unsuited I was to a celibate life.

"But what about your doctor's advice?" he said, troubled when the last candle had been extinguished and my skin felt as if it might scorch the sheets.

"Oh, I quite forgot to tell you," I said, praying hard that God might forgive me for lying. "Dr. Ives said it would be quite safe after the fifth month. It's the latest medical thought on pregnancy."

"What a splendid thing scientific progress is!" said Edward with that wry humor I loved so much, and after that I no longer had to worry about the torments of chastity.

The next morning I was overcome with guilty terror in case I had hurt the baby, but Thomas seemed as active as ever, and I soon decided that it was a mistake to believe every word the doctors said. What did doctors know anyway? Besides, it was quite true that they were always changing their minds about the best way to treat their patients.

Fortunately I was soon diverted from my guilty conscience, for on the morning after Edward's return Mr. Bull requested an audience with his employer, and I knew he intended to give Patrick a bad report.

"Edward," I said as he finished his second cup of tea and prepared to rise from the breakfast table, "might I have a word with you alone before you go to the library to see Mr. Bull?"

"Of course." He dismissed the footmen and smiled at me. "What is it?"

"It's about Patrick. Edward, he was a little naughty after you left, but I persuaded him to behave better, and since then his conduct has been exemplary. I merely wanted you to know that before you interviewed Mr. Bull."

"I see," he said. A neutral expression had crept into his eyes, but I decided to ignore it.

"Oh, and, Edward, while we're discussing Patrick, I've just remembered something else I wanted to ask you!" I said brightly. "Dearest, Patrick does so miss his friend Mr. Stranahan. I do realize that Mr. Stranahan's education shouldn't be interrupted, but might he not come home for a little vacation soon? Patrick would be so pleased, and I myself would be delighted to receive him."

"So that," said Edward, needle-sharp, "was the condition Patrick made for his reformed behavior."

"Well . . ."

"The answer to your request is no. Derry misbehaved himself severely, and I have forbidden him my house for three years not only to punish him but to separate him from Patrick. I see absolutely no reason to revoke that decision, nor do I intend to do so."

"I see," I said. In the face of such a dogmatic assertion of authority there seemed little else to say. At least, I thought, I could tell Patrick that I tried.

"And, Marguerite, I would be obliged if in future you would refrain from taking sides in matters that are of no concern to you."

"There was no question of taking sides," I said unhappily.

"No?" He gave me a cool, hard look. "I'm glad to hear it. It would have put our relationship on an awkward footing, and I fail to see why either of us should be needlessly distressed. So please—no more misguided intercessions on Patrick's behalf. Concern yourself solely with me and with your child."

"Yes," I said. "Of course. But I can't completely cut myself off from my stepchildren."

"Nor would I wish it. But to be a stepmother is difficult at the best of times, and to be a stepmother of grown children when one is only eighteen years old is a trial indeed. It would lessen your difficulties if you stayed in the background as much as possible whenever controversies arise."

"Very well," I said. "If you wish." And as I did my best to accept his advice I could not help but think it would suit me very well to be detached toward Katherine even if I found it hard to be detached toward Patrick.

I did think Katherine was very tedious. While we remained at Woodhammer it took little skill to avoid her, but early in the new year we returned to London, and there my troubles began in earnest. It is easy to avoid someone in a mansion the size of Woodhammer Hall but a very different matter to avoid that someone in a compact townhouse. Katherine mooched around behind her widow's weeds like a bad actress in a Drury Lane melodrama, and by the beginning of February I was already wondering how much longer I could bear her dreary presence in my house.

The straw that finally broke the camel's back came when Edward decided it was necessary for him to make one of his lightning visits to Cashelmara. There was no question of my going, but since Edward was taking Patrick with him for a lesson in estate management, I did hope that Katherine would decide to accompany them.

But Katherine had other ideas.

"Crossing the Irish Sea in February would be detestable," she said, and when I suggested she might like to see her sister Annabel, who lived in the Cashelmara dower house, she replied haughtily that she had had nothing to say to her sister since Annabel's unfortunate second marriage.

"I see," I said with a sinking heart. "So you'll stay here."

She gave me a cold look. "If that is so objectionable to you," she said after a small, deadly pause, "I can make arrangements to stay in Kent with my husband's parents."

"Oh no, no, no!" I exclaimed guiltily, thinking what a splendid idea this was. "Of course you mustn't leave us, Katherine!"

"Why not? It's perfectly obvious that you wish to be rid of me."

That gave me a nasty jolt. Was I really so bad at concealing my feelings? I made a rapid survey of my past conduct and thought not. "I absolutely deny . . ." I began with spirit but was interrupted.

"Besides," said Katherine, "you evidently fail to realize that I find our joint presence under one roof just as unendurable as you do. Christian charity alone prompts me to pity, not to condemn, you for being debased enough to permit yourself any intimacy whatsoever with a man my father's age, but nevertheless I find your condition quite repulsive. Indeed I can hardly look at you without feeling faint with nausea."

Anyone who has ever suffered from violent jealousy can hardly fail to recognize the symptoms in others. I said in a surprised, meek little voice, "You're jealous!"—not an intelligent remark, I do admit, but I was still reeling from her furious onslaught and was at first too stunned to shriek abuse at her in return.

"Jealous!" she exclaimed, drawing herself up to her full height and giving me her most hoity-toity look.

"Jealous!" I hurled back at her, beginning to recover. "You're jealous of my place in your father's affections!"

"What a disgusting slander!" She spoke with exquisite precision; her face might have been carved out of stone. "That's quite untrue. I have no idea what place you hold in my father's affections, but I know very well what place I hold there. I'm his favorite daughter. I always was. Oh, I know Nell was the one he treated as a companion, but that was only because she was so much older than us and he came to rely on her when Mama was ill. But even Nell married beneath her—even Nell disappointed him in the end! But I never did. I was the one who made the brilliant match. He told me on my wedding day how proud he was of me, and that made everything worthwhile, those horrible two years of marriage, those dreadful long winters in St. Petersburg. Oh, it would be impossible for someone as vulgar as you to understand how miserable I've been! But throughout it all my place in Papa's affections has remained unchanged. Wasn't that proved when he came all the way to St. Petersburg to bring me home? I knew he would come. I'm his favorite daughter, you see, and there's nothing whatsoever you can do about it."

This was more than I could endure. She was insufferable.

"And I'm his wife!" I shouted. "And there's nothing you can do about that either, you cold, selfish, beastly creature! How dare you drag him all the way to St. Petersburg just to prove to yourself that he would come if you moaned loudly enough for help! How dare you deprive us of our first Christmas together! If you think he adores you so much you should have heard how cross he was at having to journey all the way across Europe in order to do what he at least merely regarded as a tedious duty!"

"You wicked, unprincipled little liar—"

"How dare you call me that!"

"And how dare you say Papa doesn't love me!" screamed Katherine, her stony façade crumbling into a dozen heartbroken lines, and she ran sobbing hysterically from the room.

I was so surprised to learn that she was capable of shedding tears that for a moment I stood motionless, staring after her. But when my anger began to cool I tried to weigh the situation, much as I would have calculated a move at chess. Either I could wash my hands of her and hope she left the house as soon as possible, or I could make some attempt to convince her that I was not the debased monster she thought I was. My first instinct was to begin washing my hands, but then it occurred to me that perhaps I had been a little unkind in revealing Edward's reluctance to go to her rescue. There was no doubt how miserable I would have felt if after Francis had rescued me from some unhappy situation I had learned that he had actually longed to remain behind in New York with Blanche.

I gave Katherine half an hour to recover her composure, and then I tapped on her bedroom door.

"Katherine," I said when we were face to face again, "I think we've both been silly. You've been silly in seeing my marriage to your father as disgusting when in fact it's really rather romantic, and I've been even sillier in avoiding you all these weeks when ever since my marriage I've been longing for a companion of my own age. We may have nothing in common and any attempt at friendship may fail dismally, but I would at least like to try to be friends. Could we not start again and treat each other with less prejudice and more—" I groped for inspirational words and cunningly plucked a favorite phrase from her own repertoire—"more Christian charity?"

Just as a donkey will step forward to reach a carrot, so Katherine was unable to resist the temptation to display virtue. "I'm sure no one is more willing than I to behave in a Christian fashion," she said grandly after recovering from her astonishment; but remembering her jealousy, she added, "I'm not surprised to hear you have missed the companionship of people of your own age, but you should have thought of that before you married Papa."

"Oh, I know," I said earnestly, wondering how far my patience would extend despite all my good intentions. "I know. But how I envy you, Katherine! Even though you've been away for two years you must know so many girls of our age in London!"

"I do indeed have innumerable acquaintances of that sort," said Katherine, still very grand, "but I am, of course, too low in spirits to pay calls at present."

"And my condition is too far advanced. But perhaps later, in the spring . . ."

"I dare say I might consider leaving a card or two in June," said Katherine. "You might accompany me if you wished."

"Oh, I should so like that!" I said at once. "Thank you very much, Katherine."

So the first cordial overtures were made between us, and by the time Edward returned from Cashelmara, Katherine and I had become civil to each other. We were still far from being bosom friends, but we did take strolls around the garden together after breakfast, and in the evening when we had exchanged comments on our favorite fashion magazine she would even offer to play the piano for me. She played beautifully. In fact she was one of those girls who seem to excel in everything they try. The world calls such behavior accomplished, but I merely call it maddening.

"Katherine sews so exquisitely," I said to Edward. "You should see her embroidery! And she plays the piano even better than

Blanche does, and as for her sketches . . ." I was going to say that her sketches were as gifted as Patrick's but thought better of it.

"It's very good of you to take so much trouble with Katherine," said Edward gratefully. "I was afraid you might find her very dull."

There was a slight pause before I said, "Katherine's not dull. Just a little shy."

"Shy! She always seems perfectly poised to me—but what a pity it is she's so mechanical and stiff! Eleanor always used to say Katherine was exactly like a little wax doll."

There was another longer pause. "Oh?" I said at last. "A wax doll? Yes, that does tell me something about Katherine, but it tells me a great deal more about Eleanor." I stood up slowly and wandered over to the drawing-room window to look out upon the square. I always moved slowly now because I was such an awkward shape. Outside the trees were bare and snow was falling from a leaden sky.

"Parents often make rash remarks when their children exasperate them," said Edward lightly, giving me a kiss that at once made me forget Katherine. "It's hard work being a parent. But you'll find that out for yourself soon enough."

"I guess I will," I said, leaning against him with a huge sigh, "if Thomas ever decides to arrive. Do you realize that I'm beginning to believe not only that I've always been this shape but that I always will be?"

Three weeks later Thomas entered the world.

IV

Thomas was small, only six pounds, but very active. He had no hair, bright blue eyes and a pouting mouth. Chaucer would have described his complexion as choleric. I thought the infant was quite the finest specimen I had ever seen, and within a second after I had set eyes on him I was captivated.

"Look how lovely he is!" I said proudly to Edward, and as the baby squalled I added, marveling, "See how strongly he cries!"

"Admirably energetic," said Edward gravely, but he was smiling, and when he kissed me I was sure no woman could have been happier than I was then.

The birth had been easy, so my recovery was rapid. Indeed I wanted to get well rapidly for reasons which, when considered in the light of my distaste for celibacy, were logical enough, but when at the end of May Dr. Ives said I might once again live a normal life I found it took longer than I thought to return to normality. The early part of summer was not a comfortable time either for Edward or for me, but eventually matters began to improve, and when Parliament rose at last Edward decided it was time for me to make my long-delayed first visit to Cashelmara.

"How exciting!" I said, genuinely intrigued to see the place he regarded as home. "I can't wait to visit Ireland at last!"

"I've been looking forward to taking you there for so long," he said, delighted by my enthusiasm. "We can go there alone, just you and I, and stay for a couple of months. I'll send Fielding off immediately to make the travel arrangements."

"What about Thomas?"

"Oh, Ireland wouldn't be healthy for an infant his age. Nanny and Nurse can take him to Woodhammer, and we can join him there in October."

"How difficult!" I said. "I'm so sorry, dearest, but that really wouldn't suit me at all. Do you think we could possibly come to some other arrangement?"

He looked blank. "Eleanor always thought it was better to leave the younger children in England."

"But I'm not Eleanor," I said, "am I?"

"I'm well aware of that," he said quickly, realizing too late that he had made a mistake. "But having seen my favorite child die in Ireland—"

"Yes, that must have been a dreadful experience but as far as illness goes I'm something of a fatalist. It's quite true that Thomas could become ill in Ireland, but he could equally well become ill at Woodhammer Hall—and then how would I feel if I were three days' journey away from him at Cashelmara?"

"You're implying that Eleanor—"

"No, dearest, I'm not implying anything. Please don't think I'm criticizing Eleanor. I'm simply pointing out that I'm different from her, that's all. And please don't think either that I couldn't bear to be parted from Thomas for a single day. I'd love to go alone with you to Ireland and have a second honeymoon, but let's agree to part from Thomas for two weeks, not two months. Nanny and Nurse can bring him to Cashelmara to join us."

"Then the other children must join us too," he said, instinctively trying to be fair.

"Of course!" I said. "Why not? But we'll have our two weeks alone together first."

130

"You'll have your cake and eat it, you mean!" he said, laughing, and when I saw he was finally in agreement with me I could only heave a vast sigh of relief that a marital quarrel had been averted before it had begun.

V

Patrick had said that Cashelmara was the end of the world—but what a stupendous ending it was, with those great mountains ripped from the black earth and flung in a jagged circle around the ragged edges of the lake! When the carriage reached the top of the pass high above the valley and I could look down at last upon Cashelmara I was dazzled by such flawless beauty but at the same time intimidated by it. I had never seen such scenery before. Lakes and valleys—yes, New York State is full of them, but it is also full of trees, and here in Connaught the landscape was so bare that the soft edges and gentle lines I had always associated with rural landscapes did not exist. To me, a city dweller, there was something frightening about those great bare mountains towering above us like slumbering animals, the vast lonely stretches of bog and moorland, the shifting clouds forming and reforming as if manipulated by a hidden hand in that unending sky.

"That mountain over there is called Devilsmother," Edward was saying. "It's the source of many local legends. And then going from west to east you can see Knocklaur, Benwee, Laynabricka, Skeltia . . ." He talked of the mountains as if they were people. "And behind them, although one can't see it from this angle, is Maumtrasna, the tallest of them all. The county line runs along the mountain tops, and over there is Mayo. The local name for this area is the Joyce country after the tribe of that name. Connemara, the area we've seen since leaving Oughterard, overlaps with the Joyce country, yet is considered separate from it."

Connemara, Oughterard, Mayo—my head was ringing with Irish names. It was my third day in Ireland. On the first we had arrived in Dublin and spent the night as guests of the Lord Lieutenant at Dublin Castle. The next day a train had taken us across the country to the luxurious Railway Hotel at Galway, and this morning we had left Galway in a hired carriage for the forty-mile journey to the door of Edward's home. So by this time I had spent several hours staring at Ireland, from the grandeur of Dublin Castle to the simplicity of a peasant's cabin, and the more I saw the more I realized that certain previous ideas of mine had been ill-founded.

One hears a great deal about Ireland in New York. The city swarms with Irish-Americans who are only too pleased to talk about Ireland whenever they have the opportunity, and like many other families of standing we had had our Bridget in the kitchens and our Kitty in the scullery, both loud in singing the praises of their native land. I had heard of the innumerable shades of green and the darling little thatched cabins and the dear little leprechauns dancing over the bog. But nothing I had heard had prepared me for the poverty, the filth, the beggars, the mud huts and that ruined, blasted countryside which looked as if it had been ravaged by some catastrophic war. The farther west we traveled the worse it became, until suddenly the great famine of the Forties was not just a legend of another decade but an evil that still lingered amidst the splendor of that alien, mystical land.

"Edward," I said, remembering the darker Irish-American memories of Ireland, yet anxious to be tactful to him, "I know you're a good landlord and have done everything in your power for Ireland, but why can't other English landlords follow your example?"

"There are a great many good landlords," said Edward. "One simply hears more about the bad ones, that's all."

"But if there are numerous good landlords, why is Ireland in such a sad and impoverished condition? I mean . . . well, why do the English find it necessary to—to keep Ireland? Might not the Irish be better off if they governed themselves?"

"My dear," said Edward, "if you were living in luxury in a fine house and you found a beggar in residence on your front doorstep, what would you do? Would you ignore him with the excuse that it is his right as an individual to fend for himself without assistance, or would you take him into your house and try to feed him and alleviate his suffering?"

"Well . . ."

"We have a moral duty to Ireland," said Edward strongly. "We have a duty to make amends for past wrongs and a duty to improve present conditions. It's useless for the Irish secret societies to talk of independence. The plain fact of the matter is that without England's assistance the Irish would all starve and Ireland would be a wilderness."

"But, Edward," I said, "I realize, of course, that I'm just an ignorant foreigner, but haven't the Irish already starved and isn't Ireland—this part of Ireland—already little better than a wilderness?"

"Contrary to popular Irish opinion, England did a great deal to help Ireland during the famine, though I agree it wasn't enough. We have to find the solution for these periodic famines, and the solution will never be found while the peasant population exists entirely on a vulnerable source of food such as the potato. If they can be given an incentive to do more with their land than plant a row of potatoes . . ." And he began to talk about land reform. ". . . Give the peasants more of a stake in their land. . . . at present they have no incentive to improve it. . . . after the famine I experimented—gave my best tenant a leasehold for fifty years. . . . amazing the difference in his outlook once he had security of tenure, but leaseholds of that nature are almost unknown in Ireland—not so profitable immediately to the landlord, but in the long run . . ."

It was as he talked that I glimpsed the most hidden reason for his dedication to Cashelmara. It was because it was a challenge. I could picture him so well in his younger days, seeking fresh worlds to conquer, bored by problems that never taxed his abilities to the limit, and then being presented with his estate after the famine, ruined, ravaged and seemingly beyond redemption.

Meanwhile we had left the road, and the carriage had passed through a gateway up a long, winding wooded drive.

"And this," Edward said at last, shining-eyed, "is my home."

It was an old-fashioned place, plain to the point of starkness, but if one likes yesterday's architecture I suppose it was all very fine. Personally I like a touch of Gothic, but my tastes in such things have always been very modern.

"White houses are always so elegant," I said, wanting to be truthful as well as complimentary, but I could not help but notice how the elegance was blurred by the weeds in the drive and the chipped stone steps. I thought of Woodhammer, immaculately preserved and well kept, and it seemed to me that the two houses personified the difference between England and Ireland, the one rich and comfortable, the other scarred by past tragedy and neglect. "Is there a nice garden behind the house?" I said for lack of anything else to say.

"Oh, the Irish don't believe in gardens," said Edward happily. "There's a lawn, and in my father's day there were several shrubberies, but I plowed them up to grow vegetables. One must use every available square inch of arable land in Ireland, you know."

I wondered how I could have thought of him as an Englishman. No Englishman would ever have plowed up a shrubbery.

"I'm sure you'll soon feel quite at home here," he said, but I had never in my life felt such a foreigner, and England in retrospect began to seem as cozily familiar as America.

However, when one is nineteen one is very adaptable, and I was determined to find Cashelmara a pleasant place to visit even while I privately thanked God I did not have to live there twelve months a year. My good intentions were helped by the servants, who were all very friendly. The majority of them spoke little English so that true communication was impossible (I quickly abandoned any attempt to explain the words "dusty" and "dirt" to the housemaids), but they smiled so readily and appeared so full of good will that I forgave them everything except the warming pan which leaked in my bed. But even then Hayes the butler explained the leak with such imaginative zeal that I was charmed into keeping my temper. I had long conversations with Hayes and with his wife, who acted as housekeeper, not only because they were the only people in the house who spoke comprehensible English but because they continually said how much they admired my American accent. After my months among the English, who had always been kind enough not to refer to my deficiencies of speech, such compliments were nectar to me.

Presently Edward's nephew George, a pompous little man, rode over from his house at Letterturk, and after that one or two other squires called, Mr. Plunket of Aasleagh, Mr. Knox of Clonbur and Mr. Courtney of Leenane. Their wives, elderly ladies clad in the fashions of ten years before, were so interested to meet me that I began to believe my arrival was the most exciting event to have overtaken them in a decade, and when we repaid the calls I saw still more of Ireland, from George's house at Letterturk on the reed-fringed shores of Lough Mask to the famous coaching inn at Leenane that faced the fjordlike waters of Killary Harbour.

"Should I visit the poor?" I inquired of Edward two weeks after our arrival. He had been busy touring the estate with his agent MacGowan, and I had become bored of reading, toying with the chessboard or taking solitary walks to the little golden beach on the western edge of the lough as I waited for Thomas to arrive from England.

Edward was pleased. "Well, there are indeed one or two better-kept cabins that you could visit if you wished, and it would certainly be a popular gesture among the tenants if you did pay a visit to the chief spokesmen in the valley."

"Who would they be?"

"Sean Denis Joyce and—but I think I've told you about young Maxwell Drummond."

The history of the local factions was unbelievably complicated, but Edward explained to me that Mr. Drummond, whom he wished to send to Agricultural College, was related through his mother to the O'Malley clan and that the O'Malleys and the Joyces were the two most numerous families in the valley.

Mr. Drummond lived with two maiden aunts in a neat white-washed cabin almost big enough to be called a farmhouse. There was a potato patch behind the house, a courtyard strewn with chickens and piglets to one side and a manure heap planted blandly outside the front door. To my surprise the manure did not smell. It was mixed with soil from the bog, and this soil contained a chemical, so Edward told me, that negated the natural odor. Inside the cabin was not particularly clean (I can still remember the hen roosting in a bucket that hung on the wall), but it was immaculately tidy. To my astonishment I even saw three books that had been dusted and placed on the table to impress me. One was a Bible (in Latin), one an English grammar (with uncut pages) and one was a well-thumbed work called *Legends, Myths and Other Histories of That Venerable Country Ireland*.

"My father was a reading man, my lady," said young Mr. Drummond, who was about my age and clearly unafflicted by shyness. "I myself could read by the time I was five years old—and isn't that the truth, Aunt Bridgie?"

Aunt Bridgie said it was the truth, so it was, and the Holy Mother of God alone knew what a wondrous sight it was to see a childeen scarce five years old with his nose in a book of mighty learning.

"And I've traveled, my lady," said Mr. Drummond. "I've seen other sights beyond the Joyce country, for my father was an Ulster man, and he went home during the Hunger to County Down, where there was more hope of food and work. It's all through Mayo I've traveled and Sligo and Leitrim and Cavan and Monaghan and Armagh—the whole breadth of Ireland I've seen, and one day I'll see it all again, so God help me I will."

"Mr. Drummond is altogether too bumptious," I said disapprovingly later to Edward. "He never stopped talking about himself the whole time I was there."

Edward looked amused. "He's a cut above the usual Connaught peasant and he knows it," he said. "If that means he has an inflated opinion of himself, I'm not about to discourage it. It makes him ambitious, and God knows there are few enough among my tenants who have any ambitions to improve either themselves or their lands."

And the very next day he summoned Mr. Drummond to Cashelmara to offer him the chance of a year at the Royal Agricultural College in Dublin. When I returned from my visit to the leader of the Joyce family Mr. Drummond was in the hall.

"God save you, my lady!" he exclaimed with such a blast of Irish charm that I was almost swept off my feet, and I saw then to my surprise that he was not so unattractive as I had at first supposed. His best clothes did not fit him properly, but his aunts had trimmed his black hair for the occasion and his swarthy skin had a scrubbed look.

"I'm going to Dublin!" he said, stars in his eyes. "To be sure Lord de Salis is the noblest landlord ever to draw breath on Irish soil!" And somehow when he smiled at me radiantly it was impossible not to smile back and wish him well.

"I don't truly care for Mr. Drummond," I remarked afterward to Patrick. "He's so uncouth and uppity, but nevertheless there's something fetching about him. I can't quite describe it. I think my favorite novelist would call it 'earthiness.'"

"Earthiness!" scoffed Patrick with a bitterness quite foreign to his nature. "Yes—the earthiness of the dung heap! You have very strange taste, Marguerite, if you think Drummond fetching. Wait till you see my friend Derry Stranahan! Then you'll see Drummond's no more fetching than the pigs he keeps."

I finally discovered that Drummond had had a hand in Mr. Stranahan's banishment and that Patrick was ill disposed toward him in consequence.

Katherine had elected to remain in England to visit her husband's family, but Patrick and Mr. Bull had traveled to Cashelmara with Nanny, Nurse and Thomas. I was delighted to see Thomas again. He had grown even during the two short weeks we had been separated, and I spent much time in the nursery encouraging him to inch around on his forearms like a little seal. He had splendidly strong back muscles and an adventurous spirit.

"I wonder if Annabel will come to see him," said Patrick, watching Thomas's antics admiringly. "Has she called yet?"

"No. Edward says she won't call either and that I'm not to call on her. It's such a pity, isn't it? I'd like to meet her."

"I'll try and coax her to come," said Patrick. "I shall tell her how nice you are and how silly she's being."

Annabel and her second husband occupied themselves by breeding horses, a popular Irish pastime. Since she had remained implacably opposed to her father's remarriage, I was not surprised when Patrick had no success in persuading her to call, but at last, acting on the assumption that she was probably as curious to see me as I was to see her, I became determined to find some solution to our impasse. After commissioning Patrick to do some sketches of Thomas, I purchased a puppy, one of the Knoxes' litter of Irish setters, and sent both the sketches and the dog to Clonagh Court with my compliments.

Annabel called and left a card the very next day.

The day after that I left my card at Clonagh Court.

"I thought I told you not to call on her!" exclaimed Edward when I dutifully informed him of the news.

"But she called on me first!" I said, producing her card as evidence.

"Why didn't you tell me?"

"I didn't want to upset you, dearest."

The next day I received a letter which said, "My dear Cousin Marguerite, thank you for the setter and the sketches of the baby. Both appear to have considerable character. I am not as a rule interested in infants but trust that one day Thomas and I will meet. Your cousin, Annabel Smith."

Immediately I wrote back: "My dear Cousin Annabel: I should be most happy to effect an introduction between you and Thomas. I am At Home on Tuesdays. I remain, your affectionate cousin, Marguerite Marriott de Salis."

Having thus maneuvered ourselves into a relationship, no matter how formal, we were then able to satisfy our mutual curiosity without loss of face on Annabel's part and without fear of Edward's wrath on mine.

Two days later, Annabel cantered up the drive, hitched her horse's reins carelessly to the nearest tree and strode up the steps to the front door.

VI

"I suppose you think I've behaved monstrously to you," said Annabel half an hour later as we returned to the drawing room from the nursery, "and I have, of course. But sometimes Papa aggravates

137

me so much that I stop at nothing to aggravate him in return. In fact when I look back it seems I've spent most of my life being angry with him for some reason or another. But men can be so extraordinarily tiresome, can't they?"

"Women too," I murmured vaguely as she paused for breath.

"Oh, women!" said Annabel. "Women are so much put upon in this world they have a perfect right to be tiresome, but men have no excuse at all, as I said to my first husband the day I decided to leave him—though I never did leave him. I was younger then and more of a coward. Oh, he was a tiresome man! I can't think why I married him. No, that's not true. I know exactly why I married him. I wanted to escape from Woodhammer Hall. Woodhammer! Ugh! It was like a tomb—no, a shrine. Louis's shrine. I suppose Papa has told you all about Louis."

"Poor little boy."

"Stuff. He was an absolute menace and so abominably spoiled! I know one's not supposed to speak ill of the dead, but frankly I'd rather speak ill than speak lies, and it's about time someone did speak truthfully about those dreary years at Woodhammer after poor Mama went into seclusion. Of course I was devoted to Mama, who was the most beautiful and courageous person, and naturally I'm devoted to Papa too even though he's so tiresome, but how dared they behave as if Louis's death had rendered them childless? They had four surviving daughters and an infant son. Why didn't they count their blessings? Of course Louis's death was a tragedy, I'm not denying that, but they should have paid more attention to the living instead of perpetually mourning the dead. I never could understand why they thought Louis was so exceptional anyway. I was just as clever as he was and just as good-looking too, if the truth be told. But of course Papa has always regarded women as inferior beings. It must have been so dreadfully trying for Mama."

"But it's obvious he had a profound admiration for your mother's intelligence! And he has some really radical ideas about women's education."

"Papa? Radical? Good God, if he's a radical I'm a horse thief! However, don't misunderstand me. I know Papa is a very remarkable man, and I'm sure no one admires his political career more than I do. But I find him so tiresome because I can never make any headway with him at all unless we have a row, and family quarrels, as I'm sure you know, Cousin Marguerite, are always so appallingly exhausting."

138

There was a knock on the door. "Excuse me, Mrs. Smith, begging your pardon," said Hayes apologetically, poking his nose into the room, "but—"

"My father's back from Clonareen?"

"It's coming up the drive he is, ma'am, at this very minute."

"I must go." Annabel leaped to her feet, grabbed her riding crop and began to pull on her gloves. "I'm delighted to have met you at last, Cousin Marguerite, and I must thank you for receiving me after so much awkwardness. The baby's a dear little creature. I'm very glad I was able to see him."

"But surely won't you stay—"

"Oh no, better not or Papa and I will almost certainly have another row. Perhaps you could give him my love, though, as a preliminary peace offering after all these months when we haven't been on speaking terms."

"Yes, of course. But—"

"Do call at Clonagh Court and meet my husband before you return to England. Papa has probably told you that Alfred is dreadfully common and vulgar, and so he is, but he's such a nice man, so amusing, and he's never, never tiresome. I'm at home on Wednesdays."

"Wednesdays. Yes. But, Cousin Annabel, your father has said only complimentary things about your husband. He's truly pleased that you're now happily married."

"Is he? Well, why on earth couldn't he have told me so?" said Annabel crossly. "Really, he's even more tiresome than I thought he was!" And sweeping out of the room without allowing me time to reply, she hurried downstairs to avoid meeting her father in the hall.

VII

"Well, I'm glad she was civil to you," said Edward when he heard of Annabel's visit. "She can be so disagreeable and tiresome. When I think of all the trouble she's caused me in the past—"

"But it's clear she's deeply attached to you, Edward."

"I wish it were clear to me," he said bitterly, but after that he thawed and confessed his affection and said I might call at Clonagh Court if I wished.

But I did not call on Annabel immediately. I thought it would be a mistake to rush matters, and, besides, there would be plenty of time in the future to further our acquaintance. So I waited until the end of my visit to Cashelmara before I took the carriage to the far end of the lough to return her call, but although I had chosen the right day I found no one at home. The master and mistress, I was told, had gone to the horse fair at Letterturk and would not be back till dusk. Concluding that either Annabel had forgotten her promise to be at home or that the horse fair had been too tempting to resist, I left a card and returned to Cashelmara.

Three days later I was once more setting foot on English soil.

We had not been cut off from the outside world at Cashelmara, for every day a stable boy was sent to collect the newspaper which arrived at Leenane on the "car" from Galway, but I had felt so far removed from the hub of world events that the news had had as little meaning to me as the news from a distant planet. However, all that was changed once we arrived at Woodhammer, and I was reminded again of the gigantic upheavals grinding through my country and leaving bloody trails of disaster in their wake. Thomas had been born during the bombardment of Fort Sumter in April. Two days later had come Lincoln's call to arms, and after that followed news of more secessions—Virginia, North Carolina, Arkansas, Tennessee—until I could almost hear the noise of tearing, like splitting cloth, as America was ripped in two. Even the good news, the news of the slave states that had turned their backs on secession, was mangled by news of the rout of the Federal troops at the battle of Bull Run. I was flung into a great panic when I heard about this, but Francis wrote, "It won't happen again because we shall be better prepared next time and because the finest general in the whole of the United States is to be given charge of the Army of the Potomac." And that was when I heard for the first time the dismal clang of the name George B. McClellan.

By this time, like Francis, I had recovered from my initial distrust of Lincoln, and now that the war had broken out there was no question about which side I felt was in the right. But for me, living in England, one of the most intolerable aspects of the war was that the English attitudes toward it were so preposterous. For a start no one had any idea why the war was being fought. Most people thought it had something to do with state interference and the infringement of property rights, and the English have very set views on property and how far the government may interfere with it. Even the people who were sympathetic to the North thought the issue was purely concerned with slavery and had no inkling of the constitutional issues

140

involved, but at that time these people were in the minority, since public opinion favored the South.

In vain Edward explained to me wryly that when confronted by a dispute the English notoriously sided with the underdog. In my fury this explanation simply wasn't good enough for me. I knew perfectly well that England had become resentful of the Northern United States and had begun to regard them as a rival in world affairs. The prospect of that rival being pulled down a peg or two was far too delightful not to be savored, but I thought it revealed all the less attractive qualities in the Anglo-Saxon character.

However, despite the distressing news from America and the exasperating attitudes of the English, it was pleasant to be back at Woodhammer, and I was delighted when we soon became so busy entertaining visitors that I had no time to be bored with country life. Among the acquaintances whom Edward invited to share the hunting with him was his closest friend, Lord Duneden, whose younger married daughter I found particularly congenial. Lord Duneden's situation resembled Edward's before our marriage. He had been a widower for some years and was toying with the idea of finding a new wife. I even wondered if he might follow Edward's example and marry a much younger woman, for he was unusually attentive to Katherine, but Katherine herself quickly scotched that suspicion by saying I read too many frivolous novels and had too lively an imagination.

"Besides," said Katherine, who was enjoying the privacy of her widow's weeds, "I shan't want to marry again for a long time—and even if I did I would prefer to marry a man who is not half bald and elderly-looking."

I could not say that Lord Duneden was too old for her, since Edward was even older than he was, but I did agree he had little hair and was inclined to be stout. "But he has great charm," I said, "and he's very kind."

"Perhaps," said Katherine with studied indifference, and after that we did not discuss Lord Duneden any more.

We had a very happy Christmas at Woodhammer. Thomas learned to haul himself to his feet by clinging to the bars of his crib, and Patrick did a splendid sketch of him glaring ambitiously at the rail. Patrick was so good with Thomas. The three of us used to spend much time playing together in the nursery, but although Edward too visited Thomas every evening to say good night he did no more than pat the baby's head and watch him for a moment or two.

"Thomas will be more interesting to you when he's older," I said, aware that I could hardly expect Edward to follow Patrick's example and romp with the baby on the nursery floor. "What fun it will be when he can walk!"

"Children grow up too quickly," he said, smiling at me. "You should enjoy his infancy while it lasts."

"Oh, I'm enjoying it! But I'm ready for Thomas to be more than a baby now, especially since . . ." But I stopped. I wanted to say, "Since there'll soon be a new baby for me to enjoy," but for some reason I was tongue-tied.

"Since what?" he said naturally, but when I still could not explain he guessed the news and gave me a kiss. "And what is his name?" he asked, amused. "And when is he coming?"

"At the end of June, I think," I said, disarmed by his good humor and feeling less awkward. "But he doesn't have a name yet because you must choose it. I was so autocratic in deciding upon Thomas."

"No," he said. "You choose the name."

"Why?" I cried. "Don't you want to choose it? Does the baby's name mean so little to you?" And in a fit of emotion so common to me when I was pregnant, I burst into tears.

"My dearest Marguerite!" He was shocked to the core. "What a thing to say!"

"Then choose a name!" I sobbed and hurled myself against his chest in a positive orgy of weeping.

"David," he said at once, "after my brother. I was very fond of him, and I remember you said you liked him when he visited New York."

I was reassured. I managed to say to him, "You're pleased?"

"Of course," he said, holding me tightly and stroking my hair. My face was still pressed against his chest, and I could not see his expression.

"It won't make any difference to us," I said, "will it?"

"Good heavens, in what way?"

"Well, with Thomas . . . it was difficult sometimes . . . before . . . and especially afterward . . . wasn't it?"

There was a pause. Then he said, "It was nothing." And when I tried to deny this he added sharply, "You must think me very selfish if you think I'm reluctant for you to have children."

"But . . ."

"Every woman has a right to have children."

"And every husband has a duty to provide her with them? Oh,

Edward, don't let's talk about rights and duties! If you don't want the baby—"

"My dearest Marguerite," he said, gentle but very firm, "you can rest assured that if I hadn't wanted this child I would have told you so long before he was conceived. Now please, no more of this nonsense or I shall become very cross with you indeed."

I did feel much better when he said that, and I at once began to kiss him with a great passion. I was always very passionate when I was pregnant, but that was a great deal more pleasant than suffering from morning sickness or fainting spells.

After Christmas I did not go to Cashelmara with Edward but returned to London, where my doctor confirmed my condition and gave his usual tedious advice to lead a quiet life. Presently Edward returned to London, the Queen summoned Parliament, and in no time at all winter had brightened into spring. Since the beginning of my pregnancy I had felt in excellent health, but in early June when I had less than a month of waiting before me an event occurred that was to prove very disturbing: Edward's daughter Madeleine abandoned her cloister and wrote to ask him if she could come to stay.

Chapter Three

I

I had imagined Madeleine to be as virtuous as a heroine in a Radcliffe novel and as fanatical in her religious devotion as the earliest of the Christian martyrs. I had never met a nun before. Edward refused to discuss her since she had given him great offense first by becoming a Roman Catholic and second by entering the cloister, and even when she announced her intention to return to the world his only comment was "Thank God she's come to her senses before she's too old to find a husband."

"Do you intend to let her stay here?" I said, uncertain how far he meant to forgive her.

"Of course," he said. "It's my duty to give an unmarried daughter a roof over her head, but if she thinks I'm going to treat her as the father treated the prodigal son, I'm afraid she'll be greatly disappointed."

Not liking to ask him any more questions, I turned to Katherine for information, but Katherine at once assumed her remotest expression and said there was little she could tell me.

"But she's only a year older than you!" I protested.

"We had nothing in common," said Katherine and added with a flash of her old jealousy, "She was Grandmama's favorite. That was why she became so fanatically religious."

"Grandmama," I learned, was Edward's mother, a fussy old lady who had supported the most Popish branch of the Anglican faith and displayed a talent for narrow-mindedness and longevity.

"She even outlived Mama," reflected Katherine, "and when Papa went abroad after Mama's death Grandmama came to Woodhammer and made us all pray daily for consolation in our bereavement."

"Wasn't that awful!" exclaimed Patrick fervently. "So boring!"

"Madeleine liked it," said Katherine. "That was when she turned to religion. Papa said afterward it was all Grandmama's fault."

"I can't imagine Edward having a mother," I said. "Did they get along?"

"Get on," murmured Katherine conscientiously. I had recently asked her to help me pinpoint my most frequently used Americanisms. "Yes, they did. She was devoted to him."

"She was a nice old thing really," said Patrick.

"And Madeleine resembles her?" I said hopefully, but they both looked doubtful.

"Fanaticism is such poor taste," said Katherine, and Patrick added, "It's not really very jolly to be told one's doomed to hell-fire and damnation, you know."

At this point I had serious misgivings about this monster of a stepdaughter, and by the time Madeleine arrived from her Irish convent I was so nervous that I hardly had the courage to remain in the drawing room to receive her.

Fortunately Edward was with me. When she was shown into the room he said a cool "Welcome home, Madeleine," but despite his harsh words earlier he did give her a kiss. "May I present . . ."

I looked at her disbelievingly. No one had told me how fetching she was. I use the word "fetching" deliberately, because she was neither handsome like Annabel nor beautiful like Katherine, but she had that special soft, curving winningness that many men find irresistible. She was small, as small as I was, and a little plump. She had steady blue eyes, softly waving fair hair and an ineffable expression. No girl could have looked sweeter or more biddable.

"How do you do, Cousin Marguerite," she said, casting an interested but not hostile glance at my ballooning waistline, and closed her small rosebud mouth with such an air of finality that I wondered if she ever intended to say another word to me again. She turned to her father. "It's so good of you to receive me, Papa," she said politely, "but if all goes well, I hope I shall not be a burden to you for long. I have applied for a position nursing the sick at the East End Charity Hospital run by my order, and I intend to begin work there as soon as possible."

"But I thought you'd left the order!" said Edward, outraged.

"Yes, I have. I decided I wasn't suited to be a nun either in the cloister or out of it. I found such strict conformity too difficult. However, the order still wishes to help me, and when I decided to be a nurse—"

"But of course you can't be a nurse! I've never heard such a ridiculous idea in all my life!"

"I hardly think Miss Nightingale would agree with you, Papa."

"Never mind Miss Nightingale!" shouted Edward, in a great rage by this time. "I absolutely forbid it!"

"Yes, Papa, I dare say you do, but as always my duty to obey God must prove stronger than my duty to obey you."

I would never, never have dared say such a thing to Edward. I closed my eyes in anticipation of his wrath, and far away I heard a thin voice say tremulously, "Cousin Madeleine, you must be so tired after your long journey and I'm sure you must be anxious to rest. Do let me show you upstairs to your room." It was a surprise when I realized the thin voice belonged to me, but Madeleine remained undisturbed, and Edward at least made no attempt to interrupt. Maneuvering her from the room before his temper could explode, I rushed her upstairs while I talked continuously about the new wallpaper in her room and the train journey from Holyhead and would she like a little refreshment, as it would be so easy to order tea.

"How very kind," she said, regarding me with compassion, "but I can wait till dinner for refreshment." And as I sank down exhausted upon the bed she said soothingly, "You mustn't mind Papa and me, you know. He's quite used to me being the exact opposite of Katherine."

"Opposite?" I said weakly. "Katherine?"

"Of course! Katherine believes the world would end if she were not a dutiful daughter, and I believe the world would end if I were. By the way, since I'm certain Papa is already speculating about a possible husband for me, could you be kind enough to inform him that I have absolutely no intention of marrying either now or at any other time? Thank you so much."

"But—"

"Will you take me up to the nursery presently to see little

146

Thomas? I adore babies! In fact one day if I have the means I should like to establish a foundling hospital."

"How very commendable, but . . . well, in that case, wouldn't you like to have babies of your own?"

"Without being married?" said Madeleine with every appearance of seriousness, and then burst into such peals of laughter that I could not help but laugh with her. "Pray don't misunderstand me," she said at last. "Marriage is a sacred and blessed institution uniquely fitted to the human race, but God never intended it to be for everyone, did He? Such a very simple truth but tragically so often overlooked by women taught from the cradle to put the dictates of society above the will of God. Yes, it *is* pretty wallpaper. How interesting to see some modern notions in decoration! One of the nicest things about being American must be that one isn't weighed down by centuries of obsolete ideas."

And after that encouraging remark all trace of awkwardness between us vanished until soon I was even wondering how long I could persuade her to stay with us at St. James's Square.

II

But my delight at having Madeleine to stay was dampened daily by Edward's inability to keep his temper with her. Madeleine was hardly at fault; she always adopted a pleasant, polite manner that, unfortunately, Edward found all too difficult to emulate.

"If you had a husband and half a dozen children you wouldn't feel any need to work in a hospital tending lice-infested bodies, Madeleine," he said to her after she had gently reproved him for talking of suitors, and to me in private he added angrily, "If only I could make her stop all this hospital nonsense! If she gave her mind to it she would soon meet some suitable fellow and settle down."

He simply did not understand. The situation should have been eased by the fact that Madeleine did not expect him to understand, but Madeleine's placid acceptance of his disapproval was infuriating to Edward. I saw clearly then that Madeleine was the daughter who baffled him most. Annabel he could understand; they were alike, and though Annabel had angered him in the past, he continued to speak of her with affection. Katherine he could tolerate; she was always so anxious to please him that he found it easy to be kind to her. But Madeleine he could neither understand nor tolerate, and had it not been for the fact that I was in my ninth month and that they were

147

both loath to upset me, I believe they would have quarreled hope-lessly within a week of her arrival.

But I liked Madeleine. I liked someone who was interested when I wanted to discuss David's imminent arrival, and I liked someone who shared my absorption in Thomas's progress. I am not, I hope, one of those boring women who can normally talk of nothing but their children, but when one is nine months pregnant one's mind is neces-sarily filled with little else but thoughts of cribs, diapers and rattles, and Madeleine seemed to understand this more readily than anyone else. I found her a comfort, and I wanted her to stay.

Katherine became huffy, but I told her not to be so silly; she was not in the least interested in babies, and I knew I was boring com-pany for her at that time.

"But I cannot think why you should be such friends with Made-leine," said Katherine, jealous as ever, and added despairingly as if she were a small child, "I've never had a true friend before and Madeleine has always had so many!"

"Oh, for heaven's sake, Katherine!" I said crossly. "Why on earth can't I be friends with both of you?"

There was no answer she could possibly make to this, of course, and presently she did become more sensible, but I thought it was sad she and Madeleine should be indifferent to each other when there was only a year between them in age. I thought nostalgically of Blanche. That spring she had married a rich young man whose family had an estate near Philadelphia, but although she wrote ecstatic letters describing him, I thought he sounded dull, and when she sent me a picture I saw that he was barely half as handsome as Edward. However, since she seemed happy enough I found it easy to be happy for her—and when Francis wrote to say it was not quite the brilliant match he had wanted for Blanche I could not help but feel happier still. I loved Blanche dearly and was certainly no longer jealous of her, but I am, after all, only human.

"I do hope they'll be happy," I said to Edward on Blanche's wedding day. "I hope they'll be as happy as we are."

"I hope they'll be half as happy as we are," said Edward, whose hostility toward Blanche had mellowed with the years, "and even that is wishing them exceedingly well."

Edward was especially kind to me at the end of my pregnancies because he knew how much I hated the last days of stoutness, weari-ness and general immobility.

"If only David would come!" I said, sighing, but David was late, and when at last he did arrive I wished he had been later still.

Thomas's birth had been so easy and I had been so excited by his entry into the world that I could say with truth afterward that I had enjoyed the experience. I had even thought at the time what a fuss some women made about nothing. I did realize I had been fortunate, but in all the months before David's birth it had never occurred to me that I would not be equally fortunate a second time. In my ignorance I had had no idea that one woman can have two totally different experiences of bringing a baby into the world.

David was a breech birth. Had it not been for the fact that I was attended by the best doctor and midwife in London, he would probably have been born dead. Maybe I would have died too. I certainly thought I was dying. Madeleine stayed with me throughout—no one wanted her to be there, but she was willing and I was insistent—and at the end I believe I even asked her for the last rites of the Roman Church. Instead she gave me her rosary beads to bite on—a far more sensible gesture—and I knew then that she would make a perfect nurse.

I fainted soon after that, and although I regained consciousness before the birth, the doctor administered the controversial drug chloroform, which brought me the most miraculous relief from pain. In fact later I was angry that he had not used it sooner, but doctors are wary of interfering with the natural process of childbirth, and he told me to be glad he had resorted to the drug at all.

David was much larger than Thomas and looked quite different from his brother. Directly after he was born I felt no desire to see someone who had caused me so much trouble, and even when I did see him I might have felt indifferent if he had been a mere red-faced bundle of bones in a swaddling cloth. But David, fortunately for us both, was a beautiful infant, pink, white and serene, and within a day or two I could no longer find it in my heart to blame him for his agonizing entry into the world.

Naturally it took me some time to recover. For several weeks I spent my days either in bed or else reclining on a chaise longue, but I was in good spirits. I read copiously, wrote to my family in enormous detail, began a new volume of my journal and tried to catch up with current events. I never had the slightest interest in current events during pregnancy, but now I busied myself in studying the progress of the dreadful war again and working myself into a rage about

England's dismal attempts to remain neutral. How can a country be neutral when it builds warships for the side it secretly favors? I thought it was very poor behavior on England's part, and I said so to Edward during one of our numerous discussions on the subject.

But the war was not the only subject we discussed. When I was well again we became concerned with a more personal matter, and before we went to Woodhammer for the autumn Edward said to me, "I'm sure you'll want more children later despite this unfortunate experience with David, but might it not be best for the sake of your health to postpone your next pregnancy for a while?"

"Postpone it forever if you wish," I said with a shudder, trying not to remember the smell of chloroform and the crunching of Madeleine's rosary beads between my teeth. "I'm perfectly satisfied with my two boys."

He was careful not to comment, but I sensed his relief.

"What do I have to do?" I said in curiosity, my mind roaming among solutions that ranged from chastity belts to black magic.

"Good God, nothing at all," he said as if I had made some shocking suggestion. "I shall do what has to be done."

"What's that?"

"It's not necessary for us to discuss it further," he said. "It's not a subject on which a woman needs to be well informed."

No promise of black magic could have alarmed me more, and in fact when I was finally enlightened I did not care for the innovation and had to remind myself severely that the alternative lay with chloroform and rosary beads. However, presently I became accustomed to the change, and after a while I thought nothing of it—which just goes to prove one can reconcile oneself to an inconvenience if one has a strong enough incentive.

Madeleine would not go with us to Woodhammer. I begged her to come, but she said she had postponed the pursuit of her vocation for long enough, and now that I was well again she had no further excuse to stay with me.

"But I can't bear to think of you working yourself to the bone in a horrible hospital in the worst part of London!" I cried in despair and added like a true New Yorker, "And you won't even receive any money for it, only your board and lodging! It's so unfair!"

"It's not unfair at all," said Madeleine, serene as ever. "I shall be learning while I work."

"But if you could only study at the Nightingale Training School, how much more suitable it would be! I know you have no money, but I could lend—"

"Marguerite, you know Papa would never permit it, and I won't have you quarreling with him. I only hope I can leave here without quarreling with him myself."

She could not. She announced her intention of leaving, and when Edward tried to stop her they began to argue. Madeleine was sweet, demure and utterly implacable, while Edward became in rapid succession irritable, angry and absolutely livid.

"Thank God your mother isn't alive to see this!" he shouted at last.

"Please, Papa," said Madeleine, "don't you think it would be wiser not to bring up the subject of my mother? I might become too angry."

"Is this the prelude to some fanciful accusation?"

"Certainly not. I've no intention of pointing out to you what you already know—that you treated my mother abominably and ruined her health with your disgusting and selfish demands."

"That's a lie!" Edward was ashen.

"It's the truth! All your boasts about a happy marriage—what a sham! All your grief after she died—what hyprocrisy!"

"I loved her—"

"Yes—and it was your example of a husband's love that made me decide I never wanted a husband! I didn't want to be a victim like my mother!"

"You don't even remember your mother as she was! You were only six when she had her nervous collapse after Louis died."

"And for the next six years I had to watch her sinking to the grave as the result of your carnal excesses! No, don't interrupt me. We'll say nothing more about it, because whatever we said would be irrelevant. With God's help I've long since learned to forgive you, but please, if you wish me to keep a civil tongue in my head, be good enough not to fling my mother's name in my face in that fashion. Now, if you have nothing else you can profitably say to me, I shall leave your house and pursue my calling as a nurse."

"Pursue what you want, but don't expect me to give you one penny of my money! After what you've just said you can beg in the streets for all I care!"

"I doubt if that will be necessary," said Madeleine, "since the order will provide me with the essentials of life. Good day, Papa."

"Wait!" I cried, quite unable to stop myself by that time even though I knew it was foolish of me to interfere. "Madeleine . . . Edward . . ." I groped for words, tried to find some solution. "Edward, nursing does have a new respectability nowadays. Would it really not be better if Madeleine had a little money so that she could pursue her vocation at its most respectable level?"

"My dear," said Edward in a voice of steel, "you would oblige me considerably if you would refrain from comment in the circumstances. If the scene is distressing to you, you have my permission to withdraw."

I stumbled out of the room.

Later after Madeleine had left the house with the shabby bag that contained her meager possessions, he said a great many things to me. He said he realized I had meant well and had thought I was acting for the best; he said he was aware of the time and trouble I had spent befriending his daughters; he said he was neither ungrateful nor unappreciative. But when I took sides in a family argument and showed beyond any doubt that I was not in agreement with him I was doing a grave disservice to our marriage.

"I'm not saying you should be hypocritical," he said. "I'm not asking you to voice opinions you don't hold. I'm simply asking you to be silent when there's a conflict between myself and Eleanor's children. You complain loudly enough about England's poor show of neutrality in your civil war, Marguerite, but you're very far from excelling in neutrality yourself! And you should be neutral on these occasions. I don't want my second marriage to be tainted with echoes from the first."

His argument was persuasive, yet I could not wholly accept it. However, I said nothing further for fear the discussion might become too acrimonious, and anyway it was impossible for me to remain angry with him for long. That autumn he took me abroad again, this time to the south of Europe, and we spent two months traveling around the Greek islands. We had planned to spend part of that time in Italy, but Rome was still echoing with Garibaldi's revolutionary rhetoric, and Edward thought it wiser to avoid territories that were so politically unstable. I did have a brief glimpse of Venice, where we took the boat to Athens, but beyond the enthusiastic decision that I would return there one day, my journal is sparse in recording my impressions of that gorgeous fairy-tale city. I devoted pages to Greece (now all contained in my red leather journal, Volume, III, entitled "Sojourn in the Islands of Greece, 1862"), and on rereading my account, I can see that I soon recovered from my reluctance to leave the boys for such a long time in order not to disappoint Edward.

I was right to go with him. We were very happy, and in our intimacy with each other far from the distractions of our everyday life I came closer than I had ever come before to understanding the complexity of his character. It occurred to me for the first time that he was not truly suited to be a family man; he was far too restless and independent to welcome the ties of home life, and although he was happy enough to be married, he was happiest of all when his wife was more of a mistress than a domestic partner. I thought then of what Madeleine had said about conforming to the dictates of society, and it seemed to me that despite the lip service Edward paid to such rules he was at heart a very nonconforming person indeed. Whenever he was obliged to be conventional—in the role of paterfamilias, for example—he was at his least attractive and at his most ill at ease. He was at his best when he was free of all the trappings his position had cast upon him. I had seen him at his best in New York, when he was a foreigner outside his normal surroundings, and I saw him at his best now when we were alone together far from home.

It was then that I at last began to understand what Eleanor had meant to him. She too had liked to travel; she had shared all his interests, certainly far more of them than I did. Perhaps she too had been at her best in a world beyond the structure of her daily life. She would have been the companion Edward needed, a true kindred spirit to share his adventures, and once he had found her neither of them would have had any need for anyone else. A son to inherit the title, of course, perhaps a daughter to look after them in old age. But no one else. Anyone else would have been an intrusion.

"But I love you just as much as I ever loved Eleanor, Marguerite," he said, "and sometimes so much more."

All quarrels seemed very far away when he said that. In fact by the time we returned to England I was firmly of the opinion that we could not quarrel again for as long as we lived, but Edward decided that we should spend Christmas in Ireland, and it was then, on my second visit to Cashelmara, that I first became acquainted with his ward Derry Stranahan.

III

I took a great fancy to Derry. He was nearly twenty-one, just as I was, and good-looking in a dark, lithe, graceful manner that was very attractive. He had a curious accent, Irish with strong English overtones, which he must have acquired from Patrick, enough charm to lure a dozen birds from any bush and a needle-sharp wit. It never occurred to me not to like him, and, besides, I was secretly intrigued by the manner in which he had sown his wild oats. Women do tend to look twice at a man with a colorful romantic past, and I was no exception.

That Christmas he came home from Frankfurt after his years of banishment and was permitted by Edward to spend a month at Cashelmara before he went to Dublin to read for the Irish bar.

"I'm honored to meet the lady of the house at last," he said, bowing very low to me, and it was hard to believe he had ever been a peasant's son living in some smoky cabin along the road to Clonareen.

I saw little of him at first. I was too busy making arrangements for the Christmas celebrations, and he was out most of the day with Patrick on some adventure or other. He did not spend Christmas with us. Edward insisted he visit his kin at Maam's Cross, and he departed gloomily on Christmas Eve—"to sleep under the one bed with the pigs, the hens and six of the youngest children, I shouldn't wonder," he remarked, but Edward said it was his duty to visit his family at Christmas, even if they were only cousins, and Derry knew better by this time than to incur Edward's disapproval.

After his return on Boxing Day he soon reduced Patrick and myself to tears of laughter with an account of his experiences, and since all my Christmas calls had been paid and received I fancied he sought my company more often. This made me nervous, for Edward was always quick to spot any young man who paid me the most innocent attention, but eventually I realized with relief that Derry's interest was not in me but in my constant companion, Katherine.

Katherine liked Derry too. She had not seen him since before her marriage, when he had been no more than a boy, so it was as if she, like myself, were meeting him for the first time. Of course she did not say she liked him—she was far too reserved for that—but I noticed how often she smiled in his presence and how she never rebuffed him when he made deliberate efforts to charm her.

I was secretly delighted. There seemed no reason not to be; I was always reading romantic novels in which two such people fell in love as a matter of course. Katherine had been widowed for two years now; she was wealthy, beautiful and eligible. Derry was far below her by birth, but he was thoroughly presentable and his prospects were excellent. Also he knew how to circumvent Katherine's shyness, and Katherine in her turn was the perfect audience he needed for his witty stories. The one would complement the other and vice versa. Surely nothing could have been more suitable.

To make matters even more interesting from a romantic viewpoint, it soon became clear that Katherine had a second suitor. After Christmas Edward's friend Lord Duneden visited us from Duneden Castle, which lay eighty miles east of Cashelmara, and having been mildly attentive to Katherine since the earliest days of her widowhood, he now became more attentive than ever. As Katherine was an expert at not betraying her emotions, poor Derry was soon in a terrible taking.

"To be sure Lord Duneden's a great nobleman," he said, confiding in me despairingly at last, "and he has such wealth and position as I could never lay my hands on in a thousand years, but, Lady de Salis, I do have some advantages he has not. Do you think Miss Katherine—Lady Rokeby, I should say—is quite unaware of them?"

He had cornered me at the top of the stairs, and we were standing in the gallery that enclosed the circular hall. I had just returned from a second call at Clonagh Court to see Annabel but had still not managed to meet the elusive Alfred, who always seemed to be away from home either buying or selling a horse. But Annabel and I had spent a civil half hour together, and I fancied that next year she might even bring herself to spend Christmas with us if we returned to Cashelmara for the occasion.

"What do you think, my lady?" said Derry earnestly, his dark eyes febrile with anxiety, and because I was in a good mood and his attraction for Katherine was so romantically pleasing to me, I could not help but say, "Why, Mr. Stranahan, I'm sure your advantages are every bit as telling as Lord Duneden's."

"You don't believe she cares for him?" he said with a passion that I could only regard as thrilling, and added, just like the hero in one of my novels, "You think I might dare to cherish a little hope?"

"Well, Mr. Stranahan," I said, "that is really not for me to answer." But of course I answered him with a smile and made sure he was left with the understanding that Katherine favored his suit.

I was so excited about this fully-fledged romance I had nurtured so carefully that I could not resist dropping a hint of my excitement to Edward.

We had descended from the nurseries, I remember, after saying good night to the children, and were walking down the corridor to our apartments to change for dinner. His nephew George was journeying from Letterturk to dine with us that night, and I was so absorbed in wondering if I had been too rash in putting curry on the menu (God alone knew how the Irish cooked curry) that I barely listened to Edward grumbling about his other protégé, Maxwell Drummond. Young Mr. Drummond had offended him very deeply. After only a brief attendance at the Agricultural College he had run off with the daughter of one of the masters and had brought her back to the valley as his wife. Seemingly unaware of how monstrously he had repaid Edward's charity, he had called that morning to ask if he could rent the ruined Stranahan farm, Derry's old home, which adjoined his property. Edward had promised to rent it to him for a nominal sum after he had completed a year at the Agricultural College, and Mr. Drummond, despite everything, still expected him to make good his promise.

"Insolent young fool!" growled Edward for at least the tenth time. "If he rents the Stranahan property he'll pay me a fair rent for it. That'll teach him not to ruin his prospects in future! I'm only surprised that the girl hasn't already left him now that she knows she's been reduced to a peasant! Imagine a young man like that marrying a schoolmaster's daughter! Absurd!"

"But so romantic!" I sighed, wrenching my thoughts away from the curry at last. "Of course it would help if they had money—I do realize that. But, Edward, supposing they did have money. Supposing Mr. Drummond could somehow keep his wife in suitable style. Would a slight difference in social station be truly significant?"

"Marguerite, I don't know how such matters are in America, but I assure you that here the difference in rank between Mr. and Mrs. Drummond is very far from being slight."

"But supposing the difference was between someone like Derry Stranahan and . . . and Katherine?"

We were in our apartments by this time. He had been about to tug the bell rope to summon his valet, but he stopped with his hand in mid-air.

"Derry?" he said slowly. "And Katherine?"

"Oh, Edward!" I said happily. "It's so exciting. I'm sure they're dreadfully in love! Of course Derry is a little younger than she is, and I know by birth he's far inferior to her, but he's been well educated and shows such promise and after all he *is* your ward."

"He is not my ward," said Edward. "I have never accepted him as a member of my family and I certainly never intend to. He's an Irish peasant's son to whom I have exercised a certain amount of charity—often greatly against my better judgment—and if that has given him ideas far above his station I'm afraid he's about to face a considerable disappointment."

I was dumfounded. "But . . ."

"Marguerite, have you encouraged this fancy of his?"

"I . . . well, no—that is to say, at least not in any particular manner."

"Have you encouraged Katherine to think of this boy as a possible suitor?"

I swallowed. "Not exactly, but . . ."

"Can you conceivably have been so foolish as to think that I could ever approve of such a match?"

"Well, I . . . I thought Derry was your ward. I did not realize—I did not quite understand . . ."

"No," he said, and I realized with fright that he was very angry. "You did not understand. You knew that I had been obliged to send Derry abroad because of certain immoralities which I have no intention of describing to you in detail, and you knew that I have in the past disapproved of his influence over Patrick. You knew too that it was only out of kindness that I permitted him to spend this month at Cashelmara before his departure for Dublin. You knew all this and yet you assume I would welcome Katherine forming an attachment for him! And worse than that you have the effrontery to say you 'did not understand' that I would disapprove of the match!"

I said, stiff-lipped, "I did know of Derry's past misbehavior, of course, but I thought that was all forgiven and forgotten. And since he's so sincerely attached to Katherine . . ."

"I doubt that very much," said Edward. "He's merely anxious to get his hands on her money so that he won't have to earn his daily bread."

"I can't help thinking you're being a little cynical, Edward."

"And I can't help thinking you've been unbelievably naïve!" he cried, losing his temper. "And worse than that, you have as usual succeeded in meddling in my children's affairs and taking their part in direct contradiction to my wishes!"

"I didn't know this time I was contradicting your wishes," I faltered, "but if I've given you offense I'm very sorry. It won't happen again." And before he could hurl another angry word at me I fled from the room. I wept as I ran down the corridor and I wept as I scrambled up the nursery stairs, but I did. I had to pause to compose myself before I tiptoed into the night nursery to be alone with the children.

Thomas was already asleep, his red hair tousled and his snub nose pressed sideways upon the sheet, but David was awake and cooing softly to himself as he watched the flicker of the nightlight. He smiled serenely as he saw me. I picked him up. He gurgled, pulled my hair lovingly and lay, fat and placid, in my arms.

"Dearest Baby," I said, "you're really much too stout." Then I wept over him so emotionally that I thought in alarm that I must surely be pregnant again, but afterward I felt better, very calm and self-possessed.

Replacing David gently in his cradle, I tiptoed out of the nursery and went resolutely downstairs in search of Katherine.

IV

"Pray don't be so distressed, Marguerite," said Katherine. "Naturally you could not be expected to know Papa's feelings on the subject. I too thought he regarded Derry as a ward."

"I should never have encouraged you if I'd dreamt—"

"I don't think you did encourage me particularly. Anyway," said Katherine calmly, "it hardly signifies now. Naturally I would never consider a marriage that would distress Papa."

"Oh, but . . ." I said and bit my tongue.

"In a way this simplifies the situation," said Katherine. "I shall marry Lord Duneden. He is not very handsome, but as you once remarked, he's charming and kind and I expect I shall be quite happy."

"But, Katherine," I said, so horrified that I found I had to speak after all, "you mustn't marry someone you don't love! Why should you marry Lord Duneden—or anyone else—just now? Wait a little longer. There'll surely be other suitors before long, and I'm certain at least one of them will appeal to you just as much as Derry."

"I doubt if any of them would be so suitable as Duneden. Papa thinks so highly of him and they're such old friends. Duneden has an Irish estate, just as Papa has, and a house in London, and he too is active in parliamentary matters. Papa would be very pleased if I married Duneden."

I could not let this pass. I tried to, but it was beyond my powers of self-restraint. "Katherine," I said. "You're a widow. You're your own mistress. You've already married once to please your father—but

158

that was when you were eighteen and knew no better. You've admitted to me you weren't happily married. Why must you make the same mistake again when this time there's absolutely no need for you to please anyone but yourself?"

"I could not please myself," said Katherine, "if I displeased Papa." She was wooden, impeccably correct. I remembered that her mother had referred to her as a wax doll, and suddenly I was dreadfully angry—but with whom I was angry I was not entirely certain.

"You're a fool, Katherine," I said. "Do you really think marriage with Duneden will make Edward love you any better?"

She froze. I saw the wintry look in her eyes and knew I had lost her. Afterward, looking back at the entire disaster with the wisdom of hindsight, I decided it was then that my married life began to go wrong.

Chapter Four

I

I did not at first realize that my marriage had entered a new phase. The seeds of discord had all been sown by the time Katherine married Lord Duneden that spring, but none of them might have taken root if I had been more mature and Edward less influenced by my mistakes. We had quarreled over Madeleine, we had quarreled over Katherine, and had Annabel not taken such care to lead her life well apart from us we might easily have quarreled over her too. Certainly the stage was set for us to quarrel over Patrick, but the stage need never have been used if a number of unforeseeable circumstances had not merged to draw us all remorselessly from the wings.

The first of these circumstances was Edward's change of attitude toward me. He was perfectly justified in regarding me as a meddling child after the hash I had made of Katherine's romance, but his mistake was that he continued to treat me as a meddling child long after Derry had been packed off to Dublin to begin his legal studies and long after Katherine had so delighted him by marrying his best friend. He recovered from his anger, of course; the only fortunate aspect of Edward's temper was that it seldom lasted long, but afterward he behaved toward me exactly as if he were a father saddled with a wayward child whom he was obliged to discipline with affection. I knew then what it was like to be one of his children. He was sufficiently kind and concerned to make one truly wish to please him, but no matter how hard one tried to please he was always just beyond the edge of one's emotional reach. One was conscious of him making great efforts in the name of duty, but the very fact that he acted out of duty was enough to chill all intimate communication. His kindness and concern lacked spontaneity; when examined they fell apart at a touch. He was a private person and, despite all his talk of loneliness, very self-contained. Because he could withdraw for long periods to absorb himself in his work, he assumed other people did not need him any more than he needed them. It wasn't easy to be Edward's child, and it was very hard indeed to be his wife when one was treated like one of his children.

I began to be restless and dissatisfied.

My mistake was that I concealed it. My horror of quarrels had increased with the years, so that when Edward began again, as he had in the early days of our marriage, to instruct me how to behave at dinner parties and to tell me which charities I should support or which books I should read to broaden my outlook, I merely accepted the advice without complaint. But by this time I had my own ideas on these subjects, and I considered that I had already discovered the best way for me to approach his elderly friends on social occasions. Such poise as I had acquired had come because I never made any attempt to be other than myself. When Edward started telling me what I should say to each guest I felt he was trying to mold me into someone else, and my poise suffered in consequence. I began to dread each dinner party in case I displeased him by a careless word, and my position became increasingly burdensome to me.

Matters might have come to a head sooner if our physical ease with each other had dwindled, but at first, once the bedroom door was closed, our intimacy flourished more strongly than ever. I was becoming just as obsessed as Katherine with the desire to please him, and in bed at least I knew I could please him to exhaustion. Unfortunately I became so anxious to please him that I was seldom able to relax sufficiently to allow him to please me, and although for a long time I was able to accept this with equanimity, in the end I began to feel resentful and disturbed.

Once again I said nothing. I did not dare. It was all very well for Edward to tell me frankly how delighted he was that I enjoyed that side of marriage, but if I had attempted to tell him that I could be enjoying it more and that my lack of enjoyment was partly his fault, I knew he would have been horrified. I did not quarrel with this. I am not one of those crusading females like my countrywoman Miss

Bloomer, who thinks women should say what they like to men and even wear trousers while they say it. I know that the differences between men and women necessarily merit different orders of behavior, but I must confess that as the months passed and my relationship with Edward drifted into darker waters I did wish that a woman had the right in certain circumstances to talk frankly to her husband.

How long we might have drifted along together in this unsatisfactory state if events had not intervened to exacerbate it I have no idea. But during the two years which followed Katherine's marriage to Lord Duneden in the spring of 1863, Edward began for no apparent reason to suffer from impotence so that our relationship in the bedroom, always one of the strengths of our marriage, finally ground to a halt.

II

It began insidiously, as many of the worst troubles often do. He had one failure; then all was well for a time, but presently there was another and yet another and after that he withdrew from me to absorb himself utterly in his work. He spoke in the House, he sat on committees, he worked on a new thesis, he lectured at the Agricultural College in Dublin, he toured a model farm in East Anglia and he made one of his lightning visits to Cashelmara to ensure that no one was slacking in his absence. He was busy night and day, and so was I. I paid dozens of calls, organized a charity ball, ordered a new spring wardrobe for myself, tried to teach David to talk and kept myself remorselessly up to date with current events. I followed every detail of the Civil War as if it were taking place in my own back yard, until there was nothing I did not know about Robert E. Lee and his invasion of the North. I dragged myself through each dreadful detail of the defeats at Fredericksburg and Chancellorsville, lived each splendid hour of the triumph at Gettysburg, and throughout the summer of 1864 I was with Sherman on every step of his march to the sea. Francis began to write jubilant letters, and English sympathy, dimly impressed by Lincoln at last, began to veer toward the North. But as usual the English were too absorbed in themselves to do more than veer. Everyone was talking of the evils of child chimney sweeps, and presently I was following the parliamentary debates on the bill to end their abuse. I read a great many newspapers in those days, and when Edward returned from Cashelmara he remarked how well informed I was.

Matters improved between us for a short time after that. But then to my dismay our troubles began afresh, and this time, contrary to his usual habits, he went nowhere but spent most of the day and night in the library. He said he was working on a new thesis. Outwardly he was very polite to me, but in the atmosphere of awkwardness that lay between us I felt him withdraw completely from me into isolation.

I did not know what to do. Worse still, I had no one to whom I could turn for advice. There are some matters that one simply does not discuss with one's best friends or even, if one is lucky enough to possess one, with one's mother. I was alone. I tried to tell myself that all would be well, that our difficulties would pass, but to my horror we seemed only to sink into a deeper morass of estrangement. Presently Edward abandoned the item he always used to prevent me from conceiving children. He did not ask my permission. He simply stopped using it, and when I summoned the courage to object he blamed the item for his troubles and said it was a constraint to him. I became desperate. I did not want another child, and my fear of conception made me reluctant. I tried to hide my reluctance, but of course he sensed it, and when eventually it made no difference to us whether he used the item or not he turned around and blamed me for our unhappiness.

It was at this moment, when my relationship with Edward was at its lowest ebb, that Patrick was sent down from Oxford.

It was the February of 1866. In America the war and Lincoln had died bloody deaths, but Francis was already writing that there was a lot of money being made in the North during those days of Reconstruction; he himself had fared very comfortably during the war after the initial panic had receded from Wall Street, and if I were to return home for a visit he could promise me the royalest of welcomes. But of course such a visit was impossible. Edward was far too busy to contemplate the long journey to America, and it would not have been at all proper for me to go without him. I did not even suggest it, because I knew he would have been justified in refusing his permission, but by 1866 I was even wondering if the limited separation might have done us good.

Separation seemed to have improved his relationship with Patrick. In the spring of 1864 Edward had sent his son on a Grand Tour of Europe with Mr. Bull, and in the autumn of that year Patrick had gone up to Oxford. During his first year all had gone well, and Edward had been greatly pleased. I doubt that Patrick learned much, but I suspected he enjoyed his freedom from supervision. However, halfway through the Trinity term of his second year he was sent down for what was described in the official letter as "persistent drunken, disorderly behavior, refusal to attend to any academic work, and frequent incidences of truancy."

Edward was furious. To make matters worse, Patrick was in debt. Gambling had made a great hole in his allowance, and Edward had to go to Oxford himself to settle all the unpaid bills.

A day later he came home in the blackest of rages and told me he had given Patrick two hundred pounds and forbidden him to enter any of his houses for the next twelve months.

"He's not getting one penny of an allowance from me either," he said grimly. "He can manage on two hundred pounds for a year and see how he likes it. And, Marguerite, if he should come to St. James's Square to beg money from you, you're to have nothing to do with him, do you understand? Nothing whatsoever. He's thoroughly disgraced me with his weak, despicable behavior. My God, what a son for a man in my position to have! If Cashelmara were not entailed I would cut him out of my will." And striding off to his study, he slammed the door with a crash that made all the porcelain rattle in the saloon.

I said nothing. I said little to him those days on any subject that could conceivably make him lose his temper. I merely kept out of his way as much as possible, and presently when he departed for Cashelmara I was relieved to be on my own. I flung myself once more into a whirl of social activity, and every spare moment of my time I devoted to the boys. Thomas was nearly five years old and so active that I feared poor Nanny found him a terrible handful; even I, loving him dearly as I did, felt exhausted after a mere half hour in his company, but David was still delightfully placid, round and serene as a small buddha and quite indifferent to Thomas's attempts to galvanize him into a more energetic playmate.

"That stupid baby," said Thomas crossly. "He'll never grow up properly, never. And he's so *stout.*"

"I like being stout," said David. He was three now and spoke very precisely in a mellow contralto. "Nanny is stout too. I like Nanny."

David had a thatch of hair so fair it was almost white, pink cheeks, blue eyes and a dimpled chin. It never ceased to amaze me that I, who was plain, could ever have produced a child like David.

Dearest baby, I thought as David smiled at me seraphically, but I managed to restrain myself from being too doting. I suffered from a temptation to spoil both children those days and supposed it was because I was so often frustrated in my desire to show affection toward others.

It was barely a month before Patrick turned up at St. James's Square. Edward, who had returned from Cashelmara by this time, had set out in the brougham to keep some appointment, and I was already at my davenport in the drawing room where I attended to my daily correspondence. I had just written the last of a batch of dinner invitations when the butler announced that Patrick was in the hall.

My heart sank. I had known this was bound to happen, just as I knew now that Patrick would be full of faith, convinced that I could not possibly turn him away.

"Lomax," I said to the butler, "my husband has, I believe, given you certain instructions about Mr. Patrick."

"Yes, my lady. But Mr. Patrick was so insistent that you would see him that I felt it my duty—"

"Quite. Kindly tell him I'm not at home, if you please."

"Yes, my lady."

As soon as he had departed I laid down my pen, rushed across the room and flung up the window. I waited. A minute passed before Patrick emerged slowly from the house, his head bent and his shoulders drooping.

The instant Lomax closed the front door I leaned over the sill and whispered loudly, "Patrick!"

He spun around. I put a finger to my lips. "Wait in the gardens," I told him in a low voice and rushed off to find my hat and cloak.

It was a mild springlike day. In the gardens in the center of the square the crocuses were blooming beneath the trees and the daffodils were nodding in the breeze. I left the house, and as I crossed the road Patrick ran toward me, his arms outstretched in greeting.

It is hard to describe what I felt then. I looked at Patrick, and for the first time he no longer seemed a mere boy. His face lit up when he saw me, and my heart turned over. He was not Edward and never would be, but I saw Edward in him, a younger, happier Edward, very gentle and affectionate; and as I looked upon his face, which was so painfully familiar to me, and upon his long, strong, perfect limbs, I felt a terrible desire I scarcely knew how to control. I stood there completely at the mercy of a dozen conflicting emotions, and ironically it was my helplessness that saved me. As I could neither move nor speak, all the initiative passed to Patrick, and I saw in three seconds that he, despite any illusion of mine to the contrary, was quite unchanged.

"Marguerite!" he exclaimed, hugging me as warmly as any brother would hug a favorite sister. "How wonderful to see you again—and how good of you to see me after all!" He released me and gestured to one of the benches overlooking the lawn. "Let's sit down."

I nodded. Sitting down on the bench, I clasped my hands tightly and watched the crocuses bob in the spring breeze.

"Oh, Marguerite," said my stepson, "I'm in the most awful hole, I really am. I've only got one and sixpence, and I'm staying in the most beastly little tavern east of Soho and the bed has crawling things in it. My stockings are in holes, and I don't know how to mend them and I've no idea what to do about my dirty shirts and I haven't had anything to eat since yesterday when I bought a muffin in Tottenham Court Road. Could you possibly tell Papa that I'm dreadfully sorry for everything and that I'll turn over a new leaf and do whatever he likes? I'll never go gambling again, I swear it, if only he'll forgive me and let me have another chance. Please, Marguerite. Please ask him for me."

I groped for words. I did not dare look at him. I was immensely aware of his thigh three inches from the edge of my cloak.

"I lost the two hundred pounds he gave me," said Patrick, "I thought if I could turn it into a thousand I could live very comfortably for a year—and, do you know, I did win pretty considerably to begin with . . ."

A squirrel danced among the daffodils. A black cat emerged from the shrubbery and sat down to wash its paws.

". . . so then I went to Ireland, and Annabel lent me some money, but she gave me such a wigging that I didn't like to go back to her again. I called at Duneden Castle, but that wretched Katherine wouldn't even see me because I'm in Papa's bad books, although Duneden gave me a fiver to send me on my way. So then I went to Dublin and stayed with Derry for a while, but, God, I couldn't sponge on him forever, could I? I mean, it simply wouldn't have been right! Derry has only just enough money for himself anyway because Papa's so beastly tight with his allowances, and although Derry wanted me to stay I knew I couldn't. I got back to London yesterday, and, oh Lord, Marguerite, I don't know what will happen if you don't help me. What on earth am I going to do?"

"I'll speak to Edward," I said.

"Oh, Marguerite . . ." He gave me another hug. I felt his thigh and the left side of his chest and the strong muscles of his arm. "You're so good to me," he said. "You've always been so good to me, Marguerite."

I stood up. I began to walk away. I felt as if I were being stifled by heat.

"Can't you stay longer?" he pleaded from behind me. "I would so love to talk to someone for a while."

"I shall talk to you later," I said, "after I've spoken to Edward. Where did you say your hotel was?"

"It's in Mercer Street, off Seven Dials, but don't go there, Marguerite. It's a horrid place, not at all fit for a lady."

"I'll send word to you there," I said and quickened my pace before he could again beg me to stay. I said nothing else. I did not even return his disappointed goodbye. I merely hurried into the house as fast as I could, and when I was in my room I tried to imagine how I would summon the courage to speak to Edward about his son.

III

Edward returned to the house soon afterward. I was still in my room, and the first indication I received of his return came when I heard the door of the dressing room open, although even then, until I heard him clear his throat, I thought it was the valet, Pierce. Presently I heard a succession of small sounds, the clink of a glass followed by the gurgle of liquid trickling from a bottle. I was puzzled. What could he be doing? As far as I knew he was not one of those secret drinkers whom one hears about from one's gossiping friends. I remained where I was, baffled but inert, until without warning he opened the communicating door and entered the room.

He did not see me at first, and because he thought he was alone he made no effort to straighten his back, square his shoulders or walk briskly in his normal fashion. He walked slowly and he walked with a limp. He was stooped. The stoop made him look oddly short, and because he bent his head I noticed for the first time that his hair was quite gray. His face was lined with tiredness, his brows drawn together in an ill-tempered expression, and he looked old.

I had never seen him look so old, and before I could stop myself I was comparing him with Patrick, remembering every nuance of Patrick's youth and health and vitality.

He saw me. A great change came over him at once. He straightened his back and quickened his pace, but that cost him an effort. I saw the effort reflected in his face before he erased all telltale expression and gave me one of his polite smiles.

"I'm sorry," he said. "I had no idea you were resting or I wouldn't have disturbed you. I'll go back to the dressing room."

He was gone, but I was already on my feet. I followed him into the dressing room just as he lowered himself onto the couch.

"Edward . . ." I began but found I could go no further.

He stood up, stiff and straight, and waited courteously for me to speak.

I thought of a dozen things to say but rejected every one of them. I was still fumbling desperately for words when he said unevenly, "I suppose you wish to talk about Patrick. I understand from Lomax that he called here this morning."

"Yes, he did." I was so nervous that words failed me again, and to my horror he added, still in that same uneven voice, "I saw you walking together in the square, and rather than embarrass you by arriving at an inopportune moment I told Lacy to drive past the house and take me to my club. I hope you said all you needed to say to each other."

I immediately fell into such a panic that I could only stare at him in fright. My face felt as if it were on fire.

"I noticed how he put his arm around you when you were sitting on the bench," he said. "I'm sure all the servants enjoyed that too from their grandstand position at the hall window."

If I had been entirely innocent I could have defended myself very capably from such an insinuation no matter how frightened I was, but my guilty thoughts made me behave as if I had committed some appalling indiscretion.

"Well, I've been expecting this to happen for some time," he said casually, as if he could scarcely have cared less. "After all, what else could I have expected? I've no idea whether there has been any gross impropriety between you and Patrick in the past, but that hardly matters. If you haven't misconducted yourself with Patrick there must surely have been someone else by this time. Very well. I accept it. How could I possibly blame you when I've been such an inadequate husband for so long? Of course I could fly into a rage and behave like some monster in a melodrama—and no doubt many men in my position would pride themselves on behaving in exactly that fashion—but I am, I think, a practical man and I hope I'm not so dishonest or so proud that I can't admit the failure is mine and not yours. I'm sorry. I should never have married you. It's not right to expect a young girl to remain happy long with a man my age, and I can see now that I was expecting too much of you. Well, so be it. You've given me six years of the most perfect happiness, and it would be a poor reward indeed if I now proceeded to bring you nothing but misery and dissatisfaction. Turn elsewhere if you must, but . . ." He stopped. He was no longer looking at me. He was still composed, but he had to look away. "But not to my son," he said quickly. "Don't turn to him. I'll try not to mind about anyone else. I love you and I want you to be happy. Nothing else matters except that."

And nothing else did matter. Patrick no longer mattered, younger men no longer mattered, no other man on earth mattered any more. I said, laughing through my tears, "Oh, you silly, *silly* man!" and then I kissed him, slipping my arms around his neck and clasping him to me with every ounce of strength I possessed. I think he cried too, but I was determined not to see because men are so peculiar about tears and Englishmen are the most peculiar of all. I said, "So long as you love me I don't care. There hasn't been anyone else, and there never will be so long as you really and truly love me."

"I love you," he said.

"Then everything's well."

"Everything?"

"Oh good heavens," I said, "isn't there more to loving someone than merely romping around in a double bed?"

He laughed. I had not seen him laugh for such a long time, and I felt as if I had met him afresh after some painful absence. All constraint died between us. Our fingers touched, our hands clasped, and soon I had all I wanted and so did he until our isolation on the dark borders of estrangement was no more than a dead memory.

He awoke before I did. When I opened my eyes he was watching the sunlight stream through a gap in the drapes, and his brows were drawn together again in a frown.

"What's the matter?" I said at once.

He quickly wiped the expression from his face. "It's nothing. My leg has been giving me some pain lately. This morning I saw the doctor again, but although I took a dose of the new medicine he gave me it doesn't seem to have done much good."

"So that was what you were doing in the dressing room earlier! I heard the medicine being poured from the bottle." I kissed him and eyed his leg anxiously. "How long has it been troubling you?" I asked, and suddenly I understood everything, his past difficulties in bed, his uncharacteristic reluctance to travel, his preoccupation, his moods of ill-humor. I was so horrified that I sat bolt upright in bed. "Edward, you don't mean to tell me you've had this trouble ever since—"

"The pain's spasmodic," he said. "It doesn't trouble me all the time. I saw no need to tell you about it."

"But, Edward, you know how I detest martyrs!" I felt both angry and upset. "Why in God's name didn't you tell me from the beginning?"

"I didn't want to talk about it."

"But why?"

"Because I didn't want to seem old to you," he said and added with wry humor to take the edge from his bitterness, "When I was young I hated old people who constantly moaned about their aches and pains."

"I can't imagine you moaning about anything. Don't be so silly! Anyway, what's so shameful about a few aches and pains? I could understand your secrecy if you suffered from some embarrassing disease common among elderly gentlemen, but—"

"It's not simply 'a few aches and pains,' " he said. "It's arthritis. You remember that painful fever I had not long after Katherine's wedding?"

"Yes, but . . . you recovered from that."

"I was better for a time, but then the pains began to recur." He paused before saying, "The doctor says little can be done," and something in his voice made me feel cold.

After a pause I said firmly, "Well, you don't die of arthritis, do you?"

"No," he said, "not as far as I know." But when I realized he was thinking of the living death that life in a wheelchair would mean for him I felt very frightened. My fear must have shown in my face, for at once he said cheerfully, "For the moment it's just an inconvenience, and there's no reason why it should soon become radically worse. Dr. Ives was optimistic when I saw him this morning."

"Why did you go to him? He should have come to you!" I exclaimed, and then, understanding: "If only you hadn't been so secretive!"

"Yes, I can see now that was a mistake." He watched me dress, but when he made no effort to leave the bed I knew he was waiting for me to leave the room so that he could take as much time as his stiffness demanded. I was just struggling into my top petticoat when he said unexpectedly, "What did Patrick have to say for himself? You may as well tell me."

"For heaven's sake, I'd clean forgotten." I was amazed that all thought of Patrick should have slipped from my mind. "Edward, he's destitute and unhappy and he wants very much to be forgiven. He promises passionately to turn over a new leaf—"

"Yes, he's very inclined to make passionate promises of that nature. Go on."

"He says he'll do anything you want."

"That's all very well, but I've no idea what I want to do with him. I suppose he had better live quietly at Woodhammer until I can buy him a commission in the Army. At least he's not likely to get into debt at Woodhammer."

"But, Edward . . . do you truly think Patrick is suited to a career in the Army?"

"What else can I do with him? He must have some sort of occupation. I disapprove of young men leading idle, useless lives."

"Perhaps if you made him responsible for some of your property he might become interested in estate management."

"The time will never come," said Edward bitterly, "when Patrick is interested in estate management."

I was putting up my hair. Concentrating hard on pushing the pins into the right places, I said carefully, "I'm sure all will be well eventually with Patrick, Edward, because he's at heart a very . . ." I could not think of the appropriate word. "I mean, I know he's been wild, but don't all young men have to sow their wild oats? And Patrick is young, Edward, young and . . . immature." I had pinned my hair incorrectly. The chignon collapsed beneath its hairnet and I had to start again. "Patrick's a very peaceful person at heart," I said suddenly. "Peaceful—that was the word I wanted. I think he would like nothing better than to be responsible for an estate like Woodhammer and live there quietly with his wife and children. Yes—think how good Patrick is with children! Thomas and David adore him. He's certain to want children of his own one day, and once he marries and settles down . . ." I had pinned my hair well this time, by some miracle. Now that chignons were no longer worn low on the neck it was harder to dress one's hair even if one had been accustomed to doing so. If the conversation had been less private I would have summoned my maid. "Patrick must get married," I was saying. "Not immediately, of course, because he's still so young, but in a year or two. Yes, that's it. Patrick must marry a nice pretty girl who knows her own mind and can care for him while keeping him well organized. Patrick needs to be cared for and organized. I know exactly the sort of girl he should marry—"

"Marguerite!" said Edward sternly, but when I spun around in fright I saw that he was smiling. "When are you going to learn not to meddle in other people's lives?"

"But I have such good intentions!" I pleaded, laughing with him, and ran across the room into his arms.

Later he said to me, "You may well be right about Patrick. Certainly nothing would please me more than if he settled down and took an interest in the estates." He hesitated but managed to add indistinctly, "I'm sorry . . . what I said earlier . . . very stupid of me."

"It doesn't matter," I said. "I love you very much and I know now that you love me. But, Edward, in the future tell me whenever you're in pain from the arthritis. Don't keep it to yourself and be noble, because how can I help you when you refuse to let yourself be helped?"

"Very well," he said, smiling at me. "I shall complain from time to time. I'd promise you anything, Marguerite, even that."

We parted. Feeling more lighthearted, I ran joyously upstairs to the nursery, and it was not until I looked into the dressing room later and saw the medicine bottle by the ewer that I felt the coldness come upon me again. I tried to dismiss it by leaving the room at once, but for the rest of that day I was haunted by that word "arthritis" and fancied we stood on the brink of a darkness which stretched as far as the eye could see.

Chapter Five

I

It gave me a great shock when I realized I was pregnant. It was true that I had been obliged to risk pregnancy several times since Edward had discarded the means that prevented conception, but I had always escaped unscathed, and I suppose I had assumed irrationally that my luck would last forever. Also after our reconciliation I had been so concerned that he should no longer suffer from impotence that my concern had left me little room to worry about anything else. I still knew next to nothing about the forbidden subject of anticonception and saw no way I could find out more, for no reputable doctor would have discussed such a subject with me without my husband's permission, and none of my friends seemed to be any wiser than I was. So I had merely continued to hope for the best; but the best had eluded me at last, and now there was nothing to do except resign myself to the inevitable.

It was hard. David's birth had left a deep scar on my memory, and the thought of facing such an ordeal again was terrifying to me. It might have been easier to scrape up some courage if I had longed for another child, but I was perfectly content with my two boys.

My spirits sank to a very low ebb.

I did not keep my condition a secret from Edward but told him as soon as I suspected what had happened. I thought it would cheer him by making him feel more youthful, and sure enough he seemed delighted and said it would be pleasant for me to have another baby now that Thomas and David were almost ready for the schoolroom.

I smiled and said yes. I had no intention of betraying my true feelings because I knew it would upset him if he thought I was angry. I did not want him to be upset. It was very important to our married life that he should not know I had no wish to bear him any more children, because he might think that I did not love him enough and then our troubles would begin afresh.

However, I was not nearly so clever at being a secret martyr as he was, and when one day he found me crying in my room I broke down and poured out my heart to him unmercifully.

"Well, I did wonder if you were truly pleased," he said at last in such a sensible voice that I immediately felt better. "I knew you were never anxious for another child. But, Marguerite, does David's birth necessarily mean that you're certain to have another unpleasant confinement? What does Dr. Ives say?"

"He says that I was unlucky with David and that there's no reason why I should be unlucky again."

"In that case—"

"But I don't believe a word he says!" I wept.

"That's easily solved," said Edward, still supremely sensible. "See another doctor and, if you like, a third. Get other opinions and perhaps you'll feel more confident."

I wept a little more, but he had really left me nothing to weep about. I dried my eyes on his handkerchief and made a great effort to be calm.

"That's an excellent idea," I said firmly. "Why didn't I think of that myself? How stupid I've been!" But I felt my eyes fill with tears again. Clenching the handkerchief into a tight ball, I tried to will the tears away. "I'm sure I shall love the baby very much when he comes," I sobbed, and despite all my efforts at self-control I burst into floods of tears.

"We must think of a name for him at once," said Edward with cunning. "You know how you always said you liked to think of Thomas and David as people long before they were born. If you could think of the new baby as a person it might be easier for you."

"Oh yes," I said, dabbing my eyes uselessly with his sodden handkerchief. "A name. Oh dear, I can't think of any at all! Think of a name, Edward."

He offered me a second handkerchief. "Perhaps Richard?" he suggested. "That was the name of the uncle who left me Wood-hammer Hall, the uncle who had such an influence on me when I was growing up. If you like the name—"

"Richard. Yes. Yes, I do like it very much," I said rapidly, and somehow after that I did find it easier to resign myself to my ordeal.

II

Of course it was a girl.

I had an easy delivery. It was all over in three hours. Dazed, I said to Dr. Ives, "There must be a mistake. It can't be born already." But Dr. Ives merely smiled the supercilious smile that made me want to slap him, the infant wailed plaintively and the midwife, bored that the birth had been so uninteresting, said tartly, "You've got a daughter at last, my lady."

My heart sank like a stone. It was an instinctive reaction, for I had never stopped to analyze why I had no desire for a daughter, and I did not understand why I should feel so dismayed.

"It can't be a girl," I said desperately. "It's a boy. We've chosen the name. It's Richard."

"There, there, my lady," said Dr. Ives soothingly. "We all have our little disappointments. Try to rest and recover your strength."

I did sleep, but when I awoke my relief that my ordeal was over was immediately soured by the knowledge that Richard was a girl. I lay clutching the sheet, my eyes staring at the ceiling, my senses hardly aware of my physical discomfort, and racked my brains to decide what I should say to Edward. Later when the nurse returned to the room to give me another glimpse of the baby my spirits sank even lower. The infant was unremittingly plain. She had a bright red complexion, a large bald head and a puny body.

"Ah yes," I said, hiding my despair as best I could. "Very nice. Thank you, Nurse."

The baby had just been returned to the cradle when Edward came in, and the nurse withdrew so that we could be alone together.

After we had embraced he said, smiling, "So all was well?"

"Oh yes!" I said with an attempt at gaiety. "Dr. Ives is the most aggravating man, but I've no doubt he's very clever. I never dreamt that the birth would be so easy."

"Thank God for that," he said, kissing me again.

"Thank God," I agreed, holding his hands tightly.

There was a pause.

"Well," he said lightly, "I suppose we must start considering names again."

"I'm glad you mentioned that," I said rapidly, "because I have a splendid idea. Edward, why don't we call her Nell? It's pretty and it's short—I've often felt annoyed that I myself have such a long name—and I thought you might like her to be called after the daughter you loved so much. What do you think?"

He looked startled. "That's very generous of you, my dearest, but—"

"It would be so nice," I interrupted, the words tumbling from my lips, "if she could be named for your favorite daughter. I should like that very much."

"Yes, so would I, but, Marguerite, Nell was a mere abbreviation of the name Eleanor, you know, and people might think it odd if I called my second wife's daughter after my first wife."

"Oh heavens," I said, "why should I care about that?" It occurred to me as I spoke how much I had grown up since the early days of my marriage when Eleanor's name had been anathema to me. "Besides, Eleanor never used the name Nell," I pointed out, "and Nell will never use the name Eleanor. I don't see why people should think it odd."

"Well, if you're certain . . ."

"Quite certain. Oh, Edward, do you mind very much that it's not a boy?"

"My dearest Marguerite, of course not! I do realize you must be somewhat disappointed, but speaking for myself, I'm simply glad that you and the infant are safe and well. That's far more important to me than the baby's sex."

The great burden of my anxiety lifted. When he said anxiously, "Are you very disappointed?" I was able to answer with truth: "No, I'm glad to have a daughter. I'm really very glad indeed."

III

The baby did not thrive. At first she cried a great deal, just as Thomas had cried early in his life, but Thomas had gained weight fast despite his discomforts and no one had worried about his health. We all worried about Nell. Dr. Ives used to come to the house regularly to see her and the nurse stayed on so that the baby could have special care. As soon as my lying-in was over I spent most of my time in her little room off the nursery.

"Is the baby ill?" demanded Thomas.

"No, darling, just a little delicate."

"When will she be able to play with us?" said David.

"Not for a long while yet. But some day she will."

She gradually lost the red-faced complexion of the newborn infant. Her skin became pale and had a curious transparent quality that made her seem ethereal. She had blue eyes, prettily shaped, and soft down on top of her head. I thought she might be fair-haired one day. I often pictured her growing up and thought how nice it would be to choose patterns for her little dresses; later she could look through my fashion magazines with me. Perhaps she would be cleverer with a needle than I was, but that would hardly be difficult. The boys would go away to school eventually, but now I would no longer be so upset by their departure because I would still have Nell at home.

In March, two months after her birth, she began to cry less often. She also began to cough.

"When will the baby start to smile?" asked Thomas.

"Later, darling, a little later. When spring comes."

"Will we be able to take her for walks then?"

"Oh yes, because babies love to go out in the sunshine. She'll smile and laugh a lot then, you'll see."

I tried my hand at sewing again and made a little dress for her to wear when she was older. The material was lovely, pink silk with a layer of white muslin, and I embroidered little roses around the hem. I spent hours on the embroidery. I would sit by her cradle while I sewed and marvel at my newfound devotion to the needle. The London Season was fast approaching, but I had no interest in social engagements and had temporarily given up all my charity work.

"I shall take it up again later," I said to Edward. "When Nell's stronger I shall go out more."

I ordered a new perambulator because I did not want her to have anything second-hand. The perambulator that had served Thomas and David now seemed too shabby, and so did all their early toys, which I had kept in a box in the attics. I bought her a beautiful doll. I had such fun choosing it. I thought how splendid it was to go into a toy shop and look at dolls instead of inspecting the endless parade of woolly animals and tin soldiers.

Spring came. Nell was very good now. She never cried at all. I kept telling everyone how good she was.

"She still doesn't smile yet," said Thomas.

"Oh yes, she does," I said. "I often see her smile."

"I think poor Baby's cough is a little worse, my lady," said Nurse. "This morning—"

"No," I said, "it's better. I told Dr. Ives only yesterday how much better it was."

And at the end when the square was a mass of pink blossoms and the spring sunshine was streaming through the nursery windows onto the toys she would never see, all I said was "It's so nice to have a daughter. We shall have such fun together when she grows up."

She died an hour later.

IV

I went to my room and stayed there for a long time. The house was hushed and still. Once I heard Thomas talking too loudly and Nanny hissing "Shhh!" but after that there was a deep silence, and I supposed she had taken both boys for a walk. I went to the window, but when I saw no sign of them I looked instead at the pink blossoms and green leaves and thought how pretty the square was in the spring. It was a beautiful day.

I changed my clothes. I put on a black dress and sat looking at myself in the glass. All the freckles had faded from the bridge of my nose, but that was because I had been out so little lately.

Edward knocked on the door. When he came in he said, "I wondered if you still wanted to be alone."

I shrugged. I did not know. I felt confused and could think of nothing to say.

He sat down on the bed beside me and held my hand. "Marguerite, I . . . I know there's nothing to say that could make any difference, but—"

"Yes?"

"At least it wasn't one of the boys. You see . . ."

I leaped to my feet. Rage made me dizzy. The room swam in a mist before my eyes. "Don't you dare say that to me!" I shouted at him. "Don't you dare treat me as if I were a second Eleanor who cared as little as you do for all your unloved daughters!"

"I only meant—"

"Unloved!" I screamed at him. "Unloved! No wonder I never wanted a daughter after seeing the kind of women your daughters have become, Katherine thinking of love as if it were a prize awarded for good behavior, Annabel choosing to fight with you rather than be ignored, Madeleine turning to your religion-crazed old mother because you weren't there when she needed you—you and your daughters! Why, it's a wonder I even dared have sons, considering the way I've seen you treat Patrick sometimes!"

He was so white that his face seemed almost gray. He said, faltering, in a voice that did not sound like his voice at all, "I'm sure I've always tried to do my duty as a father."

"Your duty!" I said in a fury. "Your duty! Edward, where children are concerned it's not enough simply to do your duty! You think you're so ill-used because your children have failed you, but the real truth is that they are ill-used because you have failed them."

I stopped speaking. The room was deathly quiet, but I did not stop to listen to the silence. I ran out, slamming the door with a bang that echoed through the silent house, and rushed upstairs to the nursery. Nanny and Nurse were still out with the children. The door of Nell's little room was closed, but I went in, picked her up and held her in my arms while I cried. After a while I remembered she was dead. Shocked that I had disturbed her, I kissed her, replaced her carefully in her cradle and drew the sheet over her once more. I wondered in panic if I were going mad, not remembering, being so confused, saying so many cruel things to Edward. I returned to the nursery, but before I could leave I heard him coming up the stairs. He moved very slowly, and I knew his arthritis must be troubling him again.

He had suffered a great deal from arthritis that winter, and I had sensed his relief when first my pregnancy and then Nell's short life had kept me so occupied.

When he reached the landing he paused to recover his breath. I could hear his labored breathing before he opened the nursery door and entered the room.

I noticed again how he had aged. He always moved his legs awkwardly now, and only pride kept him from carrying a cane inside the house as well as outside. His hair was quite silver, but that only made him look more distinguished. Not even he minded the silver hair.

He did not speak at once but merely stood by the door. I was unsure whether he was still out of breath or whether he had difficulty choosing his words.

At last he managed to say, "You misunderstood me."

I said nothing.

"When I said 'At least it wasn't one of the boys,' I meant that the younger a child is the easier it is to bear the loss. Loss of a child is always intolerable, but when the child is no longer a baby, when there have been years, not months, of precious memories . . . I'm sorry. I phrased my thoughts very clumsily."

"You did," I said. "Yes."

"But, Marguerite, I too was upset."

"Yes," I said. "I expect you were in your own way. But you never thought she'd live. No one truly thought she'd live, did they? I expect they thought it was pathetic when I bought the doll and the new perambulator."

"We all admired your courage. I'm sure no one thought—"

"I thought she'd live if I bought things for her," I said. "It was silly of me." I moved to the window. "I wish the boys would come back."

He came closer to me. I noticed how his hand shook before he placed it on my arm. "Perhaps you would like to go away for a while —a month or two on the Continent—"

"No, thank you," I said. "That won't be necessary. I'm not Eleanor and I've no intention of ignoring the children—or you— while I indulge in a nervous collapse."

He said nothing. The silence lasted a long time.

Finally I said, "Edward, I'm sorry I'm saying all these hurtful things to you, but I simply can't help myself. Please forgive me."

"It's the shock," he said. "I understand." He put his arm on top of the chest of drawers and shifted the weight from one leg to the other. There was another silence.

"What can I do?" he said at last. "Is there anything I can do?" And I knew he was asking not only what he could do for me but what he could do for his children.

"I should like to go to Woodhammer," I said. "The countryside will look so lovely in the spring. And, Edward, I want all the children to come to stay with us, and I especially want you to forgive Madeleine so that she can come and stay as well."

"Madeleine will never come. Neither will Annabel."

"Yes, they will. Madeleine will want to see the boys and Annabel will want to see her daughters. We can invite them down from Northumberland for a visit. How long is it since you've seen your granddaughters, Edward?"

"It would all be too much for you—such a large gathering."

"I mustn't spend months grieving for Nell," I said. "I must have some important event to plan and prepare for. Why, of course!" I exclaimed, inspired, suddenly seeing how I could make some small amends to him for my unkind words. "We shall have a family party to celebrate our wedding anniversary, but we won't hold it at Wood-hammer. We'll go to Ireland. It'll be the best party that I've ever organized, and we shall hold it at no other place but Cashelmara."

Chapter Six

I

We came at last to Cashelmara, to that eerie beauty mingled with the memories of death and decay, to the wild alien fastnesses of the Joyce country where Edward had been born. It was May. The grass was lushly green after the winter rains, and the earth smelled clean and fresh and full of promise. After those dark winter months in London I felt my spirits rise, and as soon as we were settled I arranged for the family to assemble for our anniversary celebration.

The first to arrive was Patrick. I had not seen him for over a year, for as the result of his disgrace he had been banished to Wood-hammer while I had been confined to London both before and after Nell's birth. To my relief Edward had abandoned the idea of a military career for him, but he had refused to give his son any responsibility and Patrick had been obliged to occupy himself entirely with his artistic pursuits. That suited Patrick very well, naturally, and he wrote to me occasionally saying how happy he was. I suspected he had not in the least wanted to come to Cashelmara, but he turned up dutifully a week after our arrival, and Thomas and David fell upon him with great glee. Seeing how glad he was to be reunited with them, I remembered my schemes for him to have children of his own, and when a letter from Francis arrived enclosing a photograph of my niece Sarah, I found I could not resist indulging in the most delightful speculations.

Sarah. Seventeen years old now and surely, if her photograph did not lie, the belle of every future ball. It was the first picture I had seen of her with her hair up, and she looked amazingly sophisticated. Her resemblance to Francis tantalized me. She had inherited his unusual good looks, and as I stared at her picture I felt a great longing to rediscover the niece I had left behind in New York seven years before. My desire to see Sarah was probably heightened by the fact that in resembling Francis she also resembled Blanche, and Blanche, to my grief, was no longer alive. The previous summer I had received word that she had died in childbirth. The news had upset me profoundly, particularly since I myself was in dread of my confinement at the time, but Edward had been very kind, offering to take me to America at the earliest opportunity. Not that the opportunity would ever come; I knew that now. His arthritis made long journeys an ordeal for him, and no matter how much I wanted to see Francis and Sarah I knew I could never leave Edward even if he gave me permission to go alone.

"I say!" said Patrick with the most gratifying enthusiasm when I showed him Sarah's photograph. "What a gorgeous creature! Can't you invite her to England to visit us, Marguerite?"

"She's still a little young at present," I said. "But perhaps in a year or two . . ." My mind skipped nimbly ahead, visualizing Sarah begging Francis to take her to Europe, Francis unable to resist the request because he doted on her so much, Sarah and Francis both coming to England and staying with us at St. James's Square. My mind ceased to skip and leaped forward instead to keep pace with my romantic imagination. Patrick and Sarah would meet, fall hopelessly in love, marry. I should have Sarah with me in England, Francis would, of course, be unable to resist visiting Europe frequently to see us both, Patrick would be splendidly settled and quite out of reach of any irrational weakness of mine . . .

"She's rather fetching, isn't she?" I said casually to Patrick. After seven years in England I had quite mastered the cunning use of the understatement. "I thought you would be interested to see her latest portrait since I speak of her so often." And then I dropped the subject like a hot biscuit before either of us should burn our fingers.

II

Everyone came. Katherine arrived with her husband, maid, portmanteaux and diamonds, Madeleine arrived alone dressed in navy-blue serge and carrying a shabby black bag, and Annabel arrived on a splendid chestnut mare with the elusive Alfred reluctantly in tow. Annabel was pleased to see her daughters again at last. Their paternal grandparents with whom they lived in Northumberland had refused to permit the girls to stay at Clonagh Court, but Annabel promptly rode to Cashelmara to see them. A shock awaited her. She had been thinking of them as little girls in the nursery, but Clara was now fifteen and Edith a year younger, both quite old enough to treat their mother coolly and look down their aristocratic little noses at her husband. Poor Alfred! Her was really such a nice man, and he could not help feeling ill at ease at Cashelmara. I'm sure I should have been just as ill at ease if I had been in his shoes, and finally I could not resist resorting to my usual brand of meddling.

"You're being most uncharitable," I said severely to the girls. "Does Mr. Smith beat your mother? Does he oppress her and make her life miserable? You ought to be thankful that she has a kind, considerate husband who makes her happy, and as for your mother herself, I don't think your attitude toward her is at all justified. I know she was wrong to leave you, but she's sorry for it now and I think the least you can do is try to be pleasant to her even if you can't forgive her yet for what she did. Anyway, it's most un-Christian to harbor grudges and treat your mother as if she were a nasty smell. Didn't your grandparents take you to church in Northumberland? Your behavior doesn't reflect well upon the way they've brought you up."

This put the girls to shame, just as I had intended, and to my satisfaction they did try after that to make amends. They were not bad girls, but I could not help thinking it was a pity they were not more like their mother, whom I found increasingly companionable. Clara was very pretty and just the tiniest bit dull, while Edith—poor Edith!—was plain and lumpy and seldom had more than two words to say for herself. However, I knew what it was to suffer in the shadow of a pretty older sister, and fourteen is a difficult age.

Meanwhile I continued to meddle happily in other fields and thought my meddling highly successful.

"Oh, Edward, promise me you won't talk to Madeleine about getting married!" I begged him, and he assured me with a laugh that he had already resigned himself to Madeleine's spinsterhood.

"And to the nursing?" I demanded at once.

"Well, if I'm to forgive her by welcoming her to my house I suppose I must resign myself to that too," he said reluctantly, but in fact he was very civil to Madeleine, and since she herself was as serene as ever despite her sordid existence in London's East End, they did manage not to quarrel with each other. Madeleine earned a little salary now, so she was not entirely impoverished, but her hands were roughened by hard work, and I often wondered how she endured such a life, particularly since she could have lived in the luxury that suited Katherine so well.

"Edward, you will be nice to Katherine, won't you?" I said. Oh, I did meddle! My long nose inched its way into everyone's affairs, and I could not remember when I had last enjoyed myself so much. But Edward did not need to be reminded about Katherine. When she arrived he kissed her warmly and told her with great admiration that he had never seen her look so beautiful.

"Papa is somewhat changed," Katherine observed wonderingly. "I declare he has become quite mellow with age."

"Like an elderly lion," said Patrick, and I could see he was already sketching the lion in his mind's eye. "A lion who's tired of hunting and wants to lie in the shade and snooze."

"Edward," I said tentatively later, "about Patrick's future . . ."

"I have it all arranged," he said, smiling at me. "Patience!"

So I restrained myself with an effort from meddling further with that subject and cast all my energies into organizing the family dinner party that was to take place on the evening of our wedding anniversary, the twentieth of June.

As it was such a special occasion, Thomas and David were allowed to stay up and dine with us, but since this brought the number to thirteen the concession did create difficulties.

"If only George didn't have to come!" I said, but Edward said that George, as his only nephew, had a right to be there. Finally I solved the problem by inviting Lord Duneden's two married daughters and their husbands. They were special friends of mine, as well as being Katherine's stepdaughters, and Edward had known them since birth. This brought the numbers to seventeen, a clumsy total, but at the last moment Alfred Smith excused himself from attending on account of a touch of fever, and this reduced us to the splendid number of sixteen.

Instinct told me then that the evening would be a success, and so it was. To this day I can remember walking into the dining room at Cashelmara and seeing all the Georgian silver gleaming in the soft candlelight and the long red velvet curtains glowing like some sumptuous backcloth behind a richly decorated stage. I can remember Hayes, in a gale of excitement, opening the champagne and tiptoeing reverently around the table to fill the glasses, and, best of all, I can remember Patrick rising to his feet to propose the toast. I was so proud of him because he did not stammer but spoke as if he had labored long in preparing the speech and even longer in memorizing every syllable.

". . . and I'm sure Papa will not mind," he concluded, "if I ask you all to drink especially to Marguerite, who has drawn us all together for . . . " He hesitated for the first time, stopping before he could say "for this family occasion" and instead merely repeating "who has drawn us all together." At that point Annabel said "Hear, hear!" in a very Annabelish fashion, Madeleine smiled at me fondly and Katherine abandoned her haughty mien to regard me with childlike affection.

I felt quite overcome.

Patrick was saying, "So let's all drink to Papa and Marguerite on this their seventh wedding anniversary!" And as everyone raised his glass David's mellow contralto was heard saying, "Mama's face is exactly the same color as a tomato, and it doesn't at all match the color of her hair."

Everyone laughed. Thomas looked peeved that he had not made the remark himself, but the next moment his vanity was appeased when Patrick summoned him to present the family gift. It was a salver, inscribed in memory of the occasion, and after we had inspected it admiringly Edward rose to his feet to reply to the toast.

He thanked his children for coming to Cashelmara; he thanked them for their present; he thanked me "for more than could ever be expressed in words," and just as David was watching my tomato hue again with interest Edward said to his eldest son, "I would like to drink a toast to you too, Patrick, in belated celebration of your coming of age. Now that you're grown up I shall look forward to ceding part of your inheritance to you to administer as you think fit. It's a great comfort to me at my time of life to know that I have a son upon whom I can rely for help."

Poor Patrick was immediately far more overcome than I was. I saw the tears in his eyes and prayed hard that Edward would not notice, but fortunately he was already looking at the others as he raised his glass.

"I shall do my very best to help you, Papa," Patrick assured him when he had recovered his poise. "Which portion of Woodhammer did you intend me to administer?"

186

"Woodhammer?" said Edward, surprised. "Oh, I wasn't thinking of Woodhammer. You know the estate there well enough already. I was thinking that now is the time when you should learn more about Cashelmara."

I saw Patrick's expression and my heart sank. I tried to kick him to warn him not to object, but I only succeeded in kicking Annabel instead.

"Good God!" said Annabel. "There's a colt under the table!"

"Oh, Annabel!" I exclaimed feverishly. "Do tell Edward about that colt you bought the other day at Letterturk fair. It was such an amusing story!"

Annabel needed no further encouragement. The situation was temporarily saved, but later after the gentlemen had joined the ladies in the drawing room I said privately to Edward, "Dearest, I can't tell you how happy I am that you've decided to put so much trust in Patrick. I'm sure he feels very honored and pleased. Of course he'll find it a little lonely here at Cashelmara, especially after we leave for England, but if he had company for a little while I've no doubt the prospect wouldn't seem so intimidating to him. Couldn't Derry come to stay for a week or two? After all, Derry's acquitted himself so well in Dublin, hasn't he, and you never truly blamed him for that wretched business with Katherine which was all my fault. And now that Patrick's grown up . . . well, the situation is so different, isn't it, from the days when he was just a boy and easily led into mischief? I dare say too that Derry is quite settled down now that he's been called to the bar. Surely it wouldn't do any harm if he visited Cashelmara—don't you agree?"

Of course he agreed. Edward was not going to disagree with me on that night of all nights, and once again I preened myself on my successful meddling and thought how clever I was at managing my family's affairs.

III

Derry arrived two weeks later on the morning after Katherine and Duneden had departed. Madeleine had long since returned to her hospital, and because Edward was anxious to attend the closing sessions of Parliament we intended to return to London ourselves the following week. However, I wondered if he would be fit enough to travel, for after the party his arthritis had troubled him so severely that he had been unable to ride around the estate. Patrick had been obliged to go out alone with MacGowan, and Edward, who had been looking forward to instructing his son, had been frustrated in his desire to accompany them.

Another matter frustrated him too. When the pain was bad during our times alone together there was nothing he could do except dose himself heavily with laudanum and wait for the pain to pass.

"You mustn't worry on my account," I said at once when he became upset.

"But what are we going to do?" he said. "How are we going to manage? What's to happen to our marriage?" He was so weakened by the pain that he could no longer fight the despair.

"Everything will be well," I said, "as long as you trust me. If you can love me enough to do that, I shall love you more than enough not to miss what we had before."

He looked at me. I saw his cynicism and his worldliness battle with his immense desire to believe, and suddenly I was filled with a rage such as I had not known since my unhappiest days in New York, a rage against fate for having meted out unfair treatment. If Edward had been over seventy I might have been more resigned to his ill health, but he was still a long way from seventy and his mind remained active and young.

"Promise me!" I said fiercely to him, trying not to think of those endless twilight years that stretched ahead of us. "Promise me you'll trust me!"

"I promise," he said, the effects of the laudanum blurring his voice to a whisper, and he fell asleep with his hand curled peacefully in mine.

It was the very next day that Derry Stranahan arrived. Both Annabel's daughters almost swooned when they saw him, for they had lived a secluded life with their grandparents in Northumberland and had never before been confronted with such a good-looking young man. But Derry had learned his lesson. Not even his worst enemy could have accused him of flirting with Clara, whose prettiness he obviously admired, and as soon as he set foot in Cashelmara his behavior was impeccable.

Thomas and David became disgruntled because Patrick spent all his spare time in Derry's company, but I could hardly complain to Patrick about that when I had imported Derry solely to make Cashelmara tolerable to him. I did think it was a pity that Patrick could not even spend half an hour a day with his brothers, but perhaps I had come to take his devotion to the boys too much for granted. Naturally it was more fun for him to be with Derry, and I decided to hold my tongue on the subject during the two weeks of Derry's visit.

The days passed. Our life at Cashelmara remained uneventful until at last on one morning in early July Maxwell Drummond jogged up the drive in his donkey cart to make a mockery of my painfully constructed family peace.

IV

Maxwell Drummond, uncouth and brash, his boots ringing insolently on the marble floor of the hall—I was standing upstairs in the gallery as he demanded to see Edward, and as I watched I remembered how he had disgraced himself in Edward's eyes by abandoning the opportunities of the Agricultural College to run off with a schoolmaster's daughter.

"My lord's unwell," Hayes was saying guardedly. "He'll not be receiving visitors today, Maxwell Drummond."

I will not write the word Drummond used to describe this statement. To say that the word was coarse would do injustice to its gross vulgarity.

"It's the truth, so help me!" cried Hayes indignantly.

"—— the truth," said Drummond. "I'm staying here till Lord de Salis sees me, Robert Hayes, and you'd best tell him I'm here before that bastard Derry Stranahan walks through this hall or else it's a murder you'll be witnessing, and may God forgive me if I lie."

I found myself at the head of the stairs. When Hayes looked up I saw the relief in his eyes. "My lady . . ."

"I'll see Mr. Drummond, Hayes."

Drummond gave Hayes a smug look and bowed low to me. "God save you, my lady."

"Good morning, Mr. Drummond," I said in a chilly voice and swept ahead of him to the blue morning room which was set aside for receiving people of lesser quality.

The room was damp and cold. Outside a mist was creeping down from the mountains and pushing clammy fingers toward the lough.

"Well, Mr. Drummond," I said when we were alone, "my husband is unwell, but perhaps I can help you. I understand you wish to make a complaint about Mr. Stranahan."

"Himself, my lady," said Drummond. "My lady, I'm a peaceful man and I'm not uneducated and I can accept any situation as long as it's fair and just, and to be sure Lord de Salis is the fairest

189

landlord west of the Shannon, which is why I know this time there must be some mistake. I can take a great deal from Ian MacGowan, the mean Scots bastard, because at bottom it's an honest man he is and him only trying to do his job as best he can, but I'll not be taking a tinker's curse from that son of a tinker's bitch Roderick Stranahan, and that's my last word on the subject."

"Mr. Drummond, if you would kindly come to the point I would be greatly obliged—"

"Giving himself such airs! Pretending to be such a gentleman when everyone knows he used to play barefoot in front of that hovel down the bohereen from my own home—when everyone knows it's the worst drunkard and gambler his father was from here to Clonareen—"

"Mr. Drummond . . ."

"My lady, is it the truth that Lord de Salis has given Mr. Patrick all the land on the north shore and told him to do as he likes with it?"

I stared at him. I did not answer.

"And is it the truth that Derry Stranahan won't be returning to Dublin because Mr. Patrick has turned the land over to him to treat as he pleases?"

Some small noise made me whirl around. Neither of us had heard the door open, but now as the floorboard creaked I saw we were not alone. On the threshold, leaning heavily on his walking stick, stood Edward, and one glance at his face told me he was in a towering rage.

v

"Leave us, Marguerite, if you please," said Edward, and I left them. I ran all the way to the hall and caught Hayes as he emerged from the dining room.

"Hayes, do you know where Mr. Patrick is?"

"To be sure, my lady, he was riding up the drive to the stables a whileen past."

I rushed down the passage to the side door and tore through the rain to the stables. There was no sign of Patrick, but as I turned to run back to the house he rode into the courtyard with Derry. They both waved when they saw me, and then I saw their expressions change as they came nearer.

Patrick dismounted quickly. "Marguerite! For God's sake, what's the matter?"

I was too angry and too sick at heart to care what I said. "You fool," I said to him, my voice shaking. "You stupid fool! How dare you turn over your new responsibilities to Derry! Your father gave that land to you as a gesture of confidence and generosity. How dare you wash your hands of it and throw that gesture back in his face!"

"Lady de Salis," said Derry smoothly as Patrick stared at me in stupefaction, "you must have a very rough justice in America if you treat a man as guilty before you've even given him a fair hearing."

"I've heard enough to realize this is all your fault!" I shouted at him, enraged by both his coolness and his criticism.

"Then you haven't heard enough," said Derry, still smooth as glass, "for the fault's not mine but yours."

"How dare you suggest—"

"You brought me here. You implied you wanted me to help Patrick."

"I implied no such thing! I simply wanted Patrick to have some companionship because—"

"Ah, it's so touching how concerned you always are for Patrick's welfare!" said Derry, and as I saw the malice glitter in his eyes I was shocked—as if I had picked up a precious stone and seen vermin crawling in the earth beneath. "It's lucky your husband's old enough to be blind to your most private philanthropies, isn't it, Lady de Salis?"

I stared at him. For a second I glimpsed a truth that lay far beyond the borders of his insolence, and then the glimpse vanished before I could identify it, and my anger took control of me again.

"Mr. Stranahan," I managed to say, "it is quite beneath my dignity to argue with a man—I cannot say a gentleman—who has addressed me as you have just addressed me. I find your behavior rude, insolent and altogether quite intolerable, and I shall certainly inform my husband that as far as I am concerned you are no longer welcome at Cashelmara. Good day." And turning my back on them, I stumbled through the mud toward the house just as the mist thickened in the courtyard to chill me to the bone.

VI

There was an appalling quarrel.

I tried not to listen, but I had no choice. The quarrel filled the house.

Drummond was dismissed, and from the window of the gallery I watched him saunter down the steps to his donkey cart. He was whistling, and his swagger grazed my raw nerves. After a long interval Derry too left. I was in my room by this time, but since this faced the drive I saw him wait with his baggage for the trap to come from the stables to the front door. When he left he never once looked back, so I did not see the expression on his face.

Meanwhile Edward had turned to Patrick. Unable to bear to listen to their shouting, I retreated to the farthest reaches of the west wing, the part of the house reserved for guests, and in the last bedroom I closed the door, sank down on the window seat and stared across the straggling vegetable patch to the wet darkness of the larchwoods.

At last when I nerved myself to leave I returned to my room with the intention of remaining there in seclusion, but as soon as I opened the door I saw with a shock that Edward was there. I was in such a state of apprehensiveness that I might well have panicked by bolting from his presence if I had not realized he was in pain. He was sitting on the edge of the bed and dosing himself with laudanum.

"Oh, there you are," he said, perfectly calm. "I was about to ask your maid to look for you. Marguerite, there's a doctor in Westport. I forget his name, but he attends Lord Sligo now and then at Westport House. Could you write the note to send for him? I feel so unwell that I don't believe either the arthritis or Patrick's imbecility can be entirely to blame."

"Of course!" In my distress I forgot all my apprehension. "I'll send for him at once. Do you have a fever?"

"I don't think so, but there's a damnable pain in my stomach. My digestion has been playing me tricks lately for some reason or other." And with a terrible passion he added, "God, how I hate growing old!" and covered his face with his hands.

I kissed him. "I'm sorry you've been so troubled when you're unwell," I said unsteadily. "It's all my fault, I know, for pressing you to give Patrick more responsibility."

He shook his head, let his hands fall from his face. "No, your idea was sound. The fault was mine. I turned a blind eye once too often to Derry Stranahan."

"If only Patrick hadn't abdicated his responsibilities in that fashion—"

"He said he wanted only to please me. He said he was afraid he wouldn't be able to manage the work successfully, so he asked Derry to help him. He said he hadn't intended me to know he was afraid of the responsibility."

"And Derry had no motive other than kindness?" I could not help but be skeptical, sure enough Edward answered bitterly, "Derry intervened out of greed and the desire to revenge himself on those who caused his expulsion from the valley years ago. He was trying to extort money from Drummond and the O'Malleys."

"I confess I've been greatly deceived by him," I said after a pause. "He hides his true feelings much too well."

All Edward said was "He's no damned good." He was staring hard at the floor, and his clenched fists dug into the mattress at his sides.

"Edward, please have faith in Patrick. I know it's a lot to ask after everything that's happened, but—"

"Patrick's a good boy," he said unexpectedly, surprising me so much that at first I wondered if I had heard him correctly. His voice too sounded unlike him. It was strained, curiously subdued. "He's like my father," he said. "My father was a delightful man. I wish you could have known him. He and my mother were devoted to each other. He said to me once, 'I can't recommend matrimony too highly.' I can very clearly remember him saying that."

I could not quite follow the drift of the conversation and supposed the laudanum was making him wander in his speech. However, I seized the opportunity to say, "And I'm sure Patrick will say the same thing to you when he himself marries and settles down."

"Marries . . . settles down . . . yes," he said, and now I knew the laudanum was affecting him, for his words were starting to slur. "Best thing for him . . . a good boy, no son of mine could be . . . other than that."

"I'll send for the doctor at once," I said gently and tugged the bell rope to summon his valet.

A quarter of an hour later when the summons for the doctor was on its way I began to comb the house in search of Patrick.

VII

I found him at last in one of the disused glasshouses. He was sitting on an upturned box in a corner among the weeds, his elbows on his knees, his head in his hands. He looked up as I pushed open the door and then looked away as if he could not bear to meet my eyes.

"It would be better if we didn't talk," he said at once. "I know you have a low opinion of me."

"Oh Patrick!" I felt bereft, and suddenly all my anger vanished and I had to fight the urge to console him too lavishly. "I'm sorry I lost my temper," I said rapidly. "I said things that shouldn't have been said, and no doubt Derry was quite right in accusing me of not giving you a fair hearing. Edward has explained to me that you acted only to please him."

"I don't suppose he'll ever forgive me, but—"

"But he will! I know he will! Patrick, do you know what would really please him more than anything else? If you were to marry, Patrick, if you were to marry and settle down—at Woodhammer, of course. I'm sure I could arrange for that."

"But, Marguerite, I don't know any girl I'd want to marry! It's all very well you talking of marriage, but the girls I meet are either shy little things—and that don't suit me, because I'm shy myself—or else they fancy me because I'm six feet two and look pretty well on horseback and have a title and fortune to look forward to one day. And that don't suit me either, because I know they're not one scrap interested in what I'm really like."

"Oh, those English girls!" I exclaimed passionately. "Either blushing like ineffectual roses or else trying you on for size as if you were a new fashion from Paris! If only you could meet an American girl. American girls are so unstultified, so fresh, so . . . so *interested* in their suitors! I wish so much that you could meet my niece Sarah. If I could write to Francis and persuade him to bring Sarah to England for a visit—why, of course! Patrick, I've just had the most marvelous idea! Why don't *you* write to Sarah? She knows all about you, because I so often mention you in my letters, and I know she would be thrilled to receive a letter from you yourself. If you could establish a correspondence I'm sure she would soon be anxious to cross the Atlantic!"

"But would it be proper for me to write since we haven't been introduced?"

"I'll write to Francis and say I've given you permission to address her."

"But what would I say?"

"Well, for a start," I said, "you could say how delighted you were to see her new photograph and how much more delighted you would be to see her in person."

He looked at me in admiration. "You're so deuced clever, Marguerite!" he said, smiling at me despite all his troubles. "You're the most ingenious girl I ever met!"

Meddling would have been a better word to describe my machinations, but of course I much preferred to think of myself as ingenious. Blushing with pleasure, I smiled back at him.

Some people never learn.

Chapter Seven

I

We did not leave Cashelmara.

Edward's arthritis eased, but his stomach ailment troubled him to such an extent that he was obliged to abandon his plans to return to London. The doctor from Westport, diagnosing an ulcer, prescribed a regimen of mild food, but Edward did not care to be told what to eat and sent instead for his doctor in London. To his annoyance he was still prescribed a mild diet, but this time he was allowed a little brandy after dinner and a glass of wine with his meals. I strongly suspected that Dr. Ives told Edward only what he wanted to hear, but I said nothing. I wanted Edward to be well; I wanted to leave Cashelmara. We had been there for nearly two months, quite long enough for me to enjoy that eerie beauty, and now I was longing for civilization, for the brilliant clamor of London or the picture-book coziness of Woodhammer Hall.

But we stayed at Cashelmara. The grass grew lushly by the way-side of the road to Clonareen, and the gorse and heather bloomed yet again on the hillside above the larchwoods. There was a spell of fine weather. The mountains shimmered in a gray-blue haze around the dazzling azure of the lough, and below the house the Fooey River dawdled more idly than ever through the bog to the golden strand of the western shore.

Patrick longed to leave Cashelmara even more than I did. He used to talk yearningly of Woodhammer, but although he did once suggest that he might go ahead of us to England, I told him in no uncertain terms that I should take it very ill if he did. Now was his chance to make amends to his father, I told him heatedly. Now that Edward was bedridden it would mean so much to him if Patrick, not Mac-Gowan, reported directly to him on estate matters.

Patrick looked contrite. He promised to do his best, and when he so meekly acquiesced to my bullying I was aware of my feelings for him undergoing a subtle change. I saw clearly then that I could only truly love a man whose will was stronger than my own. I did love Patrick, but now at last I succeeded in loving him as a brother, for I knew him much too well to love him in any other way. It was Edward I respected, Edward I loved. All through that summer I knew I loved him better than I had ever loved him, and at last when autumn too was gone and the leaves had vanished from the trees I knew I loved him even better than that.

We had not left Cashelmara.

He had been confined to his bedroom for a long time, but although in the beginning he had complained he did not complain any more. On his better days he would dictate letters to his secretary; afterward we would play chess endlessly and keep careful account of the games won and lost. On the bad days I would read aloud to him or simply sit sewing while he lay on his pillows. The drugs made him drowsy, and often he would be able to doze to escape the pain.

I brought the children to see him every day. If he felt well he would talk to them very kindly, taking an interest in even the smallest of their activities, but if he was troubled by pain I simply let them stay long enough to say good night. We often talked of their progress. Thomas was taking lessons from a governess and could already read fluently, while David, not to be outdone, was learning his alphabet.

Shortly before Christmas Edward said, "I wish I could see them grow up. I mind missing that very much."

"Yes," I said. "It's a pity." I was making a velvet jacket for David—it was odd how I took up sewing in the sickroom—and I was trying to thread the needle when I spoke. The jacket was already a most peculiar shape, but David was so chubby.

We had not spoken of the future before, and I wondered whether Edward might change the subject, but after a while he said, "I want you to be as I remember you best—very bright and joyous—always living life to the full. I disapprove strongly of the dreary drawn-out traditions of mourning to which widows are now expected to conform, and I've never had any patience with people who claim to be wedded to a memory. If those people had really enjoyed the state of matrimony so much they would seek to return to it with another partner, so I would regard it as a great compliment to me if you chose to remarry."

"How unconventional," I said, thinking fleetingly of Madeleine, "but what good sense!" After a moment I was able to smile at him. I had given up trying to thread the needle and was sitting motionless, the little velvet jacket in my lap. I knew then that I would never finish the jacket, because the sight of it would always remind me of Edward talking of a future in which he himself had no part to play.

"Well," I said, putting the jacket aside, "if I ever find another man who can match you—which I doubt—and if that man wants to marry a plain, skinny, bossy, meddlesome foreigner—which I doubt even more—I shall seriously entertain the idea of remarriage, I promise you."

He smiled. We were quiet for a time, but later just before he fell asleep he said, "It takes courage not to pretend. I'm grateful."

I wanted to reply that I was only following his example, but somehow the words refused to be spoken, and we never mentioned the future again.

Christmas came. We celebrated it quietly, but in the new year Katherine and Duneden came to stay and George began to call more frequently from Letterturk.

Edward had one hemorrhage, then another. His London doctor returned to remain constantly in attendance, and toward the end of January I wrote to Madeleine to suggest that she too come to stay.

I became very busy. The guests had to be looked after; the housekeeper needed to be instructed with great thoroughness to ensure that hot food and hot water were always available at the appropriate times. This feat would have been difficult enough to accomplish at Woodhammer, but it was twice as difficult at Cashelmara, where half the servants were often absent at a wake and nobody ever remembered to wind the clocks to ensure punctuality. I found that household matters took up an increasing amount of my time as more guests arrived in the house, and although I knew it was important that the children should not be overlooked I did not spend as much time with them as I would have liked.

I wanted to spend every available second with Edward.

He was very thin, his flesh shrunk to the bone of his huge frame. He could not eat. He slept fitfully, and drugs gave him only the most fleeting relief from pain.

I remember everyone being distressed. I remember everyone being reluctant to go to the sickroom, and I could not understand that because I wanted to be there continuously. But I no longer took the children to see him. He was too ill, and I had no wish to make an ordeal of their daily visit.

I remember the chessmen covered with dust and the newspaper lying unread on the bedside table. I remember the view from the window and the patterns of light and shade in the room and Edward's hair a dull white on the furrowed pillow.

I remember at the end praying for more time and yet praying too for Edward's sake that no more time would be left.

I remember hissing to Patrick, the nails digging into the palms of my hands, "Don't you dare cry! Don't you dare stand sniveling at his bedside like a schoolboy!"

I remember everyone asking me questions, should they visit the sickroom, was he well enough, what should they do. I remember finding answers, being very brisk and practical and competent. The house was hushed and still, the voices muffled as if it were all a dream.

I remember saying calmly to Thomas and David, "Papa's very ill and he wants to say goodbye to you before he dies. It's sad, I know, for you to have to say goodbye, but he's in such pain here that he'll be far better off in heaven, so you must try not to grieve too much."

David said, "When will he come back from heaven?" and Thomas, who was older and wiser, began to cry.

I allowed the boys to see him only briefly because I did not want to upset them too much, but he did so want to see them one last time.

At the end all he said to me was "Be happy." And to Patrick he said, "Take care of Marguerite and your little brothers."

And then the end came at last, and the crimson dusk blazed darkly on the shining waters of the lough.

II

For a long time I could not sleep at all. I kept thinking of the past and all our finest hours, and at some isolated moment before dawn on one of those sleepless nights I knew, just as one often knows a fact for no logical reason, that I would never remarry. I thought about it often before the funeral, and the more I thought of it the more convinced I became that I was really most ill-suited for marriage. I was too strong-willed for most men, and I did have that very aggravating meddlesome streak. I wondered vaguely if I would eventually summon the nerve to take a lover. I did not fancy the idea of perpetual celibacy any more than I fancied the idea of marrying a lesser man than Edward, and I thought Edward might have approved of a discreet affair or two. He was always very pragmatic about such matters.

I was quite calm. I organized the entire funeral. There was a great amount to do, but I had plenty of time because I had given up trying to sleep. I simply had no desire to do so, and oddly enough I found I did not miss it at all.

I had known many people would come to the funeral even though the February weather was so uninviting and Cashelmara so remote, but I had visualized as mourners only those people among Edward's enormous circle of friends and political acquaintances. I had never dreamed of his tenants gathering to pay their respects, for wasn't he a Protestant landlord, one of the most hated class in Ireland, and hadn't he felt guilty for years because he had turned his back on his Irish estate during the famine?

"Ah, but he waived his rents, my lady," said Sean Denis Joyce, and one of the older O'Malleys said, "There was never an eviction during all the years of the Hunger," and someone else said, "And when it was over he came back and he gave us new seeds for our potatoes and our oats and still he waived his rents till our crops were grown and we could pay again."

"He was a great man, my lady," said Maxwell Drummond with a gentleness I would never have expected of him, "and we are all, every one of us, in his debt."

They came by the hundreds up the road from Clonareen. They gathered in the drive peacefully with not a man drunk among them, and when the coffin left the house they followed it all the way uphill to the very door of the chapel through which we, the Protestants, walked alone. But afterward at the graveside, just before I fainted, I was aware of the crowd around us stretching back into the larchwoods, and the intense yearning quality of the silence, so restrained and so un-Irish, was broken only by the soft clicking of rosary beads.

I was so surprised when I felt faint. I had had no idea I might be on the verge of illness, and although I knew that the lack of sleep must have been bad for me I had assumed I would eventually sleep when I could no longer do without it. It did not occur to me that I was clinging to consciousness in order to savor every last second of my life with Edward, but when I saw the coffin lowered into the grave I suddenly thought: I'm alone. My life with him is finished.

Then I fainted.

When I recovered my first words were "I want Francis." That surprised me too, because I had long learned to stand alone without needing anyone except Edward, but of course my desire for Francis was natural enough now that Edward was no longer there.

"Edward's dead," I said. His family was clustered around me anxiously, and I could see him in every one of them; he was behind all their eyes. "But none of you knew him," I said. "That was sad. I was the only one who knew him, wasn't I?"

Someone found some smelling salts. There was much fussing and whispering, but all noise faded until it was a mere murmur like the distant drone of the sea and I was beneath a vast unending sky. For one brief moment he was with me. I could see his hair, dark and only lightly tinged with silver, just as it had been when we had first met, and I could see his blue eyes and I knew that he was smiling although I could not quite see his smile. I said very clearly, just so that there should be no mistake, "I couldn't possibly ever love anyone else." And then the sky went black and the sea roared over my head and I knew that when I woke again I would be able to cry.

III

I cried for a long time. I had to stay in bed because I cried so much. Dr. Ives was kind but insistent. I had to lie in bed with the shades drawn and sip chicken broth at dinner and eat a boiled egg every day for breakfast. Most of all I had to have absolute quiet so that I could sleep. I had a vague impression of everyone walking on tiptoe and never daring to speak above a whisper.

Nanny brought the children to see me when I asked for them. Poor little boys! They had just lost their father and looked as if they thought they might lose their mother too. I hugged them so hard that they squealed, and I regret to say I wept over them too, but they were very good about that and David said my tears tasted delicious, almost as nice as lemonade.

Edward's other children were very kind. Madeleine even forsook her hospital to nurse me, and although Duneden was obliged to return to London Katherine stayed on at Cashelmara. But it was

Patrick who cheered me most. He worked diligently with MacGowan on estate matters, as if he knew that was the best way to please me, and looked after Thomas and David as devotedly as if they were his sons. I no longer had to worry about them being neglected once I knew that Patrick was caring for them so well.

In March I heard from Francis. He wanted me to visit America so that I could recover from my grief among my own family. If I did not wish to travel unescorted, perhaps my stepson would be kind enough to accompany me. I was assured that the new Lord de Salis would be quite welcome at my old home on Fifth Avenue.

"Dearest Francis!" I wept, overcome by such magnanimity. I considered it most noble of him not to be prejudiced against Patrick when he had disliked Edward so intensely and thought it showed how unselfish he could be when my happiness was at stake. However, soon I realized that his benign attitude toward Patrick sprang not only from a desire to please me but from a desire to please Sarah too.

Patrick heard from Sarah on the same day that I received my letter from Francis. They had been corresponding for six months by this time, and to my great delight Patrick, never a willing corre-spondent, was anxious to answer each letter from Sarah as soon as it was received. Sarah wrote excellent letters. Patrick showed me each one because he admired them so much, and when she wrote to second her father's proposal that we should visit New York he needed no encouragement from me to accept the invitation.

"Let's go as soon as possible," he said to me happily. "I'll arrange estate matters with MacGowan here and Mason at Woodhammer and give the London lawyers the necessary powers to act for me in my absence. A journey abroad would do us so much good, Marguerite! Of course, I know you're in mourning and should probably live a quiet secluded life for at least a year, but—"

"Oh no," I said. "That wouldn't be at all what Edward had in mind for me." It felt strange to say his name. I wanted to cry but managed not to. "By all means let's set out for America as soon as possible. I believe I want to go home again more than anything else in the world."

IV

We left at the end of May. We managed to acquire the necessary staterooms on the new Cunard liner *Russia,* which was already renowned for its comfort and luxury, and once the reservations had been made I felt well on the road to recovery. In fact by the time we reached Liverpool and boarded the ship I fancied the sea air had completed the restoration of my health, and after I had given unpacking instructions to my maid I left my stateroom and went on deck to join the rest of my family.

There was no sign of the boys, who were evidently exploring else-where with Nanny, but Patrick was staring intently at the crowded quayside. He was leaning forward, his elbows on the rail, but when I called his name he straightened his back and turned to me with a smile.

"You looked very preoccupied," I said lightly to him. "What were you thinking about?"

"Well, as a matter of fact," he said, "I was thinking about Sarah. Marguerite, I'm going to marry her, I'm sure of it. I know I shall fall in love with her, and then I'm going to get married, settle down, turn over a new leaf just as Papa would have wished—"

"I do hope you won't be disappointed in Sarah," I said nervously. "You should wait till you meet her, Patrick, before saying all those things."

"But thanks to those marvelous letters of hers I already feel that I've known her for years! I'm so deuced excited—and grateful to you, Marguerite. You do realize how grateful I am, don't you? You've had such an influence over my life. If it hadn't been for you God alone knows where I'd be now, but you've influenced me for the better, you've made me what I am today, and . . ." He stopped. Below us in the milling crowds at the far end of the quay something had caught his attention. A second later I saw his face blaze with excitement as he leaned over the rail.

"At last!" he cried in delight. "I thought the boat would sail before he arrived!" As I stared at him blankly he added with a laugh, "I told him when we were sailing, and he said he'd cross over from Dublin to see us off. Wasn't that nice of him?" And leaning even farther over the rail, he shouted the appallingly familiar name at the top of his voice.

I looked down upon Derry Stranahan.

When I looked back at the rail a second later Patrick had gone. He was racing to the head of the gangway, and Derry too started to run as he dodged feverishly through the crowds. He was some distance away from me, but I could see his black eyes blazing in his white, tense face.

They met at the foot of the gangway. Everyone stared as they embraced, and no one stared harder than I. They laughed, gestured, embraced again. For a long time I could not see Patrick's face; I saw only the peculiarly naked joy smoothing all trace of sophistication from Derry's expression, and then as Patrick finally turned back toward the gangway I looked upon his face and realized at last—too late—that of course he was exactly the sort of man who should never marry.

Part Three

PATRICK
Loyalty   1868–1873

. . . unfortunately Edward II was weak and wilful. The king was expected to be the mainspring of government, and Edward had no head for business. . . . He took pleasure in music and in un-aristocratic occupations such as rowing, play-acting, driving, racing, thatching and digging. But it was not so much the unkingly nature of these diversions which quickly alienated the magnates, as his inordinate affection for the young Gascon adventurer, Piers Gaveston.

England in the Late Middle Ages
—A. R. MYERS

Chapter One

I married Sarah in New York in June of 1869, a year to the day after we had first met, and after a short honeymoon at her father's country mansion I took her to Cashelmara. It was then that our troubles began in earnest.

Nothing good ever happened to me at Cashelmara.

However, until then I'd had no cause to moan about the way life had treated me, for I was fit as a fiddle and not bad-looking, and I had a title and a bit of money and all that sort of thing. I was young too, twenty-three when I first set foot on American soil, and so with my youth, health, looks and fortune I was hardly what you might call unlucky. Indeed my friend Derry Stranahan used to say that I was the luckiest bastard in the whole damned world, and I must admit that on my wedding day I had never felt more inclined to agree with him.

Derry always said that marriage was a very sorry end for a man who enjoyed his freedom, but I never enjoyed my freedom much, and while I was still in my teens I began to think how pleasant it would be not to feel obliged to cut a dash with the opposite sex on every social occasion and not to feel compelled to give the required response when a lady of easy virtue offered to unlace her corsets. I didn't dislike women, but I was shy when I was growing up and found I could enjoy a woman's company only when I knew she had no wish to pursue me to the altar or the bedchamber or both. This makes me sound deuced vain, chased by every female in sight, but you see, I was so damned lucky with all my advantages that I really did feel a trifle persecuted sometimes. But to tell the truth I was the very reverse of vain and found my good fortune such an embarrassment that I often wished I'd been born a pauper with a clubfoot.

"Never mind the clubfoot," Derry would jeer. "If you'd been born a pauper as I was, you wouldn't need any extra curse to help you savor the delights of misfortune."

I would laugh when he said that, and he would laugh too, for he was a great one for joking about the unequal way fate had treated us. Derry joked about everything, you know, even about things no soul would dare joke about, and when I was with him nothing mattered, the world was bright and clear and sparkling, for nothing could ever upset me so long as I was with Derry Stranahan.

I suppose we were like brothers, but no two brothers could have been so different from each other. Yet because of that difference we complemented each other until sometimes it seemed we were like two sides of the same coin. When we were apart I believe he was as lost without me as I was without him—although of course he would never have admitted that. Derry hated sentimentality.

Soon after I arrived in New York Sarah said with curiosity, "Tell me more about Derry Stranahan." So I talked and talked for an eternity, but even as I spoke I knew I was somehow failing to describe him. I heard myself reciting the prim facts of his life history, and all the time I wanted to say, "Look, this is one of the most exciting people you'll ever meet. He's had the devil of a life and all kinds of ghastly things have happened to him and he doesn't give a damn for anyone or anything."

"There's only one thing I care about," Derry had said long ago, "and that's this: I never want to smell famine again. I never want to smell the potatoes rotting in the fields, I never want to smell the reek of putrefied potato pits, and never, never, never do I want to smell the stench of famine fever."

I wanted to explain this to Sarah, but all I succeeded in saying was "His family all died of typhus in the epidemic that followed the famine. Derry caught it too, but he survived. He was six years old at the time."

And at the back of my memory Derry was saying, "There was vomit everywhere and everyone's eyes were open, but no one could see. The baby's swollen stomach seemed to have burst, and my mother was as stiff as an iron pole and her tongue was hanging out and the lice were crawling out of her hair."

"What a miracle that he lived!" exclaimed Sarah, marveling at the story.

". . . and I lived," said Derry's voice from the past. "I should have died, but I lived, and thanks to your father's charity I've been clothed and fed and educated. God must have chosen me, marked me out for fame and fortune, otherwise why didn't He let me die with the others? There must be a reason for it. God wouldn't have let me go through all that if He hadn't had some purpose in mind."

To say Derry was deeply religious would be an exaggeration, but he was fanatically superstitious about observing his religion, as if he thought God would look on him with disfavor if he did not go to Mass at least three times a week and make confession every Sunday. He treated God exactly as if God were some heathen idol which had to be regularly appeased in order that some terrible catastrophe might be averted. A crisis arose when Derry became old enough to confess certain unpalatable sins at confession, and for some time I watched with interest as his fear of God wrestled with his fancy for feminine flesh. I was rather sorry when feminine flesh triumphed, for I had been brought up on boys' stories where the hero is always as chaste as Sir Galahad, but since Derry could do no wrong in my eyes I did my best to alter my idea of a hero from Galahad to Lancelot.

"Well, after all," said Derry, justifying his behavior with his own brand of superstitious logic, "God must intend me to make women happy or to be sure he'd be delivering me from temptation instead of forever throwing it in my path."

But to be certain not to give God offense, he went to Mass after each fornication and lighted all sorts of candles in the church for his dead family.

He didn't talk about his family except when he was drunk, and then he would talk about them continuously. He would begin by saying how much he had loved them all and then gradually he would begin to abuse them. I could understand him abusing his father, who had obviously been an awful scoundrel, but I thought it was a bit unfair of him to abuse his mother. After all, it wasn't her fault that she had died, but to hear him talk you'd think the poor woman had more or less wilfully abandoned him to starve.

"My mother too died when I was six," I often pointed out, "but I don't hold it against her." In fact I could hardly remember my mother. I had been brought up by a thin tight-lipped Nanny who was always declaring morosely that "boys are more difficult than girls" and by my sister Nell, who was kind but distracted. I know now that she was worrying about how long she would have to keep house for our father and whether she would ever be free enough from family duties to get married, but at the time I had merely sensed she wasn't happy trying to fill my mother's place in the household, and I had always tried to keep out of her way as much as possible so as not to make her any unhappier.

"Poor little boy," said Sarah mistily, her imagination giving my childhood an aura of tragedy it really didn't possess. "You must have missed your mama very much."

Well, I couldn't exactly say I hadn't missed her a scrap, could I? But the truth was I had felt nothing at all when Nanny had told me my mother was dead, and even to this day I think of my mother with neither love nor hate but with utter indifference. However, I always take care to conceal this because I know it's shameful.

"And your father?" said Sarah sentimentally. "Tell me about your father, Patrick."

This was much easier. I felt so relieved to escape from the subject of my mother and speak truthfully again.

"My father was a wonderful man," I said, and as I spoke I could remember him so clearly, not as he had been at the end of his life when illness had enfeebled his magnificent physique but as he had been years earlier in my childhood, huge, powerful and Godlike, his footsteps making the nursery floor vibrate, his strength emanating from him in waves of awe-inspiring vitality. I remember once seeing him mount a horse merely by putting a hand on the saddle and leaping into it. When he smiled at me I felt as a soldier must feel when he receives a medal from his sovereign, and when later people began to say of me, "How like his father he looks!" my heart would almost burst with pride. I used to gaze in the looking glass and, marveling at the magic of heredity, tick off on my fingers one feature after another. Same blue eyes, same wide forehead, same hairline, which receded slightly above the temples, same firm straight nose, same—no, not the same mouth; my father had a thinner upper lip than I did. And not the same chin; his was more prominent than mine and he had a squarer jawline. My jaw was more fine-drawn and in fact, if considered dispassionately, matched my other features better than his did. Well, one can be an awful Narcissus when one's young, there's no doubt about that, and I mention all this now not to boast about my looks but to show what a striking man my father was and how grateful I felt to be at least a little like him.

"My father was devoted to me just as I was devoted to him," I was saying proudly to Sarah. "Oh, I know I used to grumble because he was so strict, but he was only strict because he cared so much about what happened to me. He explained it all to me once. He beat me because he cared. Lots of fathers ignore their sons altogether, you know, and don't give tuppence what tricks they get up to, but my father wasn't like that one scrap. I was so lucky to have a father like that, but then I've always been so deuced lucky." And I went on telling her how lucky I was, but all the while I was talking I was gazing at her in admiration and hoping against hope that one day I'd be luckier still.

II

Sarah's father, Francis Marriott, lived in a gorgeous, chunky building that looked as if it might have been made out of gingerbread. There was a cobbled courtyard, a massive flight of steps to the front door and a blank array of dark windows below a turreted roof. From one end of the gilded gutters to the other, gargoyles, cherubs, satyrs and griffins leered at one another in exotic profusion.

"I should like to live in a house like that," said my little half-brother David, who was unashamedly sentimental and loved anything that reminded him of his favorite fairy tales.

"How much did it cost to build?" inquired my other little brother. Thomas had a mathematical mind and already kept careful accounts of his pocket money.

"That's a very vulgar question, Thomas," said Marguerite, who had become daily more English since she had left this same house eight years before to become my father's second wife. "I haven't the slightest idea of the answer, nor is it necessary for you to know." And when she smiled at me across the top of his sandy head I remembered Derry's theory that Marguerite was secretly in love with me—which was awful nonsense, of course, because she had been devoted to my father, everyone knew that, and in fact she had been so prostrated by his death that this visit to America to see her family had been planned with her convalescence in mind. Derry never liked Marguerite. I can't think why. I always liked her very much; in fact,

I was fonder of her than I was of any of my sisters, and I believe she was just as fond of me as she was of her brother Francis. She was a marvelous girl, very bright and bobbish, if you know what I mean— not pretty but smart as freshly polished silver with its glitter and hidden strength and sharp pointy edges. Certainly apart from Derry there was no one whose company I preferred to hers, and on the voyage from Liverpool to New York I had looked forward to many companionable hours with her while we promenaded on the main deck or whiled away the hours in the grand saloon.

Never had I been more disappointed. She was busy each day with the boys, for David suffered from seasickness and Thomas was always what Nanny described as a "handful." Marguerite hardly left either of them alone for a minute, and by the time evening came and the boys were safely stowed in their bunks she lost no time in retreating to her own stateroom to recuperate. To make matters worse, the sea was pretty choppy most of the time, and I knew Marguerite was a nervous passenger. I didn't blame her, because I was nervous myself. It's all very well for people to say gaily that ocean travel is as safe as houses these days. They're the people who always take care to stay on shore and run no risk of disaster whenever some great hulk of a liner has "disappeared without trace." It might have helped if the steamship companies themselves had put out some word of reassurance, but their brochures spoke only of the gilded saloons and luxurious staterooms and all the splendid food that passengers could eat in the most delightful surroundings. The word "safety" was never mentioned, and neither was seasickness, discomfort and boredom.

However, I don't want to paint too black a picture of the journey, and since I myself didn't suffer from seasickness I really shouldn't complain. I had a fine stateroom, rather small, but at least my bunk was slightly bigger than a coffin and there was enough room for an armchair. The main screw of the engine was hellishly noisy (even though the *Russia*, a new boat, was supposed to have improved the noisiness; God alone knows what the previous ships must have been like). However, one did get used to the noise, although the vibrations were harder to ignore. The public rooms were very lavishly appointed, and I thought the food was pretty good even though I was told by the experienced sea salts that as far as menus went Cunard couldn't hold a candle to any of the ships in the old Collins line. I felt like saying, "Yes, but at least the Cunard ships stay afloat," but of course I didn't, for it would have been tempting fate, and since the

Collins supporters were all Americans such a remark might have started one of those nasty arguments about nationality. Besides, since the Collins line was defunct any arguments would have been pointless.

Toward the end of the voyage the weather improved, much to everyone's relief, and Marguerite began to look less green. In the hope of luring her to stay up late for a chat I raised the subject of my marriage (she had always been dead keen for me to marry), but now to my surprise she showed no interest in the subject and even went so far as to tell me it would be much better if I postponed marrying until I was at least thirty years old because marriage did so tie a man down. This was such a complete reversal of all her earlier advice to me that when I'd recovered from my astonishment I couldn't help remarking on such a brisk turnabout.

"I've changed my mind," she said—very snappishly, I thought. "A woman's entitled to change her mind now and then, isn't she?"

Well, it was very unlike Marguerite, and I didn't know what the devil lay at the bottom of it, but in the end I attributed her attitude to lingering seasickness and tried not to be too down about her snappishness.

My first impression of New York was that it was a magnificent place to approach by sea.

"There's Sandy Hook!" exclaimed Marguerite, bobbing up and down like a jack-in-the-box by this time. "And the white houses beyond those lovely sands over there belong to Rockaway Beach and Fire Island. Oh look! You can see the hotels of Coney Island! How clear it is today—and there's the Quarantine Station in the lower bay . . ."

But I was more interested in a glowering headland and the enormous network of fortifications ahead. Everyone says New York is impregnable, and I'm quite sure they're right. I'd never seen so many guns in all my life. The whole shore was lined with them.

"Staten Island!" sobbed Marguerite in ecstasy. "The Narrows. And oh look, Thomas, David, look at all the little boats in the Inner Bay!"

We chugged into the great harbor, the city straight ahead of us, Brooklyn on our right and Jersey City on our left. The Hudson River stretched north as far as the eye could see, and the color of the water would have put even the Bay of Naples to shame.

"The light is Italian," I said, fascinated. "It's not English at all."

"Well, of course it's not English!" cried Marguerite, rabidly patriotic by this time, and hung over the rail as if she could already see her brother waiting at the docks.

He was there, of course. He came hurrying to meet us, and Marguerite ran into his arms so fast that I was surprised she didn't trip over her skirts. I must say that Cousin Francis, a sporty-looking old cove, did seem awfully pleased to see her. He was pretty civil to me too and patted the boys on their heads and said what fine fellows they were.

"Dearest Francis!" said Marguerite, mopping up her tears with his very own silk handkerchief. Being an American handkerchief, it was almost as big as a tablecloth.

New York is a jolly sort of city, rather plain but with lots of spunk, like a terrier puppy. I don't care for cities myself, but I should imagine that if you do like them you would easily find New York exciting. Certainly I was excited by the time I entered the drawing room of that house on Fifth Avenue, but that was because I knew I was at long last going to meet Sarah.

I can see that drawing room now. The "shades" were drawn to keep out the oppressive summer heat, and three little black boys in livery stood around waving enormous fans. Unfortunately they were of little use to me as I was already so hot that my shirt was sticking to my back and the sweat was almost washing away my trousers.

Sarah wore a lilac gown. Her skin, untouched by that savage foreign sun, was creamily pale so that her heavily coiled hair seemed unusually dark. She had brown eyes, but they were such a light shade of brown that they seemed golden. They were extraordinary eyes, wide-set and with a slight upward slant that emphasized her high cheekbones. Her mouth, straight and rich, was a luscious shade of red. She had an unbelievably small waist, slender shoulders and a long and lovely neck.

She was gorgeous. I instantly forgot all the pale simpering English roses who came out each season in London, forgot all the overeager misses on the boat and even forgot how to say a simple "how do you do."

"Allow me, my dear Patrick," said Cousin Francis Marriott in his plummy voice which reminded me of a bad actor playing Macbeth, "to make the formal introductions. Of course since you've been corresponding with each other for some months introductions are hardly necessary, but . . ." He waffled on for a while about God knows what, but finally he stopped talking and I managed to say something like "Um. Well . . . delighted, Miss Marriott. Cousin Sarah, I mean. Yes. How are you?" I was red as a lobster by this time, and so hot that I couldn't conceivably have been any hotter even if, like a lobster, I had been flung into a pot of boiling water.

She looked me up. And she looked me down. The ice at the North Pole was never half as cool as Miss Sarah Marriott in New York City on June the eighteenth, 1868.

"I'm delighted to see you in person at last, Cousin Patrick," she said with a casual, graceful formality. "Welcome to New York. It's considerably hot, isn't it?" She gave me no time to reply but glided neatly past me to meet my little brothers, and I saw only her straight back and that lush opaque hair coiled above her long lovely neck.

My embarrassing gaucheness had meant nothing to Sarah Marriott. She was eighteen years old and had already received proposals from a Russian prince, a California millionaire and an Italian count. She was one of the great beauties of New York society, so accustomed to wealth that fortunes were meaningless to her, so used to admiration from supremely eligible men that my speechless wonder was almost beneath her notice. I knew at once that she was spoiled and pampered; I knew at once that she was enjoying giving all her suitors a hell of a fine run for their money; I knew too that I had about as much chance of success as a donkey in a steeplechase for thoroughbreds—but I didn't care. All I cared about was that for once in my life I didn't have to be embarrassed by my good fortune because for once in my life, as far as Sarah Marriott was concerned, I was no more than one of a crowd.

III

I couldn't believe it when she said she would marry me. We were sitting in the garden under a shady tree, and Sarah was drawing a pattern on the gravel path with her parasol. The weather was still unspeakably hot, but three weeks had passed since I had arrived in New York and I was more used to the climate by this time. We were discussing the merits of dogs and cats. Sarah had a nasty overbred Pekinese called Ulysses (after General Grant, who was running for President that year) and desperately wanted a white cat, which she planned to call Omar Khayyam. She was just saying how she hoped her father would give the creature to her when I heard myself announce, "Sarah, I'd like to give you anything you want. You wouldn't possibly want to marry me by any chance, would you, because I'd be awfully thrilled if you did."

She burst out laughing. I suppose it *was* rather a silly way of proposing, but I'm not much good at acting parts and making flowery speeches, and at least I said exactly what I felt.

"That's the best proposal I ever had!" she exclaimed, still laughing. "Have you spoken to Papa?"

"No, I didn't know I was going to propose. That's to say, I thought I'd wait. I mean . . ."

"If you hurry you can catch him before he leaves for Wall Street."

"You mean you—"

"Oh yes," she said. "I'd love to. I was afraid you were never going to ask me, and we've known each other almost a month. I'd practically abandoned hope."

"But why—all your other suitors . . ."

Sarah yawned and fanned herself. "You're different from the others. You talk to me as if I were human instead of an illustration in a picture book. And you've never once tried to slobber kisses all over me when you've thought no one was looking. I can't bear men dribbling affection like spaniels."

"May I kiss you now?"

"Very well, but don't slobber."

I did my best not to. Sliding my arms around her waist, I kissed her once on each cheek and once briefly on the lips. She relaxed in my arms, her body pressed against mine and suddenly I felt as if I had had two drams of poteen and was as strong as an ox. I moved back sharply, but she hardly noticed my withdrawal. She was already talking again in her low, oddly accented voice, saying that she would be glad to be married because her mother didn't understand her and her brother Charles was away in Boston for so much of the year and no company for her at all, and as for Papa, well, she guessed it would nearly kill her to leave him, but. . . .

"He'll always think of me as a child," said Sarah, "and I'm not. I'm grown up and I want to *be* grown up. I want to have my own house and my own life, even if it means I have to be separated from darling Papa."

"Cousin Francis Marriott is in his mid-forties and thinks himself an awful swell," I had written to Derry soon after my arrival. "He drinks two bottles of port a day, fancies himself as a first-rate driver of a four-in-hand and loves to talk about 'The Street,' which is where the Americans do their financial business. Marguerite told me he hates England, but *he* tells me he now has profitable connections with a large mercantile firm in Manchester as the result of the North of England's pro-Unionist sympathy during the Civil War, and Cousin Francis' heart is where the money is. Also Sarah is dying to visit Europe and she loves everything English (it's become the fashion for American girls to yearn for the Olde Worlde). So since Cousin Francis dotes on Sarah so much he doesn't dare be too anti-European or anti-British for fear of offending her. Marguerite says she would never have believed that her brother could be so sub-servient to a woman and is quite annoyed that Cousin Francis should dote so on Sarah, but I think Marguerite is jealous because he was always more like a father to her than a brother and Sarah more like a sister than a niece. Marguerite even seems to disapprove of my admiration for Sarah and keeps trying to interest me in other girls. I must say, I do think Marguerite's behavior is a little odd. However, Sarah's mother approves of my conduct, so I really have nothing to worry about.

"Cousin Amelia is large, seventeen stone at least, and has three chins, an enormous bosom and large, sad, cowlike eyes. I can't see how Cousin Francis could even begin to claim his marital rights amidst all that flesh, but I've heard he has a string of mistresses scattered through the town. New York is a great town for kept women and what the Americans call 'houses.' Prostitutes aren't allowed to solicit on Broadway but walk along very fast with their eyes on the ground—a most curious sight. They're called 'Street Walkers,' and if they can get a customer they beckon him into a side street where the police don't interfere. Then there are places called 'concert saloons' where there's no classical music but an awful lot of gin, and dance houses where the dancers are quite the dregs of humanity."

I tried to make it sound as if I had witnessed these colorful places with my own eyes, but in fact I had only heard about them from Cousin Francis one evening after the ladies had withdrawn from the dining room and he was comfortably launched on his second bottle of port. He had undertaken to warn me against visiting such places, since thievery was common and disease rampant.

"But you would enjoy the gambling here," I noted to Derry. "It's against the law in the state of New York, but nobody cares about the law as far as gambling's concerned, least of all the police. There are gambling houses within a block of Broadway and many more over on the East Side and down the Bowery in the lower-class neighborhoods.

The great American game is faro. The first-class houses are usually honest, very sumptuous in their furnishings and attended by well-mannered Negro servants, most of them ex-slaves from the South. Oh God, that Civil War! As a topic of conversation it's still second only to President Johnson's impeachment, and, talking of the impeachment, to hear Cousin Francis waffling interminably about the dangers to the Constitution is worse than being forced to read about the latest plans afoot at Westminster for Parliamentary Reform! But I mustn't say a word against Cousin Francis, who's really been most hospitable to me, and I suppose if he's going to be my father-in-law I'll have to get used to all his boring speeches about politics."

Derry's letter in reply to my lengthy discourse on Sarah's family, street walkers and faro arrived soon after Sarah had accepted my proposal.

"Re Marguerite," he began in legal fashion. "It's clear as a spring dawn that she's jealous of Sarah—but not for her place in your cousin Francis' affections. You're very dense sometimes, Lord de Salis.

"Re Cousin Francis and Cousin Amelia: How could two such frightful people have produced the Sensuous Sarah? What's her brother like? Since you don't mention him I suppose he's away pursuing his studies at Harvard, or whatever their colonial imitation of Oxford is called.

"Re your passion: Well, you always were subject to strange whims. I regard it as part of your charm, but truthfully, Patrick, honestly—you're not seriously entertaining this mad idea of marrying an American girl, are you? It seems a damned tragedy to marry when you're only twenty-three, and it's not as if you're in my position and have to marry for money (by the way, my latest heiress went to England and is now engaged to some nincompoop called Lord George Swindon-Cunningham). Besides, if you have to marry at twenty-three, why the devil choose an American girl? That step-mother of yours has been influencing you again or I'm a Dutchman, but I'll say no cross word against Marguerite, because if she's opposed to your interest in Sarah I suppose we must be allies. Well, fate can make strange bedfellows—which reminds me, American tastes in bedroom matters seem pretty droll, although by God if ever I found myself in bed with an American woman I'd gag her first so that she wouldn't say anything to distract me. The accent would put me off so, and besides American women are always so damned managing that I wouldn't put it past them to give directions to the man of their choice when lying on their backs with their legs apart. For God's sake come back to England before you do anything silly. Yours, etc. DERRY."

I was amused but also annoyed. The allusions to Marguerite didn't upset me, for Derry was always talking nonsense about her, but his remarks on American women—which were a comment, no matter how indirect, on Sarah—irritated me immensely. In fact I was so irritated that I even complained to Marguerite that Derry had cut up pretty rough about the idea of my marrying an American girl.

"And what on earth's he going to say when he hears I'm now engaged?" I added in gloom.

"He'll get used to the idea," said Marguerite sharply, and added in a milder, more persuasive tone, "After all, I've got used to it, so why shouldn't he? For a while I wasn't anxious for you to marry Sarah, I admit, but now . . ."

I brightened. "You really approve?"

"Yes." She hesitated before saying positively, "Yes, I do. I was confused for a time, but now I'm sure it's for the best. Quite sure," she repeated as if there still remained some doubt about it, and then she smiled and said she was sorry she had been so short with me lately.

I smiled too. Nothing could have pleased me more than this hint that we were to be friends again, and when she saw I was cheered she said encouragingly, "Derry's next letter will be full of congratulations, you wait and see. He won't want to quarrel with you."

She was right, but I spent many anxious days awaiting his verdict, and when the letter finally came I was almost too nervous to open it.

"My congratulations to you," he had written agreeably. "Your speed took me by surprise, but evidently Sarah has made marriage seem irresistible to you! However, I hope you don't intend to remain in America till your wedding next June. Now that you're engaged there surely can't be any danger of her running off with some other fellow, so why don't you come home for a visit? Don't forget that Absence Makes the Heart Grow Fonder—or, to be a trifle more vulgar, Abstinence (in moderation, of course!) makes the Ardor— but you can guess the rhyming adjective. If you come back for Christmas, think what a jolly time we could have together at Wood- hammer Hall! You know how much I've always wanted to see Woodhammer. Well, I must stop. Forgive me for writing only a short letter, but I have a brief to prepare for tomorrow, and I'm already burning the midnight oil. My best wishes to the future Lady de Salis. Yours, etc. DERRY."

This was all very well, but after I had recovered from my relief I began to feel in the deuce of a quandary. The truth was that the idea of Christmas at Woodhammer did seem appealing, for I was already exhausted by America. But I didn't see how I could possibly leave Sarah. For a start I didn't want to leave her, but it was really more complicated than that. It would be more accurate to say I didn't dare leave her. I knew she loved me, but she was so ravishing and so desirable that I was terrified she might slip through my fingers even though we were now engaged. If I returned to England for even the briefest of visits she could always say afterward, "Well, you left me—you went away. You couldn't have loved me much, so how can you blame me for having turned to someone else?"

Derry might be unaware of the danger, but I could see it all too clearly.

"Well, of course you must stay!" said Marguerite firmly when I confided in her. "We'll all stay."

"But I know you want to return before the end of the year." There had never been any question of Marguerite remaining permanently in America. She was determined to live in London so that Thomas and David could grow up to be Englishmen, just as my father would have wished.

"Oh, it's not essential that we should return then," she said at once. "After all, these are exceptional circumstances. We'll stay until next summer and then Thomas and David can be page boys at the wedding while I can sit in the front pew and enjoy myself."

"I suppose we could all go back to England in December and return again next spring."

"Much too upsetting for the boys," said Marguerite. "That dreadful long sea voyage, all those thousands of miles—no, it would be much better for us to stay here for the extra months."

"I suppose it would, yes. But don't you think this hot weather is unhealthy for children?"

"We'll be going upstate next week to Francis' house in the Hudson Valley. Oh, you'll love our house on the river, Patrick! I know you don't like cities, but you'll feel so much better in the country. And later on . . . well, there's no need for you to stay in New York all the time, is there? You should really take advantage of being on this side of the Atlantic and see as much of America as possible. Yes, that's it! You can take a tour, just like Mr. Trollope did, although I shouldn't go to the South, as they say it's still a wasteland from the war. But Francis has friends in Boston and Washington and Philadelphia, and of course you must see the Great Lakes—perhaps Chicago . . ."

American women can indeed be very managing sometimes. I began to wonder if there was more truth in Derry's letter than I'd dared to admit.

"But what on earth am I going to tell Derry?" I said, embarrassed as usual by my good fortune. It seemed so unfair that I should be idling away my time touring America while Derry was slaving away in some poky legal chambers in Dublin with no prospect on the horizon but a solitary Christmas at his lodgings.

"Tell Derry you can't bear to leave Sarah, of course," said Marguerite, giving me a look that plainly told me I was being unintelligent. "What else do you need to say?"

That was a good question. I spent several hours trying to think of the answer, and in the end I became convinced that if I could only compensate him in some way for my absence both he and my conscience would be appeased.

"Dear Derry," I wrote carefully at last. "I've got myself into a tricky position here and don't see how I can return to Woodhammer for Christmas—or indeed at any time between now and my wedding day. I've tried to press for an earlier wedding date, but apparently it takes them months to get ready, and anyway Cousin Francis is playing the clinging papa and insisting on a year's engagement. However, since it seems I've no choice but to reconcile myself to a long absence from home, I wonder if you would accept an important commission from me. Could I engage you in your professional capacity and ask you to keep an eye on affairs at Cashelmara? I don't have to worry about Woodhammer because Mason is such a good steward, but you know how matters slide downhill at Cashelmara if no one visits the place at regular intervals. If you could keep an eye on the servants and see they don't spend all their time drinking poteen and having faction fights, I'd be awfully grateful.

"By the way, I heard from Annabel this morning. Clara and Edith are actually staying with her at Clonagh Court now. Those stiffnecked old grandparents of theirs finally expired within a month of each other at their ghastly morgue in Northumberland, so they can't keep the girls from Annabel any more. As I'm their nearest male relative the Court of Chancery has appointed me their guardian, which is rather jolly, and as soon as the family attorney wrote to tell me so I asked Annabel to liberate the girls from Northumberland. Annabel already had, as it turned out, but I'm sure she has no idea what to do with two nubile daughters, so why don't you call with some suggestions? Clara told me once she thought you were a terrific Heavy Swell, and since Annabel thinks pretty well of you too you may have some luck with an heiress at last! Good hunting anyway. Yours, etc. PATRICK."

"Dear Patrick," Derry wrote back promptly in reply, "why you should want to consign me to a fate worse than death (becoming Maxwell Drummond's neighbor again) I can't think, but since I am, God help me, a native of that part of the world, and since I'm bloody sick of working like a dog in damp dark chambers for a pittance and since I'm pretty well fed up with life at the moment (why the *hell* can't you come home and we can have some fun?) . . . well, to cut a long list of grievances short, yes, I'll take your wretched commission if you'll pay me one hundred pounds a month (a man can't live a decent life on less than a thousand a year, and we both know that) and give me a power of attorney so that I can deal with your affairs properly. You're a great deal too trusting with that Scots bastard MacGowan, and I wouldn't be surprised if he was robbing you right and left. Look how he leased my father's old lands to that devil Drummond for twenty pounds a year! I remember very well your father saying he wanted Drummond to have the land for a nominal rent, so where do you think those twenty pounds went? Not into your father's pocket, you can be sure of that. Those Scots are all alike. They can never bear to part with money—either their own or anyone else's. Cursed Black Protestants the lot of them.

"Dear God, what fun it'll be to set foot in Clonareen again and start discussing the merits of celibacy once more with Father Donal! Make sure you write at once to your London lawyers so that I can have my power of attorney as soon as possible, and then I'll take care of Cashelmara as well as if it were my very own. Yours, etc. DERRY.

"P.S. Good news about Clara. What sort of income has she got, do you know? I suppose she can do pretty much as she likes with it when she marries. Maybe if all goes well I'll be spending my Christmas at Clonagh Court! Are you sure you can't come home and join us?"

But I didn't go home. I remained in America with Sarah, and it was to be many months before I saw Derry again.

IV

I dreamed about Sarah that night. I dreamed that she was riding down the road to Clonareen, the road that followed the shore of the lough amidst the blazing yellow of the gorse. She rode a white horse and wore a black riding habit, and in her left hand she carried a long curling riding whip. She rode slowly past the stone-walled fields on the hillside above her, but when she reached the ruined cabin which had once been Derry's home she left the road and guided her horse up the deserted bohereen to the front door.

Derry walked from the ruins to meet her, his hands outstretched in greeting.

I was watching from behind one of the walls, just as I always did, and as I peered through the familiar crack in the crumbling stonework I saw that she was facing him amidst the weeds which had long since pushed their way through the earthen floor.

Sarah laid aside her riding whip. I saw Derry help her as she began to discard her clothes, but she wore nothing beneath her habit but a shining silk petticoat with a fragile bodice. Derry began to ease the petticoat from her body; he had stepped in front of Sarah so that it was impossible for me to see her, and I could not see his face either, for he had his back to me. But I knew from the quick disdainful way he pulled off his own clothes that he was excited. He shrugged off his shirt. I saw the familiar long line of his neck, and presently as he peeled off his drawers I saw the muscles in his legs gleam as the light reflected on the strong sinews of his thighs.

He began to kiss her. Eventually he pulled her to the ground, and suddenly the earthen floor dissolved into a sparkling clover field and the sun's hot light was streaming from a blistering sky. His hands moved over her flesh. I saw his body molding itself into hers until her breath was coming in great harsh gasps for air. I saw her mouth gape wider, her back arch, and then without warning the earth moved and I was falling endlessly into a bottomless pit.

I woke up.

I awoke so violently that at first I couldn't remember where I was or who I was or what the devil I'd been doing. A second later when I realized I'd been dreaming I was able to sink back thankfully on the pillows, but my heart was thudding like a piston and I felt as wet as a drowned dog. Presently I lighted a candle and sponged my limbs with cold water from the ewer. My hands were unsteady. I kept thinking to myself, What a damnable, damnable dream, and I wished I had a small glass of poteen at hand to smooth the memory from my mind.

Well, it was only a dream, and when I awoke next morning I could even smile at its absurdity and wonder why on earth I should have been so upset. Dreams never mean anything, everyone knows that nowadays, and I certainly wasn't superstitious enough to believe I had been dreaming of the future. In retrospect the most tiresome part of the dream was that I could barely remember Sarah's part in it, only Derry's, but dreams are notoriously illogical.

Pushing all thought of the dream resolutely from my mind, I turned with relief to Sarah, who as usual was talking about our distant wedding.

"Papa says," she was remarking dreamily, "that he's going to give me the very finest wedding that money can buy."

I can never understand why Americans are so fearfully interested in money. I'm not in the least interested in it myself and think it's an awfully boring topic of conversation.

"Tell me more about London," Sarah was begging for the ump-teenth time. "How many dry-goods stores are there? I like to go shopping. Is there a store as fine as Lord and Taylor or as vast as Stewart's?"

Americans have this curious notion that one should be able to purchase everything under one roof and therefore the bigger the shop the better. They set great importance on size and are continually talking about how big things are.

"Can I have as many gowns as I like? I never wear the same ball gown twice, you know. Papa says my dress bills are positively ruinous."

The cost of the wedding was going to be positively ruinous too, but no one seemed to care about that. The guest list reached five hundred with no end in sight, and so many wedding presents streamed into the house that I thought I would have to engage a fleet of ships to transport them across the Atlantic.

"I like weddings," said my little brother David, who had never been to a wedding but was already an incurable romantic. "People wear nice clothes and there's organ music and singing. Nanny told me all about it."

Thomas looked at him pityingly before tugging at Marguerite's sleeve. He tugged at Marguerite's sleeve very often and usually when she was smiling at David. "Mama . . ."

"Yes, darling?"

"When are we going back to England?"

"After the wedding."

After the wedding. It was like some date so remote that I would never live to see it. Meanwhile Marguerite had arranged a series of short visits for me, and I found myself traveling by train first to Boston, then to Philadelphia and finally to Washington. I liked Philadelphia best; the Schuylkill Valley is so pretty, and above the city the river is just like an English river, lazy, winding and not too wide. I did not care for the Hudson, which Sarah admired so much, because it was so un-English in its width and surrounding rocky heights. It reminded me of my visit to the Rhine during my Grand Tour, and I always felt lukewarm toward anything German after Derry had been banished to Frankfurt.

I disliked Washington (there's something so depressing about a town that is being painstakingly created instead of being allowed to evolve naturally) and thought the atmosphere of the place was as dispiriting as the endless unfinished streets stretching into the marshy wilderness; but Boston had much more warmth of personality, and I took a great fancy to the little villages of New England with their green-shuttered, white-walled wooden houses.

"Isn't America wonderful?" said Sarah enthusiastically after I had returned from my last journey and was reflecting on my travels.

"Very remarkable," I said at once, having discovered by this time that Americans have to be constantly reassured what a fine country they have, but to be honest I didn't think the scenery could hold a candle to the sights I had seen either in England or in Europe.

"Do you think New England is like Old England?" asked Sarah, eager for my impressions.

"Well, not really," I said, "although it's quite delightful, of course."

"But in what way is it different?"

"Well, England—Old England—is rather more 'lived in,' if you know what I mean."

She had no idea what I meant, and finally I gave up trying to explain. "After all," I said, "you'll see it soon enough for yourself. After the wedding."

But that was still a long way off.

Then suddenly it wasn't such a long way off after all. It was next month, next week, tomorrow, until finally, still hardly able to believe my amazing good fortune, I walked down the aisle of St. Thomas's

Church with Sarah and stepped out into the brilliant sunshine of that June afternoon. The crowd cheered and threw rice. The champagne flowed like water at the Marriott mansion on Fifth Avenue, and seven hundred and fifty guests gathered to wish us well.

No marriage could have had a more auspicious beginning.

V

I admit I was a little apprehensive about the honeymoon. It was not that I was inexperienced, but to be quite honest I've always thought that sexual intercourse is a very overrated sport, not nearly so much fun as carving or drawing or even splashing watercolors on an inviting blank page of a sketchbook. However, a man can't very well say—even to his best friend—that he'd rather chisel a piece of wood than bump a piece of flesh, and God knows I had no wish to be different from anyone else. I was different enough already with all my advantages, and the least I could do was behave like an average man whenever I had the opportunity.

Anyway, it wasn't so hard to conform. In fact I often think I liked women a great deal better than Derry did, for he was always cursing them for some reason or moaning about his need to go to bed with them so often. One day I even said to him, "Why do you chase women so if you dislike them so much?" But he got very annoyed at this and said no one liked a piece of skirt more than he did, and what the devil did I mean anyway? "I'm a man, aren't I?" he added truculently, and when I laughed and said there was no denying that he thawed a little and said he liked women well enough but they were deuced irritating creatures when all was said and done and as far as he was concerned they were good for one thing and one thing only.

"Well, you certainly practice what you preach," I said hastily. "There's no doubt about that."

It was Derry's misfortune that he lived in a country where chastity is rated very highly, but even in the rigidly moral Catholic climate of Connaught there was always the impulsive maiden who could be talked out of waiting for a wedding ring or the lonely widow who was secretly pining for consolation. Derry was so acute he could spot a woman's willingness at fifty paces, even if her face were veiled, and although I was at first horrified by the risks he ran my admiration for his nerve finally overcame my horror.

In the beginning I was too young to join him in these exploits (I was three years his junior), but Derry was generous and usually let

226

me watch. The first seduction I witnessed appalled me, but after Derry had sworn the woman had enjoyed it I became less squeamish. In fact I would have been quite happy to prolong my role of observer indefinitely, but at last I realized Derry would think it odd if I continued to enjoy women in this secondhand way, and when one day he invited me to join him I hadn't enough nerve to refuse. To my relief I soon found out that there's no truth in the maxim "Two's company but three's a crowd," and later I did try an exploit or two on my own. However these proved such nerve-wracking affairs that if I hadn't dosed myself liberally with poteen beforehand I might have turned tail and fled. I'm really very shy, you see, although no one ever believes that because I'm six feet two and look as if I ought to be as brave as a lion. It was only when I was with Derry that I forgot to feel shy. He gave me such confidence and—well, it's hard to explain, but I was always quite a different person when I was with Derry Stranahan.

But Derry wasn't going to be with me on my honeymoon.

I didn't intend to drink so much at the wedding breakfast, but champagne is such a deuced dangerous drink and those flunkeys kept filling up one's glass when one wasn't looking, and before I knew where I was I felt I just wanted to lie down in some quiet corner and go to sleep. However, I managed to keep my eyes open, and finally after numerous delays we left the reception and were driven across the town to the Hudson, where we boarded Cousin Francis' yacht. We then sailed all the way up the river to his country house, where we were to spend the first two weeks of our honeymoon, and by the time we crossed the threshold it was after dark and I had already made a vow never to touch champagne again. Mumbling an excuse to Sarah, I sank down on the dressing-room couch and drifted thankfully into oblivion.

When I managed to open my eyes it was seven o'clock in the morning, my head felt as if it had been split by a blunderbuss and there was no sign of Sarah.

I crawled off the couch. I was still fully dressed; evidently my man had been too tactful to disturb me. I stared numbly at my surroundings. Beyond the window a meticulously watered lawn stretched like a carpet to the glassy waters of the Hudson and across the river the humps of thickly wooded hills towered gloomily toward the cloudless sky. It already felt too hot, and I had a useless aching moment of longing for Woodhammer Hall.

I wondered if the water in the washstand pitcher was safe to drink. My tongue felt as if it were coming apart at the seams. After peering around for the bell rope I decided that if I waited an instant longer to assuage my thirst my tongue would certainly drop out, so I scooped up some water and drank. I felt better. I drank some more and then, summoning my courage, I tiptoed to the door that led into the main bedroom, listened carefully to the silence on the other side and reached out to turn the handle.

But the door opened before I could touch it. A second later Sarah was facing me across the threshold.

She was wearing a long white night dress buttoned up to the neck, and there were violet shadows under her eyes.

We looked at each other guiltily. It took me a moment to realize she was feeling just as guilty as I was.

"Patrick . . ." She rushed forward, flung her arms around my neck and burst into tears. "Oh, Patrick, forgive me. I didn't mean it. I didn't mean to drink more than one tiny glass of champagne, but . . ."

Enlightenment dawned. I suddenly saw the funny side of the situation and began to laugh.

"Well, really!" said Sarah, taking offense when her passionate apology failed to produce the equally passionate reassurance that was necessary. "I fail to see why you should be so amused!"

"Don't be angry, Sarah—please." I was still laughing and could only speak in gasps.

Fortunately my laughter proved infectious. The situation was saved when she too began to laugh, and she looked so lovely standing there in that chaste white nightgown that I gave her a kiss and drew her toward the bed.

She drew back at once. "Not in daylight!" she said, shocked, as if I had suggested some unspeakable perversion.

"Heavens no!" I agreed fervently, very much aware of my aching head and champagne-sodden body. "But I would so like to lie down for a while with you in my arms and doze and talk and recover together. It's still too early to think of breakfast, so there's no hurry to get up."

Sarah shuddered. "I declare I should swoon if I saw a breakfast tray!"

We started to giggle again like children, and although we both felt so groggy I knew she was as happy as I was. I undressed partially, keeping on my trousers and shirt so as not to embarrass her, and presently we were lying tranquilly in each other's arms and recalling as much as we could remember of the previous day.

"It was such a lovely wedding!" said Sarah. "I did enjoy myself!"

After we had agreed that it was the nicest wedding either of us had ever been to we both dozed, and by the time we awoke again it was eleven o'clock and we felt more in the mood for breakfast.

"I'm so happy!" exclaimed Sarah as we breakfasted outside on the terrace and watched the peacocks strut across the lawn. "What fun it is to be alone together with no one telling us what to do! I love honeymoons!"

I was in no mood to drink much at dinner, but I did because I knew it was necessary. Afterward, not wishing to dally in the drawing room, I suggested an early night, and Sarah raised no objection. We went upstairs, undressed in our separate rooms and dismissed our servants. So far so good. I joined Sarah in the main bedroom, complimented her on her primrose yellow nightgown, slipped into bed and blew out the light. Again so far so good. Unfortunately once the light was out it became obvious that we had gone to bed too early, for the room was still light.

"Let's not kiss until it's dark," said Sarah.

But I knew that any delay might spell disaster for me. The effects of the evening wine wouldn't last forever. "What's wrong with kissing in daylight?" I said truculently.

"It just isn't romantic!"

"Who says it's not romantic?"

"I say it's not!" In the dim light I saw her mouth harden stubbornly. "I want to wait till it's dark."

"You're so used to getting what you want, aren't you?" I said, panic bowling me to the brink of losing my temper. "Well, this is the wrong moment for you to expect to get what you want, because this is where I get what I want for a change, so don't try and stop me and don't say another word or I'll send you straight back to your damned papa."

"Patrick!"

"And believe me, he won't be at all pleased to see you!"

"How dare you say such a thing!" she cried in fury. "And how dare you swear in front of me like that!" But there was excitement in her eyes, and I suddenly realized that my aggressive behavior, normally so foreign to my nature, had appealed to her. I pulled her quickly toward me, and although she protested her resistance didn't last long. We kissed very passionately. My body moved hard against hers, and I was aware not only of urgency but of my small secret core of fear. I knew I had to be quick or God alone knew what might happen, but my fingers were so stiff and a great heaviness seemed to be weighing on my limbs and all the bedclothes kept getting in the way.

"Patrick, don't do that."

"Stop telling me what to do!" I yelled, remembering Derry's suggestion that American women would be all too willing to give a man instructions, and suddenly the thought of Derry gave me confidence, just as it always did, and I knew I was going to be safe.

It was over. Relief swept through me, streaming into every muscle of my body. Rolling away from her, I lay limply, the sweat blinding my eyes and my heart thudding in my chest, and so absorbed was I in the aftermath of the experience that I did not at first realize that Sarah was crying.

I felt more guilty then than I had ever felt in my life. I can't bear to hurt people or see them in pain.

"Sarah, forgive me." I tried to take her in my arms, but she pushed me away. "Sarah, I didn't mean—I was simply so anxious . . ."

She was struggling out of bed. She was sobbing openly now and her eyes were swollen with tears.

"I'm so sorry," I said uselessly. "I'm so sorry, Sarah." I followed her from the bed, but she turned and pushed me away again, her clenched fists shoving hard against my chest. I felt sick with distress. I could only stare at her dumbly until at last she said, her voice shaking, "I want to be alone for a while."

"Yes. If you like. Of course." I groped my way to the door of the dressing room. "Shall I come back later?"

She didn't answer, and presently, seeing no alternative, I left her.

I lay awake for a long time in the dressing room before I managed to sleep. I wanted to get up early so that I could slip back into bed with Sarah before she could wake and remember she was angry with me, but I slept until my man came into the room to draw the curtains.

Even before I opened my eyes memory was returning to me in thick suffocating waves.

I waited a long time before entering the bedroom, but when I heard Sarah dismiss her maid I took a deep breath, knocked softly on the door and forced myself across the threshold to apologize again.

But Sarah gave me no chance to open my mouth. As I stopped

awkwardly she jumped to her feet, ran across the room and flung her arms around my neck.

"Oh, Patrick, are you dreadfully angry with me?"

"Me?" I said, hardly able to speak for shame. "Angry? No, of course not. I thought perhaps you—"

"Oh, I'm very well," she said, giving me a quick smile. "Very well indeed. Shall we go downstairs?"

"Sarah, about last night . . ."

"I don't want to talk about it," she said with another quick smile, her voice clear and level.

"But—"

"I just don't want to talk about it, Patrick."

I stared. Her smile faded. She turned away before the expression in her eyes could betray her, and I heard her say in a muffled voice, "Does it have to happen often?"

I still felt almost too full of guilt to speak. "Not if you don't want it to."

"I see," she said and added in a calm, sensible voice, "I quite understand, of course, that it has to happen sometimes, and you needn't worry that I won't always do my duty, Patrick, because I want to be a good wife to you and I do love you so much, truly I do." She was crying by this time, and I was so upset that I could only take her in my arms and mutter some platitude—God knows what it was—and at last she blinked back her tears and plucked up enough courage to ask when it would be necessary to repeat the experience.

"Oh, not for another month at least," I said, wanting only to be kind, and so it was that I made no further attempt to touch her until we were three thousand miles away from New York beneath the black slate roof of Cashelmara.

VI

It was July when we arrived at Cashelmara. The wild fuschia hedge was in bloom behind the vegetable patch, and beyond the tousled lawn the beds were bursting with potato plants. It was a totally utilitarian garden at Cashelmara. My father had been indifferent to flowers and thought of soil only in terms of crop rotation, manure and research into the prevention of the blight.

My original plan had been to extend my honeymoon by making a leisurely tour of Europe and returning in the late autumn to settle at Woodhammer Hall, but after a year's absence from home I found I had no inclination whatsoever to potter around the Continent for a few months. Sarah was disappointed when I suggested postponing our tour, but she was too eager to see England to protest for long.

"Will we stay in London before going to Woodhammer?" she demanded, but I explained no one ever stayed in London during August.

"It'll be July when we arrive!"

"Well, as a matter of fact I thought we might visit Cashelmara before we go to England," I said. "The liners stop at Queenstown, and we could travel to Galway by train."

"But I thought you said you hated Cashelmara!"

"Yes, it's a tiresome sort of place, but my father would have thought it was my duty to go there once a year to see that all was well, so I may as well get it over with before we settle at Woodhammer. Besides, I'm awfully anxious for you to meet my friend Derry Stranahan."

"I'm sure I should like that very much," said Sarah, resigning herself to the Irish visit more gracefully than I had dared hope. "I guess it would be educational for me too to see a little of Ireland."

Quite an education, I thought, remembering Cashelmara with a suppressed shudder. However, even Cashelmara was inviting, since Derry would be there to greet us, so I promptly wrote to tell him we were on our way. I also wrote a similar letter to my favorite sister Annabel, but I saw no reason to announce my intentions to anyone else. I've never had two words to say to my sister Katherine or my cousin George, and as for Marguerite, who was by this time in London with the boys, I knew Cousin Francis had already written to tell her of our plans.

My father had left his London townhouse to Marguerite for life with a reversion to the boys and had provided liberally for his second family by bequeathing them various financial interests, but both estates had been left to me. No doubt he would have left Cashelmara elsewhere if it had been possible, but most unfortunately for me it was entailed in favor of the eldest son, and there was some difficulty (which I had never quite understood) about barring the entail. I was to learn more about this difficulty later, but when my father died all that mattered to me was that I was master of Woodhammer Hall. My father knew there was no place on earth I loved better than Woodhammer, and he was too kind and too just to deprive me of it simply because some obscure legal mumbo-jumbo had yoked me to those awful acres in Ireland.

I thought of my father often after we had landed in Ireland, and I thought of him even more as we traveled north toward that unspeakable wilderness he had called home.

"Is all Europe like this?" Sarah asked, appalled, knowing the answer was no but so horrified by the streets of Queenstown that she craved reassurance.

"Of course not!" I said firmly. "Ireland happens to be the most backward and poverty-stricken country in Europe, that's all. Try not to notice the beggars, darling."

"But the smell!" exclaimed Sarah, very chalky, and ordered her maid to find her a bottle of cologne.

"The worst beggars are always to be found in Queenstown," I said. I had no idea whether this was true or not, but I had to try to cheer her up somehow. "All the scum come here to emigrate."

"But if they can only afford to dress in rags how can they afford to emigrate?"

"The landlords often pay the passage. It's a cheap way of clearing the land and getting rid of them," I explained, remembering stories about the coffin ships of the famine but not knowing whether those ships still plied their human cargo across the Atlantic. The truth was that I knew very little about Ireland apart from the fact that most of the Irish are shiftless drunkards, and no visit to Cashelmara had ever encouraged me to learn more. It was not that I hated the Irish. On the contrary I felt sorry for them, for I was sure that if I had been condemned to live in a country like Ireland with nothing to do all day but watch rain pattering upon a potato patch I would have quickly become a shiftless drunkard too.

"The weather!" exclaimed Sarah. "The mud!"

"Yes, I know," I said unhappily. "I'm sorry it's such an awful journey, darling, but it'll be better in Galway, I promise you. There's a very good hotel by the railway station."

Well, it was a good hotel by Irish standards, but by New York standards I suppose it did leave something to be desired.

"The food!" cried Sarah after one mouthful of her dinner, and later protested, "Patrick, is this supposed to be coffee?"

"I can order tea."

"I can't abide tea," said Sarah, very sorry for herself by this time, and I knew she was wishing she was back in New York.

The dreadful journey progressed inch by inch. A hired carriage took us without incident from Galway to Oughterard, but from Oughterard every mile led us deeper into a harsher, darker world. I had never paid much attention before to the mud cabins or the ditches where the less fortunate inhabitants of County Galway lived, but now I was so conscious of Sarah's horror that I felt I was seeing them all for the first time. I found myself praying: Please, God, not another mud hovel, but the next moment we would round a corner and come across not one hovel but two with the usual bunch of half-naked children rooting among the manure heap and the reek of pig offal mingling with the peat smoke.

"But why is Ireland like this?" said Sarah desperately. "Why doesn't someone do something about it?"

"Well, the English do try," I said loyally, "but the Irish like to be this way. They're hopeless. The country's hopeless. I mean, look at the country. Just look at it."

Sarah shuddered.

It was indeed very ugly. Huge mountains, bald as eggs, rose from a wasteland of black bog and empty moorland, and as we drew closer to their shadowed valleys the desolation wrapped itself around us in suffocating folds.

"Patrick, I don't want to go on," Sarah burst out wildly, in a fearful state by this time. "I can't. Tell the driver to turn back."

"Darling, please . . ." I put my arm around her and gave her a kiss. "Look," I said with hideously false jollity, "the sun's coming out at last! And we're nearly there. It's just over the top of the next hill."

I somehow managed to soothe her, but she still hid her eyes to blot out the view from the windows. By this time we had left the main road and were journeying upward through a narrow gulley to the pass. The sun did indeed manage to shine feebly for two minutes, but it disappeared again as soon as the carriage lurched to the pass's summit and we could look down on the valley below.

"There's the lough," I said brightly to Sarah. "It's called Lough Nafooey, which means Lake of the Winnowing Winds. And there's Cashelmara. Can you see the white house over there amidst the trees?"

Sarah took one look at the valley and hid her eyes again. "It's all shut in," she whispered. "All those mountains in a circle. It's all shut in."

"The mountains won't seem so bad when we reach the house. It's really a very nice house," I added, trying not to sound too glum, but to be honest I was getting a little tired of Sarah's appalled expression, and I did wish she would buck up a bit and stop teetering on the brink of hysterics. God knows I didn't care for those bald lumpy mountains either, but after all there's plenty of wilderness in America; I mean, Ireland's not the only place on earth where you can go for miles without seeing a trace of civilization.

She must have heard the note of irritation in my voice, for she did make an effort to be sensible. After she had blown her nose and wiped away a tear she said she supposed the scenery wasn't really as frightening as all that. "It's just that it's so different from anything I've seen before," she said tremulously, and I knew she was thinking of the hustle and bustle of Fifth Avenue and all the horses careering down Broadway.

The carriage zigzagged laboriously to the floor of the valley, crossed the stone bridge which spanned the Fooey River and set off over the bog that fringed the lough's western shore. We could see Cashelmara clearly on the hillside ahead of us, and suddenly I realized that despite all the trials of the journey I was excited. I no longer cared about the rain and the mist and the damp. I forgot the ugly landscape and the exhaustion of travel and the ordeal which was Ireland. Slipping my arm from Sarah's waist, I stood up as best I could in the cramped interior of the carriage and leaned out of the window to see if there was any hint of a royal welcome lying in wait for us.

The carriage reached the gates of Cashelmara and swayed through the larchwoods up the long curling drive.

I saw him as soon as we rounded the last bend. He was standing on top of the steps with the front door open behind him, and when he saw the carriage he waved languidly and sauntered down the steps to the drive. He wore wide-check trousers and a Prince of Wales pea jacket and looked no end of a Heavy Swell.

"Hurrah!" I yelled, beside myself with delight at seeing him again, and on an impulse I flung wide the carriage door, jumped out and dashed up the drive toward him.

He started to laugh. He was always so casual, so debonair. Of course he laughed.

"Derry!" I shouted. "Derry, you old bastard!"

He waved again, still very languid. "Bastard yourself!" I heard him drawl. He was always so cool, you see, that I never expected him to be other than unflurried, but suddenly he was running too, and when we embraced at last and he said, still laughing, "You damned fool, what the devil took you so long?" I saw to my amazement that his black eyes shone with tears.

Chapter Two

I

We must have seemed as garrulous as a couple of fishwives as we stood there talking nineteen to the dozen, and we were so pleased to see each other again that neither of us noticed the carriage creak to a halt before the front door. It was only when I saw Derry's glance flick past me that I realized Sarah was watching us. The coachman had helped her down and she was standing very still, the damp breeze plucking limply at her veil. She looked not only beautiful but exotic against the drab dark background of the woods, and I felt my heart almost burst with pride.

"Sarah!" I exclaimed, overjoyed that I was at last able to introduce the two people I loved best. "May I present my friend Roderick Stranahan! Derry—my wife!"

They faced each other, and the chill between them struck me like a slap in the face. It was Derry's fault. He looked her up and down as if she were one of his damned women, and Sarah responded by looking down her nose at him as if he stank of the sewer. Derry laughed. The scene at once plunged deeper into disaster, and Sarah, turning her back on him with studied rudeness, said haughtily to me, "Patrick darling, is it really necessary for us to remain out here in the rain? You and Mr. Stranahan may be content to chatter away with no thought for my comfort, but I'm very cold and exceedingly tired and I want to go indoors at once."

"Of course," I mumbled, red to the ears with embarrassment. "Forgive me. This way." I offered her my arm, but she was so angry that she ignored it, picked up her skirts and climbed the steps unaided.

All the servants were clustered in the hall to catch a glimpse of the new mistress of the house. Twenty pairs of round eyes became rounder, and twenty necks craned forward with a flexibility that would have put a herd of giraffes to shame. Hayes the butler, a thin, reedy man in his fifties, began to make one of his famous speeches of welcome, but in the middle of his rapturous lyricism Sarah said petulantly to me, "Patrick, I have the most ferocious headache. I must lie down at once or I declare I shall faint right away."

Having begun by feeling angry with Derry, I now began to feel angry with her again. Hayes *was* an old bore when it came to speechifying, but it took so little to please him, and I thought she might at least have had the courtesy to hear him out. I said awkwardly, "Hayes, forgive us, if you please, but my wife is exhausted by the journey and must rest at once. We both thank you from the bottom of our hearts for such a magnificent and moving welcome."

(You have to exaggerate always when speaking to the Irish; no exaggeration is ever too much for them to endure.)

Hayes looked disappointed, but chivalry helped him to assume a solicitous expression. I was told that all was prepared for us, and after thanking him profusely again I took Sarah upstairs to the apartments which were set aside for the master and mistress of the house.

"What!" said Sarah. "No fire? And hasn't the room been aired? I thought the butler said all was ready for us!"

"I'll ring for the maid," I said hurriedly and gave the bell rope such a tug that it nearly came apart in my hands.

"And I must have hot water," said Sarah. "At once. I feel chilled to the bone."

I sighed. To ask for hot water immediately at Cashelmara was like asking for champagne at a country inn.

"Well, I think I'll leave you now," I said uncomfortably after I had given the order for hot water and the maid was busy lighting the fire. Sarah's own maid had arrived, and the footmen were busy heaving the enormous array of American luggage up the curving staircase. After pausing in the dressing room long enough to wash my hands and face in cold water, I hurried along the gallery to the drawing room, but Derry wasn't there. I went downstairs, looked in the saloon, which was also empty, and then crossed the hall to the library.

That too was empty, but I lingered, remembering my father. There was a huge desk which occupied much of the floor, and I thought of all the times I had entered the room and seen my father sitting there, his back to the window, his elbows submerged in a sea of papers. The top of the desk looked strangely naked now. On an impulse I sat down in my father's chair and surveyed the room. The books made it gloomy, but there was a fireplace of Italian marble which I liked, and above the mantel was an arresting portrait of my mother. I stared at her dark eyes and thought how odd it was that we should have had any connection with each other. But it was a good portrait. I thought I might wrap it carefully and put it in one of the attics so that it would not deteriorate in the damp Irish air, and I was just planning the picture I would paint to replace it when I noticed the miniature of my brother Louis peeping at me from behind the inkwell. Louis had died when I had been three months old, but my father had spoken of him so often during my childhood that I had come to think I had known him all too well. Leaning forward, I took the miniature between my thumb and forefinger and dropped it firmly into the bottom drawer of the desk. I had wanted to do that for a very long time.

The door opened. Derry drawled, "God, it looks odd to see you sitting there!" and we laughed together before I remembered the scene in the drive.

"Derry, why the devil did you treat Sarah like that?" I demanded crossly. "I must say I thought you were damned uppish with her."

"But Jesus Christ, Patrick, didn't you see the way she looked at me?"

"I—"

"Oh, very well and I'm sorry!" he interrupted, all impatience and good humor. "I'll smooth her over at dinner, I promise, and make amends somehow, but Lord, Patrick, what a chilly piece of skirt! Doesn't she freeze the balls off you in bed?"

"Stop it," I said.

He laughed. "Ah come, Patrick! Aren't you going to tell me all about your life between the sheets?"

"Not this time." I wanted to feel angry with him but only succeeded in feeling ill at ease. "Sarah's my wife. She's not just a piece of skirt, as you put it."

238

"Oh God, a romantic!" he drawled, strolling over to the window with a yawn.

When I said nothing he turned; our glances met, and I glimpsed some fleeting indefinable expression in his eyes. The next moment he was saying lightly with a smile, "Don't take offense. I was only joking, and you know how I love to joke about anything under the sun, Patrick. Have we been apart so long you don't remember all my worst faults? Listen, I admit I'm jealous, for I've never seen a creature half so ravishing as she is, and that's the truth of it. You're a devil of a lucky man, Patrick, but you always were lucky, weren't you? I never knew anyone luckier than you. Sit down, there's a good fellow, and let's order some whisky to lift you back on your toes after your journey, for I've so much to talk to you about that upon my honor I scarce know where to begin."

I began to feel better. Of course it was natural he should envy me such a beautiful wife, and since he had been honest enough to admit his envy I resolved to forgive him for his misbehavior toward Sarah. Accordingly after Hayes had brought us whisky and water and we had settled ourselves in the armchairs that flanked the fireplace I asked him genially how matters had been faring at Cashelmara. "I didn't have a letter from you for over a month before I left America," I added, trying to make this a mere comment, not a complaint. "I hope nothing was wrong."

"Didn't you get that letter I wrote about your cousin George?"

"No . . . Oh Lord, has George been interfering again?"

My cousin George, the only son of my father's only brother, lived in a hideous house at Letterturk, five miles away, and spent his time either shooting innocent fowl or else watching not so innocent foxes be torn to pieces by disgusting packs of hounds. He was twenty years my senior and as bossy as a nanny goat.

"Damnation!" said Derry. "The letter must have missed you. I did wonder if it would get to you in time. Well, to cut a long story short, I've decided I'd like a change of scenery, Patrick my friend. When do you intend to leave for Woodhammer?"

"As soon as possible," I said fervently. "We came here only to see you. Yes, why don't you come and stay at Woodhammer for a while? That's a marvelous idea. I'll call on Annabel tomorrow and ask if she'll let the girls come to stay with us too. Of course it'll be a bore to have Edith, but I can hardly invite Clara on her own."

"You'll not find Annabel agreeing to part with either of them. She made it clear to me last month that she has other plans for Clara."

"No! Really?" I could hardly believe it. It wasn't like Annabel to be snobbish, for her own second husband wasn't half as presentable as Derry.

"I had a little disagreement with that husband of hers," Derry was saying carelessly. "He's a nasty little weasel and no mistake. He didn't like me playing up to Clara, and when he called me a cheap fortune-hunting tinker's bastard—well, didn't I have to tell him what I thought of jockeys who prefer riding horses to riding women? I had to say something to defend myself, didn't I, and besides I really admire Clara. She's pretty as a picture and so sweet-natured I declare I'd think of marrying her even if she hadn't a penny to her name, but of course after I'd insulted Smith Annabel flew into a fine rage and told me never to darken her door again."

"Oh dear," I said unhappily. Because I was fond of both Annabel and Derry, it was painful to think of them at such odds with each other. "But, Derry, where does George come into all this?"

"Well, after the row with Smith the next thing I knew Cousin George was puffing over from Letterturk to say Annabel had complained I'd been getting above myself or some such stuff. He stood on the carpet about two feet from where you're now sitting and breathed fire like some nasty overfed dragon—not about Clara, if you please, but about MacGowan. Yes, MacGowan, the Scots bastard! He said he—George—had been exercising considerable restraint for many months, but Annabel's complaint was the straw that had broken the camel's back. And when I asked him what I'd done all he could say was that I'd upset MacGowan!"

"But—"

"So I said, 'Of course I've upset MacGowan, the dishonest, thieving rogue! Thanks to my power of attorney I've been able to twist the purse strings out of his hands and put him back in his place!' After all, MacGowan's supposed to be an agent, not a malevolent despot. So then Cousin George goes purple and says his uncle always thought highly of MacGowan, and when I point out—respectfully, mark you—that the late Lord de Salis was no longer in this world, Cousin George flies into an even dizzier tantrum and mutters some dark threat about an interview with you when you come home. He *is* a boring little man—and so damnably rude too!"

"Oh dear," I said unhappily again.

"Never mind," said Derry soothingly. "If I can't have Clara, to be sure I've no wish to stay here at Cashelmara. Cousin George and

240

MacGowan can go to hell together for all I care and Maxwell Drummond with them."

"Don't tell me Drummond's been bothering you too!" I cried in despair.

"He'd bother the Queen herself if he had the chance. It was nothing, no more than a tempest in a teapot that arose when I decided to raise the rent he pays for my father's old lands. Twenty pounds was such a ridiculously low figure, and since I'm sure most of it went straight into MacGowan's pocket . . . well, I was only trying to straighten out your affairs, Patrick! But of course Drummond hasn't paid a penny of the new rent and says he won't pay either till he's seen you in person."

"Now at last I'll have the chance to evict him!"

"You might be able to take my father's old lands away from him, but you'll never evict him from his own property, for he's not a tenant at will—he's a leaseholder. He has a fifty-year lease on that hovel and the surrounding acres, so you can't evict him whenever you please as you would any other tenant. If he failed to pay the ground rent you might get a chance, but the ground rent's so low he'll always be able to raise the money to pay."

"But everyone in Ireland is a tenant at will! How the deuce could Drummond have a leasehold property?"

"Because your father—God save his soul—had all those eccentric ideas about improving the lot of the Irish. He granted the leasehold to Drummond's father after the famine as an incentive to improve the land, and Drummond inherited it. He'll be your neighbor till the day of judgment, Patrick—or the year nineteen hundred, whichever comes first."

This was all such gloomy news that I poured myself some more whisky. "I wish to God we were at Woodhammer," I said fervently.

"When can we leave?"

"I'd better give Sarah a day or two to recover from the journey. Perhaps at the end of the week."

There was a knock on the door, and Hayes entered with a letter. The silver salver on which it lay was an interesting shade of yellow. Mellow saffron, I thought, remembering the labels on my set of watercolors.

"This has just arrived from Letterturk, my lord."

"Oh my God," I said. "It's from Cousin George. He didn't waste any time, did he?"

"Burn it unopened," advised Derry as Hayes withdrew.

But I had a morbid curiosity to see what George had written.

"My dear Patrick," he had begun paternally. "First of all may I welcome you home from America. My best wishes to you and your bride. I look forward to meeting her soon." Having thus disposed of the formalities, he launched himself into a new paragraph and adopted a more florid style. "Much as I regret to do so, I feel bound by honor and duty . . ." Cousin George was always feeling bound by honor and duty. Many were the times I'd wished they would strangle him. ". . . to inform you that there has been trouble at Cashelmara for some months now and this is, in my opinion, due solely to the meddling presence there of Roderick Stranahan . . ."

"Oh Lord," I said in disgust after skipping to the last paragraph, in which George threatened to call on me the very next day to discuss the situation. I passed the letter to Derry. "Look at this!"

"I don't need to look at it," said Derry. "I can imagine what it says." He pursed his mouth into the shape of a prune, lifted his nose as if an unpleasant smell lay beneath his nostrils and became Cousin George. "Can't stand that fellow Stranahan!" he barked. "Always knows how to get the better of me! Damned insolent young puppy, b'God!"

I laughed till I felt weak. "Encore!" I pleaded at last. "Encore!"

Derry sank his chin upon his chest, frowned mightily and assumed a dour expression.

"MacGowan!" I gasped in delight.

Derry recited in MacGowan's clipped lowland accent, "My name is MacGowan, I'm sober and mean; I don't smile, I don't laugh and I don't drink poteen."

I was laughing so hard by this time that I hadn't the breath to beg for more, but Derry was all too anxious to continue the performance. He stood up. He patted his hair and pulled it down over his ears. Then he took off his octagon tie, undid the top buttons of his shirt and pulled the linen away from his neck to give an illusion of bare shoulders.

"Patrick darling," he minced in Sarah's well-modulated American accent. "I want this, I want that, I want simply everything."

He stopped. I was about to protest, "Hey, steady on! Cousin George and MacGowan but not Sarah!" when I felt the draft from the open door whisper around my ankles as Sarah watched from the threshold.

Derry said quick as a flash, "Lady de Salis, thank God you're here! I was trying to cheer Patrick up with a little mimicry, but I swear he's so exhausted that it's been nothing but a losing battle. Well, if you'll both excuse me, I'll go and dress for dinner."

Within ten seconds he had slipped past Sarah, closed the door and disappeared.

"How dare you!" exploded Sarah, shaking with rage. "How dare you let him mock me like that!"

"I was just about to cut up rough about it when you arrived." Fortunately the whisky made me calm. "Besides, he didn't mean any offense, I'm sure. Darling, is anything the matter? I thought you were going to have a bath."

Sarah promptly burst into floods of tears and sobbed something about the servants not understanding a word she said and that she wished she was back home in New York.

"My poor Sarah . . ." I did indeed feel very sympathetic and did not in the least begrudge the next half hour spent appeasing her. When hot water had finally been squeezed from the kitchens I made her promise to retire to bed immediately after her bath. "I'll have some dinner sent up here," I said, inspired, "and as soon as I finish eating I'll come upstairs to sit with you."

Well, I did mean to go upstairs, but Derry and I started to kill a bottle of port together, and before we knew what was happening we were looking at two empty bottles and the grandfather clock in the corner was chiming midnight.

"Bedtime," I said, trying to sound firm and only succeeding in sounding surprised.

"Lord, I wish I was in your shoes," said Derry, "and had Sarah waiting for me upstairs. Share her with me, you lucky bastard."

"Don't be a bloody fool," I said kindly. For once he was even drunker than I was. "And don't tell me you're lonely, because I'm sure there's some kitchen maid whom you've been using as a warming pan these past months."

"What do I care about kitchen maids?" he said morosely. "What do I care about warming pans? I could die tomorrow and no one would care." Derry always talked about death when he was drunk, and when he was thinking of death he'd often say to me, "Ain't life grand?" as if amazed that death could ever have such a miraculous counterpart. He was very morbid on the subject, but no doubt that was because he was a Catholic and the after-life was mapped out for him with such chilling precision. Personally I think Protestants are more sensible in keeping notions of the after-life comfortingly vague. I mean, I absolutely believe in God, but I don't think anyone goes to hell unless they're really wicked, and I doubt very much that heaven is full of angels and cherubs. That would be so awfully boring. I picture heaven as being like an idyllic garden, full of flowers and trees and friendly animals, for after all, if God made man in His own image, why shouldn't He have made Eden in the image of heaven? It all seemed perfectly logical to me and a great comfort when I thought about death—which wasn't often, only when Derry reminded me of it.

"*I* should care if you died tomorrow," I said, patting him on the head as I heaved myself to my feet. "Well, good night, old fellow. Sleep well and do try not to be so down."

My candle wavered unsteadily as I crossed the circular hall, and hot wax stung my fingers. Muttering a curse, I clambered up the stairs and wove my way along the gallery to the door of my apartments.

My man was waiting up for me patiently, so I at once stripped and dived into my night shirt. By the time I had finished with the chamberpot behind the screen he had whisked away my clothes, so I dismissed him, to our mutual relief, and plowed over to the communicating door.

I had expected to find the bedroom in darkness, but to my horror the bedside lamp was turned up high and Sarah was propped against the pillows with a book in her hands.

"Where were you?" she demanded at once in a shaking voice.

Oh God, I thought. I suddenly felt very tired and not a little befuddled. The pillows on my side of the bed gleamed at me invitingly.

"You promised you'd come upstairs directly after dinner! I've been waiting for hours."

"I'm sorry," I said helplessly. "I didn't notice the time." I slid into bed and leaned forward to give her a kiss, but she turned her face away.

"I suppose you were too busy gossiping with Mr. Stranahan!"

"Well, why not?" I said, aggrieved. "He *is* my best friend. Do be quiet, Sarah, and let's both go to sleep! I'm too tired to cope with tantrums."

"Tantrums! Aren't I entitled to be angry? You've treated me abominably ever since we've set foot in this dreadful place!"

"We'll be leaving in a day or two." I snuggled into the pillow and savored the luxurious texture of the fine Irish linen.

"Not with Mr. Stranahan, I hope!" she said, sitting bolt upright in bed.

Instinct told me that if I once admitted this I would be doomed to a sleepless night. Summoning all my energy, I sat bolt upright too and did my best to be masterful. "Sarah, you're tired and over-wrought," I said severely. "Stop whining at me, put out that lamp and go to sleep."

"I'm not whining at you!" She flung her book halfway across the room, and I thought how beautiful she looked when she was angry. Her eyes glittered, her cheeks glowed and her hair, unplaited that night, streamed over her slender shoulders in a turbulent cascade. "How dare you say I'm whining at you!"

"You're whining, moaning and being altogether most objection-able," I said, losing my patience with her. "Be quiet this instant!"

She slapped me across the face.

I stared at her. A second later she struck me again, and after a long silence I realized I was going to make love to her. I moved roughly at first because I was afraid she would fight, but there was no fighting. She lay back on the pillows and let me do as I pleased, and afterward she even took my hand and held it shyly as if to show me all was forgiven. I felt a deep rush of affection for her. Taking her in my arms, I held her so tightly that she gasped, and although neither of us spoke I knew we were both happy.

So I had a good night's sleep after all, despite my fears, and it was not until I awoke the next morning that I started to wonder how on earth I was going to tell her that Derry was coming with us to England.

III

As matters turned out I didn't have to tell her immediately, for soon after breakfast a hastily scribbled note arrived from my brother-in-law Alfred Smith to say that Annabel had had a bad fall from a horse and could I come at once to Clonagh Court.

Sarah looked sulky, as if poor Annabel had deliberately inconve-nienced her, and said of course she was much too tired still to con-sider even the smallest of journeys. "I did hope we could spend the morning alone together," she added, "but I do understand that if Annabel is injured seriously you must visit her at once."

I was too worried to pay much attention to her sulks. Alfred had not been explicit in his note, and I at once imagined Annabel with a broken back and less than an hour to live.

"Come with me," I begged Derry, in a great state by this time, and he said sympathetically that he'd ride to Clonagh Court with me, although it would be better if he went no nearer the house than the gates.

So we set off together down the road to Clonareen, and despite all my anxiety I felt my spirits lift. It was a fine morning. The dew on the wayside grass sparkled, and my tenants smiled at me from their fields or from the doorways of their cabins. Derry pretended not to notice a soul, but after all he did have his dignity to maintain, and it was awkward for him since he had once been one of their number. I was too preoccupied by responding to my friendly reception to pay much attention to the looks which were thrown at him, although I do remember thinking it was a pity people had to be so jealous.

Our journey was still proceeding in this mildly pleasant fashion when we rounded a bend in the road and saw ahead of us none other than the valley's prize troublemaker, Maxwell Drummond.

Derry always claimed that Drummond was descended from Scotsmen, and Drummond's father had indeed come from Ulster, where many Scots have settled, but to me Drummond was Irish to the backbone, stubborn as the donkey that pulled his cart and a thousand times more aggressive. He had wide shoulders, wide enough to make the rest of his body look disproportionately thin, a thick neck and a broken nose; I thought he was quite the ugliest looking cove I had ever seen. His one redeeming feature was that he didn't smell as much as he used to, for his wife, a schoolmaster's daughter accustomed to more refined odors, was obviously strict in keeping a supply of soap in the house.

He drew his donkey cart onto the verge to let us pass and gave me a peremptory nod. "Welcome home, Lord de Salis," he said. He had a brogue as thick as sour cream, but he chose his words like an Englishman. "I hope you've come here to put your house in order." And he gave Derry such an insolent look that it was a wonder Derry didn't leap from his saddle and start thrashing him.

But Derry was much too debonair to descend to such crassness. He merely yawned, made a great business of watching a cloud drift across the sky and said idly to me, "We'd best hurry, Patrick, if we want to reach Clonagh Court before the rain starts."

"I hope God'll be sending enough rain to drown you, you bastard," said Drummond, "for it's no peace we'll have in this valley till He

246

does. Good day to you, Lord de Salis," he added as an afterthought, giving the donkey a taste of the switch, and the beast began to plod forward past us along the verge.

"Just a minute!" I said angrily. I wasn't going to let him get away with insulting any friend of mine. "If you think Mr. Stranahan chose the thankless task of managing my affairs in this valley, you're quite wrong! He has better things to do with his time than persecute people like you. He'll be leaving with me for England at the end of this week, and—"

"God save you, Lord de Salis!" cried Drummond, interrupting me with the most infuriating glee. "I knew you'd see the light of day and remove that villain from Cashelmara as soon as you returned! No son of your great and mighty father, may the Lord bless and preserve his memory, could have done other than that. I wish you joy of England, Derry Stranahan, but to be sure I'd rather set foot in purgatory than scrape even the smallest tip of my little toe on Saxon soil."

The donkey broke into a trot. The cart spun lightly away in a shower of mud that spattered Derry's clothes, and I shouted a curse after Drummond, which he unfortunately failed to hear.

"Damned impudence!" I yelled. Even my horse was dancing with rage.

"Forget him, Patrick! Let him go to the devil and be damned, for he's not worth your anger!" Derry was already smiling in contempt, and when I tried to protest he merely hunched his shoulders, turned down his mouth at the corners and said in Drummond's brogue, "To be sure it's doomed to eternal hell-fire he is, the black rogue, with not a soul to buy him a Mass from the priesteen."

I smiled too then—he was so clever with his mimicry—and for a moment nothing mattered because we were out riding together and the sun was shining and it was good to be alive.

"Ain't life grand?" said Derry.

It was only then that I thought of death, just as he always did when life seemed especially good, and my anxiety rose once more as we rode on to Clonagh Court.

The house lay on the southeastern tip of the lough half a mile outside the straggling settlement of Clonareen. At the eastern end of the valley there is a large expanse of lowland marking a break in the ring of mountains. The break in the circle is not visible from either Cashelmara or the western pass into the valley because of the spurs of the southern mountains, but the plain stretches beyond Clonareen to the shores of Lough Mask and the little towns of Letterturk, Clonbur and Cong. Clonagh Court, the dower house my father had built for his mother, stood on rising ground in the shadow of the mountain called Bencorragh and faced the plain. My grandmother had deliberately chosen this view because after years of living at Cashelmara she had declared she was tired of looking at the lough and the mountains.

In the paddocks in front of the house a number of horses were grazing docilely. I wondered which of them had been responsible for Annabel's fall, and suddenly I felt very much upset, for Annabel was really awfully jolly, and although I had never known her well (she had been grown up when I was still in the nursery) I liked her far better than my other two sisters, Madeleine and Katherine. I think she liked me too. In fact she had even said once that I was a much finer fellow than our brother Louis, which I thought was pretty decent of her because everyone used to talk of Louis as if he were a child saint. But Annabel would have had no time for child saints. She was much too honest and sensible for that.

Reaching the house, I tethered my horse to a convenient tree and fended off the half-dozen dogs that were barking furiously around my shins. The front door was open—it always stood open at Clonagh Court—and I saw my brother-in-law Alfred Smith was already hurrying to meet me. He wore a patched jacket, filthy riding breeches and no necktie of any description. His short dark hair stood on end, reminding me of a hairbrush.

"Christ," he said. "I'm bloody glad to see you. Come in."

"Is she . . ."

"No, she's not dead, but she's concussed something shocking. Mrs. O'Shaughnessy, Danny and Millie and me have made her comfy as possible, but she needs someone else to look at her, and how the hell do I get hold of a doctor when there's no dispensary for God knows how many miles? Mrs. O'Shaughnessy and Millie can't go, and Danny's rheumatics is so bad he couldn't even get on a horse unless he was lifted by a rope and pulley, and I don't want to go because I want to stay here with Annabel. Christ, you should see her. She just lies there, pale as a lily," said Alfred with a startling venture into poetic language. "I can't stand to see her so quiet-like and dead to the world."

"I'll ride to the dispensary at once," I said, glad that there was something I could do.

"Well, I know you're on your honeymoon, but maybe if you could

248

send someone . . . Then there's the girls. Clara and Edith. They're in such a state, poor little things. If you could say a word to them—they'd be ever so happy to see you, I'm sure."

It's an ill wind, as they say, that blows no one no good. I had a word with my nieces, and after I had given my handkerchief to Clara I suggested they both spend a day or two at Cashelmara, where my wife would keep them company.

"But we couldn't leave poor dearest Mama!" cried Clara, who was a nice girl and very tenderhearted.

"Why not?" said Edith, who was the exact opposite of her sister in every respect and always seemed as cross as a bear with a sore head. "She left us for years. Why shouldn't we leave her for a day or two? Besides, she's not dying, and at present she doesn't know whether we're here or not."

"Oh, you're so hard, Edith!" exclaimed Clara reproachfully, but when I said my friend Mr. Stranahan was at the gates to escort them to Cashelmara she followed Edith upstairs very quickly to pack her bags.

I hardly needed to ask Derry if he was willing to fulfill the role of escort. The girls, accompanied by their old nurse, who still looked after their clothes, jogged off in the pony trap and Derry rode beside them with an expression that would have suited any self-respecting cat confronted with a bowl of cream.

Their departure left me free to find a doctor. No one seemed to know where the nearest dispensary was, although the housekeeper thought there might be a doctor at Cong. That was nearer than Westport or Galway, but it was still thirteen miles away, and finally I halted at Clonbur to make inquiries from Willie Knox, the local squireen.

I must say Knox was very obliging. As soon as he heard what had happened he offered to ride himself to fetch a retired doctor at Letterturk, and since I could trust him not to stop at a wayside shebeen, get drunk and forget his mission (as many an Irish servant would have done), I accepted his offer and rode back to reassure Alfred that help was on the way. I took a look at Annabel, but she was still unconscious and had a nasty gray-white complexion that I found most upsetting.

"I'll come back later," I told Alfred, "but I think meanwhile I'd better go back to Cashelmara and help the girls settle down."

"I wish your sister was here," said Alfred. "The nurse, I mean, not the lady at Duneden Castle."

That struck me as being a good idea. "I'll write to Madeleine," I said, "although by the time the letter reaches London Annabel will probably be on her feet again."

"Either on her feet or in her coffin," said Alfred bitterly and kicked at a table leg to relieve his feelings. I remember liking him for the first time when he did that because I had always thought, in common with everyone else, that he had married Annabel for her money and now I saw that perhaps he really might have been in love with her after all.

I was starving by the time I reached Cashelmara and felt I could have drunk at least a gallon of beer to quench my thirst, but to my horror I found a most unpleasant reception awaiting me. Sarah was on the verge of hysterics because I had inflicted the girls on her without warning, MacGowan was glowering in the hall as he waited to give in his notice, and last but not least my cousin George de Salis of Letterturk was dancing up and down the saloon like a turkey cock as he demanded to see me without delay.

IV

I dealt with George first. I had no choice. I was scooped into the saloon before I had the chance to escape.

"You'll ask Stranahan to leave, of course," he said as soon as he could. "You're not going to harbor him under the same roof as your innocent young nieces."

"For God's sake, George!" I protested. "The girls are chaperoned by their old nurse as well as Sarah. You surely can't think that anything improper could happen."

Unfortunately Cousin George could. "I happen to know for a fact that Stranahan has designs on Clara."

"But you surely don't think he'd seduce her!"

"I wouldn't put anything past him," said George darkly. "Look here, Patrick, you've no choice. That rogue's got to go."

"Don't dictate to me like that!" I shouted at him. I'm normally a placid, even-tempered fellow, but it was half past two and I'd had no lunch and my favorite sister was at death's door and I simply wasn't in the mood for Cousin George. "You're not my father, so stop talking to me as if you were, you interfering old mule!"

He goggled at me as if he were a goldfish hauled from his bowl. Then he exploded. He said I was "ungrateful," an "insolent young puppy," and he wouldn't be a bit surprised if I came to a "deuced rotten end." He was glad my father wasn't alive to see the "shambles" resulting from my "prolonged neglect of my duties." God only knew what a "disappointment" my father had found me.

"That's a bloody lie!" I yelled at him. "My father was proud of me! The trouble with you is that you're jealous—jealous because your father was the younger son and mine was the elder, because I have Cashelmara and Woodhammer and all you have is that rat-infested hovel at Letterturk!"

"How dare you say such a thing!" He was purple as a hyacinth. "My concern for Cashelmara springs from the purest of motives!"

I laughed in his face.

"Very well!" he shouted at me. "If you won't take advice I'll hold my tongue and you and young Stranahan can go to the devil as fast as you please!"

Derry at this point would have made some devastating witticism, but I was too exhausted to care that I hadn't had the last word. As soon as George had stormed out of the house I collared Hayes, told him to bring beer and sandwiches to the library and collapsed into the chair behind my father's desk.

Hayes turned up ten minutes later with a tankard of ale, a carefully sliced loaf of bread and a plate covered with dollops of butter and cheese.

"For God's sake, Hayes, isn't there any cold meat?"

"There was a wondrous fine chicken leg, my lord, but no one's seen it in a whileen. My lord, Ian MacGowan would see you now, if you please."

"Find that chicken leg," I growled, attacking the bread with a single-minded concentration that excluded consideration of all other subjects, and Hayes fled.

When he dutifully returned some time later he reported that the chicken leg had vanished from the face of the earth. He even had the gall to mention fairies. After that, having a craving to talk to someone hardheaded and practical, I demanded to see MacGowan. "And bring me more beer!" I yelled wrathfully after Hayes as I wondered, not for the first time, how any Englishman could live in Ireland and retain his sanity.

MacGowan marched into the room, bid me a sour good day and told me he wished to leave. With a great effort I repressed the urge to reply, "Go and good riddance" and instead sank my teeth into a mushy hunk of cheese. Why the Irish can't make decent hard cheese is a mystery known only to themselves.

"My lord," MacGowan was saying, "Cashelmara is not big enough to contain two agents, the one undoing all the other's hard and loyal work. It's not my place to criticize you for appointing Mr. Stranahan to a position of authority here. I may only say that he has made my position untenable. Therefore with your permission, my lord, I respectfully submit my notice and will leave at your earliest convenience."

The meal had revived me. I at once realized that MacGowan's resignation was the last thing I wanted if I intended to leave soon with Derry for Woodhammer Hall. MacGowan might have his faults, but he could in his own fashion keep the estate running evenly. If he left I might have difficulty finding a replacement, and worse than that I would be obliged to stay at Cashelmara for God knows how long before the man could be engaged and instructed. Better the devil you do know, I told myself firmly, than the devil you don't.

"MacGowan," I said, "Mr. Stranahan and I intend to leave shortly for England. I'm sorry your position here has been difficult. That wasn't what I intended, and I promise you that from today you can manage matters exactly as you see fit. I appreciate very much the efforts you've been making on my behalf during my long absence and would be pleased if you would accept an increase in salary of . . ." I hesitated. I suddenly realized I had no idea what his salary was. My lawyers in London sent him the remittance each month.

"My brother in Scotland who is agent for the Marquess of Lochlyall has twenty-five pounds a year more than I do," said MacGowan with typical Scots cunning. He sounded so gloomy that not even his worst enemy could have accused him of being insolent in suggesting the figure before I did.

"Well, we're not in Scotland, are we, MacGowan?" I said. "But nonetheless I think you've certainly earned an extra twenty-five a year." As soon as I said that I realized he had expected me to beat him down to fifteen. To cover my confusion I said hastily, "Talking of your family in Scotland, how's Hugh?"

Hugh was his son. He was a year younger than I was, and I had not seen him since he had left Cashelmara ten years before to attend a school in Glasgow. Shortly afterward Mrs. MacGowan, a fierce woman who looked as if she might have won a prize tossing the cabre, had left her husband and settled with relatives in Glasgow to be near her son. No one had ever known what MacGowan had thought of this arrangement, but remembering Mrs. MacGowan, one could only assume he had been relieved to see the last of her. He lived alone in a neat stone house on the other side of the Fooey River and was reported to keep a sack of gold hidden in the privy.

"Hugh is doing very well, thank you, my lord," said MacGowan, almost sociable now that he had the extra twenty-five pounds adding a golden glow to his future. "My brother in Scotland has arranged for him to be an apprentice on the Lochlyall lands and is instructing him in the details of estate management."

"How nice," I said. "Do remember me to Hugh when you next write, won't you?" But in fact I had never cared for Hugh Mac-Gowan, whom I remembered as a tough, sullen little boy always spoiling for a fight or else sulking because I preferred Derry's company to his, and I didn't care a jot that I was most unlikely ever to see him again.

Meanwhile MacGowan was suitably appeased, Hayes reappeared with more beer and I was beginning to feel I might possibly survive the day. I still had to cope with Sarah, but to my relief I found she had calmed down and was doing her best to be hospitable to my nieces. Derry in turn was making a great effort to charm her, and although she still insisted on being cold toward him I did feel that the situation was not so far beyond redemption as I had earlier feared. Presently I found I even had a moment to write to Madeleine to ask for her help, and to save time I sent a stable boy to take the letter immediately to the mail car at Leenane.

Having dealt with all the crises at Cashelmara, I was able to return to Clonagh Court, but barely had I crossed the threshold when the housekeeper came sobbing down the stairs to tell me my sister had died.

v

I cried and Alfred cursed, but she was gone. At last I mopped up the tears which I had shed as furtively as possible, and Alfred stopped swearing. It was very quiet in the house after that.

"Have a drink," said Alfred finally and produced a huge bottle of pale poteen.

"Thanks," I said, so we sat down together and started drinking. He told me all about himself. He had had six brothers and seven sisters, and he thought he had been born in a stable on Epsom Race Course, but he wasn't sure. His father had been a groom for old Lord Rustington (the father of Annabel's first husband), and as Alfred was the oldest son he had followed in his father's footsteps. Fortunately he had turned out to be the right size for a jockey, and after that he had been as happy as a king and had even been able to keep his parents from destitution in their old age. His brothers were either dead or in Canada, and his surviving sisters had all kinds of husbands and offspring—he couldn't remember how many. He had never thought he would be a husband himself because he only liked tall girls and tall girls had always thought he was too small. Annabel had been the only woman who had ever been halfway decent to him. He had liked her so much he had even been prepared to overlook her being a baron's daughter. He had never been cowed by the aristocracy anyway. He had rubbed shoulders often enough with them at the race course, and they weren't anything special, just different.

"Have some more poteen," he added as an afterthought and snatched my glass from under my nose.

"This is awfully powerful stuff," I said hazily as he poured me another tumblerful.

"It's bloody old," said Alfred. "That's why it's so bloody pale. They make it in a shebeen not far from here, but I swore blind I'd never tell a soul where it is in case the magistrates get wind of it. Well, as I was saying . . ."

He said a great deal more, describing his early years in loving detail, and then I too embarked on my life history. We talked far beyond sunset, and finally after we had sworn eternal friendship with each other we fell asleep at the dining-room table. When I next opened my eyes Alfred was still snoring opposite me, the morning sun was high in the sky and if a priest had walked through the door I would immediately have asked for the last rites. In fact we were both of us so ill that I was quite unable to leave Clonagh Court that day and could only just manage to write a note to Sarah to say I had been obliged to stay with Alfred to make arrangements for the funeral.

The next few days were as confused as a nightmare and far more harrowing. I was relieved that Derry was at Cashelmara to look after the women, for it was as much as I could do to stay at Clonagh Court and look after myself and Alfred. I tried feverishly to make funeral arrangements, but when I despaired of ever being able to arrange anything in that godforsaken corner of the world I had no choice but to swallow my pride and ask Cousin George for help. He at least had the advantage of being a native of the district, and he did eventually succeed in organizing a proper English funeral. I have no prejudice against Roman Catholics, but Irish funerals are so awfully un-

English, and I knew Annabel would have wanted to be laid to rest with the minimum of fuss.

The grave was dug in the little plot beside the family chapel at Cashelmara. The parson was summoned from Letterturk, where the nearest Protestant church stood, and a few select mourners gathered, the Knoxes of Clonbur, the Courtneys of Leenane and the Plunkets of Aasleagh. After a short plain service the coffin was lowered into the ground and the ordeal, to my great relief, was over.

I had quite forgotten the letter I had written to Madeleine, and when she arrived the next day I was astounded to see her. She had taken an outside car from Galway and had walked the three miles to Cashelmara from the Leenane road. Naturally after such an arduous journey she was even more offended that I hadn't waited for her before holding the funeral.

"How was I to know you would even come?" I said, aggrieved. "You never wrote, and besides I had no idea how long my letter would take to reach you."

"Well, it's done now," said Madeleine, annoyed, "but I must say I think the entire incident from Annabel's fall to her funeral has been grossly mismanaged. Why didn't you send for a proper doctor instead of that old man at Letterturk?"

"Because there wasn't a doctor for miles!" I cried heatedly. "No one around here even knows where the nearest dispensary is!"

"That's a scandal. An absolute scandal. I shall do something about it."

"Do," I said, relieved that Ireland, not I, was now being blamed for the tragedy.

"I shall open a dispensary in Clonareen," announced Madeleine. "I'll go to the Archbishop for money—I'll even go to the Pope if I have to—and you can donate the land, Patrick, in Annabel's memory and arrange for a little house to be built where I can treat patients."

If that was the price I had to pay for placating Madeleine, I supposed I would have to pay it. Madeleine always looked as if she would never have the heart to say boo to a goose, but underneath that soft exterior she was as tough as old boots—as my father had discovered when he had tried to stop her becoming in turn a Roman Catholic, a nun and a nurse. For some reason which was beyond my understanding, Marguerite liked her the best of my sisters.

"Marguerite was most upset not to be informed of Annabel's accident," Madeleine was saying severely to me. "I went to see her before I left London. You should have written to her, Patrick! That was very remiss."

"But Annabel wasn't dead! I mean, when I wrote to you—"

"It must have been obvious that she was at death's door. Have you written to Katherine?"

"Not yet."

"Patrick!"

"Well, I knew she'd be in London and would think it too far to come for the funeral."

Madeleine gave me a withering look from her china-blue eyes and said politely, "I shall write to Katherine immediately. Will you be here if she decides to come to Cashelmara?"

"No, I'm going to Woodhammer," I said thankfully. "Sarah and I are leaving the day after tomorrow."

"But what are you going to do about Clara and Edith? You're surely not going to leave them with that wretched Smith?"

"Alfred Smith," I said angrily, "is a jolly nice fellow and I won't hear a word against him."

"The word 'wretched' was simply intended to convey commiseration. You'll let him stay on at Clonagh Court, of course? Good. I'm glad you intend to be charitable. Now, about the girls . . ."

"They're coming with us to Woodhammer."

"An excellent solution! After all, no matter how much one would wish to be charitable one can only admit that Clonagh Court has been the most unsuitable environment for them, and besides I hear from George that it would be advisable for Clara to be separated from Derry Stranahan."

"Derry's coming with us to Woodhammer," I said, too incensed to hide the fact from her. "And if he wants to marry Clara I certainly shan't stand in his way."

Madeleine was motionless. She looked up at me with an inscrutable expression and finally said, "I see. Well, of course, it's not my business to interfere, but I can't help but think you're misguided."

Half an hour later Sarah was rushing up to me in a towering rage to say that if Derry came with us to Woodhammer she would take the first boat back to New York.

VI

I did manage to pacify her, but it was damned uphill work, and I had to tell her at least twenty times how I would do anything in the world to make her happy.

"But I must help Derry just this once," I pleaded. "If he can get things settled with Clara it would mean such a lot to him, and after all . . . well, he *is* my oldest friend, darling. Do try and understand."

"But it'll be months and months before he marries Clara, and we shall have to have them and that dreadful Edith with us for all that time!"

"But, darling, I thought Clara would be nice company for you!"

"Why can't *you* be nice company for me?"

"Well, I'd love to be, but you must admit it's been deuced difficult lately."

"Don't make excuses! You don't love me. You can't love me or you'd take me to Europe."

"Woodhammer's much nicer than the Continent," I said, kissing her. "Wait and see." I thought I was talking reasonably enough, but at length I realized that if I wanted to prove to her she was loved I would have to do more than talk. I made an effort; Sarah was coaxed to bed and all was well once more. At least by the time we left Cashelmara we were still on speaking terms.

I won't attempt to describe the journey to Woodhammer. Suffice it to say that to traverse Ireland, cross the sea and journey by a series of irregular railway connections to Warwickshire with three females, a bunch of servants and a mountain of luggage is enough to prostrate any two men in the prime of life. Derry and I arrived looking very white around the gills, and I don't think I've ever in my life been more relieved to see dear old Woodhammer slumbering in the sunshine amidst all that beautiful, orderly, civilized English countryside.

Home, I thought thankfully and only just managed to control myself from weeping for joy. Derry, who deplored sentimentality, kept giving me suspicious looks, but Lord, how good it was to be back at Woodhammer again! I had been born at Woodhammer, spent all my childhood there; it was part of me. People had entered my life and left it—parents, brothers, sisters, servants, friends—no one ever seemed to stay very long, but Woodhammer! Woodhammer was always there. Woodhammer was continuity, security, warmth, comfort and peace. Generation after generation of de Salises had lived and died there; I liked to think of that. It wasn't that I was much of a one for history, but I enjoyed thinking of my ancestors growing up as I was growing up, encircled by Woodhammer's mellow walls. When I was very young I had asked the people in charge of me where I had come from, and after being fobbed off with explanations about the stork I had at last heard the right words from the cook. She had said, "Why, you come from Woodhammer Hall, dear, just like every other little de Salis," and from then on I no longer cared about storks. I knew who I was and I knew where I had come from. I was a de Salis of Woodhammer Hall, and Woodhammer Hall was the center of the universe. So when my father was away, as he was most of the time, and when my mother died after secluded years in which I scarcely saw her—when my nanny observed yet again that boys were more difficult than girls and my sister Nell became more distracted than ever—I no longer minded because I had my home and I loved my home with all the passion I never had the chance to lavish on other people.

And what a beautiful home it was! It was an Elizabethan house, shaped in the traditional E, with tall stately chimneys and weather-beaten walls and odd windows that didn't match one another. It faced an expanse of parkland laid out by order of one of my eighteenth-century ancestors, but behind the house was a fascinating Elizabethan garden with a maze to rival Hampton Court's and several walled arbors where flowers bloomed throughout the summer and the grass was very smooth and short and green. There were other eighteenth-century features—an orangerie and a rather frightful gazebo—but I liked the Elizabethan garden best, and it was there that I first became interested in planting flowers and watching them grow.

And inside the house—oh God, I can see that hall still, panel after panel of exquisite oak, and beyond the huge fireplace with the crossed swords over the chimney piece, beyond the far corner of the immense Persian carpet, rose the staircase, *my* staircase, the finest staircase in all the world, the wood hand-carved by Grinling Gibbons with such a brilliance that I couldn't look at it without experiencing that great thrill which always overwhelms me when I see a work of art so superb that no words can describe its splendor. It was that staircase which first inspired me to turn to woodcarving, and for a long time now I had enjoyed working with wood more than anything else.

There was a great deal of carving at Woodhammer, though none matched that splendid staircase. The paneled rooms were warm and serene, the maze of winding corridors mysterious, the priest's hole endlessly fascinating. It was a wonderful place for a child growing up, and nothing pleased me more than to think that when I had children they would grow up there too.

Of course I never said that to my father because I knew he

wouldn't understand. He came from the one generation of the de Salis family who hadn't been brought up at Woodhammer Hall. My poor father! He had been born at Cashelmara, stark, terrible, brand-new Cashelmara, chillingly symmetrical, architecturally perfect and spiritually null. Built in a wilderness, devoid of the sense of times past which I found so comforting at Woodhammer, impregnated by the damp mind-numbing Irish air and surrounded by the hostile alien Irish peasantry, it was at once terrifying, depressing and repugnant to me. Whenever I came home to Woodhammer after even the briefest of visits to Cashelmara I always wanted to go down on my knees and thank God for once more delivering me from evil.

Thank God! I thought fervently, running true to form, and as I looked at the servants drawn up in neat quiet lines, Ireland at last seemed as remote as a South Sea island and Cashelmara no more than an unpleasant memory fading to the back of my mind.

I was just shaking hands emotionally with the steward when some-one came hurrying down the staircase. Glimpsing the glow of red hair, the flash of light reflecting on pince-nez and the sweep of a smart, dark, fashionable dress, I felt my heart lift in joy a second time.

"Marguerite!" I shouted. "What a marvelous surprise!"

But Marguerite didn't even smile at me. She was looking at some point beyond my right shoulder, and just as I was realizing that my enthusiasm was unreciprocated, Sarah shot past me as fast as a fox breaking covert and flung herself weeping into her aunt's out-stretched arms.

Chapter Three

"The solution," said Marguerite firmly, "is quite obvious." Dear Marguerite, she really did have the most splendid talent for organizing other people's lives. "You and Sarah must have more time alone together."

We were in the long gallery at Woodhammer an hour later. Sarah had been soothed and put to bed, the girls were also recuperating from the journey, and Derry had not yet emerged from his room. I had been about to seek sanctuary in a quiet corner, preferably in the attics among my woodcarving collection, when Marguerite had pounced on me, clutched my sleeve so that I couldn't escape and maneuvered me to one of the sofas that faced the view across the terrace to the Elizabethan garden. There was no choice but to surrender. After listening gloomily as she talked of Sarah's distress I cheered up only when she added, "Of course it's not entirely your fault, I do realize that."

"Isn't it?" I said hopefully.

"Heavens no. I'm not so blind that I can't read between the lines of Sarah's letters which she wrote pleading for help and begging me to come here to Woodhammer. However, I did think a quick visit wouldn't be amiss in the circumstances."

"I'm awfully glad to see you. Why don't you send for the boys and stay a month or two? I can't see why you left them in London."

It was then that Marguerite imparted her pearl of wisdom that Sarah and I needed more time alone together. "That's why I'm determined to keep my visit very brief," she explained. "I thought I would just come here to collect Clara and Edith and take them back to London. They can come with me when I take the boys to the seaside at Bournemouth."

"But . . ." I began and stopped.

"Oh, I do understand!" said Marguerite at once. "You're so kind and generous, Patrick, that it never occurred to you not to take those girls under your wing, but really at present it would be much more suitable if they lived with me."

I felt both wary and confused. "That's very decent of you, Marguerite, but—"

"There's some difficulty?" said Marguerite, lynx-eyed.

"Not exactly, but you see Derry's awfully taken with Clara, and he was so looking forward to seeing a little of her."

"Excellent!" said Marguerite. "Why not? I'm sure he's always wanted to see London, and a clever young man like Derry can always find well-paid congenial work."

"Um," I said. I honestly didn't know what to say. I tried to be frank. "Well, I've been looking forward to spending some time with Derry myself, actually, but I dare say it's more important that he follow Clara to London. He's pretty spoony about her, you know."

"Wonderful!" said Marguerite. "I love a romance!"

"You approve?" I couldn't help sounding surprised. "Everybody else seems to think it's monstrous that Derry should even look at Clara."

"I think it's high time Derry followed your example and settled down," said Marguerite firmly. "Besides, one must be practical, mustn't one? Derry has plenty of talent and ambition, but we all know that talent and ambition alone aren't enough to ensure success. He needs a rich well-connected wife in order to make his mark in the world, and Clara, like any other young girl, needs a handsome, charming, clever young husband. What could be more suitable?"

"Good Lord, Marguerite!" I exclaimed in wholehearted admiration. "Why on earth isn't everyone as sensible as you are? Life would be so much simpler and more comfortable. So you've forgiven Derry, have you, for all that bother at Cashelmara before Papa died?"

"It's not at all Christian to harbor grudges," said Marguerite blandly. "Now, Patrick, after we've all left Woodhammer and you and Sarah are alone together, do remember how much she depends on you at present. She has a new country to adjust to as well as a new way of life, and it's inevitable for her to feel insecure at first. You will remember that and make allowances for her, won't you?"

"Yes, of course. Poor Sarah, of course I will. I didn't mean to leave her alone so much in Ireland, but what with Annabel's death and the funeral—"

"It must have been very trying for you," said Marguerite sympathetically. "Never mind, I'm sure you can make amends to Sarah very nicely now that you're home in England at last."

I did indeed feel relieved at the prospect of being on equable terms with Sarah again. After I left the long gallery I was about to go to her apartments to see if she felt better when I remembered Derry and decided to drop in first for a word with him.

"Oh, my God," he said as soon as I mentioned Marguerite's name. "I wondered how long it would be before she started influencing you." But after I had told him that Marguerite was in favor of the match he thawed and said maybe the news wasn't so bad after all. "I'd rather stay here at Woodhammer," he said, "but I suppose since I've made the effort to come to England I might as well see something of London. Anyway I can't afford to let Clara slip through my fingers. Supposing she meets some other man who fancies her once she settles in town?" He shuddered at the thought before adding, "When will you and Sarah be coming up to London?"

"Lord, I've no idea. I hadn't thought about it."

"You don't think Sarah's going to be content for long with a quiet country life, do you?" he said, laughing.

"I hope she'll like it for a while at least," I said unhappily. I had been looking forward to several peaceful months at Woodhammer before I fulfilled my promise to take her abroad in the spring.

"Don't fool yourself, Patrick. She won't rest till she sees those city lights! Why don't you bring her up for a week or two soon?"

"Well . . ."

"Hell, Patrick, what am I going to do with myself in London if you're not there to show me around?" he protested, amused, and when he put it like that I at once thought of all the marvelous times we could have together gambling in Mayfair, carousing in Soho and riding hell for leather through the dust of Rotten Row.

"Well, it might be rather jolly," I said reluctantly.

"Of course it would be, and Sarah will be the first to admit it. I'll wager you five guineas that within three days after we've all gone to London she'll be clamoring to follow hard on our heels!"

It was actually five days, not three, but once Sarah began to speak of London with that certain longing note in her voice I knew I should have no peace until I had agreed to take her up for a visit. However, I did try to postpone the inevitable. I again pointed out that no one was in town during August and that it would be much more sensible to stay in the country until the end of September.

"But no one is in the country either!" objected Sarah, and I had to admit there was a certain amount of truth in this, as all our neighbors had departed for Scotland to shoot grouse. However, I succeeded in postponing the visit to London until early October, and after that I settled down to savor Woodhammer to the full. Unfortunately Sarah, I soon realized, was quite unable to savor it with me, and I found it hard to enjoy myself when I knew she was pacing up and down the long gallery as she wondered how to pass the time. The trouble was not only that Sarah couldn't bear to be alone. Remembering Marguerite's remarks about Sarah's dependence on me in a country that was foreign to her, I could make allowances for her desire to be with me every single minute of the day. The main trouble was that she had no hobbies. You would think I'd have realized that in New York, but she had always been so busy there with all her social obligations that I had never seen her at a loss for something to do. But it was a very different story at Woodhammer. She did sew, but after half an hour she would put the embroidery aside in boredom; she did read a novel or two, but she could only face a chapter a day, and unlike Marguerite, who read voraciously and dipped into all sorts of books, Sarah was uninterested in literature, current events or politics. I didn't hold that against her, for I wasn't interested in them either, but at least I did have other pursuits and Sarah had none.

I took her for walks, rides and drives. I did my best to give her the constant entertainment she needed, but I was longing to spend time alone with my woodcarving, and when I had no chance to work during the day I began to stay up at night so that I could be by myself. However, I needed my sleep as much as she did, and I suppose she was justified in being annoyed when I retired several times during the day for long snoozes.

By the time October came I was almost as anxious as she was to leave Woodhammer, and having come to the conclusion that I would have time to myself only when Sarah was totally absorbed in city life, I wrote with a frantic eagerness to Marguerite to ask if we could stay with her at St. James's Square.

Derry by this time was doing pretty well for himself. He had lodgings in Westminster, and Marguerite had actually managed to get him a good position as a clerk in the Colonial Office. Being a member of the Irish bar, he was not able to practice law in London, but this didn't trouble him.

"I never did want to be a barrister," he said. "That was your father's idea, not mine. Still, there's no doubt a law qualification can open doors into other fields, and I shall see if I can't get a seat in Parliament once I'm married to Clara. They say that even now, despite all the reform, it's only a question of knowing the right people and having a bit of money to spend on the election."

His romance with Clara was progressing very smoothly, and he thought he might propose at Christmas. In fact he was so cheered by his prospects that he even found a good word to say about Marguerite and confessed grudgingly that she had been pretty useful to him since he had arrived in town.

"And how do you like London?" I asked, thinking how well he had settled down, but he made a face and said he supposed it was a fairish sort of place, although to be an Irish Catholic in London was surely as bad as being a black man in America in the days before the Civil War.

"But now you're here I won't feel such a stranger," he said, relieved, and added anxiously, "How long are you going to stay?"

I had no idea, but presently Sarah began to say we couldn't trespass indefinitely on Marguerite's hospitality and why didn't we buy a house of our own? I had to admit this was good sense, so we began to spend long days house-hunting. I found this very tedious, but Sarah loved every minute of it, and after we had selected a house in Curzon Street she launched herself with great zest into the task of choosing the furnishings. Since this occupied her from dawn till dusk I was at last able to do some carving and produced an American chipmunk, which was a failure, and a frieze of squirrels, which was more successful. I used pine, which is a soft wood, and worked the knots into the background of trees, leaves and acorns. I felt much happier after that. By the time I had finished the frieze Sarah was still occupied with the house, so I had more time to devote to making Derry feel at home in London. There was a new club, the Albatross, which had recently opened in Park Street, and I arranged for us to be admitted as members. Some fellows I had known up at Oxford were members, and remembering the fun we had all had together in the old days, I was sure Derry would enjoy running with their set. The club was supposed to have some vague political purpose, I believe, but no one ever talked about politics. One could dine there and the brandy was good and there was always a game in progress, so it was a pretty sporting sort of place. Derry thought it was awfully jolly.

By the time Christmas came I was enjoying myself so much that I no longer pined for Woodhammer as I usually did when I was in London. In fact I was only surprised that I had not enjoyed London more in the past, although that was really easy to understand when I remembered that I had never been in London with Derry before.

I did toy with the idea of spending Christmas at Woodhammer, but finally I reconciled myself to remaining in London, where Sarah had arranged to give a huge house-warming ball on New Year's Eve. I must say, Sarah did do that sort of thing very well, and everyone, from the Prince of Wales down, was tremendously impressed. The house looked fit for a king, and although there was a certain flamboyance in the furnishings which hinted at an American mastermind, there was nothing tasteless about Sarah's choices. I supposed it had all cost quite a bit of money, but after all a man in my position has to have a decent house in town, as I told Fielding when he mentioned to me that the bills were beginning to come in. I had retained Fielding, my father's secretary, to deal with the charitable letters that were addressed to me and see that the bills were paid; he worked in conjunction with the family lawyers, who gave him the necessary supervision. As a matter of fact I was rather annoyed when he mentioned the bills for the house, since the purpose of my employing him was to save me the bother of thinking about that sort of tiresome detail. As Derry said to me once, one of the nicest things about having money is not having to worry about counting it.

In the new year Derry proposed to Clara and was accepted, so to celebrate we went to the club and he won damned nearly five hundred pounds at loo. "What a celebration!" I marveled as we drank champagne together, and Derry said his luck was beginning to turn at last; he could feel it in his bones. The next day he gave up his position at the Colonial Office and said he was going to be a gentleman of leisure till he married.

"Well, why not?" I said, so once we were both gentlemen of leisure we had even more time to enjoy London together, and after he had paid his call on Clara the day was ours to do as we pleased. I didn't have to worry about Sarah, because she was so busy with her calls and her dressmaker, and besides Marguerite had said to her once in front of me that it was natural that I should want to help Derry celebrate the last days of his bachelor life. The only slight upset occurred when I realized we would have to postpone our visit to the Continent to the autumn since the wedding was to be in the spring, but Sarah accepted that with good grace because it enabled her to be in London for the entire Season.

I decided to give Derry a house as a wedding present. After all, he was marrying a rich wife, and I couldn't let him go to the altar empty-handed; it would have been so bad for his self-respect. I bought a nice little house just around the corner from us in Clarges Street, and Clara was awfully thrilled about it. Derry became embarrassed about how he was going to furnish it, and when I added the cost of the furnishings to my present Fielding became hot and bothered again about the bills. I was becoming rather annoyed with Fielding. I began to think seriously of dismissing him and employing a younger man.

Derry had been right in thinking his luck was on the turn, for all through the early months of that year he had the most prodigious luck with the cards. I got pretty envious, I admit, especially when I went through a patch of losing heavily, but the nice thing about gambling is that even when you're locked in a losing streak there's always the possibility that your luck will change with the next hand of cards, so you need never get too down for long.

Spring came. I wondered if either of my sisters would come to the wedding, but they didn't. Madeleine was busy building her dispensary at Clonareen (I had been obliged to finance that in the end when there was a difficulty with the Archbishop about the money and the government had declined to accept responsibility for the project), and Katherine flatly refused to receive Derry, let alone celebrate his wedding.

"I cannot find it in my heart to congratulate Clara on marrying the son of an Irish peasant," she announced in that maddeningly priggish manner of hers, and after that there was nothing I could do except marvel to Derry that I should possess such a sister.

"Oh, I'll not worry about Lady Duneden," said Derry with the light, scornful smile he reserved for those who had offended him, "for it's plain to see she's jealous of Clara marrying a man who's forty years younger than her own husband and a whole heap more fun."

I thought that was probably true, although Katherine always seemed perfectly happy with Duneden, and even Marguerite confessed that the marriage had worked out better than she had dared hope. Katherine had no children, although I believe she had suffered a miscarriage or two, and Duneden treated her as if she were the crown jewels, rare, priceless and almost too sacred to handle. Old men can make such fools of themselves sometimes, as Derry said on more than one occasion.

Well, I gave Clara a magnificent wedding. There were five hundred guests, for Clara was well connected on her father's side as well as her mother's, and despite Katherine's standoffishness plenty of people wanted to wish the bride well. Besides, Sarah and I had cut such a dash in town that any wedding we sponsored was certain to be well attended. So Derry and Clara were married with great ceremony at St. James's, Piccadilly, after a small private service at the Church of the Jesuit Fathers in Farm Street, and after they had left for six weeks in Italy I barely had the chance to miss him since Sarah and I were immediately plunged into the whirl of the London Season.

"How exciting it all is!" exclaimed Sarah radiantly and ordered twenty-five new ball gowns to celebrate her *joie de vivre*.

It was an amusing summer in its own way. Court circles were still unbearably dull, of course, and the Queen reached new heights of unpopularity every day, but the Marlborough House set was smart as fresh paint and kept life bowling along at a brisk pace. Certainly I like a bit of fun as much as anyone else, and when Sarah was such a success I was not only proud but relieved to see her so happy. I couldn't help regretting on our first wedding anniversary that there was still no sign of a son or daughter, but since Sarah never complained I didn't like to say anything on the subject. Privately I began to hope that a pregnancy would provide the excuse to postpone the visit to the Continent again, but that made me feel guilty, as I was sure Sarah would be disappointed. I could only hope instead that the dubious international situation would provide me with the excuse I needed when autumn came. The tedious Bismarck was on the warpath again, and all the Frenchies were in the devil of a panic.

When Derry and Clara returned from their honeymoon in early August they joined us at Cowes, where the yachting season had begun, and presently when it was time to leave I invited them to come with us to Woodhammer.

"You did *what!*" exclaimed Sarah when I mentioned the invitation.

"Well, you know how bored you get at Woodhammer. I thought—"

"I'll be even more bored with you out all day with Derry while I have to entertain that horrid simpering little Clara! Besides, haven't you forgotten that we've been invited to Scotland to stay with—"

"We're not going to Scotland," I said. "We're going to Wood-hammer."

"But—"

"We're going to Woodhammer." I'm an easygoing fellow in many ways, but I'm perfectly capable of sticking to my guns if my mind's made up.

"Very well," said Sarah, a spot of color burning in each cheek. "But not with Derry and Clara."

"But dash it, Sarah, they've got nowhere else to go and they can't possibly stay in town in August."

"I won't have them at Woodhammer!" cried Sarah violently. "I've put up with them long enough!"

"How can you possibly say that when they've scarcely been back a week from their honeymoon?"

"Haven't I had to put up with them ever since we left Wood-hammer last October and came to London? I'm absolutely sick of you and Derry living in each other's pockets! Marguerite said I must make allowances for you both before he got married, but no matter what she says I'm not making allowances for you any longer!"

I was dumfounded. I had no idea she felt so strongly, and I couldn't help feeling she was being a little unreasonable. After all, a man's entitled to have his best friend to stay occasionally, isn't he? Feeling in need of some sympathetic help, I turned as usual to Marguerite, but to my surprise she was very cool and said it was time I left Derry to fend for himself.

"You've done everything a friend could do and more besides," she told me bluntly. "Now it's up to him to lead his own life for a while and not depend on you any further. Let him find someone else to ask him out of town."

"But I'm the only real friend he has. I do have some sort of obligation."

"Yes, you do!" said Marguerite with such strength that I flinched. "But your obligation's not to Derry. It's to Sarah." And she gave me a look that would have bored a hole through a two-inch mahogany plank.

"Very well," I said resignedly, seeing it was useless to argue with her. "Perhaps you're right, but I've already invited Derry to stay. How can I turn around now and tell him not to come?"

"Since you're the only friend he has," said Marguerite, "I'm sure he'll be all too willing to make allowances for you if you apologize to him and say you've been obliged to change your plans."

Well, it was damnably awkward, but fortunately I happened to hear that a small estate two miles from Woodhammer called Byngham Chase was to let, so I was able to suggest tactfully to Derry that Clara might think it fun to have her own little place in the country that summer. I had to tread carefully, though, because I didn't want to hurt his feelings, and meanwhile Sarah was kicking up an awful rumpus at the thought of having the Stranahans for neighbors. Since she hadn't complained about having them as neighbors in London I couldn't see why she should make such a fuss, but to soothe her I began to talk of our approaching visit to the Continent, and soon she was mollified enough to look at maps and guidebooks. A Franco-Prussian war was still very much in the offing, so I told Sarah it would be wiser to postpone a visit to Paris, but I saw no reason why we couldn't go to Italy by sea. I liked Italy better than France anyway. I liked the quality of the light and the shapes of the cypress trees, the palazzos and the paintings, the marble and bronze, the wine and the laughter and that lovely lissome language.

"Wait till you see Florence," I said to Sarah hungrily and discovered to my surprise that I was really quite keen to go. Accordingly I wrote to my lawyers to say I needed funds for a three-month sojourn abroad, and on the day before we were due to leave London for Woodhammer Mr. Rathbone of Rathbone, Armstrong and Mather called upon me unexpectedly in Curzon Street.

Mr. Rathbone was not a crusty old man, as family attorneys so often are. He was still in his thirties, with rather a swell's taste in clothes and long Dundreary whiskers. "But young Rathbone is very sound," my father had said after old Rathbone had died. "He's well suited to follow in his father's footsteps."

For some reason the memory of this remark had always set my teeth on edge, although whenever I saw Rathbone I did try not to let it prejudice me.

"Lord de Salis," he announced after presenting his compliments to me in the usual manner, "I'm afraid I have business to discuss which—alas!—must necessarily be of a delicate and painful nature."

I hadn't a notion what he was talking about, so I told him I had a luncheon appointment in half an hour and perhaps he wouldn't mind if he stated his business quickly.

"Of course, my lord," said Rathbone. "The business relates, sad to say, to your lordship's pecuniary situation."

"Oh yes," I said, stifling a yawn. "Did you arrange the funds for my visit to Italy?"

"My lord," said Rathbone, "it appears that for the moment there *are* no funds for your proposed visit to Italy."

Well, I knew at once he was mad. I mean, there I was, sitting in my house in Curzon Street with Woodhammer Hall, Cashelmara and an income of God knows how many thousands a year, and he was telling me I couldn't rustle up a bit of change to take my wife for a holiday.

"Your lordship owes your bankers a considerable amount of money," said Rathbone.

"Well, what of it? Isn't that what bankers are for?"

"Lord de Salis, there comes a time when even bankers must draw the line. And in addition to the bankers there are, it unfortunately seems, the moneylenders. I have had a visit from a Mr. Goldfarb of Bread Lane."

"Oh, that concerns gambling debts," I said. "I issued a lot of paper to the fellows at the club, and when I had to make good the notes Mr. Goldfarb helped me out. He's a friend of Captain Danziger, the club secretary, and was very obliging to me actually."

"Even Mr. Goldfarb cannot be obliging indefinitely, my lord."

"Wait a minute," I said, deciding I had had enough of his tom-foolery. "I dare say I have spent quite a bit of money this year, but I'm not a poor man and I can't see why my creditors should be making such a deuced fuss. There must be plenty of men in London who are worse in debt than I am."

"I dare say, my lord, but I can hardly advise you to join their ranks. I think it essential that you should reduce your debts before they grow extensive enough to become a severe drain upon your property. That's why I cannot, in good conscience, recommend that you take a costly journey abroad with your wife at this time."

"Well, I'm sorry," I said, "but I can't disappoint my wife. I must have the money. Go to some other banker and get it."

"My lord, I doubt if there is a banker in London who would advance you money at the moment without some sort of lien on your estate."

"Well, give them a lien or whatever they want! For God's sake, Rathbone, haven't I made myself clear?"

There was a pause. "Your lordship is instructing me to mortgage Woodhammer Hall?" asked Rathbone politely at last.

"What!" I leaped out of my chair.

"There's no other way to get the money, my lord. Your debts are too severe."

"No one's touching one brick of Woodhammer Hall!"

"Well, no one can touch Cashelmara, my lord," said Rathbone, "because of the entail."

"But entails can be barred—especially in Ireland! Wasn't there some act of Parliament passed after the famine to make it possible for almost anyone to bar an entail to get rid of an estate?"

"The Encumbered Estates Act doesn't apply to Cashelmara, my lord."

"Why the devil not?"

"Because the ultimate remainder in fee tail is to the Crown. To put it in other words—"

"Yes, for God's sake do."

"When Queen Elizabeth granted the estate to your ancestor with the provision that it should descend in the male line, there was also a provision that if ever that male line should cease the estate would revert to the Crown. This has the effect of creating an unbarrable entail, a rare but not altogether unknown situation. The Duke of Marlborough, for instance—"

"I'm not interested in the Duke of Marlborough!"

"Very well, my lord. Then I shall merely repeat that, bearing these circumstances in mind, I must advise you that Woodhammer is your only negotiable estate."

I sank back into my seat again.

"Quite apart from this visit to the Continent, my lord, I think it would be advisable to pay off at least thirty thousand pounds of your debts or else no matter how quietly you live you will barely be able to pay interest on the principal sum outstanding. Perhaps if you were to sell this house in London—"

"No," I said. I tried to imagine what Sarah would say if I did. "Out of the question."

"Then perhaps if you sold some of the Woodhammer lands—"

"Never!" I said fiercely.

"Well, in that case, my lord, it might be best to consolidate your debts by taking out a mortgage on Woodhammer Hall, and if you're still set on going to Italy I dare say there would be a little money to spare after the mortgage has been arranged."

But the thought of mortgaging Woodhammer was repugnant to me. "There must be some other way," I said stubbornly.

"Not if you refuse to sell any property, my lord," said Rathbone, "and not while Mr. Goldfarb is exacting forty percent interest on his loan. If you won't reduce your debts you must at least consolidate them and pay a civilized rate of interest to a reputable source."

I searched feverishly for inspiration. Francis Marriott would probably lend me money, but I didn't want to go begging to my father-in-law. But there was Cousin George. He was sitting childless on a tidy little fortune. And there was Katherine's husband Duneden. He wasn't exactly a pauper either. I didn't want to go begging to my cousin and brother-in-law any more than I wanted to go begging to Francis Marriott, but they were at least English gentlemen, and I knew they would understand that a fellow can have a bit of difficulty now and then.

"I'll raise the money by some other means," I said abruptly. "I'll let you know as soon as I've made the arrangements. Good day, Mr. Rathbone." And having thus terminated the interview firmly, I summoned the butler to show him to the door.

II

I didn't tell Sarah about Rathbone's visit. I saw no need to mention any difficulty before we went abroad, although common sense told me that on our return I would have to say a cautionary word or two about extravagance. However, my first task was to inform not Sarah but Cousin George and Duneden, so after gritting my teeth I faced the ordeal of writing the necessary letters. I kept my tone casual and tried to avoid sounding desperate while simultaneously making it clear that I was in an awkward situation. I had of course borrowed money before from time to time, but never from my cousin and brother-in-law and never in such large amounts, and I was very nervous as I waited at Woodhammer for their replies.

I had to wait two weeks, and even before I finally received their joint letter I had suspected that the two of them were conferring with each other. Duneden was at his country estate eighty miles from Cashelmara, and Cousin George would have thought nothing of blustering over from Letterturk for a council of war.

"My dear Patrick," George had written, the tone of his letter so cool that I knew he had been writing at Duneden's dictation. "Lord Duneden and I are in receipt of your letters of the 23rd, and since I have had the pleasure of dining with him today we found ourselves in a position to discuss your situation in detail. However, we agreed that there remain many details unknown to us, and we should be obliged if you would contrive to see us at the earliest opportunity in order that we might discuss the matter further. Might I suggest that we all meet at Cashelmara at the end of the week of August the fifteenth? Pray let me know your inclinations on the subject so that we may make the necessary arrangements. I remain your affectionate cousin . . ."

There was no choice but to go. I told Sarah that a crisis had prompted MacGowan to send for me, and she was very sympathetic. In fact she even offered to go with me, which I thought was damned decent of her since she disliked Cashelmara so much, but of course I insisted that she remain in England. Fortunately, as Marguerite and the boys were due to stay with us, I didn't have to insist very hard. But to Derry I could be more frank. I had already told him about the grisly conversation with Rathbone, and now it was a relief to confide to him my dread of the approaching interviews.

"I don't care about George," I said. "I could face George any day, but Duneden is a different kettle of fish altogether. I wish to God now that I hadn't dragged him into it, but I could never have got such a large sum of money from George alone and there was no one else I could have approached. God, Derry, I wish you were coming with me! I'm nervous as a kitten and I don't mind admitting it either."

"I'll come if you like," he said straightaway. No man could have been a better friend than he was. "I don't give a tinker's damn about that gray-bearded old goat and that shabby overgrown bullfrog." And he gave such an amusing imitation of Cousin George admonishing me that I couldn't help laughing, and once I'd laughed I did feel much better about facing my ordeal.

"No," I said, scraping up my courage. "I got myself into this mess and I must get myself out of it. It would be quite unfair to drag you into it as well. Stay with Clara and make a novena for me or do one of those other jolly Catholic things you enjoy so much."

He protested, but I was firm, and the next morning, wearing my best brave face, I departed on the dreary journey to Ireland.

It was raining when I reached Cashelmara, and the house was as damp as the inside of a grave. Huddling over the library fire, I drank a great quantity of hot brandy and water before I could face the journey upstairs to my room, but the next morning my nose was running and I felt very sorry for myself. It was still raining. The lough was the color of smoky glass, and the mist lay heavily on the mountains. Having nothing better to do, I huddled over the library fire again with more hot brandy and water, and then just as I was beginning to feel better Cousin George and Duneden arrived and I again felt as sick as a pauper in prison.

It had not occurred to me to question why the meeting was to be held at Cashelmara instead of at Duneden Castle or Letterturk Grange, but I discovered the answer soon enough. My inquisitors wanted to interview MacGowan, inspect the books and determine whether the estate was being administered to my best advantage.

"Frankly, Patrick," said Duneden in his politician's voice, "I find it hard to believe you could have lived so far beyond your income that you now need a loan of such gargantuan proportions."

"I had many heavy expenses this year," I said in my best meek voice.

"What kind of expenses?" demanded Cousin George at once.

I knew it was no good talking about a run of bad luck at cards or Derry's wedding, so all I said was "Good Lord, George, you don't expect me to provide an inventory, do you? Talk to Rathbone if you need details like that, and personally I can't see why you need to know such details anyway."

"My dear Patrick," said Duneden, sounding just like my father, "you are asking us to supply you with a considerable sum of money. In return I think we're entitled to know something of your financial affairs."

"Yes, of course," I muttered, anxious to smooth him over. "I do realize that. Very well, where do we begin?"

Well, we had the devil of a day. MacGowan was summoned, the books were produced and every penny of income from the estate was investigated. The next three days were spent riding around the estate (rain fell continuously) and inspecting matters in person. Cousin George thought the rents were shockingly low, for in many instances they hadn't been raised since the early Fifties, and Duneden too said it was a mistake not to have the rents set at a realistic figure.

"Once the Irish become accustomed to having a roof over their heads for a pittance," he said, "they'll fight tooth and nail against a more equitable arrangement." And Cousin George added, "If you give them an inch they'll expect a mile for the rest of their lives. Besides, it's for their own good. You won't help them if you go bankrupt, Patrick, and I saw too many ruined estates after the famine not to know how the tenants suffer in those circumstances."

Despite all this it was grudgingly agreed that MacGowan was honest and had done a reasonable job in the circumstances.

"Very well," said Duneden after MacGowan had been instructed to implement a new scheme of rents, "so much for Cashelmara. Now we must adjourn to Woodhammer."

I tried to protest, but I might as well have saved my breath, for they had me by the short end of a rope and we all knew it. So I was placed in the embarrassing position of having to explain to Sarah why my kinsmen were looking into my affairs, and the whole wretched process of investigation began all over again.

The ironic part was that I had always been so sure nothing ever went wrong at Woodhammer, but it turned out that old Mason, the steward, had become very slack and profits had dropped sharply. Also there was some sort of national slump in agriculture. I didn't understand why, but Cousin George blamed bad harvests and Duneden blamed the rising power of the United States and I'm sure they were both wrong. Anyway, after we had spent a week at Woodhammer Duneden announced to my horror that we must journey to London to talk to Mr. Adolphus Rathbone of Rathbone, Armstrong and Mather.

It was impossible to stop him. Two days later I was sitting in the morning room of my house in Curzon Street and listening in despair as Rathbone talked blithely of townhouses, society weddings, dispensaries in the west of Ireland, umpteen new ball gowns and last, but unfortunately not least, Mr. Goldfarb of Bread Lane and his ruinous rates of interest.

To cap it all Duneden had by this time heard gossip that I had once dropped three thousand pounds in a single night at the Albatross, and after that I knew I could expect nothing but a raw deal.

By this time I was in a state of mingled anger, resentment and humiliation. I was livid that they had seen fit to pry into my affairs and although I admitted they had a right to know how matters stood I still felt that between gentlemen a loan should be either given or refused with no questions asked. It was only because they were kinsmen that they had dared assume this monstrous right to pry. I was also furious that they should humiliate me before my lawyer and my servants by treating me as if I were a mere child who couldn't be expected to keep his house in order. I knew I had behaved stupidly; that went without saying. But everyone makes mistakes, and I didn't see that my stupidity made me the feckless rogue they clearly thought I was. The only reason I played along with them was because I really did need the money, but in the end I even began to wonder if such treatment at the hands of my relatives was too high a price to pay.

The hour of reckoning came on one fine morning in the drawing room of Duneden's house in Bruton Street. Duneden, possibly aware that his lack of a blood relationship with me made his high-handed attitude all the more inexcusable, had made the gesture of appointing Cousin George as his spokesman.

"Well, Patrick," said Cousin George, pompous as ever, "we have finally reached a decision."

Damn handsome of you, I thought furiously but managed to assume a politely inquiring expression.

"We have decided to lend you the money."

Relief streamed through me. "That's very decent of you both," I said sincerely. "Thank you very much."

"On certain conditions," said George, not even bothering to acknowledge my words of appreciation.

Here we go, I thought.

"First of all, it's quite obvious that you should live quietly for the next two years until your debts are considerably reduced."

"Yes, of course," I said. "Well, I'm sure I shan't mind spending most of the year at Woodhammer." I tried not to think how much Sarah would mind and told myself that I could always take her to London for visits.

But Duneden, damn him, knew exactly what I was thinking. "Woodhammer's too near London, Patrick," he said at once. "And London presents you with too much temptation to spend money. I'm afraid we must advise you to close Woodhammer for at least two years and let the house in Curzon Street to supplement your income. Your cousin and I will hold the title deeds of the townhouse as some sort of security against the large sum we shall lend you. In my opinion it would be better not to sell the townhouse, as you would never recoup the enormous expenditures you have lavished upon it. Better to hold on if you can and trust that the value of the property will rise in due course."

"But look here!" I said, alarmed. "If I can't live in London and you won't let me live at Woodhammer, where the devil *do* you expect me to live?"

I knew the answer, of course, before I had finished speaking. It was the first time I had ever truly known the meaning of the phrase "chilled to the bone."

"Cashelmara, of course," said Cousin George, surprised. "Where else?"

I opened my mouth to say "Never!" but closed it again. Better to play along with them for the time being. Now was hardly the moment to tell them that even the strongest cart ropes in the world could never drag me to Cashelmara to live.

"Well, I can't pretend I wouldn't rather live at Woodhammer," I said after a deadly pause, "but if I have to live at Cashelmara I suppose I must. Are there any more conditions attached to your loan?"

Duneden had taken over the role of spokesman. "You must give us your word that you won't indulge in any form of gambling either now or at any time during the next two years."

"Very well," I said. "I know I've been stupid about that. I'll give you my word. Now when can I have the money?"

"There's one other condition which hasn't yet been mentioned."

"Yes?" I said, trying not to sound too exasperated. "What's that?"

"We absolutely insist that you neither see nor communicate with Roderick Stranahan at any time in the future."

There was another pause. The morning sunlight slanted onto the rich Axminster carpet, and below the open window in Bruton Street two landaus rattled past toward Berkeley Square.

I stood up. There comes a time when a man has to take a stand, and although I know I have many faults I know too that I have one great virtue which no one has ever questioned.

I'm always loyal to my friends.

"In that case, gentlemen," I said, "we have nothing more to discuss. Keep your money. I won't sell my friendship with Roderick Stranahan at any price, not even for the sum you propose to loan me."

That shook them. They looked at me as if they could hardly believe their ears, and in their dumfounded expressions I found my revenge for all their prying and preaching and dictatorial demands.

"Of course you're not serious," said Duneden at last.

"You can't afford not to do as we say!" blustered Cousin George, putting his foot in it as usual. I can think of no other remark that would have made me more determined than ever to refuse his money.

Duneden's eyes were as gray as the rainy lough at Cashelmara. He did not resemble my father in looks, yet he reminded me of him very much. And suddenly for no apparent reason I was remembering a conversation I had had with my father long ago when he had warned me about the ways of the world and told me all kinds of repulsive facts about sexual matters. I could never think of that conversation without feeling sick, and I felt sick now as I looked into Duneden's eyes and saw in them a veiled expression which at first I could neither define nor understand. Then I realized he was pitying me, and I was so angry that I forgot to feel sick. I might have made a mess of my financial affairs, but no man had a right to look at me with contempt, least of all a man who had offered me a loan under such monstrous conditions and given me the hell of a life for damned nearly three weeks.

"To the devil with both of you," I said, returning his contempt, and allowed myself the luxury of telling him in no uncertain way what he could do with all his filthy money. Then I turned my back on them, walked out of the house and took a cab all the way to Temple Bar.

Half an hour later I was confronting Rathbone in his chambers at Serjeant's Inn and telling him to mortgage Woodhammer Hall.

Chapter Four

I

Once the deed was done I felt in better spirits and discovered with relief that there was really nothing so horrific about a mortgage after all. Indeed Rathbone was very pleased and said I had taken a major step out of my troubles by enabling my debts to be consolidated.

"But even so, my lord," he warned me, "it's imperative that you live carefully for a while if you want to avoid having to sell any land."

"Yes, of course," I said soothingly. "I do understand that." I was so relieved to be free of Cousin George and Duneden that not even the thought of future economies could upset me. After I left Rathbone I sauntered back to my house through the sunlit streets, and that same day I returned to Woodhammer to tell Sarah joyfully that our troubles were over for the next few months.

"So we'll be able to go abroad straight away!" I said, kissing her affectionately. I was so glad I didn't have to disappoint her by abandoning our plans.

Well, we did have a marvelous time on the Continent despite the fact that the Franco-Prussian War was in full cry by this time, and since Paris was under siege I had no choice but to stick to my plan to sail straight to Italy.

"If only we hadn't postponed our visit so often!" said Sarah, trying to sound merely regretful but succeeding in sounding accusing as well. "Now I'll never see the Empire in all its glory. Everyone says Paris will never be the same again."

Fortunately, to my great relief, Italian society opened its doors to us as soon as we stepped onto Italian soil, and once we were showered with invitations to country estates, town mansions, operas, theaters and salons, Sarah soon recovered from her disappointment. She was a great success; she had a new wardrobe for the occasion, and although in truth I did get a little tired of our exhaustingly sociable life in Rome, Venice and Florence, I was proud to see her stunning all those foreigners with her elegance. However, finally we managed to snatch a few quiet days by the northern lakes, and I painted some amusingly splashy watercolors of Como and Maggiore. In fact I would have been quite happy to paint all day long if Sarah had not complained that I was neglecting her, and her restlessness reminded me that I still had to explain to her about the sort of life we would be obliged to lead in the future.

I broke the news to her on the cross-Channel steamer as it chugged through the choppy December seas on the way to Dover. We had traveled home through Switzerland and the new state of Germany, and still avoiding poor starving Paris (I must say, I felt as anti-Prussian as the Prince of Wales by that time), we had boarded the steamer at Ostend.

"Sarah darling," I said tentatively, "we have to try to save money during the next few months until my affairs are straightened out. I know it's an awful bore, but now that Woodhammer is mortgaged I've simply got to be careful. You do understand, don't you?"

"Yes, of course," said Sarah. "I'll cut down the guest list for our New Year's Eve ball."

I began to feel uncomfortable. "Well, the fact is, Sarah, I think we'd better cancel our plans for the ball this year. You see—"

"Cancel the ball!" She looked at me as if I were mad. "But how can we do that? People expect us to repeat last year's success!"

"I can't help that. We have to go down to Woodhammer, I'm afraid, and lead a quiet country life for a while. In fact I think I really should let the townhouse for twelve months."

"Let the townhouse!" She couldn't have looked more horrified if I had suggested she ride naked down Curzon Street.

"Well, maybe I won't let it," I said unhappily. I did hate to disappoint her. "But we must restrict our time in London, Sarah, because it costs us so much money."

"Oh, stop talking about money!" burst out Sarah, in a great tantrum by this time. "I wasn't brought up to pinch pennies, and I don't see why I should have to begin now just because you chose to go on a series of gambling sprees with Derry Stranahan!"

"It's got nothing to do with Derry."

"It's got everything to do with Derry!" she blazed. We stood there by the window of the enclosed deck, and beneath our feet the boat rocked as uncomfortably as our own marriage. Sarah's eyes were tawny and her mouth was set in a hard angry line. "And I'll tell you this," she said. "I'm not staying at Woodhammer while he's just across the river at Byngham Chase, and I'm not staying in London while he lives just around the corner in Clarges Street. I despise and detest him. I always have and I always will, and if I'd known before I married you that I'd have to see him every day of my married life you can be sure I'd have broken off the engagement and stayed in America."

"My God, I wish you had!" I cried, turning my back on her in a rage. We were so angry that we refused to speak to each other during the remainder of the journey to London, and when we reached Curzon Street at last I slept in my dressing room as I always did when she was indisposed.

The next morning I told her we would be leaving for Woodhammer at the end of the week.

"You can do as you please," said Sarah. "But I've already told you I won't go to Woodhammer while Derry's at Byngham Chase. If you leave London I shall go to St. James's Square to stay with Marguerite. That should avoid any gossip for the time being."

I was so furious with her that I almost said, "Go ahead—I don't give a damn!" but I had my pride, just like any other man, and I knew no husband ought to stand by meekly while his wife dictated her plans to him. "You're not staying here in London!" I said resolutely.

"Try and stop me!" retorted Sarah.

We both arrived on Marguerite's doorstep at almost the same moment. I had rushed out and collared a hansom while Sarah had waited for the brougham to be brought to the door, so fortunately I did have a ten-minute start. I had just managed to explain to Marguerite about Sarah's complete lack of understanding of my financial situation when Lomax announced Sarah's arrival.

"Oh my God!" I groaned.

"Wait here," said Marguerite, resourceful as ever. We were in the drawing room. "I'll receive her downstairs. Now, Patrick, calm down, be patient and whatever you do don't dare interrupt us."

I paced up and down the drawing room for half an hour. When Marguerite finally reappeared I was in such a state that I could hardly summon the words to ask her what had happened.

"At least I've managed to explain to her about your financial difficulties," said Marguerite, subsiding into the nearest chair, "although I can't explain to her why you have to see so much of Derry. You and Sarah will have to compromise with each other, Patrick. Sarah says she would be willing to stay next year at Woodhammer if you in your turn would see less of Derry. But how you're going to do that when Derry's perpetually on your doorstep, I've no idea."

"And I've no idea," I said bitterly, "how Sarah is going to live all the year round at Woodhammer without driving us both mad."

"If only—"

"Yes?"

"Nothing. I was only thinking what a pity it was that she doesn't have a baby yet." She fidgeted uneasily with her sleeve before changing the subject. "Derry should have some sort of occupation," she declared. "If he did, perhaps he wouldn't depend so much on you for company. Didn't you say he wanted to be a member of Parliament? Perhaps if he brought Clara up to town after Christmas I could arrange for him to meet one or two people who might take an interest in him."

"I dare say he'd like that," I said gloomily. "But meanwhile I still don't see how I'm going to persuade Sarah to go down to Woodhammer."

"Why don't we all go down there for Christmas?" suggested Marguerite. "I think Sarah would come if I agreed to go with her, even though Derry's still at Byngham Chase."

This proved to be an acceptable compromise, but I still thought Sarah was being unreasonable, and I resented her implacable antagonism to my best friend.

"God, women are the very devil, aren't they!" exclaimed Derry as we went riding together at Woodhammer on Boxing Day. "Always complaining about something or other!"

"Clara doesn't complain much, surely?" I said, surprised.

"Don't you believe it! She's always moaning about how ill she feels now she's pregnant. Well, it gives her something to grumble about, I suppose, poor child."

"But you and Clara are happy, aren't you?"

"To be sure we are—why not? Being married ain't so bad when all's said and done, and I'll be as proud as a dog with two tails when Clara has the baby."

I was silent. I didn't grudge him one ounce of his good fortune, but I couldn't help feeling a little envious of his meek loving wife and the baby coming in the spring. Sarah and I were on speaking terms, but she was so chilly when we were alone that I was still spending every night in my dressing room, and I had begun to wonder if she would ever present me with a son and heir.

However, she did thaw considerably once the Stranahans had accompanied Marguerite back to town. We began to share a bed again, and soon we were both hoping that she might be following in Clara's footsteps, but again we were disappointed. One day in March I came indoors from a ride and found her crying in her room.

"Never mind," I said after I had learned what the trouble was. "Our luck's bound to turn soon. It's just a question of being patient."

"I'm tired of being patient!" cried Sarah, tears streaming down her face. "How can I go on being patient when Mama keeps sending baby clothes from America and even that stupid little Clara gets pregnant on her honeymoon . . ."

But Clara lost the baby. It was born early and lived only a few hours.

"Better luck next time," wrote Derry philosophically, but I knew he was down because he barely mentioned politics. There was some talk of his standing as a liberal candidate for a Lancashire borough in the next election, and he was very bucked about it.

"If only we could go back to London!" wept Sarah. "I'm sure I'll never have a baby when I'm so unhappy down here!"

"My poor Sarah . . ." Well, a man doesn't like to see his wife unhappy, does he? I mean, I had to do something to cheer her up, so I said I'd take her to London for a couple of weeks. It was April, the entire London Season lay ahead, and since we had lived so quietly for five months I thought both of us were entitled to a reward.

I didn't mean to go gambling with Derry. I really didn't. But you know how it is after you've split a bottle of champagne with your best friend and a few other fellows are cutting the cards and everyone's so damned pleased to see you back in town. And I did mean to steer clear of loo, which is such a silly game that no sensible man would touch it with a coachman's whip. Nor did I mean to touch poker, that monstrous heathen game, but there was an American at the club that night and you know how the Americans are about poker. And you know too how it is when you win twenty pounds straight off and someone calls for soda and brandy and the card room's so warm and comfortable and cozy.

I meant to stop when I was winning; I had it all worked out. I was determined to leave as soon as I was fifty pounds to the good, but then I had the very devil of a hand and lost a little, not much, just a couple of pounds, and of course after that I had to go on. I mean, I had to, didn't I? You know how it is when the pale-yellow light glows alluringly on the green baize cloth and a fellow snaps the cards in his fingers and you have a whole new round coming up. Anything can happen, can't it? You know you're going to win eventually, so you simply have to go on. And someone orders more brandy and soon nothing matters, nothing can touch you, you're beyond all pain, all despair, because nothing matters except the cards and the pattern they make when they fall and the clink of coins or the whisper of paper money as the winnings are pushed back and forth across the table.

I had to go on.

It was dawn when the game broke up. I felt numb, as if someone had slammed me over the head with a gun butt, and it was Derry who found the hansom to take us to Curzon Street.

Before we parted he said, "You can have back the money I won, if you like."

"Don't be a bloody fool," I said. "I lost more to the other fellows than I did to you. Besides, what do I care? I'm not a pauper and I'll get it all back. I'll have a lucky streak soon, you'll see."

So I stayed the whole summer in London while I searched for my lucky streak, and Sarah was so delighted that she even overlooked my regular outings to the Albatross with Derry. When she ordered a new summer wardrobe and redecorated the first floor of the house, I hadn't the heart to stop her, and anyway I knew my luck at cards was sure to turn any moment. It did too. For one glorious week I could do nothing wrong at the card table, but even before I could count my winnings my luck had slipped through my fingers again. Well, it had been such a damnable short lucky streak that I was sure I'd find it again in a day or two, so I kept playing. But to my horror disaster followed disaster, and by the time we withdrew to the country in August I had already told Rathbone to sell the townhouse and arrange for a second mortgage on Woodhammer Hall.

I told Sarah I would rent a townhouse for the following summer. It was the only way of pacifying her, but when in October I had to refuse her suggestion that we should give a Christmas ball at Woodhammer we quarreled bitterly and were on bad terms for some weeks. Derry was still pursuing his political ambitions in London, so I spent most of my time by myself in my attic workroom. Carving soothed me. I tried to make an elaborate bowl of flowers in the manner of Grinling Gibbons, but the stems were too stiff and the petals looked heavy as lead. Disappointed by the failure, I found I could no longer shut out my troubles, and indeed by this time Sarah's sourness had become so unpleasant that I wrote to Marguerite to ask her if we could spend Christmas with her in London.

It was in London—at the Albatross, of course—that I heard about the railway shares. Everyone was talking about them and saying what a marvelous investment they were. Everyone knew fortunes had been made in America with the development of the railways, and this new company, floated in order to build a railway from San Diego to Tucson, was reckoned certain to quadruple any investor's money.

Derry had put a lot of money into the scheme, and not wanting to be left out, I borrowed two thousand pounds from my old friend Mr. Goldfarb of Bread Lane. Everyone said that I was wise and that the opportunity was too good to be missed.

Everyone.

The crash came in April when the company went bankrupt. We were still in London. I had already rented a townhouse because I thought that with several thousand pounds' profit on my investment a temporary home in London was the least I could afford. But now all hope of profit was gone, my borrowed money was lost and Mr. Goldfarb was again paying visits to Rathbone at Serjeant's Inn.

I got a bit desperate then. It was understandable after all because I really was in the devil of a hole. Derry would have helped me out if it had been possible, but he too had lost all his money in the crash and was now utterly dependent on Clara's trust funds.

Borrowing another two thousand pounds, this time from a Mr. Marks of High Holborn, I set off once more for the card table.

It was my only hope, you see. And somehow . . . well, it's hard to explain, but I was absolutely certain that I would win and make everything come straight.

A month later, knowing Woodhammer was lost unless I swallowed my pride, I once again sat down to write to Duneden and my cousin George.

III

I dreamed of my house slumbering amidst its lush parkland. I dreamed of the house I loved, those warm mellow walls and tall chimneys and the orderly reassuring formality of the Elizabethan garden. I dreamed of that glowing wood paneling and my ancestors in their ruffs and the massive strength of the mahogany furniture. And last of all I dreamed of the staircase, the sublime carving by Grinling Gibbons, whose work meant more to me than any masterpiece by Michelangelo or Leonardo or Raphael. I saw each fragile leaf, each delicate cluster of berries, each gossamer-thin tracery of flowers in full bloom. I could try all my life to carve as he carved, yet no spark of his gift would ever be mine. But that staircase was mine, and no one was going to take it away from me; no one was going to deprive me of my home. But the thought that I was the de Salis who might lose Woodhammer forever was so painful that my mind refused to dwell upon the house as a whole and clung solely to the staircase, which in its beauty and grace represented all that my home meant to me.

Duneden said, "You're obviously quite unable to handle money. I refuse to lend you a penny unless you hand over complete control of your financial affairs to your cousin and myself. We shall pay you a monthly allowance."

That beautiful staircase. I could see the golden light of evening slanting through the long windows and blazing fiercely upon the wood Gibbons had transformed.

"Woodhammer must be closed, the farmlands leased and the staff replaced by a caretaker."

I saw the dust falling on those curving leaves, but that didn't matter because the leaves would still be mine.

"You must live at Cashelmara. No lavish entertaining, no visits to London . . ."

I saw the fruit, ripe and luscious. How could wood ever look like that? But he had done it; it was a miracle. My throat ached with the wonder of it and the tears stung behind my eyes.

". . . and no communication whatsoever with Roderick Stranahan. So long as you observe all these conditions we're prepared to help you. Flout any one of them and you can go to the devil as fast as you please, and neither your cousin nor I will lift a finger to stop

286

you. This is your last chance. Have I made myself clear? Your very last chance."

So I saved my staircase. I saved the wood which Gibbons had carved. I saved that one link I possessed with a talent so grand that I could not think of it and remain unmoved. I won.

But it was a terrible price I had to pay.

"Damn them both to hell!" cried Derry. His black eyes blazed with rage. "Why should they dictate to you like that? What have I done to them that they should be so set against me? Is it a crime for a man to better himself? If it is, they should be set against your father for giving me an education and a roof over my head! Why should it be a crime for me to be friends with you? I have no parents, brothers or sisters. Aren't I entitled to at least one friend? Have I ever taken anything from you that you haven't pressed me to accept? Could I help it if you've always had so much more to give me than I've had to give you? Well, see here, Patrick, I'll pay you back now for any unfair advantage I've taken of you. I'll put my own money aside to help pay your debts."

"But . . ."

"Oh, I know I've no money except Clara's income at present, but just wait! Once I get elected I'll be on the right road, and when I'm appointed to a junior position in the government I'll have a salary and you can have every penny I earn."

Of course I told him what I thought of that nonsense, but I was touched by his offer and felt even more bitter toward Cousin George and Duneden.

We didn't say goodbye.

"What's the point?" said Derry, cool again after his rage. "We'll see each other again sooner or later when your money's straight, and let's hope it's sooner rather than later. So no drawn-out farewells, there's a good fellow, because you know how damnably bored I am by sentimentality."

We parted. He walked off down the street, and I stood outside the Albatross and stared after him. I felt so low that I couldn't face telling Sarah about the grisly future which lay in store for us. Instead I called at St. James's Square and asked Marguerite if she would break the news to her.

"Marguerite, couldn't you come to Ireland with us for a while?" I concluded in despair. The very thought of Sarah in Ireland with nothing to do except watch the rain fall was enough to fill me with panic. "If you were at Cashelmara to help Sarah settle down . . ."

Marguerite said nothing.

"Please," I begged her. "It would make all the difference. Please."

Marguerite said suddenly, "Patrick, you can't always be relying on me to smooth over your troubles with Sarah, you know. This is your marriage, yours and Sarah's, and when all's said and done you're the only two people who can keep it stitched together."

"Well, I dare say—yes, I'm sure you're right, but, Marguerite, this is such a crisis that I don't see how I can begin to keep things stitched together unless you help us. God, when I think of living all the year round at Cashelmara . . ."

"It may be a blessing in disguise," said Marguerite unexpectedly. "Perhaps you can spend more time together now."

"Yes, but—"

"All Sarah needs is a little attention, Patrick. Do you think she would spend so much money to make you notice her if she didn't feel she must constantly make an effort to avoid being overlooked?"

"But I've paid her every attention! I've almost bankrupted myself to give her what she wants!"

"Are you sure you really know what she wants?"

"I know exactly what she doesn't want, and that's to live for twelve months of the year at Cashelmara! Marguerite, please, if you've got any pity at all—"

"Oh, bother the pair of you!" said Marguerite crossly. "I feel quite put out. Very well, I'll speak to Sarah and I'll come to Ireland for a while to hold your hand, but I don't want to hear you complaining about each other from morning till night. If you do I'll leave. I'm tired of being caught in the middle of your marriage and being obliged to mediate between you all the time."

I was much too relieved to mind her ill-humor. Indeed so relieved was I that after she had departed to see Sarah I stayed to talk to my little brothers, whom I had neglected during my recent troubles. They were no longer so little. Thomas was eleven years old, lanky and argumentative; he fancied himself very strong and liked to practice wrestling with me. His lunges and thrusts were based on a theory relating to the law of gravity, and he had each step committed to paper as an equation. David, almost ten, was not in the least interested in wrestling, but he did enjoy playing cricket; he liked to pretend to be a fieldsman while I batted and Thomas hurled the ball at me in a fever of energy. David's chief interest, however, was music. He had just built an opera stage in papier-mâché and was planning to stage excerpts from *The Marriage of Figaro* by making puppets and singing each of the major roles.

"You will come, won't you?" he said after inviting me to the gala performance. "You won't send an excuse and stay away?"

I felt guilty when he said that. Hastily I promised to attend and added that I would be seeing far more of them soon when we were all at Cashelmara.

I never found out what Marguerite said to Sarah, but although Sarah was red-eyed for two days afterward there were no scenes or tantrums. On the day of our departure from London I managed to say to her, "It'll only be for a short time. We'll be back in London soon, I swear it." And when she nodded speechlessly, not looking at me, I took her hands, held them tightly and said I'd do my best to make her happy at Cashelmara.

"I shall do my best to make *you* happy," she said, subdued, her answer coming as such a surprise that I dropped her hands and stared at her openmouthed. "I know I haven't been very . . . dutiful lately. Marguerite said you wouldn't have gone gambling so often if you'd been contented at home."

Well, I hadn't thought of it in that light, but I must say I did think Marguerite was very understanding.

Sarah didn't mention Derry's name, and when I remembered my conversation with Marguerite I realized she hadn't mentioned him either. But Marguerite always was the cleverest girl I ever met. I only hoped Sarah could learn to be more like her once we were finally alone together at Cashelmara.

IV

I had been dreading the return to Ireland so much that it was a pleasant shock to find life wasn't as bad there as I'd feared. I did make good my promise to my brothers to spend time with them, and as always I enjoyed Marguerite's company. My niece Edith had fortunately stayed in town with Clara, so Marguerite had not been obliged to bring her to Cashelmara. I don't mean to be unkind about Edith, but I must admit I did find her a difficult girl and I admired Marguerite enormously for being so patient with her.

"Edith's not a bad girl," explained Marguerite when I raised the subject, "but she's very prickly. Of course she pretends she doesn't want to get married, but that's because she's afraid no one will ask her. I'm sure she would never have stayed with Clara unless she was anxious to remain in town until the end of the Season. She knew she wouldn't meet any young men here at Cashelmara."

"One could go for days without meeting *anyone* at Cashelmara," I said gloomily, and it was true. I did visit my brother-in-law Alfred Smith, who was still at Clonagh Court, but he was in such a low state that he was hardly good company. He said he found the valley too lonely without Annabel and was thinking of going back to Epsom to seek a position as a horse trainer. He asked for a loan to help him settle in England and didn't quite believe me when I explained I had barely a penny to my name. I suggested Cousin George might help him, but after that there was an awkwardness between us and I didn't call on him again.

The only other person with whom we exchanged visits was my sister Madeleine. I was afraid she too would ask me for money, but fortunately the Archbishop had woken up at last, and she also had a dozen charities supporting her little dispensary. She was even planning a hospital wing, and knowing Madeleine, I felt sure it would soon be built. Some people always manage to fall on their feet.

"Now, Sarah," said Marguerite busily after we had visited Madeleine and seen the ghastly sight of the ailing Irish lined up outside the dispensary, "here's a charity right on your doorstep and well worthy of your attention. Why don't you do a little work to help Madeleine? As soon as the hospital opens you could go there every week to take flowers and food."

"I'll have them sent," said Sarah quickly, "but I'd rather not go myself." Visiting the poor had always been abhorrent to her, and the only charity work she did consisted of attending charity balls. I didn't blame her one scrap. We can't all be like Florence Nightingale—or Madeleine, who remained utterly serene amidst the repulsive diseases flourishing in the squalor of poverty.

The summer days drifted limpidly past. I took my brothers rowing on the lough and riding over the mountains. Once we rode all the way to Leenane and had a meal at the inn while we watched the boats bring in the seaweed that provided a livelihood for many of the peasants who lived on the shores of Killary Harbor. On another day we rode to Letterturk, although I refused to see Cousin George, and to Clonbur, where we called on the Knoxes; later we rode as far as Cong to inspect the ruins of the abbey. The boys were good company. I enjoyed Thomas's energy and enthusiasm and was surprised by David's eye for beauty. I began to suspect that David was like me not only in looks but in his inclinations, and the more time we spent together the more I wished I could have a son exactly like him. But that would remind me of Sarah's childlessness, and the sadness would seep through me, just as the mist used to seep through the woods when the clouds hung low over the valley.

Sarah had found no new interest to occupy her time. She would spend hours writing to her family (I became very nervous of what she might be saying in those letters, but she swore she was only writing to console her father, who had been in poor health). However, although Marguerite tried to persuade her to begin a journal, Sarah refused with the excuse that her life was so dull there was no event she wished to record.

"That still doesn't prevent you from writing to Francis, I notice!" remarked Marguerite. I must say Marguerite did try hard to find new occupations for Sarah, but all her suggestions about charity work, journals and other such time-passing devices fell on deaf ears. Sarah did make efforts to be "dutiful," as she called it, but how is a man to enjoy making love to his wife when he knows she hates every minute of it? In despair I stopped sleeping with her again, and as the summer passed and I spent more time with my brothers I saw her less and less.

It was in mid-August that Marguerite said to us casually, "The boys and I must be thinking of leaving soon. I've promised to be in Yorkshire with the Fenwicks at the beginning of next month, and I would like to spend a week at St. James's Square before traveling north."

Sarah and I were immediately plunged into a fearful panic, but although we begged her to stay she refused.

"I've enjoyed my visit here," she said firmly, "and I know the boys have enjoyed it too. You've been so good with them, Patrick. But no visitors should outstay their welcome, and we do have other commitments."

They left. We were on our own at last at Cashelmara, and as we stood on the front doorstep and watched the carriage roll away down the hill Sarah broke down and wept, and I felt exactly as Robinson Crusoe must have felt when he first found himself stranded on that abominable desert island.

v

"Why don't you sleep with me?" said Sarah.

"I didn't think you wanted me to," I said.

"I don't."

That hurt. I knew she preferred to sleep alone, but still her words hurt.

"Then why did you ask why I don't sleep with you?"

"Because we must sleep together."

"But I thought you said—"

"I want a baby," said Sarah, crying. "I want a baby, and how am I ever to have a baby if you don't come near me, never kiss me, never touch me, never, never, never do anything . . ."

Then the most damnable disaster overtook us. I tried to make love to her and couldn't.

"Why can't you?" said Sarah. "Why not?" She was crying again.

"Be quiet," I said.

"But I don't understand."

I had to leave the room. I couldn't listen to her nagging any more. I went downstairs and got drunk and fell asleep at the dining-room table, and when I awoke I went outside into the tangled garden to watch the sun rise.

I think it was then that I decided to become a gardener. I sat on a mildewed bench on one side of a weed-strewn patch of undergrowth and saw smooth green lawns, blazing flower beds and a series of winding walks through the woods amidst the rhododendrons and azaleas. I could build little terraces and design arbors. There could be a fountain, perhaps a pond with water lilies and a statue or two, pure white marble in the shadow of cypress trees—an Italian garden. It would remind me of Florence and happier times. I didn't know anything about gardening on such a large scale, but I was sure I could learn. It would be more fun than woodcarving too, because whenever I carved wood I knew anything I produced would be so very far from the perfection of Grinling Gibbons. But a garden . . . I would no longer have to worry about how to pass the time at Cashelmara. I wouldn't have to worry about anything. I would need only to think about flowers and trees and shrubs, about earth and stone, light and water. And I would make a wonderful garden at Cashelmara, a garden so beautiful that people who came after me would say, "This garden was created by Patrick de Salis" and my name would be synonymous with beauty and art and peace, and *that* would be my immortality. It wouldn't matter if I never had a son; it wouldn't matter if I failed at everything else I undertook. I would make a great garden at Cashelmara and create a work of art out of a wilderness.

I spent much time thinking about my plans, and after I had walked a dozen times around the walled acres attached to the house I withdrew to the library to sketch my ideas on paper. It was then that I discovered the gardening books. I had never noticed them before, but I had always assumed that none of the books in the library could possibly interest me. The gardening books were in the small alcove at one side of the fireplace, and when I examined them I found my grandfather's name, Henry de Salis, written neatly on every fly leaf.

I became passionately interested in my grandfather. I searched the attics, and when I found a portrait of him I took it downstairs to the library. I had long meant to remove my mother's picture from its position over the chimney piece, and now I was able to replace it with the portrait of the stranger I had never known. He was a plain man with mild blue eyes and an innocent expression. The portrait was indifferently painted, but it meant more to me than that elegantly executed portrait of my mother with her overpowering beauty and grace.

Sarah couldn't understand it, but then Sarah couldn't understand anything I did nowadays. We had muddled along together hopelessly for a week or two after Marguerite had left, and then, thank God, a diversion had arisen when Katherine asked if she might visit us.

Of course we both begged her to come (Katherine, of all people!) because anyone's company was preferable to being alone with each other at Cashelmara, so Katherine journeyed from Duneden Castle to spend September with us. Duneden didn't come, but that was no surprise since I knew he despised me, and besides I knew Katherine was only at Cashelmara because it would have been socially incorrect not to have acknowledged the presence of her brother and sister-in-law less than eighty miles from her country home.

When Katherine left I did try to make love to Sarah again, but it was no use, even though I was primed with just the right amount of poteen. It began to rain endlessly at Cashelmara, hour after hour, day after day, and there was nothing I could do in my garden. I browsed among my grandfather's books and dreamed of what I would do when spring came, but all the time I was aware that first I must endure Christmas, a Christmas alone with Sarah, for Marguerite had long since promised to spend that Christmas with Katherine, and although I too hoped for an invitation no word reached us from Duneden Castle.

Alfred Smith had departed for Epsom; Madeleine was already

planning a Christmas dinner for all the shiftless peasants who were willing to pretend to be starving in order to get a free meal. We were alone.

On the fifteenth of December I rose at dawn, dressed and padded downstairs to the library.

"Please come," I wrote to Derry. "Cousin George and Duneden can go to the devil for all I care, for I'm so down I don't even mind about Woodhammer any more. It's pretty dull here as you can imagine, and I would so like to have a merry Christmas. I do hope Clara is recovered from her ill health. Sarah is quite well. We look forward to seeing you both. Please, please come. Yours, P."

It was a poor letter, but there was nothing else I felt capable of saying. Anyway I sealed it, saddled a horse and rode off with the letter to the inn at Leenane, where the mail car was due to call later in the day. The sun came up as I rode past the tip of the lough and crossed the stone bridge over the Fooey River. As my horse toiled uphill to the top of the pass, I looked back over my shoulder and saw the mountains were black against a pale pink sky.

I was within a mile of the road that ran from Galway to Leenane when I saw someone riding toward me.

I knew at once who it was. How I knew I've no idea, for it was barely light and he was no more than a black-coated figure on horse-back, but I knew. He knew who I was too, for we both spurred our horses to the gallop at one and the same moment. The mud flew from the hoofs, the wind sang in my ears, and then the next moment we were laughing, reaching out to grasp each other's hands, and Derry was drawling in that cool voice which was so painfully familiar to me: "Ain't life grand?"

Chapter Five

I

"It was damnably dull in London after you left, Patrick," said Derry after we had recovered from the splendid shock of seeing each other so unexpectedly. "Besides, I drew the ace of spades so often at cards I was sure I'd sicken and die if I stayed in England." He glanced over his shoulder as if he expected to see death smirking at him, and when I laughed he protested, "But it's a deadly business being an Irishman in London. You English are such a stiff-necked crowd!"

"I hadn't noticed anyone being stiff-necked toward you."

"Well, to be sure everyone was friendly to me when you were there, but once you were gone the prejudice against me was disgraceful. Watermill and Huntingford wouldn't accept my IOUs, and that bastard Danziger as good as asked me to quit the Albatross. He said there'd been a complaint I cheated at cards—cheated, by God! It's a pity there were no witnesses to our conversation or I'd have sued the shirt off his back for slander."

"But who—"

"Oh, how should I know who lodged the complaint? It was Steele, I dare say. He owed me a couple of hundred and didn't want to pay up when I needed his cash to settle my debts. But what does it matter who ran rusty on me? The lie was soon passed around that I'd been booted from the Albatross for cheating at cards, and soon no one in politics would touch me with a ten-foot greased pole. So much for my ambitions! That was what the ace of spades meant, I've no doubt—my death as a rising politician!"

"But that's monstrously unfair!"

"So it may be, but I don't care any more. I thought I'd go back to the bar and settle in Dublin. I've left Clara at St. James's Square with Marguerite. I thought I'd cross over first to find somewhere to live before I brought her to Ireland. But once I set foot in Dublin it seemed a shame not to take the train to Galway, and when I reached Galway . . . well, I took an outside car as far as Oughterard and then the horse went lame and we were all stranded, but I managed to hire this horrible nag, who can barely put one hoof in front of the other—"

"You mean you've ridden all night from Oughterard?"

"It was either that or bed down in some flea-ridden hovel!"

"You poor old fellow, you must be exhausted! Let's get home as quickly as possible."

"Well, I'll not make things awkward for you. I haven't forgotten how you're placed with that rogue at Duneden Castle, but I can't see the harm in such a short visit. What's your news? How's Sarah?"

I shouldn't have told him but I did. I told him the whole story, only omitting that Sarah had twice reduced me to impotence, and afterward when he said lightly, "Holy Mother of God, women are the very devil, aren't they?" I found my loneliness less oppressive. "What we men have to put up with!" said Derry, his black eyes sparkling with impudence, and I laughed, for life looked good to me again and even my worst troubles seemed trivial now that I had Derry once more by my side.

II

As soon as Sarah saw Derry she went straight upstairs to her room and wrote to Cousin George. She didn't have to wait long for a response. That same afternoon George thundered over from Letterturk, stormed into the library where Derry was drinking soda and brandy with me and announced that I had broken my word, b'God, and I'd be sorry, wait and see. The whole scene was so ludicrous that Derry couldn't resist caricaturing George in his presence, and George became so enraged that I honestly thought he was going to have an apoplectic fit.

"I leave tomorrow for Duneden Castle!" were his parting words as he hurled himself from the room.

"Hell hath no fury like a squireen scorned, b'God!" barked Derry

296

after him, and George, who hated to be called a squireen, was so incensed that he had to step back into the room to say that Derry was without doubt damned to hell for all eternity.

"I'll make it comfortable for you when you arrive," said Derry, having the last word as usual. "*Au revoir.*" And we both burst into gales of laughter even before he had left the room. I suppose we were a little unkind to George, but I did so resent his heavy-handed efforts to dictate to me.

"Jesus," said Derry, wiping his eyes, "now the cat's properly among the pigeons and no mistake. I'm sorry, I should have held my tongue."

"I'm glad you didn't. I'm sick to death of Cousin George."

"How important is his money to you at present? I mean, what exactly is your financial situation?"

I wasn't sure myself, but I did my best to explain. "He and Duneden paid the debts I incurred last summer," I said, "and they've promised to pay the interest on the Woodhammer Hall mortgages each year so long as I live quietly at Cashelmara and have no communication with you. If we all keep this up for three years I will have saved enough money to pay off the second mortgage and my income will be in a healthier state again. I might even be able to afford to live at Woodhammer and go up to town occasionally. But meanwhile all the Cashelmara monies go directly to George and Duneden, who pay me a monthly allowance."

"What do they do with the surplus? Do they invest it?"

"I've no idea. I suppose so."

"Do you receive the interest on the investment?"

"I shouldn't think so, since they're paying the interest on the mortgages. That wouldn't be fair, would it?"

"Patrick, I swear no man was ever half as trusting as you are! Does Fielding still work for you? Perhaps he'd know more about the situation."

"No, Fielding was dismissed as an economy. All the bills go to Duneden, and I suppose his secretary sees the tradesmen are paid."

"But Jesus, Patrick, you've put yourself entirely in the hands of your worst enemies, and they could be swindling you out of hundreds a year!"

"Well, it was either that or lose Woodhammer," I said glumly, "and even though they're my worst enemies they are at least English gentlemen."

"English gentlemen!" scoffed Derry. "English gentlemen swindled me out of a political career and a fine life in London! I'll tell you, Patrick, I'd rather meet six members of the Molly Maguires armed to the teeth than a brace of English gentlemen armed with a power of attorney! How much is the annual interest on the Woodhammer mortgages? I'd be willing to wager that with a little careful rearrangement and some shrewd investment you could safely pay the interest, wipe out the second mortgage and still save money—and all without a whisper of help from Duneden and Cousin George!"

"Well, I don't know," I said doubtfully. "I'm not much good with money."

"But I am," said Derry. "I've learned the hard way how to count my pennies. Oh, I know I made a mistake about that damned railway, but even the sharpest fellows make mistakes now and then. I'll help you, Patrick. Don't turn a hair if those two English gentlemen make a fuss. Clara and I can come and live here at Cashelmara, and I'll make you a rich man again if it's the very last thing I ever do."

III

Duneden and George tore up the deed which gave them their power of attorney and declared the trust set up to "save me from myself" was irrevocably destroyed.

"We've done all we can for you," said Duneden. "We can do no more."

Thank God, I thought. I wanted to say it aloud, but somehow I had no chance before he and George walked out. I watched them go with enormous relief, and afterward Derry shared a bottle of champagne with me to celebrate the return of my independence.

The next problem was Sarah.

"I refuse to live beneath the same roof as Derry," she said stonily. "Either he goes or I go."

I tried to imagine whose side Marguerite would take and had an uncomfortable feeling it might be Sarah's. Besides, I didn't want to lose Sarah, particularly now that I was in charge of my own affairs again and feeling more of a man. Despite her threats I doubted that she would leave me for good, since her pride was too great to tolerate the disgrace attached to a deserting wife, but I did fear she might go to London for a prolonged stay with Marguerite. I disliked the thought of being a husband who couldn't keep his wife at his side when he wanted her, and I disliked even more the possibility that my friendship with Marguerite might suffer in consequence. Accordingly I was anxious to soothe Sarah, but I had no idea how I was going to begin. I really did need Derry's help in organizing my financial affairs, and the last thing I wanted to do was to kick him out of the house.

"But why should there be any difficulty?" said Derry, unruffled as ever. "Clara wants a home of her own just as much as Sarah does. Why don't we live at Clonagh Court now that Alfred Smith's gone back to England? It's three miles away at the other end of the lough, and Sarah needn't see either of us if she doesn't want to. On the other hand it's near enough for you to visit us as often as you like."

That did seem to be an ideal solution. Sarah could no longer protest that she was forced to endure Derry's company, and when I was careful to spend every evening with her she could no longer complain of being neglected. I still didn't sleep with her—I hadn't quite enough courage yet to try that again—but I felt I was taking steps in the right direction and might resume our relationship in the bedroom when a suitable opportunity presented itself.

Meanwhile I had other problems to overcome. Derry had organized my money very neatly, using my surplus income to cover the interest on the Woodhammer mortgages. He had been careful not to offend MacGowan by interfering with estate matters, and since the rents had recently been overhauled there was little he could have done in the way of reform. The four of us, Derry and Clara, Sarah and I, lived modestly but comfortably in our respective homes, so really I had no complaint to make except that I couldn't see how I was ever going to pay off either one of those mortgages. But Derry soon invented a scheme.

"There's money to be made in forestry," he said and told me a long story about an Irish peer who had made a fortune out of planting a few trees on his estate. "I think it would be worthwhile consulting a forestry expert," he suggested. "He could tell us which part of the estate would be suitable for a plantation, and it wouldn't commit us to any expenditure. If we decided not to go ahead all we'd lose is the man's fee."

That sounded reasonable to me, so I wrote to the Royal Agricultural College in Dublin and presently they recommended to me a Mr. MacDonald, who had pioneered experiments in forestry in the Scottish Highlands.

It was plain to see that he was appalled by the treeless wastes of the Cashelmara estate, but he did think an area was suitable for a small plantation. Halfway down the lough the road to Clonareen curves inland to follow the spur of Leynabricka, and the land which slopes upward at this point does possess a layer of topsoil above the usual bare rock. Since the soil was too poor and the slope too steep for all but the most primitive farming, I hardly thought it would be much loss to clear the land of the few potato patches that had been optimistically planted there and tell the peasants to go somewhere else. Derry said there was still plenty of abandoned land where they could resettle themselves if they made the effort, and the rest of their tribe in the valley would see they didn't starve.

"In fact you'd be doing them a favor by evicting them," said Derry, "for that land wouldn't support a tinker's goat if it could help it, and there's some far better land on the south side of the lough which they could farm in conacre."

So I decided to proceed with the scheme. I was rather taken with it by this time, for Mr. MacDonald had spoken lyrically of his Scottish successes, and it did seem a jolly idea to make money by planting trees.

My only worry was that I had no idea where I was going to find the money to make the initial investment. The seedlings had to be bought, planted and nurtured, and after all the bills were paid I didn't have a penny to my name.

"Perhaps I could sell some heirlooms," I said to Derry, although I hated the thought of parting with the beautiful Georgian silver and even doubted that I was legally entitled to do so. I wished I could have pawned all Sarah's useless jewelry, but that was out of the question. I had to tread so carefully with Sarah.

"Don't sell anything," said Derry, producing the perfect solution with his usual ease. "Why bother? You've got a rich father-in-law ailing on the other side of the Atlantic. Write and remind him that he can't take his money with him when he departs for the next world."

This seemed reasonable, particularly since I had never asked Cousin Francis for a penny before, but somehow the idea of writing to him was not attractive and I found myself putting off the task for a day or two.

"Let's clear the land first," I suggested to Derry, so I summoned MacGowan, explained the forestry scheme and asked him to issue the necessary eviction notices.

"There'll be trouble, my lord," said MacGowan at once in his gloomiest voice.

I repeated Derry's suggestion that the tenants should resettle themselves on the south side of the lough.

"That land's no better than a bog now, my lord," said MacGowan.

300

"It was different in the old days, but the river changed its course and there was no alternative but to abandon the fields there. That's why the land has never been resettled."

"Well . . . send the tenants to America or something," I said on inspiration. "They live in such squalor that they'd probably jump at the chance to go."

"If you want them to go they'll want to stay," said MacGowan, and having produced this depressing insight into the perverse nature of the Irish peasant, he added in what can only be described as a voice of doom, "They're all O'Malleys, you know."

"I don't care who they are," I said, much irritated by this time, and then remembered with a sinking feeling that the O'Malleys' champion was none other than my old enemy Maxwell Drummond. "Oh Lord!" I muttered. "What a bother! Well, perhaps we'd better pay them compensation."

"That would prove very expensive, my lord, and set a dangerous precedent. Every evicted tenant afterward would demand compensation from you and you'd soon find yourself in all kinds of trouble."

"Oh. Well . . ." I was utterly nonplussed by this time. "I'll talk to Mr. Stranahan about it," I said at last, knowing Derry would find a way out of the difficulty somehow. "He'll deal with the matter for me, I dare say."

But Derry saw no way out except to stand firm when the O'Malleys protested. "They can fend for themselves!" he exclaimed. "And as for MacGowan saying the land on the south shore is useless, I don't believe a word of it. All they need to grow are potatoes! They don't need the best acreage in the valley for that."

"But what if Drummond makes a fuss?"

"I can deal with Maxwell Drummond," said Derry, and I knew that like a true Irishman he was already thirsting for a fight. "Leave him to me."

Well, I did, but I didn't like it, and as the weeks passed I liked it less and less. I did manage to extract the money from Cousin Francis, although he wrote me the devil of an uppish note about it, but I had no chance to put my forestry scheme into operation because it proved impossible to clear the land. Derry handed out the eviction notices, MacGowan retreated into glum neutrality and all the O'Malleys banded together, marched to the very front door of Cashelmara and demanded to see me. When I refused, thinking it would be a loss of face on my part to negotiate with such a rabble, two windows were smashed and Sarah was in such a state that I felt I had no choice but to send for Maxwell Drummond. But Drummond, damn his insolence, now refused to see me. In a carefully written letter he told me there could be no negotiations while Derry remained at Cashelmara.

"Don't listen to him!" said Derry, incensed. "What right has he to talk of negotiations and lay down the law to you! You've signed the eviction orders, Patrick. Stand by them! If you retreat now you'll never hear the end of it."

That was all very well, but trying to suppress Irish discontent is like trying to stop an old bucket from leaking water—if you block one hole the water bursts out somewhere else. We did finally manage to evict the tenants but not before the sub-inspector at Letterturk had ordered all the police at his command into the valley and not before the eviction machines had wrecked the mud cabins almost over the inhabitants' heads. I thought after that the worst trouble would be over, but never was I more mistaken. The troubles had barely begun. My cattle, which grazed docilely in the meadows by the Fooey River, were mutilated. One of my favorite setters, Polonius, disappeared and was discovered a week later sitting bolt upright on the altar of the chapel; he had been decapitated and his head was resting neatly beside him. Worse still, the chapel had been desecrated. The altar reeked of urine and all the pews had been slashed with knives.

By this time I was thoroughly enraged and very deeply upset. I would never have embarked on the forestry scheme if I had known it was going to result in such unpleasantness. I hadn't wanted to offend anyone, and how was I to know the O'Malleys would take a few evictions so hard? I only wished I could abandon the idea without delay, but of course that would have been the crowning ignominy, and Derry rightly refused to hear it.

So I tried to stand firm, but life became so deuced uneasy that I was soon seriously worried that I was exposing Sarah to real danger instead of mere unpleasant discomfort. The last straw occurred in early March when Sarah's carriage was pelted with rotten eggs as she drove home from Clonareen after calling on Madeleine.

I was so distressed that I promised to take her at once to London.

"But the money!" wept Sarah, mindful at last of our need to be thrifty.

"We'll use some of the money your father sent us," I said promptly, "and we'll stay at St. James's Square with Marguerite."

I felt relieved once the decision had been made. "You and Clara had better come too," I said to Derry. "It's no good staying here."

"I've got to stay," he said. I'd never seen him so determined. "You leave, by all means, and take both the women to London—it would be a relief for me not to have to worry about Clara—but I must see this thing through to the end. It's really a personal matter between Drummond and myself, you see, and I'll not give in until I have him in jail for conspiracy, trespass, breach of the peace and a dozen other outrages. Let me once nail Drummond for you, Patrick, and I swear the valley will be as safe again as the Garden of Eden before the Fall."

I didn't like leaving him alone at Cashelmara. I wanted to recall the police so that a constant watch would be kept on the house, but Derry refused to consider it.

"That would make it look as though I'm scared," he said, "and why should I be scared of a bunch of smelly peasants? I've got a gun, and if they drive me to prove my marksmanship I'll show them I'm man enough to look after myself. Don't you worry about me, Patrick. I'll write and tell you as soon as Drummond's behind bars."

I said I would return as soon as the women were safely in London, but he shook his head. "This is my chance to do something for you, Patrick," he said. "I put you into this damnable corner. Now it's up to me to get you out of it."

No man could have been fairer or more honest than that; no man in adversity could have had a better friend. I left him reluctantly, but I no longer felt guilty about leaving him because I was convinced that this was what he wanted. Accordingly I wrote to the sub-inspector at Letterturk to request an armed escort, and when he responded a day later I left the valley with Sarah and Clara.

I had never in my life felt more glad to leave.

IV

It was amazing how much Sarah changed once we had turned our backs on Ireland, and the closer we drew to London the more I noticed the difference in her. Sulkiness and boredom had made her plain at Cashelmara, but now she was beautiful again, brimming with that brilliant sparkle I remembered so well, and it was impossible for me to remain unaffected by her recovery. I no longer felt it needed an act of courage to go to bed with her again. All it needed was a successful visit to the theater and a late supper alone together at the house in St. James's Square; all it needed was for me to see her in a new gown with amethysts at her throat, her thick hair coiled elegantly upon her head and her eyes tawny above her high cheekbones.

And later when we were alone and she kissed me to show her willingness, all our unhappiness dissolved, my failures might never have existed and I had a tantalizing glimpse of what our marriage might have been—and could still be if we could only give it half a chance.

"I do love you, Sarah," I said. "I really do. I'm going to turn over a new leaf in the future and everything will be quite different, I swear it."

We talked of the future, and when Sarah said in despair, "If only we didn't have to live at Cashelmara!" I promised I would take her to New York for a visit. I thought perhaps Cousin Francis would invest some money for me on the New York Stock Exchange, and once he had made enough money to enable me to repay his loan and wipe out the second mortgage I could afford to live at Woodhammer again and visit London during the Season. After all, Cousin Francis had made his own fortune a dozen times over; why shouldn't he make a little fortune for me, especially as his daughter's happiness was at stake? It all seemed very logical to me, and when Sarah proved thrilled at the prospect of a visit home, Marguerite said approvingly that the long voyage across the Atlantic would be like going on a second honeymoon. So we set a date in May, and while Sarah wrote dozens of excited letters to her family to warn them of our plans I booked our passages and paid for them with more of the money Cousin Francis had loaned me for the forestry plantation.

Three days before we were due to leave I received a letter from Derry.

I had been receiving letters from him every week, and when this final letter arrived I thought it would be no different from the others, a catalogue of new "agrarian outrages," examples of Drummond's slipperiness in avoiding prosecution and a determination to quell the O'Malleys at all costs. But this letter was a plea for help. He had changed his mind about having the police keep watch on Cashelmara (I knew then that the situation must have become very serious), but the sub-inspector, who was hand in glove with Cousin George, had spitefully refused his request for aid.

"I'd go to Letterturk myself," Derry wrote, "and shake that nincompoop till his teeth rattled, but matters have come to such a pass here that I daren't leave the house alone and there's no one I trust enough to take with me as a bodyguard. I'm giving this letter to MacGowan and have promised him a reward if it reaches you, so no doubt his avarice will encourage him to take it to Leenane for collection by the mail car. Can you come as soon as possible to wake up the sub-inspector? You know I would never have asked you unless I really felt it was necessary, but that devil Drummond will see me in hell yet unless I do something desperate, although God knows if I go I'll be damned if I don't take him with me."

I had no choice. He was looking after my affairs for me; he was doing everything a loyal friend could do. What sort of a friend would I have been if I had ignored his appeal for help and steamed off on a jolly voyage to New York? A man does have certain responsibilities, and although I wanted to fulfill my promise to Sarah I saw no way it could be done without betraying Derry's trust. I had a moral obligation to help him.

"Let Derry fight his own battles!" blazed Sarah.

"Well, he's tried but he's obviously in a deuced dangerous situation."

"He chose it!"

"Yes—to help me! To enable us to be in London together! How can I refuse now to help him in return?"

"I don't believe he needs help!" cried Sarah, in such a towering rage that she became irrational. "He just wants to get you back! He's jealous thinking of us alone together and he's determined to get your attention!"

I tried to be patient. "Darling, just because you'd feel jealous if you were at Cashelmara and Derry and I were in London there's no need to assume Derry would feel the same way. You can't assign your own feminine jealousies to a man like Derry."

"Oh, can't I! Why not? He's always been jealous of me, always, from the very beginning!"

"Absolute nonsense. Look, Sarah—"

"Patrick, if you cancel our voyage to New York now and go to Ireland, I'll never forgive you. Never. It'll be the end of our marriage."

"Don't be so melodramatic and ridiculous! Just because there's a serious crisis at Cashelmara—"

"It's got nothing to do with Cashelmara!" she shouted at me. "It's all to do with Derry! You've had to choose between us and you've chosen him!"

Well, what can one do with a woman who twists the truth in such a demented fashion and compounds her madness by making such hysterical statements? I decided I must keep my dignity and allow her time for her anger to cool, so I shrugged my shoulders and headed in resignation for the door.

I never reached it. My refusal to argue maddened her still further, and she grabbed me by the wrist. I turned to protest. She tried to hit me, and in an effort to smother her flailing hands I made a half-hearted attempt at an embrace. It was only when she recoiled from me in disgust that I finally lost my temper.

"Damn you!" I blazed. "You spoiled, selfish bitch!" I said other words too, words she had never heard before, and suddenly the anger had faded from her eyes and I knew she was frightened.

Now it was my turn to recoil. I couldn't stand to see her quivering like a jelly. There was sweat on her forehead and she smelled of fear, and I was nauseated by her. I looked at her round breasts and they were ugly to me. I looked at her long neck and it was grotesque.

"What a miserable creature you are!" I said bitterly. "What use are you to any man?" The rage was flowing through me like a stream of molten lead. I felt overpowered by it, pressed by its weight into a different, darker mold. I no longer had any control over what I said, and it was as if a stranger were talking in my voice. "You think you're so beautiful and desirable," I said, "but you're not. You're sexless, a failure, no better than a unicorn, the biggest swindle ever made on a man who walked down the aisle to the altar."

She began to cry. I had a blurred impression of watery eyes and straggly hair and was again so nauseated that this time I had to leave the room. But she came after me. She was sobbing noisily by this time, and she went down on her knees and clung to the hem of my jacket as she begged me to stay.

I pushed her away, ran upstairs and vomited. I expected to feel better after that, but I didn't. My brain was numb; I couldn't think clearly. All I could tell myself was: It wasn't me. I didn't say those things. It was someone else.

Someone I didn't want to know.

I summoned my man, told him to pack my bags. Marguerite tapped on my door later, but I refused to see her.

I took the afternoon train to Holyhead, and the next morning I crossed the sea to Kingstown. It was evening when the Dublin train drew into Galway, and I felt so exhausted that I had no choice but to go to bed at once at the hotel on Eyre Square.

The headache was gone when I awoke next morning, but it soon came back. I couldn't eat any breakfast and hadn't the heart to make the effort to hire a private carriage, so I took the outside car which left daily for Clifden. I was alone. Not wanting company, I had left my man in London, and so there was no one to look down their nose in disapproval as I sat down between a priest and a farmer's wife. The car grated along through the pastoral country to Oughterard, and then after that the trees died, the meadows gave way to bog and in the distance rose the huge naked mountains of Connemara and the Joyce country.

I left the car at Maam's Cross where the roads to Clifden and Leenane diverge and managed to hire a horse from one of Derry's distant relatives who lived there. The wretched animal refused to hurry no matter how much I urged him, so it was well over an hour before I left the Leenane road and headed uphill through the gulley to the pass between Knocknafaughey and Bunnacunneen.

It was unseasonably hot, and I had seldom seen the valley look more tranquil. Even the lough's ragged edges seemed smooth, and on the hillside across the valley stood Cashelmara, shimmering mysteriously in that unnatural brilliant light.

He must have seen me coming from a long way off, for when I had passed the tip of the lough and my horse had begun to climb again I saw him running down the dark drive to the gates.

He raised his hand, waved joyfully. I knew that if I had been within earshot he would have said, laughing, "Ain't life grand?" and suddenly I knew who I was again and none of my troubles mattered any more.

He began to unlock the gates with the giant key. I was still some way off, but when the gates swung open I stood up in my stirrups to call a greeting.

He never heard it. He came rushing out toward me, and before I could speak I saw the dazzling flash of sunlight on naked metal and heard the clatter of his gun as it fell unused from his hand.

He had stopped. For one long moment I saw him standing there very straight and proud, his eyes sparkling, his hair blowing lightly in the soft wind, and then he keeled forward, slipping from his knees to the mud road at his feet.

The knife shone in his back as obscene as an inverted cross.

When my horse refused to gallop I slid from his back and started to run. I ran and ran, the sharp stones rough beneath my city shoes, and the sun streamed down upon the valley from that hot and steamy sky.

I reached him. He was conscious. We looked at each other, but neither of us spoke, and the stranger inside me mocked us, saying we had never really talked to each other at all. As if to deny it, Derry made a great effort to speak, but it was too late. He was beyond all

307

speech, and as I pressed him closer to me his face stiffened, his eyes grew darker and the blood ran from his mouth as he died.

V

I never saw the man who killed him. He must have been hiding among the large boulders above the road, and afterward it would have been easy for him to slip away out of sight around the corner of the walled grounds. I saw no one but Derry.

But I went after Maxwell Drummond. I summoned all the magistrates. I summoned the sub-inspector. I wrote letters to everyone concerned with law enforcement in County Galway. I even wrote to the Inspector General of the Royal Irish Constabulary and the Secretary of State and the Lord Lieutenant at Dublin Castle. And when people shrugged and said outrages were all too common nowadays I wrote to Gladstone at Westminster and said that what was needed in Ireland was not the secret ballot or land reform but law and order.

"We are the leaders of the civilized world," I wrote, the words spinning dizzily from my pen, "and yet here on our very doorstep is this unspeakable country where the inhabitants are worse than savages and murder is so commonplace that it has ceased to be an atrocity and is treated as a way of life. Why can't something be done about it? Why do we have to suffer this intolerable situation?"

Mr. Gladstone in his reply explained that Ireland was indeed a grievous cross for the English to bear, but as good Christians it behooved us to improve the lot of the Irish in order that they might be led from the dark waters of their discontent into the paths of enlightenment. In other words he had the insufferable nerve to say that the solution to outrage was to mollycoddle the Irish in order to make them happier.

"I'd like to shoot every O'Malley from here to Clonareen," I said fiercely to George when he and his brother magistrates and the sub-inspector were at last assembled at Cashelmara. "For a start you must imprison Drummond. He's the one responsible. Imprison him and beat him till he confesses."

They all looked at me blankly. I started to shout at them, accusing them of sympathizing with the murderers, and when they tried to interrupt I cursed them till I was too exhausted to curse any more. After that I found myself alone with George, who said I was making a shocking exhibition of myself and must pull myself together at once.

"Not until I've found the murderer and seen him hanged!"

"My dear Patrick," said George, "I may as well warn you, you'll never find him and neither will anyone else. Drummond was at Leenane at the time of the murder. Half a dozen witnesses can vouch for his presence there. There's not even a chance that we could prove he was a conspirator, and as for proving which O'Malley threw the knife . . . well, you'd fare better if you tried to prove the world was flat."

"But there must be witnesses! If we offer a reward surely someone will come forward!"

But all George said was "Have you never heard of Ribbonism?"

I had but I must have looked blank, for he said in explanation, "Ireland is riddled with secret societies like the old Ribbon Society of the Forties, and all of them are busy fostering agrarian outrages in a continuing war against the landlord. The society which flourishes in this valley calls itself the Blackbooters, and no matter what anyone says to the contrary I'm convinced they're supported by none other than the Irish Republican Brotherhood."

"Oh, the Brotherhood—the Fenians—no Englishman could take them seriously!"

"Scoff if you wish, but mark my words, you'll find no one willing to collaborate with the authorities in a case like this, for any collaborator would be subject to the most savage reprisals. You'll never find a soul willing to testify on the subject of Stranahan's murder."

"Then what do you suggest I do?" I said in a great rage. "Sit back and let my friend's assassin live happily ever after?"

George said nothing. His silence maddened me. I said, "Don't think I won't get even with Drummond one day. I won't forget and I won't forgive and one day I'll see him hanged."

I knew then that it didn't matter who had thrown the knife. All that mattered was that Drummond had arranged it.

But there was nothing I could do except bide my time and bury my friend as best as I could. It was no easy task. I knew his grave would have been desecrated at Clonareen, and when I decided to bury him in a quiet corner of the family churchyard by the chapel at Cashelmara I couldn't find a Catholic priest who would say a Mass by the graveside. Father Donal said he was crippled by a pain in his leg, and when I offered to send the carriage for him he said he had a fever and begged to be excused.

That was when I really began to believe George's talk about the power of those rural secret societies, but fortunately Madeleine came to my rescue. I will say for Madeleine that she was always very good at doing the impossible. She bribed the Archbishop's private chaplain to journey to Cashelmara, and although the poor man was terrified out of his wits and obviously expected to be murdered in his bed, I was at last able to give Derry a funeral according to the rites of his own church. I wished Clara could have been there, but of course I had to forbid her to come because I could never have forgiven myself if anything had happened to her.

Thinking of Clara made me remember Sarah, and after the funeral, when I had no choice but to face the fact of Derry's loss, I became increasingly aware of my loneliness. A lassitude overcame me. I suppose it was the aftermath of shock, but I made no attempt to leave Cashelmara and shrank from going to London until I knew how I would be received. I still could not bear to think of our quarrel in detail, but eventually I wrote asking her to forgive me and saying that when I returned to London I did hope she would consent to talk matters over.

She did not reply. Presently I wrote again and said I was coming to London to take her to America as I had promised. I thought that at least would prompt some response, but when I heard nothing I suspected her letters were being intercepted by ill-wishers. At that point I sent for MacGowan. I was tired of living in an armed fortress, tired of troubles created by malcontents determined to make my life a misery. I told MacGowan to do whatever had to be done to put matters right with my tenants, and when he asked about the forestry plantation I told him I had abandoned the scheme and the O'Malleys could go back to their land if they wished.

I waited another week in case there was word from Sarah, but when none came I wrote a third letter. For the first time I tried to face the memory of our quarrel, and after many drafts I wrote, "My darling Sarah, I know I said unforgivable things to you when we quarreled, but none of them was true. Looking back, I feel that I never said them and that they were said by someone else. Whoever that someone was he's gone now and I'm myself again. I'm no longer the man who made you so unhappy. I'm the man who loved you and married you and loves you still. Please give me another chance. All I want is to make you happy and prove I love you better than anyone else in the world. Please write. I shall leave here and come to you as soon as you send word that there's a chance of me being forgiven. All my love, PATRICK."

I waited. The days dragged past. Eventually in despair I wrote to

310

Marguerite. Was Sarah determined to remain unforgiving? Had she perhaps already left for America? Was she ill? Dying? Dead?

"Please write," I begged Marguerite. "Please, please write."

I felt so isolated. Despite MacGowan's overtures of peace to the O'Malleys I still thought it unwise to wander far beyond the grounds, so I didn't go riding or boating or paying calls on my neighbors. Instead, as my lassitude ebbed, I began to work on the garden. I had decided to shape the lawn so that it resembled a lake surrounded by flowers and shrubs. Lawns, I had read, could provide a satisfactory visual substitute for water, and although I hoped later to build a lily pond I had decided to place that farther uphill on a plateau in the woods. The pond would be part of my Italian garden, linked to the "lake" garden by a long flight of steps. When the trees were cleared the view would stretch over the roof of the house to the lough and the mountains, and I could then frame the view by building some sort of pavilion—an Italian teahouse, perhaps, or a ruined temple. The garden would be Tuscan, not Renaissance, the design based on Petrarch's idea of what a classical Roman garden might have been like, and the emphasis would be not on flowers but on water and stone. And to border my Tuscan garden . . . well, I thought a topiary might be fun. I liked the idea of shaping trees, molding them into different shapes, cutting, nurturing, experimenting.

I loved my garden already, although it was still a wilderness, and in my distress it proved to be a solace to me. I cut the lawn and edged it; then I found a rusty roller in one of the greenhouses and began to roll it up and down, up and down over the coarse bumpy turf.

The servants all thought Derry's death had unhinged me, but I took no notice, and presently when the lawn showed no marked improvement I wrote to the Royal Agricultural College for information about grass seed. If my lawn was ever to resemble a lake it was no use wasting more time on a patch of land that was more of a clover field than a grassy sward.

Still no word came from Sarah.

One gray afternoon I was outside digging up all the clover when Hayes tiptoed from the house to say that visitors had arrived.

"Visitors?" I said blankly. I straightened my back, rolled down my shirt sleeves and wiped the sweat from my forehead. "Who?"

Hayes peered at the card on his salver. "A Mr. Rathbone of London," he pronounced, rolling his "R" like a Frenchman.

I stretched out a muddy hand and snatched the card from him in disbelief. My first thought was that Sarah was petitioning for divorce. As far as I knew she had no grounds, but I could see no other explanation for Rathbone's journey to Ireland.

"To be sure he's come as an escort," said Hayes helpfully. "These would be difficult times for a lady traveling alone, I'm thinking."

"What lady?" I said, startled.

Hayes looked at me with that compassionate wariness that kind people reserve for the hopelessly insane.

"Why, your lady, my lord," he said. "Your wife, may the Virgin and the Holy Saints protect her."

I left him and rushed across the lawn.

VI

Rathbone was in the morning room. He was alone.

I said two words—"My wife?"—and he, still rising to his feet, answered, "I believe she went upstairs to your apartments, my lord, to refresh herself from the journey."

I raced upstairs, tripped on the top step and hurtled against the wall so hard that I damned nearly dislocated my collarbone. Then with my heart beating like a bass drum I stumbled down the gallery and burst across the threshold of the bedroom.

She was there. She was very pale, and as we stood staring at each other I sensed a new stillness about her, a poise and gravity that were unfamiliar.

"Sarah?" I whispered uncertainly and wondered for one bizarre moment if I was hallucinating.

She took a step forward and tried to speak, but no words came. Her eyes filled with tears.

"Sarah . . ." I could hardly speak myself. "You've forgiven me?" I said, still not daring to believe it. "You've come back?"

She nodded. The tears began to stream down her face, and suddenly I realized with shock that they were not tears of distress but tears of joy. "Oh, Patrick," she said in a strange, quiet voice. "Patrick, it's like a miracle. I'm going to have a baby."

Part Four

SARAH
Passion   1873–1884

The beauty of the royal pair . . . excited universal admiration; for the bridegroom was the handsomest prince in Europe, and the precocious charms of the bride had already obtained for her the name of Isabella the Fair.

Lives of the Queens of England
—AGNES STRICKLAND

Chapter One

I

He was born in December, just before Christmas, and weighed exactly eight pounds.

"Francis!" I whispered adoringly as soon as he was placed in my arms.

"Edward!" said Patrick equally adoringly at one and the same moment.

We never could agree about anything.

"I really think you should give way to Patrick this time, Sarah," said my aunt Marguerite, the peacemaker. "After all, the baby is heir to the title, and it would be more suitable, by English standards, if he were named for Patrick's father, not for yours."

I would never have followed Marguerite's advice so often except that she was always right. I can't bear people who are always right, but Marguerite was always right in such a clever way that I still loved her just as dearly as if she had been my sister (and probably a whole heap better). So I gave in to Patrick for the umpteenth time (oh, it does so aggravate me to give way when my heart is set on something!), and the baby was christened Patrick Edward after his father and grandfather in the chapel at Cashelmara.

The champagne had hardly vanished from our glasses at the luncheon afterward when Patrick and I were squabbling about whether Baby should be addressed as Patrick or Edward.

"Patrick would be nicer than Edward," I said. I have always thought Edward is an unbearably stuffy English name.

"No, we can't call him Patrick," said Patrick. "It would be too confusing."

"But Edward is so stiff for a little boy!"

"We can call him Ned."

"Ned!" I was horrified. "Just like a donkey! Oh, Patrick, we can't!"

"I like it," said Patrick with that mulish expression I had come to know and dread, "and Neddy is the nickname for a donkey, not Ned. If you spoke English properly you'd know that."

"How can you say I don't speak English properly?" I exclaimed, amazed by his nerve, for he was always using the most dreadful slang, and my speech was far more proper than his was. Besides, to be frank, I have always thought the well-bred American accent is far more pleasant on the ears than the languid drawl of the London drawing rooms.

After this squabble Marguerite said to me in private, "Sarah, give way to Patrick absolutely with this child, and then you can do exactly as you wish with the next, can't you see?"

"If there ever is another baby," I said bitterly. I had not intended to say that, but I was feeling so cross at the prospect of Baby being called after a donkey that I let the words slip out.

"Of course there'll be another baby!" said Marguerite sharply. "Don't be foolish, Sarah. You've had this golden opportunity to make a fresh start in your marriage, and I can't believe you could be so shortsighted as to let the opportunity slip through your fingers."

That appealed to my pride, of course, and also her words put the silly squabble in its true perspective so that I felt ashamed. What did it truly matter what Baby was called? He was there—that was the important thing—and he was thriving, and he was without question the most beautiful baby in the world. All mothers say that about their babies, I know, but Ned really *was* the most beautiful baby. Everyone said so, not just me.

"Your luck's changed, Sarah," said Marguerite to me before she left Cashelmara for London in the new year. "I really believe all's going to be well between you and Patrick now, but whatever happens in future don't forget that there are three things you must never do. Never complain about the lack of money, never refer to past disasters, and never, never, *never*—"

"—mention the name Derry Stranahan," I said wearily, trying not to sound impatient. Four and a half years of marriage had at least taught me a little wisdom, and I had no intention of making the mistakes I had made when I was a bride of nineteen. "I know, Marguerite, I know. You've said all that to me before."

"Some things should be said more than once," said Marguerite, but she saw I was annoyed and added quickly, "Don't think I'm prejudiced. I've been just as stern to Patrick as I've been to you. In fact," she continued, smoothing a layer of praise over the unpalatable advice, "when I remember Patrick's neglect of you in the past, Sarah, it's a wonder you've remained faithful to him. You've behaved very well, and you've certainly earned the right to some happiness now."

I like to be praised. Certainly nothing would have been pleasanter for me than to have smiled warmly and murmured a gracious word of thanks, but her praise was misplaced and I knew it. So instead of smiling I blushed—and I seldom blush, for I've not the complexion for it—and muttered in embarrassment about ballroom flirtations in London.

"But you never went to bed with anyone, did you?" said Marguerite sharply, and that flash of coarseness stunned me so much that before I knew it I was telling her the truth. I had never told anyone the truth before, never. There are some subjects that are so unmentionable that it's difficult even to think of them, let alone put them into words.

"You never went to bed with anyone, did you?" said Marguerite, and I said, shuddering as I spoke, "Heavens, no! It's bad enough having to go to bed with Patrick! Why should I ever want to go to bed with anyone else?"

And as we stared at each other in the silence that followed I saw to my stupefaction that I had shocked her far more than she had shocked me.

II

I often wonder whether circumstances or heredity play the biggest part in making us what we are. I have always believed myself to be a victim of circumstances and that my life began to go wrong when I made an unfortunate marriage, but why did I make such a marriage in the first place? Because I was brought up to believe that the highest pinnacle of achievement for a girl consisted of marriage with a rich, young, good-looking aristocrat? Or was it because I was my father's daughter and placed too much emphasis on luxury? Or could it even—horrible thought!—have been because I was also my mother's daughter and always longed to please people by "doing the right thing"?

One fact at least is certain: Nothing in my childhood had prepared me for an unhappy marriage. Oh, I know I was extravagant and willful and spoiled half to death by a doting father—how clearly I can see that now! But I was loved. Loved too much, perhaps, cossetted to excess, protected from the harsher realities of the world by a gold-plated cocoon, but loved nonetheless, and for many years while I was growing up the thought that I might ever exist in a world where I was unloved simply never crossed my mind.

"Everyone is so happy in your family!" Patrick said to me wistfully when he first came to New York, and it was true. Papa and Mama were fond of each other; certainly they never quarreled in front of us, and although I found out years later from Charles that Papa had kept a mistress, I think it must have been an arrangement that suited not only Papa but Mama as well. Charles, two years my senior, was more studious and serious-minded than I was, but that was only fitting, since he was the son and heir and there was a certain responsibility on his shoulders. I thought that Charles was gorgeous and was utterly devoted to him. So was Mama. I suppose that was why Mama and I were so often at odds with each other when I was growing up, although since I was Papa's favorite it was only right that Charles should be hers.

However, to give credit where credit is due, I must admit that Mama suspected what no one else, least of all me, suspected—that marriage would turn out to be a rude shock for me. Mama always gave the impression of being lazy and stupid, but that was merely because she was fat. In fact she had plenty of common sense and was most industrious in her social activities, but she suffered from timidity and never quite had the strength to stand up against Papa and myself when we were at our most autocratic. But I knew she was worried about me before the wedding, because she steeled herself to talk about Unmentionable Matters, and that must have been a great ordeal for Mama, who was always the soul of propriety.

"I wish you weren't going so far away after you're married, dearest." I can hear her say that now. I can still see that anxious expression in her large brown eyes. "I do wish you were to be living in New York."

"I'll have Marguerite with me in London," I said impatiently, thinking she was making a great fuss about nothing. I had long since made up my mind that Patrick and I were going to live happily ever after, just as all the best people did, and I saw no need for Mama to be living within arm's reach of my home.

"But Marguerite is only eight years older than you are," Mama was saying, "and besides . . ." She and Marguerite had never been the best of friends, but of course she couldn't say this. ". . . besides, there are times when a girl needs her mother."

"Oh yes," I said, stifling a yawn. I was very missish, thinking I knew everything. "Well, you can come and visit us in London."

"Not for a while," said Mama. She was so sensible always, never permitting herself any illusions. "Your papa's always so busy, and anyway he dislikes Europe. In a few years, of course, we shall visit you, but then you'll be settled and won't need me so much."

"Mama, I'm sure I shall manage perfectly well! I can't see why you should be in such a fluster."

"Well, it's very hard for two people to live together, Sarah, and although Patrick's so kind and gentle he may seem very unkind to you at first." And she told me all about the Marriage Act—she spoke of it as if the initial letters were capitals—and as she spoke she became redder and redder, but she went right to the end almost without pausing for breath. Looking back, I can only admire her courage, but at the time I thought she was beastly to tell me so many horrible things, and when she had finished all I said was an insolent "Oh, I've known all that for years!" which was an absolute lie because, having been brought up in a gold-plated cocoon, I wouldn't have known that men differed from women below the waist if I hadn't seen Charles naked when we were very young. Even the classical statues in the mansions on Fifth Avenue always sported fig leaves in the right places.

I thought about the Marriage Act all the way through the wedding ceremony, and the more I thought of it the more convinced I became that I would like it—just to spite Mama, who had made it all seem so revolting. In fact by the time I left the church with Patrick I was very cheerful and had decided that the Marriage Act couldn't truly be so great an ordeal or no couple could possibly hope to live happily ever after.

I remember feeling angry with Mama for frightening me so much, and when the time came for me to leave the wedding breakfast my farewell kiss to her was cool.

Poor Papa was dreadfully affected by my leaving and wept, which upset me very much. I even began to wonder whether he was crying at the thought of me submitting to the Marriage Act, and that made me feel nervous again so that I resented his distress.

So by the time we reached Papa's summer mansion where Patrick and I were to spend the first weeks of our honeymoon, I felt both angry and resentful; I didn't even feel in the mood to kiss Patrick, and yet when he was too drunk to do more than sleep through the wedding night I felt just as angry with him as I had felt with Papa and Mama. Indeed when I look back the emotion I remember best from my entire married life is that anger which began on my wedding day, that dull, smoldering resentment I could neither explain nor understand, the feeling that somehow, somewhere along the way, I had been cheated and short-changed. Often I was unaware of the anger; sometimes it would erupt during a quarrel, but usually it was dormant, a small core of discontent ceaselessly eroding the walls of my elegant, gold-plated cocoon.

Needless to say, the Marriage Act was just as awful as Mama had warned me, only worse. At first I couldn't think how I was ever going to endure it, but fortunately Patrick seemed no more anxious for intimacy than I was, and so the Marriage Act became a monthly chore which we steeled ourselves to face because we both wanted children.

I am uncertain how long it was before I found out that not all women thought as I did. It was before we started mingling with the Marlborough House set, because I can remember that by then I barely raised an eyebrow at their activities. Perhaps my enlightenment came when we first settled in London and I met some young English wives who liked to gossip about other people's adulteries. I was very shocked to think such wickedness existed, for I had been protected from the New York decadence, and when I arrived in England in the late Sixties society was so arranged that immorality among the upper classes was heavily swathed in discretion. It was true that the Prince of Wales had already embarked on the career that was to make his set the fastest in Europe, but nonetheless the sobriety of the Queen and her court dominated the national morality so that at first I did not realize there was often a considerable gap between what many people said and what they actually did.

Of course I had instinctively known that no "good" woman could truly enjoy the Marriage Act. But it came as a shock to me to discover not only that some apparently "good" women chose to live

320

like courtesans but that genuinely "good" women either didn't mind the Marriage Act or else merely thought it "a bit of a bore."

That was when I first realized that there might be something wrong with me. Long before Patrick said to me in a rage that I was as sexless as a unicorn and an utter failure as a wife, I was as ashamed of my abnormality as a cripple would be ashamed of a deformity. My only consolation lay in the fact that no one knew about it except Patrick and Marguerite—and I was quite determined that no one else except those two people would ever know. This precluded all possible love affairs, and although I often met attractive men, the thought of watching their admiration turn to disillusioned disgust was so chilling that I had no difficulty in behaving coldly whenever the occasion demanded.

It never occurred to me that there might be other women who found it as hard as I did to be a dutiful wife. It never occurred to me that because no one boasts of failure there might be other women who concealed their troubles just as fanatically as I did. Thinking myself quite alone, I simply bore my cross as best as I could—and that wasn't easy, especially during my worst quarrels with Patrick. Everyone, even Marguerite, thought Patrick was kind and gentle twenty-four hours a day, but there was a darker side to his nature, particularly when he was drunk, and at such times he had a very violent temper and a very cruel tongue.

"You're such a damned hypocrite, Sarah!" I remember him saying once. "You beckon a man on and then when he's eager for you you turn into a lump of ice. There's a very vulgar word which describes a woman like you, but knowing your horror of vulgar language, I'll save it until you try to seduce me with kisses and then fly into hysterics as soon as I lift your skirt. Knowing you, I doubt if I'll have long to wait."

"Knowing you," I said, "and your reluctance to lift my skirt I'm sure we'll wait forever."

That exchange led to a fully-fledged quarrel until he called me the name he had in mind and several others besides. He was always very coarse when he was angry, and although I knew it was weak of me to be so sickened by rough language, I couldn't help myself. Any conversation relating to the Marriage Act made me feel physically ill.

After a scene like that I would usually make some excuse to sleep alone for a few days, but this in the end proved no solution to our troubles. It was hurtful to me when Patrick welcomed my suggestion, humiliating for me later when I was obliged to remind him that we both wanted children, nightmarish when in desperation I had to try to seduce him. Despair overwhelmed me not merely because I wanted a child but because I wanted Patrick himself—because I longed to end the loneliness that engulfed me whenever he turned his back—but as time passed and I found it increasingly hard to decide whether I was more unhappy with the Marriage Act than without it, I even began to wonder if I could scrape up enough courage to leave him.

But that would have been madness. A woman who leaves her husband has no place in society, no future. She is ruined, and although I knew I could bear the burden of a failed marriage in private, the idea of displaying that burden for all the world to see was unthinkable. Anything, I thought, anything at all would be better than that.

So I tried to keep myself very occupied in order to take my mind off my troubles. That was easy enough in London, where there were always so many people to see, but in the country . . . The very thought of country life filled me with dread.

"Your trouble," said Patrick, "is that you have no interests. In fact you're no damned good at anything except spending money, looking decorative and flirting behind potted palms."

He often made me cry, but I would always try not to cry in front of him. I would cry when I was alone, and I would cry especially when he said I was no good at anything because I knew it was true. Patrick was so much more artistic than I was that I shied away from painting and sketching, and although I did play the piano I had no gift for it. I did a little reading and a little sewing, a little of this and a little of that, but as Patrick had made all too clear, my accomplishments were no more than mediocre.

Yet I felt sure I was gifted at something, if only I could find out what it was. I thought about it a great deal, and gradually as one childless year succeeded another I came to realize that I wanted a baby not merely because it was expected of me but because I was sure I would have a talent for motherhood. I began to pray constantly for a baby. I had never been deeply religious before, being too much preoccupied with myself to take more than the conventional notice of God, but then I did become very religious, and by some extraordinary miracle my prayers were answered when Ned was born.

I knew as soon as I held him in my arms what my talent was. It wasn't simply motherhood. It was loving. I looked down at my son and loved him as passionately as I had loved my father and brother, and the one thought that remained with me long afterward was: If I could only meet a man whom I could love as I might have loved my husband, I would love him with such a passion that he could not help but love me a little in return.

III

After Ned was born Patrick and I made all sorts of vows and promises to each other to mark the mending of our marriage. These were preceded by confessions in which we admitted all our past faults and regretted them. No couple, I swear it, were ever more determined to reform than we were.

"I love you very much, Sarah," said Patrick, "and I'm going to turn over a new leaf now, I promise you."

I was moved enough to echo this promise, and settling down together harmoniously, we began to turn over our new leaves.

It took me some months to recover my health after Ned was born, but neither of us minded the excuse this gave us to sleep apart. However, eventually we no longer had an excuse to avoid each other at night, and as soon as the Marriage Act reared its ugly head again I realized that all the good intentions in the world could be useless when attempting to cure the incurable.

But I said nothing. I could at least pretend to reform, even though the pretense was hard, and besides I was older now, wiser. In the past I had complained too much, but that at least I could change. I had been sullen and bad-tempered also, the antithesis of a meek, submissive wife, but that I could change too. I wanted so much to live up to my promises, and because he was living up to his I felt I doubly owed it to him not to disappoint us both.

We fell into the habit of reserving one night a week, Friday, for the chore of marital intimacy. People might laugh at this, but for us it was easier to have this set habit because then we knew exactly where we were. We knew that on the other six nights of the week we could relax with each other, and this improved our relationship very much. On Friday, knowing what lay ahead, we could prepare ourselves accordingly. We would drink a great amount of wine at dinner, I drinking almost as much as he did, and then we would retire early to avoid enduring hours of suspense in the drawing room. The wine softened my pain and sometimes killed it altogether so that I could reach that much-longed-for state in which I could close my eyes, think of something else and not mind at all. When it was over relief would make us cheerful. We would lie in each other's arms and talk for a while of this and that, and I was really very happy then, convinced that it was better to live with the Marriage Act than without it and glad that we were both able to make the effort to be so intimate with each other.

In fact my worst difficulty after Ned was born was not in adjusting to my marital duties again but in resigning myself to living where I wanted to live least, amidst the numbing remoteness and stupefying isolation of Cashelmara. By this time I was prepared to tolerate living in the country; I had Ned to occupy my time, and I prided myself that I had passed beyond the stage of being a social butterfly who wilted when deprived of a daily diet of balls, evenings and dinner parties. I could have lived at Woodhammer Hall in Warwickshire—indeed I could have settled down anywhere in the English country-side and reconciled myself to our inability to afford to live in London. But Cashelmara. It was one of the few subjects on which Patrick and I were in complete agreement.

"I know this is a ghastly place," said Patrick when we were making our vows to reform, "but we simply must endure it for two or three years. Duneden and Cousin George have agreed to take over my financial affairs again now that Derry's dead, and they tell me that if only we can live quietly in Ireland for a while we'll eventually be able to afford to go back to Woodhammer. So if you could possibly be patient, darling . . . I hate to ask you, but . . ."

Of course I promised him that I would be patient.

But it was hard. I was uncertain what I detested most about Cashelmara, but it was probably the silence. At Woodhammer the countryside was full of small sounds ranging from birds singing to otters plopping into the river, from stoats rustling in the bushes to the distant sound of a railway engine on a clear day. But at Cashelmara there was nothing. There were woods planted around the house, but I seldom saw a bird and never once caught a glimpse of a wild animal. During the great hunger of the Forties all the wildlife had been killed for food, and although the animals were said to have returned they kept themselves well hidden. No sound came from the lough. The Fooey River glided noiselessly across the bog between sandy banks, and even the rain fell so softly that it never drummed against a window pane or spattered in a water butt.

I can still hear that silence. If anyone says silence is inaudible, they have never heard the silence at Cashelmara. It was a living silence, unearthly and unnerving, but I never mentioned to Patrick

324

how much it oppressed me. If he could endure Cashelmara without complaint, then I could too.

He had some extraordinary idea of making a garden out of the wilderness behind the house, and that spring he became quite eccentric about it, working all day at digging the earth, leveling the ground, cutting down trees and sometimes even transporting trees to other places. He employed four men to help him, but the Irish work for a pittance, so even his cousin George couldn't call this extravagant. George did call it odd, though, for Patrick to work alongside them as if he were a navvy, and I confess I found it not only odd but humiliating. However, again I said nothing. Patrick didn't criticize me for my absorption in Ned, so I didn't criticize him for his absorption in his garden. After all, both of us needed some diversion to make life at Cashelmara endurable.

In the summer Marguerite returned with her boys for a visit and was full of praise for Ned's progress.

"He's very acute," she said admiringly. "Anyone can see that."

"Marguerite says Ned is very 'cute," I said proudly to Patrick. Of course I had known this from the day he was born, but it was very pleasant to hear someone else admit it. And indeed Ned did look 'cute. He would sit up straight, and his eyes were very bright in his small shining face. He had blue eyes, fair hair and pink cheeks.

"The picture of health," said my sister-in-law Madeleine approvingly. Madeleine called on us every week from Clonareen, where she was in charge of the dispensary, and had been a great comfort to me in my confinement. I had been dreading having a baby in a place as remote as Cashelmara, but when Madeleine had assured me I would have no difficulty I was so impressed by her confidence that I became confident too. She had just persuaded a retired doctor from Dublin to come to Clonareen to help her. Dr. Townsend was well into his sixties, but it was impossible to persuade a younger man to settle in such a place, and I suspected that the only reason Dr. Townsend had come was that he had been too overwhelmed by the force of Madeleine's personality to refuse. She had met him during a visit to the Archbishop, and it was reported that Dr. Townsend had never been the same since.

"But Madeleine will never marry," said my other sister-in-law, Katherine, pityingly. "She's much too eccentric for that."

I liked Katherine. She had marvelous taste in clothes and always wore the most ambitious hair styles, which made me positively green with envy.

"The entire secret," said Katherine, "is to have a French maid, my dear. After that everything follows as night follows day."

I wondered how much it would cost to have a French maid but didn't dare ask. My own maid was a London girl, clever with her hands, conscientious but unimaginative. I often missed Lucy, the maid I had brought with me from America, but she had married soon after we had settled in England, and my wardrobe had suffered in consequence.

"I can't think what you see in Katherine," said Patrick. "But whatever it is I wish you wouldn't. She makes you discontented."

"No, she doesn't!" I protested, but it was true. Katherine, so beautiful, so elegant, living the life I would have liked to lead, political hostess, society matron, wife of an influential and respected peer. "I suspect I make Katherine discontented," I said defiantly to Patrick. "She has no child." And all the time I was thinking: Mustn't complain, mustn't nag, mustn't wish life was just a little more exciting and we could live anywhere in the world except Cashelmara.

Patrick's brothers liked Cashelmara, but for two growing boys it probably seemed an exciting place, with endless uncharted territory to explore beyond the boundary walls and the prospect of a different expedition each day. Marguerite gave them an unusual amount of freedom to do as they pleased, which everyone said was a very foreign way to bring up children, but I thought the results proved her justified, for the boys were well mannered without being dull and lively without being a nuisance. I did not care greatly for Thomas, who was a sharp-nosed, red-headed child with too high an opinion of himself, but David was delightful, full of imagination and a rambling old-fashioned charm. Presently he overcame his dismay at no longer being the baby of the family and even offered to take Ned for a walk in the perambulator.

"Silly!" said Thomas, who thought all babies far beneath his notice.

"Not at all," said David, who was twelve years old and often sounded at least sixty. "To push a perambulator in Patrick's garden requires great courage and considerable fortitude."

This, unfortunately, was all too true. Patrick had plowed up the lawn and was busy creating what he called an Azalea Walk that would link the lawn with the chapel. The mud, mess and destruction were so appalling that whenever I wheeled the perambulator I simply took Ned down the drive to the gates.

326

I spent so much time with Ned—too much time, his nanny probably thought, for I always wanted to help with his bath and dress him in his clothes and brush his hair with the little silver brush. Both Patrick and I were forever visiting the nursery, and I was never happier than when we were both sitting on the nursery floor with Ned amidst all his toys.

I wrote ecstatic letters to my family. "Darling Mama and Papa, everything is well here and we're all so happy . . ." and "Darling Mama and Papa, when are you coming to see us? I know I wasn't anxious for you to visit us when we had all our troubles, but those days are quite gone now . . ." and "Darling Mama and Papa, Patrick and I are so anxious that you should visit us at Cashelmara . . ."

It was in June when the black-edged letter came from America. It was addressed to Patrick, and Charles had asked him to break the news to me as gently as possible. Papa had died at the end of May after a short illness, and there would be no likelihood of Mama visiting Cashelmara for many months to come.

IV

I was so distressed that I wanted to rush back at once to New York, but Patrick and Madeleine both pointed out that since Papa had already been buried by the time the letter reached Cashelmara it was too late to think of attending the funeral.

"Besides," said Madeleine practically, "imagine a long sea voyage with an infant!"

"We could leave Ned here, of course," said Patrick doubtfully.

"Oh, I couldn't bear to leave him behind!" I cried and burst into a torrent of fresh weeping at the thought of it.

Marguerite fortunately was at Cashelmara. It was a comfort to me to be able to talk about Papa to someone who had loved him as much as I had, and presently when I felt better I wrote to Mama and Charles to explain that it was impossible for me to face the long sea voyage at that time. I also begged Mama to reconsider her decision not to visit Cashelmara, but she wrote back explaining that her own health was so indifferent that her doctor had forbidden her to travel. As for Charles, he was so involved with business matters that it would be a long time before he could leave New York. Papa's fortune had suffered severely during the Wall Street crisis of '73, and his failing health had hindered his attempts to reconstruct his financial affairs before his death.

Because of these misfortunes I hardly expected to receive a large legacy—or indeed any legacy at all—but despite all his troubles poor dearest Papa had still managed to scrape together fifty thousand dollars for me. Considering Papa had spent most of his life being a millionaire, this sum was hardly a fortune, but to us, crushed by debt as we were, the legacy seemed enormous, and we were both immensely cheered. Patrick did say with reluctance, "I suppose we should put all the money toward paying off our debts," but I wouldn't have it. After all, Papa had intended the money for me to spend as I pleased, and although I was willing to contribute to paying our debts I didn't see why the debts should swallow every penny of the legacy.

"But, Patrick, just think!" I said, giddy as a starving man at the sight of a feast. "Fifty thousand dollars! Surely can't we spare a little of it to have a month or two in London?"

"And Woodhammer," said Patrick longingly. "We could pay off the second mortgage, open the house again—"

"Entertain," I said. I was already buying ball gowns and engaging a French maid. "Oh, Patrick, just a month in London before we go down to Woodhammer!"

"Well, of course you can have your month in London!" he said, kissing me. "You've been so wonderful, Sarah, these last few months. A month in London is the least you deserve."

I wept for joy. We kissed again, very passionately this time, and afterward so intoxicated were we by the prospect of escaping from Cashelmara that we whirled in waltztime around the drawing room as Patrick sang "The Blue Danube" at the top of his voice.

v

Need I describe what happened in London? Shouldn't it have been perfectly obvious to us that despite all our vows and promises London was a place in which neither of us could be trusted?

"Oh, but everything's quite different now," I said to Marguerite when she tentatively dropped a word of warning. "We're both so much wiser than we used to be."

Yes, I really said that. I went to London, beautiful, exciting, feverish London, with its overwhelming, unending brilliance, and I really believed I knew better than to be extravagant. I believed it even when I began to buy new clothes, because surely in the circumstances new clothes were justified after those long dreary months of penny-pinching at Cashelmara. Didn't I deserve a reward for all those occasions when I had never complained? So I ordered gowns, gorgeous gowns lavishly trimmed with flounces and puffings and flowers, and day dresses in satin and Jap silk, designed in two shades of the same color, apple green and moss green, pastel blue and sulky blue. Oh, they were so luscious! I ordered a shawl mantle and a three-decker cape and three sealskin jackets. No, I can't explain why I bought three except that they were all a little different and all so ravishingly beautiful, and wearing any one of them made me feel very special and happy. Then I bought muffs to match and three pairs of long kid gloves and a Dolly Varden hat with "follow-me-lads" streamers and ten pairs of high-heeled shoes. By this time my old underclothes seemed desperately shabby, and I couldn't rest until I had an entirely new supply of petticoats and silk stockings. And then there were the little lace caps, the chemisettes, the fichus and the berthas—all so lovely and all making me feel like a queen. And Patrick, dearest Patrick, gave me jewelry because he said he was so proud of me: He gave me a long emerald necklace, and of course it was so stunning that I simply had to buy earrings to match. All our friends were so glad to see us again, and everywhere we went people said what a handsome couple we were and how glad they were to find us both so happy.

"Oh, Patrick!" I said as the allotted month in London neared its end. "How can we ever endure to return to Cashelmara when the time comes?"

Yes, I said that. It was dreadful, but I said it. And I said more too, words I'm too ashamed to repeat about how I hated pinching pennies and hated living in the country and I could never be truly happy unless I was living in town.

That night Patrick slipped out of our rented townhouse after I had gone to bed. He did that every night for five days, and I knew nothing about it until one morning I went downstairs to breakfast and discovered he was missing.

He returned at two o'clock that afternoon. By that time I was frantic with worry and on the verge of summoning the police, but pride alone stopped me. I thought the police would at once assume they were dealing with one more unfaithful husband and his hysterical wife, but I was convinced Patrick hadn't been unfaithful, just as I was convinced he hadn't been gambling. Infidelity was hardly a vice of his, and as for gambling—hadn't he promised to reform?

He came back very quietly, his face gray with exhaustion, his eyes bloodshot, the reek of brandy clinging to him like an invisible coat of armor. He looked at me as I rushed down the stairs, but he did not speak.

"Where have you been?" I demanded, distraught, glancing over my shoulder to make sure the footman was no longer in earshot. "How dare you stay out all night! I've been worried half to death!"

He did not answer but moved past me up the stairs.

"Patrick!" I grabbed his shoulder and shook it. I was still more angry than frightened, and when he wrenched himself loose so roughly that I nearly fell downstairs I lost my temper. "Stop it!" I cried. "What's the matter with you? Stop it at once!"

"Be quiet!" He was upstairs by this time, and when I ran after him he dragged me into the drawing room and slammed the door. Then he started cursing. He said that I was spoiled and rotten, that all our troubles were my fault.

"You drove me to it!" he shouted at me in the voice he used only when he was very drunk. "Breaking all your promises not to be extravagant, making such a fuss, complaining about Cashelmara! You drove me to it!"

"To what?" I screamed at him, but I already knew. My anger vanished. I was terrified.

"To winning back all the money you've spent!" he yelled back at me, and even before he launched into his long rambling explanation I knew that he had lost all we had and far more besides.

He talked and talked. He relived every hour of his past five nights of gambling. He explained how he had won and how he had very nearly won and how he had almost won and how he would have won "if only."

"And it's your fault," he repeated again when there was nothing left to say. He was crying. His face was crumpled with grief, and huge tears blurred his eyes so that he looked blind. "It's all your fault."

I opened my mouth to deny it, but the words were never spoken. Denials were no use. I wanted to hurl abuse at him, but that would have served no purpose either. As I stared at him in silence I knew only that we were back again on the razor's edge of disaster and that my entire future depended on what I said next.

I thought of Ned and the other children I wanted, and finally my pride too came to the rescue, reminding me of the bitter humiliation of having to admit to the world that my marriage had ended. I thought of nineteen-year-old Sarah Marriott marrying her rich, titled, handsome young Englishman, the splendor of that social success, the glory of being the bride of the season, the heady prospects awaiting in a dazzling future. I can't bear to fail, I thought fiercely, I won't.

"Patrick," I said, "let's not talk about it any more at present. You look dreadfully tired. Why don't you sleep for a while? You'll feel better once you've had some rest, and then we can talk about everything calmly and decide what we must do." And making an enormous effort, I sat down on the arm of his chair and kissed him on the forehead.

His response was so pathetically grateful that I was appalled. He clung to me, saying he despised himself, he was no good, he had always known he was no good, he had always been stupid and foolish, failing at everything he undertook.

"That's silly talk," I said, trying not to sound as chilled as I felt by this outburst of self-pity. "Think of all your gifts. Think of Ned. How can you be a failure when you have a son like Ned?"

He said he didn't deserve Ned, didn't deserve me, we were too good for him.

I did feel sorry for him, but I was still repelled by his abject humility. I had to remind myself forcibly that he had given me a child, which I had wanted more than anything, and that he really was a kind, gentle and affectionate husband. Plenty of women would have envied me. But then all those dreadful thoughts began to run through my head again—supposing I leave him; no, I can't, I'd be ruined; supposing I reconciled myself to ruin; no, I can't, because if I left him I would have to give up Ned; there's nothing more despicable than a deserting wife, all the judges say so; remember that case in the paper only the other day.

"I do love you, Sarah," said Patrick, still crying like a little boy, and after a pause I said, "I love you too." I didn't know by this time whether that was true or not, but I thought it ought to be true if I were to stand by him. "You must go to bed now, Patrick," I repeated. "You must get some rest," and while I spoke I was thinking, I'm trapped. There's no way out. None.

He was docile as a child as I led him to bed, and presently after his valet had been summoned I returned to the drawing room. Rain was falling. The tree in the tiny garden was lushly green. For a long time

I stood watching by the window, and as I stared the anger began to burn in me again, and my nails dug like pins into the cold palms of my hands.

VI

He had to sell Woodhammer Hall. It was already mortgaged so heavily that no further mortgages were possible, and his cousin George, Katherine's husband Lord Duneden and Rathbone the family attorney all agreed that Woodhammer must go.

We were back at Cashelmara by this time, but Patrick returned to England to take one last look at the home where he had spent his early years. No one would give him the money for the journey, but he pawned some silver. He was away two weeks, and I was just beginning to worry when he reappeared. He looked ill, and his clothes were in a dreadful state because he had not been able to afford to take his valet.

"What were you doing all this time?" I said sharply and added with dread, "Did you gamble again?"

"No, I only stayed at Woodhammer," he said. "I didn't go to London." He produced some sketches. There were twenty-four of them, all of Woodhammer, and at least six were devoted to the intricate carved staircase in the great hall. "My staircase," he said, and I quickly made some excuse to leave the room before he could start to weep again. It was not that I was unsympathetic, for I knew how fond he had been of Woodhammer, but being too close to tears too often myself those days, I needed someone I could lean upon, not someone who would lean upon me.

The days passed.

It was so quiet at Cashelmara.

Patrick devoted himself to his garden with a new intensity and seldom left the grounds, while I made an effort to organize my own life into some form of time-consuming routine. I paid calls scrupulously, took the carriage to Aasleagh, Leenane and Clonbur, and in return I received calls from the Plunkets, the Knoxes and the Courtneys. Conversation consisted of children, the Protestant church and what could be done for the poor. Patrick flatly refused to see anyone, so there was no question of giving dinner parties even if I had been tempted to do so. I saw little of Patrick myself. Our intimacies on Fridays had ceased, he often missed meals, and the place where I was most likely to see him was the nursery. It seemed that Ned was the only person he still wanted to see.

I wrote more often to Charles and Mama in America. I wrote to Marguerite in London. I even began to write a journal, something I'd vowed I would never do, but it's amazing what one tries when one is desperate to be occupied. I knew matters would improve when Ned was older, but at that time he still slept in the morning and afternoon and was always in bed by half past six.

And all the while there was that silence, the endless numbing silence from which there was no escape, no release.

I must occupy myself, I said over and over again. Must keep busy. Must fill up all those empty hours or I shall go mad.

One day I walked to the chapel along the new Azalea Walk, not because I wanted to pray but because I had nothing else to do, and halfway along the walk I felt as if I were suffocating. The silence seemed to crush me in pounding waves until in a panic I tried to scream at the top of my voice, but no sound came. This terrified me. I thought I really was going mad, so I ran all the way back to the house and ordered the carriage to the door. I thought that the doctor who helped Madeleine could prescribe me some soothing medicine, but when I reached the dispensary I found he had gone to Letterturk to collect some medical supplies due to arrive that day from Dublin.

"But what a delightful surprise to see you, Sarah!" purred Madeleine before I had a chance to explain my troubles. As soon as she had seen me she had assumed my visit to be a charitable gesture. "I always hoped you would come to us one day. Would you care to have some tea in my office before you inspect the ward?"

I was in such a state that I was quite unable to tell her that illness still repulsed me as much as it ever had and that I had no intention of visiting the sick in order to pass the time. I merely followed her into her office, a tiny room no bigger than a pantry, and sank down on a wooden chair as she called to one of the village girls to make tea.

"I would have brought some flowers," I said faintly, "but the garden . . ."

"You brought yourself," said Madeleine. "That's much more important." She shifted some papers on the little table and removed a basket of eggs from the other wooden chair. "You chose a splendid time to come. I've just finished with the last patient in the dispensary and was about to write a letter to the Archbishop before I looked at the ward."

"I hope—I mean, there's nothing infectious, is there? I have to think of Ned."

"Of course. No, there's nothing of that nature. We have only nine beds, you know, so we only take the patients who are dying and have no families to tend them. At the moment we have one malignant growth, two liver disorders and the rest are starvation cases which have gone too far to be cured. We did have three consumptives, but they're gone now, God rest their souls." She was just crossing herself absent-mindedly when there was a knock on the door. "Come in!" she called at once.

A young woman came into the room. She was older than I was but perhaps still less than thirty. Her neat black dress and gentility of manner led me to assume that Madeleine had imported her, like Dr. Townsend, from Dublin.

"Here's your tea, Miss de Salis," she said to Madeleine with a smile.

"Ah yes, thank you so much. Sarah, allow me to present to you one of my most devoted and valuable volunteers, Mrs. Maxwell Drummond. Mrs. Drummond, this is my sister-in-law, Lady de Salis."

I recognized the name Maxwell Drummond but was at a loss to imagine how this well-spoken, well-mannered young woman could have married a rogue who, according to Patrick, was not only the chief troublemaker in the valley but also the man responsible for Derry Stranahan's murder.

"How do you do, Mrs. Drummond," I said, trying not to look too amazed.

"Well, my lady, I thank you," she said civilly, dropping me a small curtsy, but I noticed she did not look at me when she spoke.

"Mrs. Drummond's youngest child is the same age as Ned," said Madeleine, taking no notice of either my confusion or Mrs. Drummond's embarrassment. "Stay and have some tea with us, Mrs. Drummond. There's a stool behind the bag of meal in the corner."

"I wouldn't wish to intrude, Miss de Salis."

"You wouldn't be intruding," said Madeleine in her sweetest, mildest voice. "You would be refusing an invitation."

Mrs. Drummond had evidently worked long enough for Madeleine to recognize an order when she heard it.

"That's very kind of you, Miss de Salis," she said. "I'll just be fetching another cup for myself."

"Of course," said Madeleine benignly, watching her as she left the room. As soon as we were alone she said to me, "I feel so sorry for

334

that girl, Sarah. She is, as you can see, educated and refined—
actually a Dublin schoolmaster's daughter—but she made the ghastly
mistake of running off with Drummond, and—do you know
Drummond?"

"Good heavens, no! Patrick wouldn't allow me within a mile of
him!"

"Well, he's very uncouth—that would perhaps be the kindest way
of describing him. And immoral," said Madeleine, pursing her small
mouth. "However, it's not for me to judge him—I leave that to
God—but at least I've been able to help that poor girl by providing
her with an interest and a little companionship. Fortunately her
husband's two maiden aunts live at the farm, so she has help in
minding the children and can spare a few hours each week to help me
here at the dispensary. She told me just the other day how much she
enjoyed . . ." Mrs. Drummond's footsteps sounded outside. By the
time the door opened Madeleine was already inquiring after Ned's
health.

I looked at Mrs. Drummond with fresh eyes and thought how
fortunate I was. When I remembered that Cashelmara was a fine
house, even if it was lonely, and that Patrick had always been faithful, I felt ashamed of myself for making such heavy weather of our
recent misfortunes.

"How many children do you have, Mrs. Drummond?" I asked,
anxious to be friendly toward her.

"Six living, my lady, thanks be to God, four girls and two boys."

"And your youngest—the one who's the same age as my baby?"

"That's Denis, my lady. He was born last December."

We discovered that Ned and Denis had been born within three
days of each other, and a fascinating conversation followed as we
compared notes on our infants' progress. Madeleine, to her great
credit, appeared to find the conversation just as fascinating as we did.
It was only after we had all drunk two cups of tea that she suggested
it was time at last to inspect the ward, but by then I was in such a
cheerful frame of mind that I would have inspected anything without
complaint.

"I do hope you'll be calling here again before long, Lady de Salis,"
said Mrs. Drummond after I had smiled at each of the nine patients
and wished them well.

"But of course I will!" I said at once and turned to Madeleine in
time to see her satisfied expression.

335

Before any of us could say more, Dr. Townsend arrived from Letterturk, and Mrs. Drummond retreated to the kitchen to supervise the preparation of the midday soup.

"You'll do us the honor of lunching with us, I hope, Lady de Salis," said Dr. Townsend, who was lean and spry and looked nearer fifty than seventy, but I thought of Ned having lunch in the nursery and said that unfortunately I was unable to stay. I was about to take my leave of them when there was a crisis in the ward nearby. A patient shrieked for help, and when Madeleine and Dr. Townsend rushed to the rescue I was left alone in the hall.

The hall was large, since it served also as the waiting room for those who came to the dispensary, and bare save for the rows of stools placed against every whitewashed wall. I was standing at the end farthest from the front door, but as I waited for Madeleine I began to move slowly around the room, pausing only to read the religious texts which hung on the walls between pictures of the Virgin and Child. I was just wondering how many of the Irish could read and how many of the ones who could read would appreciate such sentiments as "Blessed Are the Poor" when there was an interruption. At the other end of the hall the front door burst open, and a gust of clammy air made me draw my cape more tightly around my shoulders as I waited for the door to close.

But the door stayed open. A man was in the hall, his back to the light. He wore filthy trousers, muddy boots and a smelly jacket.

Mrs. Drummond's voice exclaimed behind me, "Max! What brings you here? Is something wrong at home?"

And as she darted forward he slammed the door, cutting off the light behind him, and I looked for the first time upon the face of my husband's enemy, Maxwell Drummond.

336

Chapter Two

I

He was tall, but his shoulders were broad enough to make him appear shorter than he was. He had long untidy hair, very dark, sideburns that needed trimming and a clean-shaven chin and upper lip. His eyes were even darker than his hair.

"Max . . ." Mrs. Drummond was blushing, deeply embarrassed by my presence. She groped for the appropriate phrases of introduction. "Lady de Salis . . . my husband . . . Max, this is . . ."

"Well, to be sure it is," he said. "Haven't you just said so? Good afternoon, my lady. Eileen, you'd best come home. Sally's twisted her ankle and it's defeating even Aunt Bridgie's favorite poultice."

"I'll come at once." Mrs. Drummond looked distraught as well as confused. "I must fetch my shawl and tell Miss de Salis I'm leaving. Shall I ask Dr. Townsend to come with us?"

"Jesus, no! Sally wants her mother, not a doctor!"

"I only thought—"

"Where's your shawl?"

Mrs. Drummond withdrew without another word, but I saw her bite her lip as if it were an effort for her to keep silent. She did not look at me. When she was gone I began to draw on one of my gloves.

There was a silence. He was watching me. My other glove slipped from my fingers and fell to the floor, but although I waited for him to pick it up he did not move. I was going to pick it up myself when I glanced at him first.

His nose looked as if it had been broken more than once in the past, and his jaw was very square.

I remembered the glove. It was still on the floor. I looked at it as if it presented some insoluble puzzle and felt the color, hot and moist, creep up my neck toward my face.

And I never blush. I've not the complexion for it.

He went on watching me.

I turned, walked briskly to the ward. "Madeleine!" I called. "Madeleine, are you there?"

Madeleine was still stooped over the patient. "One moment, Sarah, if you please," she said, not looking up, so I moved slowly back into the hall again.

He was still waiting there, and my glove still lay like a question mark upon the floor.

I retrieved the glove, drew it on. What was Mrs. Drummond doing? Why didn't she come back with her shawl? Moving to the nearest religious text, I began to read it, but suddenly I was gripped by a compulsion to look over my shoulder.

He smiled at me.

"Oh, Max, I'm so sorry to be keeping you waiting . . ." Mrs. Drummond was rushing back into the room, but I scarcely saw her. She was talking, but her words made no sense to me.

He left. Mrs. Drummond said goodbye to me and I think I said goodbye to her. When they were gone I waited for a minute in the empty hall, and then I went outside without saying goodbye to Madeleine and told the coachman to drive me home to Cashelmara.

II

All the way home I told myself: I won't think about it any more. But when I did think about it I told myself: It was nothing. I remembered all the men who had smiled at me in the past, and when I lost count I shrugged my shoulders and tried to think of something else.

On arriving home, I felt so hot and sticky that I decided to have a bath. To have a bath in the middle of the day at Cashelmara was like asking for an earthquake, but eventually at three o'clock the bath had been filled with hot water and I was washing myself scrupulously with the last bar of the expensive soap I had bought in London. It was only later when my maid was helping me into my tea gown that

I remembered not only that I had had no lunch but that I had missed having lunch with Ned in the nursery.

I had tea with him instead, and presently Patrick came in from the garden to give Ned rides on his back across the nursery floor. I was just watching them contentedly when the thought slipped into my head: I wonder when I'll see him again. And the thought with all its implications disturbed me so much that I had to scoop Ned off Patrick's back and squeeze him very tightly to blot the memory of Drummond from my mind.

After dinner that night I said to Patrick, "I'd so like another baby. Do you suppose . . . perhaps . . ."

So we resumed our Friday nights together, but no baby came, and at last, unable to face the Marriage Act any longer without a respite, I asked if we could suspend the Friday ritual for a month. I said I hadn't been feeling well, and he said he was sorry to hear that and he did hope I would feel better soon.

It was impossible for him to disguise entirely the enormity of his relief.

Meanwhile I visited the dispensary once a week, but I never saw Drummond again, although I found myself becoming well acquainted with his wife. In early December I even called on her with a little present for Denis, but word quickly traveled to Cashelmara that Lady de Salis had visited the Drummond farm, and Patrick was so angry that I realized the visit had been a mistake. Fortunately Marguerite and the boys spent Christmas with us, so we were obliged to patch up the quarrel, but the awkwardness lingered and we continued to sleep in separate rooms.

Spring came, summer passed and never once during all my weekly visits to Clonareen did I set eyes on Maxwell Drummond. The memory of him had become blurred in my mind, but always when I went to Clonareen I was filled with an anticipation I acknowledged but made no attempt to dwell upon, and the anticipation made tolerable the emptiness of life at Cashelmara, the stifling boredom of embroidering sheets for the dispensary, paying calls, writing a page a day in my journal and struggling unsuccessfully to take an interest in household affairs.

I had another blow in the fall when I heard from Charles that Mama had died. I had not realized until then how much I had been counting on her to visit me as soon as her health had recovered, and the news of her death plunged me into the lowest of spirits. I wrote to

339

Charles, begging him to visit Ireland, and was bitterly disappointed when he again said that it was quite impossible for him to leave his business interests at that time. Crisis after crisis continued to rock Wall Street, and years later I learned from Charles that when Mama died he had been on the verge of bankruptcy. He did suggest that Patrick and I should visit New York instead, but of course we were even closer to penury than he was, and I was too proud to tell my brother that we couldn't afford to cross the Atlantic to see him.

Winter came again and with it Ned's second birthday. We had a little party for him. Cook's children came and Hayes's granddaughters, and there was a luscious sponge cake crowned with butter frosting and two blue candles. Patrick had made Ned a rocking horse, and the nursery reverberated with Ned's squeals of delight as he rocked himself to and fro.

It was on Christmas Eve that I took two hampers of food to Clonareen, and after leaving the first for the sick at the dispensary I called on the parish priest to leave the second for the poor. Madeleine did not think highly of the priest and said he was uneducated, superstitious and no better than the peasants of his flock, but I thought he was delightful, far superior to the sullen villagers who watched my carriage pass through Clonareen every week to the dispensary. He was passionately interested in America, and on the few occasions when we had met he had asked me all manner of questions about New York.

"I've brought some food, Father Donal," I called to him as he came out of his cottage to meet me. "Perhaps you would be kind enough to distribute it among the poor tomorrow."

"God save you, my lady!" he said with great chivalry, helping the coachman lift the hamper down from the box. "May all the saints in heaven smile down upon you in your charity." Having dispensed with the gratitude, he then asked me if I would do him the honor of stepping across his threshold for a sip of tea.

I had never been into his home before. Our previous meetings had all taken place at the dispensary, but I saw no reason why Patrick should object to my being polite to the local priest, and Madeleine would surely have approved, despite her low opinion of Father Donal's capabilities. So I descended from the carriage and allowed myself to be ushered across the threshold of a poky little cabin that smelled of soot and turf and various other odors I thought it wiser nòt to try to identify. I wanted to produce my lavender-scented handkerchief but had no wish to give offense. Father Donal led me to the best chair in front of the hearth, and I sat down gingerly on the hard wooden seat. Thoughts of lice and fleas flitted through my mind as Father Donal's housekeeper, after curtsying to me at least four times, pushed two smelly dogs away from my feet and placed a pot of water to boil above the fire.

Father Donal was already talking about New York. A hen, which had been nesting in a niche on the wall, laid an egg.

"Praise God!" exclaimed the housekeeper, crossing herself. "And she broody these past two days!"

"And is it really the truth, my lady," said Father Donal, "that the Lady Chapel of St. Patrick's is decked in cloth of gold and jewels the size of hen's eggs?"

There was a knock on the door.

"I'm not in, Kitty," said Father Donal, "unless someone's dying, and if it's already dead he is, tell him I'll come later."

"Faith, Father," said Drummond, opening the door before Kitty could reach it. "That's a fine welcome to give an old friend."

His glance swept the room. When he saw me I managed to incline my head to acknowledge him.

"As you can see, Max," said Father Donal reprovingly, "it's distinguished company I'm keeping at present."

"Yes. So I see. Good day, Lady de Salis," he said, still standing on the threshold.

I tried to say "good day" in return but could not. I felt very sick. I even wondered if I was going to faint.

"Didn't you see my lady's carriage at the door?" Father Donal was saying crossly.

"I saw it," he said. He turned aside. "I'll come back later."

"If there's something urgent . . ." called Father Donal, his conscience pricking him.

"It was nothing," said Drummond. "Nothing at all."

He was gone. The door closed. It was over.

"I've never seen Max so strange!" said Kitty, making the tea.

"Ah, Max never had any manners nor ever will," said Father Donal tartly. "I must be begging your pardon, my lady. I hope you'll not complain to your husband that you met Maxwell Drummond beneath my roof."

"Of course not," I said. The sickness had passed, but it was still difficult to breathe evenly. Fortunately Father Donal began to talk about St. Patrick's again, and by concentrating hard I managed to say yes and no in the right places. The tea helped. By the time my cup was empty I knew I would be able to stand without feeling dizzy.

"God go with you, my lady," said Father Donal, escorting me outside to the carriage. "A merry Christmas to you and Lord de Salis and the honorable Master Patrick Edward."

"Thank you," I said, knowing my Christmas was already ruined, and all the way to Cashelmara I wondered how close I was to madness by being so affected by the sight of a man I hardly knew.

III

I drank a large amount of wine at dinner that night, and afterward, feeling drowsy, I retired for an early night.

I had a dream. Drummond was in it, but he was a long way away. He was weeding a potato patch in a field by the lough. Then Patrick came and showed me some flowers from the garden. They were beautiful. "It's Friday," he said. "Had you forgotten?" So we went upstairs to bed. The candle went out just as I slipped between the sheets, and I was smitten with such terror that I cried out. A match flared, the candle was lit again—but I dared not open my eyes for fear whose face I would see above me. "Only Patrick," I said, "no one else but Patrick, because no one else must ever know." But I knew Patrick wasn't in bed with me any longer, because he had gone to his separate room. "No!" I screamed, my eyes still shut. "No!" But I was too late. Someone was laughing, mocking me for my failure, blaring my defects to the world.

"No, no, no!" I screamed again and woke on the verge of hysteria. I scrabbled for a match to light the candle, and all the time I was shouting for Patrick. At last he emerged from the adjoining room, and as the match flared in the darkness I could see he was tousle-haired, yawning and bewildered.

"My dear Sarah, what on earth's the matter?" he demanded, but when I sobbed that I had had a fearful nightmare he said "There, there!" very kindly and took me in his arms. "What was it about?"

"Nothing. I don't remember." My body was still trembling. "Patrick . . ."

"Hm?" he said, stifling another yawn.

"I must have another baby. Please."

"Why not? It'd be awfully jolly. I don't know why you have to sound as if I'd strictly forbidden it. After all, it wasn't me, you know, who begged for a separate bedroom a few weeks ago."

342

"Yes, I know. I was at fault, but—"

"Yes, you were. Well, never mind. We'll try again if you like. We'll go back to our Fridays."

"But, Patrick . . ."

"Now what's the matter?"

"I thought . . . well, must we wait till Friday? Can't we . . . isn't it possible to—to begin tonight?"

"For God's sake, at this hour? With you on the verge of hysterics and me half asleep?"

I saw at once I was being unreasonable, but tears still pricked humiliatingly behind my eyelids. "I'm sorry," I said. I tried to speak levelly and made a great effort to compose myself. "I simply didn't think. Forgive me."

"Of course." He kissed me with great tenderness. "I'll stay with you for the rest of the night," he said, slipping into bed beside me. "Then you won't be too frightened to blow out the light. Nightmares are beastly things, ain't they?"

He was asleep almost as soon as his head touched the pillow, but I lay awake for the rest of the night, and when dawn came I was still remembering how Maxwell Drummond had looked around the room for me when he had opened the door of Father Donal's cabin in Clonareen.

IV

I thought of Drummond for months afterward, all those long dreary months when I never became pregnant, the first nine months of 1876. I saw him twice during that time, once in May when I glimpsed him in the distance heading for Letterturk and once later that summer when I glanced out of the window of the dispensary and saw him pass by in his donkey cart. I allowed myself to invent elaborate fantasies. At first I merely pictured meeting him and having a long polite conversation. The meeting place would be at the dispensary or in the main street of Clonareen or even by his farm, which stood above the road to Cashelmara. Then gradually the fantasies changed. The meeting place would be in some wild remote mountain fastness—a ruined cabin, perhaps. We would still talk politely, but now our conversation would be on a less formal level. I imagined him taking my hand in his and holding it while he looked searchingly into my eyes. Wasn't that what always happened in the romantic novels that Marguerite lent me whenever she came to stay? The pastoral retreat, the clasped hands, the promise of undying devotion . . . It would be a Hopeless Love, of course, and Nothing Could Come of It. We would part for the last time and he would kiss me, perhaps briefly on the lips but more likely lingeringly on the brow. Heroines were always having their brows kissed. There was something very comforting about that. No sweaty embraces, no naked indignities, no stabbing pain. I waded deeper and deeper into my fantasies.

I thought I would change in the autumn when I discovered I was pregnant, but the daydreams lingered on. All winter I was confined to Cashelmara; all winter I dreamed of Drummond, until at last in the spring my second son was born to save me from the torment of Drummond's constant presence in my mind.

We didn't think the baby would live. He was so small and frail that he had no strength to suck milk, and after he was born he lost so much weight that he was no more than a tiny pile of skin and bones. I heard the midwife say to Madeleine, "It's often better if they die," and this upset me so much that I flew into a rage and banished the woman from the house. I was determined that he would live. I devoted all my time and energy to him, and in the months that followed there was certainly no time to moon after Drummond.

The servants reminded one another that Patrick and I were cousins—distant cousins, but no one bothered to remember the distance—and said that between cousins the blood often runs thin. All those old wives' tales, all that ghoulish enjoyment of impending tragedy, all those whispers whenever my back was turned—I hated them all.

We called him John. I had wanted to call him Francis, but in the beginning when it seemed inevitable that he would die I decided to save my father's name for a son who was as healthy as Ned, and John was one of the few names that both Patrick and I found unobjectionable.

But John didn't die. He drank more and more milk from the tiny silver spoon that could slip into his mouth and soon he was strong enough to suck from a bottle. One day he smiled at me, and then nothing mattered, neither Cashelmara nor all our misfortunes, because my baby was thriving at last and everyone, from Nanny to the scullery maid, said that it was all due to me that he had lived.

"When will the baby be big enough to play with me?" demanded Ned on his fourth birthday in December.

"In a while," I said, hugging him. I felt guilty because during

344

those anxious months I had been too preoccupied with John to give Ned my usual attention. "Next spring he'll start to walk and then he'll be much easier to play with."

But John was late in walking, and by the time spring came he could barely sit up. His health was still delicate, and I was plunged into anxiety every time he sneezed. But he was a lovely baby. He was dark-haired and fine-boned and his eyes were an unusual shape.

"He may not grow up quite as other children do, you know, Sarah," said Madeleine to me when John still showed no signs of walking.

"Of course he will!" I said angrily. I felt hurt that she should make such a comment just because John wasn't as quick as Ned had been at that age. "All he needs is enough love and care and attention."

Madeleine never mentioned the subject to me again, but Marguerite, when she came for her summer visit with the boys, was most reassuring.

"Oh heavens!" she said. "David was so fat when he was John's age that I thought he'd never do anything except sit on the floor, but look at him now!" So I looked at David, who was sixteen by this time, still a little stout but undeniably mobile, and felt much happier.

It was in September, when Marguerite was still at Cashelmara, that we received word from Duneden Castle that Katherine was ill with a lung inflammation and had asked to see us.

"I'm not going unless she's dying," said Patrick firmly. He could barely endure to be in the same room for longer than five minutes with Katherine's husband. "I'll stay behind with the children if you want to go with Marguerite and the boys."

"I'm taking the children with me," I said at once.

"Oh no, you're not! John's not strong enough to travel, and Ned would be bored to tears at Duneden Castle. Damn it, Sarah, why do you always try to keep the children to yourself the whole time? They're my children as well as yours, you know! You couldn't have had them without me!"

"More's the pity," I said before I could stop myself, and the next moment we were having our worst quarrel in months. As usual it was Marguerite who suggested the appropriate compromise: John stayed behind with Nanny at Cashelmara, while Patrick and Ned came with me to Duneden Castle. "For after all, Patrick," said Marguerite sternly, "it would really look very poor if you didn't come, and

Katherine would hardly have asked to see us if she hadn't felt very ill indeed."

Patrick conceded gloomily that she was right, so we made our preparations to leave as quickly as possible. But we weren't quick enough. By the time we reached Duneden Castle a distraught Lord Duneden told us that Katherine was sinking fast, and within three hours of our arrival she was dead at the age of thirty-eight.

V

"Oh Lord," said Patrick glumly after we had begun to recover from the shock, "now I'm really in the soup."

We were in our apartments before dinner. Beyond the windows a dank mist hid the flat green Irish countryside and clung to the ivy-clad walls of the castle. I was thinking so hard of Katherine that at first I didn't hear what he said, and even when he repeated his words they made no sense to me.

"What do you mean?" I said, startled.

"I was hoping to touch Duneden for a loan, but I can hardly ask him in these circumstances, can I? It's all deuced awkward."

"A loan!" The word gave me such a jolt that I forgot Katherine altogether. "But, Patrick, I thought we were doing so well financially since John was born! You were even talking of taking me to America the year after next!"

"That's true," he agreed heavily. "I was."

"But what's happened?"

"Don't get hysterical, darling."

"I'm not hysterical! I simply want to know what the trouble is!"

"Well, it's the beastly harvests," said Patrick. "It was a rotten one last year and apparently it's a rotten one this year, and the tenants can't pay their rents and . . . well, I'm beginning to feel the pinch, to put it mildly. If I had another source of income there would be no difficulty, but I'm dependent now on Cashelmara for every penny I get, and Cashelmara's not exactly the richest of Irish estates at the best of times."

"Why can't the tenants be made to pay their rents? They must have some money saved!"

"What little they had went after the first bad harvest, and Mac-Gowan says it's pointless to expect them to produce what they don't have. Sarah, you don't understand how poor these people are. They grow potatoes for themselves and wheat and oats for sale to pay the

346

rent. If the crop fails they have nothing. MacGowan says I should thank God the potato hasn't failed as well, because if it did everyone, including me, would be damn well destitute."

"But there must be something you can do," I said desperately. "If it's a question of a loan, perhaps George . . ."

"George is just as dependent on his tenants as I am, so I'm sure these are bad times for him too. No, Duneden was my only hope. Well, perhaps after the funeral . . ."

It was a very awkward situation, and I didn't in the least want to know any more about it; but after the funeral Patrick begged me to be with him when he broached the subject with his brother-in-law, and when I tried to refuse he insisted that he would have more chance of success if I was there. I was sure he was wrong, and since I had been profoundly upset by the funeral, I was in no mood for a distressing interview, but to avert another quarrel I did as he asked. We saw Lord Duneden alone on the morning we were due to leave for Cashelmara, and the interview was every bit as humiliating as I had known it would be.

"How dare you mention such a subject at such a time!" said Lord Duneden. He was an old man now, well past seventy but with great presence and dignity. "And how dare you expect to conduct such a discussion in front of your wife, who should know nothing of such matters! Have you no pride at all? It's quite obvious you have no sense of propriety!"

Patrick stammered apologies mingled with references to the bad harvests, but Lord Duneden cut him off with an incisive movement of his hand.

"I've done with you," he said. "I've helped you all these years for one reason and one reason only—that you were Katherine's brother. But now Katherine's dead no power on earth is going to make me help you again. Leave my house this instant, and never return as long as you live."

There was nothing else to be said. I was so covered with shame that I could hardly summon the strength to leave the room, and afterward, not trusting myself to speak to Patrick, I went straight upstairs to Marguerite.

"But the solution is obvious," she said, surprised after I had poured out my troubles to her. "You must close Cashelmara at once to save every penny you can and come to stay with me for a few months."

"But, Marguerite," I said, almost in tears at her generosity,

"London . . . I don't think we could . . . you know what happens to us there."

"Well, as it happens," she said, "I was thinking of buying a small place in the country. I've made a little money with my investments lately, and I've been thinking for some time that I'm tired of living in London all the year round. It would be nice if I found somewhere in Surrey and used the house in St. James's Square only for the Season."

"Surrey's so close to London," I said fearfully.

"I have every intention of finding a house a long way from the railway station," said Marguerite, and so it was settled. Thomas and David were delighted with the idea, and even Patrick himself, once he had recovered from the interview with Lord Duneden, remarked buoyantly that it was an ill wind that blew no one no good. As for me, my joy at escaping from Ireland for a few months was soured only by the knowledge that we would be living on Marguerite's charity, but since this clearly didn't trouble Patrick I supposed it was foolish to let it trouble me.

In fact by this time I was feeling utterly exhausted. I had identified myself strongly with Katherine in the past, and when I had looked upon her dead face it was as if for one horrifying moment I had been looking at myself. I had no choice then but to admit how terrified I was of the future, for it was so obvious that there could be no security in beauty and youth and every conceivable material advantage life could offer. Nothing saved you in the end from the passing years, from growing old and from the grave.

I was very disturbed for some days, and when Patrick pawned more silver so that MacGowan's wages could be paid during our absence it was hard for me to make preparations for the move. But once I began I was soon so busy that I had no time to visit the dispensary, and I heard that Eileen Drummond had had a new baby only when Madeleine visited us at the end of October, three days before we were due to leave.

"At least the Drummonds don't have to worry as much as some do about the bad harvests," Madeleine was saying, and she embarked on some complicated explanation about a leasehold which gave them security of tenure. "And Drummond's a shrewd farmer," she was saying. "He'll scrape by somehow and feed the extra mouth in the family."

"Madeleine," I said before I could stop myself, "I would so like to send a little gift for the baby. Perhaps if I gave you something now . . ."

"I'll give it to Mrs. Drummond when I next see her," said Madeleine approvingly. "A very good idea, Sarah."

"You mustn't tell Patrick. There was such trouble when I visited Mrs. Drummond once, do you remember?"

"The sins of the husband should not be visited on the wife," said Madeleine firmly, so I went upstairs and fetched three dresses that John had worn when he was newborn. I had made them myself from the finest silk and had embroidered the smocking in blue.

Two days later I was taking John for a walk in his perambulator when Maxwell Drummond turned his donkey cart through the great iron gates of Cashelmara and came jogging steadily up the drive toward me.

VI

I was alone. Ned was helping Patrick in his final hours of gardening before the move, and Nanny was in the nurseries packing the last of the toys.

"Good day, my lady," said Drummond as the cart halted in front of me. He jumped down from the driver's seat, his head bare, his hair overgrown at the back, his sideburns reaching to his jaw, and in his hands were the three baby dresses I had sent to his wife.

"We'll not be needing your charity, so I'm returning your son's old clothes to you," he announced, tossing the dresses over the side of the perambulator, and turned as if to climb straight back into his donkey cart.

Anger helped me find my tongue. "Mr. Drummond," I said, surprising myself by the firmness of my voice, "I sent the dresses to your wife as a token of good will toward her, and you needn't talk as if I had nothing else to do with them except throw them away. John wore the dresses so seldom that they're as good as new."

"They're still as good as new," he said, swatting flies from the donkey's back, "for we've had no use for them."

"But—"

"The baby's dead," he said, swinging around to face me. "Eileen was thanking you for your gift but felt she must return it."

I was horrified by my lack of understanding. How slow and stupid he must have thought me! I swallowed and tried to speak, but he was the one who spoke first.

"It's better this way," he said. "I'll have enough trouble feeding six children through the winter, and the baby wouldn't have had enough to eat."

I thought of Eileen and the poor dead little baby and nearly choked with rage. "How can you say such a thing?" I cried. "Babies eat so little."

"Enough to force others to go without."

"But—"

"You know nothing," he said. "You don't know what hunger means, and if it's telling me you are that it's better to see children die by inches than die quickly without suffering, I'll be asking you to hold your tongue and mind your own business."

"Mr. Drummond—"

"Ah, sure I know what you're going to say! You're thinking: 'And is it complaining he is and he ten times better off than anyone else in this valley!' But I'm kin to the O'Malleys, and there's none so poor in all the valley as they are, and is it for me to be sitting in comfort in my snug little home while all my kin starve? And don't be telling me I could send my wife and children to her family in Dublin, for her father won't have her in his house since she was wed, so she's chained here the same as the rest of us. But you! Why should you be caring? You can go to England, you can escape. Faith, I swear I can hear your husband arranging the whole beautiful scheme! It's closing the house he'll be, putting all the servants out of work, telling Mac-Gowan to organize the evictions, leaving the sinking ship as fast as a pack of rats—"

"Stop it!" I shouted at him. I was trembling with rage and thoroughly unnerved by his violent lack of respect. "Stop it!"

John began to wail in his perambulator.

"See what you've done!" I cried, upset beyond all endurance, and burst into tears.

"Holy Mother of God," said Drummond, exasperated. "Here, Baby." He patted John's head, and as John looked up at him mistily I regained my self-control.

"That will do," I said in my coldest, sharpest voice. "Good day." I tried to push past him, but the perambulator wheel had jammed in a rut and I couldn't push it free. I struggled uselessly as Drummond stood by and watched.

"Help me, can't you?" I said breathlessly, ready to burst into tears again. "Help me!"

"Oh, is it help you're wanting?" said Drummond. "And don't

350

ladies always say please when they ask for help from a gentleman?"
And as I raised my hand to slap him he caught my wrist with a
laugh, said very gently, "I'm sorry," and smiled straight into my
eyes.

In the perambulator John started to cry again, but I never even
looked at him.

Drummond's fingers tightened on my wrist.

What would have happened next if MacGowan hadn't come
clattering up the drive on horseback I hardly dared to think. But he
did come up the drive, and Drummond turned abruptly to face him.
John was still crying. Picking him up, I hugged him tightly and he
smiled at me from the folds of his shawl.

"Move that cart," said MacGowan tersely to Drummond, and to
me he added with his customary courtesy, "Good day, my lady."

"Good day, Mr. MacGowan."

MacGowan turned to Drummond again. "What are you doing
here?"

"That's my business." He was already coaxing his donkey to face
the gates. "If you move that skin-and-bone bag of tinker-bred horse
flesh you happen to be sitting on, I'll be taking myself off. Good day
to you, Lady de Salis."

"Good day, Mr. Drummond," I said and watched him wordlessly
as he led his donkey down the drive toward Clonareen.

Chapter Three

1

"Marguerite, I must talk to you," I said unevenly.

We were in London, in the drawing room of her house in St. James's Square on the night of our arrival. Patrick and his brothers were still lingering in the dining room, and although I knew they would be joining us I was unable to restrain myself any longer from confiding in Marguerite. Very fortunately Edith, Patrick's niece, who lived with her, was away on a visit to her sister Clara, who had recently remarried, and so I had Marguerite to myself.

"I simply must talk to you," I repeated, suddenly aware that I had no idea how to begin my confession, and began to roam around the sofa to the fireplace. Beyond the window the lamplighter was touching the lights in the square, but although normally I would have paused to watch this entrancing sign of civilization I was in such a state that I barely remembered I had not seen a lamplighter in years.

"I noticed as soon as you arrived that you were in a great gale," remarked Marguerite, seating herself in her favorite chair and putting her tiny feet up on an embroidered footstool, "but I put it down to the fact that you were seeing London again after such a long absence. Sarah, you will be prudent, won't you? About being in London, I mean. I do wish you and Patrick could have gone straight to the new house as we had originally planned, but Mr. Rathbone says conveyancing is always a very slow business, and—"

"Marguerite, have you ever met Maxwell Drummond?"

"Drummond? The farmer? Yes, I have. He was a protégé of Edward's for a while."

"What did you think of him?"

The expression changed in Marguerite's eyes. "Why, I thought he was rather dangerous," she said after a pause, "and altogether too big for his boots."

"Oh. I see."

"Why? Do you like him?"

"Not in the least," I said rapidly. "I can't endure him. But I can't stop thinking about him either. It's the most extraordinary and peculiar thing. It makes no sense at all, but whenever I meet him—"

"I see," said Marguerite. She had smoothed all expression from her face. Her blue eyes regarded me with blank intelligence from behind her pince-nez.

"I mean, it's not even as if he's handsome. He's really quite ugly and he's dreadfully rude in his language. I've had only one conversation with him, but—"

"I see," said Marguerite again. "Only one conversation."

"It was the fifth time I'd seen him." I described the first meeting at the dispensary, the two glimpses in Clonareen, the encounter at Father Donal's cabin and finally the conversation in the drive at Cashelmara. I talked very fast, scarcely pausing for breath, and the word "Drummond" reverberated again and again until the very air seemed to hum with his name. "And each time I see him—"

"Quite," said Marguerite.

"I simply can't understand it. If he were good-looking . . ."

"Such things often have nothing to do with good looks."

"If he were a man of my own class . . ."

"That would, of course, be much simpler," said Marguerite. "You could have an affair with him and be on the road to recovery in no time at all."

"Marguerite!"

"My dear Sarah, don't bother to look so shocked! We both of us know what goes on in the world, and I see absolutely no reason why either of us should have to pretend to the other that we don't."

"But I couldn't possibly even think of . . ."

"Couldn't you?" said Marguerite. "Then perhaps you're not so badly smitten as you think you are. Never mind, the discussion is quite irrelevant since you obviously can't have an affair with a man who's little more than a peasant. Even affairs, after all, have their conventions."

"But what am I to do? I've been thinking of him continuously ever since I last saw him!"

"Try and see your infatuation for exactly what it is—an infatuation. You may think you can't be infatuated with his appearance, but in fact his appearance must be exactly what you find so fascinating. You hardly know him well enough to be infatuated with his noble soul—if he has one, which I doubt."

"But—"

"Heavens, Sarah, you must have suffered from infatuations before! Didn't you write and tell me once when you were fourteen that you were madly in love with your dancing master?"

"It's not like that" was all I could say.

"My dear, I'm afraid it is."

"No, you don't understand." I had never said that to her before. I could hear the stubborn edge to my voice and she heard it too, for she said quickly, "Oh, but I think I do understand! I've had my infatuations too, you know, and very troublesome they were at the time, but I did eventually recover. One simply has to be as patient as possible and wait for them to die a natural death."

"It's four years since I first saw Drummond," I said. "If it's an infatuation, shouldn't it have died a natural death long since?"

"It's lasted so long because you've seen him so seldom. Familiarity breeds contempt. If you saw him every day for a month you'd wonder soon enough what you could have seen in him. Sarah . . ."

"Yes?"

"Is he aware of your feelings?"

There was a silence.

"Lands' sakes, Sarah, you haven't knowingly given him any hint—"

"There was no need," I said. "He's always known, just as I have."

"How can that possibly be so! You're dramatizing the situation, Sarah, making a romance out of it."

"I can't help it if it's true," I said and suddenly found myself crying.

"There, there . . . I'm sorry." Marguerite sounded both alarmed and upset. "I didn't mean to be unkind, but . . . Sarah, you must be sensible about this, you really must. I know you're not as happy with Patrick as you might be. I know it must be dreadfully tempting

354

for you to look at other men, but Sarah, not at men like Drummond! It would be a disaster for you, can't you see that? Patrick would leave you instantly. There would be no question, as there might be if you had an affair with a man of your own class, of Patrick being complaisant or even making the effort to cover up your indiscretions. You would be divorced, disgraced, a social outcast. The children . . ."

Far away in the hall we heard Patrick's laughter and the sound of footsteps on the stairs.

"You'd never see the children," said Marguerite. "Never."

There was nothing else to say. I had no choice but to stop thinking of Drummond—and yet I went on thinking of him, and throughout the happy months that followed I found I was quite unable to rid myself of that terrible longing to see him again.

II

Marguerite must have said something to Patrick after our conversation, for he was very loving toward me, and for the first time in months we started sharing a bed again. By the time the new year came I suspected I might be pregnant. There had been a small but telling increase in my waistline, and I thought what a relief it would be if all temptation to buy a new wardrobe of fashionable clothes was removed by the promise of a ballooning figure. We were living a quiet life in London and seeing hardly any of our old friends, but I knew all the old temptations were there and so did Patrick. However, he avoided his gambling haunts, and I avoided extravagance, so perhaps we had finally learned a little wisdom after our disasters. Patrick was still mesmerized by his garden at Cashelmara and kept rearranging it on paper. He never carved wood now but browsed interminably among ancient gardening books and took Ned on a series of expeditions to the botanical gardens at Kew.

In January he was diverted by the garden of Marguerite's new house at Mickleham, a tiny picturesque village in the Surrey Hills south of London. Marguerite had bought the Queen Anne mansion which lay beyond the inn, and the garden consisted only of untidy lawns and enormous cedar trees. Little could be done to improve the garden at that time when the ground was hard with frost, but Patrick lost no time drawing up plans for a rose garden, two shrubberies and a pair of matching fountains flanking a gazebo.

"But, Patrick, this would cost a fortune!" protested Marguerite when he began to talk of building the fountains in Italian marble.

"Yes, but think how beautiful it would be!" he exclaimed. "It would be a monument to you, Marguerite."

"How awful—just like a graveyard! No, Patrick, I'll have the shrubberies and as many flowers as you can manage but no fountains, no gazebo and absolutely not one square inch of Italian marble."

As we began to settle down, I helped Marguerite with the delightful task of ordering the remainder of the furnishings. A visit to Brighton and the royal Pavilion had given me an entirely new attitude toward interior decoration, and to Marguerite's horror I became enrapt with ornate furniture laden with serpent motifs. "Eye-catching but impractical," she said hastily. "Comfort must come first." And along came the lounging chairs, the conversation sofas, the footstools and the whatnots. However, we did agree on a series of delightful floral wallpapers for the reception rooms, and this choice satisfied Marguerite's taste for modern furnishings as well as my passing fancy for the exotic.

The January days raced past. Thomas and David returned to their school at Harrow, and Ned, who had been enjoying their company during the Christmas holidays, began to mooch around glumly on his own.

"When are we going back to Cashelmara?" I heard him ask Patrick, but Patrick had no idea. He heard once a month from MacGowan, who reported that conditions had worsened on the estate, and occasionally we heard from Madeleine that people were flocking to the dispensary, while the workhouse at Letterturk was overflowing with the destitute. But in the spring she wrote, "Everyone is optimistic about the crops this year, and the potato fields are healthy. By autumn, God willing, it will be possible for you to return to Cashelmara."

A day or two later MacGowan wrote to say he was still doing his best to extract rent from the tenants who could pay but had been obliged to evict three families who had been deliberately withholding their rent money. "It's politics that's to blame," he added tersely. "So long as that rogue Parnell tells the peasants they have a moral right to refuse to pay rent there'll be no peace either here or anywhere else in Ireland. The Blackbooters meet in Clonareen every Sunday and openly admit their alliance with the Brotherhood, except now the Brotherhood calls itself the Land League. The priest's in it up to the neck, so it's no use looking to him to give moral guidance.

356

These are grievous times for a loyal hard-working agent, my lord, with abuse and rotten eggs hurled from all sides and my own servants afraid to work for me in case the Blackbooters take reprisals. Even Hayes and his wife have been told to leave Cashelmara, and Hayes is so scared I have no doubt but he will run at the first sign of trouble. If he goes I shall request the police to mount a guard on the house, but it will take extra money to keep them there, so I must warn your lordship of the expense in advance. Your lordship should also know that agents are fleeing their estates right and left except those that have been offered extra inducement to stay. I remain your lordship's humble, obedient and loyal servant, IAN MACGOWAN."

I sold a pair of diamond earrings so that Patrick could respond to this blackmail. I personally thought the letter was monstrously insolent, but Patrick said all would be lost if MacGowan left the estate, and so the money was sent. I didn't dare object when Patrick hinted that we could sell some jewelry, for I was too afraid that if I refused he would resort to gambling to try to win the money he needed.

Apart from this disturbing letter from MacGowan the summer passed peacefully. Ned helped Patrick in the garden, all the local gentry beat a path to Marguerite's door, and Thomas and David, when they returned from school, went on long riding expeditions up Box Hill or along the Mole Valley. Thomas was eighteen now. He had improved in looks, but he was still gauche in many ways and seemed either not to care to make sociable conversation or to have no gift for it. He was greatly interested in the study of medicine and fancied his talent for dissecting mice. In contrast David was sociable in the extreme, easygoing and easy to talk to. Of the two brothers it was he who took the greater interest in Ned. He would take him for walks across the meadows to the river or drive him in the pony trap to Dorking to explore the shops.

Ned was going to be six that December.

"Bright as a button," said Nanny fondly.

"Ever so tall for his age," said the nursemaid who was to help Nanny with the new baby.

"Dear little boy!" said Cook.

"We're very lucky, Sarah," said Patrick.

"I know," I said. "I know."

I kept telling myself how lucky I was.

"Some people are born lucky," said Patrick's niece Edith, who had

357

unfortunately returned from her sister Clara's house in the spring. I could not bear Edith. She was twenty-six-years old, unmarried and the sort of female who gave the word "spinster" a bad reputation.

"I can't think how you tolerate her living with you," I said to Marguerite in a great sulk soon after Edith's return. "You must have the patience of a saint."

"Well, one must make allowances," said Marguerite mildly and talked about what a hard life poor Edith had had, neglected by her mother and overshadowed by her pretty older sister. "Poor Edith! I know exactly what she wants, but for the life of me I can't see how she's ever going to get it."

"What she wants is a good box on the ears," I said, "and she'll get it too if she's not careful."

Fortunately Edith went up to town to stay with friends of Marguerite's as soon as the Season began, and she remained in London until July.

In August, just as Edith was moaning that no one had invited her to the yachting at Cowes, my new baby arrived. She was a girl, very pretty, with a pink and white skin and perfect little features.

"You're so lucky, Sarah!" said Marguerite, whose own daughter had died in infancy.

"How lucky we are, Sarah!" exclaimed Patrick, thrilled. "Two boys and now a girl. How well we've arranged things!"

He wanted the baby to be called Eleanor.

"After your mother, I suppose," I said, considering the suggestion.

"Oh, I wasn't thinking of my mother," he said—not surprisingly, for Patrick never did think of his mother. Despite his claim that he remembered her fondly, I had long ago realized that his attitude toward her was entirely negative. "I was thinking of my sister Nell, who brought me up."

I thought Eleanor was a pretty name, and we were so astonished to find ourselves in agreement that we even had the energy to choose a second name, Marguerite, before the baby was christened.

It was the day after the christening that the grim letter arrived from MacGowan. "The rain never ceases," he wrote tersely, "and it seems the oat crop will never ripen. The turf crop is all but lost. Despite all my earlier hopes this has been a bad summer, my lord."

Grimmer news was to follow. We had written to Madeleine to tell her of Eleanor's safe arrival, and her reply arrived soon after Mac-Gowan's letter. After congratulating us she wrote, "The potato has failed and the stench of the rotting potato plants is beyond belief. The people sit numbly looking at the blackened fields. This is one more terrible cross that God has sent the Irish to bear. Pray for us."

We did not hear from her again, but Marguerite began to raise money for the poor at Cashelmara by a series of charitable ventures, and Edith and I found ourselves working side by side to help her. Edith enjoyed charitable ventures. Organizing them gave her an excuse to be bossy and officious. I kept my temper as best I could, but I was relieved when the last parcel of clothes had been dispatched to Father Donal and the last farthing had been sent to the dispensary at Clonareen.

"I don't know how much longer I can endure staying in the same house as Edith," I confided to Patrick in an agony of exasperation. "If only matters could improve at Cashelmara!"

As if in answer to my wishes, MacGowan reported in October that there had been a change of fortune. The rains had ceased, the crops had ripened and the turf might still be saved if the fine weather became prolonged. As for the blight, it was not universal, and potatoes were being sold in Letterturk for fourpence a stone.

"I have told the police they need no longer guard Cashelmara," he added, "for I have no doubt that that coward Hayes will be back from his relatives in Dublin now that matters have eased. I advise you strongly, my lord, to dismiss Hayes from your service. Such disloyalty should not go unpunished. I myself put a high value on the virtue of loyalty, as your lordship well knows, and firmly believe that God punishes the idle, the shiftless and the untrustworthy. May He in His Mercy bring the Irish to True Repentance by submitting them to this season of Famine and Pestilence. I remain, my lord, ever your humble, obedient and loyal servant . . ."

"He sounds positively Cromwellian!" exclaimed Marguerite, horrified after Patrick had read the letter to us, but Patrick pointed out that MacGowan had always had fanatical religious leanings and that Scots Presbyterians were notoriously attracted to the idea of a stern God punishing the shiftless Irish.

"I wonder why Madeleine doesn't write to tell us things are better," I said a day or two after we had received MacGowan's letter.

"I expect she's still very busy," said Marguerite, who was drawing up a guest list for a charity ball she intended to give in London in the new year. The starving Irish had become a very popular cause, and

Marguerite had every hope that the Prince of Wales himself would attend.

"Aunt Madeleine only enjoys writing about bad news," remarked Edith, pausing during her embroidery of quite the ugliest sampler I had ever seen. "Now that the news is good I'm not surprised we don't hear from her."

"You're the one who can't bear to hear good news," I said before I could stop myself. "We all know you hate to hear of anyone who's happier and luckier than you are."

"Certainly I can't bear people who brag about their good luck in such an immodest fashion!"

"Edith!" said Marguerite, stern as a governess. "Sarah! Stop being so childish!" And she added severely to me after Edith had marched out of the room, "Sarah, you must know by this time that to mention the word 'luck' to Edith is as dangerous as waving a red rag at a bull!"

Luck, luck, luck. One bazaar, one sale of work, one tea party. So lucky. One walk with my beautiful new baby, one hour playing with my affectionate, loving John, one brief kiss for Ned before he dashed into the garden to play cricket. So much luck. One luncheon with the rector, two dinner parties with local families, one embrace from a handsome husband who told me how much he loved me. Lucky, lucky, lucky.

"Patrick," I said in November, "we can't go on indefinitely staying on Marguerite's charity. Don't you think that now the situation has improved we should go back to Cashelmara?"

When I looked at Patrick I saw the relief mingle with his enthusiasm. "Well, I hadn't liked to suggest it," he was saying, "because I thought that in spite of Edith you were happier here with Marguerite, but to tell you the truth I'm anxious to get back to Cashelmara too. I have a new scheme for the garden . . ." And as he began to talk about his garden again I thought how odd it was that having detested Cashelmara so intensely in the past we should now both feel drawn back there by compulsions beyond our power to control.

III

Marguerite protested so strongly when we announced our plans to leave that we immediately invited her to come with us and spend Christmas in Ireland.

"We would so love to repay you for all your hospitality," I begged her. "Can't you give us an opportunity to begin as soon as possible?"

"But are you sure you're not going back too soon? You won't see much rent before next spring."

"There are one or two pictures I can sell to tide us over," said Patrick, "and MacGowan's recent reports have been very optimistic. There's no difficulty, Marguerite."

"Well, if you're certain . . ."

"Positive."

"Then I'll come. But it's odd," Marguerite said, puzzled, "that we haven't heard again from Madeleine."

We decided to leave at the end of November. Thomas and David would still be at school, but Patrick wrote to tell them to travel to Cashelmara with Edith as soon as their term ended. Edith, thank God, had embarked on another visit to Clara, so there was no question of her coming to Cashelmara immediately; but even without Edith and the boys we were to be a large party, and several days passed before Patrick had made all the travel arrangements.

"Home!" said Ned, skipping for joy. "We're going home!"

His excitement was infectious. Even I became so excited that I forgot the oppressive silence of Cashelmara, the mist, the rain and the damp, and thought only of the sunlight sparkling on the waters of the lough and the mountains shimmering in a purple haze. Eagerness, bizarre but undeniable, took possession of me, and by the time we left at last for Cashelmara I was in a fever of anticipation.

Holyhead, a rough crossing to Kingstown, the awkward journey between Kingstown and Dublin with the baby screaming and John crying and all the servants distraught. A night in Dublin, a cheerful start to the station, the long dreary journey west to Galway, another night in a hotel and then the hired carriages, shabby and noisy, which were to take us those last miles to the gates of Cashelmara.

The horses were changed at Maam's Cross. The weather was sunny and mild, and despite the appalling journey I felt my spirits rise.

"Why don't we see any people?" said Ned. "Why are all those cabins in ruins?"

"All the people have gone to America, dear," said Nanny. "It's nicer for them there."

"But why did they pull down their homes before they left?"

"I dare say the landlord did that, dear, when the naughty people didn't pay their rent."

"Why didn't they pay their rent?"

"They didn't have enough money."

"Why not?"

"I've never known any child to ask as many questions as Ned does," I said to Marguerite with a smile.

"Thomas was just the same. I must say, the countryside is extraordinarily deserted. I've never seen it as empty as this before."

It was late afternoon by that time, and it was later still when the carriage edged through the pass above Lough Nafooey and we looked down upon Cashelmara.

The walls were as white as a bleached skull.

That was when the nightmare began. We went down into the valley, past abandoned cabins and ruined fields, and not a living creature moved as far as the eye could see. And all the time, facing us across the valley, stood Cashelmara, macabre Cashelmara, its windows blank as black holes in a lifeless white body.

"What's that smell?" said Ned.

None of us recognized it. But the odor grew stronger and stronger until I was scrabbling in my handbag for my lavender bottle, and suddenly Ned said, pointing outside, "What's that?"

It was a blackened, putrid mass lying in a ditch. Nanny took one look and jerked Ned away from the window. As I fought the urge to vomit I noticed her face had turned gray.

"What was it?" said Ned as the carriage creaked past.

Nobody answered him. John, who was sitting on my knee, buried his nose against my breast.

"What was it?" persisted Ned. "I want to know."

"Sarah," said Marguerite, thrusting her smelling salts under my nose.

"Aunt Marguerite . . ."

"It was a dead body, Ned. It's gone now."

"Was that where the smell came from?"

When there was no answer he tried again. "Was that—"

"We won't talk about it any more, dear," said Nanny, recovering herself. "Sit down, there's a good boy."

"I wish Papa was in this carriage," said Ned. "He always answers every single question I ask."

I was still unable to speak.

We reached the gates of Cashelmara at last, and the trees rose darkly on either side of the carriage.

"The drive's covered with weeds," said Ned.

The carriage rounded the last curve. We were face to face with the house.

"Oh, look!" exclaimed Ned, horrified. "Who did that?"

The front windows were broken. The door sagged drunkenly on its hinges. The air of dereliction clung to the walls in an aura of ruin.

"So MacGowan allowed the police to go home too soon," said Marguerite grimly. "Sarah, Patrick did write to MacGowan, didn't he, to tell him which day we would be arriving?"

"Of course he did!" I was almost too appalled to speak. "And I wrote to both Hayes and his wife to tell them to prepare the house for us because MacGowan said they were returning from Dublin."

But when we entered the house there was no sign that we had been expected. The furniture still lay beneath the dust covers, and on venturing through the green baize door to the servants' quarters, we found the kitchens empty, the pantry stripped of all food, the floors covered with mice droppings and mildew. Of Hayes and his wife there was no sign.

"What are we to do?" I whispered to Marguerite. We were alone in the kitchens. Patrick was combing the rest of the house for some sign of life, and the children and the servants were waiting in the hall.

It was the only time I had ever seen Marguerite at a loss for words. She stood stock-still in the middle of the scullery, her face blank, her glance traveling quickly over our dirty deserted surroundings.

"We'll have to stay here," she said at last. "For tonight at least. It'll soon be dark and the children are tired."

"But I can't send the children to bed with nothing to eat!"

"We'll take one of the carriages to Clonareen. Madeleine must have some food at the dispensary. We can take some food for tonight and set out for Galway tomorrow morning." She closed the door of the pantry with an air of finality and turned her back on it. "Obviously MacGowan didn't get Patrick's letter," she said after a moment. "I wonder if Madeleine's long silence means that she also hasn't heard from us. Well, we'll soon find out. Let's go back to the hall."

"I suppose Hayes and his wife never came back from Dublin," I said as we opened the green baize door again. "I merely assumed that since MacGowan said conditions were improved—"

"I think we misunderstood MacGowan," said Marguerite. "It may be true that the crops are saved and that potatoes are for sale in Letterturk, but I think the change of fortune has come too late for many people in this part of Ireland."

Patrick was coming downstairs as we entered the hall. He reported that the house was deserted, and when Marguerite repeated her suggestion of seeking help from Madeleine he immediately offered to set out for Clonareen.

"No—wait, Patrick." Marguerite lowered her voice so that the servants wouldn't hear. "It would be better from the point of view of morale if you stayed here and took command, just as the master of the house should. That little nursemaid looks as if she might have hysterics any minute. Keep her busy—keep them all busy. They'll be much less likely to panic if you're here. I'll go with Sarah to see Madeleine."

"But supposing you and Sarah meet a bunch of marauders on the road!"

"I doubt if we'll meet anything except more rotting corpses, but anyway the elder coachman has a blunderbuss."

"Well, if you really think it would be best . . ."

"I do. Come on, Sarah."

We told Nanny and Nurse to take the children upstairs and make them as comfortable as possible in the nurseries, and then I explained to Ned where we were going and promised we would soon be back. By that time I had given up trying to invent an excuse to stay behind. I couldn't let Marguerite go on her own, and it did seem best that Patrick should remain at the house to take command.

The senior coachman didn't in the least want to drive another three miles to Clonareen, but when Marguerite said there would be no food for anyone unless he did he reluctantly scrambled up onto the box again. The younger coachman was assigned the task of finding fodder for the horses, and when we left he was staring hopelessly at the empty stables.

Fortunately Marguerite was right about the marauders. We met no one on the road to Clonareen, although as the journey progressed the light faded and the air turned much colder. I was glad I had my heaviest sealskin jacket to wrap around me as I stared out of the window at the deserted countryside, but I still found it hard to stop shivering.

"I must remember to ask Madeleine for some arsenic," said Marguerite. "I know she always keeps a supply at the dispensary, and there's nothing better for killing vermin. I'm afraid the mice have colonized Cashelmara very thoroughly in your absence, Sarah."

I shivered all the more. "I'm not staying there one hour longer than I have to! Marguerite, if you want to go straight back to

England while we stay in Galway, I wouldn't blame you in the least."

"Nonsense! Of course I shall stay until you've sorted everything out. You'll need help recruiting some suitable servants and ordering the dispatch of all the necessary foods. To set Cashelmara back on its feet is going to be the most exhausting undertaking, and you'll need every scrap of help you can get."

The smell of rotting flesh prevented me from replying. This time I found my lavender bottle immediately, and Marguerite already had her smelling salts in her hand.

It was still twilight when we reached Clonareen, but the main street was empty. The dirty hovels straggled to the crowded grave-yard, and beyond the church the hulk of the dispensary loomed large in the uncertain light. When the carriage halted, the silence screamed in our ears. Not a dog barked, not a bird sang, not a tomcat yowled in the dusk.

"Everyone must be dead," I whispered, struggling with my panic.

"I think I can see a light in the dispensary." Marguerite was already poised on the edge of her seat. "Why doesn't the coachman open the door?"

It was then that we heard the noise. It was a whispering, almost a twittering, as if a group of birds without voices were trying to sing. The smell reached us a moment later. It was different from the reek of putrid flesh, yet it was still the smell of disintegration. When Marguerite turned ashen I too leaned forward to peer out of the window, and what I saw so appalled me that at first I could not believe my eyes.

We were looking at the living dead, scarecrows who might once have been men and women, half naked, sexless, gray-skinned. There were small scarecrows too with grotesque swollen stomachs, and one woman was carrying a dead baby with a blackened tongue.

The noiseless chattering, senseless and inhuman, began again. Skeleton arms stretched toward us in an appeal for alms.

"Marguerite . . ." My voice was far away, distorted as if I were at the end of a long corridor.

"Stay here," she said. "I'll go."

"No, don't!" I was terrified for her, terrified for myself. "We'll go back to Cashelmara!"

"We must see Madeleine." Marguerite's face was white and set. "We've come all this way. We've got to see her."

"But . . ."

"Give me all the coins you have."

I was so terrified that I could no longer argue with her. I did as she asked. Black spots began to dance before my eyes.

When she opened the door the stench was so overpowering that she almost lost her nerve. I saw her hesitate. The coachman was sitting riveted to his box and would not come down, so she had to scramble unaided to the ground. I saw her fling some coins at the mob, and as they scattered she ran lightly to the door of the dispensary.

The door opened. I saw a room full of people before I fainted.

When I opened my eyes again Marguerite was coming back. The twittering was louder, and as she threw down the rest of the coins the crowd ignored them and pressed closer to beg for food. But Marguerite was empty-handed. She pushed past, stumbling as they grasped her coat, and suddenly there was a mighty explosion as the coachman fired his blunderbuss in the air. The crowd fell back in fear. Heaving as hard as I could, I thrust open the door and dragged Marguerite into the carriage.

She was so white that the freckles stood out on the bridge of her nose like dark blotches. She was trembling as she collapsed onto the seat beside me.

The carriage moved forward with a jolt. The twittering nightmare receded slowly into the dusk.

After a long while she managed to say, "The ward . . . the little ward with nine beds . . ."

"Yes?"

"There were forty people in it and all of them were dying."

"Of hunger?"

"Of fever," said Marguerite. "Famine fever." She clenched her hands tightly in her lap. "Madeleine had no food but soup. I didn't take any. It would have been wrong. She hadn't received our letters, and she said she had had no time to write any herself. She and Dr. Townsend haven't had a proper night's sleep in weeks. The fever came to the valley a month ago from Letterturk, and people have been dying like flies. Madeleine said that if she'd known we'd even dreamt of returning . . . " She stopped.

The carriage plodded on beside the long lough. The horses were so tired they stumbled often and the carriage swayed sickeningly on the narrow road. It was quite dark by this time and the stars were shining.

"We can leave now," my voice said. "At once. As soon as we get back."

366

"It's too late for us to leave," said Marguerite. The long silence had enabled her to recover herself, and when she spoke she sounded as crisp and practical as she always did. "But Nanny and Nurse must leave with the children as soon as they wake in the morning, and they must leave in the other carriage and with the other coachman."

"But . . ."

"The fever travels on the clothes, Sarah. We may both be carrying it at this minute. We can't risk seeing the children again until it's certain we're safe." After a pause she added, "Edward's favorite son Louis died of fever here at Cashelmara thirty years ago. We mustn't let history repeat itself."

The very idea was so appalling to me that I could not speak again for the rest of the journey and found my tongue only when on our arrival we found that Patrick had been busy in our absence. Fires had been lit in the nursery, library and kitchens, and Patrick himself was chopping wood as vigorously as any artisan. The kitchen fire looked so cheerful that I thought I might stop shivering if I knelt beside it, but I was chilled to the bone and my mind remained numbed by the horrible experience in Clonareen.

The very next morning the children left for Galway on the first stage of their journey back to England.

When I had finished crying I found that Patrick had taken one of the horses from the remaining carriage and ridden to Letterturk to buy food. None of us had slept that night. Patrick, Marguerite and I had huddled in the chairs before the library fire, while his valet and our maids had rested as best they could before the fire in the kitchens.

"We must keep busy, Sarah," said Marguerite. "Tell the servants to unpack the clothes upstairs while we start taking off all the dust covers down here."

"But, Marguerite . . ."

"We're going to be here at least a week and we must have something to do."

There was no arguing with her, and when Patrick arrived back from Letterturk he found Marguerite industriously sweeping the hall while I was folding discarded dust sheets into neat piles.

"Heavens above!" exclaimed Marguerite. "Look at all that food!"

"Isn't it odd? There was plenty for sale in Letterturk, but George said when I saw him that the poorer people have no money at all—

their last article of bedding is pawned to the gombeen man—and so they can't even afford fourpence for a stone of potatoes."

"But that's monstrous!" exclaimed Marguerite. "How can famine exist in a country where there's plenty to eat? I shall write to the *Times* at once and expose the situation. There must be some very muddleheaded thinking at Westminster! Any administration that permits a situation like this must be criminally negligent."

"But the English are trying so hard to help!" protested Patrick. "Think of all the money that's being raised at present!"

"Yes—but where is it? What happens to it? Why isn't it saving people from starvation? It's a scandal," said Marguerite, having whipped herself into a fine rage by this time, "an absolute scandal."

Her intensity was characteristic but too frantic to be normal. I sensed her repressed fear and had to struggle to fight my own panic.

"We must keep busy," she was repeating. "Let's try and cook. I've always wanted to. How do you suppose one cooks a potato?"

"You boil it until it's soft," said Patrick promptly. "It takes about half an hour."

"How on earth do you know that?" I said, amazed.

"I was always in the kitchens at Woodhammer when I was little," said Patrick happily. "I know all about cooking. It's great fun."

I restrained myself from saying how extraordinary he was. I was too hungry to do more than urge him to cook us a meal immediately.

Summoning the servants from their labors upstairs, we divided one of the loaves to take the edge off our hunger while more food was cooking. Patrick boiled eggs and potatoes together for the same length of time and was disappointed to discover how hard the eggs were. However, we were all so hungry that we ate everything, and when Marguerite's maid offered to cook one of the chickens Marguerite promised her an increase in salary.

The last egg had just been eaten when MacGowan, having seen the smoke from the chimneys, arrived to find out what was happening. He looked not only stupefied to see us but shocked to the core to see Patrick in his shirt sleeves by the kitchen range.

"If your lordship had written to tell me you were coming . . ."

As we had suspected, he had not received Patrick's final letter. He began to apologize for the broken windows, the damaged front door and the missing livestock, and he was still explaining how the police had left despite all his attempts to bribe them when Marguerite said fiercely, "MacGowan, why did you send reports that matters were improving in the valley? It's obvious everyone's on the brink of starvation."

"No indeed, my lady, with all due respect. The starving people are mostly O'Malleys, and they were always too shiftless to do more than tend a potato patch. This is God's judgment on their idleness and sloth, my lady."

"Don't talk of God's judgment to me!" cried Marguerite in a fury. "It's English negligence, not God's judgment!"

"That must, of course, be for your ladyship to decide," said Mac-Gowan sulkily. "But the Joyces and the O'Flahertys have their crops now, and although it's not a fine harvest it is at least an average one and they'll pull through. All the reports of famine are much exaggerated, and if your ladyship knew the Irish as well as I know them, your ladyship would also know the Irish love to make a fuss over their troubles. To tell the truth they welcome it because it gives them a chance to complain about the English."

"Absolute stuff!" said Marguerite. It was so unlike her to be so rude that we all gaped at her. "I've seen starving people dying of famine fever. How dare you tell me they welcome it!"

"It's God's judgment, my lady," said MacGowan again, "and God's will. My lord, with your permission I beg leave to withdraw."

"Yes, very well. No, wait. MacGowan, we must have some servants—a cook, a couple of maids. Employ some women without delay, could you, and send them here as soon as possible."

"I'll do my best, my lord, but these peasant women know no more than how to cook a potato, and they wouldn't know what the word 'clean' meant. I'll have to send to Galway for decent Christian servants."

After he had gone Marguerite said in a trembling voice, "Patrick, you've got to dismiss that man. He's intolerable."

"Marguerite . . ." He saw she was overwrought and tried to take her in his arms, but she pushed him away.

"Don't come too near me."

"You're not going to get fever," he said gently. "Plenty of people are immune to it, you know. One often hears stories of people who nurse the sick and yet never sicken themselves. You'll be safe and everything will soon be well again."

"Nothing will be well unless you dismiss MacGowan" was all she said as she turned away from him. "He's going to bring us trouble, I'm sure of it. I can feel it in my bones."

369

"I'll dismiss him later when everything's returned to normal, but I can't dismiss him now. I need him."

Even Marguerite had to admit this was all too true. MacGowan, heavily armed, made the regular expeditions to Letterturk to buy food. He would set out at different times to avoid the risk of ambush, and during the week that followed he managed to find an old woman who would cook for us and two young girls who would wash floors and light fires. All the local cats had been eaten, so the mice were still rampant in the house, but Patrick built traps for them and soon I could go to sleep without fear of finding a mouse in bed with me when I awoke.

Presently the scarecrows came to stand in the drive. They were not violent, but they refused to go away even after we had distributed what food we could spare. They would stand for hours and hours in the cold and only disperse at nightfall.

"We must start a soup kitchen," said Marguerite. "I believe soup is easy to make, and a little of it goes a long way."

So the soup was made, and one of the maids, who had had the fever in the past, was put in charge of the distribution.

"What can we do next?" said Marguerite, still aflame with energy as I longed to collapse with exhaustion. "I know—the nurseries! We can prepare them for the children's return. That'll cheer you up, Sarah. Let's get the dusters and take them upstairs right away."

We had been doing all our own dusting, as the maids had been too burdened by the heavy work to spare time for the lighter cleaning, and Marguerite had attacked the work with great zest. I can see her now, her wiry hair tucked neatly under a cap, an apron tied tightly around her tiny waist, her spectacles anchored firmly to the bridge of her thin nose. She had abandoned her pince-nez a year ago after complaining that she could see nothing at all whenever it fell off and that she was too old to be blind for vanity's sake. The spectacles did make her look older, but she was still so petite that she looked far younger than her age, which was thirty-seven. Only her hair, mellower now than the startling carroty red of her teens, hinted that she was closer to middle age than one might have guessed.

However, there was nothing middle-aged about her dusting, and so I was surprised when later in the day nursery her energy seemed to flag. I was in the middle of wiping the dust from Ned's rocking horse when she stopped work and began to open all the windows.

"What are you doing?" I said, startled. It was a chilly day and the upstairs rooms were very cold.

"Don't you feel hot?" said Marguerite.

"Not in the least."

"I think I'll go downstairs and see if that new pot of soup is ready. Then I can step outside for a breath of air. I won't be long, Sarah."

When she didn't come back I went downstairs to look for her, but no one had seen her in the kitchens.

I went to her room. "Marguerite?" I said, tapping on the door. "Marguerite, are you better?" And then as I opened the door I smelled the stench of sickness and saw the pool of vomit on the floor.

We tried to get the doctor. Patrick rode to Clonareen at once, but Dr. Townsend had died of fever that same morning, and Madeleine was alone at the dispensary with her sick and her dying. Someone said there was a doctor at Letterturk, so Patrick rode there to fetch him, but he too was dead and no one knew where another doctor could be found. Meanwhile, all the Irish servants had left us except the one who had already had the fever, and Marguerite's maid was in such a stupor of fear that she refused to go into her mistress's room. I could not ask my own maid to go, and I refused to leave Marguerite's care in the hands of the poor illiterate servant girl who remained at the house.

"But surely someone else can nurse me, Sarah," whispered Marguerite. "I know how you feel about illness."

"It was the thought of illness that frightened me," I said. "But now that I'm face to face with it I don't mind."

"But you mustn't come too near."

"Dearest Marguerite," I said.

"I want you to be safe, Sarah. Please go. I shan't blame you a bit. Please."

"No."

"But . . ."

"Never."

She suffered dreadfully. There were headaches so painful that she would scream in agony, dizziness, nausea and vomiting. The eruption occurred on the fifth day, a dark blotchy red that covered her entire body and led to hemorrhaging beneath the skin.

Patrick had ridden to Galway for a doctor, and I knew he would be away for some time.

There were days and there were nights. I sponged away the fever as best I could, changed the linen often and did everything I could to make her comfortable. I no longer noticed the smell. I sat with her

371

hour after hour, and presently I no longer noticed anything except Marguerite. Sometimes I remembered my children and thanked God they were safe, but I no longer wondered if I myself would live or die because I had accepted the fact that the choice was not in my hands. I was living daily with the unthinkable, so I no longer thought but merely held Marguerite's hand as if I could hold her back from the brink of that darkness which had terrified me all my life.

Marguerite's maid sickened but she lived. I always felt bitter about that afterward. I could only look at her and think: She lived. And I never forgave her for living, just as no doubt she never forgave me for begging her mistress to spend Christmas with us at Cashelmara.

From Galway Patrick sent the letter to Thomas and David, but of course it never reached them in time.

It began to rain at Cashelmara. The larchwoods were black against the winter sky, and above the house the tower of the chapel was iron-gray among the bleak trees.

The end came, the delirium before the final coma. She talked a great deal of her husband Edward, and when Patrick arrived back from Galway she mistook him for his father and said how wonderful it was to see him again and that she had missed him more than anyone had ever guessed. She talked of Thomas and David too, and sometimes it was as if she were telling Edward about them, for she said that he mustn't be impatient with Thomas's passion for medicine because it was so important to let children do what they were best suited to do and not to expect them to be replicas of their parents. Sometimes she talked of London and Woodhammer and even of New York, and once she spoke of her honeymoon on the Continent, but always she spoke of them to Edward as if he were at her bedside and she could see him more clearly than she could see us.

The doctor Patrick had brought from Galway could do nothing.

It was before she slipped into unconsciousness for the last time that the delirium ebbed and she recognized me. I was alone with her. Outside the sun was rising and the room was filling with a pale white light.

"Sarah, I've felt so guilty," she said, and the shock of hearing her speak in a lucid voice was so immense that I was struck dumb. I realized I had let go of her hand as I dozed in the chair, and that so frightened me that I clasped the hand quickly and pressed it in mine.

"So guilty," she repeated. "All my fault." Her voice was gone; her whisper was very faint. "I urged him to get married and you've both been so unhappy."

I shook my head. "We're happy now." I groped for words. "Everything's well—the new baby . . ."

"Such a waste," she said. "Such a pity."

"You mustn't feel like that." I was so distressed but could think of nothing else to say.

. There was a long silence, and then just as I was wondering if she had fallen asleep she said in a strong, clear voice, "Be very careful, won't you, Sarah?"

She never spoke again.

An hour later I noticed that she was no longer breathing. I held my own breath to listen, but no sound broke the silence and I knew I was alone.

I was still holding her hand.

After a while I looked upon her face and saw that she seemed very young, much younger than I, and her features were strangely unfamiliar, as if they belonged to someone I had never met.

I was still sitting by the bed when Patrick slipped into the room and asked how she was.

"She's dead," I said. "Marguerite's dead." And I went on looking at her stranger's face and I went on holding her familiar hand.

It was he who cried. He said very violently, "The people I love best always die," and then he pressed the palms of his hands against his cheeks as if he were a small boy and began to sob as if his heart would break.

IV

We buried her beside her husband in the family graveyard. It was a clear day, mild for the time of year, and the white surplice of the parson from Letterturk fluttered gently in the soft wind. Thomas and David had arrived the day before, Cousin George had ridden over from Letterturk Grange and Madeleine had somehow managed to leave the dispensary to attend the service. There were no other mourners. People were too frightened of fever, and all Marguerite's many friends were far away in England.

I didn't cry. I watched the coffin being lowered into the grave and knew there was no God, and that shocked me because everyone believed in God, didn't they? It simply wasn't done not to believe or, at the very least, not to pretend to oneself one believed. But I no longer believed, and that was really very awkward, because if I didn't believe in God I couldn't blame Him for Marguerite's death, and someone had to be blamed, I saw that very clearly; someone had to take the responsibility.

Someone scattered earth on the coffin. It was Sarah Marriott, Sarah de Salis, Lucky Sarah who had always had everything she could possibly want. She had wanted Marguerite to go to Cashelmara for Christmas, and of course Marguerite had gone.

No, it wasn't my fault. I'm not to blame. I didn't want to go back to Cashelmara. It was Patrick, talking of his garden. I didn't want to go.

But you asked. "Oh, Patrick, we really can't go on living on Marguerite's charity . . ." You thought of Maxwell Drummond and you asked to go back.

"Sarah." Someone was talking to me. The coffin was covered with earth. The clergyman had closed his book. Everyone was walking away. "Sarah . . ."

"I want to be alone for a while," I said to whoever it was. "I want to think."

"But you mustn't stay here . . . must come back to the house." It was Patrick. I could smell the whisky on his breath, and I wrenched myself free.

"No."

"Sarah . . ."

"Leave me alone!" I shouted at him and ran away across the graveyard to the door of the chapel.

It was dark inside but quiet. I sat down, listening, but now the silence was no longer oppressive but comforting to me. I was thinking clearly at last, my thoughts sensible and logical. No more Drummond. The very sight of him would repulse me since he was responsible, no matter how indirectly, for Marguerite's death, and once I had accepted that I saw no reason why my marriage shouldn't be tolerable. I could have at least three more children at three-year intervals. That would take up nine years. I was now twenty-nine, so by the time I had the other children I would be thirty-eight. Perhaps I could have one more. Then I would be past forty, which would be dreadful, but it would be time to enjoy the older children's maturity. It would be fun when Eleanor was old enough to be presented—all those parties and dances—but who was she going to marry? I would have to see that we were leading some form of acceptable social life by that time. It was no use Patrick thinking we could continually live like recluses while he worked like a navvy in his wretched garden. We must at least present Eleanor at Dublin Castle—no, that was really too provincial; it would have to be London, and we would find the money somehow.

All manner of schemes swept through my mind. I had always taken a defeated attitude toward Cashelmara, but there was no reason why it couldn't be made into a smart and fashionable house. Marguerite had always thought its style hopelessly out of date, and indeed when I myself had first seen Cashelmara I had thought it a plain white lump of a building, but there was something about those long straight lines, that extraordinary symmetry, that had gradually mesmerized me. Its beauty was not of today, but that didn't matter. It was the beauty of a thousand yesterdays and perhaps of a thousand tomorrows, timeless Cashelmara, geometrically perfect, splendidly stark. It was a beauty that repelled me, but I thought I could at last see how it could be put to my advantage. With a little attention to the rooms, some inexpensive but imaginative refurnishing, well-ordered grounds . . .

Perhaps Patrick should be encouraged in his gardening after all. Grounds were very important. When people came to stay they would find a beautiful exotic garden awaiting them, while beyond the boundary walls there would be opportunities for shooting and fishing. If the Prince of Wales could visit the Brownes of Westport, why should he not eventually come to Cashelmara? Of course money would be a problem, but in normal times Cashelmara yielded an adequate income, and if I took the trouble to learn about money . . . Yes, that was it. No more leaving household matters blithely to the nearest inefficient housekeeper, no more expecting Patrick to spend money with any inkling of wisdom, no more announcing haughtily that I hadn't been brought up to count the pennies. Beggars couldn't be choosers. I certainly hadn't intended to be an impoverished member of the Anglo-Irish aristocracy, but since I was I must, for my children's sake, make the most of it. If I could somehow enable my children to have every possible advantage despite our misfortunes I wouldn't feel I had endured those misfortunes for nothing. The children were all that mattered now, I could see that, and I wanted them to have nothing but the best. No children were going to be happier than my children, and no children were going to be more fortunate.

And my marriage? Well, Patrick and I would rub along somehow. Why not? Other couples did, so why shouldn't we do at least as well as all those others?

It never occurred to me to doubt that this was possible, but I can see now that I was closing my eyes to the one truth that should by that time have been painfully obvious—that Marguerite alone had kept Patrick and myself together and that without her our marriage was doomed.

Chapter Four

I

It was less than three weeks after Marguerite's death that Hugh MacGowan, the agent's son, came to Cashelmara.

My children were still with Nanny and Nurse at Marguerite's townhouse, and although I was longing desperately to see them again I didn't dare sanction their return. In the valley the fever was waning, but in other parts of the country it continued to rage, and it was thought that the outbreaks would continue through the winter until the potato crop brought an end to the famine.

After Marguerite's funeral I wanted to return to England until conditions at Cashelmara improved. I couldn't bear the thought of not seeing the children until the spring, but Patrick rightly pointed out that we should wait until the new year to make certain we were all free of fever. Meanwhile Marguerite's boys were still with us. Thomas was in his first term at Oxford, while David had begun his final year at Harrow, but after their mother died it was clearly impracticable for them to return to England for the few days that remained of their terms, so they stayed with us over the Christmas holidays. It was a comfort for them to be with Patrick, and Patrick in his turn derived comfort from them.

For my part I was still beyond comfort. I found it impossible to cry or grieve in a normal fashion and instead immersed myself so thoroughly in household matters that I retired to bed exhausted each night. I continued Marguerite's soup kitchen, tried to train the new servants, made efforts to keep the house in some sort of order. Meanwhile Patrick went to Galway to buy horses, grooms were engaged, the carriage was repaired and the stables lost their derelict appearance. The new grooms accompanied MacGowan on his expeditions to Letterturk to buy food, although MacGowan said they would be of little use in an ambush since they would probably side with the attackers.

"Patrick," said Thomas shortly before Christmas, "have you noticed that MacGowan's mad?"

We were all in the morning room after breakfast. The musty smell of damp still clung to the room, but the fire was blazing in the grate and I was loath to leave my sewing to investigate activities in the kitchens. I had found a bolt of silk in one of the attics and was making a little dress for Eleanor.

"Aren't you exaggerating a little?" said Patrick vaguely to Thomas. He was standing by the window and staring at his misty, tangled garden.

"Of course I'm not exaggerating! I should have thought it was quite obvious that MacGowan's as mad as a March hare. He's become a religious maniac."

"I must say," said David, looking up from his volume of Tennyson, "I do think it's rather wicked of him to keep telling the Irish the famine is their fault because they're papists. It's so awfully tactless, isn't it?"

"They say he's going to evict all the O'Malleys," Thomas said abruptly. "He says he's God's instrument and God punishes the idle. Patrick, I thought you were going to be lenient about evictions between now and next summer."

"Well, I expect MacGowan knows what he's doing," said Patrick. From the expression in his eyes I knew he was thinking of his garden and was only half listening to what Thomas was saying.

"Marguerite wanted you to get rid of MacGowan," I said to jolt him.

Her name hung in the air long after I had spoken it. They all turned to look at me, and then David bent over his poetry again, and Thomas, shoving his hands into his pockets, turned away toward the door.

"She did, didn't she?" said Patrick, his garden forgotten. "How angry he made her! Perhaps I'd better have a word with him after all about the evictions."

378

At this point the subject was dropped, and I thought no more about it until we all met that evening in the drawing room before going down to dinner. Patrick was the last to appear.

"You were right about MacGowan, Thomas" were the first words he said as he entered the room. "He's quite mad. He talks about nothing but the wrath of God and the Day of Judgment and eternal hell-fire for Catholics. I don't know what the devil I'm going to do."

"Get rid of him, of course," said Thomas promptly.

"Well, I tried to—although God knows the last thing I want to do at this moment is hunt for a new agent—but he simply wouldn't listen. God, what *am* I going to do?"

"But of course you must dismiss him!" I said, exasperated. "How can you leave estate affairs in the hands of someone who's insane? Unless you do something soon you'll have a riot on your hands in no time at all."

"But, my dear Sarah, after thirty years' service—"

"Yes, it would be cruel to dismiss him so abruptly," mused David. "Besides, perhaps the insanity is only temporary. Could you suggest that he consult a doctor?"

"MacGowan doesn't need a consultation!" exclaimed Thomas. "He needs a strait-jacket!"

"But Patrick doesn't have the power to commit him to a lunatic asylum."

"Then he must get hold of someone who has! Doesn't MacGowan have any relatives?"

"There's a son," I said, remembering. "He's an agent on some Scottish estate—Lochlyall Castle, isn't it, in Wester-Ross?"

"I could write to him, I suppose," said Patrick doubtfully.

"I'd write without delay if I were you," said Thomas.

"I think he should at least know that his father seems to be unlike himself at present," I said, watering down Thomas's dogmatic assertions to make them palatable to Patrick. "Then even if he doesn't wish his father to be committed to an asylum he can at least assume the responsibility for his father's welfare."

Patrick heaved a sigh. "Well, I suppose that really would be the best thing to do," he agreed with reluctance, and so it came about that ten days later on a dark misty afternoon Hugh MacGowan arrived at the gates of Cashelmara and rode up the long winding drive into our lives.

Patrick had ridden with the boys to Leenane to leave some letters for the mail car, and I was alone by the drawing-room fire with my sewing. I was embroidering the little dress for Eleanor by this time. I can see it still: pink rosebuds on white muslin over pale-blue silk. I was pleased because it looked so pretty.

"Excuse me, m'lady, your honor," said Kathleen, the younger of the two precious housemaids, as she poked her head around the door, "but there's a Mr. MacGowan asking for you, but it'll not be Mr. MacGowan but someone else."

After I had deciphered this announcement I told her to show Mr. MacGowan into the blue morning room and inform him that I would see him presently. The blue morning room was the room set aside for receiving guests of lesser quality. It lay at the end of a little passage that led to the servants' quarters, and after I had put aside my sewing I went downstairs hoping that my message had been delivered correctly and that I wouldn't find Mr. MacGowan still waiting in the hall. But Kathleen for once had been intelligible. The hall was empty, and when I entered the blue morning-room I found the stranger there waiting for me.

He turned as I came into the room. He had been looking out of the window, and as I glanced past him I saw that the clouds were hanging low over the mountains and the rain was brushing lightly against the pane.

"Mr. MacGowan?" I said. "Good afternoon. My husband is out at present, but I'm expecting him to return very soon. I'm sure he'll be glad to see you. He's been most worried about your father."

"I'm sorry to hear that, Lady de Salis." He moved forward, took my extended hand politely and gave a small bow. As he straightened his back I looked at him more closely. Although not strikingly tall, he was above medium height and not an ounce of superfluous flesh marred his muscular frame. He wasn't dark but he wasn't fair either. At first glance I thought his coloring made him nondescript, but then I noticed that his gray eyes were very steady, giving him a peculiarly intent expression, and that there was some element in his presence that commanded attention. He had thinning brown hair, a pallid complexion and a wide brutal mouth.

"This must be your first visit to Cashelmara for a long time," I said to him.

"I was a boy of thirteen when I left," he said, "and that's twenty years ago."

380

He was well spoken, very civil. He had a Scottish way of clipping his words, but his accent was slight, and apart from his voice I could detect no resemblance to his father.

"Perhaps you would care for some refreshment while you wait for my husband," I said after a moment.

"No, thank you, my lady. I lunched with my father less than an hour ago." And he smiled slightly, relaxing the muscles about his mouth.

For some inexplicable reason I turned away. I was just opening my mouth to say, "I'll ask my husband to see you as soon as he comes back," when I heard laughter in the hall and knew that Patrick had already returned from Leenane.

"I'll tell my husband you're here," I said abruptly, but the grooms in the stables must have already passed the news to Patrick, for even before I had finished speaking the door was opening as Patrick himself walked into the room.

"Good afternoon, Lord de Salis," said Hugh MacGowan.

"Hugh! My God, I wouldn't have recognized you!" He tossed aside his riding crop so carelessly that it fell from the chair to the floor and strode forward with his hand outstretched. "How are you? Welcome back to Cashelmara!"

"Thank you, my lord."

"Sit down and make yourself comfortable! God, it's good to see you again—it seems only the other day since we were boys together!"

"Indeed, my lord." He was still standing. He was very quiet, very polite. "My lord, before we start remembering the old days I would prefer we discussed the reason for my visit. I trust you will understand if I say that I'm so concerned about my father's position that I've at present no desire to reminisce about the past."

"Well, of course," said Patrick uneasily. "Yes, I quite understand."

"I'll leave you, if you'll excuse me," I murmured tactfully, but to my fury Patrick said at once, "No, there's no need for you to go, darling. This is more of a social call than a business appointment, despite what Hugh has said, and besides, he's one of my oldest friends."

I knew immediately that he was nervous of telling his old friend unpleasant news, and when I looked at Hugh MacGowan I saw that he knew it too. He was watching Patrick with his peculiar intentness, and I saw the muscles tighten again about his mouth.

"I would prefer to leave," I heard myself say, and then as I glimpsed Patrick's expression I added with a note of false gaiety, "Oh, very well. I'll be happy to stay if you wish." And I sat down on a chair by the door with every appearance of willingness.

Patrick and MacGowan were still standing.

"Do sit down, Hugh," said Patrick.

"I'd rather stand."

Patrick looked taken aback by this show of hostility but recovered himself quickly. "Very well," he said in a level voice. "Now, in regard to your father—"

"I understand you want to dismiss him," said MacGowan.

"I did suggest that he might retire, yes. You see—"

"He's served you and your father for thirty years," said Mac-Gowan, "yet you'd kick him out without a second thought."

"No indeed! There would, of course, be a generous pension."

"My father's work is his life. He's not yet ready to retire."

"But I really feel—"

"What you feel isn't good enough, Lord de Salis," said Mac-Gowan. "It's simply not good enough."

There was a deathly silence. I was so horrified by the man's insolence that I couldn't speak. My mind screamed at Patrick, Answer him! Throw him out! But Patrick was as stunned as I was and could do no more than stare at MacGowan in stupefaction.

"My father is unwell," said MacGowan quietly at last. "He's been working himself to death for you, dealing with a famine-ridden estate and tenants who do nothing but listen to the leaders of the Land League. Do you know nothing of what goes on in Ireland? Does it mean nothing to you that Ireland's political troubles are the worst they've been this century and that the entire country's on the border of anarchy? Charles Stewart Parnell makes speeches telling the Irish peasants to pay only rent they consider fair, but you don't give a straw about Charles Stewart Parnell, do you? You're too busy idling away your time in England, so it's my father who has to carry the entire burden of tenant rebellion, it's my father who has to decide that mass evictions might after all be unavoidable, it's my father who has to sleep with a gun by his bedside every night because he has the courage and the moral conviction that he must be loyal to his employer. Yet all you can do when you come back from England is loaf around here and tell my father he must retire! He deserves your gratitude, my lord, not your contempt, and it's a poor reward for all his loyal service to talk of compulsory retirement and 'generous' pensions."

"But—"

"He's suffering only from exhaustion. Give him a month's rest and he'll be as fit as he ever was."

"I—I don't see how you can be certain of that," said Patrick, stammering in his confusion. "I mean, I think he's rather ill. Besides, he's not getting any younger. I really do think it would be best if—"

"There can be no retirement," said MacGowan.

"But I can't continue to employ a lunatic!"

"Don't call my father a lunatic!"

"And don't come here dictating to me!" yelled Patrick. I was never so glad to see him lose his temper. I was still sitting riveted to my chair, still unable to speak. "Get out of my house and take your crazy old father back to Scotland and damn you both to hell!"

Everything happened very quickly after that. I was still looking at Patrick with relief, and Patrick, trembling with anger, was turning toward me when MacGowan grabbed him by the arm, spun him around and struck him a terrific blow across the mouth.

I screamed. I leaped to my feet just as Patrick righted himself after reeling against a high-backed chair.

"Patrick!" I screamed again, rushing forward instinctively, but he pushed me away.

"Keep back," he said to me through his teeth and swung his fist at MacGowan's jaw.

MacGowan dodged, lunged and tried to throw Patrick to the floor by a quick shift of weight, but Patrick was strong enough to drag MacGowan after him as he fell. They began to wrestle, their bodies locked together, their breath rasping like animals, and as I wrenched open the door they both saw Patrick's discarded riding crop at one and the same moment.

Paralyzed, I stopped on the threshold, but although I tried to scream a third time no sound came. MacGowan had grabbed the crop. I waited, not knowing at first what I was waiting for but finally realizing I was waiting for Patrick to wrest the crop from him. He could have done it. I knew he could have done it. He was taller than MacGowan and surely he was stronger, but all the fight drained out of him—I saw it happen—and MacGowan began to lash out at the prostrate body on the floor.

"Stop, stop!" But it was I who was shouting at MacGowan, not Patrick. Patrick never spoke, and suddenly his silence was blistering in its eloquence.

Memories flashed through my mind. Patrick reminiscing with

bizarre nostalgia about the beatings he had received from his father. Patrick's stimulation when I had struck him during one of our early quarrels. Hadn't I found out long ago that if I wanted to excite him I had to be violent as well as passionate? I had never stopped to think about this before, and now that I did I knew why. It was because such behavior made no sense. Impossible for anyone to enjoy being an object of violence, impossible for anyone to welcome it.

Yet the impossible was happening before my eyes. I stared, unwilling to believe what I saw, and even when I believed I remained unable to interpret it. It was beyond my understanding, outside the realm of my experience, and because of this the scene took on a new dimension of terror and repulsion.

I backed away, stumbling against the doorframe, and the next moment I was running away down the passage. It was as if I were moving in a nightmare, that familiar nightmare where one's feet are weighted with lead and the long corridor is never-ending and some unnameable horror lies in the darkness left behind. My mouth opened. I was shrieking for Thomas, for David, even for Hayes, who had never returned from Dublin, and my voice reverberated in my ears as crazily as if I were falling down some bottomless shaft.

The last thing I saw before I fainted was the housemaid's white, terrified face receding from me as I collapsed onto the cold marble floor of the hall.

When I recovered consciousness Thomas and David were with me, the housemaid had fled and I seemed to be lying in a pool of poteen.

"Drink some of this, Sarah. I can't find the brandy, but Patrick drinks this, so it must be safe." It was David. I found myself half sitting, half lying in his arms, the glass of poteen two inches from my nose. I pushed the glass away and tried not to faint again.

"Here comes Patrick," said Thomas far above me and then exclaimed in a horrified voice, "For God's sake, Patrick, what the devil's been going on?"

I opened my eyes wider. The scene ceased to be a blur and became etched in harsh, painful lines. Patrick had a bruise below one eye, a cut lip and a red weal across his cheek, but he was smiling. MacGowan was unmarked. He was smiling too.

"Patrick," I said. I suddenly realized I was on my feet, although I had no idea how I arrived there. I was still leaning heavily on David. "Patrick . . ."

"My poor Sarah, whatever's the matter? You'd better go upstairs

384

and rest. Oh, by the way, Hugh, allow me to present my brothers. Thomas, David, this is Hugh MacGowan. You'll stay to dinner, Hugh, won't you?"

"Patrick," my voice repeated before MacGowan could reply. "I don't understand. The quarrel, the fight . . ."

"Fight? Oh, for God's sake, Sarah, that was just a spot of horse-play! That was all it was, wasn't it, Hugh?" he added, and as MacGowan smiled I saw that Patrick was gazing at him with that mesmerized enthusiasm he had once reserved exclusively for my old enemy, Derry Stranahan.

III

For months Marguerite and I had worried about my ability to stay faithful to Patrick. It was ironic to think that when my marriage finally collapsed the infidelity was Patrick's, not mine.

It took me a long time before I realized what was happening. I wasn't totally blind. I saw from the beginning that Hugh was going to take Derry's place, but it was because I assumed Hugh would be no more than a second Derry that I closed my eyes to the situation long after they should have remained wide open. There was another reason too for my slowness, for in the new year I went to England at last to see the children and sort out Marguerite's effects, and I was away from Cashelmara for some weeks.

"I'd like to come with you, of course," Patrick said. "But I really think I have a duty at present to stay here."

It would indeed have been awkward for him to leave. Hugh had offered to quit his post in Scotland in order to help his aging father at Cashelmara, but first he had had to return to Scotland to wind up his affairs there, and if Patrick too had left at that time the estate would have been quite untended. The elder MacGowan had gone with his son—"A holiday," explained Patrick, "to improve his health"—and for a month Cashelmara was without an agent.

I went to London. I saw my children. I wrote long dutiful letters to Patrick asking if I should engage a governess or tutor for Ned and saying how well John could walk now and how pretty Eleanor was when she smiled. David had returned to school, but Thomas came up to town every weekend from Oxford to help me sort through Marguerite's possessions. When I had finished with the house in St. James's Square I went down to Surrey. It was painful to return to the house at Mickleham where we had spent so many happy months, and yet in confronting the pain I was at last able to grieve in a more normal way for Marguerite and I spent many hours weeping in my room.

As if mirroring my pain, Thomas wanted to sell the house at Mickleham, but David refused to allow this. Evidently the happy memories that were so hard for Thomas and myself to bear were a solace to him, and at last in deference to his feelings the house was not sold but let for a short period to a family who had just returned from India. The townhouse was retained. The boys regarded it as home, and although Patrick had invited them to live with us at Cashelmara they were old enough to prefer a home of their own.

"Besides," said Thomas, "Ireland's no place for an Englishman these days what with the Land League and the agrarian outrages and all this talk of Home Rule."

"Ireland's such a delightful place to visit," said David, anxious that I shouldn't take offense, "and I would certainly like to spend part of each year at Cashelmara, but . . ."

"Not all the year," I said. "I understand."

Patrick too said he understood. He was answering my long dutiful letters as soon as they reached him, and this surprised me, for he was a poor correspondent. Presently he told me that Hugh had returned from Scotland and would often have dinner with him after they had toured the estate together.

"Hugh's frighteningly efficient," he wrote, "and hard as nails about money. I can't believe how lucky I am that he wants to come and work here."

This pleased me very much. If Hugh was going to make Patrick a rich man again I was going to be the last person to raise any objection.

"Old MacGowan's better now," wrote Patrick in March, "but he and Hugh don't really get on together very well, and so I've invited Hugh to stay at Cashelmara until Clonagh Court is rebuilt. I thought Clonagh Court would suit him rather well. Of course it's been empty since Derry and Clara lived there, and the wretched Irish have chopped down all the doors to use for fuel, but nevertheless it does have distinct possibilities. Hugh says I can't afford to renovate it immediately, however, so that's why I invited him to stay at Cashelmara. He can have the guest rooms in the west wing, and I don't think he'll really get in our way at all."

My way, I thought. But I was impressed by Hugh's grasp of what

Patrick could and could not afford, and I agreed that in order to keep a first-class agent at Cashelmara it was vital to provide him with a first-class home.

Meanwhile, I was making my preparations to return to Ireland. A governess had been engaged for Ned; Mr. Rathbone, the family attorney, had been seen for the last time; and Patrick wrote to say that there hadn't been a new case of fever in the valley for three weeks.

". . . and I've just had a letter from Edith." he added, concluding his letter with bad news. "She's quarreled with Clara and wants to know if she can come to stay. It's deuced awkward, isn't it? Now that Marguerite's dead, it would hardly be appropriate for Edith to live alone with the boys at St. James's Square, and if she's quarreled with Clara she has nowhere else to go unless I invite her to Cashelmara. I suppose I'll have to invite her, but I know it'll be an awful bore for you, darling, and you'll probably be furious. But what else can I do?"

I thought of Marguerite saying, "Poor Edith . . . one must make allowances," and I did my best to dredge up the dregs of my charity.

"Yes, you'll have to invite her," I wrote back to Patrick with reluctance, and soon Edith arrived at St. James's Square to join me on the journey to Ireland.

I'll say this for Edith: She could never mention Marguerite's name without tears springing to her eyes, and when I saw this my heart did soften and I made all kinds of resolutions to be patient and friendly toward her.

But I still found this hard. Edith was cross because she hadn't had an invitation to spend the Season in Town, and she resented the prospect of being marooned at Cashelmara.

"It's not marriage itself I care about," she said to me in her querulous voice, "but a girl ain't worth sixpence unless she's married, Sarah, we both know that. And, besides, I'd like a home of my own and the freedom to come and go as I please. Personally I think most men are very silly creatures and I never did care for children, but I've got my self-respect, just like any other girl, and I don't see why I should be a failure and Clara a success just because Clara paints herself up and simpers at the right moment. Heavens, you should see how much Clara rouges! I think it's disgraceful. I never thought the day would come when I would have to admit to anyone that my own sister would stoop so low."

I had to tolerate this tedious conversation throughout the entire journey to Ireland, and by the time I arrived at Cashelmara I was wondering not only how I had endured the journey but how I was going to endure the approaching summer. In fact I was so sick of Edith that I was even more pleased than I thought I would be to see Patrick again. He hugged me very warmly and said how much better I was looking, and then he hugged all the children and gave Ned a pick-a-back ride around the hall. Amidst the excited squeals of joy I barely noticed Hugh watching from the gallery, and it was not until some minutes later that Patrick called him down to present him to Edith and the children.

Of course I soon realized that they were living in each other's pockets, out together all day and dining together every evening, but I decided immediately that I wasn't going to complain. I was twenty-nine years old now, not a spoiled, petulant bride of nineteen, and I prided myself on being mature enough to cope with my husband's intense friendships with people of his own sex. So when Patrick said to me guiltily, "I suppose you resent me spending so much time with Hugh," I said at once, "Not at all, darling. I expect you've missed the boys since they went back to England, and it's nice you've found a good friend to keep you company."

I thought how proud Marguerite would have been of me. No scenes, no tantrums, just a serenity which came from an adroit handling of an awkward situation. Of course it *was* awkward that Patrick had decided his best friend should be his Scottish agent, but it was really no more awkward than when Derry had been his best friend, and that was a situation I knew all about, that was a road I had traveled before, and a problem that is familiar isn't nearly so difficult to solve as a problem outside one's experience.

Also, my marriage was at a different stage by this time. In the early years I had wanted Patrick's company every hour of the day and night, but now that we were leading our separate lives I was no longer inclined to lose my temper merely because he preferred someone else's company to mine.

Yet Hugh was very different from Derry. I knew this, still, with a misunderstanding that seems in retrospect almost deliberate, I went on assigning him Derry's role. I had hated Derry, but now unexpectedly I found myself sympathetic to his memory. I remembered his wit and his gaiety, his good looks and his charm. I could understand why Patrick, after a lonely, gloomy childhood, had

388

chosen Derry for a friend, but what I found impossible to understand was why he had chosen Hugh to take Derry's place. Hugh was always so self-effacingly courteous to me that I never summoned the energy to dislike him, but still I thought him not only humorless and passionless but also unremittingly dull.

"But he's really quite clever," said Edith. "Oh, not a gentleman, of course, but he's remarkably well educated for a mere agent, and those Scots are always so hard-working. I wonder why he's never married."

"Well, he's so plain a woman would have to be desperate to look at him more than once," I said snappishly. Edith always made me snappish, and after ten minutes in her company I found myself saying things I would normally have shunned.

"But he's very masculine," said Edith, "don't you think?"

I said I really hadn't thought about it and excused myself from her company by saying I wanted to look over my household accounts. Cashelmara was fully staffed again by this time, but although Hayes and his wife had eventually crept back from Dublin to resume their posts as butler and housekeeper, Hugh, like his father, had insisted that they be dismissed. I was sorry, for Mrs. Hayes had always been agreeable and Hayes himself had long seemed a part of Cashelmara, but it did at least give me the chance to act as my own housekeeper and evolve an efficient system for running the house. At first I found it very difficult. Irish servants are notoriously unwilling to be efficient, and I began to despair of ever living in an organized household, but gradually I learned from my numerous mistakes until at last I had some idea how much food cost, how many tenants paid their rent in food, how much the servants could be expected to do and how many funerals and wakes would keep them from doing a full day's work. In fact I was so busy, dividing my time between household matters and the children, that it was not until early June that I found out exactly how matters stood between Patrick and Hugh MacGowan.

It all happened very simply. George called late one morning from Letterturk, and when I received him he told me he had come in response to a note from Patrick. He didn't mention what message the note had contained, but I suspected it had been a request for a small loan. Patrick wouldn't have dared ask for a large one, but only money could have driven him to invite George to lunch.

I knew nothing about this invitation, but I concealed my ignorance from George and sent Flannigan to find Patrick. Flannigan was the new butler from Dublin. He always seemed to walk on tiptoe and possessed a large paunch and impeccable credentials.

"I hope Patrick hasn't forgotten he sent for me," said George, sensing my ignorance and beginning to pace in annoyance up and down the room. "I postponed an important engagement to ride here to see him."

Flannigan chose that moment to enter the room and say that Patrick was nowhere to be found.

"Let *me* go and look for him," I said, acutely embarrassed by this time, and escaped upstairs as fast as I could. I looked in our apartments, and when I found them deserted I went to the bathroom. There was only one bathroom at Cashelmara, an innovation I had achieved with great difficulty some years ago when an engineer had been coaxed from London to install a bath and a water closet, and although the plumbing was always breaking down it was at least an improvement on the medieval conditions I had found on my first visit to Cashelmara. Convinced that Patrick was there (Flannigan would have had too much delicacy to invade a bathroom), I rattled the handle noisily and was most surprised when the unlocked door swung open to reveal an empty room. I went to the nurseries. No one was there, for the children were all outside in the garden. I was just beginning to feel baffled when I remembered the sitting room of Hugh's apartments and hurried down the long passage to the west wing.

"Patrick!" I called, knocking on the sitting-room door, but there was no answer. I looked in. Again the room was empty, the curtains blowing lightly in the breeze from the open window, and I was about to hurry back to the gallery when I heard Patrick laugh.

I spun around. Across the room, twenty feet away from me, was a door that led into the adjoining bedroom.

I should have stopped to think then, but I didn't. It was so much easier not to stop, not to think, not to face reality. So much easier to remember George pacing angrily up and down the morning room, so much easier to say to myself in relief, So Patrick's here after all. So much easier to cross the room, to knock and open the bedroom door without waiting for a reply.

"Patrick . . ." I began, and then everything ended, all my illusions, all my false hopes, all my desire to preserve the pathetic shell of my marriage.

I looked upon the truth, and the truth was terrible to me.

Not one of us spoke. The scene should have remained a clear

390

tableau etched forever in my mind, but so appalled was I by what I saw that now when I look back all I can recall is the bed bathed in the brilliant sunlight of that summer morning and the smile of amusement tightening the corners of MacGowan's wide, brutal mouth.

Chapter Five

I

Patrick said, "We'd better talk, hadn't we?" and I was dumb; I could think of nothing to say. I had forgotten entirely about George waiting downstairs. Hours later I heard he had left in disgust when neither Patrick nor I appeared to lunch with him, but meanwhile I could think of nothing but my discovery.

We were in my room. Mauve silk counterpane, mauve silk bed draperies, satinwood furniture, all so delicate and pretty, and beyond the window was the familiar view of the lough shimmering in the heat of a summer noon.

Patrick said something about being sorry and I must believe him but he hadn't wanted to hurt me.

I laughed. I must have been even more distraught than I thought I was.

"No, Sarah—please . . . listen. I know you won't understand, but—"

"I understand perfectly," I said. "I've been very naïve and very stupid. I suppose this has been going on for a long time. With other men."

He shook his head. "There's been no one else."

"No one else since Derry, you mean!"

Again he shook his head and again he said, "There's been no one else."

"I don't believe you," I said. I was trembling. I could feel my self-control slipping out of my reach, and the next moment before I could stop myself I was saying terrible things, cruel things, calling him warped and depraved and disgusting, but all the while I shouted at him he stood quietly, not saying a word in his own defense, until his passive acceptance of my abuse infuriated me even more than an outburst of temper. At last I stopped. There was nothing else I could say, and in the silence that followed I felt no longer enraged but baffled, humiliated by that passiveness I now recognized as dignity. I wanted to cry but the tears refused to come. I wanted to understand why I should feel so annihilated, but all I understood was my isolation, my helplessness and my overwhelming sense of failure.

After a while I managed to say, "If I were being rejected for another woman I could begin to look for reasons, I could fight, try to change myself, try to win you back. But this . . . there's nothing I can do. I'm rejected for being something I can't help and can never change."

"You are what you are," he said, "and I am what I am. And I discovered a little while ago that I would rather be what I am than pretend to be something I'm not."

"But—"

"Oh, you needn't worry. I'll act the right part to the rest of the world, but I'm not acting parts to myself any more, that's all. That's finished."

The pain had spread to the front of my head. I tried to think clearly, but it was too difficult.

"Listen, Sarah," he said. He had drawn up the stool from the dressing table and was sitting facing me. His eyes were very blue. "Don't let's deceive ourselves any more. Our marriage was finished long before this. We've made each other very unhappy very often and you know that as well as I do. If it weren't for the children we could think of our marriage as eleven wasted years, but the children make up for almost everything, don't they, all those quarrels, all those fights, all that bickering. Now, there's no question of divorce, we both know that, and there's no question but that for the children's sake we must go on living under the same roof like any other married couple, but the time has come when we have to acknowledge to each other that we're entitled to our separate private lives. I shan't mind if you have lovers. I shall only mind if you fail to be as discreet as I intend to be with Hugh."

I said so quickly that I stumbled over my words, "You can't mean you're going to continue seeing Hugh."

He looked at me as if I were mad. "But of course I am," he said, amazed. "What did you think?"

"But you can't . . . you wouldn't . . ."

"We won't embarrass you. No one will ever know."

"Of course they'll know! They'll find out!" I was so appalled that again I had difficulty in speaking. "Patrick, if you continue to live with that man—"

"Sarah, he means all the world to me. I'm not letting him go."

"Then I'll leave," I said. I felt strong suddenly. I stood up. "I'll take the children. I'll divorce you."

"Don't be a fool." He stood up too. He was losing his quiet passiveness at last, and his mouth was set in a stubborn angry line. "Do you think I'd ever let those children go?"

"You're not fit to bring up children!" I began to walk toward the door.

"Sarah, listen to me." He caught my arm and spun me around to face him, but I wrenched myself free.

"Let me go!" I grabbed wildly at the door handle. I was gasping for breath, my eyes blinded by tears.

"No . . . wait . . . " He gripped my wrist again, but he was too late. The handle turned, the door swung wide.

And there on the threshold stood Hugh MacGowan.

II

There was no time to scream. There was hardly time to gasp. Patrick exclaimed in relief, "Thank God you're here! Why didn't you come straight in?" And I heard MacGowan say in his pleasant, even voice, "I thought Lady de Salis should at least be given the chance to see reason without undue persuasion."

He was closing the door, turning the key in the lock. I took one pace back from him, then another, but it wasn't until he turned to look at me again that I realized I was terrified.

"Please sit down, Lady de Salis," he said. We were always so polite to each other, he addressing me with the formality appropriate for his employer's wife, I addressing him with the cordiality due to a friend of my husband's. It was true I had thought of him privately as "Hugh," but it wasn't until that day, when I became obliged to use his Christian name, that my private thoughts labeled him simply "MacGowan."

394

"I think it's time you and I had a talk together," he was saying, and backing my way to the bed, I sat down on the edge.

He watched me. His gray eyes were intent, his head tilted slightly to one side, as if he were making some complex calculation. I noticed that his arms didn't hang loosely but were stiff at his sides, while his fingers curled toward the palms of his hands.

"First of all," he said, "I'm going to tell you what you're going to do. Then I'm going to tell you why you're going to do it—or, in other words, I'm going to explain to you what will happen if you don't do exactly as you're told."

I managed to look at Patrick. He was standing by the window and examining his thumbnail. The early-afternoon sunlight, slanting into the room, made his hair seem fairer than it was.

"Are you listening to me, Sarah?" said Hugh MacGowan.

Anger gave me courage. "How dare you address me as Sarah!" I said furiously, "And how dare you tell me what to do!"

"Be quiet." He never raised his voice, but I saw his knuckles shine white in the dim light by the door. "Talk to Patrick as you wish, but never make the mistake of thinking you can treat me as you treat him."

There was a silence before he moved slowly to the foot of the bed. My fingers closed on a fold of the bedspread and held it tightly.

"There's going to be no scandal," he said at last. "Do you understand that, Sarah? No scandal. And that means no divorce. We're all going to come to an arrangement. It's going to be a very civilized arrangement, Sarah, and if you behave sensibly there's no reason why you should find it intolerable. Quite the contrary. You'll continue to be mistress of Cashelmara and you'll continue to live with your children—and what else do you want? Not, surely, a loving husband insisting on his marital rights—or a lover insisting on sharing your bed. Of course, as Patrick has already said, you can have a lover if you want one, but let's not be hypocritical, Sarah. Since we're all being so honest with one another let's admit that you have your deficiencies as a woman and that you're unlikely to suffer a broken heart merely because you sleep alone every night."

He stopped. I felt sick. I felt the color stain my neck, and all I could think in an agony of humiliation was that he knew, Patrick had told him; he knew what a failure I was and despised me for it.

"Of course we shall all have to make our little sacrifices to ensure that the arrangement works well," he was saying, "but on the whole I think Patrick and I will have to sacrifice more, in the name of discretion, than you'll have to sacrifice. You'll merely have to sacrifice your pride, Sarah, and considering you really have so little to be proud of, I don't think that's asking too much of you."

There was a pause. He relaxed slightly, unclenching one of his fists and tracing a pattern with his finger on the post at the foot of the bed.

"Do you understand me so far, Sarah? Good. Now let me explain what will happen if you should be misguided enough to try to undermine our arrangement. For instance, if you should complain to your sister-in-law Miss de Salis, or Patrick's brothers, or even your own brother in New York—or, worse still, if you should try to leave with the children or seek legal advice or take any step that would result in scandal—well, that really wouldn't be at all advisable, Sarah. Believe me, that would be most foolish. You should always remember that Cashelmara is very . . . remote. Unpleasant things can happen in remote places, particularly to people who break their word or go back on a bargain—and there's going to be a bargain, Sarah, make no mistake about that. You're going to give us your word that you'll do everything possible to preserve the *status quo*. You've no choice. The cards are stacked against you, and if by some extraordinary chance you managed to reach the divorce court you'd soon find out that you'd be the one who suffered most. A deserting wife, perhaps a little manufactured evidence of adultery, and what would you say to the judge? 'Please, my lord, my husband's indulging in unmentionable vices with another man'? Who's going to believe that? There's not a soul in England or Ireland who can testify that Patrick has previously indulged himself in this way, and as for myself . . . well, I intend to marry once I've moved to Clonagh Court—that's one of the sacrifices I shall make to sustain this arrangement of ours—and a judge will think twice then before believing any hysterical accusations you might be foolish enough to make. But you wouldn't be so foolish, would you, Sarah? I do give you credit for some intelligence, and besides, I should be so angry if you broke your part of the bargain. You do understand that, Sarah, don't you? I should be so very angry."

He was standing over me. I was staring blindly at the carpet, but I was aware of nothing but his right fist clenched six inches from my face.

"We mustn't have any scandal, must we, Sarah?"

"No," I said.

"It would be so bad for all of us. Particularly for the children."

"Yes."

"Good. I'm glad we're in agreement. Now give me your word you'll do everything possible to preserve our arrangement."

"I . . . give you my word—"

"Go on."

"—to do everything possible to . . . preserve the arrangement."

"You'll ostensibly continue to be a devoted wife to Patrick. You'll make no complaints."

"Yes."

"I want your word, Sarah. I want to hear you promise."

"I promise."

"Yes?"

"Devoted wife . . . no complaints."

"Very well." He touched me. I cried out with the shock, and when he saw my terror he smiled. "That's better," he said, tilting my chin up so that I was forced to look him in the eyes. "I like a woman to be meek and submissive." His fingers tightened on my face. I would have cried out again, but I could barely breathe. "Now listen to me," he said, his smile vanished, his voice low. "You keep your promises, for I swear to God that if you break them I'll hurt you in places where not even your maid would think to look."

He released me. I fell back on the bed and the room spun dizzily before my eyes.

"Is there anything you want to say to her, Patrick?"

There was a silence, the silence of Cashelmara, intense, empty and cruel.

"Very well, we'll go. Goodbye, Sarah. Remember what I've said."

I remembered. I remembered night after night and day after day, and as I tried in despair to see some way of escape from the locked strait-jacket of my marriage, the nightmare of MacGowan's "arrangement" stretched ahead of me as far as the eye could see.

III

A week passed. They left me well alone, and whenever I did see MacGowan he was always so scrupulously polite to me that I could almost believe I had imagined the scene in my room. At last when I could think of the situation dispassionately I even found myself agreeing with him that there should be no scandal that would affect the children's future. I had decided after Marguerite's death that the children's future was to be my future also, and it seemed increasingly important to me not to put that future in jeopardy. The children were all I had, my one success amidst many failures, so they must, whatever happened, come first. What did Patrick's private life and my own humiliation matter when weighed against the children's welfare? It was vital for the children to have two parents who were outwardly on good terms with each other. Any hint of divorce, with all its implications about unnatural vice . . . No, it was unthinkable. Better MacGowan's arrangement than that, and besides once MacGowan moved to Clonagh Court I would hardly see him.

Perhaps the arrangement wouldn't be as bad as I had feared. My humiliation would exist, but at least no one would know about it.

Ned wouldn't know. Ned with his bright hair and eyes, his boisterous, inexhaustible energy so different from John's timid liveliness. People said it was strange that John spoke so little, but he could talk, I knew he could, and he was so affectionate, quite different from Ned, who was always dashing off on some expedition and never had time for more than a passing hug. All John needed was time. Marguerite had understood, telling me those stories of how late David had been in walking.

I did so miss Marguerite.

"Baby's coming along nicely, my lady," said Nanny as I helped Eleanor stagger across the nursery floor. "I think she'll walk before she's a year old." Eleanor looked like Ned because of her bright hair and eyes. She was going to be so pretty, and I could hardly wait for her to grow a little older so that I could order lots of dresses for her, silk and muslin and organdy, and hats, lovely straw hats with pink streamers and little bonnets for the Sunday services at the chapel. I could so clearly see us all strolling up the Azalea Walk, my fingers resting lightly on Patrick's arm, the children hand in hand—and no one would ever know.

In September MacGowan arranged for work to begin on Clonagh Court and announced that he intended to move there in the new year.

Thank God, I thought, and began to pine for the new year as a convict in prison might pine for the day of his release.

"Sarah," said Edith at the beginning of October, "I wonder if I might speak to you for a moment."

Edith wore an olive-green handkerchief dress, very fashionable, and a multitude of fussy carnation-red trimmings which matched her rouged cheeks. At first I thought she had been daring enough to revive the bustle, but then I realized she was merely ill-corseted.

"Yes, of course, Edith," I said, pausing in my letter to Charles.

Edith and I had succeeded in avoiding each other with greater success than I had dared hope for that summer, and I had even forgotten when we had last had "words."

Edith sat down. We were upstairs in the room I had converted into a little boudoir, or sitting room, for myself. I had felt the need for a private retreat of my own, and although I had expected Patrick to object he had approved of the idea and had even told me I could refurnish the room if I wished. But I hadn't wanted to be extravagant. I had merely brought some old furniture down from the attics and ordered the reupholstering of the Grecian sofa and chairs and the refinishing of the Carlton House writing table. I had sufficiently tired of the exotic tastes of the Prince Regent to judge them decadent, but Cashelmara had influenced me subtly again, and just as I no longer found the house ugly, so I now found the turn-of-the-century furnishings more attractive than the efforts of modern craftsmen and their machines.

"I have some important news to tell you," Edith was saying.

"Oh? How exciting! Do tell me." I thought perhaps she might have had an invitation to spend Christmas with Clara. They had patched up their quarrel and were corresponding regularly again.

"I'm going to be married," said Edith.

There was a silence. I looked at the fire in the grate and the mist beyond the window and my unfinished letter to Charles before me on the writing table.

"But how lovely, Edith!" I said. But it wasn't lovely at all. I saw my coming freedom vanish and my jailer no longer in retreat but stationed permanently outside my prison cell. "And who is the gentleman I must congratulate?"

She told me. I tried to think of something to say.

"The *younger* Mr. MacGowan, of course," said Edith, smiling as I groped for words.

"Of course," I said, and all the time I was wondering how much she knew and whether there was any chance of making her change her mind.

"We'll be married in the new year. Clonagh Court will be ready by then, and I dare say Hugh will have made it comfortable. However," said Edith, giving me another smile, "I expect we shall be often at Cashelmara."

I said nothing. There was a pause.

"I can see you think I'll be marrying beneath me," said Edith, but she didn't sound dismayed.

"Of course I think you're marrying beneath you," I said. "Hugh MacGowan's hardly a man of your own class."

"Ah well," said Edith, very coolly, "if he's good enough for Patrick, he should be good enough for me, don't you think?"

There was another silence.

Edith was still smiling, and as I realized how intensely she disliked me a series of vistas into the future, each more appalling than the last, began to flash before my eyes.

"Please don't worry, Sarah," said Edith. "I declare I shall be a positive paragon of discretion. Of course I shall expect one or two little favors now and then but nothing you can't easily manage. For example, I shall expect to have regular invitations to Cashelmara, and I shall expect to move in your social set. Patrick tells me you're full of plans for the future because you're anxious for the children to move in the right circles." She paused. "Oh, come, Sarah, don't be difficult about this! You can't cut me after I'm married, you know. Hugh wouldn't like that at all. In fact he thinks it's a very good thing that I'll be living so near you. He thinks you need a companion of your own age—someone to cheer you up when you feel low-spirited, someone to . . . well, someone to keep an eye on you. So thoughtful of him, don't you think?"

I put down my pen. Watching the flames in the grate, I said, "Edith, I don't think there's anything else we need say to each other at present. If you'll excuse me, I would like to finish this letter to my brother."

"Dear me," said Edith. "We're rather uppity all of a sudden, aren't we? Hoity-toity!"

"Edith, I can't believe you really want to marry a man like that."

"Why not? I'm tired of being left out, passed over, pitied and forgotten! And I like Hugh. He's the only man who's ever given me credit for any intelligence. 'I need a clever, exceptional wife,' he said, 'a woman capable of handling an unusual situation with the maximum of efficiency and discretion. I want a partner,' he said, 'someone I can trust, someone who can share my ambitions.' "

"He's marrying you simply to conceal his relationship with Patrick," I said.

"You're quite wrong. He likes me just as much as I like him."

"I should think it's the idea of a rich wife that he likes. Your money would compensate him for the tedium of being obliged to share a house with you."

"How dare you say such a thing!"

400

"Why not? It's true. It *is* tedious to have to share a house with you. My God, I should know!"

"You wicked, evil-tongued slut!" shouted Edith. She was red in the face, and her protuberant eyes glittered with rage. "You'll be sorry you said that!"

"And you'll be sorry you didn't stay a spinster," I said. "God only knows what kind of a marriage you'll have."

She didn't answer. She had already stormed out of the room, and as the door slammed behind her I began to tremble at the thought of her complaining to MacGowan.

IV

"That really wasn't very sensible of you, Sarah," he said. He entered the room without knocking, and the shock of seeing him so suddenly jerked me to my feet. The fashion magazine that had arrived that morning slipped through my hands to the floor, but I made no attempt to pick it up.

"Sit down," he said.

I sat down on the edge of the window seat and stared at him mutely.

"If you want me to treat you with the minimum of courtesy," he said, "you'd better mend your manners toward Edith."

"Yes. I'm sorry."

"So you should be. You can apologize to Edith in the drawing room before dinner tonight, but don't do it before Patrick and I join you. I want to hear your apologies for myself."

"Yes."

"And if you ever make the mistake of being so rude to Edith again . . ."

"I won't."

The door closed. He was gone, the unspoken threat lingering behind him. At last when I had stopped shivering I went to my bedroom, took a shawl from the chest and drew the folds tightly around me before I tiptoed downstairs. Patrick was in the garden. He had spent so many summer days there that the sun had lightened his hair, and in a moment of irony I realized that although he had always been a handsome man he was even more striking now at thirty-five than when he had proposed to me twelve years earlier. The change lay not merely in the fact that his physique was enhanced by his obvious good health and that his eyes seemed unusually blue in contrast to his sunburned skin. The difference ran deeper than that. He seemed to have a new self-assurance, and as I watched him working rhythmically his movements seemed not only graceful but full of the purpose he had lacked when he had been no more than an ingenuous and idle young man about town.

He was wearing his gardening clothes—old trousers and boots, a faded tweed jacket—and in his hands was a twig broom he was using to sweep the autumn leaves from the weedless expanse of lawn. Ned and John, each equipped with little twig brooms, were busy helping him, and on the stone seat on the far side of the lawn Nanny was knitting beside Eleanor's perambulator.

"Patrick," I said, "may I have a word with you, please?"

"Of course." He was smiling at Ned, who was staggering across to the wheelbarrow with his arms full of leaves. "What is it?"

"A word without the children."

"Papa, is it time to light the bonfire yet?"

"In a minute. I'm just going to show Mama the new sundial in the Italian Garden. You stay with John and make sure he doesn't toss all the leaves out of the wheelbarrow."

We crossed the lawn, and he led me up a path to a new clearing in the woods where stone balustrades enclosed a long deep pit that would eventually be filled with water. At the far end in the center of a paved square stood the block of stone that he had transformed into a sundial.

"What's the matter?" he said, pausing to run his fingers over the familiar stone, and in that casual gesture I saw how calm he was, how relaxed and unconcerned. I was clasping my shawl around me so tightly that my fingers ached, and the air was so dank in the woods that I had begun to shiver again. The fallen leaves bore the faint, moist scent of autumn, and above us the sun was already sinking in the late-afternoon sky.

"Edith has told me about her engagement," I said. I had to be very careful, since every word I said would be repeated to MacGowan. "I'm glad for her, since she's so anxious to be married, and I hope she'll find this marriage will give her what she wants. But, Patrick, you know Edith and I have never got along. Why, you yourself have said at least a dozen times how difficult she is! Yet now she's talking of seeing a great deal of me after she's married, and I just don't know what I'm going to do. How am I ever to avoid quarreling with her? We're so unsuited to be friends. I think perhaps Hugh doesn't quite realize how unsuited we are."

"Hm," said Patrick, still fingering the sundial. I noticed a button was missing from his tweed jacket. "Well, you'd better do as Hugh says."

"I know, but . . ." I stopped, kept calm, tried again. "Patrick, I'm being put in a very difficult position, can't you see that?"

"Well, why don't you talk to Hugh about it?"

"Because . . ." The nails dug into the palms of my hands. "Patrick, I'm terrified of Hugh. I think one day he's going to seize on some excuse to hurt me, and I'm afraid he's going to find the excuse he needs in my behavior toward Edith. I shall try as hard as I can to be civil to her, but . . . supposing I made a mistake—gave her offense. Patrick, you wouldn't let Hugh hurt me, would you? I mean . . . you don't hate me enough for that?"

"Of course I don't hate you!" he said, astonished, and laid a gentle, comforting hand on my arm. "And I don't see why you should be so worried about Hugh. He wouldn't hurt you unless you deserved it. He's very fair and just, and . . . well, I trust him to do whatever's right. He's awfully sharp, you know, and not at all the kind of person who makes mistakes."

"We all make mistakes," I said. I was beginning to feel ill. I had to lean against the sundial to support myself.

"Oh, if only you weren't so prejudiced against Hugh!" he exclaimed with a mixture of irritation and impatience. "If only you could see him as he really is! He's so clever and interesting—and he loves the land, just as I do, although he doesn't know much about flowers. Trees are his great interest, and he's made some marvelous suggestions for my topiary. In fact, he's the only person who's ever really understood about my garden. We talk about it for hours and hours, and . . . Sarah, you're not listening."

"I must sit down for a moment."

"But why can't you understand that your view of Hugh is distorted? Why can't you admit it? It's foolish to be so obstinate!"

"You're the expert in obstinacy," I heard myself say, but he did not answer, and presently when my dizziness had passed I looked up and found I was alone.

It was very quiet.

After a long time I went back to the lawn. Nanny had taken John and Eleanor indoors, but Ned was helping Patrick stoke the bonfire. I watched them, and when Ned waved I thought, What am I to do? But there was no answer, only Ned's bright smile and the acrid tang of smoke, and at last, seeing no alternative, I returned to my room to dress for dinner.

Chapter Six

I

In December Thomas and David arrived to spend Christmas with us, but since they had problems of their own, neither of them noticed immediately that anything was wrong. Thomas wanted to leave Oxford and study medicine in London, and David, who was eighteen, wanted Patrick's permission to visit the famous opera houses of the Continent. After that he would go up to Cambridge and write librettos while he studied English literature.

"But, David, librettos—the stage—is it really suitable?" I asked, worried, but Patrick said firmly, "I should do exactly as you wish, David, and if your librettos ever match the standard of W. S. Gilbert, I'd be awfully proud of you. Have you ever thought of translating the Johann Strauss operas into decent English?"

"But he's so difficult to translate! How do you translate a song where all the characters simply stand around singing 'Dui-du'?"

"Good God!" exclaimed Thomas fervently. "Thank heavens I at least have had the sense to choose a practical profession!"

"But, Thomas—medicine!" I could not help saying anxiously. "It's hardly very aristocratic. What would your mother have said?"

"I think she would have been very pleased," said Thomas. "She always encouraged my interest in anatomy and pathology. I know medicine is a middle-class profession, but I don't care, and as for leaving Oxford without a degree, I don't care about that either.

What's the point of giving up two more years of my life to obtain a piece of paper which will be worthless to me? I must study either at London or at Edinburgh. Oxford's no use to me. It's too old-fashioned."

"I loathed Oxford," said Patrick sympathetically.

"Then may I leave?"

"Why not? Do whatever you feel is best. I say, maybe Hugh knows about the medical school in Edinburgh. Why don't you ask him about it?"

But Thomas never asked. After their personal problems had been so happily resolved he and David became more observant of the situation at Cashelmara and soon began to regard MacGowan with suspicion.

"You don't really like him, do you, Sarah?" demanded Thomas.

I shrugged. "He's Patrick's best friend, so I must do my utmost to try."

"But surely Patrick can't remain entranced with him indefinitely!"

"Perhaps not," I said, and indeed this was the hope that sustained me during my worst moments of depression. Most love affairs didn't last. Why should this one be any exception to the rule? I would watch them daily for any sign of friction, but the only disagreement I saw occurred when Thomas and David left and Patrick for some reason began to drink heavily.

"You're a fool to start drinking before noon," I heard MacGowan say to him.

"You only say that because of that damnable Presbyterian upbringing you had."

"I say it because I care about your health," said MacGowan, and this was clever of him, for Patrick was sentimental enough to be touched by this show of concern. Handling Patrick was child's play to MacGowan, and for a while Patrick did restrict his drinking to the evenings.

February came. Edith was so busy putting the final touches to the interior of Clonagh Court that I seldom saw her, and the wedding date had been set for the middle of March.

"Marriage may be the making of poor Edith," said Madeleine during one of her calls to Cashelmara. She had been calling more frequently because she had at last succeeded in finding a new doctor to help her in the dispensary. Her success was all the greater since Dr. Cahill was a young man and had been trained in London as well as Dublin. "Of course MacGowan is most unsuitable, but Annabel married beneath her when she married Smith and so both her girls were set a poor example. However, I have every intention of being charitable in the circumstances, and it will certainly be pleasant to see Clonagh Court occupied again. I remember so well when my dear grandmother was alive . . ."

My thoughts drifted away. Madeleine often spoke of her grandmother, and Marguerite had once said the old woman had been an unfortunate influence. If only Marguerite had lived . . .

"And did I really smell whisky on Patrick's breath when he kissed me or was it my imagination?"

"I . . . don't know, Madeleine. I didn't notice it myself."

"Is anything troubling him?"

"Not as far as I know."

"Is anything troubling you?"

"No, Madeleine. Nothing."

"You've been looking a little strained these past few months. I wondered . . ."

"It's just that I find the task of housekeeping so demanding. There's always so much to do."

"Now that Patrick's situation has improved you should engage a housekeeper."

"No, we must save as much money as we can. The children . . . the future . . ." And I talked on and on about the future, because it was so much easier than to talk of the present.

For we lived in troubled times. I had been so wrapped up in my personal worries that I had found it difficult to pay attention to the troubles around me, but now for the first time in years I was surrounded by newspapers and continual discussions of politics. MacGowan watched public events closely, and Edith, whether through natural inclination or because of a desire to impress him, followed them as intently as he did. MacGowan, of course, had an ulterior motive. He and his father, who still helped him on the estate, dealt daily with a hostile, truculent tenantry, and every inflammable word uttered by Parnell, Davitt and Dillon stoked the fires of discontent. MacGowan's job made it vital for him to know what was happening, and because of this I found myself hearing all about the Land League, Parnell's organization bent on reform of the Irish land system, and all about Parnell himself with his band of sixty Irish members of Parliament at Westminster clamoring for Home Rule. Parnell, Dillon, Sullivan and the other leaders of the Land League had all been arrested the previous year and charged with conspiring to prevent a payment of rents, but in November after a twenty-one-day hearing the jury had failed to agree.

"A black day for us agents," said MacGowan grimly later, and began to talk of the Boycott case. Boycott, an agent who lived less than forty miles from Cashelmara on the shores of Lough Mask, refused to accept the rents his tenants were prepared to offer, but when he began his evictions, he found himself shunned by the community to such an extent that he had to bring in volunteers from the north to save his harvest for him. A military guard had to protect the volunteers, and the cost of the entire disaster amounted to ten times the value of the crop saved.

"My God!" exclaimed Patrick, much alarmed by this inability to control a united tenantry. "Supposing that should happen here!"

"Impossible," said MacGowan shortly. "Can you imagine the O'Malleys ever uniting with the Joyces for more than five minutes at a time? Besides, the Land League in this valley consists of no one but that ridiculous old secret society the Blackbooters, headed by that oaf Maxwell Drummond."

It gave me such a shock to hear Drummond's name on his lips that I barely heard Patrick warn him to be careful.

"After all, remember what happened to Derry," he concluded anxiously.

"Derry Stranahan lived by his wits, not his fists," said Mac-Gowan. "If he'd believed in the value of less talk and more action he'd be alive today."

"But Drummond had him killed, Hugh!"

"Damn it, Patrick, I could knock the devil out of Maxwell Drummond with one hand tied behind my back! All I hope is that one day he'll give me the opportunity to try."

It was said that altogether, counting the police as well as the military, there were seven thousand men keeping the peace in County Mayo at that time, and Cashelmara was on Mayo's doorstep, just south of the border which ran along the summit of the mountains behind the house. No wonder the Queen, opening Parliament in January, announced that the social condition of Ireland had assumed an alarming character. That was an understatement, and when in February the House of Commons sat for a record sitting of forty-one hours to discuss a new bill for the protection of life and property in Ireland, we knew even Westminster was echoing with the clamor of rebellion. My few remaining friends in London wrote begging me to return to England before I was murdered in my bed, and I wondered in alarm if I should take the children to stay at the house in St. James's Square.

"What do you think, Hugh?" said Patrick.

"No, Sarah must stay here at present," said MacGowan at once. "If you let your wife run away you'll be telling the Irish that you're frightened of them. She's got to stay."

"Very well, but maybe the children . . ."

"Patrick, if anyone's going to get a bullet in the back it certainly won't be the children. It'll be me."

I immediately began to pray for a timely assassination, but there was no bullet in the back, and on the twelfth of March MacGowan and Edith were married quietly in the chapel at Cashelmara and departed to live at Clonagh Court. As I had guessed, I was still far from free of them. Edith called every day. No watchdog could have been more tiresome, and she and Hugh continued to dine at Cashelmara at least twice a week. However, there was no denying that the situation had improved, and when in the spring Edith asked if she could accompany me on my few social calls I accepted the suggestion without protest. It was still impossible to entertain guests at Cashelmara, for our English friends shunned any idea of a visit to Ireland and our Irish neighbors were reluctant to travel after dark, but I did persist with the formality of calls. They provided a welcome change from the rigors of housekeeping, and once spring had arrived it was pleasant to escape from the house.

We traveled always with two armed footmen, and I never saw any of the peasants except at a distance. I never caught a glimpse of Drummond, but that didn't matter because I seldom thought about Drummond now. For me he had died with Marguerite, and my friendship with his wife seemed as remote to me as those far-off times when I had journeyed every week to the dispensary in the hope of seeing him.

The summer passed. Ned's governess gave notice, which pleased Ned very much, and Patrick advertised for a tutor for him. John celebrated his fourth birthday and blew out all the candles on his cake with pride. I still worried about his health, but there was no doubt that he had grown up very much in the past year. He could say real words now, not many, but he understood everything that was said to him. So did Eleanor. Even before her second birthday her chatter filled the nursery until I began to worry that she might be too precocious.

"We shall soon have to engage another governess specially for her," said Patrick, laughing, and at such times when we shared our pride in the children I knew that all my struggles were worthwhile and that no sacrifice was too great to make. "I only hope I manage to find a good tutor for Ned."

"Get a Scots tutor," said MacGowan. "Scottish education is second to none."

"I don't want Ned to have a Scottish accent!" said Patrick, teasing him, but MacGowan, who had no sense of humor, merely remarked that the accent of an educated Scot was minimal.

"Your father has a marked accent."

"My father is an uneducated man."

I never quite understood MacGowan's relationship with his father. They worked well together, the old man regarding his son with grudging deference, and MacGowan was certainly a dutiful son, calling every week at his father's house; but I had seen too much of Hugh MacGowan not to wonder whether a deep-rooted contempt might lie beneath his faultless good manners. He seldom spoke of his father; his mother, who was still alive in Scotland, was never mentioned. The only hint he gave of his past life with his parents was when he remarked to Edith after she had said something to annoy him, "I hope you don't intend to turn into a nagging wife, my dear, because I assure you I despise henpecked husbands."

However, as Edith herself pointed out to him smartly, he was hardly the sort of person to become a henpecked husband.

I had no idea whether Edith was disappointed in her marriage, but she didn't complain, so I supposed that for the time being she was satisfied. Yet I noticed that MacGowan paid very little attention to her, even when she talked so intelligently about politics, and if I had disliked Edith a little less I might have felt sorry for her.

At Westminster the Irish Land Bill was being discussed ceaselessly, and when Parliament rose in August, Thomas and David came to Cashelmara to bring us firsthand news of London. Thomas was studying medicine in London by this time, and David, who was to go up to Cambridge in October, was busy writing not librettos but a detective story.

"I like writing stories even better than writing librettos," he confided to me. "Wouldn't it be jolly if I could get it published?"

" 'Extraordinary' is the word you want," said Thomas, who thought all novels frivolous. "Not 'jolly.' Sarah, does Patrick usually drink as much as this or is he simply in a convivial mood to celebrate the start of our visit?"

"He must be celebrating your arrival," I said, smiling at him, but my smile felt stiff and awkward.

"Well, I wish he wouldn't celebrate quite so hard. The amount of port he drank after dinner last night horrified me. I cut up a liver recently that had belonged to a down-and-out who had died in the casual ward of the Marylebone workhouse, and if Patrick could have seen the state that liver was in I'm sure he'd never touch port again."

"Don't be revolting, Thomas," said David severely. "You've developed such a nasty habit of telling everyone your corpse stories. Personally, I'm not in the least surprised that Patrick's drinking so heavily. I'd take to drink myself if I had to tolerate MacGowan's company as much as Patrick does. I'm sorry they're still such bosom friends."

"So am I," agreed Thomas. "My God, if I didn't know Patrick as well as I do I'd say the friendship bordered on the unnatural."

"What a beastly thing to say!" exclaimed David, so embarrassed by my presence that he blushed pink. But I suspected the idea wasn't new to him.

"Oh, for God's sake, I didn't say it *was* unnatural, did I? All I said was that if we didn't know Patrick as well as we do know him . . ."

But they did know him so very well. Patrick drank and acted his part, and I found myself drinking too as I acted mine. I had little glasses of Madeira at odd times during the day and always took an extra glass of wine at dinner.

"Sarah," said Thomas, finding me alone by the decanter in the dining room on the day before they were due to leave, "what *is* going on in this house?"

"Nothing," I said. I looked at the decanter. "I've been having headaches lately and the wine seems to help."

"Have you seen a doctor? There's a marvelous new drug for headaches nowadays, and . . . Sarah, is something wrong?"

"No—no, I simply worry about things too much. I worry in case we can't get a tutor to come here and I worry in case the servants decide to give notice and I worry in case Nanny decides she can't bear to live in Ireland any longer."

"I do see that the political situation must be very nerve-wracking. If you could come to London—"

"No, I can't. It's impossible. MacGowan said . . ." I stopped, but it was too late.

"MacGowan," said Thomas. "MacGowan this, MacGowan that. Always MacGowan. He controls every single item in this house, doesn't he?"

"It's for the best, Thomas. Patrick needs someone strong to organize his affairs."

"I can't believe it's for the best that MacGowan should walk into this house as if he owns it and tell you and Patrick what to do."

"I can't talk about that, Thomas. You must talk to Patrick."

But Thomas hadn't quite enough nerve for that. Patrick was sixteen years his senior and the idol of his childhood, and although Thomas had enough courage to ask certain questions he hadn't at that time enough courage to want to hear the answers. So nothing was said, and soon he and David went away to London with the promise that they would return for Christmas.

But they didn't come back. They made an excuse. They had had a very special invitation from Marguerite's best friend . . . Christmas in Yorkshire . . . didn't see how they could refuse . . . they did hope Patrick and I would understand.

Patrick did understand and got drunk. I had stopped my surreptitious drinking after the boys had left, but Patrick, to MacGowan's fury, had gone on. After the boys' letter had arrived Patrick had drunk two bottles of port and MacGowan had found him in a stupor in his room.

"You bloody fool!" MacGowan yelled. Although my own room lay between Patrick's bedroom and the boudoir I could hear every word he said. "Get up!" I heard blows being struck, but that made me feel ill, so I ran away upstairs to the nurseries. By some great stroke of misfortune George chose that afternoon to pay his annual call, and when I was summoned from the nurseries to receive him I was so distraught that he noticed at once that something was wrong.

"My dear Sarah, is there some trouble . . . anything I can do?" His voice was so unexpectedly kind that I looked at him with new eyes. I had always dismissed him as a crusty old bachelor who had as little use for Patrick as Patrick had for him, but now I saw that once his bluff manner was discarded he had a gentle face and shy, anxious eyes. "If there's any difficulty . . . hope you feel you can confide . . . always thought you were such a splendid girl, so much better than Patrick deserved . . . don't like to see a pretty woman upset."

I was crying. It was because he said I was pretty. I wouldn't have cried otherwise.

"Excuse me . . . quite overwrought . . . not myself at all . . ."

"Patrick must take you away from here. There's too much stress. You must go to London, take the children. I'll give Patrick the money if he can't pay."

"You're most kind, but . . . we have to stay." Mustn't mention MacGowan. "Patrick says—"

"Patrick don't have a mind of his own nowadays, if you ask me. Madeleine says it's disgraceful how he allows himself to be pushed around by his Scots agent, and I think it's worse than disgraceful. It's a scandal, by God. It's even worse than when that insolent puppy Stranahan had a free rein."

"I can't . . . it's not my place to criticize . . ."

"Of course it isn't. You're a loyal and devoted wife to Patrick, anyone can see that. But all the same, I think something should be said to him. I'll say it myself, if it comes to that. God knows I've never shirked doing my duty, no matter how unpleasant that duty might be."

"No . . . Cousin George . . . please . . ."

"Don't you worry your pretty little head any more, my dear. I'll talk to Patrick."

"No!" I shrieked at him. I was on the verge of hysteria. "He'll think I've been complaining—there'll be a frightful scene. Please, Cousin George, please, please say nothing!"

He did finally agree to hold his tongue, but I could see he thought I was misguided, and his compassion was stronger than ever.

"Always feel you can call upon me for help" were his parting words as he squeezed my hand. "All you need do is send word to Letterturk Grange."

Strangely enough I did find his words reassuring. It made a difference knowing that there was at least someone who might help me if matters became intolerable, but meanwhile, as so often happened after a stormy episode, there was a lull in which life returned to normal. Patrick, bruised and subdued, gave up drinking, Edith developed a chill, giving me a week's respite from her company, and the children began to talk longingly of Christmas.

For the children's sake we always took an immense amount of trouble to make Christmas at Cashelmara a festive occasion. We decorated a fir tree in the hall, just as the Germans did, and Patrick spent hours making colored paper chains to hang on the nursery walls. Cook and the kitchen maids began to prepare a staggering array of cakes and puddings, and the largest goose was duly slain in the yard. I wrapped the presents, labeled them and placed them around the tree, where on Christmas Eve we would join the servants in singing carols and on Christmas morning unveil all the surprises in those tantalizing parcels.

After that the parson, Mr. McCardle, would arrive at Cashelmara and hold a service in the chapel before he returned to conduct the Christmas service for his Protestant parishioners at Letterturk. We held services in the chapel only twice a month now, to keep up appearances, but of course it was unthinkable that there should be no service on Christmas Day.

I still managed to enjoy Christmas that year because I spent all my time in the children's company, and they were so happy and carefree and gay.

After Christmas came New Year's Eve. I hated New Year's Eve with its images of vanishing time and life slipping past into oblivion, and now when the future looked so bleak the last day of the old year seemed more unbearable than ever. I thought how different things would have been if MacGowan hadn't disrupted our lives. Eleanor was two and a half, and I could be thinking of having another baby. There would be something to look forward to and I wouldn't feel so crushed by a sense of waste and futility.

If I could only have another baby!

I continued to think about it. I thought about it endlessly, and soon it was an obsession. Perhaps I wasn't in my right mind; perhaps all the strain of those past months had affected me more than I realized, but in the end I thought, Why not? I've kept my part of the bargain, so why shouldn't I have a reward? How can MacGowan object when a new baby would keep up appearances so admirably? Why shouldn't I have something to look forward to?

"No," said Patrick. "Absolutely not."

"Why?" I tried not to cry.

"Because I have to pretend to enough people in the world already and I don't want to have to pretend to any more."

"But for my sake—"

"It would be quite wrong for us to bring another child into the world," he said with that stubborn expression I knew so well. "You want a child for all the wrong reasons, Sarah."

The immensity of my disappointment made me cruel. I said scornfully to him, "You only say you don't want a child because by this time you probably couldn't even beget one if you tried!'' and he went very white before he turned his back on me and walked away.

It was less than ten minutes before the door of the boudoir opened again. I was flicking through the pages of a magazine, but I was far too upset to notice the pictures that flashed before my eyes.

"Don't tell me you've had second thoughts," I said bitterly without looking up, and then a shadow fell across the couch, and I knew it was MacGowan who had entered the room.

II

"Don't look so alarmed, Sarah," he said, strolling to the hearth and leaning one elbow casually on the chimney piece. "I come bearing good news. Patrick's told me that for certain reasons you're anxious to go to bed with him again, and I thought you'd like to know that I at any rate have no objection."

I stared at him. He stared back, and for one brief moment I sensed his overpowering jealousy and rage.

"So Patrick's changed his mind," he said. "He's going to spend a night with you after all."

When he saw me struggling to understand, he smiled. "Wasn't that what you wanted?"

"I wanted a baby," I said. My lips were stiff.

"Of course you do. And you were worried in case Patrick was incapable of giving you what you wanted."

There was utter silence.

"Come, Sarah, there's no need for you to worry about that, you know! Worry about conceiving, if you wish—haven't you always found conception difficult?—but don't worry about Patrick. I'll see that he's capable."

I tried to speak. Nothing happened.

"Still worried? Well, of course, it *is* unlikely that one night chosen at random could result in a pregnancy, but never mind, there are other nights, aren't there, and if you're so obsessed by this ludicrous idea for another child . . ."

"No," I said.

"You're not obsessed? Ah no, I understand. You mean my imaginative solution to the problem doesn't appeal to you. What a pity! I like the idea myself. When one is obliged by society to live what that society is pleased to call a 'normal Christian life,' the promise of unconventional amusement tends to give rise to the most disproportionate excitement. Bizarre, isn't it? One wonders what would happen in a society in which there were no rules to break. Doubtless everyone would quickly die of boredom."

"Stay away from me."

"Not while you tear up Patrick's self-respect and fling it in his face, you bitch!" All trace of blandness was wiped from his face, and I saw the violence shimmer in every line of his frame.

"I didn't mean what I said."

"Oh yes, you did," he said. "I know your kind—a little sarcasm here, a cutting remark there. You destroy a man by inches."

"I—"

"Shut your mouth. You've had your say, and one day soon, by God, I'll make you pay for it."

There was no time to scream. He was gone almost before he had finished speaking, and the door banged behind him with such a blast that all the ornaments rattled in the alcoves and the curtains shivered in the gust of air that rushed through the room.

After a long time I stood up, found the paper knife in my writing-table drawer and slipped it under my petticoats until it lay hidden in the top of my stocking. I did feel safer after that, although I don't know why, because I was sure I would never have the courage to use it, even in self-defense. I wanted to write to Charles, but I knew I mustn't. I might be weak enough to beg for help, and if MacGowan intercepted the letter . . . No, that wouldn't do at all. I had made a mistake, and now there was a crisis, but I would simply have to endure the crisis until it went away. MacGowan had threatened me often enough before, but he had never yet made good his threats, and there was no reason he ever should so long as I appeared suitably cowed. So that evening before dinner I apologized to Patrick in front of MacGowan, and then I apologized to MacGowan too, for safety's sake, and Patrick said, embarrassed, that he didn't want to talk about it any more.

I locked my bedroom door every night for the next two weeks and even dragged the chest across the doorway as a barricade, but no one disturbed me. Presently my fear ebbed. I stopped carrying the paper knife in my stocking, and the next day when Patrick told me he would be spending that night at Clonagh Court I decided there was no need to lock my bedroom door.

That was a mistake. They came back. It was long after midnight, and I was enjoying my first deep sleep in two weeks. They came to my room, both of them, and once MacGowan had locked the door there was no escape.

At first I thought that MacGowan meant only to hold me down while Patrick raped me. I thought MacGowan's mere presence would be enough to excite Patrick and humiliate me.

I was very naïve.

They lighted the lamp—or at least Patrick must have lighted it, because MacGowan was pinning me to the bed as I twisted and screamed. Patrick was drunk, not drunk enough to be unsteady on his feet but drunk enough to talk a lot in a loud voice. At first I couldn't hear what he was saying, but then I must have stopped screaming, for I heard him say something about a demonstration. I didn't know what he meant, but when I tried to ask him no words came.

That was when MacGowan said that I must stop thinking of Patrick as my husband and start realizing that Patrick belonged solely to him. Since I was apparently so determined not to recognize this they had no choice but to force me to face the truth.

"And the truth is that this is the only way I can go to bed with you now," said Patrick. "The only way." And the next moment it was he who was pinning me to the bed while MacGowan, moving behind him, tugged something from his belt.

It was a whip. It had an ornate silver handle that glittered in the lamplight.

Still I didn't understand.

MacGowan was pulling at Patrick's clothes, and the glitter of the whip was blinding. Squeezing my eyes shut, I tried to scream again, but Patrick's mouth closed wetly on mine and his breath was fetid against my nostrils. I wanted to vomit because the stench of liquor was so strong, but I couldn't even retch. All I could do was listen to the whip. I could shut out the sight of it, but I couldn't stop my ears, and although the blows never touched me I felt every one of them in Patrick's shivers of ecstasy.

He became unbearably excited. His weight shifted as he gasped for breath, and his rough undisciplined movements made me rigid with pain. No past marital act had been so painful before. I almost fainted with the pain of it; in fact I believe I would have fainted if only I hadn't noticed that I could no longer hear the whip.

My fear sharpened just as Patrick glanced back over his shoulder, and the expression on his face so appalled me that I lost the last shreds of my self-control. I thrashed out, hysteria making me strong enough to wrench one arm free, and the next moment the lamp crashed to the floor. The flame died in the sudden down-draft, the glass smashed and for an instant all was confusion in the darkness.

MacGowan cursed me. Patrick in his distraction could no longer contain his excitement, and I felt him go limp with a shudder. The bed creaked as I struggled afresh, but even though Patrick had by this time withdrawn himself his body was now slumped leadenly on mine to pin me once more to the mattress.

MacGowan struck a match.

I looked across the flame into his eyes.

That's the part I'll always remember. That's the part I'll carry with me to the grave. What came afterward is blurred now, mercifully dulled by the passage of time, but even today I can still hear that match being struck and see MacGowan watching me above the single steady flame.

For one clear second I saw myself as he saw me, the rival, the constant menace, the one person who might conceivably take Patrick away from him. I saw how my desire for a child would have seemed a ruse to him, a trick to divide them and bring Patrick back to me. And lastly I saw how in disrupting the scene before he had had the chance to gratify himself with Patrick I had driven him to an unprecedented pitch of rage.

He never spoke.

The match burned his fingers, and he shook it out and struck another. Then he lit a second lamp and brought it closer. Patrick was still lying spent on top of me, but MacGowan shoved him off so violently that he fell from the bed to the floor. Patrick barely protested. He was already half asleep, and although I screamed, begging him to protect me, my screams fell on deaf ears.

No one heard. No one came to save me. And as MacGowan moved soundlessly toward me I knew it was no longer Patrick he wanted for his partner in sodomy.

Chapter Seven

I

When I recovered consciousness my only thought was that one day I would kill him. I had no idea how or where or when I would kill him, but that didn't matter. All that mattered was that one day I was going to take my revenge on Hugh MacGowan, and I was going to take such a revenge that he would wish he had never come to Cashelmara, never ridden up that long winding drive into our lives.

The lamp was still burning in the darkness, and I was alone. It was very cold in the room, and in the first aftermath of shock I shivered, but when the rage began to burn inside me I no longer noticed the cold. The rage grew and grew. Soon it was such a huge virulent force that I hardly knew how to keep it in check, and its power frightened me. I thought: I'm going mad. But then I realized the rage was generating its own peculiar strength, and the strength enabled me to say to myself: If I go mad, MacGowan wins. He'll send me to an asylum and I'll never see the children again.

The very thought of such a failure infuriated me. I at once made up my mind not to fail, not to go mad. I had to win, and to win I had to survive.

I started to think about survival.

MacGowan must believe me to be thoroughly cowed, so I must play the part of broken victim so convincingly that no trace of my

418

rage showed. With Patrick I could allow a moderate amount of anger to show; that would be natural in the circumstances, but with Mac-Gowan I must appear to be completely crushed. Then he would think I was no longer a threat to him, and once he thought that I could take advantage of his overconfidence and escape.

Escape would be very difficult and very dangerous, especially since I couldn't possibly leave the children behind. But I would have to escape somehow, have to think of a way. Of course if MacGowan were to die—but the police would arrest me at once for murder, and an arrest, like madness, would mean the loss of the children and the end of everything.

I checked myself. What was I doing even thinking of murder? The shock must have temporarily unhinged me. Only people who were insane or wicked committed murder, and I wasn't going to go insane—I'd already made up my mind about that—and I certainly wasn't wicked either.

But I wanted to kill him. I wanted my revenge.

Mustn't think about that at present. Think of one thing at a time. Think first of survival, and save all thought of revenge until later when I had safely escaped from Cashelmara.

I stayed in my room all that day, and when Patrick sent me a note to say he wanted to talk to me I refused to see him. I wanted very much to see the children, but they were so innocent and I felt so unclean. Finally I took a series of baths. I bathed that evening and the next morning, and then I had a third bath after lunch and a fourth before dinner. After that I stopped for fear my behavior would be thought too eccentric, but I was at last able to face the nurseries, and when I saw my children again I felt not only much stronger but also more determined than ever to play the waiting game I had chosen for myself.

I went downstairs. I saw Patrick face to face. I controlled the shaft of hatred which twisted through me at the sight of him. That all took great strength, of course, but my strength was still growing, nurtured by my rage, and its growth was amazing to me. Soon I felt not only strong mentally but strong physically as well, strong enough to cope with all the domestic problems that continually arose among the servants and more than strong enough to nurse John night and day through a lung infection. In fact the only irregularity in my health lay in the absense of my monthly indisposition, but that, of course, was merely the result of the shock I had suffered.

MacGowan kept his distance from Cashelmara. Patrick avoided me whenever possible, and I went through the motions of leading my normal daily life. I even thought I might resume my calls, and when Patrick forbade it I was so startled to be thwarted in the role I was playing that I at last allowed him to have a few minutes of private conversation with me. Stammering in his awkwardness, he reminded me of the troubled world we lived in, and as he spoke I remembered Parnell's arrest the previous October and the Land League's suppression by proclamation a week afterward.

"But that was long ago," I said. "Months ago. All the trouble must have stopped now."

"On the contrary the discontent's only been driven underground and it seems to be simmering more fiercely than ever. There were windows broken at Clonagh Court last week, and Hugh never goes out alone on the estate now. Sarah, about Hugh . . ."

"I refuse to discuss him." I was startled by the violence in my voice, and in alarm I made a great effort to steady myself. I mustn't let him sense the full extent of my rage.

"Sarah, I'm sorry. I never thought . . . never dreamt . . . he would lay a finger on you himself."

I didn't trust myself to speak, so I said nothing. He looked at me pleadingly, and to shut out his face I closed my eyes—and suddenly, like a nightmare, I saw the match flare in the darkness, MacGowan's eyes above the steady flame.

"All I wanted was to show you what kind of man I am."

"You succeeded," I said.

"No, you don't understand. Please listen to me for a moment, Sarah."

Opening my eyes, I glanced at my hands. MacGowan's sickening image faded; I no longer felt dizzy.

"You see, all my life—until I met Hugh—I was trying to be what other people wanted me to be. I tried to be the son my father wanted, the brother Marguerite would have admired, the husband you were looking for—and yet I wasn't any of those people, and the harder I tried to be what I wasn't the worse mess I made of my life. But when I met Hugh—can't you understand, Sarah? I knew who I was at last. I grew up. I wasn't a statesman or a politician—or even a society rake—and I certainly wasn't the husband you wanted. But that didn't matter because I'd grown up enough not only to recognize who I was but to accept it. I was just an ordinary sort of fellow

420

who liked gardening—and if I'd only been an artisan or even a modest country squire this wouldn't have mattered a scrap. But my great bad luck was that not only was I born into the wrong class but I was born into the wrong century and country as well. If I'd been born two or three thousand years ago in Greece my relationship with Hugh would have been perfectly respectable and no one would have thought twice about it."

"I see," I said "You're not vicious, depraved and degenerate after all. You're simply unlucky. What a comfort for us all!"

"Sarah, I know you're entitled to be angry and I know you won't believe me, but what happened the other night wasn't what I intended to happen. I wanted only to show you that I was finished with trying to be what other people—including you—wanted me to be. I wanted you only to be an onlooker, but I was drunker than I should have been, and when I started to get excited—"

"You thought what fun it would be to rape me while Hugh raped you. Oh no, I forgot. Hugh doesn't have to rape you, does he? You submit with the greatest enthusiasm. Well, I'm quite unable to follow your example, Patrick, extraordinary though this may seem to you, and now I'm afraid you really must excuse me. I must talk to Flannigan about the new bill from the wine merchant in Galway."

"Sarah, it won't happen again, I swear it. Please—let's try and forget the disaster ever happened. Let's go back to where we were before."

It amazed me that he should think this was possible. I looked down at the floor again so that the expression in my eyes wouldn't give me away.

"For the children's sake, Sarah."

I was fighting for control over my rage. It was a hard fight, but I won. I didn't shout at him, "Don't dare mention the children in the same breath as your perversions!" but said instead without any particular expression, "Very well, Patrick, but all the same I'd prefer not to see Hugh again—at least not for a while. I'm sure you understand."

"Oh God, he's coming to dinner tomorrow night! Look, please be sensible about this. You've got to face him sooner or later, so . . ."

So MacGowan had at last decided to see how submissive I was in his presence. For one exquisite moment I fondled my dreams of revenge, but then I pulled myself together and gave Patrick the answer he wanted to hear.

"Very well," I said stonily. "I'll receive him—but only to keep up appearances for the children's sake. And in future I'd prefer it if you dined at Clonagh Court instead of bringing him here."

He said he would, but I knew the promise was meaningless. He was clearly thinking in relief that I was consenting to a return of the polite relationship that had existed in public between the three of us, and that consent would have negated any request that MacGowan should stay away from Cashelmara. No doubt he thought the request was merely a matter of form, a sop to my injured pride.

I turned my back on him before the rage could show in my eyes and went to talk to Flannigan about the wine merchant.

Spring was coming. After I had seen Flannigan I went upstairs and, to keep calm in spite of my rage, examined my wardrobe to decide which of last year's clothes could be altered to conform to the current fashions.

I began to try on my summer dresses.

How strange! None of them fitted me. Of course I was over thirty now and couldn't expect to keep my figure forever, but how could I possibly have put on so much weight? I knew I had been eating well, but I had been very busy, and surely one only became fat if one was inactive. Perhaps—horrible thought!—I was going to grow as stout as my mother had been.

I thought about my mother the following night when MacGowan came to dinner. All day I had been revolted by the thought of seeing him and repulsed by the submissive role I knew I had to play, but when we were finally face to face the familiar strength came to my rescue again, and I found I could control my feelings so long as I didn't look him in the eyes. If I once allowed myself to do that I would see the match flare again in the darkness, so I spent most of the time watching the carpet and took care to speak only when I was spoken to.

But MacGowan spoke only to Patrick. He spent dinner talking about the techniques of forestry, and as I pretended to listen to him I thought of Mama saying there were times when a girl needed her mother. And then I thought of long white dresses and promises of eternal devotion and what a dishonest charade a wedding was, futile, unreal and even a little fantastic. I tried to remember my wedding gown but could not.

So odd about those summer dresses.

"My dearest Sarah!" exclaimed Madeleine on her first visit to Cashelmara for some weeks. "Is it too soon to congratulate you?"

And I thought: If I don't believe it, it won't happen.

But I knew, even as I told Madeleine she was mistaken, that I had no choice but to believe.

II

At first I was very calm. I thought of knitting needles and falling downstairs and drinking a glass of gin—all those horrifying old wives' tales about which I had heard during the course of my married life. I wouldn't have the baby. I couldn't have it and stay sane—and my fear of madness overwhelmed me again so that for a long time I could do nothing but shudder uncontrollably. When at last I managed to stop shuddering I gave way to self-pity and wept. I had to give up all thought of escape for the next few months. To escape with the children was difficult enough, but with the added complication of pregnancy—no, I would have to wait. I started to weep again. There was no God after all. Supposing I died as the result of trying to get rid of the baby. The thought of trying to get rid of it both frightened and repulsed me. More tears. I cried and cried endlessly in my room.

And then at last when there were no more tears to shed I suddenly thought: Poor, poor little baby.

I remembered too who had wanted the child. Not Patrick. Not MacGowan.

Me.

Why should I be so stunned to realize I was pregnant? Didn't I always get what I wanted? I had wanted a baby. I had been so consumed by my own selfishness that I had scoffed at Patrick when he had suggested it would be wrong to bring a child into the world we shared at Cashelmara, but Patrick had been right, I knew that now, and the responsibility for the entire disaster could rest on no other shoulders but mine.

I cried a little more, but for the baby this time, and after a very long while, dry-eyed, I was able to think: I shall love it better than any of the others in order to make amends for what I've done. I tried to imagine the baby and hoped it would be a girl, dark, as I was, and not like Patrick at all. I wouldn't think of Patrick when I looked at her, and whatever happened I would never, never look at her and think of the match flaring in the darkness, MacGowan's eyes watching me above the single steady flame.

No, I wouldn't think of that because I would love her so much that it would no longer matter how she was conceived. My love for her would protect us both against that past obscenity; in fact perhaps

God had sent her to me with the intention of dulling the terrible memory of that night. Of course! That was it. The baby was not a disaster at all but a foretaste of the victory I would one day win over MacGowan, for what could be more of a triumph than my indifference to MacGowan's memory and my joy not only in accepting the baby but in loving it with all my heart?

I closed my eyes. I felt very tired, but I was at peace with myself, and I knew then without any doubt that I was going to survive.

III

I never told Patrick I was pregnant. I altered all my dresses, telling the seamstress to make them unfashionably full, but he never guessed why I was hiding my figure and anyway we seldom saw each other. Occasionally we would meet in the nursery, and once in July he joined me in the drawing room when Madeleine came to tea.

"And are you hoping for a son or a daughter this time, Patrick?" inquired Madeleine kindly as she accepted a second slice of boiled cake.

I couldn't blame Madeleine. I had long since told her she had been correct in suspecting my pregnancy, and naturally she would have assumed that Patrick was looking forward to the baby's arrival.

Patrick said nothing. He simply looked at me, stood up and walked out of the room.

"Heavens above!" exclaimed Madeleine, shocked.

"He—he didn't want the child," I said, nervous in case she questioned me further, but all she said was a stern "One cannot go against the will of God."

As soon as she had gone I searched for Patrick. I thought he might be in the garden, but finally I discovered him sitting at the dining-room table with a jug of poteen.

"You might at least have pretended to Madeleine to be glad!" I exclaimed furiously. "God knows, you're the one who continually insists on keeping up appearances!"

"I'm sorry." When he looked up I saw he was just as appalled as I had been when I had first realized my condition. "But God, what a damnable thing to happen!"

"It's not the baby's fault. You can be as indifferent as you please toward it, of course, but speaking for myself, I shall make an extra effort to love it just as much as the others."

"That's the least we can do in the circumstances, I would have thought."

424

I hadn't expected his feelings to match mine. After a pause I said, "Well, I suppose I should be thankful that you take that attitude. I thought that since I was the one who wanted the baby you would turn on me now and blame me for what's happened."

"Do you think I'd be drinking like this if I thought I was blameless?"

His unexpected sharing of responsibility lightened the burden of my guilt. For a time I felt better, but presently I became afflicted with ailments that had never bothered me during my previous pregnancies. My ankles began to swell uncomfortably; I suffered from spasmodic pains and an odd discharge that made me fearful of miscarriage; I felt tired and unwell.

Dr. Cahill began to call twice a week from the dispensary and told me that not only must I rest as much as I could but in no circumstances must I consider any form of travel. It was soon after he gave me this advice that MacGowan declared Nanny should take the children away from the valley until after Eviction Day.

Ireland had been in a ferment all summer since Parnell's release in May and the assassinations in Phoenix Park. The assassinations had shaken even MacGowan, and after the deaths of the new Chief Secretary for Ireland and his Under-Secretary not even Parnell's denial of all knowledge of the deeds could make us feel secure again. At Westminster the government had tried to clamp down on Irish unrest, but Ireland was like the proverbial pot of water boiling on the hearth; the longer one clamped down the lid, the more likely the lid was to blow off. In the valley the tenants had refused *en masse* to part with their rent money, and MacGowan had ordered the wrecking machine and a detachment of soldiers from Letterturk to begin evictions on the first of September.

I had not seen MacGowan since Patrick had discovered I was pregnant, and I did not see him now. He merely told Patrick that although he didn't anticipate serious trouble at Cashelmara, there was no harm in taking sensible precautions in regard to the children. That month we had all been horribly shocked by the "Maumtrasna murders," the massacre of an entire family, and MacGowan's suggestion was his way of admitting that the days were past when he had been the only one of us in danger of murder.

"You'll want to go with the children, I suppose," said Patrick to me uneasily.

"Of course I do," I said dryly, "but I can't, even if Hugh were to permit it."

"I expect he would let you go to stay with Edith at Clara's."

"Patrick, I can't travel anywhere. Have you forgotten?"

He had. He had been drinking more than ever in recent weeks and often did not remember what was said to him.

The children departed with Nanny and Nurse to spend a month by the seaside at Salthill, and without them the house seemed like a morgue. I tried to occupy myself with sewing new dresses for the baby and planning how I could alter my winter wardrobe, but time passed slowly, particularly since I was confined to the chaise longue.

Dr. Cahill continued to call, and once a week Madeleine managed to accompany him. She had increased her visits to me as soon as I had become unwell.

"I'm glad the children have been sent away, Sarah," she said on the thirty-first of August. "There's bound to be trouble tomorrow when the evictions begin, and although I'm sure there'll be no damage to Cashelmara there might be an unpleasant demonstration that would be bad for the children. Patrick will be here with you, of course?"

"I suppose so, yes."

"Good, then there's no need for you to worry."

The first of September dawned. It was a clear day, and as soon as I awoke I knew it was going to be hot. Hot weather didn't suit me because of my ankles, so I knew I would have to stay indoors in an attempt to keep as cool as possible.

I was still lying in bed and forcing myself to eat some breakfast when Patrick tapped on the door and looked in to inquire how I was. I immediately suspected that Madeleine had harangued him about my state of health, for he would never normally have sought me out in that fashion.

In response to his inquiry I told him shortly that I felt much the same.

"Oh." He tried to think of something else to say, and in the silence that followed I could almost hear Madeleine declare sternly, "Sarah must be treated with the greatest possible consideration." At last he said awkwardly, "Would you like me to bring you some flowers?"

I couldn't have cared less about flowers, but I was as anxious as he was to provide an excuse for his escape. "Yes, please," I said. "That would be very nice."

He wandered off in relief and reappeared an hour later with an enormous bouquet and two large vases.

426

"Shall I arrange them for you?"

"I'd be grateful if you would. I'm not supposed to stand, and it's so trying to arrange flowers when one's sitting down."

It was the longest conversation we had had with each other for some time. It took such an enormous effort to be calm and polite. My head was already aching with the strain of it.

He began to arrange the flowers with great attention to detail, and as I watched him I sensed we were both thinking of MacGowan.

"I wish I could go down to Clonareen to help," Patrick said at last, trimming the stalks of the gladioli, "but Hugh told me very firmly that I should keep out of the way."

I didn't answer. I was thinking how MacGowan had been avoiding me since Patrick had learned of my pregnancy, and I was picturing him not only nauseated by the news but maddened when he realized there was nothing whatsoever he could do about it. The image of MacGowan enraged yet powerless was so pleasing to me that I smiled.

". . . and I do wish the Irish wouldn't be so difficult," Patrick was saying. "Heaven knows I don't want to evict anyone, but what else can one do with people who don't pay their rent? If I were rich and had other sources of income I wouldn't mind so much, but I've simply got to have my rents, and anyway it's not as if the tenants can't afford to pay. That would be different. But why should I suffer just because they decide to withhold their rent for political reasons? I can't help the way the land's distributed in Ireland! That was all arranged centuries before I was born, and how can I alter it and still make both ends meet?"

"I'm sure Mr. Parnell could give you an answer," I said. By this time my thoughts were dwelling again on the distant prospect of revenge, even though I still had no idea how my revenge would be achieved. I smiled again.

"Parnell!" Patrick was exclaiming. "An Anglo-Irish Protestant landowner, just like me! My God, the fellow's a traitor to his class." He rearranged the last sprig of greenery and added as he left the room, "I do wonder how Hugh's getting on."

It was a long time before I saw him again.

In the afternoon I slept for two hours, and when I awoke I rang for tea. I had sent my maid on a shopping expedition to Galway to buy the materials I needed for two winter day dresses, and Flannigan had accompanied her in order to inspect the account books of the wine merchants who sent us such unbelievable bills. When no servant appeared in response to my bedroom bell I immediately thought: With Flannigan away they've all gone to the nearest wake, and I realized with a sigh how much I had come to rely on Flannigan with his heavy breathing and tiptoeing walk.

Since I was unable to summon help I had no choice but to go downstairs and find out what was happening. That took an effort, but I was feeling well after my rest and my ankles were hardly swollen at all. Finding some slippers, I wrapped a peignoir tightly around myself and went downstairs to the hall.

There was no one to be seen.

"Terence!" I called. "Gerald!" But no footman answered, and at last I moved reluctantly down the back passage to the green baize door.

The kitchens were deserted. They should have been full of people preparing dinner, but there was no one there. I stood transfixed, remembering how Marguerite and I had found the kitchens abandoned in the famine of '79. Abandoned kitchens meant disaster. Turning abruptly, I walked out the back door into the kitchen yard and moved past the privies, past the small vegetable garden and through the orchard to Patrick's beautiful lawn.

"Patrick!" I called. "Patrick, where are you?"

There was no reply. The sun shone and all his flowers swayed in the breeze. I didn't want to walk far, for my slippers were too flimsy and Dr. Cahill had strictly forbidden exercise, but I couldn't go back to the house without finding Patrick.

I called his name again, and when no one answered I looked in the glasshouses, struggled up the path to the Italian Garden and peered through the windows of the unfinished teahouse. I would have gone up the Azalea Walk, but that was too far, and anyway I could think of no reason why he might have gone to the chapel. My ankles were starting to swell again. Knowing I had to rest, I returned to the house and went to the library in the hope that he was dozing on the couch.

The library was empty, but there was a note beneath the paperweight on the desk. I sat down and read it. "Sarah, I've gone to Clonareen after all. I couldn't stand waiting here and wondering if Hugh was safe. See you later. P."

I stared at the note for a long time. At last when I felt stronger I returned to the kitchens, bolted the back door and locked the side door that led into the garden. Then I went back to the library, sat down on the window seat and began my long wait for Patrick's return.

IV

After a while I felt dizzy, so I lay down for an hour on the couch. I wanted to lock the library door, but there was no key, and as I rested I kept hearing small noises, probably the mice pattering in the wainscoting. The mice were such a nuisance. I would have to get more arsenic from Madeleine.

I tried to think about the baby. I had privately named her Camille, but I was sure Patrick would hate that. We had never agreed about any name except Eleanor, and even then he became cross when I pronounced it in the American way. But I wasn't very American any more. It was thirteen years since I had left New York, and as soon as I had arrived I had made great efforts to be thoroughly English. Marguerite had been so amusing with her stories of how hard she had found it to settle among the English, but I hadn't found it difficult at all. Of course Marguerite's trouble had been that her marriage to an elderly man had cut her off from people of her own age. I remembered how sorry I had always felt for her because she had married someone old. What misplaced sympathy! I tried to remember Patrick's father, but that was difficult because I had only met him years and years before when he had visited New York. I had been so young at the time, but I could remember someone very tall, someone who had cast a long shadow, someone aloof and powerful and remote. I had been rather frightened of him for some reason, I never knew why, although sometimes I thought I could see that long shadow cast across my future, and that didn't make sense because he was dead.

I got up once more and moved slowly to the window. The ground sloped so sharply below the house that I could look over the tops of the trees to the lough, and when I opened the window and leaned out over the sill I saw a puff of smoke far off at the other end of the valley. Did they burn the cabins after they had wrecked them? I didn't know. I tried to imagine myself as an Irish peasant woman, eight months pregnant, with an idle husband, three children and no roof over our heads. How did such people live? What did they think about? Of course they had no expectation of a comfortable life and they had their religion for solace, but . . .

I thought of Parnell making speeches at Westminster in his cultured English voice. Supposing Parnell was right in his demand of Home Rule for Ireland? According to the newspapers, many Englishmen thought he was. That was what the Irish never remembered. They always thought all the English were villains and implacably opposed to any change in the government of Ireland. And I? What did I think? But politics had never interested me, and I had always found it so comforting to retreat behind the maxim that women and politics don't mix. But this wasn't simply politics any more. This was my husband letting his agent turn women and children out of their homes to starve; this was my household abandoning me because the servants all knew there was going to be trouble; this was me, eight months pregnant, being left entirely alone at Cashelmara.

Mustn't think about that. Think about something else. That smoke at the end of the valley—could it possibly be Clonagh Court? No, surely not. Perhaps if I went upstairs I could see better.

It was Clonagh Court. I was sure of it. I knelt on the window seat of my bedroom and tried not to panic, tried to think sensibly about what I should do. Perhaps I could hide in the chapel. No, it was too far, all the way uphill along the Azalea Walk. I couldn't face it. I was feeling ill again. Must find something to eat. I went downstairs, but I felt so dizzy in the hall that I had to sit down on the bottom step of the staircase and wait till the dizziness had passed. Then I returned to the library, the nearest room, and lay on the couch. I don't know how long I lay there, but I must have slept, because when I opened my eyes again it was twilight, the long twilight of an Irish summer evening, and I heard the sound of horses' hoofs galloping up the drive.

I ran to the window, saw who it was and rushed to open the front door.

Patrick was unhurt. He dismounted as soon as the horses were halted at the foot of the steps, but MacGowan's coat was streaked with blood, and one arm hung uselessly at his side.

"Quickly, Sarah!" gasped Patrick. "Call Terence and Gerald and tell them—"

"The servants have gone," I said. I leaned against the doorpost to ease the weight on my feet.

"What do you mean? Gone where?"

"I don't know."

"Christ Almighty! Well, don't waste time standing there gaping at us. Get some brandy, for God's sake!"

"Get it yourself," I said and went to sit down again on the stairs.

Through the open door I saw him help MacGowan down from the saddle. MacGowan never made a sound, but I knew he was in pain

430

because when they entered the hall all he did was look for the nearest chair.

"Come into the library." They disappeared for a moment before Patrick returned to the hall.

"Damn you!" he exclaimed to me in a fury. "Won't you even lift a finger to help a man with a bullet in his arm?"

I said nothing, and the effort of keeping silent was so intense that I had no strength left to rise to my feet. Yet the thought of the bullet was pleasing to me. I smiled as Patrick turned abruptly and went into the dining room.

"Christ, is there no more brandy?" He returned to the hall in a worse rage than before. "Where's the key to the cellar?"

"Flannigan has one," I said coolly. "The other is upstairs in the top drawer of my writing table." He was already climbing the stairs when I added, "But there's no more brandy. You drank it all."

He looked angrier than ever and ran on upstairs to bring lint and bandages from the bathroom closet.

When he reappeared he carried not only the medical supplies but a jar of poteen that had lain hidden in some secret cache. He neither spoke to me nor looked at me, and it was hard to believe that a few hours before he had been bringing me flowers and inquiring conscientiously about my health.

He dressed MacGowan's arm. I heard him say things like "Looks like a flesh wound. If I bind it up very tightly . . . Have some more poteen. Sorry, did that hurt? You must see a doctor . . . soon as possible."

MacGowan spoke only once. He said, "One day I'll ruin that bastard Maxwell Drummond," and the ugly lowland Scots accent was so strong in his voice that he sounded a different man from the well-spoken agent who ruled Cashelmara.

I wanted to go upstairs now that I was no longer alone in the house, but after those long nerve-wracking hours of solitude I derived a curious comfort from the presence of other people—even those two people—and I was still sitting on the stairs five minutes later when I heard the murmur of sound far away.

The front door was open. As soon as I reached the threshold I saw the torches flaring downhill by the gates and heard the distant tramp of marching feet.

"There are people coming up the drive!" I ran into the library and the words tumbled from my mouth so fast that I hardly knew what I said.

431

Patrick went ashen. "Are you sure?"

"Look!" I dragged him to the window and pointed into the gathering dusk.

He spun around to face MacGowan. "We can ride up the Azalea Walk past the chapel and escape into the mountains. Do you think you can get back on your horse?"

MacGowan nodded and levered himself to his feet.

"You're not leaving me," I said to Patrick. The newspaper account of the Maumtrasna murders flashed sickeningly through my mind and made me forget the pride which would have forbidden me to turn to him for help. "You can't leave. I'm alone here."

He was busy helping MacGowan. "I've got to go with Hugh."

I stared at him wordlessly.

"They'll kill him if they find him here. I've got to help him get away."

"Let him get away by himself!"

"He's injured."

"He's well enough to ride!"

Patrick simply shook his head and helped MacGowan to the door.

"Patrick, you can't leave me alone here. I'm eight months pregnant. I'm having your child. Please stay. You've got to stay. Please!"

"They won't harm a pregnant woman."

"But a savage mob, bent on violence . . ."

He took no notice. I went on pleading with him, I even wept, but I might not have existed. All he cared about was MacGowan.

They had barely scuttled away on horseback around the side of the house when the mob swept around the last curve of the drive and howled across the gravel sweep toward me.

I turned and ran. I was so frightened that I didn't even stop to close the front door. I tried to barricade myself in the library by dragging a chair across the room, but the chair was too heavy for me, and when the pain shot through my body I sank in terror onto the couch. The tears were streaming down my face. I hugged the baby as if I could will it to stay in my body, and oddly enough this futile gesture gave me courage. Rage at Patrick's desertion flooded through me, and with the rage came the familiar strength so that when I heard the front door crash open and the hoarse voices shouting in Irish I stood up, wiped the tears from my face and moved behind the huge desk before turning to face the intruders.

Someone kicked the door open. A torch flared. Noise blasted across the room, and the smell of smoke and unwashed bodies slapped me across the face. My strength abandoned me suddenly. A great sickness churned in my stomach, and even as a bearded ruffian yelled something unintelligible at me the room faded before my eyes and I slipped thankfully over the edge of consciousness into the dark.

V

When I awoke I was aware first of the silence. The room was full of people; I could smell them and dimly see their distant faces, but nobody spoke. Yet someone was close to me. I was no longer alone.

Then someone spoke. The Irish was soft and low, a dying language and yet so very beautiful, and the next moment I felt the cold rim of a glass against my lips and the fire of poteen as it burned my throat. I choked, gasped. An arm tightened around me, and closer than the unwashed bodies, closer even than the reek of poteen, I smelled the faint raw tang of carbolic soap and the barest nuance of tobacco.

"You're quite safe, my lady," said Maxwell Drummond.

I looked up. He was there. His eyes were grave.

"Let me move you to the couch."

Someone took the glass from my hand. I felt myself lifted from the floor and placed gently on the upholstered velvet. Across the room the army of peasants spilled across the library threshold and filled the hall, but still not one of them moved and still not one of them spoke.

"My lady, there are questions I must be asking you." I looked up at him and he stopped. After a long moment he said, "Where's your husband?"

"He . . . left." My voice sounded higher than usual but surprisingly strong.

"With MacGowan?"

"Yes."

"Which way?"

"Past the chapel," I said, "and up into the mountains."

He turned to his followers and gave orders in Irish again. Suddenly everyone was moving, and the silence was broken by the murmur of a hundred voices and the clatter of boots on the marble floor of the hall. I closed my eyes, overcome with relief that I was to be left alone, but when I opened my eyes again I saw that although the mob had left Drummond himself was still there. I had never thought he would stay, and the shock of seeing him was so great that I started violently.

433

He made a gesture of reassurance. "I won't hurt you. Are you in pain?"

"No, just a little weak . . . probably because I haven't eaten . . . not since lunch. All the servants have gone. I was going to get myself something to eat, but . . ." I couldn't remember what had happened, but I knew it no longer mattered.

"You mean you're alone in the house?"

"Yes."

"Your husband knew that?"

"Oh yes," I said and found that didn't matter any more either.

"Sweet Jesus, what a creature! If I didn't see your figure with my own eyes I'd think he was masquerading as a man." He finished the poteen and set down the glass with a bang.

"MacGowan drank from that same glass less than half an hour ago," I said.

"You told me a little late, didn't you? And me already poisoned!" We smiled at each other. I felt well suddenly and very strong.

"I want to get even with MacGowan," I said.

"I'll drink to that." He poured himself some more poteen and handed me the glass. "We'll both be drinking to it," he said, so I took a little sip from the glass, not much, for I was afraid of choking on it again, and when I handed the glass back to him he raised it and said with a laugh, "To the blackest Black Protestant that ever came out of Scotland—may he fry in hell!" And when I laughed too he said, "I'll make you a present one day. How would you like that?"

"What sort of present?"

"A long rope necklace, nothing fancy to be sure, but with Hugh MacGowan's private parts dangling at the end of it."

He laughed again, and the most extraordinary part of all was that I laughed too. It never occurred to me to be shocked. The suggestion with the images it conjured up was so delightfully absurd that I giggled like a schoolgirl, and suddenly I knew there was no longer any doubt that I would get my revenge. My spirits soared. I couldn't remember when I had last felt so excited, and all I wanted was for him to stay.

But of course he couldn't. He had to go.

"I must bring some food for you before I leave," he said. "How will I be finding the kitchens?"

I tried to give him directions, but he only said, "Holy Mary, I'll need a compass or I'll be lost forevermore!" and disappeared with a candle into the hall. He was gone no more than five minutes. When

434

he came back he carried a loaf of bread, half a chicken and a pitcher of milk, all crammed precariously on a small silver salver.

"If it's a butler you're wanting," he said, "I'll not apply for the post. What's the use of a little tray this size?"

"That's only for leaving calling cards."

"Well, I called," he said, "and in my own way I've left my card." He looked around the room. "This is a fine house," he said, "a house fit for a king. I always did admire Cashelmara." He poured some milk for me into the glass which had held poteen and after a moment added, "I'll see that Miss de Salis knows you're alone here and she can come with the doctor to make sure all's well. But no harm will come to you between now and then, that I promise. Are you sure there's no pain?"

I was looking at the laugh lines about his mouth and at the corners of his eyes, but suddenly I could no longer see them, for he had moved too close and his face had slipped into a different focus. He was sitting on the couch beside me, and I saw only his straight, narrow upper lip as the palms of his hands slid gently behind my head.

I parted my lips even before his mouth closed on mine. I had never done that before, but then I had never liked kissing, so moist and messy and later jerky and rough. But now I wanted to be kissed, and to my surprise everything became very smooth and firm as my whole body relaxed in his arms.

My mouth was free again. I felt him straighten his back, and I squeezed my eyes tight shut to summon the will to say goodbye. But he postponed all goodbyes. He leaned forward again, and as his hands moved upon my neck and shoulders I couldn't believe I had once thought him uncouth. It was almost as if he knew how repulsive I found emotional violence, but of course he'd never know that. I'd see he never looked at me with pity and contempt when he discovered what a failure I was.

Tears blurred my eyes. He withdrew, but I felt so bitter and confused that I scarcely noticed. By the time I was able to look at him again he had risen to his feet and was looking down at me.

"Is it crying you are," he said, "and you the bravest woman I ever met! Tears are no use. It's not tears that'll get you even with MacGowan." He stooped over me again and tilted my face to his. "I wish you a safe confinement," he said, "and a speedy recovery. And when you've returned to health—" he paused, his eyes inches from mine—"I'll come looking for you."

He didn't wait for my reply. He left the room, and I heard his boots ring out as he crossed the hall; but I was strong still, and I no longer minded being alone in the house. I drank a little milk and ate some bread and meat, and after a long while I remembered how I had blamed Drummond for Marguerite's death and how convinced I had been that the very sight of him would repulse me.

It was five hours before a distraught Madeleine arrived with Dr. Cahill, but I didn't mind the long wait. I merely lay on the library couch and thought of Maxwell Drummond, and whenever I remembered the necklace he had promised me I felt my lips curve involuntarily in a smile.

Chapter Eight

MacGowan escaped. He and Patrick found their way over the mountains into the Erriff Valley, where MacGowan took the first passing outside car to Westport, while Patrick, with MacGowan's horse in tow, rode the other way to the inn at Leenane.

The servants crept back to Cashelmara. Madeleine, who had decided to stay with me until all danger of a miscarriage had passed, reprimanded them until they all wept for shame and then packed them off to Mass in Clonareen to assuage their guilt. One of the grooms was delegated to ride to Letterturk after Mass to fetch George.

George reported that Clonagh Court was a gutted ruin and that the elder MacGowan's house had been attacked with the thoroughness of a wrecking machine. Hugh had sent his father to Galway the day before, so the old man was safe, but three peasants had been killed in the fight with the soldiers, and the captain of the military detachment came to Cashelmara to say his men had suffered numerous injuries.

The police arrived to make arrests, but George said no, better not; God alone knew what might happen if there were arrests now on top of evictions and shootings, and it would be best to let matters quiet down before taking any further steps.

"We've got to consider Sarah's health," he said to Madeleine. "We can't risk any further violence at Cashelmara at present."

"I wouldn't have thought George would have been so sensible," said Madeleine to me afterward. She herself had deplored the evictions and had repeatedly told Patrick not to take MacGowan's advice.

"Of course," said George, "Patrick is quite unbalanced on the subject of MacGowan."

"We won't talk about that in front of Sarah," said Madeleine.

"Why not?" I said. "I know better than anyone how unbalanced he is."

Neither of them would meet my eye. "We must speak to Patrick, George," said Madeleine to him after a pause.

"I wonder if you'll have the opportunity," I said bluntly. "It would be suicide for MacGowan to come back to the valley at present, and Patrick will want to stay with him."

They looked at me doubtfully. I could see they were thinking that the shock had affected my reason.

"But, my dearest Sarah, of course he'll come back!" exclaimed Madeleine, shocked. "I know Patrick has behaved very badly, and you can hardly be blamed for feeling bitter, but he does at least have a conscience. Besides, quite apart from you and the baby, he has no choice except to return to Cashelmara. He has no money and nowhere else to live."

I still thought Patrick would go with MacGowan, but I was wrong. He came back. He rode home that evening from Leenane with MacGowan's horse in tow and refused to see anyone until the next day. He might have stayed longer in seclusion if Drummond hadn't arrived with Michael Joyce, the new patriarch of the most influential family in the valley, but they wanted to present certain demands, and George, who was still at Cashelmara, refused to receive them on Patrick's behalf.

I didn't see Drummond. I was resting in the boudoir and discovered that he was at Cashelmara only when George came upstairs to consult Madeleine, who was keeping me company.

"Patrick will have to talk to them," he said, worried. "If we send them away today, they'll be back tomorrow. To think that the Joyces and the O'Malleys should be united for once! Ever since I can remember they've always been at each other's throats! Well, at least MacGowan's brought unity to the valley, even if he hasn't brought peace."

"I'll fetch Patrick," said Madeleine, putting aside her sewing. "Sarah mustn't be troubled by all this." So she left the boudoir and walked through my bedroom to the door that linked my room with

Patrick's. I didn't hear him answer her knock on the door, but when she entered the room I did hear her say, "How disgusting! How could you bring yourself to touch whisky at this hour of the morning?" and Patrick yelled at her to leave him alone.

"Dear me," said George, hurrying to Madeleine's rescue.

There was a violent quarrel.

"I'm not seeing that bastard Drummond!" shouted Patrick.

"Damn silly thing to say!" exclaimed George. "Excuse my language, Madeleine, but really—"

"Please, George," said Madeleine, "now is hardly the time to worry about my sensibilities. Patrick, you must talk to Drummond and Joyce. You're not in a position to do otherwise, and if you can't see that you're more of a fool than I thought you were."

"Shut your bloody mouth," said Patrick. That was when I knew how drunk he was, for he would never normally have talked to a woman in that way.

"No, I won't!" said Madeleine strongly. "I've shut it for long enough, thank you very much, and now I think it's time I said something. You must pull yourself together, Patrick. You've become an absolute disgrace, drinking so heavily, abandoning your pregnant wife, hero-worshiping that man MacGowan in such a humiliating fashion—"

"Don't preach to me! Get out!"

"Yes, I will preach to you! It's my moral duty both as your sister and as a Christian. What would Papa have said if he could have seen you like this?"

"Never mind Uncle Edward," said George practically. "Thank God he's dead and didn't live to see this debacle. It's what other people say that matters now, and I might tell you, Patrick, that your private life is becoming subject to the most unfortunate rumors from here to Dublin—and to London too, for all I know."

"For God's sake, what does that matter now? Hugh's gone, isn't he? I'm here with my pregnant wife, aren't I? Well, *aren't I?*"

"You must give us your word MacGowan will never return. That's what Drummond and Joyce want, and if you don't give them what they want I'll not answer for the consequences."

"Patrick, you have a duty to Sarah and your children and your unborn child—"

"I simply want to be left in peace. I want to work in my garden. I want the children to come back."

"Then . . ."

"Oh, tell Drummond and Joyce what you like! What do I care so long as you all leave me alone!"

"Of course he was disgracefully drunk," said Madeleine to me after George had gone downstairs to see Drummond and Joyce. "I would have said more to him, but I didn't think that in his condition it would have been of any use."

"No use at all," I agreed wearily.

I didn't see Patrick alone until two days later. Madeleine had by that time returned to the dispensary, and George, after promising Drummond and Joyce that a new moderate agent would be engaged to replace MacGowan, had retreated in exhaustion to Letterturk. Since the valley was quiet again I decided to consult Patrick about recalling the children.

"I've already recalled them," he said. "I wrote to Nanny yesterday."

"Why didn't you tell me?" I exclaimed angrily, for I had stayed awake the previous night worrying about whether it was too soon to send word to their hotel in Salthill.

"I didn't want to talk to you."

"Yes, but . . ." Some bleakness in his manner attracted my attention. It was unlike him. "Patrick, you must make more effort, you really must, or the children will suspect all's not well between us."

As soon as I spoke I thought: After the baby's born I'll leave him. I'll take the children and go to Dublin—or London—to seek legal advice. Now that MacGowan's gone I don't have to be terrified of escape any more.

But then I thought: With MacGowan gone life at Cashelmara would at least be tolerable. I'll never forgive Patrick, just as I'll never forgive MacGowan, but although I despise and detest him I'm not afraid of him, and no doubt I could arrange matters so that we seldom had to talk to each other. And for the children's sake I've got to avoid scandal, got to avoid divorce. If it's at all possible I must try to stay, and besides . . . wasn't Drummond going to come looking for me when I was well again?

"Patrick," I began reasonably, but he interrupted me.

"I'm tired of lying," he said. He was drinking again. It was only eleven o'clock, but he was drinking soda water and some of the brandy Flannigan had brought back from Galway. "I'm tired of caring what people think."

"But you must care what your own children think! Think of

Ned—nearly nine years old now! If he should ever guess the truth—"

"He'll find out. One day."

"But he mustn't! How can you say that so calmly?"

"Because my values are different from yours. Because I don't want my son to say of me one day, 'My father was a wonderful liar and a superb actor whom I never really knew at all.' I want him to say, 'My father loved me and he was honest with me—and that's all that matters.' "

"You're drunk again!" I said furiously, but because MacGowan's expulsion had given me new heart and because I now wanted Patrick's cooperation I smothered my anger and contempt and made another attempt to approach him. "We've got to try to keep up appearances, Patrick," I said reasonably, choosing a phrase he had often used to me. "If we give up now it'll mean our past efforts have all been for nothing. Promise me you'll make a fresh effort—for the children's sake."

"I'll promise you anything you like," he said, "if you would only leave me alone."

Fortunately his spirits improved after the children returned, but the prolonged bouts of heavy drinking had taken their toll on his appearance. He looked older, his face more lined, his complexion more blotched, his eyes more bloodshot. With MacGowan's departure he had lost interest in his garden, and the lack of exercise had made him put on weight so that his splendid physique was now showing the first signs of ruin. He still had the self-assurance MacGowan had given him, but without a sense of purpose he seemed to sink deeper into apathy, and whenever the children were absent he was morose and hostile. However, in their presence he did make an effort to be his old self, and when I saw this I thought with relief that the children might still be spared the shame and disgrace of a divorce.

The baby came.

I was very ill. Unlike my previous experiences, the birth was long and difficult, and afterward I lost so much blood that I was unconscious for hours. No one could tell me until much later about the tumors, and even then Dr. Cahill was so busy assuring me that they weren't cancerous that I found it hard to understand what had happened. No one had expected me to live. Dr. Cahill had been obliged to use a surgeon's knife, and had it not been for the fact that he was a young man and had been trained in London as well as in Dublin I'm sure I couldn't have survived. Even despite his modern knowledge I developed an infection, and for days afterward I was aware of nothing but the heat and pain of fever. But at last one morning I was better and could remember that long ago I had had a baby.

"A little girl, Sarah," said Madeleine, who had been nursing me faithfully. "Very pretty. Dark, like you, and not a bit like Patrick."

I asked if she was expected to live and could hardly believe Madeleine when she said yes.

"You're saying that to protect me," I said, but when the infant was shown to me I saw she was a healthy pink. "How lucky," was all I could say as I sank back on the pillows. "Always so lucky." But I could say no more, for I was too weak.

It was not until weeks later that Madeleine told me I would never have another child. She explained it in medical terms, but I had never understood much about the feminine parts of the body, so I simply nodded and tried to look interested. At first I didn't feel in the least disappointed, for I had no intention of ever bearing Patrick another child, but after a while the fact of my sterility weighed upon me and brought me to tears on more than one occasion when I was alone in my room. I did tell myself I had no right to complain since I had four beautiful children, but still the thought would flit through my mind that I wasn't fully a woman any more and a great sadness would descend like a lead weight across my heart.

To raise my spirits I would think of Drummond. But a long convalescence stretched ahead of me, and I had no means of knowing when I would see him again.

The baby was christened at Christmas when I was well enough to walk. Naturally Patrick balked at the name Camille, and naturally I balked at his choice of Louisa, so we were at a complete deadlock within an hour of the clergyman's arrival.

"Try something simple," suggested Madeleine, stepping into Marguerite's role of mediator. "Jane, perhaps, or Joan."

"Not Joan," said Patrick and I in a rare moment of unison, so the baby was christened Jane, much to the disappointment of the other children, who thought the name far too ordinary.

"Guinevere would have been nice," said Ned, who had been reading about King Arthur.

"Buttercup," said John, who liked flowers.

"Victoria after the dear Queen," said Eleanor, precocious as ever, and cast a sidelong glance at her father, who said with a laugh that she was quite the cleverest little girl he had ever met.

I wondered if she would be cleverer than her sister. Poor little baby, I would think each time I kissed her, and then I would kiss her again to make sure she knew she was loved.

Poor little Jane.

Thomas and David came for the christening and spent Christmas at Cashelmara. They made no secret about how glad they were to see MacGowan gone and a new agent living in old MacGowan's stone house, and Thomas said too how glad he was that Patrick had given up drinking.

But he hadn't given it up. He was simply better at concealing it, for the bills from the wine merchants only lengthened and the expense became a larger and larger item in the household accounts.

I heard once from Edith, at Christmas. She had rented a house in Edinburgh, and MacGowan was living there with her. He had had trouble with his injured arm and it still wasn't healed. However, the doctors in Edinburgh were excellent, so at least he was receiving the best treatment. Old MacGowan was also in Edinburgh but not living with them; Hugh wouldn't have that, although he had rented some chambers for his father within half a mile of their house.

I supposed MacGowan would look for another position when his arm was better. Or perhaps he would merely continue to live on his rich wife's income. I wanted to ask Patrick if he intended to go to Edinburgh for a visit, but I had to be very careful what I said to Patrick, and in the end I found it wiser never to mention Mac-Gowan's name.

January passed. I was feeling much stronger now after my ordeal and was wondering over and over again how I could see Drummond. I thought I might take the carriage to Clonareen and call at the dispensary; that would let him know I had fully recovered. I felt no embarrassment at the thought of seeing his wife. I had always found it difficult to connect Eileen with him, and now I found it so difficult that I simply blotted from my mind the fact that he too was married with children. Besides, it was not as if I were planning some gross impropriety. I knew I would always stop short of that to prevent him from despising me, and so I saw no harm in seeing him for a few minutes now and then.

"And when you're well again," Drummond had said, "I'll come looking for you."

But MacGowan came looking for him first. He came riding over the hills from Letterturk with a huge detachment of troops and all the police in County Galway, and before the sun had set on the valley

443

that night the Drummond farm had been burned to the ground and Drummond himself had been flung into the county jail.

Eileen Drummond took her children to Dublin, where her parents still lived. Madeleine lent her the money. I wanted to help her too, but I didn't dare.

"How good it is to be back!" exclaimed MacGowan, sitting down in the chair at the head of the dining-room table. "Flannigan, bring a bottle of champagne!"

Flannigan gave notice the next day.

The shock of MacGowan's return had a curious effect on me. I felt lightheaded, and from time to time I was able to look down upon myself as if from a great distance and watch the puppetlike figure who was pretending to be the lady of the house.

"There's absolutely no need for you to trouble yourself about the household accounts any more, Sarah," said Edith. "Hugh wants me to do it. He says you're too extravagant and spend too much money on clothes. You're to have an allowance, and Hugh says you must be very careful not to exceed it."

The other servants started to give notice, and when Edith replaced them with the humblest of the valley girls, the quality of service deteriorated. But this, I was told, would be a mere temporary inconvenience until the estate was set right and Clonagh Court rebuilt.

Meanwhile the MacGowans would remain in Cashelmara.

Ned's tutor left, and when a new one arrived he remained less than a week. Even Nanny gave notice when Edith tried to reduce the supply of fuel for the nursery fires, and the notice was withdrawn only when I broke down in tears and begged her to stay.

Strangely enough the fright of Nanny threatening to leave had a beneficial effect on me. It shook me out of my state of shock, and once the shock was gone my rage started to burn again. I was careful to conceal it, but now I was quite clearheaded enough to realize that something would have to be done. Obviously I could do nothing but bide my time until the MacGowans had returned to Clonagh Court, but after that . . . The difficulties of escape haunted me again. I couldn't leave Cashelmara without the children, yet with the children it was impossible to leave. Cashelmara, as MacGowan had once said, was so remote. Even if we took no baggage we would still need a carriage, and carriages needed horses, grooms and coachmen before

444

they could embark on a journey. It didn't take much imagination to visualize the commotion of departure. To sneak away hurriedly in the dead of night with four children could only end in failure, for even if we managed to leave the grounds without Patrick stopping us we wouldn't have a chance of reaching George's house in Letterturk. Word of our flight would reach Patrick within the hour. He would ride after us, summon MacGowan . . . If we were indeed lucky enough to reach Letterturk Grange, there would be nothing George could do to prevent Patrick from removing the children and taking them home. And what would happen to me? Well, no doubt Mac-Gowan would think of some appropriate solution.

The match flared in the darkness. His eyes watched me above the single steady flame.

I felt ill. My fear and hatred of him rose in my throat like vomit until I felt I would suffocate, and my brain became so clouded that I could no longer dwell on plans for escape. Perhaps when the Mac-Gowans had returned to Clonagh Court I would be able to think more clearly.

Patrick ordered the finest Connemara marble for his lily pond, and all through that terrible summer his garden was a brilliant mass of blooms. I can see the rhododedrons, vast, sprawling and exotic, their colors rich against the lush leaves of the trees, and all the way along the walk to the chapel the azaleas blazed with a fire eerie in its intensity. The beds around the lakelike lawn were dense with color too, and I remember gazing day after day at the red trumpets of the flame nasturtiums, the dazzling blue of the gentians, the multicolored fantasy of a whole border of anemones, the pale perfection of the graceful lilies. The magnolia tree flowered too that year, and in the kitchen garden the peach trees drooped to the ground beneath the burden of their luscious fruit. I had never before seen such a beautiful garden. Patrick worked so hard, caring for his flowers until they seemed to have some mysterious entity of their own, while up on the hillside the altar cloth rotted in the chapel and the pews lay caked in dust.

It was in June that I learned I was to have no respite from the MacGowans. They decided they would live permanently at Cashelmara, and with that decision my desperation drove me to consider leaving Cashelmara without the children. But I knew I couldn't leave them behind unless I had some assurance that I could get them back with legal help. If only I could consult a lawyer and find out what my legal position was! And as I wracked my brains to think how this could be done, it occurred to me that here at last was a situation where George could give me active assistance.

I wrote him a note. I gave it to Madeleine when she came to tea, and that was a great accomplishment for Edith watched me like a hawk and longed only for me to make some mistake that she could report to MacGowan. But I slipped the note to Madeleine after I had upset tea all over Edith's new dress, and Edith was in such a state that she never saw Madeleine grasp the note without a change of expression and slip it into her coat sleeve.

I wrote to George: "I had resolved to remain here for the children's sake, but matters are at such a pass now that I think it would be far worse if they remained at Cashelmara than if I took them away. However, I dare not leave openly for fear of what MacGowan might do to me if I tried. I know I am a danger to him because I can testify about his perverted behavior with Patrick, and if the matter is brought before the courts there must be at least a chance that I can not only bring them both to ruin but also deprive Patrick of custody of the children—something which Patrick has always dreaded. Yet before I attempt to leave I *must* find out my exact legal position, and since I cannot escape from the valley I have no choice but to ask you if you would see an attorney on my behalf. I know it is a great deal to ask, particularly since you cannot approve of the scandal resulting from a divorce, but dearest George, I no longer care about the scandal. I'm far too desperate for that. Please, please help me. In particular be sure to ask the attorney if, by appearing to condone the situation here, I have lost my grounds for a divorce. I cannot leave only to find that the children are denied me, for I would never dare return to be with them. Words cannot express how much I fear and loathe MacGowan.

"Please believe me when I say there is no use in reasoning with Patrick. He will never, never give MacGowan up. And please, I beg of you, be very careful to destroy this letter as soon as you have read it and never breathe one word about my request for help."

In this at least George obeyed me. He must have destroyed the letter, for no word of it reached MacGowan's ears, but despite all I had said he could not believe Patrick would refuse to give up MacGowan once scandal threatened. I suppose George was shocked because I had put into words what he himself had long suspected, and the shock must have impaired his judgment, for he came to Cashelmara to reason with Patrick one last time.

Patrick and MacGowan saw him in the morning room, and when I had eluded Edith by saying I had a headache I waited in the shadows of the gallery in the hope of seeing the expression on George's face when he left. I was frightened in case he betrayed I had written to him, and all I cared about was finding out whether or not I was safe.

But I never saw George again. I heard voices raised in argument and seconds later a heavy crash followed by silence.

"He fell," said MacGowan hours afterward to Dr. Cahill. "It was very unfortunate. A stroke perhaps? A touch of apoplexy? It seemed as if he lost his balance, and before we could catch him he struck his head on the fender."

Dr. Cahill revealed that George had long suffered from high blood pressure and diagnosed that a spasm of dizziness had caused the fall. ". . . and the fall against the fender killed him. Most unfortunate accident. No one in any way to blame . . ."

I said nothing. I didn't know what to believe, although I was sure Dr. Cahill would have spoken up if he had suspected George's head injury had not been caused by the fender. I wanted to believe in the possibility of an accident because I knew I would be less frightened if I did, but night after night I would dream of MacGowan's strong arm and awake sweating with fear.

I wondered if I could send word to Thomas and David but decided I couldn't. Too dangerous, both for me and for them. Could Madeleine help? But she was so religious. She might simply tell me that, unfortunate though it was, I had a moral duty to stay with my husband in any circumstances. Perhaps Charles . . . No, Mac-Gowan mailed all my letters to America, and I was sure he read them first. I could ask Madeleine to mail a letter, but did I dare risk passing a letter to Madeleine again?

By this time I had given up the idea of seeking legal advice before I took any radical step, but I still didn't trust the law to restore the children to me if I were to leave Cashelmara on my own. I knew what the law thought of deserting wives, and I knew too that Mac-Gowan would engage the best lawyers to discredit me and vindicate Patrick. In the circumstances I thought it would be foolish to assume that I would be automatically granted custody of the children.

So I was back where I'd begun. I knew I had to escape and I knew I had to take the children with me, but I still couldn't see how I was ever going to do it.

In July Drummond was tried in Galway and sentenced to ten years in jail.

Drummond would have helped me. If Drummond were free . . .

There must be some way, I thought. There must be.

In September two political prisoners escaped from a jail near Dublin, and the newspapers said the Irish National League had bribed the jailers to ensure the escape. The Irish National League was a new organization that included members of the dissolved Land League as well as all sections of the Home Rule Party. If I could somehow talk to Mr. Parnell . . . MacGowan and Patrick had both testified against Drummond at the trial. If I could show someone high up in the National League that Drummond's trial, arrest and imprisonment were the result of a personal feud . . . But I dared not write to Mr. Parnell and I couldn't escape to see him. I was almost as much of a prisoner as Drummond was in the county jail in Galway.

"God save you, my lady!" said Father Donal when Edith and I met him one day during a morning call on Madeleine, and suddenly I remembered Patrick talking about the Land League and old Mac-Gowan writing sourly, ". . . and the priest's in it up to the neck."

"Good morning, Father Donal," I said, smiling at him, and that same night I summoned all my courage and said to Patrick in front of the MacGowans, "I wonder if you could arrange for Father Donal to call here to see me? I've been thinking for some time about becoming a Roman Catholic and I would like to take instruction."

I saw MacGowan look at me. But I never looked him in the eye nowadays, so I was careful not to arouse his suspicions by suddenly giving him a bold stare. I merely kept my voice low and glanced meekly at Patrick, exactly as I always did, and across the dining-room table I was aware of MacGowan relaxing in his chair, his suspicions lulled.

"But how commendable, Sarah!" he said dryly, mocking me. "And how unlike you!"

"Yes . . . I know." I tried to smile, as if I were humoring him. I sometimes did that and I knew he wouldn't think it unusual. "But ever since Jane was born I've been thinking more and more about my religion." I thought this was a clever touch. After a brush with death many people take to religion with unexpected fervor.

"I dare say that could be arranged, Patrick," said MacGowan genially. "You can write to Father Donal for Sarah, if she wishes. Edith, perhaps you too would be interested in learning more about the Roman Church."

448

Edith opened her mouth to protest but thought better of it. "Well, it'll be a diversion, I suppose," she remarked offhandedly and gave me a pitying look.

Edith lasted four hours of instruction, during which Father Donal talked long and earnestly in his delightful Irish voice about everything under the sun except his faith, and then before his fifth visit I overheard her say to MacGowan, "Do I really have to endure any more instruction from Father Donal?"

"Aren't you enjoying it?" he said, amused.

"On the contrary I declare he's quite the most boring little man I've ever met."

"And Sarah?"

"Oh, poor thing, she's quite in earnest. It's absolutely pathetic."

I felt giddy with triumph. I saw Father Donal alone at last, and as soon as I had made sure no one was eavesdropping I began to talk about the National League and political prisoners and Galway County jail.

Father Donal's eyes grew very round, and after a while he forgot to close his mouth, and at the end he was sitting on the edge of his chair.

"God save you, my lady," he said at last. He was so dumfounded he could think of nothing else to say. "God save you."

"I'm sure He will if we can save Drummond first. Listen, Father, I have a plan. I want Drummond to go to New York and take a message to my brother. It's very important both for my safety and the safety of my children, and it must be a complete secret because if word gets back to MacGowan I've no doubt we'll all be murdered in our beds. If the Blackbooters or the Brotherhood or whatever they call themselves nowadays could arrange for Drummond's escape to America . . ."

"My lady, there's but one problem, but pray God you have the means to solve it. It'll take a lot of money."

"How much?"

He thought about it. "It's the bribes, you see, several of them, each man asking for more than the last. Ah, it's a terrible world we live in, and the love of money is the—"

"A hundred pounds?"

"At the very least, my lady."

But I had no money, and my necklaces, bracelets, earrings and tiaras had all been sold to stock Patrick's garden and pay for the marble lily pond.

I took off my wedding and engagement rings and gave them to him. "Sell these."

He was transfixed. "My lady, you can't—"

"I want Drummond out of that jail and on a boat to America," I said. "Everything I have depends on that."

"But if your husband should be asking you about your rings—"

"He'll never notice."

"Mr. MacGowan might notice," said Father Donal.

We looked at each other. "I shall tell him I lost them," I said, "and he'll never be able to prove otherwise."

He opened his mouth and shut it again. At last he said, "I'll be praying for you, my lady—even if you stay a Protestant," he added as an afterthought. I always thought this was the most Christian remark I ever heard during all my years in Ireland and not at all typical of an ill-educated country priest.

"Perhaps one day you'll be saying Mass at the chapel at Cashelmara, Father," I said, smiling at him, and he said that would be a great day indeed and he hoped so too.

It was a considerable time before Drummond's escape could be arranged, but this eventually worked to his advantage. It was spring by the time all was ready, and I knew the spell of mild weather would lessen his discomfort as he traveled north back to the valley.

For I insisted on seeing him before he left. I would have entrusted my letter to Charles to no one else, and besides I wanted so much to see him again. It was worth the risk. The thought of seeing him made it possible for me to endure the long months of waiting, and I knew that after the meeting I would have fresh courage for the months that lay ahead.

May came, May the thirteenth, and the promise of summer breathed a magical life into Patrick's garden.

Drummond escaped. The jailer looked the other way as he filed through the bars on the window and lowered the rope that had been smuggled into the cell, and when he reached the main gates he found them unlocked and the guards asleep. And outside the Brotherhood was waiting to take him through the night to safety in the dark rabbit warren of the Claddagh.

The next night he traveled to Oughterard, and waiting for him in an isolated cabin was a hot meal and a place to sleep before the hearth.

They were searching for him by this time, but of course no one imagined he had gone north. They searched the Galway docks and

450

they combed the Claddagh and they blocked the road to Dublin, but they didn't find him.

The next night he traveled to Maam's Cross and the next to Clonareen, where Father Donal gave him clothes and money and helped him bathe, cut his hair and rid his body of lice.

The following morning before sunrise he walked up into the hills and struck westward along the valley to Cashelmara.

"There's a ruined cabin above Cashelmara," I had said to Father Donal. "It's on the mountainside about half a mile from the walls."

I was quite unable to sleep that night, and I lay awake until I could see the sky lightening beyond Clonareen. I was still terrified that something would go wrong, and when I rose I avoided lighting the candle and dressed in darkness. The night before I had selected a plain gray day dress and a pair of boots suitable for the long walk up the mountainside.

Since there was no light I was unable to put up my hair, but I brushed it in the darkness and tied it back from my face with one of Eleanor's ribbons. I knew I must look very plain, but I accepted that. Better to look plain than risk rousing MacGowan or Edith by making an elaborate toilette. Besides, I knew I had lost my looks. The strain of the past months had made me haggard, and I had been too thin since Jane's birth.

Taking a cloak, I wrapped it around me and tiptoed out of the house.

No one saw me. I made an elaborate detour around Patrick's immaculate lawn and turned uphill through the shrubbery. It was dark in the Azalea Walk, and I was so nervous that I kept stumbling as I looked over my shoulder. But no one was following me, and presently the gray ghostly tower of the chapel rose before me in the trees. I passed it. By this time the backs of my legs were aching because the path led so steeply uphill, but at last I came to the wall that bounded the grounds and the thick wooden door that led onto the mountainside. I fumbled for the key, dropped it, stooped to pick it up. My hand was trembling so much I could hardly turn the key in the lock, but a moment later the door was closing behind me again and I was looking up the bare mountainside toward the ruined cabin.

My feet slipped on the loose stones. I kept thinking: Supposing he's not there, supposing something's happened to delay him, supposing something went wrong. For all I knew for certain then was that Drummond had escaped from prison three days before and no one had seen him since.

The sky was growing lighter, and when I looked back for the last time I saw that the dawn was casting great golden fingers across the lough far below.

The doorway of the cabin was empty. I was sure then that he wasn't there, but I went on, my legs aching, gasps for breath tearing at my throat and tears pricking behind my eyes. A minute later I had to pause; I was too out of breath to continue, and then as I glanced uphill once more I saw a shadow fall across the ruined doorway and I knew with a great joyous surge of relief that he was there.

III

He had lost weight, but that somehow made him look taller. The lines were deeper about his mouth, but that made no difference to his smile. His hair seemed darker than ever, untouched by silver and shaggy from Father Donal's scissors.

He didn't speak. He didn't even move forward from the doorway to meet me. He merely stepped back a pace, and as I crossed the threshold he took me in his arms and drew me aside so that my back was pressed against the wall.

We still didn't speak. He began to kiss me. He kissed each cheekbone, each eye, my hair, forehead and nose, and finally he began to kiss me on the mouth. His hands slid from my waist to my hips, then back to my waist, and as they paused before moving upward again I knew I would do anything he wanted.

I was terrified. I managed to say in a halting voice, my eyes blinded by tears, "Please, no . . . I—I'm not a very . . . passionate person . . . so useless . . . such a failure."

There was a silence. I could hardly bear the weight of my grief, and so, unable to look at him, I merely strained my ears for the sound of his voice.

At last he asked very gently, "Who told you that? Your husband?" But when I nodded in an agony of shame he threw back his head, roared with laughter and exclaimed incredulously, "And you believed him?"

The distorted glass I had faced all my married life cracked from side to side. I found myself suddenly before a different mirror, and after that there were no words. I simply stared dumfounded at my new reflection until when at last he touched me again my tears were gone and so was the burden of failure I had carried for so long.

I was cured. For the first time in my life I began to live, and the passion burst within me in a vast and violent tide.

452

Part Five

MAXWELL DRUMMOND

Ambition 1884–1887

[Roger Mortimer was] determined, ambitious . . . without scruple
. . . reputation for bravery . . . a way with women . . . seems to
have had all the instincts of a modern gangster . . .

The Three Edwards
—THOMAS COSTAIN

Chapter One

She left him.

She left her husband, she left her home and she even left those children. Of course she had a plan for getting hold of them later, but once she saw that MacGowan would never let her leave with all four children clinging to her skirts, she set out for America alone.

I was already there, waiting for her. I'll never forget how I waited. All through that summer I waited and all through that autumn into winter. I waited until it seemed I'd been shut up forever in that hell of a city which was surely hotter than hell ever was, with the shirt clinging to your back as early as eight in the morning and the nights so stifling you'd feel it easier to suffocate than sleep. I thought I knew all about waiting after I'd been slammed into the county jail in Galway on a trumped-up charge—Jesus, that jail in Galway!—but I didn't know a damn thing about waiting until I was shoved off that immigrant boat in New York in the June of 1884.

I had a lot to learn, but I learned it fast, and all the while I was waiting, waiting for Sarah to slip through MacGowan's net, waiting for the ice to melt on the Hudson River, waiting for her fancy ship to come steaming into New York harbor in the spring. I waited until I couldn't imagine a time when I didn't have to wait, and when at last the time came and I didn't have to wait any more I went down to the docks and I saw her fancy ship come in and it was as if it was all a

455

dream, and indeed I'd have sworn blind it *was* all a dream if the river hadn't been such a smelly blue and the noise of the wharf hadn't made my ears ache. That city was beyond belief. It was a bastard place belonging to no one, a roughhouse, a free-for-all, a nightmare trip to purgatory. Dear God, I used to pray, deliver me from evil, danger and the whole city of New York. Amen.

They put the gangway down, a very smart gangway, white and shining, and the ships' officers in gold-braided uniforms were bowing and scraping over all the smart passengers, and I waited, my eyes straining to see her, my neck aching and my fists clenched and my mouth dry as forgotten bread. I waited and went on waiting, and suddenly, like a miracle, she was there.

I went crazy then. I elbowed people out of the way—New York had at least taught me how to do that—and I heard someone say, "Christ, another drunken Irishman!" (for the prejudice in that city was terrible, with so many nationalities scrambling around the bottom of the ladder of fortune). But I didn't care about being slandered, I didn't care about anything except getting to Sarah before that high-stepping brother of hers got there and swept her off to his poky little palace. I saw Charles Marriott, his flunkeys beating a path for him through the crowds, and he saw me, for he flinched as if I were scum from the Five Points. But I reached the bottom of the gangway before he did, I beat him to it, and I was the first to welcome Sarah back to her stinking, swarming, hellhole of a city. She rushed down the gangway, stumbling in her haste, and I rushed up it, and then the worst was all forgotten, the exile, the waiting, the endless, gnawing longing that soaked me in sweat night after night. I grabbed her in such a fever that it was a wonder we didn't both topple over the side into the water, and all I remembered as I crushed my body against hers was seeing Lord de Salis in court on the day I was sentenced to jail and vowing that I'd lam his lover and lay his lady or else crawl forever dishonored to my grave.

II

My enemies say I'm nothing but a felon who should have served every day of his ten-year sentence in jail. Even my wife Eileen, who's never denied I've been the victim of injustice, is probably still telling our children that I was no better than a peasant and never had a proper education. But that's all lies, for I went to the best hedge school west of the Shannon—at least we called it a hedge school because it was still held in the same barn as in the bad old days when the Saxon tyrants had forbidden Irishmen to receive a Catholic education, but in truth it was better than a hedge school and its reputation stretched to places as far away as Clonbur and Cong. Anyway, even before I went to school my father had taught me to read and write. My father was an Ulster man, and the only reason he went to Connaught was because he was the youngest of nine and there was no land left for him at his father's home near Donaghadee. Now, my enemies say he was a Scotsman, but that's a lie too; Connaught men will say that about anyone from Ulster, but sure everyone should know there were Drummonds who were bishops in County Fermanagh in days past, and my mother's family, the O'Malleys, are all descended from Queen Grace O'Malley herself of immortal fame and glory.

So I'm an Irishman to the bone, and as for my first name, which everyone thinks is such a Saxon mistake, all I can say is I was named for a good friend of my father's. He may have been descended from Scottish heretics, but he must have been a good Catholic, because my father would never have named me for a Black Protestant. Besides, I like my name. It has a ring to it and gives me a confidence which maybe I wouldn't have had if I'd been called Paddy Murphy. Eileen told me when we were courting that it sounded like a gentleman's name. I've always remembered that. It's true I was born on a humble farm in Connaught, but I was born with a gentleman's name.

Anyway the farm wasn't so humble. Eileen said it was, but it was the best farm in the valley and always was, ever since my father married high up into the O'Malley family and began to work himself to the bone growing wheat and oats instead of contenting himself with only a potato patch. We had twenty-five acres of arable land with another twenty-five acres of bog, and of the arable land ten acres were under crops and the rest was in grass. The land in grass was too rocky and hilly to cultivate, but the sheep liked it and my cows did well too. In the winter the cows would find their way down to the bog and draw up the black rushes, which had white succulent roots over six inches long—indeed, I think the cows flourished better there than they did on the grass. The bog had other uses too, for it gave me heather for bedding my donkey and an ample store of fuel, and I'll always be agreeing with those who say a little bit of bog is a great thing for a clever farmer.

In the old days the rent we paid was twenty-six pounds, being calculated at one pound per acre for the arable land and one pound for the acres of bog, but after the famine old Lord de Salis favored my father with a special grant of land at a reduced rent. It was a leasehold, which meant the land was as good as ours for fifty years, and we weren't ordinary tenants any more. Like a miracle it was, I can still remember my mother shedding tears of joy and my father exultant with poteen and singing Lord de Salis's praises to the skies.

So we lived well, even having books in the house, and Lady de Salis (the old man's second wife) would call and we were grand, not as grand as Eileen would have liked, perhaps, but grander than any other family on the estate of Cashelmara.

I was the only child. I liked that, for it meant my father always had time for me, and my mother wasn't driven wild by half a dozen others constantly under her feet. It meant too that there was always enough food and I always wore decent clothes and had a pair of shoes. So whatever Eileen may say I wasn't giving myself airs when I told her long ago in Dublin that my father was a squireen. I truly did feel myself a cut above the others in the valley for all my mother was an O'Malley and kin to half Clonareen, and when Father Donal told me in my teens that for the sake of my immortal soul I'd best marry young, was it any wonder I looked past all the peasant girls to a schoolmaster's daughter?

Eileen thought I was good enough for her when we first met in Dublin. Old Lord de Salis had given me money when he sent me to study at the Agricultural College, and I spent most of it on clothes so I wouldn't have the other students looking down their noses at me. Those Dubliners always look down on a Connaught man if they have half a chance, and sure enough despite all my fine clothes they would look at me as if I were fresh from cutting turf on the bog. I didn't like the Agricultural College. To be honest, it was a waste of time, all talk about things that didn't interest me, and when they said I hadn't enough education to profit from it I thought, Well, if it's education I need, to the devil with it, for I'm educated enough already. Didn't I know Latin and Greek from the hedge school and all the classical mythology, and couldn't I recite every detail of the Battle of Clontarf when Brian Boru (may the saints bless his glorious memory) triumphed over the Vikings? To be sure I was educated! Eileen thought I was when we read the newspapers together and discussed politics. She'd listen well enough when I'd talk of the day of Ireland's liberation from tyranny, and when I paused for breath she'd say I was certain to end up a politician at Westminster alongside the hero O'Connell.

I was staying on in her father's house in those days when she had such a good opinion of me. Old Lord de Salis had arranged for me to be lodged with the family of one of the masters because he knew it would at first be strange for me to live in a city, and he thought Eileen's father would look after me well.

But Eileen looked after me better. We had a happy marriage for a long time, although of course she wouldn't remember that now. I know it was a shock for her when she first saw the farm, but she got over that, I swear she did despite all she said later during our first terrible quarrel.

We never quarreled until the day I first set eyes on Sarah de Salis. I'd had to fetch Eileen from her charity work at the dispensary because there had been an accident at home. I remember I was angry because I felt she should have been at home instead of playing nurse in Clonareen, and then I found out she was angry too because I'd been rude to her in front of Lady de Salis. "You might at least have been civil," she said bitterly, and I yelled at her, "And you might at least have been home!" so she said why shouldn't she do some charity work, and besides it was a relief to talk occasionally to a cultured, refined lady like Miss Madeleine de Salis. "And since when has your family not been good enough for you?" I shouted at her, angrier than ever, and I told her it was time she stayed at home to pay her husband and children some attention.

"I do pay you attention!" she snapped.

"Not enough!" says I. "The only attention I ever get from you nowadays is ten minutes in the dark once a week—if I'm lucky and often I'm not!"

Jesus, we had the father and mother of a quarrel then. She let loose a whole stream of complaint, saying I was a fine one to talk, for when did I ever pay any attention to her? I was always getting drunk with the O'Malleys or making an exhibition of myself in political meetings, so when might she expect the time of day from me, might she be so bold as to inquire, or was she to be satisfied with acting as a substitute for Rosie Costelloe whenever the fancy took me? So I said Rosie Costelloe did at least give me value for money, and then—dear God, the quarrel got worse and worse and there was nothing we didn't say to each other. She called me names and I said that if I'd been unfaithful once or twice it meant nothing because I had only done it to spare her. She said how dared I say such a thing and when had she ever asked to be spared, and I said of course she'd never ask, she was too dutiful for that, but I could put two and two together as well as the next man, couldn't I?

459

That infuriated her. She called me more names. She said I was gross and coarse and she'd always regretted marrying beneath her.

"Always?" I said. That cut very deep.

"Always!" she said. "Do you think I wouldn't rather be living like a lady in a decent house in Dublin than like a peasant in this smoky little hovel?"

"This is a fine farmhouse," I said, "and we don't live like peasants."

She laughed. I never forgave her for that. We patched up the quarrel somehow, but we were a long way from the boy and girl who had run off to the altar in Dublin, and both of us knew it. If I was the rogue Eileen said I was, I'd blame her for the estrangement that existed between us long before the final separation came, but I won't do that. I want to be honest, and so I've no choice but to say the fault lay not in Eileen but in me. I was the one to blame because I couldn't forgive her for betraying she rated me no better than a peasant and because I knew that Lady de Salis would yield to me if ever I had the chance to spend more than five minutes with her alone.

III

Maybe Eileen was right during our worst quarrel when she called me a cheating son of a tinker's bitch, but I can hardly believe there's a man alive who wouldn't have wanted Sarah de Salis from the first moment he set eyes on her.

She was very, very beautiful.

It was an unusual beauty. She didn't look like anyone else I'd ever seen. She had narrow eyes that seemed dark and light at the same time because they were golden brown, and high cheekbones like the ladies on the Chinese screen in her bedroom at Cashelmara. Her skin was soft and pale, untouched by wind or rain or sun, and she had full lips, which she kept clamped together as if she was scared she'd look too luscious. It was only when she laughed that you saw what a lovely mouth she had, and when I first knew her she didn't laugh often. Her long thick hair reached to her waist when it was uncoiled, and when she was naked it was hard to believe she had had as many as four children, for she didn't have that droopy overripe look common in Irish girls past twenty-five. She had a tiny waist, magnificent hips which managed to be well curved without being over-padded, perfect breasts and long, lissome, lovely legs.

460

I always knew I wanted her, but I never believed we were exactly right for each other until she sold her wedding ring to buy me out of jail. After all—and you'll pardon my cynicism—it's easy to lust after a beautiful woman but not nearly so easy to know what to do with her after you've had what you wanted. So I used to daydream about Sarah as I milked the cows and threshed with my flail, but I never imagined more than finding myself by some miracle in a fourposter bed with her and relieving my feelings against a luxurious background of exquisite linen sheets and soft white pillows. It seemed like such an impossible daydream that it never occurred to me to wonder what would happen afterward. But I wondered when she bought me out of jail. My first thought was: What a woman! And when I remembered how months before I had sat with her in the library at Cashelmara and drunk to MacGowan's damnation, I marveled to myself: What a partner!

I saw her only once between my escape from jail and my voyage to America, and there was no fourposter bed, no fine sheets and no soft pillows. But I took my jacket and her cloak and laid them on the hard damp floor of a ruined cabin, and I never gave a thought to my old daydreams. For she was no longer just a beautiful woman I wanted. She was Sarah, brave yet terrified, full of hope yet teetering on the brink of despair, laughing for joy yet weeping because we had so little time together and neither of us knew how long it would be before I could see her again. In my daydreams I had imagined her to be willing yet self-possessed, while I'd be my usual self, taking what I wanted and enjoying the scenery as I went along—"masterful" was the word I chose when thinking about this sort of pastime, but suddenly I found out that this was no pastime and I was no master. Sarah wasn't self-possessed, nor was she even willing, for that drunken pervert of a husband of hers had given her such a low opinion of herself that she was scared to death of yielding to me, and when I saw she was scared I was scared too. I thought: Holy Mary, if I hurt her everything'll be finished. Please, God, don't let me hurt her, and so it was a terrible state I was in because Sarah was such a lady, so delicate and fragile, and I felt as rough and clumsy as if I truly were no better than the poorest peasant in the valley.

Then she put it all right. She said, "I love you. I'll never want anyone else," and when I looked at her I no longer saw a fragile lady because I knew she no longer looked at me and saw a peasant. There was no disdain, no contempt. Her consuming worry was not whether

I was good enough for her but whether she was good enough for me, and after that gentleness came easy and tenderness too and it was all very different from any experience I'd had before.

Long afterward when we could speak again she said, "I feel quite a different person," and I said I did too. I felt as if I'd stepped out of one world into another, and as I looked at her again I thought, With this woman there'd be nothing I couldn't achieve. That was when I stopped thinking of a future without her.

"Come with me now," I said to her. "We'll go together to America." But she shook her head stubbornly and said she had to wait until she could arrange for the children to come with her. She had a plan, she said, and she must stick to the plan or all would be lost. She'd been working toward it for such a long time and she couldn't give it up now. "But I want more than anything to go with you," she said, crying, and that was when I made love to her again, not quite so gently this time, and when she answered me I had a tantalizing glimpse of what our nights were going to be like when she was living with me as my wife.

But that time was far off. It was nearly a year before I saw her again, eleven months of homesickness, misery and despair for me and for Sarah eleven months of endless machinations, plotting and intrigue.

IV

The Greeks had a word for it. Nemesis. My master at the hedge school said it meant evil and bad luck and a malignant fate all rolled into one, and I never forgot that, because when I first clashed with Hugh MacGowan that was the first word that flashed into my head.

MacGowan was a small man with big ideas. I don't mean he was physically small. He was no dwarf, but he had a small, tight-fisted mind with a bunch of small, stunted passions to match. Only his ambition and greed were on a grand scale, and since they were continually gratified by his employer they were continually growing. But I stood in his way. It was a time of awakening in Ireland, the dawn of a day that belonged to Charles Stewart Parnell, and we'd all of us had more than enough of Black Protestant agents like Hugh MacGowan. Offer your landlord only as much rent as you consider fair and just, said Parnell, and if he refuses that give him nothing. Well, we offered and were refused, so whose fault was it that trouble came to the valley? We were only being fair and reasonable. It was MacGowan and his greed who were to blame for his near lynching, and I blamed none other than MacGowan when I was falsely arrested, tried before a packed Saxon jury and tossed into jail.

Of course Eileen thought I was a fool for bringing so much trouble on us. "You have your leasehold," she said. "You're secure here on this land till nineteen hundred, and all you have to pay is the ground rent. Why must you mix yourself up in these fights and bring us all to ruin?" Well, there was a time in jail when my spirits were at their lowest ebb and I thought she might have been right, but she wasn't, I can see that now. It wasn't just that I had a moral duty to stand beside my O'Malley kinsmen, who were all in trouble, though that was part of it. It was because Parnell was talking to all Irishmen everywhere, the secure ones like myself and the insecure ones like my cousins who were dependent entirely on the good will of the landlord. "Stand up and unite!" said Parnell, and what sort of an Irishman would I have been if I had stood by and never lifted a finger to help my kin when MacGowan was extorting every penny they possessed and pulling down their cabins until they were homeless as well as destitute?

MacGowan said there was a new act of Parliament that allowed us to go to court and protest if we didn't like his rents—but what use were courts to us? The courts were run by Saxons, any fool knew that, and the Saxons would be sure to side with Lord de Salis and his agent. Besides, when you're desperate and the agent's on your doorstep with the wreckers, there's no time to go begging to fancy lawyers and their fancy courts of law. Parnell knew that. That was why he threatened to test the act by bringing some sample cases before the courts; he knew the act was just a piece of Saxon deception. Parnell was a great man, even in those days back in the early Eighties. Get out of our land, he said to the Saxons, and let us govern ourselves by a Parliament of our own in Dublin, for we'll get no justice while we're subjected to your rule of tyranny from Westminster.

You'd think MacGowan, a Scot, would know all about the tyranny of the English, but he was the type who has given the Scots a bad name in Ireland. He'd have sold his grandmother if there was profit in it. All he thought about was money, even if he had to spend his life fawning at Saxon feet to get it.

MacGowan, my enemy, my nemesis—and Sarah's nemesis too, the man who ruled Cashelmara and kept her from me for all those months after I had escaped to America. I didn't know then how far he had terrorized her since he had begun to rule the roost; if I'd known I would never have let her go back to that house.

463

But she went back and I went to America, days and days at sea on a boat as crowded as Noah's Ark. Being a fugitive, I couldn't afford to call attention to myself by traveling as a steerage passenger on a decent boat, and when I returned to Galway after seeing Sarah my friends in the Claddagh had arranged for me to be taken to Queenstown and smuggled on board a terrible old tub. Jesus, after only a week at sea I felt so dirty and starved and sick to my stomach that I was afraid I'd die before I saw land again! But I didn't die, and when I was on dry land at last at Castle Garden and they threatened me with the immigrant hospital, I at once felt miraculously better. I knew all about hospitals. Hospitals were where you caught fever and died. So I wheedled my way out of Castle Garden, fobbed off all the tricksters who gathered to fleece the newcomers, shoved aside the bummers shrieking for charity and somehow found a flophouse where I could lie down until I felt better.

Three times I nearly had my money stolen while I slept. I've never known such a place as New York for thievery and wickedness; it was worse even than Dublin. But I held onto my money (and there wasn't much of it left), and when I felt recovered I bought some new clothes and a bar of soap and some powder for the vermin and headed for the nearest bath. My money was nearly gone, but there was just enough afterward for a visit to the barber. It was either that or a square meal, but I'd been hungry so long I thought I could stay hungry a little longer, and I knew how important it was that I shouldn't turn up at Sarah's old home looking like any other poor Irish immigrant just off the boat from the Old World.

Sarah had given me a letter for her brother, and as soon as I had made myself presentable I walked up Manhattan Island to Fifth Avenue to pay him a call.

Uptown New York! I could feel my eyes getting wider and wider because it was all so grand—not as grand as Dublin, of course; I wouldn't want to exaggerate. But everything was so big. Why, the race-track field at Letterturk would have fitted three times into Washington Square! And the houses! Jesus, what palaces! All the way up, side by side, were these magnificent mansions, all of them as big as Cashelmara and some even bigger. It was such a state I was in that I didn't even feel my wallet being lifted—but that didn't matter anyway since the wallet was empty. I walked on and on, staring so hard I swear I forgot to blink, and everywhere there were enormous carriages and beautiful horses and even the sidewalks looked as though they were fit for ladies in gold slippers. Now, I never liked New

York, but Holy Mother of God, if I'd had the chance to live uptown maybe I'd be thinking it was a fine place after all. I'm sure Charles Marriott thought so when he returned each day from Wall Street to his fairy-tale home on Fifth Avenue.

It took me two whole minutes before I could nerve myself to walk through the gilded gates across the courtyard and another two before I could steel myself to ring the front doorbell.

"Good morning to you," I said to the butler, who was the blackest man I had ever seen—and the loftiest. "I'll see Mr. Charles Marriott if you please."

"Mr. Marriott," said the butler, "is not at home."

"Well, if it's away from home he is," I said, "I'll wait. I have a letter for him from his sister, Lady de Salis, wife of Baron de Salis of Cashelmara, may the Virgin and the Holy Saints protect her."

I thought I sounded most respectful and polite, but that cut no ice with him because he didn't believe me. The next moment we were having a shouting match, and he was yelling at the footmen to throw me out. That was when Marriott turned up. Of course he'd been at home all the time. He came down the stairs and said, "Whitney, what the devil's going on?" And when I had the chance to wave Sarah's letter in his face he put out a soft white hand to steady the envelope so that he could see the handwriting.

After a long pause he said, "Thank you. I can see that this does come from my sister." And he fished a dollar out of his pocket and held it out to me as casually as he might to a Bowery bummer.

"Begging your pardon, your honor," I said, doing my best to keep my temper, "but I'm a friend of your sister's, not just a messenger."

He took another look at me—and I took another look at him.

He was in his mid-thirties, I reckoned, and I saw at once that he was the kind of man who lives indoors most of his life and would throw a fit if a trace of mud spattered his boots. There was a likeness in looks between him and Sarah, but you had to look hard to notice it. He had a similar long neck—it looked odd on a man—and those high cheekbones, but his eyes were a dark brown and his mouth was thin-lipped, and apart from some fairish hair dragged across his scalp he was as bald as a bantam's egg. He spoke with a funny strangled sort of American accent, and later I realized he liked to use fancy language that made him sound as if he'd swallowed a dictionary. I found out later too that in addition to his fine expensive house he kept a fine expensive wife—though the wife was older than he was and frumpy too for all her fine clothes. But that didn't surprise me. It

465

wouldn't be bothering Charles Marriott if his wife was unattractive, for to be sure he'd consider bedroom romps no more than a cheap sport for the uneducated masses.

We hated each other on sight.

"Who are you?" he said. "What is your name?"

"My name is Maxwell Drummond," I said, and as always my name gave me confidence so that I found myself speaking up to him like an equal. "I'm a squireen and my lands lie about two miles east of Cashelmara."

"My sister has never mentioned you."

"Well, if it's a mention you want," I said, "why don't you read her letter?"

I'll say this for Charles Marriott: He was genuinely fond of Sarah in his own stuffy way, and once he had read her letter it was all I could do to stop him rushing over to Ireland on the next boat to rescue her. In fact he was so appalled by what he read that he completely forgot his distaste for me and hustled me into his study, where we could discuss the situation in privacy.

"The first thing you'd best realize," I said, quite in command of the situation by this time, "is that you can't go careering around Cashelmara like an elephant in a wheatfield. Sarah said I must be sure to make that clear to you. Mr. George de Salis did that and he's now a dead man."

"But I can't believe a murder could go undetected in such a manner!"

"Why not?" I said. "It happens all the time in Ireland."

"But—"

"Look, Mr. Marriott. Sarah wants to get away with all the children. If she tries to run away, MacGowan will bring her back and punish her because it's in his interests—and Lord de Salis's interests—to keep the marriage together. Lord de Salis wants to keep the children, and neither he nor MacGowan wants the world to know about their sodomy. So if Sarah goes she's got to go with Mac-Gowan's permission, and the only way to get MacGowan's permission is to provide her with a cast-iron excuse to go—which is where you come in. I don't know just what she said in her letter, but—"

"Money. This man MacGowan's greedy for money." He still sounded dazed.

"So it's money you have to dangle before him to lead him on. You have to write to your brother-in-law and—"

"Quite," he said abruptly, and I saw he was remembering who we

466

both were. "You may rest assured that I shall do whatever is necessary. I shall keep you informed."

"Well, it's not information I'm wanting at present," I said smoothly, "although I'm sure I shall be glad of it when it comes. I need money. I've spent my last penny in bringing your sister's letter to you, and Sarah said you'd see I didn't starve." And when he started fishing in his pockets again I said, "Keep your charity, for I'm not a beggar and I don't intend to be. Give me employment and I'll fend for myself."

He looked me up and down and I could almost hear him thinking, My God, what am I to do with him?

"Can you read and write?" he said doubtfully at last.

You Saxon son of a bitch, I thought, it's easy to see you can trace your ancestry back to Cromwell.

"I went to the best school west of the Shannon," I said, "and I completed my education at the Royal Agricultural College in Dublin."

He gave a small cynical smile and said he could find me a clerical position at his house of business on Wall Street.

"Good," I said. "I'll take a month's salary in advance, and maybe I'll change my mind about the charity. How about two hundred dollars as a reward for my letter-carrying services?"

He stood up. "Look here, Drummond—"

"I'm thinking you'd better not be less than generous with me," I said. "Sarah wouldn't like it at all if she thought I was being treated as less than a friend of the family."

I watched him turn a deep dull red. When he could speak again he said with far more nasal twang than usual, "I don't know what your relationship is with my sister. I can hardly believe she has ever given you permission to call her by her first name—"

I laughed. He went redder than ever.

"—but you have no relationship with me and I'm under no obligation to give you any help whatsoever. Is that clear? I could kick you into the gutter if I chose, and let me tell you that there's no gutter so filthy as the gutter of New York City. So you'll take a month's salary in advance from me and no more, and by God, if you don't want to be a beggar by the time my sister arrives, you'll accept what you're given and be grateful for it."

I admit I never thought he'd have the guts to speak to me like that, so I was taken aback. But I tried not to show it. I shrugged and said very well, if that was the way he chose to treat a visitor to his

467

country and his sister's friend, it was for God to pass judgment on him, not I. "So I'll say thank you and we'll speak no more about it," I added. "I'm not a man that bears a grudge."

That was twisting the truth, but instinct told me to smooth him over before he went so far as to withdraw his offer of work and money.

The next two weeks were very miserable for me. Charles Marriott played his part; he wrote to Lord de Salis, asked to see Sarah and the children and reminded his brother-in-law that he was a rich man with a childless wife. I've no doubt this was wrapped up in the fanciest language, but that wouldn't have stopped MacGowan picking up the message about money. Money had been scarce at Cashelmara since the famine of '79, Sarah had told me, and MacGowan wasn't the man to take a drop in profits lying down.

So with Charles Marriott playing his part, I had to play mine and work in his countinghouse, or his office, as he called it, but I hated that and quit after a week. I was used to being my own master and spending each day in the open air, so what would I be wanting with days spent sitting on a high stool and copying out rows of figures? I didn't know how any man could live like that, and I told Charles Marriott so when I quit.

"And how are you going to earn your living now?" says he, very sarcastic.

"Why, Mr. Marriott," I said, "don't you be bothering yourself about that, for sure it's none of your bloody business."

"Well, don't come to me when you're starving," he said, and I didn't for I didn't starve.

I'd met other Irishmen by this time. There were Irish in my lodginghouse, and soon I knew the Irish bars and Irish eating places and the Irish factions and I found the job I wanted. There was this man Jim O'Malley—he must have been a kinsman of mine and both of us descended from Queen Grace herself—and he had a chophouse south of Canal Street with gambling in the back room and girls upstairs and he needed someone to keep order from time to time when the place got too lively. I picked up a gun and all there was to know about turning a fast card at poker, and soon I was doing very nicely for myself, with two new suits and better lodgings and a steak for dinner every night on the house. I was doing well, there was no denying that, but Sarah was still at Cashelmara.

Lord de Salis—writing at MacGowan's dictation, I've no doubt—

said he couldn't let four little children take that long cruel voyage to America and his wife couldn't bear to leave them behind. However, if Charles Marriott himself wanted to cross the Atlantic . . .

Charles Marriott said he couldn't possibly leave his business at present, and besides the children weren't so little and would probably enjoy a sea voyage very much. He hoped to welcome them and Sarah to New York before the end of the fall.

Lord de Salis wrote back with more excuses, and I realized with a great rage that this letter-writing was going to go on for some time. But Charles Marriott was not only patient but crafty, and he didn't give up easily or else go rushing across the Atlantic waving a big stick.

"It's just a question of time, Drummond," he said as I paid my weekly call on him to find out if there was any news. "He'll run out of excuses—or money—eventually."

Time ticked on. Jim O'Malley brought an oyster saloon off Broadway, very fashionable, and invested in a fancy brothel, and the O'Flahertys, another Irish faction, started to muscle in on him, so I was kept pretty busy. Those O'Flahertys were always a wild crowd, as anyone who's ever been to Galway City knows, and they were wilder than ever in New York, where everyone ran in factions and there was a lot of money to be made if you were in the right line of business. The only time we got any cooperation from the O'Flahertys was when the Germans began to crowd us both, but it was a funny world we lived in, at the O'Flahertys' throats all week and then trooping to Mass with them on Sunday. It made me think of home with the Joyces and the O'Malleys beating one another to pulp in a faction fight and then all mingling peacefully in church together the next morning. I thought of home a great deal, usually when I was in church or when it was raining. It rained in a hard foreign way in New York. There was no soft Irish mist, and instead of walking through wet green fields I would have to trudge through dirty, dark city streets. I hated the city. I always hated it even when I was doing well for myself, and day after day I longed for Sarah and home.

Lord de Salis said how good it was of Charles Marriott to be so interested in his estate, and if he had twenty thousand dollars to spare he might like to consider an investment. Charles Marriott said yes, he might, and he would discuss it with Sarah when she brought the children to New York in the spring.

You'd think I would have missed Sarah less as the days passed,

469

but I missed her more. I even stopped telling the priest about the wicked dreams I had because after a while I became tired of shocking him to pieces in the confessional.

"You're a married man lusting after a married woman," ran the familiar words, "so your thoughts are doubly adulterous."

"But you'll give me absolution, Father?" I pleaded, for to tell the truth I lived a dangerous life in some ways and my one dread was of dying violently before I could receive absolution for my sins. I always did my best to keep in a state of grace, but after a while the priest became angry with my adulterous thoughts and I stopped going to confession.

That upset me, for I was as religious as any other decent Irishman, and I fully expected retribution, but nothing happened except that Jim O'Malley gave me a raise and offered me the pick of the whores in his new brothel.

"Well, thank you, Jim," I said. "You're a generous man and no mistake." But of course it was the same old story. I couldn't look at another woman for more than two seconds before thinking how inferior she was to Sarah, and besides, I was terrified of the diseases you can get from city women. The sights I saw in New York and the tales I heard were enough to make anyone's hair stand on end. I've never been a man to rate celibacy more than a passing sneer, but for once in my life I was as celibate as a Benedictine monk.

That didn't make life in New York any easier for me either.

Lord de Salis wrote and said he really couldn't consent to his children going to America; it was too far. But if Sarah wanted to go without them he wouldn't stand in her way.

One Sunday morning in February I awoke and all the heat was off and it was so bloody cold that I'd have sold my soul to be sitting by a peat fire. I stayed in bed and thought of Ireland, and I don't believe I've ever been so miserable in all my life. In fact I was in such a low state that I didn't go to Mass.

Now, I thought, surely God'll reach down from Heaven and punish me. First I stop going to confession and then I turn my back on the Holy Sacrament itself. God help me, for surely something terrible's going to happen.

But nothing did. That week I won two hundred dollars at faro, and Charles Marriott said Sarah had decided to visit New York in April—without the children.

I never went to Mass after that. I wanted to, but I could no longer pretend to care about the adultery, and if I couldn't lie to myself any more I didn't see how I could hope to lie to God. All I cared about was Sarah. I didn't give a tinker's curse that we were married to other people, because our partnership was going to be greater than any marriage, and she was going to mean far more to me than even the best wife in the world meant to her loving husband.

v

We couldn't wait. She went home with her brother and I went with her, but as soon as she dared she told him she wanted to step out with me and take a little walk along Fifth Avenue. He let her go although he was very angry, but neither of us cared about that.

We went to my lodgings. I had two nicely furnished rooms off Fourth Avenue by this time—in a tenement, it was true, but there are two classes of tenements, as anyone knows who's ever lived in New York, the upper-class which is inhabited by honest respectable working people and the lower-class which is no better than a cesspool and which has given the word tenement a bad name. My tenement building was clean and well kept, and when Sarah stepped into my apartments they seemed as good as royal to me. I couldn't believe how beautiful she was. I was struck dumb and could only watch her fingers trembling as she tried to undo the buttons of her dress. Then I tried to undo the buttons, but I was in such a state they kept slipping through my fingers. Jesus, we were both so clumsy there was nothing to do but laugh, and after that we were ourselves again, and the torture of that long separation was at last at an end.

I was so out of practice that I swear if I'd been an onlooker I would have booed and hissed, but she was so passionate I was soon having another try, and after that I don't know what happened to the time except that outside it got dark.

Later, when I was lighting a candle, she asked if I'd been faithful to her, and when I said yes she said she didn't believe it and I said no, I didn't believe it either but it was true. We laughed again, but afterward she cried and begged me never to leave her, and I said I should be the one to do the begging, not her. But still she couldn't believe I loved her. I had to repeat it to her many times and prove it yet again until finally I had persuaded her to believe.

It was midnight when I brought her back to the Marriott home, and her brother was waiting up for her. It was plain to see he was furious, but Sarah embraced him and pleaded his forgiveness so fervently that he had little choice but to smother his ill-temper. Yet after she had gone upstairs he said to me, "I want no scandal about this, Drummond, for Sarah's sake. I refuse to tolerate my sister becoming the laughingstock of New York society. She can see you whenever she pleases, but don't expect to dine at this house or to attend any functions to which Sarah may be invited. Also she must spend every night beneath this roof, if you please, and next time I'll be obliged if you would kindly bring her home no later than ten o'clock. I speak not out of personal animosity, you understand, but out of concern for Sarah, and if you care a straw for her I think you'll realize that I'm talking sense."

"Oh, is it sense you call it?" I said. "I thought it was prejudice." Him and his "personal animosity"! But neither Sarah nor I had any wish to quarrel with him after all he had done to help us, so I did my best to keep a civil tongue in my head, and Sarah did her best not to embarrass him in the eyes of New York society.

Lord de Salis began to write to his wife, saying what had happened to Charles Marriott's offer to invest in the estate and when was she coming home?

Sarah left the letters unanswered for a while, but when she did write she gave evasive answers.

"My plans are plain," I said to her. "I have to stay in America until I can win a pardon from the Queen. I can't go back to Ireland till I'm pardoned or I'll be flung back into jail."

"But how can you get your pardon?" she asked in despair.

This was a question I had asked myself so often that I had a smooth answer ready. "The Clan-na-Gael will help me," I said confidently. "That's the Fenians, you know, and New York and Boston are packed with them. If I contribute enough money to their funds they'll take up my case with the hero Parnell and Parnell will take it to the Queen herself, I shouldn't wonder." I had no idea how much truth there was in this, but I had convinced myself that there was every likelihood of it coming true. I couldn't have endured New York if I had allowed myself to believe for one moment that I'd never get back to Ireland. "And when I'm pardoned," I said, sinking still deeper into my dreams, "I'll cross the Atlantic Ocean again and make Hugh MacGowan wish he'd never been born."

"If it's a question of money," said Sarah, worried, "perhaps Charles—"

"Your brother wouldn't lend me a plugged nickel," I said bitterly, "and even if he did I'd turn him down. I'll make my money my own

472

way, and at the rate I'm going I'll have it all in the twinkling of an eye."

"But how long—"

"A year."

"Promise?"

This was tricky. It was one thing to talk big to cheer her up and quite another to deceive her deliberately. "No," I said at last. "I can't promise. Something might go wrong. But I'll be trying my hardest, I can promise you that."

"It's the children," she said, twisting her hands together. "I can't bear to think how long I may have to be away from the children."

"Well, to be sure it's terrible for you," I said. I always became uneasy whenever the conversation turned—as it so often did—to her children. "But don't lose heart. Maybe we can tempt your husband to part with them after all."

But I somehow couldn't see this coming true, especially when Lord de Salis persisted to nag her. When was she coming back? Had Charles changed his mind about the money? The children asked every day when she would be coming home.

"Every day!" said Sarah, weeping. Scarcely a day passed when she didn't burst into tears at the thought of the children. "Oh, Maxwell, what am I to do? I can't bear to be apart from them indefinitely. I'm not strong enough, but I can't go back. I'm not strong enough for that either."

"You'll get those children," I said, but I was so worried that she might be on the brink of a nervous collapse that I swallowed my pride and begged for a secret audience with Charles Marriott.

"If you could go to Ireland," I said humbly to him, "if you could ask Lord de Salis to let you bring the children on a visit to America . . ."

"I could do no such thing," he said at once. "It's obvious de Salis isn't going to let those children go. They're his insurance his wife will return to him."

"And I suppose you think it would be a good thing if she did return!" I exploded, unable to be humble a second longer. "You think it would be better for her to be at Cashelmara with a pervert than in New York with me!"

"I didn't say that," he said coolly. "Obviously she can't return to Cashelmara. But I think she should return to London—or to Dublin, if the marriage falls within the jurisdiction of the Irish courts—and seek legal advice with a view to obtaining a divorce. Whichever way

473

one looks at the situation the inescapable fact remains that she'll never see those children again until she obtains custody of them in a court of law."

"But I can't go to Ireland or England until I have my pardon."

"Quite," said Charles Marriott. "Forgive me for saying so, but I can't help but feel that's a good thing. Your presence at Sarah's side could only jeopardize her chances of obtaining the children's custody. In fact, it might even jeopardize her chances of obtaining the divorce itself."

"She won't leave me."

"Are you sure of that?" he said coldly, and I wasn't. I had reached the point where I woke every morning in a cold sweat for fear she'd gone back. I knew all too well how much those children meant to her.

"We've got to get the children out here!" I said in despair. "You must go back to letter-writing again—dangle some more money in front of MacGowan's nose."

"Don't try and tell me what to do!" he interrupted furiously. "I've had enough of you giving me orders!"

So Sarah had to give him the orders instead.

"I realize now he'll never part with all four children," she said. Poor Sarah, it would have melted a heart of stone to see her saying that so calmly and trying so hard to be brave. "But perhaps we could tempt him to part with one . . . or two . . ."

Charles Marriott started to say something about going back for a divorce, but she wouldn't listen to him. "Not without Maxwell," she said, and my heart nearly burst with pride and relief. "I'm never going to be parted from him again."

Charles Marriott looked sick when she said this, but what could he say? Sarah was his sister, and no matter how much he disapproved of me he still wanted to do all he could for her. So he said, "I'll write again to Patrick and say I'm thinking of making Ned my heir. Perhaps that'll tempt him to send at least Ned across the Atlantic to see me," and so it came about that on the fourteenth of December 1885 I first met the Honorable Patrick Edward de Salis, son and heir of the eleventh Baron de Salis of Cashelmara.

Chapter Two

I

He was twelve years old, and of all Sarah's children he was the one she mentioned most. She was too good a mother to have favorites, but if she had had a favorite it would have been Ned.

"I love all my children," she said to me over and over again. "They all mean something special to me." And this was amazing, not only because it was true but because a lesser woman might have felt differently in the circumstances. For instance, the second son, John, was simple-minded, and there are plenty of parents who reckon it an insult to themselves to produce a simpleton, but I never heard Sarah say a word against him. She was full of how sweet-natured he was and never once mentioned that he couldn't read or write. But I knew that because Eileen had heard it from Miss Madeleine de Salis at the dispensary, and to be sure Miss de Salis never told a lie in her life. Then there was the younger daughter, Jane, conceived in a way that would have revolted the devil himself and a plain, uppity little thing, if Miss de Salis was to be believed. "But Jane has such a dear little face and she'll be attractive when she grows up—even more attractive than Eleanor, I shouldn't wonder," said Sarah with such sincerity that I began to wonder if Miss de Salis was a liar after all. "Of course she's a little naughty, but all children go through naughty stages."

In fact I heard more about Jane than I heard about John and Eleanor, but I still heard more about Ned than I heard about Jane.

I went with Sarah to the docks to meet his ship, although Charles Marriott didn't want me to go and told Sarah he refused to be there unless I agreed to stay away. When Sarah wouldn't hear of that they quarreled, and he stayed behind in a fine huff at his house while Sarah and I took the Marriott carriage to the docks.

Sarah was so nervous that I thought she'd faint. As the passengers began to disembark she kept talking steadily—and all about nothing in particular—and she clung to my arm as if she was afraid of toppling over in her excitement, and all the while she was straining her eyes for a glimpse of her darling boy.

The odd part was that despite her eagerness I saw him before she did. He was leaning over the rail on deck and scanning the crowd below. I'd seen him once or twice out riding with his father, and I recognized the gold gleam of his hair.

Sarah began to cry, but that was only because she was in an ecstasy of happiness. She kept saying she couldn't believe he was truly there, and when I looked down at her radiant face all I could think was: So be it. I'd had enough time to get used to the idea of Ned joining us, and although I didn't welcome the idea of sharing Sarah with anyone I knew how much his presence would mean to her. Also I'd spent some painful moments missing my own children in months past, and although I'd now accepted it would be a long while before I saw any of them again I knew what it was to long for a glimpse of one's son. By the time I met Ned I had even convinced myself I would enjoy having a boy to look after again. To be sure I realized it would be difficult for him at first to think of me as a stepfather, but I was prepared from the beginning to treat him as a son. After all, as I told myself over and over again, the poor little bastard's got the feeblest father any boy could wish for, so at least I should be able to set him the kind of example he's always been lacking.

He came down the gangway.

He was a fine-looking lad indeed, tall for his age and quite the young gentleman in the way he held his head up high. He looked a great deal like his father, but I made up my mind not to hold that against him. He moved slowly at first, almost sauntering, as if he wanted the world to know how grown-up he was, but when he saw the expression on Sarah's face he ran down into her arms.

"You've grown!" was all she could say, weeping for joy again. "How you've grown!"

He laughed. When I saw him try to disentangle himself I smiled in sympathy, for I knew no boy of twelve likes his mother kissing him too long. But when he found disentanglement difficult he yielded gracefully and gave her a warm bear hug that made her gasp in delight.

"But are you by yourself?" she said at last when she'd got her breath back. "Your father promised he'd send your tutor with you. You're much too young to travel alone."

"My tutor gave notice, and Mr. MacGowan said it would save money not to pay an extra fare, and *of course* I'm not too young, Mama!"

"Of course!" I agreed, still smiling. "You're as good as grown up."

He spun around. When he saw me his back stiffened so abruptly that Sarah let him go.

"Maxwell, I must introduce you," she said quickly to me. "May I present Ned. Ned, this is Mr. Maxwell Drummond. I expect you remember his name."

He stood stock-still.

"Hullo, Ned—how are you?" I said, and held out my hand.

He ignored it. "I'm Master de Salis to you if you please," he said icily, and, swinging around on his mother, he demanded as rudely as any tinker's brat, "When the devil are you coming home?"

II

Jesus, it was an awkward moment and no mistake, but fortunately Sarah was in such a state of elation that it was impossible for her to be upset. She said gently, "Darling, please don't be so discourteous to Mr. Drummond. He's been such a help to me since I arrived in New York."

I decided not to wait for Ned to comment on this—or indeed on anything else. "I'll wait for the baggage, Sarah," I said. "You go ahead to the carriage."

"Very well. Ned, how many bags do you have?"

"One trunk and one box," he said and turned his mouth down at the corners.

The sulky little bastard! If either of my boys had behaved like that I'd have reached for my best leather belt without a second thought.

It took a while to recover the baggage, but eventually I had a man carrying it to the Marriott carriage and was opening the door to say goodbye to Sarah.

"I'll be calling tomorrow morning as usual," I said, for I began my working day at five in the evening and my mornings were usually free. "Perhaps we can all have lunch together at Delmonico's."

If the boy saw I could take his mother to a place like Delmonico's, he'd think twice about looking down his aristocratic little nose at me.

"That would be lovely." She smiled, and her face was radiant again. I wondered if she would have the nerve to kiss me in front of her son, but she did. She had great courage and great honesty, and I never loved her more than I did then.

As I watched the carriage rumbling away over the dirty cobbles I remembered my own boys, Max and Denis, far away in Dublin, and by the time I reached my apartment I was knee-deep in the blues, as the Americans say. I drank some whisky, but all the whisky in the world couldn't have chased those blues away, and when I tried to write to my sons I lost heart because I knew they wouldn't answer. But one day I knew they'd understand why I had to fight MacGowan and risk losing all I had. One day they'd understand it was Mac-Gowan, not I, who was to blame for their homelessness, MacGowan and all those centuries of Saxon misrule and persecution.

And I went on thinking to myself in that vein until in the end I had stopped thinking of my boys and was thinking only of the revenge I would take once I got home to Ireland. That banished the blues quickly enough, and after I'd slept off the whisky I put on my gun and my best fancy suit and went off to work.

The next morning I called on Sarah.

She received me in the poky little sitting room where Mrs. Charles Marriott had insisted that I be hidden whenever I put my nose across the Marriott threshold, and I saw quick as a flash that yesterday's joyous reunion had become today's prize problem.

"I've talked and talked to him," she said, agitated after we'd kissed, "but I can't bring myself to tell him the truth. Charles says he's too young to know, but unless Ned knows how is he to understand that I'm justified in refusing to return to Patrick?"

"Wait." I tightened my arms around her and held her until she'd stopped trembling. "Let's sit down and talk this over calmly."

So we sat down on an overstuffed seat, and opposite us on the dark-red wall was a huge picture of the Hudson Valley and a stuffed fish in a glass box. The fish always seemed to be watching us, and whenever I noticed him I wondered about the bright soul who had stuffed him instead of eating him as he deserved.

"First of all," says I, holding her hand and speaking clear and sensible, "it's plain Ned must know what's going on at that house. He's twelve years old, and boys of twelve always know everything there is to know."

"No, they don't! He's never been away to school. Nobody would have talked to him about it. I'm sure he's quite innocent."

"Bull," I said. "It's not possible."

"Maxwell, you don't understand. A boy of his class . . ." She bit her lip. "Well, you may be right," she said after a moment, "but from my conversations with him since he arrived I feel certain that he has no idea what's going on. Yet I daren't ask him directly in case . . . Maxwell, I'm frightened of telling him and yet I want him to know. If only he knew I'm sure he would forgive me for everything."

"You've told him, of course, that you'll not be going back."

"Yes, but he wouldn't listen. He says I've got to change my mind. That's why I'm sure he can't understand."

"Well, it's time he did," I said. "I'll talk to him."

"But Charles says—"

"Never mind Charles. I'm not standing by with my mouth shut while some fool of a boy tells you to go back and live with a drunken pervert."

"But, Maxwell . . ." She stopped.

"Yes?"

"Perhaps it would be better if Charles talked to him. I mean—"

"Why?"

"Well . . ." But she could think of nothing to say.

"Don't you trust me?"

"Of course! But it might be easier if he heard the truth from Charles, his uncle."

"Listen," I said, "whoever breaks the news it's not going to be easy for Ned. Now, your brother has no sons and I have two and I know what to say to boys that age. Besides, your brother looks as if he'd have a hard time talking about fornication to his wife, let alone sodomy to his nephew. I'll do it, Sarah, and you needn't worry that I won't do it as it should be done."

"You will be kind to him, won't you?" she said, trying not to cry. "You will be gentle."

"He's your son," I said, "and I'd like to care for him as if he were mine." If he'll let me, I added to myself, but I didn't tell her I was beginning to have second thoughts about this high-flying little snob she'd dragged to America. Soon I was even beginning to wish I hadn't been so eager to justify his mother's behavior to him, for as soon as I parted company from Sarah I saw clearly that it was going to be the very devil of an interview.

III

I decided to keep out of his sight for a week to give him a chance to simmer down, and sure enough Sarah told me that matters had improved. Charles was taking an interest in his nephew and had spoken up in her favor. Ned had recovered from his sulks and had decided to put aside all thought of home while he enjoyed his visit to New York. Sarah spent her afternoons taking him to the zoo and Central Park and the theater, and Charles arranged for him to go riding with his friends' children, so it wasn't until Sarah told me that Ned had introduced the subject of Cashelmara again that I decided I must make my move.

"I'll take him out to dinner," I said. I reckoned he was less likely to quarrel with me if I were his host in a public place, and I knew a fine restaurant between Gramercy Park and Broadway where I could get a discount on the bill. "Let me see him tomorrow when I call, and I'll issue my invitation."

I only hoped he would agree to see me, but I knew I could trust Sarah to win him around, and lo and behold, when I arrived he came with her to the little sitting room and stood stiffly beneath the stuffed fish. This time I didn't make the mistake of offering him my hand. I just smiled and asked him how he was enjoying New York.

"Well, it's educational, I suppose," he said loftily, "but I can't say I care for cities."

"Then we have one thing at least in common," I said, "for I can't stand 'em either. Maybe you could do me the honor of dining with me one night and we can talk for an hour or two about Ireland."

He glanced at his mother. She gave him a melting look that would have made any man's head spin, and he turned down his mouth at the corners again.

"Very well," he said shortly. There was no "thank you," no "sir," not even a "Mr. Drummond." He was as insolent as a tinker's mule.

"Would tomorrow suit you?" I said, and when he nodded sulkily I said, "I'll call for you at seven" and turned to Sarah to extricate us from the interview.

"I'm going for my morning drive now with Mr. Drummond," she said to him. "Would you like to come too, darling?"

Darling said he wouldn't, thank you very much, and I was able to

480

escape with Sarah to my apartment for our usual morning pastime. I was never more relieved to get out of that house, but in no time at all I was back again, waiting for Ned to come downstairs. He kept me waiting ten minutes, and when he finally strolled into the sitting room he offered me not one word of apology.

We set off on foot for Gramercy Park.

The restaurant I had chosen was Ryan's, off Irving Place. Jim O'Malley had just bought it from Ryan, and his manager there, Liam Gallagher, was an old friend of mine. It was a high-class place, more so than Jim's other restaurants. The dining room was lighted by lamps with huge colored shades—Tiffany lamps, they were called, except that real Tiffany lamps were proper stained glass and so grand that only the very rich could afford them, and these were just painted glass imitations—and there was paneling on the walls and snow-white Irish linen on all the tables. As for the food, it was delicious, none of that French stuff drenched in sauce and reeking of garlic but straight, plain, honest fare that would make any Irishman lick his lips. There were huge steaks and thick meaty chops as well as the traditional bacon dishes, and the baked potatoes were the most luscious I'd ever tasted, so magnificent in flavor that they didn't need butter to dress them up for the palate. The greatest eating treat in New York for me was a potato at Ryan's, and my friend Liam Gallagher always saw that I was given two potatoes, not just one. The Americans are stingy with their potatoes for all they're so fine, and in fact some races in New York don't eat potatoes at all but nasty white stringy stuff they call by all manner of heathen names.

I had already warned Liam I'd be coming with a friend, and he had a corner table by the window saved for me.

"Who's your young friend, Max?" says Liam when we arrived, and I answered smoothly, "This is the Honorable Patrick Edward de Salis, son and heir of Lord de Salis of Cashelmara. Master de Salis, may I present Mr. Liam Gallagher?"

Liam looked astounded, as well he might, but recovered himself enough to bid Ned welcome and ask him what he wanted to eat.

"Is there a menu?" said Ned, lofty as ever.

Liam produced a menu and winked at me. "Steak as usual, Max?"

"No, give me the mutton chops tonight, if you please, and don't forget my potatoes."

"To be sure I wouldn't dare! A pint of stout?"

"Fine. Ned will you take some stout with your meal?"

He shook his head. Liam helpfully offered him cider, but he shook his head at that too. Presently Joe the waiter brought my drink and a basket of freshly baked soda bread still warm from the oven and a dish of butter so creamy it might have come from my own churn.

"Have some," I offered Ned.

He shook his head a third time.

My patience snapped. Right, I thought, if that's the way he wants it, so be it. So I shut my mouth. The silence lengthened. I drank some stout, ate some bread, and when our chops arrived I picked up my knife and fork without a word. By this time Ned was beginning to look uncomfortable. He was shifting uneasily in his seat, and although he tried to eat his chop he left it half finished. In the end I took pity on him. He was only a lad after all and perhaps not so bold as he wanted me to think he was.

"Pudding?" I asked briefly.

"No, thank you," he said, staring down at his platter, and I knew he had become more approachable.

I ordered cheesecake and tea. They made tea properly at Ryan's, unlike other American establishments I could name, and I always had a large pot after I'd dined there. Then as soon as Joe had brought me the order I leaned forward, moving so quickly that Ned jumped, and said to him in my quietest voice, "Your mother's asked me to speak to you about certain matters. Are you going to listen civilly or do I have to tell her you were too rude for us to have any conversation?"

He swallowed and answered with difficulty, "By all means say what you have to say."

"You call me sir when you speak to me," I said. "You're twelve and I'm past forty and by age alone I'm entitled to some respect from you."

He stared at the tablecloth. No statue could have been more still.

"Why is it so difficult for you to be civil to me?" I said. "It can't be just because your mother's my mistress, for when we first met you didn't know she and I had ever shared a bed."

He looked up as sharply as if he had been stung, and I saw the stricken expression in his eyes.

"So you know what that means," I said, watching him. "I thought you would."

Speech was beyond him. He was blushing, his mouth clamped tight shut, and I suddenly realized he was on the verge of tears. He was very young.

"Look," I said, softening my voice and doing my best to be gentle.

482

"I bear you no ill will. I love your mother and I'm going to look after her, and as far as you're concerned I'm more than willing to be friends. Now I've been honest with you, so why don't you be honest with me and tell me why you've always treated me like dirt?"

He tried to speak, but no words came.

"It's because you think I'm not good enough for your mother, isn't it?" I said. "That's the reason."

"No," he said, "it's not because of that. It's because you're my father's enemy."

I stared at him. I wasn't sure why I should feel so taken aback, but perhaps it was because I'd never imagined him caring twopence for his father's opinions. After all, a creature like de Salis . . . But maybe de Salis was cleverer than I'd given him credit for.

"I'm MacGowan's enemy, Ned," I said, knowing instinctively that I mustn't speak abusively of de Salis and deciding in consequence that MacGowan must take the brunt of all my criticism and condemnation. "My grudge against your father is that he's too easily led by MacGowan, and MacGowan's caused your mother more suffering than any woman should be asked to endure."

To my surprise he at once seemed more at ease. He straightened his back and held his head up high again.

"I know my mother was unhappy at home," he said, "but it was only because she couldn't be practical about her marriage. My father told me all about it. We had a long talk together when it became clear she wasn't coming back from America, and my father told me everything."

"Everything?" I said, confused by this time.

"Yes, sir. He said he and my mother had never been very happy together although they had both tried hard, and finally they became so unhappy that my mother didn't want to live with him any more as a wife should. He said he understood this, for he didn't want to live with her either, so it was best they lived their separate lives—although for the sake of us children they would go on being husband and wife in public and sharing a home together. But Papa said Mama wasn't prepared to let him live a separate life. She wanted him to keep on lying, but he wouldn't live a lie. He wanted to be honest. He loved Mr. MacGowan better than he loved her. He said that Mr. Mac-Gowan was the very best friend he ever had and that he always felt so happy and peaceful in his company. He said it was easy for him to live with Mr. MacGowan as a friend but impossible for him to live with my mother as a husband."

He stopped. Now I was the one who was speechless, and he, mistaking my stunned expression for disapproval, said hastily, "He said he was sorry for my mother, but it was much better to face the truth than not to face it. He said my mother wouldn't face the truth and wanted to divide the family by taking us children away from him, but he loved us all too much to let her do that. He said if she'd truly loved us she wouldn't have left Cashelmara, and if she truly loved us she'd come back. I don't think he's right about that, sir, because I know she does truly love us, but I do think she should go home. I don't mind for myself because I'm nearly grown up and I don't need a mother any more, but my sisters are very little and my brother isn't as grown up as I am. I know she doesn't like Mr. MacGowan, but he and Cousin Edith are rebuilding Clonagh Court, and Papa says that if Mama comes back she can be mistress of her own house again and he and Mr. MacGowan won't bother her at all."

"Ned," I said.

"Yes, sir?"

"I'm thinking you don't truly understand what your father was trying to tell you. It's not as if he and MacGowan never do more than shake hands, you know."

He looked blank. I saw it all then, de Salis being honest but not explicit, the boy being sympathetic but naïve. I knew I had to be very careful at this point, so I stopped to think before I spoke again. Mustn't abuse de Salis but must uncover the truth. Concede he'd been honest but show he hadn't been honest enough. Point out the hell Sarah had lived in and name MacGowan as the devil incarnate but leave it to the boy to decide what kind of a man that made his father. Go easy, be careful, walk on tiptoe.

"Supposing Mr. MacGowan was a woman, Ned," I heard myself say casually at last. "Would you still say that your father was justified in demanding your mother's return?"

"But he's not a woman," said Ned.

"Exactly," I said. "All the more reason for your mother to refuse to return home."

He looked at me. I watched the puzzled lines fade from his face until it looked very smooth and fresh and young. Then he looked away. He looked at the teapot and he looked at my untouched plate of cheesecake and he looked at the snow-white tablecloth gleaming beneath the Tiffany lamps.

"Your father was right," I said, taking care to speak in an even, neutral voice. "It's better to face the truth, and the truth is that he

484

was expecting your mother to go on condoning his unnatural love affair with his agent. The only reason your mother endured it for so long was because she wouldn't leave you children, but MacGowan made her life such a hell that it's a wonder she's still alive to tell the tale. At one stage she was so frightened of him that she used to carry a knife around with her for protection, because your father told her in all honesty—yes, I admit your father's an honest man—that if MacGowan chose to hurt your mother he wouldn't lift a finger to stop him."

I paused. Around us the restaurant hummed with conversation mingled with the clink of glasses and cutlery.

"And if it's honesty you're wanting . . ." I could no longer keep the neutrality in my voice. I wanted to, but by this time I was in such a rage at the thought of Sarah's past suffering that my judgment slipped out of focus and for five dark, blurred seconds I forgot all my efforts at self-control. "And if it's honesty you're wanting," said my voice violently, "let me tell you that the last time your father insisted on acting like a husband he had to have MacGowan in the bedroom with him before he could act like a man with your mother. So let's have no more talk of her going home to Cashelmara, for it's not angry you should be with her that she left but grateful that she stayed so long."

I'd managed to stop myself spilling out the fact that MacGowan had forced Sarah to submit to sodomy, but I still cursed myself for having said more than I'd intended. I was breathing unevenly, my fists clenched harder than ever, but Ned hadn't moved. He was staring at the napkin in his lap, and I couldn't see the expression in his eyes. His face was white and still.

"I'm sorry," I said heavily. "I didn't mean to say all that, but I wanted you to understand what your mother's been forced to suffer these past years."

The chair scraped against the floor as he stood up. His napkin fluttered to the ground.

"Ned . . ."

"Excuse me, please, sir," he said politely and ran out of the room.

I leaped to my feet, called to Joe, "Tell Liam I'll pay later!" and ran after Ned into the street.

I chased him all the way to Gramercy Park and caught up with him only when he stopped on the north side. Leaning against the railings, he gripped them with both hands, pressed his forehead against the iron bars and vomited.

Poor wretched little bastard, I thought as I kept my distance and waited for him to finish. I felt pretty sick myself, because I knew that although I'd started out so well I'd made a mess of things, and all I could do now was repeat to myself over and over again: I'll make it up to him. I'll be extra kind and nice to him. And one day, if he should ever turn to me for help, I'll give him the best help any boy could wish for.

When he had finished vomiting I offered to take him home, but he tried to run away from me again, and we had a little struggle on the sidewalk.

"I'm taking you home," I repeated. "I'm seeing you to the door. I'm responsible for you, and your mother would never forgive me if I left you to find your own way back."

He made a futile effort to hit me and then gave up. His face was awash with tears.

I thought of walking over to Broadway and taking a streetcar, but I was sure he wanted the privacy of darkness, so we headed on foot down to Fourteenth Street and around Union Square to Fifth Avenue. The child stumbled along beside me, not saying a word, but every so often I would hear him sobbing wretchedly to himself, and when we neared the Marriott mansion he tried to dry his eyes on his sleeve.

"We can wait a minute before we go in, if you like," I said, stopping by the gates, and although he shook his head violently he started to cry again, so we waited. I leaned against the wall and lighted a cigarette so he wouldn't think I was staring at him, and at last he was able to say in a small trembling voice, "I want to go home and I want my mother to come with me. I promised I'd bring her back. What's going to happen to us now?"

"I'll take you both home before long," I said. "Your mother and father will settle their differences in a court of law, and everything will be well again, I promise you."

"But I want to live at Cashelmara," he said. "I don't want to live anywhere else."

"Indeed and why shouldn't you live there?" I said. "You're the heir, and Cashelmara will be yours one day." And all of a sudden I thought: Holy Mother of God, that's an idea and a half and no mistake.

"But if my parents don't live together and I have to look after Mama . . ."

"There, there," I said, soft and gentle as lamb's wool, "we'll not be

486

thinking about that just now, for to be sure it's best we cross our bridges when we come to them."

But I was already crossing bridge after bridge. Get rid of Mac-Gowan. De Salis didn't care for either Ireland or Cashelmara, so without MacGowan why should he stay? He could go to England and live with his brothers. Of course he might need a little persuasion, but . . . We could deal him a hand that would suit us all, let him see the children occasionally, give him an allowance. Then Sarah could live at Cashelmara with the children, and I . . . Well, Ned would want someone to look after the estate for him until he came of age, and what better agent could he have than someone who knew the valley as well as I did and would look after his interests as if they were my own? I could even ask my boys to come and help me, and suddenly I could see their handwriting on a series of envelopes, Maxwell Drummond Esquire, Cashelmara, County Galway.

"I think I'll go in now, sir," said the poor wretched child at my side.

"Of course, Ned," I said kindly. "I hope our next meeting will be a happier one."

I watched him as he crossed the courtyard and toiled up the steps to the front door, but even after the butler had answered the bell I made no effort to leave. I looked up at the gilded gates and thought of Cashelmara, and every ambition I'd ever had in my life made the blood run singing through my veins.

Chapter Three

Of course Sarah and I had often discussed the future, but it had never occurred to either of us that we might live at Cashelmara. Sarah had thought her divorce settlement would enable her to buy a small country house with farmland, and I'd planned to go looking for somewhere suitable while she was seeing her attorneys. I would have liked to go back to the Joyce country where Cashelmara stood, but I saw that a fresh start somewhere else would have its advantages; and since Sarah would be making a sacrifice by living in Ireland, I thought I'd best make the sacrifice of turning my back on Connaught in favor of Ulster. I wasn't a stranger to that part of the world, for my father had taken his family there during the worst of the Great Hunger of the Forties, but I'd been little more than a baby then and my memories were blurred. But there was rich country in Ulster, I knew that, and I suspected that if I had a decent farm to run I'd make more money there than I ever made at my home on Lough Nafooey. It's not that money means everything, and anyway Sarah would have the income from the divorce settlement, but I couldn't live on her money, and besides . . . Well, I needed to make enough to afford to live like a gentleman. You can't bed with a lady and not provide decent sheets. Eileen had taught me that.

The morning after my dinner with Ned I got up early, brewed myself a large pot of tea on my little stove and sat munching the remains of yesterday's loaf. I still felt bad about Ned, but since there was no use crying over spilled milk I willed myself instead to think of my plan to live at Cashelmara. I wondered how I could put it to Sarah. I knew Cashelmara would have unpleasant memories for her, so I'd have to play that down and concentrate on Ned's future. I reached the end of the bread and spread on the last of the bacon drippings before I looked at the gold watch I'd won the other day at poker. Eight o'clock. Time to clean my gun before I went off to the Marriott house to collect Sarah.

My gun was one of the famous model P's, the colt revolver that goes by all kinds of names like "Peacemaker" and "Single-Six." They're great ones for naming guns in America. It was a .36 caliber and (being the model P) was a single-action revolver, which meant you had to cock the damn hammer manually for each shot. But the Americans swear the single-action is more accurate, and they don't hold much with the double-action kind you meet across the Atlantic. They're probably right. I tried a Smith & Wesson double-action once but was glad to pick up my "Peacemaker" again afterward.

I had just opened up my gun and was busy with the gun oil when someone tapped timidly on my door.

"Who's that?" I yelled. I felt unprotected with my gun out of action on the table, and in New York you never know what might happen next. Grabbing the bread knife, I padded up to the door, eased out the stopper that masked the peephole I'd carved in the wood and took a look at my visitor just as Sarah whispered, "It's me."

I scooped her inside. "You came alone!" I was shocked.

"I couldn't wait till you called at ten, so I told Evadne I was going early to Stewart's with my maid and took the carriage before she could say no." Evadne was her sister-in-law, Charles Marriott's frumpy wife. "Maxwell, I'm so upset about . . . What's this?"

"Oh, that's nothing. Just my gun."

"Gun!"

"Security guards always carry guns—didn't I tell you?" I was thinking how smart and lovely she looked in her fur cape and fur muff. She made me feel tousled, for I was still in my shirt sleeves and I hadn't shaved and I knew I must look just like the escaped convict that I was. "Never mind my gun," I said, wiping my oily hands on a rag. "Sit down and have some tea. I suppose it'll be Ned who's put you in such a spin." I made up my mind as I spoke not to confess to her that I had mishandled the interview. It wasn't just that I was

489

ashamed of myself; I also wanted to spare her from extra worry and anxiety.

"Yes, Ned was dreadfully upset," she was saying, "and so was I." Apparently he had asked her if I had told him the truth about his father and MacGowan, and when she had said yes he had shut himself in his room and refused to speak to her.

"Give him time," I said, realizing with relief that Ned hadn't been specific about what I'd told him. "He'll get over it. Of course it was a shock for him."

"But why is he so angry with me still?" she said frantically. "I thought once he knew the truth about his father he would at least be on my side!"

"And so he will be," I said, very soothing.

"Maxwell, you didn't tell him about—"

"About what?" I said much too quickly, thankful that I could truthfully deny disclosing the sodomy even though I'd disclosed MacGowan's presence in the bedroom, but fortunately Sarah was only referring to her love affair with me.

"Yes, I did tell him," I said, hiding my relief. "Why not?"

"Well, I—"

"Since when have you been ashamed of it?"

"It's not that. It's simply that it must have been so much for Ned to bear . . . all at once . . . don't you see?"

"I wanted him to know I loved you and was going to take care of you. Look, sweetheart, I've had a wonderful idea which'll suit Ned right down to the ground and have him eating out of our hands in no time." And I told her about my plan to return to Cashelmara.

She shuddered at first, but I'd expected that. "I hoped I'd never have to return there as long as I lived."

"Of course you did, but it's going to be Ned's one day, isn't it? And if your husband's not there and MacGowan's gone . . ."

Something in her expression stopped me. There was a glitter in her eyes, just as there always was when MacGowan's future was mentioned, and as I watched the color touched her cheeks gently and her parted lips became moist. "You won't forget my necklace, will you?" she said, and when we both laughed the passion of her hatred struck a spark in me and I wanted her.

The necklace was a private joke of ours, dating from the memorable evening we'd drunk to MacGowan's damnation and I'd promised her his balls strung on a rope like pearls.

"You and your necklace!" I teased, and reached out to take her. I

490

forgot my oil-stained hands, and soon there was oil everywhere, on her petticoats and bodice, her thighs and breasts, but neither of us gave a damn. She kept saying, "Love me. Please," and so I did, for Lord knows I needed no encouragement, and afterward she said, "I don't know what I'd do if I ever lost you"—as if I were on the brink of leaving her for another woman.

"Why should you be losing me?" I said, smiling at her. "You know you're not the careless kind!" But I knew the blues hit her hard at times and guessed that, despite all my reassurance, she was still worrying herself silly about the boy.

"You mustn't worry about Ned," I said, moving to the sink and pulling out the tin bath. "Keep him busy so he doesn't have the time to mope like a broody hen. Get Charles to hire a tutor for him. Lessons will give him something to think about." I reached for the jug and began to fill the bath with water. "Later when he's used to me I'll take him out and about a bit. I'd like that. I was thinking only the other day of all the expeditions we could make together."

"If only he can accept you . . ."

"Of course he will," I said with far more confidence than I felt. "What choice does he have? He's got to take your side, and once he realizes that he'll see he has to take me too. Then think what a nice surprise he'll have when he finds I'm not the ogre he believes I am!"

"That's true," she said, and at last she did smile. "Yes, I'm sure you're right and I'm being silly to worry."

We took a bath. The oil clung to us like dung on a cartwheel, but we enjoyed ourselves scrubbing away at the stains.

"It's a pity we're not in Charles's house," said Sarah, giggling like a girl of seventeen. "There are six bathrooms there, all with marble floors and solid-gold bath taps, and the baths are almost big enough to swim in." And the next moment she was saying restlessly, "I'm getting very tired of living beneath Charles's roof with both him and Evadne disapproving of everything I do."

"Indeed and I hate it too. How would you like to live in Boston for a while?"

"Boston!"

"Boston." I wrapped us both in a towel and paused to kiss her. "A good friend of mine called Liam Gallagher has a brother there who might be able to give me a job where I could make a heap of extra money—more than I could pick up here. If you wouldn't mind living in a small apartment . . ."

"I'd live with you anywhere," she said. "You know that. But, Maxwell, you must save your money and not spend it on me or you'll never get back to Ireland. I must try and endure staying with Charles until you have the money you need."

"I'll not stand by and see you unhappy there!"

"I'm happy so long as I can see you every day," she said, and after that we fell into the unmade bed and pulled the blankets over our heads and warmed ourselves in the time-honored way until we were so hot I hurled all the blankets to the floor. When I smoked a cigarette she had to have a puff too, and after we'd blown smoke at each other Sarah decided the fumes would smother us both, so we went into the sitting room and gave the furniture there a hard time for a while. By noon we'd broken a spring on the sofa and were as worn out as a couple of elderly donkeys, so we fell back into bed again and slept like the dead. I've heard it said the powers fail a man when he's past forty, but it's not true. If he has a woman who's as passionate as Sarah he'd be the devil of a man even if he was ninety—unless he was only half a man to start with, like that weakling de Salis.

That afternoon I paid my regular visit to the headquarters of the Clan-na-Gael in New York. The Irish Republican Brotherhood might change its name as often as a rich woman changes hats, but it was alive and thriving on American soil. Many people say the Clan is different from the Brotherhood, but as I see it for all practical purposes it's six of one and half a dozen of the other. If anyone wants to challenge me about this, let him look at it this way: Back in 1858 they began a new Irish-American version of the Irish Republican Brotherhood and they called it the American Fenian Brotherhood, or the Fenians, and their object, as we all know, was the separation of Ireland from England so that Ireland could become an independent republic. Now, the American Fenians were different from the Irish Fenians (or the Brotherhood), but both were on the same lines, and they got into trouble when they tried to invade Canada, and by the end of the Sixties they were all split into factions and the whole thing was a most unholy mess.

Finally in 1869 the Clan-na-Gael was founded, and the first thing it did was reorganize the Brotherhood in Ireland and knock their heads together to put sense in them. Well, the Clan was successful, and before you could wink twice it had swallowed up all the Fenians and all the secret societies in Ireland except one (that was O'Donovan Rossa's Irish Confederation) and was making an alliance with the political movement headed by the hero Parnell. That was what they called the New Departure, with everyone working for the same end—the Destruction of the Act of Union and the founding of a free Ireland, except Parnell hoped to destroy the act by Home Rule, and the Brotherhood—I mean the Clan—were pledged to a republic, being more extreme. And then the National Land League of Ireland was established and the Irish National Land League of America, and then the Land League was discredited by the Phoenix Park Murders, which were committed by a secret society called the Invincibles (which should have been swallowed up in the Clan but weren't), and the whole thing was renamed the National League, except it was called the Irish National League in America, and at the end of 1883 the Clan divided into two, one part retaining the old name of the Brotherhood and the other part (which was larger) adopting the initials USA.

See? It's as clear as daylight really if you think about it. Well, I don't quite know where all that leaves Ireland, but I do know it left me paying a call on the New York lodge of the Clan where I was a member.

I'd joined the Clan soon after I'd settled in New York. All Irishmen of standing joined the Clan, and besides, I could see straight away that it was the one road that might lead me to my pardon. That makes me sound very self-seeking and not interested in the Clan itself, but that's not true. It was certainly true that my pardon was of enormous importance to me, and I would have done almost anything to get it, but of course I admired the Clan's goals and ideals and was glad to support them. I'd led our local secret society the Blackbooters until it was taken over by the Brotherhood (the Fenians, I should say), and even after that I'd organized all the agitation arising from the Land League policies. I'd always been active in local politics, always been fighting for Irish freedom, so I was glad to be a member of the Clan. I was admitted to my lodge in the August of 1884 after being recommended by my friend Liam Gallagher who ran Ryan's. It was the devil of a business getting in, though, and by the time I'd been balloted for and cross-examined and sworn in I felt dizzy with all the ceremonial.

However, once I was in I had one or two unpleasant surprises. The first was that although the Clan talked very big they did very little—at least for people like me. They talked endlessly of righting Irish wrongs, but when it came down to righting the wrong of an individual Irishman they did nothing beyond promising to write to "important people" in Ireland and asking for additional "contributions" to the glorious cause. This was all very well, and I didn't mind contributing for a while, but I had no intention of contributing indefinitely. The second thing that irritated me about the Clan was that they were by this time lukewarm toward Parnell. They said he didn't go far enough, that he had no true policy for establishing a republic, that he was no more than an Englishman dazzling the Irish with fancy terms like Home Rule. What was Home Rule anyway? Not Republicanism, that was for sure. It was just another name for Saxon rule but with the rule coming from Dublin instead of Westminster.

"But if we can get Home Rule we'll be halfway to a republic!" I exclaimed, but they couldn't understand that. It was republic or nothing for them. "But the Saxons will never let us have a republic straightaway!" I said, amazed that this wasn't obvious to them. "No Saxon alive today would agree to a republic, but there are plenty of Saxons who aren't averse to the Irish ruling themselves from Dublin within the framework of the Empire, and plenty of Saxons respect Parnell—"

"Because he sounds and looks just like they do," said the Senior Guardian of my lodge grimly.

"But he's united Ireland. He's brought us all together, he's helped us get a fair deal on our rents—"

"He'll never give us a republic," said the Irish-Americans, and that, I was infuriated to discover, was always their last word on the subject. The whole trouble was they didn't live in Ireland and they didn't understand the great practical victories Parnell had won for the Irish. They were far too bound up in their dreams and theories to be practical, and it was impossible for them to see that Parnell's battles at Westminster with his eighty-five loyal MPs from the Irish Parliamentary Party brought more benefits to Ireland than all the dynamite bombs set off in London.

"Well, Sean," I said as I entered the Senior Guardian's stuffy little room in a downtown tenement (Sean wasn't his real name, of course, and I won't disclose the tenement's whereabouts). "It's me again. What's the latest news on my pardon?"

"Oh, it's you, Max Drummond," says he. "Come and look at the new bomb we're designing to blow up the Houses of Parliament."

I took a look at the drawings and said it was the finest bomb, the loveliest bomb and the most useful bomb I ever saw in all my life.

"And have you heard from the National League yet about my case?" I added civilly.

"Oh, there's grand news from the League," says he. "They say Lord Salisbury's government can't last six months, and once Gladstone's in again they'll carry the Home Rule bill and then Charles Stewart Parnell—if he's a true Irishman—can launch the True Republic and the day will dawn when every Irishman can awake and shake off the shackles of tyranny."

"Amen to that," says I, smothering the urge to strangle him. "And what about my shackles, Sean? What about the false conviction and the unjust prison sentence hanging around my neck like a tombstone?"

"To be sure that's a terrible thing, Max," he says, "and we're working hard to see you get your justice. But these things take a little time, and the Saxon devils don't know the meaning of the word 'justice' as we know it. Now, if we could send over a little more money on your behalf . . ."

"I've paid you enough money," I said. "Now you show me some results. Did the League engage an attorney to investigate my case?"

"Not yet. But once the Home Rule Bill is passed and the True Republic is born everyone will get their justice, so if you could just wait a whileen . . ."

I would have walked out, but I knew I mustn't offend him, for he was the only link I had with the National League and so, indirectly, with Parnell. I just nodded and even paid him a little more money, although I was sure it went straight into his own pocket, for he was from County Cork, and they're a devious bunch down there in the south, everyone knows that.

Then I went out and got drunk. At this rate I'd never get my pardon, never get back to Ireland, never meet MacGowan again face to face.

I had to get back. Had to. Well, perhaps if Parnell won his fight for Home Rule . . .

But he lost. They threw out the Home Rule bill. I read all about it in the newspaper. It was defeated in the House of Commons by three hundred and forty-three votes to three hundred and thirteen, and Mr. Gladstone said later he feared that "the child that is unborn shall rue the voting of that day." Rioting broke out in Belfast, the Clan swore a terrible vengeance, and my faint hope of a prompt pardon went rattling down the drain. That was when I wrote the letters. I wrote to

Parnell and I wrote to the Lord Lieutenant of Ireland and I even wrote to the Queen. Meanwhile it was July and hot as hell and Charles Marriott was talking of leaving town for his summer home in the Hudson Valley.

"He wants me to go too," said Sarah. "I won't, of course, though it would be nice for Ned."

I was late calling for her that morning because it took me a long time to word my letter to Queen Victoria, and when I arrived it was lunchtime.

"Why don't we have lunch here?" suggested Sarah, seeing I was blue and making an inspired effort to divert me. "Charles never gets back from Wall Street before three, Evadne's gone to the Island for the day to visit friends, and Ned's tutor has taken him to the Natural History Museum. We'll have the house to ourselves."

"The bathrooms too?" I couldn't resist saying, and when we laughed I felt better.

I'd never had the chance to see anything of Marriott's house apart from the pokiest of the parlors, but Sarah ushered me into a swell dining room with silver candlesticks strewn over the table and a chandelier sagging from the ceiling. I thought it all very fine, except for the meal. The cook had coddled eggs in some nasty sauce and popped a sprig of parsley on top, and the footmen served some rolls and butter instead of a vegetable.

"Jesus!" I said. "Doesn't Charles Marriott keep any meat and potatoes in his larder?"

Sarah giggled, the footmen looked at me pop-eyed and the black butler went yellow around the gills.

Well, we were in a wonderful good humor by the time we went upstairs to the drawing room, but when I tried to light a cigarette Sarah said I mustn't because Evadne would smell the smoke when she came home, so we stepped out onto a fine stone terrace for a while before I suggested we inspect the bathrooms.

"Jesus!" I exclaimed in wonder as she led me from room to room. I had to stop in every one to turn on the taps to see if they worked, but they all did. It was amazing. Then I became fascinated by the water closets and had to pull all the chains. "Jesus!" I kept saying and once or twice I said, "Holy Mary!" until Sarah was laughing so hard she couldn't speak and I was laughing with her. Finally we chose the third bathroom—there was such a crafty full-length mirror—and wallowed around in the enormous bath as merrily as two pigs frolicking in a trough. By this time I had quite recovered from the blues and was feeling in fine fettle.

"Time to explore the bedrooms," says I, wrapping a purple towel around myself, so off we went, tiptoeing down the corridor with Sarah giggling in terror in case we should bump into a servant.

"Stop!" she gasped. "I've got a stitch in my side and I can't move another step till it's gone!"

"Well, that's a problem that's easily solved," I said and carried her across the threshold of the nearest bedroom. By some stroke of luck it was the one that belonged to Charles, and I soon found out that the springs of the enormous bed would have gratified an acrobat.

"Your brother goes up a notch in my estimation," I said, trying a bounce or two.

"But we can't stay here!"

"Why not? I like it. Jesus, what a bed!"

So we stayed, but Sarah was so nervous that presently I pulled out and suggested we move to her room.

"Perhaps it would be safer," she agreed in relief, but when I asked if she was going to straighten the covers before we left she was so hot for me she said she'd do it later.

Later never came.

We were just sneaking down the corridor two hours afterward so that I could slip out of the house before Ned came home from his museum when on the landing we came face to face with none other than the master of the house.

"Charles!" exclaimed Sarah guiltily. "How early you're back today!"

"I've been back for some time," he said, giving her the hardest of hard looks. "I've been busy setting my bedroom straight—and the bathroom in the north wing—before the servants could see the mess for themselves and draw their own conclusions."

Sarah blushed. She wasn't the sort of woman who blushed easily, but when she did there was no hiding it. "Charles . . ."

"Be quiet!" he said fiercely and swung around on me. "Get out. And never show your face in this house again."

"Wait a minute!" I said. No soft-living, high-stepping New York swell was going to tell *me* what to do. "If I'm good enough for your sister—"

"You're not good enough for her," he said, never raising his voice but speaking much faster. "You're a convicted felon and you earn

497

your living by acting as a gunman for a criminal Irish faction downtown. Are you going to get out of this house immediately or shall I have my servants summon the police?"

"Charles," begged Sarah. "Please . . ."

"I'm not having him in this house any more, Sarah. It's my house and I'm entitled to refuse admittance to any man I please."

"But—"

"And how dare you bring him here and behave like a whore—no, don't pretend you haven't treated this place as if it were a bordello! Have you no shame, no sense of decency? Does it mean nothing to you that your name is now so notorious in New York society that everywhere I go I hear people whispering, 'There goes Charles Marriott. His sister is the one who amuses herself with cheap Irish scum—' "

"Why, you—"

"Maxwell!" screamed Sarah and somehow managed to slip between us before I could throw him downstairs.

"It's the truth!" shouted Charles Marriott. "All my friends joke about it behind my back. Evadne's even been slighted because her sister-in-law is little better than a streetwalker!"

"What a tragedy for you both!" cried Sarah. "Very well, I'll leave tomorrow!"

"Leave? Sarah, are you insane? This man's only after your money! He won't want the expense of keeping you!"

"Shit!" I yelled. "I'd keep Sarah even if I had to pawn my soul to the devil to pay the rent! Get out of my way and let me take your sister out of your fucking house!"

He went white at my language and tried to grab Sarah's arm. "Sarah, you're not going with that man. I absolutely forbid it. What about Ned? If you think this man's fit company for a boy that age—"

"Ned's my son!" cried Sarah. "He's not yours! And I'll be the judge of who's fit company for him!"

"I'll cut him out of my will. I'll stop the allowance I've been giving you. Not one cent of mine goes into your pocket so long as you're living with that man!"

The doorbell rang far away.

We looked down the stairs and saw the upturned faces of the gaping servants. After a long moment the butler recovered himself enough to stumble to the door.

It was Ned and his tutor, back from the museum.

498

"I'll come tomorrow," said Sarah to me in a trembling voice. "I must pack my clothes and talk to Ned. But I'll come tomorrow morning."

I said nothing, just kissed her and began to walk downstairs. Ned was looking at me, and something in his expression reminded me of someone, though I couldn't think who it was.

"Good afternoon, Mr. Drummond," he said. He had always been very polite to me after our dinner at Ryan's, but my hopes of taking him on expeditions had never come to anything. He had a talent for inventing excuses, and after a while I had stopped issuing my invitations.

"Hullo, Ned," I said, smiling at him just as I always did, and then I walked out of Charles Marriott's house for the last time and spat at the gilded gates as I stepped past them into Fifth Avenue.

Chapter Four

I

I bought Sarah a wedding ring and had it engraved with our initials and the date. All that evening I wondered if we would ever be married in church, but I didn't see how that could ever be unless we outlived our spouses, and although I could think with joy in my heart of de Salis in his coffin, I hated to picture Eileen in the grave. It was no use hoping divorce might lead to a proper wedding because God doesn't recognize divorce, everyone knows that, but if Eileen chanced to die (which God forbid) and if de Salis drank himself to damnation . . . Sarah might turn to Rome—heretics often did—and then we could be married properly before a priest. I kept thinking what a relief it would be if I could go to Mass again with a clear conscience unburdened by that terrible worry about not being in a state of grace. I'd grown used to living outside the Church, but once in a while I'd wake up in the dark and break out in a sweat at the thought of purgatory.

Well, it was no use worrying about it, I told myself when I awoke that morning after a disturbed night. I'd rather burn forever than give up Sarah, so I've no choice but to live for the present and not dwell on the future.

Besides, it was easy to forget about purgatory once Sarah arrived at my apartment.

She brought with her two trunks, two bags and Ned. "I told my

500

maid I would send for her later," she said, "and I decided I didn't need the other baggage I brought from Ireland." She wore a blue walking costume with a lot of navy embroidery up and down the front seams and a big hat with flowers in it, and with her beside me I felt as smart and grand as any lord with a ten-thousand-acre estate.

"This is a great day," I said. "Make yourself at home while I run out and buy some champagne."

So I ran all the way to the liquor shop and back, and when I returned I found Sarah polishing some glasses for us while Ned sat quietly on the edge of the sofa.

"Take off your coat and roll up your sleeves!" I said to him, for he looked so uncomfortable in his tight reefer jacket, so he shed it obediently and went on sitting quiet as a mouse in his corner. I'd been afraid he might be sulky, but he was good as gold.

"You must have champagne with us!" I said to him with a smile, and when he said "Thank you, sir" I could hardly remember how rude he had been when we'd first met. I thought: We're going to get on fine. We'll be friends in two shakes of a lamb's tail now.

"I saw my friend Liam Gallagher last night," I said to Sarah, "and he says he's sure his brother in Boston could find a job for me. He's going to write to him and find out, but I hope he's right, for I'm tired of New York and it would do us all good to start afresh somewhere else. Besides," I added, thinking of my pardon, "maybe the Clan in Boston will be more willing to help me than the Clan here."

"It's years since I was in Boston," said Sarah, "but I remember it as being a lovely old-fashioned city. I'd like to go there again." And she started to talk to Ned about Beacon Hill and Paul Revere's famous ride.

Ned nodded at intervals, and once or twice he said, "Yes, Mama," as he watched his champagne. When she had finished he asked if he could go for a walk to explore the neighborhood, and in spite of Sarah's doubtful expression I said why not, for he was old enough to look after himself and my street wasn't disreputable.

"But don't wander too far, Ned," said Sarah anxiously as he left. She tended to protect him too much, and I could see I'd have to put a stop to that. A boy must have room to breathe when he's growing up, as my father had always said to my mother when she had become overanxious with me, but the truth is that women aren't meant to have only one child to look after, for it's too hard for them to have all their eggs in one basket.

When Ned had gone I said to her, "This man Phineas Gallagher in

Boston is rich—and influential too from all I hear—so if he takes up my case maybe the Clan will give me a decent hearing, and then by this time next year we'll be back in Ireland and living as man and wife." Then I gave her the wedding ring and filled up her glass and we were very happy.

Later she said, "I'll try very hard not to be an expense to you, Maxwell. I have all the clothes I need, but I'm afraid my laundry bills might be expensive and I don't know what we can do about meals. Do you suppose I might find someone who would teach me to cook?"

"Certainly not!" I exclaimed. "The idea of it! We'll eat out while we're in New York, and as soon as we get to Boston we'll take a bigger apartment with a kitchen, and you can have a maid who can come in every day to cook and clean for us."

"But the expense . . . I don't want to be a burden."

"I'll be making good money in Boston. Everything will go well once we leave this place, I know it. Once we get to Boston our luck will start to turn."

We left New York a week later, much to our relief. The apartment was too small for the three of us, and although Ned was so quiet we hardly knew he was there, we were both uncomfortably aware of him on the sofa as we lay in bed in the other room.

"I'm sorry to lose you, Max," said Jim O'Malley when the time came for me to say goodbye to all my friends, but when I tried to give him back his gun he laughed and told me to keep it for a while.

"Take it back to Ireland with you and shoot a Saxon with it," he said, "and then send it back to me with Saxon blood on the barrel."

His father had been evicted by Lord Lucan in County Mayo during the famine, and as a boy of six he had watched the English soldiers burn his home to the ground.

"I told my brother Phineas which day you'd be arriving," said Liam Gallagher. "Are you taking the morning train?"

"Indeed we are," I said. I was secretly a little afraid of trains. "To be sure it'll be a terrible journey."

"Better a train than a coffin ship," said Liam, and I thought: Jesus, these Irish-Americans have memories like elephants. It's true that all the Irish like to dwell upon the past, and I've sworn vengeance on Cromwell's men myself often enough after a jug of poteen, but the Irish-Americans are more Irish than the Irish, as I'd noticed more than once since I'd set foot on American soil.

The train journey was just as bad as I'd thought it would be, though of course it wasn't as bad as an immigrant ship, I admit that. But we'd picked a hot day to travel, and I missed getting us reserved seats in the best parlor car. Since I'd never been on a train before I didn't know all the ins and outs of reservations and tickets and "checking" the baggage, as they call it. We did travel first-class, but since nearly all the rail travel in America is first-class that wasn't saying much, and the truth of the situation was that we had to endure a six-hour journey crammed into a long, stuffy, crowded car no better than a giant cigar.

I tried to apologize to Sarah, but she said it didn't matter a bit; she was just happy to be going away with me. I felt so proud when she said that and thought what a real lady she was, so strong and fine, always loyal and never uttering a word of complaint. Ned didn't complain either. He sat in his corner with a storybook for boys in his hands, but the car swayed too much to make reading easy, so he spent most of his time looking out of the window.

I tried not to look out of the window too often. Personally I think it's heathen as well as downright dangerous to go so fast, and if God had intended man to travel faster than the speed of a horse he would have created a nice decent animal to do the job. But a chain of cars running along little rails! It wasn't natural somehow, and who the devil wants to be averaging forty miles an hour anyway?

However, before we were even halfway to Boston I not only knew the answer to that question but wished we were averaging eighty so that the abominable journey could be over sooner. I believe there was supposed to be some sort of air-cooling system, but it didn't work, and by the time we arrived my clothes were soaked in sweat and I was sick to the stomach with all the swaying and rocking.

"We'll find a hotel for the night," I said to Sarah. "The very nearest hotel to the station."

Sarah, who was too exhausted to speak, nodded thankfully.

We stumbled down the platform. It was so hot that I wondered if I'd died without knowing it and was already tasting hell-fire. People bumped into us and shouted in loud voices, and Sarah looked so ill I thought she'd faint.

"Ned," I said, hardly able to speak myself, "take your mother to that bench over there and sit down while I find the baggage."

"Maxwell . . ." Sarah clutched my arm and pointed down the platform. "Look!"

I stared, dazed. An enormous black man, immaculately dressed, was standing facing us some yards away. In his hands was a large board on which someone had printed boldly in charcoal MAXWELL DRUMMOND.

"Holy Mother of God," I said, so weak I hardly had the strength to be amazed. "To be sure it must be a message from the Almighty Himself." I stumbled down the platform, half afraid the glorious vision would disappear, but the messenger remained firmly planted on his chosen spot and watched with interest as I staggered up to him.

"I'm Maxwell Drummond," I gasped.

"Good afternoon, suh," said the black man, raising his top hat and bowing respectfully. "Please come this way, suh."

"Wait . . . my wife . . . son . . . the bags . . ."

The black man gently took the checks from my hand and said he would attend to the bags. I started to wave frenziedly at Sarah and Ned, and as they left their bench someone tapped me on the shoulder.

I spun around. Facing me was a stout man of about my own age. He wore the best-cut coat I'd seen in a month of Sundays and he carried a silver-topped cane and he was smiling an Irish smile.

"Welcome to Boston, Max," he said brightly, his blue eyes the color of the lough at Cashelmara, and I thought: Dear God, is there ever a race that hangs together like the Irish? And the tears filled my eyes as I thought of us all, condemned to exile thousands of miles from home and yet rising from the ashes of pestilence and persecution to triumph over all our adversities. Yes, I know that was sentimental, but I'm an Irishman, and God knows I was never prouder of being Irish than when that stranger came forward in a city where I knew no one and offered me his hand to shake as he called me by my Christian name.

"My name is Phineas Gallagher," he was saying, "and indeed any friend of my brother Liam's is already a friend of mine. Come outside to my carriage and let me take you to my house on Beacon Hill."

II

I knew Liam's brother was successful enough to be well heeled, but it came as a surprise to me to find I hadn't exaggerated to Sarah when I'd told her he was rich and influential. I knew that, like Jim O'Malley, he had his finger in the gambling pie, but Liam had never mentioned the real-estate deals, the companies and corporations. Perhaps he was a little jealous, for Phineas was his younger brother and they'd both started out in America with nothing but the rags on their backs.

But Phineas Gallagher had come a long way since he'd stepped off that coffin ship. His new house didn't face the Common, for all the old gentry clung to those houses, and Boston was a snobbish place, worse than New York, but it faced a pretty square and he kept his wife and daughters in very refined style. His wife was a cheerful Irish girl not much older than Sarah, and she knew all about dainty manners and the latest smart charity to support. I thought Eileen would have liked her. The four daughters learned the piano and studied Italian and sewed samplers, just as she had when she was growing up, and I suppose that's all very well, but personally, as I said to Eileen whenever she raised the subject, I think my own girls were just as happy learning how to milk the cows and bake good bread.

The Gallagher house wasn't as big as the Marriott mansion, but it was much more fun to live in. The rooms were decorated with a magnificent slapdash gaiety. They had one parlor decorated entirely in emerald green with marble shamrocks on the mantel, and in every bedroom was a brightly colored plaster statue of the Virgin and Child. As for the dining room, it was a starving man's dream. Great big steaks the size of platters, potatoes even more luscious than those Liam served at Ryan's, black pudding, Irish sausage, cheese—soft cheese, mind you, Irish cheese, none of that hard stuff that looks like candle tallow—and buttermilk so rich a leprechaun could have danced on it. As for the whisky—"Jesus!" I exclaimed. "It's got the kick of poteen!" And almost weeping with delight at finding myself in a true Irish home at last, I quite forgot all my two-edged opinions of the Irish-Americans.

"It's a pity there's no boy for you to play with, Ned," said Sarah, but I was already thinking those four girls would do him the world of good. They were all plump—small wonder when you remember the food their mother served at table—and they all giggled a great deal, and they were all named for Irish places. It was hard to tell one girl from another, but in descending order of height their names were Clare, Kerry, Connemara and Donegal. The last two, known as Connie and Donagh, were still under ten, but Kerry was twelve and Clare two years older, so Ned did have company of his own age.

I was anxious to start work and not outstay our welcome, but Phineas Gallagher was hospitality itself and insisted we should take our time about finding an apartment. Meanwhile, he put me in charge of the gambling at his new concert saloon and promised me a salary that was nearly double what I'd been making with Jim O'Malley.

It did occur to me to wonder what he was after, but since I couldn't see I had anything he wanted I decided to accept his generosity at face value. Anyway I was sure he liked me as much as I liked him, and I thought we all got along very well together. To be sure there was a little awkwardness when it came to Sunday Mass, but he said quick as a flash as soon as he saw I was embarrassed, "I'm not a priest, Max, and I'll not be sitting in judgment on you," and that was a great relief to me, for he could easily have had strong views on adultery. Phineas had heard through Liam that Sarah and I weren't married, but his wife didn't know and neither did the girls. Our absence from Mass was taken to be because we were Protestants, so every Sunday morning I escorted Sarah and Ned to Trinity Church on Copley Square. I never went inside, of course. I might have been a bad Catholic, but I still had my principles, and no one was going to see me crossing the threshold of a Black Protestant church.

In the middle of August Phineas invited us to join him while he and his family spent a month at his villa at Newport.

"Of course we can't go," said Sarah at once when I told her about the invitation. "It really would be abusing their hospitality, Maxwell. Don't you think we might look for an apartment now?"

"What's wrong with a month by the sea?" I said. "I thought you'd like that."

"I'd rather be by ourselves," she said, "in a home of our own." And there was something about the way she glanced around our bedroom that told me the whole story.

"You don't like them, do you?" I said suddenly. "You don't like Phineas and you don't like Maura. Why?"

She was silent.

"Sarah?"

"Oh . . ." She made a small graceful gesture with her hands and turned away. "They're very kind, of course," I heard her say, "and very hospitable, but . . . Well, they're so shoddy, Maxwell! I mean shoddy in the New York sense of *nouveau riche*—"

"Thank you," I said, "but I've lived long enough in New York to know the meaning of the word 'shoddy-rich.' "

"I mean . . . well, look at this house! The ghastly taste in furnishings, the dreadful wallpaper, all those cheap, vulgar religious statues! And I find Maura Gallagher's attempts at social climbing pathetic to say the least. Just because she can afford to send a thousand dollars every now and then to her favorite charity and give those girls of hers ideas far above their station, she thinks . . ."

She saw my face and stopped. There was a silence.

"I don't mean to be unkind," she said in a rush. "I didn't mean . . ."

She stopped again. She was twisting the wedding ring around and around on her finger. "I'm sorry," she said rapidly at last. "Of course we can go to Newport if you like. I'm sorry, Maxwell. I didn't mean what I said."

"Oh yes you did!" I said. "You meant every goddamned word, you snobbish little bitch!"

She began to cry, saying over and over again that she was sorry.

"Listen to me," I said, taking her by the shoulders and shaking her into silence. "What's good enough for me is good enough for you, and if you don't see that you can go back to your blue-blooded sot of a husband and good riddance. I can always find another woman to sleep with me."

It was a terrible thing to say. I knew it was terrible, but I couldn't stop myself. I looked at her and suddenly I was looking beyond her into the past and listening to Eileen calling my fine farm a hovel, saying she'd always wished she'd never married beneath her. I felt as if someone had plunged a knife into my guts and was wrenching the blade around and around in the torn flesh.

Sarah was sobbing. Her face was twisted with grief and she was tearing her clothes, offering herself to me, saying she'd do anything, anything at all so long as I'd promise not to leave.

Sanity returned to me like a wet slap across the face. I groped for her, pulling her torn bodice back over her breasts and stroking her hair as I held her close to me. After a long while I said I was sorry. I was still holding her close, and when she stopped crying I said, "Of course I'll never leave you. Why do you think I gave you a wedding ring? It's the finest woman in all the world you are and me the luckiest man alive."

"If only we could be married," she said. She was trying to dry her eyes. "If only . . ." And she started to weep again.

I knew at once what she was thinking because she had often spoken of it before. "Sweetheart, I thought we'd agreed long ago that it's best there can be no baby."

"Yes, I know, but I should feel safer . . . more secure . . ."

"Then it's a terrible failure I've been if you can only feel sure of me with a child in your arms."

"It's not that. But I do so love babies, and I would like . . . so much . . ."

"I know." Indeed I did feel sorry for her, for I knew how much she regretted that a past sickness prevented her from having another child, but at the same time I couldn't help but secretly look upon it as a blessing in disguise. Of course if we'd had a child I'm sure I would have been pleased, but romance has a mysterious way of dissolving at the first flap of a baby's shawl, and it wasn't as if neither of us had brought a child into the world before.

"At least we have Ned," said Sarah, trying hard to be sensible. "I'm sure he'll enjoy a visit to the shore."

"We won't go for the whole month," I said. "We'll go for a week so as not to give Phineas offense, but then we'll come back to Boston and find a fine apartment." I was wondering as I spoke if Ned too privately rated his new surroundings shoddy-rich, but although I watched him closely I saw no sign of discontent. His appetite, which had dwindled in New York, had returned. He wolfed down plate after plate of that delicious Irish food, and later I heard him laughing as he played in the garden with the girls. The girls would giggle and scream and Ned would be almost rowdy.

"It's a wonderful thing to see young people enjoying themselves," said Phineas Gallagher benignly. It was the night before we were all due to leave for Newport, and he and I were alone in the dining room after dinner. "Help yourself to a cigar, Max, my friend," he added with his usual hospitality after the servants had withdrawn, "and let's have a cozy little chat together."

No cat ever crept up to a mouse as daintily as Phineas Gallagher tiptoed up to me that night.

"Let me tell you a secret," he said as we lighted our cigars and caressed our glasses of port. "I'm thinking of going into politics."

"Politics! Why, that's a grand idea, Phineas!"

"Well . . ." He sighed. "I'd like to do something with my money, and a little power never did a man much harm. Politics ain't much in America, but it would give those snobs something to think about if I became Mayor of Boston. They couldn't look down their noses at me then, could they? Now, I never thought I'd give two cents for what the snobs think, but it's amazing how your values change when you find your wife's been slighted and your little girls made to cry for

508

something that ain't their fault. It's an unjust world and no mistake."

"It's a terrible world, Phineas," I said, tucking into my port.

"What I want now," he said, puffing away at his cigar, "is to be respectable. It's my dearest wish in life. I want my darling wife and girls to be happy and treated as ladies."

"Very proper too," says I, thinking what good port it was.

"So I'm selling out of my gambling interests," he said, "and I'm selling out my share in the brothels too. My money's going to be clean, as clean as the purest money in all Boston, for politics is a low-down dirty game, Max, as we both know, and a man'll make enemies who'll stop at nothing to fling mud at him and make it stick."

I forgot the port. "You're selling out of the gambling interests?" I said nervously, thinking of my job.

"That's right, Max, but don't worry. I'll not let you down. I've taken a real liking to you, Max, and I want to do all I can to help you. Indeed I can't remember when I last met a man I liked as much as I like you."

We swore eternal friendship and drained our glasses. He filled them up. I wondered what was coming.

"Well, Max," says he when we're puffing our cigars again, "I've been honest with you and told you my dearest wish in life. What's your dearest wish, may I ask, if you'll be so good as to be honest with me?"

"Why, sure I'll be honest with you, Phineas," I said. "My dearest wish is to go back to Ireland and settle an old score with my landlord's agent who ruined me."

"There's something about a pardon, isn't there—or am I mistaken? Liam mentioned it, but perhaps he didn't get the story straight."

I told him about MacGowan and my trial. I'd never told him about it before since I'd had no wish for him to know I was an escaped convict. I'd simply told him I'd left Ireland after a dispute with my landlord. Of course I'd planned to confide in him later and seek his help, but he'd been so generous to me since my arrival that I hadn't liked to ask for too much too soon.

"To be sure that's the greatest miscarriage of justice I ever did hear!" said Phineas. "Have a little more port."

I absent-mindedly reached for the decanter.

"A packed jury, you say," said Phineas, "and your landlord and his agent sleeping in each other's beds, the terrible perverted sinners, may God have mercy upon their souls."

"Everything they did was illegal," I said, grinding out my cigar. "I was no ordinary tenant. I had a deed of leasehold to my land and Lord de Salis couldn't evict me as he could the others, but once I was taken prisoner by the military my home was set on fire. They claimed it was an accident but it was deliberate, for my deed of leasehold was destroyed and afterward Lord de Salis says he knows nothing of any deed and that I invented the story and that as I'm just a tenant like anyone else he's evicting me. I wanted to have a lawyer, but I had no money and they wouldn't let me see a lawyer anyway. There was nothing I could do but wait in jail for my trial, and when I was tried that bastard MacGowan told lies to convict me and every man on that jury was a Protestant and the judge had been born in a place called Warwick, which is in England, so he was as good as a Saxon for all he was an Irish judge."

"And a friend of Lord de Salis too, I shouldn't wonder," said Phineas.

"A friend of the family, that's for sure. Old Lord de Salis used to have an English estate in Warwickshire, and wouldn't that have been near the town of Warwick?"

"At the very least you deserve a new trial, Max. And at the most—"

"At the most I must surely be pardoned. Phineas, I never gave the order to burn Clonagh Court and I never gave the order to shoot MacGowan. It's all very well to accuse me of conspiracy, but there was no conspiracy. There was a movement with every man of us in one mind—to take a stand against that villain MacGowan and protect our families and homes. But they trumped up false evidence against me, MacGowan saw to that, because I've always been a thorn in his side and because Lord de Salis has always been against me, ever since I had a hand in banishing his first lover to Germany over twenty years ago."

"It's a clear-cut case, Max," said Phineas. "An innocent man victimized by sodomites. The dear little Queen wouldn't like it at all."

"I wrote to the Queen," I said bitterly, "but of course my letter will never have reached her. I wrote to Parnell too, but—"

"When was this?"

"After Home Rule was defeated at Westminster."

510

"Where did you send the letter?"

"To London. To the House of Commons."

"Hm. That may not reach him, but never mind. I know where he can be reached." He held out the wooden box to me again. "Have another cigar."

I knew Phineas was high up in the Clan, but I'd never guessed how high. I knew too that he had met Parnell several times during Parnell's American visit, but he had never told me they corresponded. It was reassuring to know that the Clan could keep its secrets well when it chose.

"Parnell's a great leader, Max," Phineas was saying. "It's the fashion now to be impatient with him, but if he came back to America they'd all be flocking to his side. I'll write to him for you."

By this time I was so excited I could hardly speak. I had dreamed of help on this scale but had never really believed such a dream could ever come true. "You . . . he . . . he'd listen to you?" I stammered. "If you wrote? About me?"

Phineas laughed. "Why, to be sure he'd listen, Max! I've poured a lot of my money into Ireland—didn't you know the whole Home Rule movement has been financed by American money?—and I don't think Charles Stewart Parnell has been ungrateful."

"Jesus Christ," I said weakly and gobbled down some more port to steady myself.

"He'll listen," Phineas was saying comfortably, "but it'll still take time for him to act. The Queen don't like him, as you can imagine, but Parnell has influence at Westminster and he'll find a way to take care of your case. I'll ask him to engage an attorney too to make sure your land's restored to you in full as soon as you get home to Ireland."

"But about Parnell—how can you be sure the letter reaches him? They say he never answers his letters—never even reads them."

"He reads them if they go to the home of a lady he happens to be acquainted with. Don't you worry about it, Max. The letter will reach Parnell, and eventually your case will be before the Queen. Ah, the dear little Queen! Such a lovely slip of a girl she was when she came to Dublin in forty-nine, so everyone says, and I'm sure I would have cheered her myself if I hadn't been driven out of Ireland two years before by her cursed Saxon subjects, God rot them all to hell. She's all German, you know," he added as I bellowed the required "Amen," "and it's not her fault she has to be Queen of England."

"God save her gracious majesty!" I cried. "And just think, Phineas, when she pardons me I can go back at last to my dear old home, back at last to my fields stretching down to the lough—the darling lough!—and I'll walk again down the street of Clonareen and I'll pray once more in the holy church . . ."

God, I was drunk! But so was he, for he became just as maudlin as I was. He called me his dearest friend and said there was nothing he wouldn't do to restore me in triumph to my darling valley where I could live in peace with my lady, may the Holy Virgin and the saints protect us both.

I almost wept at his magnanimity, and we had to repeat all our vows of eternal friendship.

"How can I ever repay you?" I said, moist-eyed, in a hushed voice. "My dearest friend, how can I ever reward you for your help?"

"Well, of course I'd do it all without even the whisper of a reward," says he, wiping a tear from his eye, "but since you ask, Max, my friend, there *is* one small thing you can do for me."

"Anything," I said. "Anything you like, Phineas, my dearest, kindest friend. Name it and it shall be yours."

"Well, I know it's but an idle dream, Max," says he, wiping away another tear, "but one day I'd like nothing better than to tell those snobs who call me shoddy that I have an Irish peer for a son-in-law."

I wasn't so drunk that I didn't at last understand the reason for his amazing hospitality, but I was much too drunk to be either astonished or resentful. After all, if he had turned up on my doorstep with a young baron-to-be, wouldn't I have coveted the precious heir for one of my own four daughters? It seemed a very sensible idea to me, and I was upset only because I knew very well I had no power over Ned's future.

"That's a beautiful plan, Phineas!" I cried. "But Ned's not my son. There's no control I have—"

"You're his guardian in all but name, aren't you?"

"Yes, but—"

"See here, Max. Sure, match-making's a lost art nowadays and the world's very different now from when my parents were growing up in County Wicklow, but there is such a thing as giving two young people an opportunity. Of course we wouldn't say anything to them, for if we did they'd be sure to run off in different directions, but if later I sent one of my girls over to Ireland to spend some time with you and Sarah and Ned, who's to say what mightn't happen? Sarah could teach her how to be a real lady and present her at Dublin Castle . . ."

I had one very sober thought: If I want my pardon I'd best vow to move heaven and earth for his daughter.

"Which daughter did you have in mind, Phineas?" I said with interest.

"Well, Connie and Donagh are too young, and although Clare's the eldest she's a home-loving child and too timid for a bold scheme like this one. I'd thought of Kerry. Kerry's my favorite," he added, his blue eyes misty with sentimentality. "She's brave as a lion and as bold as a boy. She'd think it a fine adventure to visit you in Ireland for a while when she's older."

I thought: There'll be no need for Ned to marry her. Even Phineas himself has admitted you can't make matches to order nowadays. Sarah and I can do our best for the girl and then she can go back to America with no harm done.

"To be sure she'd have a wonderful dowry," said Phineas. "I know a marriage settlement ties money up, but I could arrange it so you had a little money free. I was thinking you might be in a tough position, Max, when you settle down in Ireland again. After all, Sarah's a lady, the finest lady I ever set eyes on, and she'll have certain expectations which she'll look to you to provide. And nothing hamstrings a man like lack of money, especially when there's a lady at stake."

There was a pause. At last I said, "That's true."

"We could say a third now," said Phineas, "and two-thirds after the wedding."

"And if they don't marry?"

"You can keep the part I give you now."

"How much?"

"Enough to take you back to Ireland in style. Enough to square your enemy MacGowan. Enough to keep you all till Sarah gets the settlement out of her husband."

There was another pause.

"It would be a good investment for me," said Phineas, "and a stroke of fortune for you. What do you say?"

"You've dealt me a hand that suits us both," I said.

"So it's settled. Max, you're a fine upstanding man to do business with and no mistake, and I swear by the Holy Cross there's no man I'd rather call my friend! I'll have my lawyers draw up a deed so you can see I mean to stand by my word."

"Your word'll be good enough for me!" I protested, but I didn't protest too much, for after all there's no harm in having a promise in writing. I thought the deal was a good one. I'd get some money with no uncomfortable conditions attached, for I wouldn't have to pay it back when Ned eventually told Kerry he had other fish to fry.

"Of course if you change your mind once you're in Ireland about taking Kerry into your home," said Phineas, "I'll expect the money back, but don't worry, Max, my lawyers can figure that out and put it all in the agreement. That's what you pay lawyers for—to think of everything that could happen."

I made up my mind to read every word of the agreement at least three times. "Indeed and it must be wonderful to have good lawyers," I said. "You won't forget to tell them, will you, that the whole arrangement hinges on you winning me a pardon?"

He laughed. "I'll get you your pardon, Max!" He raised his glass. "Let's drink to the dear little Queen who's going to grant it to you!"

"The dear little Queen!" I cried with enthusiasm.

So there we were, two drunken Irishmen who detested all Saxons, drinking the Queen's health as if she were a cherished relative after making plans to wed an Irish girl to a boy who had nothing but Saxon blood in his veins.

"Was there ever such a splendid race as the Irish?" I exclaimed passionately to Sarah as I reeled into bed, but I couldn't stay awake long enough to listen to her reply.

Chapter Five

I

I didn't tell Sarah about the deal I'd made with Phineas until three weeks later when we had found a fine apartment for ourselves with a maid to cook and clean, just as I'd promised. Meanwhile, we had spent our week by the ocean at Newport, and Ned had had the time of his life racing around with those giggling girls all day long. The governess was very shocked and told Maura Gallagher it wouldn't do to let girls run wild in the open air all day, but Maura just smiled and said it seemed to do pretty nicely, thank you, and there was no need for the governess to trouble herself about a crowd of children enjoying some sunshine.

"They'll get very hoydenish," said Sarah. "And freckled too." But she made no other criticism, and all through that week she was charming to the Gallaghers and very passionate with me when we were alone.

Newport had once been an old-world fishing village, but now it was very grand and fashionable, full of white marble palaces that had been built by millionaires. Phineas didn't have a palace, though I'm sure he could have afforded one, but his villa was just his style, as comfortable and homelike as his house on Beacon Hill. Its gardens stretched to the rocks by the water's edge, and you could see the sea from almost every window.

I had decided I liked the sea after all. My experience on the immigrant ship had given me a distaste for it, but I soon discovered there was nothing more pleasant than taking a walk in the sea air or taking a dip in the water when it was too dark for anyone to see I'd left all my clothes by the water's edge. Everyone made such a fuss about bathing in daytime, and I never had the patience for it, for there were all kinds of rules about what you had to wear and when you could go in without giving offense to the lady bathers. The sea was warm, far warmer than the ice-cold waters of Lough Nafooey, and I'd float around peacefully while I watched the stars and thought of Ireland.

Since Newport had proved so pleasant it was easy to feel dissatisfied when we returned to city life, but our spirits rose again when we moved into our new home. I had been dreading looking for a place, for my weekly wage could hardly afford the kind of home I wanted for Sarah and I didn't want to end up in the North End with all the other Irish immigrants. But Phineas came to the rescue again. He owned a house in a side road off Marlborough Street, a fine well-heeled neighborhood, and he arranged for us to live there rent-free. It was one of those modern houses with a kitchen in the basement, a dumbwaiter in the pantry and room for five in-help in the attics, so we hardly knew what to do with all the space, but, as I told Sarah, it was better to have too much space than too little. So we closed off the attics, engaged a servant who came in daily and were very comfortable. I was anxious in case Sarah said she didn't like the furnishings, but she was so pleased to have a place of her own at last that she hardly seemed to notice them.

In fact I was so relieved that she had given the house her stamp of approval that soon after we had settled down I decided to tell her about the bargain I had struck with Phineas.

"Maxwell!" exclaimed Sarah, horrified.

"Look, what choice did I have? Anyway, Ned doesn't have to marry the girl!"

"I should think not! I mean," said Sarah, recovering herself, "the two younger little girls are very sweet and the eldest is well mannered, but that Kerry's such a little miss! I don't like the thought of being saddled with her for months."

"She'll have improved by the time she comes, I shouldn't wonder. Besides, if it means I'll get my pardon—"

"Yes, of course. That's the most important thing of all. I do understand that."

I decided that perhaps the time wasn't right for me to reveal the exact details of the financial arrangements, so I simply said Phineas had agreed to help pay for our return to Ireland as an extra reward for taking care of Kerry when the time came.

"He's being very generous," said Sarah politely, but I knew she was still nervous at the thought of me doing deals with Phineas Gallagher.

Soon after we had settled in our new home Sarah made arrangements for Ned to go to school. Phineas, who had offered to pay the fees, told her where all the snobs sent their sons, and presently the headmaster was falling over himself to welcome a pupil who had the word "honorable" before his name and a baron for a father. It had seemed best that Ned should take up his education again, for he had been moping around not knowing what to do with himself since we had left Newport. I'd certainly thought that school was a good idea, but Ned hated the prospect and got as cross as a flea-bitten mule.

"Schools are like prisons," he said, very sullen.

"If you'd ever been in prison," I said, "you'd laugh at yourself for saying that. Anyway, you're not going to board. How can you feel imprisoned when you can come home every afternoon?"

He looked more sullen than ever and turned down his mouth at the corners.

Of course Sarah worried herself silly about this and only half believed me when I said the only reason why Ned was in such a sulk was because he had never been to school before and was scared of it. She wanted to go with him to the school on his first day, but I thought he might find that an embarrassment, so I offered to go instead. No boy of nearly thirteen likes to look as though he's tied to his mother's apron strings.

He didn't want me to come, but I walked with him to the gates before saying goodbye.

"I'll give you one word of advice," I said before we parted, for indeed he did look very pale and unlike himself. "You stand up for yourself, and if anyone tries to crowd you because you're new or because you don't talk like an American, you give them hell. That was what I learned when I got off the boat in this country, and I'll pass it on to you for what it's worth. Good luck and goodbye and I'll see you this afternoon."

He came home sedately some hours later and told us in a casual, offhand way that he had two new friends and an invitation to go riding at the weekend.

"And what about the lessons, darling?" said Sarah in anxiety.

"Oh, they've got some funny ideas about English history," said Ned. "Quite backward, I'd say. And no one knows any French."

Sarah worried a little less about him after that, but unfortunately that didn't mean her worries were coming to an end. She had written to her brother asking him to forward the rest of her possessions, for winter was coming on and she was already anxious for warmer clothes, and Charles, in addition to forwarding two enormous trunks, also forwarded a bunch of letters from Cashelmara.

Only one was to her. The others were addressed to Ned.

"I can't let him see them," said Sarah, panicking. "It'd be too disturbing. They would upset him."

"Why do you say that? When you were both in New York he received letters from his father, didn't he?"

"Yes, but Patrick thought then that Ned would be home in the fall even if he didn't bring me with him. Once Patrick realized we'd left New York he'd know he'd been tricked, and I'm sure Charles would have written to tell him we'd left his house."

"So your husband now writes and tells Ned to leave you and come home. Well, what of it?" I shuffled the letters carelessly, as if they were a pack of cards. "Ned's not going to listen to him. During the last six months have you once heard him mention his father's name?"

"But Patrick will be abusing me—saying terrible things. It would confuse and hurt Ned so."

"Well, there's one way we can set your mind at rest," I said. "We'll open the letters and read them for ourselves."

Sarah didn't want to do that either, but in the end she gave way.

We read the letters in silence.

"Oh God," said Sarah when the last one had been laid to rest on the table. "Maxwell, we can't let him see these."

I didn't answer directly. "What does your own letter say?"

It was more abusive than the other letters she had received. It began by saying he had heard—from Charles—that she was my mistress and that she had debased herself so far that she could only hope to see her other children again if she returned to him immediately. He swore she would have nothing to fear from Hugh, who was prepared to treat her with all possible respect, but if she wasn't home by Christmas there would be no forgiveness and no possibility of her seeing the other children again. He would also take steps to remove Ned from her control. She needn't think Ned was safe from him just because the Atlantic Ocean was three thousand miles wide. He would engage the best lawyers to fight his case, and since he was leading an exemplary life while she was flaunting an infatuation that had scandalized New York, there was no doubt whom the judge would favor. He concluded with the usual wicked tug at her heartstrings by saying the children cried themselves to sleep every night because they missed her so much.

"Don't listen to a word he says, Sarah," I said at once. "The piece about the judge and the lawyers is all a lie to frighten you, for it's certain he can never keep his sodomy concealed if the fight's ever brought to a court of law, and sodomy's worse than adultery, God himself said so and wrote it down in black and white in the Bible. And as for the piece about the children crying themselves to sleep every night, don't believe a word of that either. Of course they miss you, but he's exaggerating the story, puffing it up so you'll be crushed with guilt."

"I know," she said wearily. "I came to terms with remarks like that months ago. I expect you're right too about the legal situation. But, Maxwell, these other letters—we can't let Ned see them!"

"Hm." I picked up one of them. "My dearest Ned, I think perhaps your mother has prejudiced you unfairly against me . . . I have a right to ask you to return and you have a duty to obey, but, Ned, I don't want to talk about rights and duties. I'd rather talk about love, and so I say if you love me as I know you once did, please come home and don't listen to your mother any longer. I won't say a word against your mother, for I know you love her too, but I know she's fallen under the influence of a man whom I can only regard as wicked and unprincipled, a man who could never be fit company either for you or for her. I know you're very wise and grown up, far wiser and more grown up than I was at your age, but, Ned, you're still too young to have seen much of the world and you may not realize that this man Maxwell Drummond will stop at nothing to further his own ambitions and that he's a man who would deal out murder and violence as casually as other men deal out a hand of cards . . .'"

"We'll show the letters to Ned," I said. "He knows me well enough by this time to see these accusations are a pack of lies."

"No," said Sarah.

We looked at each other. I laughed. "When you meet a bull face to face," I said lightly, "grasp it by the horns."

"Maxwell, this isn't a game of poker."

"And I'm not bluffing my way out of trouble! What's bothering you, sweetheart?"

"Ned's going to side with his father if he reads this letter. He'll believe every word Patrick says. You see, he's been brought up on the story—"

"That I'm the devil incarnate?"

"That you were responsible for Derry Stranahan's murder."

"Oh, is it Derry Stranahan's murder that I'm famous for!" I said, still smiling. "And me at Leenane all that day buying kelp from Tomsy Mulligan!"

"Yes," she said. "I know you were at Leenane."

"And you think I hired one of my kin to kiss the knife into Derry Stranahan's back!"

"I didn't say that," she said, very nervous, and when I laughed again she added in a rush, "I hated Derry and was glad when he died. If you arranged for his murder you can tell me so. It won't change my love for you. Nothing could ever change that. But all the same, I'd like to know the truth. Were you responsible for Derry's death?"

"Sweetheart," I said, drawing her to me and kissing her, "I swear to you on my dead mother's grave that in all the conversations I had with my kin about Derry Stranahan, the word 'murder' never once passed my lips."

She leaned against me. I could see my own face in the mirror that hung on the wall, but hers was hidden from me. I could feel the shape of her breasts as her body pressed against mine. A strand of her rich dark hair brushed my cheek.

"All the same, Maxwell," I heard her say, "I think it might be kinder if we kept these letters from Ned at present. They can only upset him. I won't throw them away—that would be wrong—but I'll wait until later before I let him read them."

"Whatever you say, sweetheart," I said and turned her face to mine so I could kiss her on the mouth.

For an hour after that we forgot the letters, but when Sarah remembered them an unpleasant thought occurred to her.

"Maxwell, supposing Patrick comes to America to bring Ned back?"

"Jesus, Sarah," I said, "they couldn't even spare the money to send a tutor across the Atlantic with Ned. By the time they save the money for the fare we'll be back in Ireland."

I privately had my doubts about this, but I thought it better to take this firm line to spare her sleepless nights. Meanwhile, it was I who found sleep hard to find. I hoped to God I'd hear about my pardon by Christmas.

That night I did my own share of letter-writing. I sent Eileen some money and told her to buy Christmas presents with it, and I wrote to my favorite daughter Sally and told her to be careful of all the young Dublin men who were sure to be chasing her by that time, and I wrote to Max and Denis, promising to rescue them from the city and take them back to the land. Then I waited for their replies, the replies that never came, and at last after I'd waited many weeks I had a letter from Eileen to say that Sally had married and emigrated to England and that the boys (but not the girls) knew I was living in adultery, may God and all his saints have mercy upon my soul.

"I hear from Father Donal's sister that it's the talk of Clonareen," she wrote, "for the servants at Cashelmara say Lord de Salis does nothing but curse the pair of you all day long. Thank God at least I'm not still in that valley with everyone pitying me and the girls all put to shame by the disgrace. I hope you can get your pardon and come home to Ireland, for I wouldn't wish exile on any Irishman, but please don't come to this doorstep unless you come as a husband who wants a reconciliation with his wife—and even then I don't know whether I could ever bring myself to forgive you, though I suppose a priest would tell me to try. But you won't come, will you? You're reaching above yourself again, just as you've been reaching above yourself all your life. You were never content with what you had. It wasn't enough for you, was it, that you were a big fish in a small pond! You always wanted bigger, grander ponds to swim in, and I suppose you think now you've got what you wanted, but all I can say is you'd best be careful, for in those grand ponds there are fish bigger than you'll ever be and they'll destroy you if you poach too often on their ground. If you had any sense you'd be content with what you had instead of swimming beyond your depth in waters where you'll never be at home."

I kept this letter to myself for a day or two and showed it to Sarah only when I realized she was eating her heart out with suspicion.

"Of course she's justified in feeling bitter," she said afterward.

"Why? Our love was dead long before I started loving you. It's a dog-in-the-manger air she has, not wanting me but not wanting anyone else to have me either."

But I didn't like to think of my girls put to shame and my boys not answering my letters and Eileen passing on her bitterness to whoever she chose. I wrote to her again. I said I'd respect her position as my wife and see she never wanted for anything once I was back in Ireland. I said I hadn't wanted to hurt or shame her, but she

521

had to realize that I couldn't help loving Sarah the way I did. It had nothing to do with ambition. It was no good treating me as a calculating monster who loved with his head instead of his heart, and it was no good trying to explain my conduct according to reason because it was incapable of reasonable explanation.

"It's like an act of God," I wrote boldly, though I knew as well as anyone that it's the devil, not God, who locks two people together in adultery. "It's no use talking of sin. To be sure I'd rather be living in a state of grace and going to Mass every Sunday, but since that's not possible it's no use talking about it. Sin's for priests to talk about and people who have never suffered temptations no man could resist."

But I didn't think Eileen would understand this, and I wasn't surprised when she didn't reply.

Eileen might not be writing, but the letters still kept coming from Ireland. Just before Christmas a package arrived from Cashelmara, and inside Sarah found some letters from her children.

They had never written to her before.

"DEAREST MAMA," John had printed, putting his R's back to front. "I CAN WRITE NOW PLEASE COME HOME I LOVE YOU JOHN."

Eleanor, who was only seven, wrote fluently in a fine script: "Dearest Mama, we do miss you and Ned so much and are longing to see you again. This is the second Christmas we have spent without you and Jane cannot even remember how Christmas used to be when you were here. I talk to Jane about you every day so that she does not forget you. Nanny says you are certain to come home soon to see us. When will that be? Please give Ned a kiss from me. With very best love from your devoted daughter, ELEANOR."

Jane sent three pictures of fat orange animals and labeled them "MY CATS."

De Salis completed the package with two letters, one very typical letter to Ned and one most untypical letter to Sarah, which it was clear he had written at MacGowan's dictation.

". . . and I feel it only fair to warn you that if you fail to return by Easter I shall apply for a decree of restitution of conjugal rights which will pave the way to seeking a divorce from you on the grounds of adultery and desertion. I would of course obtain absolute custody of all the children. I am advised by Rathbone that you would have no grounds for divorcing me since, in the event of misconduct being alleged against me, I could prove that the alleged misconduct was condoned. As for my present conduct I need only say that it is exemplary and you would find it impossible to prove otherwise. I remain your devoted and affectionate husband . . ."

"Maxwell," said Sarah in terror, tears streaming down her face, "Maxwell . . ."

"It's a bluff!" I said. "How many more times do I have to tell you he's bluffing? He'll never go through with his threats, never!" And all the time I was thinking in a rage: MacGowan, my enemy. My nemesis.

"But, Maxwell . . ."

"If they can bluff, we can bluff," I said. "Write and say you're seriously thinking about returning. Make it look as if you'll be back by Easter. I'll talk to Phineas again about my pardon."

But the National League attorneys were still pursuing my case, and although Parnell replied to Phineas' letter of inquiry he had nothing to report.

In April I said to Sarah, "Tell de Salis you'll be home in September after Ned's completed his year of school and you've spent August at Newport."

It was like a game of poker. I could almost see the green baize cloth and the deck of cards and the chips piling higher and higher, and across the table facing me was MacGowan, my enemy, my nemesis, pretending he had all the cards in the pack, daring me to call his bluff one more time.

At the end of May I left the Gallagher house and ran all the way home down Marlborough Street.

I found Sarah in a terrible state, her eyes red and swollen from crying, her hands trembling so much she could hardly show me the legal writ the de Salis attorneys had sent her to start the proceedings for the decree of restitution of conjugal rights.

"And look at the letter Mr. Rathbone's written me!" she sobbed. "Look at it!"

"And look at the letter the Queen's written *me!*" I yelled, waving the Lord Chancellor's parchment above my head. "We're going home, Sarah! We're going home!"

II

It had been a rough six months.

In the past Sarah had been the one who felt insecure, but her burden had passed to me, and during those six months it had been sitting on my shoulders like a vulture at a wake. I kept telling myself she wouldn't leave me, but I wasn't sure I was right. She was working herself into a state over those children and those threats, and I knew she was growing impatient, thinking I'd never win my pardon, believing I was lying to keep her at my side. We quarreled, made peace in despair and promptly quarreled again. The more afraid I became of losing her the more possessive I became, and the more she worried about losing the children the less eager she was to be possessed. I started to drink more than was good for me, and when I went about my work I would lose my temper at the slightest provocation. Sarah wept, I sulked and Ned spent as much time as he could at the Gallagher house on Beacon Hill.

So near, I'd think every day, yet so far. And I'd long for Ireland with such a craving that I dreamed every night I was riding down into the valley toward Cashelmara, fairy-tale Cashelmara, shimmering mysteriously like an unspoken promise, beckoning me on and on and on to the very end of my dreams.

"The dear little Queen's forgiven you at last, Max," said Phineas Gallagher.

I saw the round hall and marble floor of Cashelmara and the library with its walls lined with books and its huge square desk which stood by the window. I could remember old Lord de Salis sitting at that desk and telling me he was sending me to the Royal Agricultural College in Dublin, and I could remember him telling me later that since I'd squandered my opportunities he wanted nothing more to do with me. Old Lord de Salis was the toughest Saxon I ever met for all he was the best landlord west of the Shannon, and he was the only man who ever put the fear of God into me. I could remember him rising to his feet. He was a very tall man, far taller than I was, and he held himself very straight and his eyes were a dark hard blue, like splintered slate.

"Be quiet," he said to me. "I'll hear no more insolence from you. I could ruin you tomorrow if I chose, and don't you forget it." His voice was smooth as polished steel, and though he never raised it once I was afraid of him, for I was just wed then and my wife was already pregnant and it was a bad time to fall out of favor with my benefactor. Old Lord de Salis had been a big fish, as Eileen might have said, and he had swum in a pond on which the sun had never set—but that was all long ago now, long, long ago, and I would never look upon his face again. Instead I'd sit at that desk where he himself had sat, and around me would be his house, Cashelmara, and I would call his house my home.

"We must celebrate!" said Sarah with shining eyes, so we all dressed up and went out to dinner at Locke-Ober's, which is the grandest restaurant in all Boston. Sarah was worried that it might be too expensive, but I was determined to take her to a place where everyone would admire her beauty and know her for the titled lady that she was.

"It was a lovely dinner, Maxwell!" she said after we had washed down the prissy food with champagne, and when she smiled my heart nearly burst for joy that she was happy again after those long hard months of waiting.

We went home, we went to bed—and everything was well between us, so well it was hard to remember the bad times had ever happened. We moved together for a long while, and when I slept at last I dreamed not of Cashelmara but of MacGowan, riding away through the great gates on his way to eternal damnation.

III

"Maxwell," said Sarah, "what are you going to do with Mac-Gowan?"

It was the morning after our triumphant dinner, and Ned had already departed for school. We were in our bedroom. Sarah was arranging her hair, I was smoking a cigarette and far away in the kitchen we could hear the maid washing the breakfast dishes.

"What do you think I'm going to do with him?" I said with a smile and blew a smoke ring at the ceiling to tease her.

She smiled back at me in the mirror. "You don't trust me at all, do you?" she said.

"It's protecting you I am! A lady like you shouldn't have to bother herself with thinking of a bastard like MacGowan."

She put down her comb and turned to look at me. "I've reached the stage where I like to think of him. I've thought of him every day for years now, just as you have."

I blew another smoke ring at the ceiling and felt the bed move as she lay down beside me.

"Don't keep your plans to yourself," she said. "Let me share them."

Our glances met. The cigarette burned unsmoked between my fingers. After a pause I said, "It's better if you don't know too much. That way you'll find it easier later to act surprised and innocent."

"But—"

"Sarah, I'll be running risks. I'm entitled to say how many risks I'm not going to run, even for you."

"But can't you at least tell me—"

"Sure I can. You'll have all the revenge you've ever wanted for Hugh MacGowan."

"All?"

"All except the necklace, and I'd give that to you except there must be no mark on his body which can't be explained away by a fall from a horse."

She laughed, then shuddered. "That was always just a joke, Maxwell!"

"Was it?" I said, and she didn't answer.

After a moment I felt her shudder again. "Maxwell, I'm very frightened. I don't want you to end up in jail a second time. I'd rather MacGowan went scot-free."

"MacGowan's not going to go scot-free," I said, "and I'm not going to go to jail. Now, don't be frightened, sweetheart, for all's going to be well, I promise you. We must just be careful, that's all, and take every precaution we can. For example, I was thinking we'd best win your husband's brothers to our side, and as they dislike MacGowan that surely shouldn't be too difficult for us to manage. Why don't you write to them, tell them you're returning to Ireland with Ned and say you'd like to meet them in Galway to discuss the situation."

"Should I mention you?"

"No, they're more likely to turn up in Galway if they think you'll be alone with Ned."

So she wrote to the two young de Salis brothers, although as we planned to leave Boston before the end of the month we knew there would be no possibility of receiving a reply before we sailed.

"I suppose I should speak to Ned," said Sarah nervously. "What shall I say to him?"

"Tell him his uncles are going to be waiting for us in Galway and that they'll be helping you sort things out with his father. There's no need to say anything else. That's more than enough to reassure him."

But Ned didn't think it was enough at all, and there was an awkward moment while he decided to be mulish.

"What will my uncles say when they see Mr. Drummond?" he demanded when Sarah had hesitantly explained the situation to him.

"Darling, I'm sure Thomas and David will understand that I preferred not to travel unescorted."

"Do they know you're living with Mr. Drummond? What will they say when they find out you're Mr. Drummond's mistress? Are you going to go on living in sin openly when you get back to Ireland?"

"Ned!" cried Sarah in an agony of embarrassment. I suppose ladies don't like to hear their sons talking about such things.

"Why don't you leave us for a moment, Sarah?" I said. "Ned and I'll discuss this together."

Sarah went off obediently, and Ned looked grumpy. That was when I knew he had wanted to embarrass her.

"Well, Ned," I said pleasantly when we were alone, "the answers to your questions are: Yes, your uncles must know I'm living with your mother since your father knows, and no, we won't be indiscreet once we're back in Ireland, as we don't want to spoil your mother's chances for a fair hearing in the divorce court. Satisfied?"

"I suppose so. Mr. Drummond, I realize all you've done to help my mother in the past and indeed no one's more grateful to you than I am, but I really can't go on allowing you to inconvenience yourself on our behalf. I'm quite old enough now to take care of my mother, and I think—"

"Look, sonny," I said. "Do you want to spend the next few years growing up at Cashelmara or don't you?"

"Well, I do, of course, but—"

"Then give me the chance to deal us a hand that'll suit us both. I know you'd prefer your mother was living as chastely as a nun, but she's not and she's never likely to be—and that's not such a disaster either, for there are scores of husbands and wives who'd give their back teeth to be as happy as we are, and besides, I'm going to fight for her harder than any husband ever fought for his wife. So trust me and let's be allies, just as we should be, for if we quarrel your mother'll suffer more than we will, and to be sure that's the last thing either of us want."

"Yes, sir," he muttered, not looking at me, but I heard the respect in his voice and knew the battle was won. I was just heaving a sigh of relief when he said, "What kind of a hand are you going to deal Mr. MacGowan?"

"Oh, Mr. MacGowan's going to be leaving Cashelmara," I said.

"He's been cheating your father out of too much money. Agents can always be dismissed for dishonesty, you know."

"Who's going to dismiss him?"

"Well, I wouldn't be surprised if your uncles couldn't arrange it if they went to court and declared your father unfit, but maybe Mac-Gowan will resign of his own free will once he knows the game's up."

"Oh. I see. Yes. I won't have to see my father, will I?"

"Of course not."

"But won't he stay at Cashelmara?"

"With MacGowan gone?"

"Oh, you mean my father will go away with Mr. MacGowan and I can take my mother back to Cashelmara."

I smiled at him without replying.

"I feel better now I know what's happening," said Ned. "I'm sorry I was rude to you. I know you're doing all you can to help us."

"But of course I am!" I said soothingly. "Didn't I promise you long ago in New York that one day I'd take you and your mother home to Cashelmara, and do you think I'm not the kind of man who keeps a promise?"

"Of course I don't think that, sir," he said hastily, and we were friends again, although I'll admit he'd given me a fright with all his questions. He was a sharp lad and growing sharper every day.

We sailed for Ireland at the end of June after some busy weeks of preparation, and all the Gallaghers came to the docks to see us off. We were traveling by the best steamship, of course, thanks to Phineas' generosity, and as soon as I saw the enormous monster sitting on top of the water I knew my second journey across the Atlantic was going to be a very different experience from my first.

The two youngest little girls cried to see Ned go, and Clare shed a tear as well, but Kerry just giggled. "Don't fall overboard!" she said to Ned, and Ned giggled too. She was wearing a pink dress that made her look plumper than ever, and as she scampered about, her skirts hitched up, I could see the holes in both her stockings.

"Such a plain child," said Sarah afterward, and I had to agree that Kerry was indeed as plain as a pat of butter. But butter can be so delicious when it's served fresh from the churn.

Of course we'd never breathed a word to Ned about our plans for Kerry, and so it was a shock to Sarah when Ned said to the girl, "Come to Ireland for a visit one day."

"Sure—why not?" said Kerry. "We'll all come, won't we, Pa?"

Phineas said yes, it had always been his heart's desire to go home for a visit one day, and as soon as Kerry's back was turned he gave me a benign knowing look.

We left. The sun was shining. The shores of America faded into a hot misty haze, and then there was nothing between us and Ireland at last except three thousand miles of sparkling sea.

Chapter Six

I

I saw the Irish skies with their scudding clouds, and when the sun came up the light was soft and gentle, so different from the hard glare of a summer day in Boston or New York.

"How wonderful to see land again!" exclaimed Sarah in relief, but I couldn't speak. I saw the dark-blue hills of Clare slumbering while far away the sun shone on Galway Bay, and it was as if I was already on the road to Oughterard, heading north to Connemara and the Joyce country.

"How strange it will be to see Galway again," said Sarah uneasily, but I could no longer see anything except the blurred shimmer of light upon water beneath the Irish sky.

"Look at the meadows above Salthill!" cried Ned in wonder. "Look at the color of the fields!"

And the soft Irish rain came out to meet us, though the sun was still shining upon the mountains far away.

"Look, Mama!" said Ned. "Look at the spires . . . and all the boats . . . and the houses of the Claddagh packed together like boxes . . ."

All I could think was: God help those poor Irish-Americans who'll never look upon this sight again. I thought of Phineas and his money, and I pitied him.

"It does look pretty from the sea," Sarah was saying to Ned. "One can't see the squalor and the poverty from here."

"No man's poor who lives in Ireland," I said, and Sarah squeezed my hand with a smile and said how exciting the return must be for me.

I thought of icy winds blasting down the long straight streets of New York and dirty, stinking sidewalks reeking in the sweating summer heat. I thought of lighting a candle and seeing the cockroaches run, of lying awake in the dark and listening to the rats. I saw the drunken derelicts lying in the streets and the painted wrecks of women in the cabarets and the mutilated beggars smelling of the sewer.

"It's over," I said. "I'm home."

The reek of fish and worse was in the air, but it didn't matter, and when we reached the dockside I hardly saw the beggars or the narrow cobbled streets littered with dung. My feet were on Irish soil again and Irish voices were in my ears and, Lord, I swear there wasn't a man alive who was as happy as I was at that moment.

"I'm back!" I shouted, throwing my hat in the air. "I won! I beat them all! I'm home!" And I grabbed a flower seller who was hovering plaintively at Sarah's elbow, kissed her and gave her a gold sovereign. "Be sure and drink my health tonight, sweetheart!" I cried, seizing six bunches of violets as she almost fainted with shock. "For I'm an Irishman who's come home from beyond the grave!"

"Car, your honor?" said a carman who had seen the flash of gold and was already darting ahead of his rivals.

"An inside car!" I said grandly, clinking the gold coins in my pocket, and there I stood, every Irishman's dream, a man who had gone to America with nothing but the shirt on his back and come home with his pockets lined with gold.

"The Great Southern Railway Hotel!" I ordered the carman, and the name of the grandest hotel in Galway City rang out as true and clear as the singing coins in my pocket. Sarah clutched my arm. She was laughing, looking so pretty and smart and gay, and I felt as if I already had a jug of poteen inside me with another dancing on the table before my eyes.

"Dear Jesus!" I gasped. "I'm in heaven!"

"We're all in heaven!" cried Sarah, kissing me as the car lurched uphill to the square.

So we went to the grandest part of Galway, and there before us lay

531

the mighty hulk of the hotel with all the mashers of western Ireland going in and out of its front door.

"I want the finest suite of rooms you have," I said to the flunkey who greeted us. "I don't care what it costs, but I must have the best. And I want champagne wine, very cool, in a bucket with ice in it, and caviar in a silver dish, and six potatoes baked in their jackets with a bowl of butter."

"Yes, sir," said the flunkey, pop-eyed.

From somewhere a long way away a man's voice said disbelievingly, "Sarah?"

I swung around. Facing us was a spindly young man with carroty hair and owllike spectacles.

"Thomas!" cried Sarah in delight and ran into her brother-in-law's arms.

II

He was more than a mere brother-in-law to her; he was also her cousin, the child of her favorite aunt, and so she had every excuse for being pleased to see him, but I thought he looked a feeble little Saxon, and I didn't like the look he gave me one bit. But I knew I had to be meek and agreeable to him, so I smiled politely as I waited to be introduced.

". . . and is David here too?" Sarah was asking.

"He's upstairs. We arrived only an hour ago. Good heavens, how Ned's grown! How are you, Ned?"

More family reunions followed.

"I see Mr. Drummond has been kind enough to accompany you," said Thomas afterward.

Sarah nearly fell over herself making the formal introductions and apologized to me for being so slow.

"As if it mattered," I said, smiling at her, and wondered if young de Salis would offer me his hand to shake.

He did. My opinion of him went up a notch or two.

"Good afternoon, Drummond," he said with courtesy, and then he suggested we should all meet later after we had had time to recover from the journey.

"Dearest Thomas!" said Sarah happily as we were shown upstairs to our suite. "He's grown to look so like Marguerite."

"Never mind who he looks like," I said with relief. "He's here to meet us, that's all that matters, and that must mean he and his brother are taking your side against MacGowan."

When we reached our suite we found that it faced the square. There were gold-tasseled curtains on the windows and thick carpets on the floor, and in the sitting room the furniture was upholstered in red velvet.

"This'll do, I suppose," I said. "Is there a bathroom?"

There was. It was hardly up to the standard of the Marriott bathrooms, but I said I supposed that would do too.

"It's lovely!" said Sarah. "We can have the main bedroom, and Ned can have the smaller one on the other side of the sitting room."

The porters were beginning to bring up the bags, and the next half hour was spent straightening ourselves out. The champagne arrived with the caviar and potatoes, and afterward Ned asked if he could go out for a walk in the square.

"Sure, if you like," I answered, and when we were alone together I said to Sarah, "Look, I'm not anxious for long conversations with your brothers-in-law tonight, and besides it's certain they'd prefer to dine alone with you and Ned. Could you make some sort of excuse for me, do you think, and at the same time hint that I'm anxious not to intrude too much? I want to make a good impression on them."

"Yes, of course. What shall I say when they ask me about my plans for the future?"

"Repeat what you told them in the letter. Tell them your main concern is to obtain legal custody of the children as soon as possible. Obviously they approve of that idea or they wouldn't be here to greet you. Lead up to the idea of a divorce and see if they approve of that too. Find out what's been going on at Cashelmara. Say you're prepared to live there with the children if MacGowan and your husband could be removed. What we want is for your brothers-in-law to offer to have your husband stay with them in England."

"What shall I say when they start asking about MacGowan?"

"Talk about the legal possibilities of removing him. Talk about the legal possibilities of everything, separation, divorce, custody, control of the estate—the whole goddamned lot. There's nothing the Saxons like better than to talk long and loud about the law."

"I'm especially anxious to find out what they think about Patrick's attempt to secure a decree of restitution of conjugal rights. If Patrick really had no likelihood of winning the decree—if it really was all just another scheme of MacGowan's to drive me insane—"

"Of course it was! Didn't I tell you that over and over again?"

"Yes, but I knew Patrick must sincerely have wanted to get Ned back and hold on to the other children."

"And MacGowan made use of that sincerity so that he could have a new chance to persecute you! Well, don't you be worrying any more about Hugh MacGowan, sweetheart. Tomorrow morning I'll be taking the first car into the Joyce country."

"Maxwell, promise me you'll be careful!"

"As careful as a tinker with a crock of gold," I said, smiling at her, and while she was gone I wondered again how far the young de Salis brothers would be prepared to help us.

But the news proved good. When Sarah returned to our bedroom after dinner she told me Lord de Salis's drunkenness was much worse, and although neither of his brothers had been able to face visiting Cashelmara for some months they had heard from their sister that Lord de Salis's health had deteriorated. Both of them thought he hadn't a hope of either winning a divorce petition or being awarded custody of the children, and both said they were prepared to go to court if necessary to have their brother judged incompetent and MacGowan removed from office.

"What a surprise it'll be for them when they find out that going to court won't be necessary!" I said, kissing her, and after we had celebrated the good news I no longer wasted time worrying but fell instead into a deep dreamless sleep.

III

The outside car left Galway City at eight o'clock the next morning and bumped and swayed over the hills through the rolling meadows to Oughterard. It was raining at first, but beyond Oughterard the rain stopped, and ahead on the horizon I could see the Twelve Bens, the mountains of Connemara, rising to the skies in a single prayer. The clouds shifted and parted, the sun shone, and suddenly the little loughs we passed were blue as jewels, and the bog, brown-green and restful as a lullaby, rolled endlessly toward the hills.

The meadows were long gone now, the soft frilly fields of buttercups no more than a memory. There was nothing to distract the eye but the mountains walking toward us from the horizon, nothing but pure lines and the stillness of some magical dream and the Godlike peace of another world. I had traveled that road several times before, but never in all my life did I see it as I saw it then after three years of exile in foreign cities. If any man wants a true taste of heaven he should toil in the gutter of New York City and then journey through Oughterard from Galway into the fairest land on earth.

The mountains encircled us like a fairy ring, and I felt so safe and warm and comfortable—as if I were back in my father's house again with the peat fire smoldering on the hearth. The mountains were tall, straight and strong, and not a tree marred their shining lines. Beautiful as sharpened blades they were, and they shimmered in the sun with the radiance of naked steel.

"Your honor wanted the next crossroad?" called the carman, and ahead of me the sun was blazing on the road that led to Letterturk.

"Indeed I do," I said, "for I'm bound for Cashelmara and the town of Clonareen."

I began to walk. It was wonderfully quiet, with only the running water of the stream nearby and the occasional bleating of a sheep above me on the mountainside. I walked on and on uphill through the gulley to the top of the pass, and as I watched, the clouds shifted endlessly sending shadows chasing across the misty stretches of furze.

I came to the pass between Bunnacunneen and Knocknafaughey, and there below me like a dazzling dream lay the long, slender lough and Cashelmara.

I stopped for a long moment, and around me the wind hummed through the pass and the water cascaded over a precipice into the valley far below.

I set off downhill. I crossed the Fooey River. I walked past the gates of Cashelmara and along the lough to Clonareen, and all my kin came out to meet me and all the other families came too, even the Joyces, and when I arrived at last in the main street of Clonareen I found myself carried shoulder-high through a cheering crowd, as if everyone already knew I'd come to rescue them from their nemesis, Hugh MacGowan.

IV

Several hours later in Jeremiah O'Malley's cabin I laid my gun upon the table.

"This was given to me by a cousin of ours in New York City," I said. "His name's Jim O'Malley and a finer man you could never meet though you could travel the length and breadth of America all your life long looking. His family was evicted during the Great Hunger by Lord Lucan, God curse his Black Protestant name forevermore, and ever since that terrible day Jim O'Malley has vowed revenge."

Someone obligingly filled up my mug of poteen, so I paused to drink.

535

"So when Jim O'Malley gave me this gun," I continued, "he said to me, 'Maxwell Drummond,' says he, 'I never want to see this gun again until it's stained with Saxon blood—keep it,' says he, 'and when it's served its purpose send it back to me along with the brave man who's rid Ireland of one more of the tyrants which the Saxons have sent to persecute us.' " I paused for another taste of poteen and looked around. You could have heard a pin drop.

"So I said, 'To be sure, Jim, there's nothing I'd like better than to return the gun to you myself, but my reputation's so exalted with the Saxons that they'd never let me escape to America a second time. And besides,' says I, 'I've the chance to teach young Master de Salis how to be a good landlord, and I'll be needed in the valley to help my kin.' So he says with tears in his eyes, ' 'Tis a shame, Max, so it is, but send me the bravest man among your kin and I'll be well content.' "

I picked up the gun again, and the tallow flame flickered along the barrel. Eight heads craned forward yearningly to take a better look.

"Let me take it back to Jim O'Malley, Max," says young Tim.

"No, I'll take it," says Jerry, his father.

"No, it's for me to have the glorious chance!" begged Shaneen. "And me the youngest of nine with not even a yard of potatoes to call my own—and all that money waiting in Ameriky."

"Dear God, let me see Ameriky before I die!" sighs his brother Joe.

"Let me—"

"No, me—"

"We'll draw lots," I said. "We'll do the choosing sweet and fair, just as it should be done, and may the best man win."

So we took straws from the floor and I evened them out and Shaneen won, which pleased me, for there was so little to keep him in the valley, and for years he had talked of emigrating.

"What do I do, Max?" he asked, all eagerness, when the choice was settled.

"Be at the gates of Cashelmara before noon tomorrow, take cover among the rocks and wait for me there. But first let me show you how to use this gun."

"Jesus, what if I miss?" Shaneen said nervously afterward.

"That's impossible—you'll be too close," I said, for I knew he had a good eye and all he needed was confidence. The Brotherhood had once had guns circulating in the area, and Shaneen and I and a few others had been selected for firearm instruction. We'd gone up into

536

the mountains three times a week for target practice and would have gone every day except that ammunition had been too scarce.

Presently when the poteen was passed around again I told them I had hopes of becoming the agent at Cashelmara. "And if I'm agent," I said with a smile, "you can be sure this valley will be the land of milk and honey God promised Moses, with never a man evicted and everyone paying Lord de Salis only what's fair and reasonable."

"But how'll Lord de Salis come to be choosing you as his agent, Max?" said Joe.

"Why, Lord de Salis is going to England with his brothers to take a cure for the drink," I said, "and Lady de Salis will speak up for me, you can be sure of that."

I heard the awkwardness in the silence and saw how all of a sudden no one would meet my eye. "Dear God," I said, appalled, "you'll not be believing the wicked rumors that I've seduced Lady de Salis! And me with a wife and six children in Dublin! Lady de Salis may be the finest lady in the world and the most beautiful, but I've done no more than any other man anxious to help a lady in distress."

I saw the relief in their faces and knew I'd been right to bend the truth a little. Fighting the Saxon enemy was one thing; adultery was quite another.

"Will you be rebuilding your home and bringing Eileen back, Max?" asked Jerry.

"Sure I'll be rebuilding my home," I said. "Don't I have my children to provide for? But if Eileen decides to stay in Dublin there'll be nothing I can do to bring her back."

"Eileen always did hold herself above us," someone said.

"And maybe Max will too," said someone else jokingly, "when he's agent for Lord de Salis."

"The day will never dawn, please God," I said good-humoredly, "when I shall be ashamed to cross your threshold and accept your hospitality."

And indeed it felt so good to be back among those men who were like brothers to me that I stayed up late talking to them and fell asleep only when the dawn was breaking in the east and the last drop was gone from the last jar of poteen.

v

I borrowed a horse from Mr. O'Shaughnessy, the gombeen man (he always had the best horse in the valley), and rode down the road to

537

Cashelmara. It was eleven o'clock, the sun was high and the cool wind blew away my headache before I was a mile from Clonareen.

I reached the great iron gates. They were not only unlocked but standing wide open, and when I saw that I smiled, for I knew it was my enemy's way of flinging down the gauntlet. I rode through the gates. I wasn't afraid of ambush, for I knew he'd never dare shoot me in cold blood unless he could claim I'd provoked him to it, and surely not even a Saxon court of law could see any provocation in a man paying a morning call.

Dismounting, I hitched the horse's reins to a tree just inside the grounds and walked up the dark winding drive to the gravel sweep in front of the house. I would have ridden right to the porch steps except that I wasn't planning to leave by the way I'd come.

The gravel crunched beneath my feet. The slim windows watched me as I walked toward them.

I rang the bell, waited, and when there was no reply I pounded on the wood with my fists until Mr. Timothy O'Shaughnessy, the gombeen man's brother, opened the door a crack and peeped out.

"Why, it's Timothy O'Shaughnessy!" I said. "And the top of the morning to you, Timmy! I never expected to see you in a butler's coat!"

He tried to retreat, but I shoved my foot in the door.

"If it's Lord de Salis you're wanting, Maxwell Drummond—"

"Lord de Salis!" I exclaimed. "Whatever gave you that idea? No, Timmy, it's not Lord de Salis I'm wanting. I've come to see Mr. MacGowan."

Chapter Seven

I

He came to the library, where I was waiting for him. I never heard his soft footsteps. All I heard was the door opening, and as I spun around I found us face to face at last, MacGowan my enemy, my nemesis, the man who had ruined me and taken everything I had.

He waited by the door. I had forgotten how ordinary he looked. We were much the same height, but he was slimmer than I was and he had thinning brown hair and colorless eyes.

From the way he stood I knew he was armed.

"Welcome back," he said.

He was smiling a thin smile with his thin mouth so I smiled too. But I said nothing.

"A pardon from the Queen, I understand," he said. "I've already had word from Dublin that your land's to be restored to you in full. You made powerful friends in America, didn't you?"

"How news travels!" I said.

"Powerful friends and a well-bred bitch of a mistress. You've come up in the world, Drummond! I suppose I should congratulate you."

I saw he wanted me to get angry, so I laughed, sat down on the edge of the desk and picked up a heavy glass paperweight with a casual movement of my hand. "So you still remember Sarah," I said. "I thought you might have forgotten her by this time."

"I have a long memory."

"So have I," I said, tossing the paperweight gently up and down as I watched him, "and so has she."

He had closed the door, but now he opened it again and made a gesture toward the hall. "I'm touched that you called to pay your respects," he said, "but now if you have nothing else to say I'll ask you to leave. Mr. Rathbone, the London attorney, has a copy of your leasehold, and when a further copy has been made it will be sent to you. As for your land, you can do as you like with it, but take my advice and settle down quietly, for if you make trouble I'll have you rammed back into jail so fast your head'll spin off your shoulders. Good day."

I went on tossing the paperweight. "A brave speech," I said courteously, "but what a waste of breath!"

He left the door and moved a shade closer. "Leave this house at once, if you please."

"Well mannered too," I said. "I like that."

"I'll give you five seconds to get out."

"T - t - t!" I said reprovingly.

"One . . . two . . . three . . ." He had maneuvered himself cleverly behind a high-backed chair. Leaving the desk, I strolled along the nearest book-lined wall. ". . . four . . . five . . ."

He drew his gun, but I threw the paperweight first. He was slow on the draw by American standards, and I had plenty of time.

He dodged, but before he had recovered I was on top of him and twisting the gun out of his hands.

Jesus, but he was strong! I knocked him off balance and grabbed at his forearm, but his wrist was stiff as a ramrod. He chopped at me with his free hand, but he was already reeling against the wall, and by clinging to his wrist I locked that dangerous free arm behind his back. He kicked and shoved—and still his wrist was like steel. I tightened the lock on his other arm. By this time we were both gasping and my heart was thudding in my chest.

The steel bent at last. He gave a shout of pain and the gun clattered to the floor.

Shoving him away, I tripped him and drew my own gun.

"Not a word," I said, "or you'll get a bullet between the eyes."

He was silent. He was still breathing hard and his eyes shone with rage.

I retrieved his gun and tucked it into my belt.

"Get up."

"You bloody fool," he said. "I'll see you back in jail before the day's out."

"I'll see you on the road to hell first!" I said, speaking violently to make sure he thought I might kill him on the spot. "Get over to that desk."

"What for?" he said, trying to gain time while he figured out a way to rush me.

"Do you have a manservant?"

"Do I have a . . . What the devil's that got to do with anything?"

"Do you have a manservant?"

"I do now, as a matter of fact, yes. But why—"

"Then sit down at that desk or I swear to God I'll hurt you in places where not even that manservant of yours would think to look."

He recognized the threat he had once made to Sarah. His face became very still.

"Well, are you going to sit down or . . ."

He sat down.

"That's better," I said, lounging against the marble mantel. "Now, you're going to write a little letter. Take a sheet of that notepaper on the side there and pick up the pen."

After a pause he did as he was told.

"To the Honorable Thomas de Salis and the Honorable David de Salis," I said, "St. James's Square, London. Gentlemen . . ." I stopped to give him time to write. His pen squeaked across the thick paper. "I am writing to you to offer my resignation from the post of agent for Lord de Salis on the estate of Cashelmara."

He laughed, but I cut him short. "Go on."

He scratched away again, but he was smiling.

"Lord de Salis is too ill for me to approach him on this subject," I said, "so I have no choice but to offer my resignation to you, his brothers. I have been considering leaving Cashelmara for some time, as my lord no longer appreciates my services as he used to and now his drunkenness has reached such a pass that I can do no more but leave as soon as possible. In God's name I urge you to come and save him from himself. I shall be leaving Cashelmara at two o'clock this afternoon and will be traveling with my father to Scotland, where my wife will join me as soon as she has settled matters at Clonagh Court. I remain, gentlemen, your humble and respectful servant . . ."

He hooted with laughter again. "You don't really imagine I'll leave, do you?" he said, still scratching away carelessly with the pen.

"Sign the letter. That's right. Now give it to me and address an envelope."

"There are no envelopes."

I moved to stand behind him. "Find one."

He didn't like me breathing down his neck. He dragged an envelope hastily from the nearest drawer and picked up his pen again as I glanced at the letter to see that it was correct.

"Good," I said when the envelope was addressed. "Put the letter in and seal it."

"What exactly do you think you're doing?" he inquired, amused, as he warmed the wax. "I can't quite see the purpose of this charade. You can't make me leave Cashelmara!"

"How much do you bet?"

Hot wax dripped onto his fingers, but he didn't notice. He was looking steadily at me, and there was a pinched expression about his mouth.

At last he said in a rush, "You wouldn't dare lay a finger on me."

"I'd dare anything," I said. "I could kill you now if I chose and bury your body somewhere on the grounds. No one would be any the wiser, and your letter of resignation would explain your disappearance."

He was scared. He sealed the letter clumsily and his fingers shook. "So you're going to kill me."

"Not if you do as I say. Leave this house at two o'clock this afternoon and ride to your father's house. You can ride a horse and take your bags on a donkey—or have them sent later, whichever you like. But you must ride alone. No servant, no de Salis, no—is your wife here?"

"No, she's at Clonagh Court. Why must I ride alone?"

"You won't be alone once you get to your father's house. You and your father are going to leave this valley together, just as you wrote in that letter, and you're never going to show your faces here again. If you do—"

"You're going to kill me," he said, stumbling over his words. "I want a promise of safe passage to my father's house. I want—"

"I don't give a tinker's curse what you want," I said. "You can go where you like and do what you like when you get there, and if Lord

542

de Salis wants to join you later I'll be the first to wave him goodbye. But you're leaving this house at two o'clock this afternoon, and if you don't come out I'll send my kin in to get you and I'll not be answering for the consequences. Understand? Fine. Give me the letter and get up."

"Where are we going?"

"Why, we're going to take a little walk together," I said, softening my voice as I gave him a smile, "and we're going to have a talk about old times. Where's Lord de Salis?"

"In bed. He wasn't well this morning."

"And the children?"

"In the nurseries with the governess, I suppose."

"Very well, let's go. But remember—if we see anyone you're to say nothing. Nothing at all. I'm the one who'll do the explaining."

We walked into the empty hall.

"Open the front door."

Outside in the drive a stiff breeze made MacGowan shiver. "Where are we going?" he said again.

"The chapel."

"The chapel! For God's sake, why?"

"Oh, it's such a nice, quiet, private little place, I'm thinking," I said, "for a nice, quiet, private little talk."

When he spun to face me I saw the sweat on his forehead. "Look, Drummond. I'll do what you want. I'll leave at two. I won't come back. I'll go to Scotland and Patrick can come and live there with me. I don't care about staying in this place. All I care about is being with him. I—"

"Be quiet," I said. He revolted me. I thought of him and de Salis fawning on each other and felt the vomit heave in my stomach. "Start walking."

At the back of the house we came to the garden. I'd never seen anything like it in all my life. God alone knows what it must have cost. Huge bloated flowers festered on rich soil that would have supported a hundred starving families, and amidst the sickly riot of color were stretches of lush succulent grass where no cattle were ever allowed to feed. I thought of my country's history, the rich conquerors having so much they could afford to throw away their riches, the poor oppressed Irish locked out in the cold beyond high stone walls, and that garden was obscene to me, as obscene as the man who scuttled ahead uphill through the woods to the chapel.

The chapel was small, bare and dark, like I'd always heard it was, and it smelled of decay. I didn't feel I was in church, but that wasn't surprising since it was a Protestant place and not a true church at all.

"Take off your clothes," I said to MacGowan.

He was so paralyzed with fright he couldn't move.

"Come on," I said, motioning impatiently with the gun. "Hurry up."

"What are you going to—"

"You ask far too many questions," I said. "Do as you're told."

"You're going to torture me," he gasped, gibbering with panic.

"Shut your goddamned mouth and get out of your goddamned clothes."

He struggled out of them. I watched curiously. He was well proportioned, but his skin was dead white, like a corpse, and mostly hairless.

"Jesus," I said, "that's an unattractive sight if ever I saw one. Back up against that pillar."

When he obeyed, still gibbering, I took a length of cord from my pocket, bound his wrists behind the pillar and wove the cord around his legs.

He started to shout at me, but I took no notice. I merely sat down on a pew, put up my feet and lighted a cigarette.

His language was very colorful, but presently he ran out of curses and started whining again about what I was going to do.

I smoked my cigarette and didn't answer.

At last he lost his nerve and became hysterical. He ranted, raved, wept and writhed, and all the while I smoked my cigarette down to the butt and watched him in silence.

When my cigarette was finished I said, "Now you know what it feels like to live under the threat of violence for ten minutes. Sarah lived under that threat for five years. Think about that for a moment, would you? I'd like you to think about it."

I lighted another cigarette while he thought. He was quiet now, but every few minutes he would shudder uncontrollably. When my cigarette was finished I took a knife from my pocket and ran my finger idly along the blade.

"I made a promise to Sarah once," I said. "Would you like to know what that promise was?"

He began to whimper again. He was disgusting.

"I said that one day I'd make her a present of your—"

544

He screamed before I could finish the sentence. I waited, still running my finger up and down the blade, and when at last he had sunk into a sobbing silence I said, "But mutilation has never been one of my favorite pastimes." I slipped the knife into my pocket, left the pew and drew close to him. "Before you think you're going to escape without a scratch," I said, "let me give you this—" I lashed out at him across the face—"for all those months I spent in jail, and this—" I lashed out again—"for all the years I spent in exile, and *this*," I said, finally unleashing every ounce of my white-hot rage, "is for all Sarah suffered, for her terror, degradation and shame." And as he opened his mouth to scream I kicked him hard below the belt and slammed him over the head with the gun butt before he fainted.

I stood looking at his sagging frame for a long time, and when I was in control of myself again I cut the cords so that he sprawled face down on the stone floor. Then I dressed him, in case anyone should come into the chapel and find him before he had recovered consciousness. I wanted to leave behind nothing I couldn't explain away later, and although I could explain bruises there could be no explaining away a naked body tied to a pillar. It was only when he was dressed that I remembered his gun, tucked in my belt. I didn't want to risk it being found in my possession, and yet I certainly had no intention of putting it back into his hand. In the end I hid it, wedging it tightly under a back pew between two hassocks—not a very brilliant choice of a hiding place, but since MacGowan would be thinking I'd taken the gun with me he wasn't likely to spend time searching for it. With the gun hidden I pocketed every strand of cord, took a quick look around to make sure there was nothing I'd forgotten and then walked outside into the sunlight.

The stone wall that bordered the grounds stood nearby, and scrambling up a convenient tree, I swung along a strong branch like a monkey and landed gingerly amidst the broken glass on top of the bricks. Luckily I was wearing good heavy shoes. It was tricky getting down, for I didn't want to cut my hands, but in the end I crossed myself for luck and jumped with the prayer that I wouldn't break a leg.

I didn't. All the luck was running my way now, and within minutes I had retrieved my horse from his makeshift hitching post by the gates and was giving my cousin his final orders.

"He'll be coming presently, Shaneen," I said. "Have you marked a place to wait?"

He had. I looked at it. There were three rocks bunched together near the road but above it.

"That's fine," I said. I gave him my gun and some extra bullets.

"And the money?" he asked.

"I'll have it for you in Leenane," I said. It was true he was a kinsman and I loved him dearly, but it never hurts to be cautious about money, particularly when so much was at stake.

"Where will I be finding you?"

"By Tomsy Mulligan's kelp boat. Good luck, Shaneen."

We embraced. Then mounting my horse, I rode away downhill to join the road to Leenane.

II

At the inn I stabled my horse and went in search of Tomsy Mulligan. There was nothing as pleasant as looking up an old friend, and Tomsy and I smoked some tobacco together on the jetty while we reminisced about the day three years before when I had been a convict on the run and he had taken me by boat from Leenane back to Galway. It had been the day I had met Sarah in the ruined cabin above Cashelmara, the day she had become my mistress. I had reached Leenane that afternoon, and after Tomsy had taken me down to Galway another member of the Brotherhood had taken me in his boat to Queenstown, where I had boarded the immigrant ship to America.

"But that's long ago now, Tomsy," I said, smiling at him, "and I'm a respectable gentleman again."

Tomsy said respectability was a wonderful state for a man and began to talk about his two grandsons in the priesthood.

When I left him at last I returned to the inn and told the landlord I'd be staying the night before taking the outside car back to Galway.

It was a good afternoon for loafing around. I saw Leenane and Leenane saw me. Quite a sociable day I had, and by evening I was eating pork and black pudding and the landlord's daughter was bringing me a glass of porter.

It stayed light very late that evening, but as the dusk thickened I told the landlord with a yawn that I'd be taking a short stroll before I went to bed.

It was cool outside, and the dark salt waters of Killary Harbor gleamed beneath the night sky. The tide was high, and when I looked

546

across the jetty I saw Tomsy Mulligan's boat bobbing up and down like a black cork.

"Any sign of him yet?" I called softly to Tomsy.

"Not a word."

I waited. The tide rose higher. I was moving back toward the inn again when I heard him coming up the road.

"Max . . ."

"Yes, it's me. This way." I guided him off the road into the wood that had been planted by the inn. He gasped when I touched his arm, and I felt the soft stickiness of blood.

"Jesus Christ, what happened?"

"All's well," he said, sinking to the ground, "but I'm weak as a kitten and I think I'll sit me down for a moment."

"Let me look." I struck a match.

"Indeed it's but a graze," he said. "Don't worry, Max."

"Even a graze needs care." I gave him my hip flask. "Drink some of this," I said, and taking a clean handkerchief from my pocket, I made a bandage as best I could.

"That feels better." He drank, shivered, drank again. "Dear God, what a day!"

"Did you miss the first time?"

"Yes, but listen to what happened! Waiting I was there this afternoon after you'd gone when Timothy O'Shaughnessy—he's butler there now—"

"I know."

"Well, it's rushing out he comes in a donkey cart and drives across the bridge to old MacGowan's house as if all the fiends in hell were hot on his heels. Then later back he comes and the old man with him, and the old man has a shotgun."

"God Almighty!"

"Well, what could I do, Max? I was thinking I'd best not shoot him because if he never reached Cashelmara Hugh MacGowan would be too scared to poke his nose beyond the gates. So I let the old man pass, but sure enough it's with the old man Hugh is when he pokes out his nose at last and the two of them armed to the teeth."

"If only I'd left another man with you—"

"Faith, Max, it was nothing, for I was man enough for the two of them and all the saints are my witnesses!" He crossed himself and took another shot of poteen. "It was Hugh I took first, for I came to thinking he was the one who mattered most. The second shot it was

547

that took him, and he fell from his horse as if God Himself had smote him from on high, but then the old man was shooting at me and it wasn't so wide he shot either, as you see. But I fired again and hit his horse. The poor beast was only winged, but he ran like a demon down to the lough and the old man was thrown. At first it's shamming I thought he was, but when I looked I saw he'd broken his neck. Hugh was still alive, so I had to fire again, and oh, Holy Mary, Max, I was as weak as water by that time, and if Hugh MacGowan hadn't been the villain the devil knows he was, I'm thinking I'd have run all the way to Ameriky without firing another bullet. But I sent him to eternal damnation—I sent both of 'em, Max. I'll be a hero in the valley now, won't I? I've rid our poor suffering country of two more of the Saxons' tyrants, and to be sure one day God Himself will reach down from heaven to give me a reward."

"It'll be men like yourself, Shaneen," I said, "who'll help Ireland rise again from the ashes and drag the British Empire into the dust where it belongs. It's the truth that you're the finest patriot I ever met, and there's no greater honor a man can have than to fight for his country against tyrants which the devil alone couldn't equal for their untold cruelty to millions of innocent people."

"God save Ireland!" says Shaneen with tears in his eyes.

"God save us all. Listen, Shaneen. Here's the money you need. Tomsy Mulligan will take you down to Galway, and then you're to go into the Claddagh and find a man named Brian O'Hagan. He'll take care of you until he's arranged your journey to Queenstown and the immigrant ship. It's best you sail from Queenstown, as the police will be watching for you in Galway. The voyage will be rough, but Jim O'Malley will give you work when you get to New York. Here, I've written down his address for you, and don't you lose it."

"God bless you, Max," he says, tears spilling down his cheeks. "I'll never be able to repay you, never."

"Don't talk of repayment, Shaneen, after all you've done today. But when you get to New York light a candle for me in St. Patrick's and tell Jim O'Malley I sent the bravest man west of the Shannon to bring his gun back to town."

I walked with him to the boat and watched as Tomsy cast off. The little boat started to slip away from the jetty at once, and within seconds it was lost to me among the huge shadows of the mountains.

After a while I returned to the inn.

"It's turning damp out there," I said to the landlord. "We'll have rain tomorrow, I shouldn't wonder." And when he agreed with me I

548

went upstairs to my room and slept as soon as my head touched the pillow.

III

When I awoke next morning I couldn't believe it was over. I thought: MacGowan my enemy, my nemesis. But he was gone. The score had been settled, and I would never see his face again. I felt bereaved by the thought of it and empty, as if I'd lost something precious. I never knew until then how much my hatred of MacGowan had become a part of me, like an arm or leg, and had kept me alive during those years of imprisonment and exile. Getting even with MacGowan had lain so long across my mind that it was hard to imagine a future where my revenge didn't exist. Of course I had plenty of plans. I had to look after Sarah and her children and take good care of the estate. I was going to have my hands so full I would hardly have time to sit twiddling my thumbs, but somehow that morning I felt as listless as a sick dog and aimless too, as if I was recovering from a blow on the head. I suppose I'd wound myself up till I was tight as a drum before I met MacGowan again, and now in my triumph I had unwound myself more than I'd intended.

Still, it was a long journey back to Galway, and by the time I reached the hotel again I was feeling more like myself. I found the de Salis brothers taking tea with Sarah and Ned in our suite, and after the first flurry of excitement had died down I was introduced to David, the younger brother. He looked even feebler than Thomas. He had white skin, pink cheeks and a soft handshake.

"Well, the battle's won," I said. I didn't look at Sarah, but I was immensely aware of her. I took the letter from my pocket and gave it to the brothers. "Here's his resignation, and by now he and his father will be halfway to Scotland."

There was great excitement about this, and Sarah said breathlessly, "Did all go well? Oh, Maxwell, for God's sake tell us what happened!"

I looked at her levelly, willing her to be calm before the brothers noticed her excitement was unnatural, but David only exclaimed in admiration, "Yes, how on earth did you persuade him to resign?"

"Why, it was simple," I said. "We had a little talk and then he wrote the letter and we took a stroll in the garden together to arrange the final details. He wants Lord de Salis to go and live with him in Scotland, but I said it might be wiser if my lord took a cure first. But of course," I said politely to the brothers, "that's for you to decide."

David and Sarah started exclaiming in wonderment again, and I was so enjoying their pleasure that it came as a nasty shock when young Thomas said sharply, "I'm still waiting for a full explanation, Drummond."

I took a good hard look at him and saw he was taking a good hard look at me. So I had underestimated him.

"Believe me, Mr. de Salis," I said, speaking up respectfully at once, "it wasn't hard to persuade MacGowan to leave. He must have known he was finished in that valley as soon as he heard news of my return. I'm an important man among my kin, as you may know, and they were all thirsting for revenge as soon as they set eyes on me again. I called at Cashelmara to tell him I couldn't guarantee his safety if he chose to stay, and he told me—very smooth he was—that since he'd made his fortune out of the estate by this time he was well prepared to move on to greener pastures. He told me that to annoy me, I've no doubt. He didn't want me to think I was chasing him out, but of course it's chasing him out I was, for he had no choice but to leave."

"But of course!" cried David happily. "Don't you see, Thomas? It all makes perfect sense. Open the letter and let's see what he has to say."

Reluctantly Thomas broke the seal. "The excuse he gives is that Patrick's impossible to work for," he said later, passing the letter to his brother.

"Dear me," sighed David. "What *are* we going to do with Patrick?"

"He'll have to take a cure," said Thomas, "before he even thinks of following MacGowan to Scotland. If he thinks of it." He gave me another sharp look. I decided I didn't care at all for Mr. Thomas de Salis's sharp looks. "My brother and I will leave for Cashelmara tomorrow," he said abruptly to me. "We'll talk to Lord de Salis and to my sister at the dispensary and try to make some suitable arrangement to benefit his health."

Sarah whispered, "The children . . ."

"We'll send them to you at once. As I've already told you, David and I have wanted to remove them from that house for a very long time. Later when Patrick's better perhaps you and he can work out some suitable arrangement about custody, but at present he's quite unfit to look after them and I shall tell him so if he tries to stop them coming here to you."

"Good heavens!" exclaimed David. "Isn't it amazing how much easier everything's suddenly become now that we don't have to contend with MacGowan?"

"MacGowan would have fought me every inch of the way over the children," said Sarah. "It was a personal feud." Her voice wasn't quite even, and when I looked at her I saw her eyes were brilliant as if she had a fever. Desire stirred in me, just as it always did when I saw the passion of her hatred burning in her, but I smothered it and wandered casually toward the bedroom door.

"If you'll excuse me I'll change my clothes," I said over my shoulder. "I'm dusty as a tinker after all those hours on the road."

"Drummond."

It was Thomas. Still moving casually, I turned to face him.

"I'd like a word with you in private, if you please."

"Of course," I said. "As many words as you like, sir."

He followed me into the bedroom and closed the door. "I merely wanted to tell you," he said, "that the children are staying at Cashelmara while you continue to share this room with their mother. Forgive me for being so direct, but you're not a fool and you must realize that I do have a certain responsibility toward my nieces and nephews. Perhaps you would be kind enough to take another room— if you don't intend to return immediately to Clonareen."

"Of course I'll take a separate room," I said, deciding it was best for the moment to roll with the punches. "And you needn't worry, Mr. de Salis, that Sarah and I won't be very discreet once we're back in the valley. We don't want to do anything that might lessen Sarah's chances of getting a divorce and custody of the children."

For the first time I saw him look relieved.

"Was there anything else on your mind?" I asked helpfully, but he shook his head.

"Not at present. Thank you, Drummond," he said and went meekly back into the sitting room.

It was ten minutes before Sarah could get rid of the brothers and send Ned off on some errand. I had stripped to my underclothes and was lying on the bed to rest my tired muscles. I had closed my eyes, and when I heard her enter the room I kept them closed because I knew I'd tell her everything if I saw her and wanted her.

"Maxwell . . ."

"All's well," I said.

"Tell me."

"I will. But not just yet."

"Why not?"

"Because when your little brothers-in-law come rushing back from Cashelmara I want you to be as innocent as Eve before she met the snake."

"What a bad actress you must think me! How weak and feeble!"

"You know it's not that, but—"

"Then stop treating me as if I were made of china!"

I opened my eyes and was lost.

"No," she said when my intentions were beyond my power to conceal. "If I don't have your confidence why should you have mine?"

So I told her. I told her everything, and afterward I had her like I'd never had her before, and the violence soldered us together like a white-hot iron. When we fell apart at last she slid gasping into an exhausted sleep, but I didn't even close my eyes. I lay beside her and thought how fate could bend a person into different shapes, and then I kissed her, covered her with the quilt so that she wouldn't get cold and opened the wardrobe in search of fresh clothes.

When she awoke she was very quiet, and when she tried to put up her hair she started to cry.

I said nothing, just sat down beside her on the wide stool and put an arm around her shoulders.

"I feel so strange," she said, "as if a part of me were dead."

"I felt like that too."

"Sometimes I think he drove me mad. But I'm not mad, am I, Maxwell? At least, I'm not mad any more, and since it's all over I know I'll never be mad again. But I can understand now why you didn't want to tell me."

"I would have told you later."

"Yes—when the time was right. I'm sorry. But I promise I won't fail you. I shall be very strong and do everything exactly as it should be done."

"I know you will, sweetheart," I said. "I know it."

We said no more after that, and when she was dressed we went downstairs for dinner.

The de Salis brothers left the next morning. I did nothing about taking a separate room for myself but told Sarah to say I had done so if Thomas asked her about it. By this time Sarah could think of nothing but seeing her children again. She hardly knew what to do with herself beyond pacing up and down the sitting room in a fever of impatience and gazing from the window as if the de Salis carriage was already on the point of rolling into the square.

"They could be here in three days," she said, crossing off the days on her fingers. "A day for Thomas's and David's journey, a day to pack, a day to travel . . ."

"Don't forget de Salis might delay them by kicking up a fuss."

"But I know Thomas and David will insist—and Patrick will give way because he'll be too crushed about MacGowan to care. Oh God, how am I to wait! I shall die of impatience, I know I shall."

But Thomas came back before the end of the second day. He arrived alone, and as soon as Sarah saw him she burst into tears.

"Wouldn't he let them come?" she cried as we both tried to comfort her.

"They're coming tomorrow," said Thomas, kissing her. "There, there, Sarah, I'm so sorry, but they had to pack, you know, and Nanny said it wasn't possible for them to leave earlier."

"But why didn't you wait for them? Why did you come back so soon?"

"Because there are some things that have to be said."

There was a pause. It was early evening, and we were in the sitting room of our suite. Ned had been reading the newspaper at the table by the window, Sarah had been mending some clothes and I'd been working out my money in a notebook. Glancing around just before Thomas's arrival, I had thought what a peaceful, domestic little scene it was.

"Things that have to be said?" repeated Sarah, and I saw her fingers tighten on her needle as she picked up her sewing again.

"About the situation at Cashelmara." Thomas was still standing watching us. "Patrick's very ill. He drank himself almost to death the night before we arrived, and Madeleine is going to take him to a first-class nursing home near London. So you'll be quite at liberty, Sarah, to return with all the children to Cashelmara as soon as Patrick's well enough to leave."

"And MacGowan?" said Sarah fearfully. "Did he leave as he promised? Doesn't Patrick want to go with him?"

He looked at her but was evidently satisfied by what he saw. He turned to look at me.

"MacGowan's dead," he said.

There was a silence. Although I was watching Thomas I was

aware of Ned glancing at me over his shoulder. He had gone to the door to shake hands with his uncle and had been wandering back to his newspaper by the window.

"So it's dead he is!" I exclaimed with a delight I took no trouble to disguise. "And not a minute too soon, the thieving dishonest rogue! That's the best piece of news I've had in a month of Sundays."

"He was murdered," said Thomas.

"Well, of course he was. No villain like Hugh MacGowan ever died a natural death. And who was the hero who plunged the knife into his heart?"

"MacGowan was shot," said Thomas. "Both he and his father were killed. The murderer hasn't been found."

"May he prosper and increase," I said, sinking comfortably into my armchair again.

For a moment I thought young Thomas wasn't going to rise to the bait, but in the end he opened his little mouth and nibbled at it.

"Drummond, I can't help but feel your attitude is unfortunate. I know MacGowan was a despicable character and you had every right to bear him a grudge, but to condone murder—to make a mockery of the law . . ."

This was exactly the diversion I wanted. "That's rich," I said, "coming from an Englishman. English laws never did Irishmen one blind bit of good, Mr. de Salis. Hugh MacGowan was allowed to plunder and pillage my valley for years, and why? Because Englishmen have been plundering and pillaging Ireland for centuries, that's why—and all in the name of law and order, of justice, righteousness and religion!"

"I have absolutely no intention of getting involved in one of those political arguments which can only end with you referring me to the example of the Wretched Cromwell at Drogheda," said young Thomas with surprising spirit. "I know Ireland's suffered in the past, but Ireland should count itself lucky that it's been riding through the nineteenth century on England's coattails and not on the coattails of some country like Russia—then you really would have something to complain about! England has poured money into Ireland. The system of social welfare that exists here is far in advance of anywhere else in Europe—"

"We don't want your goddamned money!" I said. "We want our freedom!"

554

"You want to sink back into the Dark Ages," said Thomas, "and on reflection perhaps that's exactly where you belong."

"We want to live in a world where we own our own land," I said. "We want to live in a world where we don't have to live in terror of a bad harvest, we want to live in a world where men like Hugh Mac-Gowan can't rob us and beat us and evict us from the only homes we've ever known, we want to live in a world where a man can't be tried before a packed jury and jailed for crimes he didn't commit. And we want to live in a world where 'murderer' isn't just another word for 'patriot' and 'hero.'"

"Is this leading up to a confession that you yourself killed Hugh MacGowan?" demanded young Thomas, very bold and reckless by this time. "It certainly sounds as if it is!"

"Thomas!" gasped Sarah. She played it just right. She had risen to her feet, but now she sat down abruptly, as if the shock was too much for her.

"Sarah, you'd better leave us," said Thomas. "Ned, help your mother into the bedroom and stay with her till I send for you."

But Ned didn't move.

"Here, sweetheart," I said to Sarah, stooping over her and giving her hand a small private squeeze. "Let me help you."

She submitted as if she was stunned. Leaving the door open so that Thomas could see every move we made, I helped her into the bedroom and stooped to kiss her as she collapsed on the bed.

"There's nothing to worry about, sweetheart, I promise," I said in my clearest voice, "for I can prove I'm innocent, and if you wait here I'll go back and tell Mr. de Salis so."

She nodded, careful not to look at me, and I left her, closed the door and prepared to produce my trump card to flummox young Thomas.

"Mr. de Salis," I began earnestly, "I swear to you on my dead mother's grave that during all the conversations I had with my kin this week on the subject of Hugh MacGowan, the word 'murder' never once passed my lips."

"In that case," said young Thomas, bold as brass, "you'll have no objection when I ask you where you were on Tuesday afternoon."

"Indeed I have no objection! I was at Leenane. As soon as I left Cashelmara I went to Leenane to see all my old friends there. They'll vouch for me. I stayed the night at the inn and took the car the next morning for Galway."

There was a long silence. At last young Thomas said, "I see. You'll forgive my suspicions, but you had been at Cashelmara that day, and—"

"Well, it was a natural mistake to make, and you can be sure I'll bear you no grudge!"

"—and MacGowan had left a letter behind," said Thomas with a flintiness that rocked me unpleasantly. "I read it."

MacGowan my enemy, my nemesis . . . "Did he, now," I said with a smile. "And was it a confession of all his crimes?"

"It said you had extorted the resignation from him at gunpoint and that you had beaten and tortured him."

"And if that isn't just the kind of lie one would expect from such a pervert! Jesus, as if I'd ever stoop to the kind of behavior that was the breath of life to him!"

"Why should MacGowan have written the letter if what he said was untrue?"

"To have his revenge on me, of course! I'd driven him out of the valley, and to be sure he'd rather die than take the defeat lying down. Where did you say this letter was, Mr. de Salis?"

He hesitated fractionally. "I gave it to the District Inspector."

I knew he hadn't. He had wanted to question me before the D.I. even heard that I'd been back in the valley. He had his sister-in-law to think of and his nephews and nieces, and he was quite smart enough to imagine all sorts of uses for that letter.

"You've got it in your pocket, haven't you?" I said, still smiling at him. "Well, don't look so worried—I'm not going to relieve you of it at gunpoint. I don't have a gun anyway, and besides I don't care what you do with the letter. Show it to the District Inspector and let him make what he likes of it. I shall deny it's true, and the District Inspector can take it or leave it as he pleases. What does it matter now? All that matters is that I never fired the bullet that killed Hugh MacGowan, and nobody on this earth could ever prove that I did."

"Quite," said Thomas, his eyes expressionless behind his spectacles.

There was a pause while both of us decided what to say next.

"Mr. de Salis," I said, resolving to drive home my victory by shoring up his confidence in me, "please rest assured that I care for Sarah as if she was my wife and I want to do all I can to look after her and the children. Give me a chance to prove my good intentions and I swear you won't regret it. Can't we shake hands and be allies?"

He hesitated, but when I said, "You'll not hold it against me, I hope, that I've the courage to speak up for my country to an Englishman such as yourself?" he did offer me his hand. "Of course not," he said evenly. "You're entitled to your opinions. Very well, since we both want the best for Sarah and the children, an alliance would certainly be sensible. And now, if you'll excuse me, I shall retire to my room to recover from the journey. Ned, perhaps you'd like to come and see me for a few minutes before dinner."

"Yes, Uncle Thomas," said Ned from the window.

I had forgotten he had been there, listening to the entire conversation. He was still looking down at the open newspaper on the table, but as the door closed he glanced up at me.

"Well, I'm afraid your uncle thinks I'm very heartless," I said to him with a smile, "but I'd be a liar if I said I was sorry MacGowan's dead, wouldn't I?"

He said nothing. The evening sun slanted across the bones of his face, and I saw that his eyes were the color of splintered slate.

The resemblance, which I had noticed before but never identified, struck me like a blow between the eyes.

"Jesus, how like your grandfather you look, Ned!" I exclaimed before I could stop myself, and then as he smiled at me with old Lord de Salis's smile it was as if a ghost had walked across my grave.

Part Six

NED

Revenge   1887–1891

Edward was both a realist and a romantic. Brave, handsome, with magnetic appeal, a brilliant performer in the tournament lists and a model of knightly deportment, he embodied all the qualities that the young aristocrats around his throne admired. . . . [But] he had suffered greatly.

The Age of Chivalry
—Sir Arthur Bryant

Chapter One

I

I shall always remember the day I heard that Hugh MacGowan had been murdered.

For a long time I had thought of MacGowan with nothing but repulsion and loathing, but now the shock of his murder triggered older memories to the surface of my mind, and although I tried to shut them out I failed. I could see him newly arrived at Cashelmara and saying to my father, "Come riding with me but leave the child behind this time." That was when he had been impatient, not caring that I was present and heard every word he said.

But my father answered, "I always go riding with Ned on Saturday mornings. Go by yourself if you don't want his company."

People always talk as if my father never spoke up to MacGowan, but he did. And people always say that nothing ever ruffled MacGowan, that he was as cold and hard as a block of marble, but he wasn't because I saw him flush when my father reproved him, and when he looked at me I saw he was so embarrassed that he didn't know what to say.

"Very well," he said at last. "We'll all go."

But of course I immediately turned to my father in a great sulk and said I didn't want Mr. MacGowan's company on our precious Saturday-morning ride.

MacGowan was more embarrassed than ever. I remember him shifting from one foot to the other as he waited for my father to rescue the situation, but when my father said nothing he had to rescue it himself.

"I'm sorry, Ned," he said. "I had business to discuss with your father and I thought you'd be bored if you came with us, but the business can wait. I hope you'll come."

I didn't swallow that either. Children always know when they're being fobbed off.

My father squatted down on the floor beside me and looked me straight in the eyes. "Mr. MacGowan didn't mean to offend you, Ned," he said. "He simply didn't think before he spoke. We all do that sometimes, so don't hold it against him now that he's apologized. Come on, let's go or the morning will be wasted before we've been anywhere."

That evening MacGowan tried to make amends to me. He gave me some pictures for my scrapbook and talked to me about Scotland, although he soon ran out of things to say. He had no way with children, and although he tried hard to be friends with me, his shyness was a handicap to him.

Nobody ever mentions MacGowan was shy, although I have heard my mother say he was reserved, never speaking of his family or his past. In fact he was an extremely difficult person to know well and not the kind of man who made friends easily. I think that was why, when he made friends with my father, he stuck to him through thick and thin. People said it was just greed for my father's money, but it was a lot more than that. My father was everything MacGowan was not—good-looking, charming and likable—and MacGowan would have been at first flattered and then gratified by his friendship. His devotion to my father was inevitable in the circumstances, his jealousy of my mother the natural result of his single-minded admiration.

People always say my father was completely under MacGowan's thumb, but MacGowan was far more enslaved than anyone was willing to believe. Also people often confess themselves baffled to know what my father could possibly have seen in MacGowan, although to me it's obvious. MacGowan was a strong man physically, and this strength together with his sharp, shrewd brain combined to produce an aura of power that held my father spellbound. My father was susceptible to the idea of power. "He was a powerful man," he would often say of his own father, and I could see the idea of power was thrilling to him, perhaps because he himself was a gentle man and the brutality of power, being foreign to his peaceful nature, had for him the irresistible fascination of the unknown.

After my mother left home and went to America MacGowan was pleasanter to me than ever, probably because he was in such good spirits to have my father all to himself for a while, but although I no longer resented him as I once had I never really liked him. Yet sometimes I felt I almost did. When he helped me choose a tree for my little garden, for instance, he went to great trouble and couldn't have been nicer to me. Afterward, long afterward, when I was listening to Maxwell Drummond telling me my father was a pervert, all I could think of was MacGowan helping me choose the little fir tree for my garden. I was very careful to think of MacGowan while Drummond was talking because I knew I wouldn't be able to bear it if I thought of my father.

I didn't think of my father for a long time after that, and I didn't think of MacGowan either. I was like a sufferer from vertigo who sees the world tilting crazily before his eyes and can only cling with both hands to the ground beneath his feet while he waits for the dizziness to pass. So I clung to my ground, which at that moment was America, and thought neither of the future, which was too uncertain, nor of the past, which was too painful, but only of the present. The present consisted of the company of my mother and my Uncle Charles, who lived in New York. I loved my mother, and since my father was now hopelessly lost to me I was doubly terrified of losing her. That was why, when my Uncle Charles told me I could continue to stay with him after he had thrown my mother out of his house, I refused to hear of it. I was afraid he would destroy my mother for me, just as Drummond had destroyed my father, and then my world would be nothing, not even a dizzily spinning parade of events over which I had no control, but an appalling void.

My mother went to live with Maxwell Drummond, and I, seeing no alternative, went with her.

I hated Drummond, just as I hated Tiffany lamps and snow-white Irish linen tablecloths and indeed anything that reminded me of the restaurant where he had told me the truth about my father. I was dreading seeing his face when he opened the door of his rooms because I was sure he'd be hoping my mother had left me behind with my uncle. I even thought he might try to get rid of me so that he could have my mother to himself. The best I could hope for, I felt, was that he would ignore me.

563

But he didn't. He smiled when he saw I was with my mother and said I was welcome, and when he opened a bottle of champagne he not only gave me a glass but filled it to the brim. And throughout the months that followed he would say to me at regular intervals, "I love your mother and I'm going to take care of her. And one day I'll take you both home to Ireland."

My world stopped spinning dizzily. It stopped tilting at its crazy angle. "I'm going to take you home," said Drummond, and suddenly it was no longer too terrifying to look ahead. I looked into the future and saw Cashelmara, my home, the part of my past that no one could destroy, and during the remainder of my days in exile I found myself praying night after night: Oh God, let me get home to Cashelmara and I'll never ask even the smallest favor of you again.

II

Drummond took us back. He threw his hat in the air as he stepped onto Irish soil and he bought my mother six bunches of violets and I liked him so well I laughed.

Less than a week later MacGowan had been murdered, my father had been shuffled off to some nursing home to take a cure for his drunkenness and I no longer knew what I thought of Drummond any more, although I supposed I really had no choice but to go on liking him as best I could. I managed to banish my vertigo by telling myself everything would sort itself out once I got home to Cashelmara.

How can I describe Cashelmara in those days long ago when I was a child? It wasn't smart, for there wasn't enough money to maintain it properly, and it wasn't grand, just an ordinary late-Georgian mansion. There are dozens of them in Ireland and in England too for that matter. But it was very comfortable, a good family house, one might say, and it was well situated, having pleasant views from nearly every window. To be honest I must admit it would have been an unexceptional place if it hadn't been for the garden, but the garden was dazzling, imaginatively designed, splendidly stocked and emanating an extraordinary atmosphere of beauty and peace. It was the finest garden in Europe in my eyes, and my father, whom I had once loved, had created it out of a wilderness.

Two days after I had heard of MacGowan's murder I had to go to my uncle Thomas's room in the hotel in Galway and listen while he and my uncle David discussed what was to be done with Drummond.

"Do we have a choice?" I said when I was able to get a word in edgeways.

They both looked at me as if I were being very unintelligent.

"My dear Ned," said Uncle Thomas. "Drummond may think he can step neatly into MacGowan's shoes, but I'll be damned if I'll appoint him to be agent. I don't trust him an inch."

"But don't you see?" I said, bewildered, wondering why it wasn't as plain to them as it was to me. "It doesn't make any difference whether you appoint him or not. Even if you employ another man, Drummond will be the one who makes the decisions. You'll both be in England, and my mother will ask Drummond to manage the estate either with the agent or without him."

"Oh, I don't think your mother would be able to do that," said Uncle David doubtfully.

"Legally impossible," said Uncle Thomas with severity.

"Look, Uncle Thomas," I said, "I don't mean to be impertinent, but you simply don't understand. Drummond's going to do just what he bloody well likes, and my mother isn't going to stop him either. What's more, that needn't necessarily be a bad thing, so wouldn't it be better if we dealt him a decent hand instead of making trouble by standing in his way?"

"Gracious me!" said Uncle David. "You're talking just like an American card-sharper, Ned!" And Uncle Thomas added, "Don't you think it's time you started talking like an Englishman?"

"Hell no!" I said, beside myself with frustration by this time. "Why the devil should I? I'm not an Englishman. I never was and I never will be! I was born in Ireland and I grew up in Ireland and now I'm back in Ireland after two years in America and I'm telling you that once we're at Cashelmara Drummond's going to be calling the shots. He's got rid of MacGowan, just as he always planned he would, and he's using you to get rid of my father, and then he's going to settle down at Cashelmara and look after my mother—and if you don't get in his way everything might work out quite well—at least until I come of age and can take care of the estate myself. You say you can't trust Drummond, Uncle Thomas. Well, you're wrong. You can trust him to work hard and provide for my mother and her children because he's been doing exactly that for the last two years."

They stared at me. They were speechless, and I saw that my speech, littered with American crudities, had shocked them to the core.

I tried again. "Look, sirs," I said, scraping together as much of an English accent as I could remember, "I'm sorry if I've been rude, but I'm dreadfully upset. I don't want any more trouble and people fighting each other, and I'm just afraid that if you start fighting my mother and Drummond the trouble will flare up all over again and there'll be no end to it. I know you don't like Drummond, and I know you don't like him living with my mother, but can't you at least give him a chance to prove himself? He's been very good to us."

This touched them, as it was meant to.

"Poor Ned," said Uncle David. "What you must have been through."

"Well, perhaps we should give Drummond a chance," said Uncle Thomas. "Perhaps he does deserve at least that. But he's damned well got to be discreet with your mother or Sarah's going to be in deep trouble later when she seeks a divorce."

"It's all so appallingly unsuitable," said Uncle David. "For the children, I mean. Good Lord, can't you hear Madeleine's comments? She's bound to say the children's moral welfare will be endangered."

"I can't believe Aunt Madeleine would be quite such a fool," I said, forgetting myself again. "Four children live in the care of a drunken pervert and no one gives a damn, but once they're in the care of their mother, who's the best mother in the world even if she does sleep with a man who's not her husband, their moral welfare is endangered."

This created an uproar naturally. They both leaped to their feet, and although Uncle David began, "My dear Ned . . ." Uncle Thomas shouted him down.

"Look here!" he said sharply. "This sort of behavior won't do at all, you know. I'm sorry, but it won't. You're thirteen and a half years old and you should know by now that children your age should keep a civil tongue in their head when talking to their elders. I realize you're upset and that this upheaval is very distressing for you, but you'll gain nothing whatsoever by being rude. Now listen to me. It's quite untrue to say no one cared a scrap about the unsuitable environment at Cashelmara both before and after you left for America. Madeleine, David and I were extremely worried, and had Sarah not decided to come home we might well have gone to the Court of Chancery and applied for the children to be made wards of court. That would have made it possible for the children to be removed from Cashelmara and placed in the care of a guardian appointed by the judge. The only reason we were reluctant to take this step was because your father—as you may or may not remember—is devoted to his children and we found it very hard to decide whether it would be more damaging to the children to take them away from him than to allow them to remain at Cashelmara."

"You could have sent them to America to my mother!"

"Indeed we could not! Your father would have gone to court to oppose such a move, and no judge, believe me, would have consented to children being sent abroad to a deserting wife who was living in adultery."

"But—"

"Don't interrupt! And don't you interrupt either, David! I'm going to have my say. Listen, Ned. We all know that your father is at present unfit to have charge of his children. What you seem incapable of realizing is that a judge might say your mother is no more fit than your father is to have charge of them. I'm not saying he *would* say it. I'm merely saying he *might* say it. That's why it's very important to try and settle these family troubles privately and keep them out of the courts. Please don't think we're unsympathetic to your mother. We're not. We're on her side and we think your father has treated her abominably. But you must realize that she's not exactly as white as driven snow herself and that there are plenty of people, not least your Aunt Madeleine, who would be justified in complaining about your mother's relationship with Drummond. Have I made myself clear?"

"We want the welfare of all you children to come first," said Uncle David. "We only want to do what's best for you, but sometimes it's so difficult to know what the best is. In fact sometimes I feel equally angry with both Patrick and Sarah. It upsets me to think of children suffering just because their parents can't behave as parents should."

After a pause I said, "I just want to go home. That's all I want. I want to take my mother home."

That was when they told me they would be leaving the next day for Cashelmara to take my father away to England to cure his drunkenness. Once he was gone my mother would be able to go home with her children.

My brother and sisters had arrived the day before at the hotel in the company of my Uncle David, Nanny and the new governess, who was called Miss Cameron. I had not met her before, but I had known Nanny all my life, and seeing her again was just as exciting as seeing John, Eleanor and Jane.

When they arrived I was waiting for them in the hotel hall, and the first person I saw was Nanny as she hauled herself down from the carriage. Nanny was short and dapper and always wore a widow's bonnet and dozens of red flannel petticoats. The bonnet was worn in memory of the Dear Departed One, who had died in the Crimean War. They had been married only two weeks before the Dear Departed One had left to serve his country, and Nanny had been widowed at the age of twenty-one. The idea of remarriage appalled her—"Not at all proper, and the dear Queen would be the first to agree"—and although now I can wonder if such sentiments were really a compliment to her husband, when I was a child they seemed eminently noble and fitting.

Nanny believed very much in doing what was fitting. According to her definition this encompassed a belief in good manners, truthfulness, the Ten Commandments and the British Empire and excluded all foreigners (including the Irish), spiritualism and the Salvation Army. To explain her continuing presence at Cashelmara it should be understood that she had decided it was her mission in life to bring up four poor little English children condemned through no fault of their own to live among savages. However, she was fiercely loyal to my mother, despite the fact that my mother wasn't English, and when it had become obvious that my mother planned to remain in America, Nanny had been the first to spring to her defense.

"She'll be back one day," she said. "You mark my words." And when I still complained she demanded, "Do you think she would ever have left you if I wasn't here to save you poor innocent lambs from the wickedness of the world?" I had no idea then what wickedness she was referring to, but I did know she would never leave us. It wouldn't have been "fitting," as Nanny would have said. It wouldn't have "suited" at all.

"Nanny!" I shouted as she leaped spryly from the carriage, and rushing forward, I grabbed her in my arms and swung her off the ground.

"Mercy!" shrieked Nanny, red petticoats flying. "You're tall as a maypole!"

I wasn't, but I was pleased to hear her say so. "How wonderful to see you again!" I cried, giving her another twirl.

"Heavens above!" gasped Nanny. "What a nasty American accent!"

A dark head stuck itself from the carriage window. "Ned!" yelled my brother John. "Ned, I'm ten years old now—one, two, three, four, five, six, seven, eight, nine, ten!"

"Hullo, John!" I yelled back in delight. "So you became a mathematician!"

"Ladies first, Johnny," said Nanny briskly. "Don't be in such a hurry to get down! Come along, Eleanor."

I had forgotten how pretty Eleanor was, and now I saw she looked prettier than ever. Her fair hair was set in ringlets, and her violet eyes were enormous in her heart-shaped face. "Eleanor!" I exclaimed, kissing her admiringly, and waited for the familiar stream of chatter, but to my astonishment not a word was said. Eleanor hid her face in her hands and burst into tears.

"There, there, precious," said Nanny, putting her arms around her, and seeing my horrified expression, she added soothingly, "The excitement's too much for her. She's been high-strung lately. Johnny, help Jane down, there's a good boy."

"Hullo, Neddy," said my younger sister.

"Don't call me Neddy!" I growled.

"I want Mama," said Jane, just as if she were ordering an item in a restaurant. She was dark like John and had an upturned nose and a wide mouth that was capable of shaping itself into any number of expressions, most of them impudent. "I want her now—at once—and then I want to go home before Ozymandias dies of grief without me."

"Who in God's name is Ozymandias?"

"Ozymandias King of Kings," said Jane, "is my eldest cat. Why isn't Mama here to meet us?"

"But she is!" cried John. "Look!"

"Mama!" sobbed Eleanor.

"Mama!" shrieked Jane, elbowing Eleanor out of the way, and there followed a very confused and emotional five minutes on the steps of the hotel. Uncle David and I stood watching with foolish smiles on our faces, Nanny wiped away a large tear and all the passers-by stopped to sigh "Ahhh!"

"Very fitting," said Nanny when she could speak again.

The euphoria of the reunion lasted some time and was still at its peak when I had the conversation with my uncles about Drummond's future at Cashelmara. It was not until my uncles had departed to remove my father that I had the chance for any long private conversations with either John or my sisters, for my mother refused to let them out of her sight. However, on the day after my uncles' departure she was indisposed enough to stay in bed for the morning, and after breakfast Nanny and Miss Cameron announced their intention of taking the younger children to the beach at Salthill. It was only two miles away, and one could travel there by tram.

"Will you come with us, Ned?" asked Nanny deferentially, and I said I would. It was a sunny day and I liked the promenade at Salthill.

After we were safely installed on the beach with the picnic basket and other paraphernalia, Nanny produced her knitting, Miss Cameron took the girls off to look for shells and John wandered away to practice drawing numbers. The tide was low and some sand was exposed invitingly below us.

"Johnny's come on such a lot," said Nanny fondly. "He can write now, you know."

"About time too," I said. John's ill-health had made him backward, but I had never thought he was stupid.

"Miss Cameron's been good for him," said Nanny. "She took trouble, you know, when the tutors wouldn't. Mr. MacGowan engaged her because he said Scots teachers were the best, and I must say she's done wonders for John and the girls."

"Hm," I said. I had scooped away a layer of pebbles, found some sand underneath and was busy sculpting some turrets.

"Of course," said Nanny, "it's ever such a shocking thing about Mr. MacGowan."

"Hm," I said again.

"Mark you, he might have been a wicked man in some ways, but it's not for us to judge. Murder can never be right."

I stopped sculpting and stared hard across Galway Bay. The blue mountains of Clare stared back. I thought of Drummond throwing his hat in the air and buying six bunches of violets for my mother.

"A criminal can be sentenced to death and hanged," I said. "That's murder, but everyone would say it was justified."

"That's quite different, dear. The judge is allowed to give a sentence of death according to the law of the land, but judges are special people appointed by the Queen. We can't all be judges and take the law into our own hands! It wouldn't be at all fitting. Besides, remember the Commandments. 'Thou shalt not kill.' "

The vertigo had begun again. I dug my fingers hard into the sand and screwed my eyes tight shut.

"There, there," said Nanny quickly. "I didn't mean to upset you by referring to Mr. MacGowan. We'll talk about something else. I must say, it gave me rather a turn to see Mr. Drummond here with your mama, but of course a poor defenseless woman does need an escort in this wicked world. Ned dear, I don't want to say it, but I feel it's only right to warn you that some very vicious rumors are circulating about Mr. Drummond and your mother. I hope he sends for his wife as soon as he gets home."

I looked at the blue mountains again. There were three clouds above them. I stared, concentrating hard on each cloud in turn.

"Of course your mother's such a good woman," said Nanny, knitting needles clicking. "Such a devoted wife and mother always and never a shred of gossip to the contrary, which is more than one can say of many a beautiful titled lady, you mark my words. I'd always trust your mother to do what was fitting."

After a moment I said, "Will you excuse me, Nanny? I want to talk to John." I stood up, stumbling over my sculpted turrets, and walked steadily across the sand to my brother.

"Look how pretty my figures are," said John, who had reached the number nine. "Aren't figures a lovely shape?"

"I suppose they are. John, seven doesn't come before six."

"Papa's going to design the topiary again, and he says I can help him think up new shapes. I've decided to choose the shape of the number five. Eight would be nice, but it's too difficult."

"John," I said, "Papa's very ill. Uncle Thomas and Uncle David are taking him away to live in England for a while."

"Yes, that'll be nice. But he'll come back, won't he? He's promised me we can work on the topiary together."

"I'm not sure exactly what's going to happen, but Mama's going to get a divorce, and—"

"What's that?"

"John, you must know what a divorce is!"

"I don't think so. Is it a flower?"

"Good God, no!"

"I don't expect I would know about it, in that case. I only know about flowers. The west border's lovely now, all purple and white, and you should see the Azalea Walk! Papa's bought a new kind of azalea, and—"

"Didn't he tell you he was going away?"

"Of course—when we said goodbye to him. Aunt Madeleine had come to stay, so she was there, and Uncle David was there too, of course, and Papa wore a nice velvet smoking jacket, bluish, the color of those pretty dark pansies along the east border. Papa kissed me and asked me to look after the garden for him while he was away, so

I said I would. Then he wanted to kiss Eleanor, but she ran away and that made him upset. Eleanor's peculiar nowadays. But he kissed Jane and Jane kissed him twice *and* hugged him, so that made up for Eleanor. Papa gave Jane a little wooden cat he had carved. He's always giving her things, you know, and Nanny says he spoils her. Nanny's very strict with Jane, but it's no use because Jane just goes to Papa and Papa says she can have whatever she wants."

Jane had always been abominably spoiled. It was one of the reasons why she was so obnoxious, and whenever the subject was raised I always felt quite unreasonably cross.

"Jane's a little menace," I said, unable to stop myself. "She was a menace even before I went away, and now it's obvious she's worse than ever. I can't think why Mama and Papa think she's so special."

"Nanny says it's because she's the youngest. She says youngest children often get spoiled. Spoiling's common among parents, like a cold, Nanny says, and even the best parents can catch it. Nanny says it's a pity and we should feel sorry for Jane, but I don't feel sorry for her particularly because she's such a nuisance. Ned, what's a divorce?"

"It means that Mama and Papa are going to get unmarried and that they won't be living together in the future. It's a pity, but it's for the best. Papa treated Mama very badly and he let Mr. Mac-Gowan ill-treat her too."

"Mr. MacGowan's dead," said John. "I was sorry about that. He had planted some nice little trees, you know, and he showed me the seedlings. They were like baby Christmas trees. I liked them awfully."

I said roughly, "John, you're not listening to a word I'm saying!"

"Yes, I am. Mama and Papa are going to get unmarried. When will Papa come back to Cashelmara, do you think?"

"John, that's exactly what I'm trying to tell you! He won't be coming back. We're going to live at Cashelmara with Mama, and Mr. Drummond will be the agent. When Papa's better he'll live in England with Uncle Thomas and Uncle David."

"Oh, but he'll come back one day," said John. "There's the garden, you see. We're going to do the topiary together. Does Mr. Drummond like gardening?"

"I shouldn't think so."

"Well, he won't be any use if he can't garden. You'd better tell Mama to send him away."

572

"John . . ." I said, exasperated, and then gave up. I could only stare at him helplessly.

"Yes?" he said.

I made one last effort. "Mama's very fond of Mr. Drummond. He's going to take care of us all now instead of Papa."

"That's jolly obliging of him, but actually I'd rather have Papa. I don't mind if Papa and Mama get unmarried, but Papa must come back and live with us. Mama can keep Mr. Drummond if she wants, but Papa's got to come back."

"John . . ." I was floundering for words again. "Why can't you understand?" I said desperately. "You're ten years old and yet you're talking like a baby of five. What's the matter with you?"

"I'm not a baby!" yelled John, suddenly deciding to lose his temper. "I'm not, I'm not! I'm grown up and big and I'm going to fight you!" And he swung his fist furiously at my head.

"Now, now!" called Nanny warningly from across the beach.

I caught John's wrist and held it fast. "Wait, Johnny. I'm sorry if I hurt your feelings."

"Big beast!" said John, his eyes bright with tears. "Why don't you go back to America?" And tearing himself free, he stalked off across the sand to the water's edge.

Miss Cameron and my sisters were only a few yards away.

"Dear me!" said Miss Cameron, who was a tall, angular woman of about thirty-five with a slight but meticulous Scots accent. "What was all that about, pray?"

"It was nothing," I said. "Just a slight misunderstanding." I took Eleanor's hand. "Come for a walk with me," I suggested, smiling at her. "Maybe we can buy some ices."

"I want to come too," said Jane at once.

"You're not invited. Come on, Eleanor."

"Let's see if Nanny has any more of those delicious peppermints, Jane," said Miss Cameron.

"Shan't," said Jane, grabbing my free hand and digging her sharp little fingernails into my palm. "I want an ice."

"You won't get one from me. I don't like spoiled little girls who don't know how to say please and thank you."

Jane decided to throw a tantrum. Everyone else on the beach stared as Nanny came skimming toward us, and Miss Cameron clicked her tongue disapprovingly against her long white teeth.

"Run, Eleanor!" I said quickly, so we dashed across the shingle and scrambled up the steps to the esplanade.

"Nothing's going right for me this morning!" I said wryly. "First I make John lose his temper and then I send Jane into a tantrum. I hope I shan't quarrel with you as well or I shall feel very out of sorts."

She smiled but shyly, and her silence was painful to me. I could remember her when she had been little, constantly talking and laughing, always so bright and smart and cute.

"What's happened, Eleanor?" I said after a pause. "What's the matter? You're not shy of me, are you?"

She shook her head, still smiling, and clasped my hand tightly as we wandered down the promenade. We didn't find any ices, but I bought some potted shrimps from a shrimp vendor and presently we sat down on a bench to enjoy them.

At last I said, "Was it very bad at home after I left?"

She shook her head.

"Was anyone unkind to you?"

She shook her head again.

"You can tell me if they were. Did Mr. MacGowan hurt you?"

She shook her head a third time.

"Who, then?"

"Papa."

It was my turn to be speechless. I began to feel sick. "What did he do?"

"You mustn't tell anyone," she said. "Mr. MacGowan said not to tell anyone, not even Nanny. Mr. MacGowan said that if I told anyone I'd have to be sent away to a boarding school."

I felt sicker than ever. I could no longer look at my potted shrimps. "Mr. MacGowan's dead, Eleanor," I said. "It doesn't matter any more now. Nobody's going to send you away."

"Is he really dead?"

"Of course!"

"I won't be haunted by his ghost if I disobey him?"

"Never."

"I've been dreaming that his ghost comes back to haunt me," she said. "I've had horrid dreams ever since—"

"Since when?"

"Since Papa went mad," she said crying. "It was last autumn. He was helping me stick some new pressed wild flowers into my album, and he was telling me all the names in Latin and in English so that I could label them correctly. There was this lovely tall yellow flower, and when he looked at it he screamed and dropped it and said it was

574

a snake. Then he screamed again and started tearing at his clothes. He said he was being eaten by insects. Cousin Edith came in and Mr. MacGowan, and Cousin Edith dragged me out of the room and afterward Mr. MacGowan said I mustn't tell anyone."

"He did that," I said, "because if Mama had known about it she would have taken you away from Papa, and Papa at that time was trying to convince her that he could deprive her of her children unless she returned to him."

"But I can stay with Mama now, can't I? I don't have to see Papa any more?"

"Of course not. Papa's a drunkard and not fit to be in the same house as you." I still felt sick enough to vomit, and every muscle in my body was rigid with anger.

"John says Papa will come back," Eleanor was saying fearfully.

"That's not true. He won't come back. Mama's getting a divorce."

"A divorce?" I had thought I was giving her good news, but she was appalled. "Oh goodness, isn't that terribly wicked? Nanny says divorces never suit."

"It's the best Mama can do," I said rapidly. "It'll mean that you can stay with her and nobody can force you to see Papa."

She relaxed in relief. "I do love Papa, but I was so frightened of him in case he went mad again."

"I understand." I hugged her reassuringly.

"Mr. Drummond's not a drunkard too, is he?"

"No, he'll look after us well, you'll see. Everything will be fine once we're all home together again, and you won't have to worry about anything any more."

I know I comforted her when I said that, because she dried her eyes and started to eat her shrimps, and presently she even said how nice it was to have a little holiday by the sea.

I didn't tell my mother what Eleanor had said because I didn't want to upset her, and although I almost told Drummond that evening I didn't. I was too ashamed of my father to want to repeat the story, and besides, despite my favorable words about Drummond to John and Eleanor, I was still confused about him. When I went to bed that night I lay awake for a long time worrying in case Nanny should give in her notice once she realized my mother was living in adultery, and before I finally drifted into sleep I remember thinking numbly: If only John hadn't mentioned MacGowan and his little trees.

But then I slept, and when I awoke all thought of MacGowan and my father had been scrubbed from my mind. For at last it was time to go home to Cashelmara, and it seemed my long nightmare of uncertainty and anxiety was finally coming to an end.

III

I came home. But it was not as I thought it would be. The house was the same, and so were the horses in the stables, and although some of the servants were new they were all valley people and their faces were familiar to me. Even Flannigan the butler was soon to return, lured back by my mother. The view was as dazzling as I remembered, the lough set in the mountains like a precious stone in a heavy ring, and above the house in the woods the little chapel still stood bleakly above the family graves. Even the cobwebs decorating the musty pews still seemed spun in exactly the same way.

Yet everything was not the same. It was changed because my father was no longer there.

I walked in his garden and it was as if he walked beside me. I wandered across the "lake" lawn, past the blazing borders and up the stone steps to the Italian garden, serene amidst the larchwoods. All the lilies were blooming on the water, and beyond the little teahouse the view of the lough and mountains was framed in white marble. My fingers trailed across the sundial he had carved, and suddenly he was with me again, wearing his shabby work clothes, his long strong hands covered with dirt and his eyes very blue in his tanned face. I could remember wanting to carve yet having no talent for it, but he hadn't minded my failure. "You'll be good at all the things I was never good at," he had said, smiling at me, and when I had said, "But I want to be like you," he had said that wasn't important because the most important thing of all was that I should be myself. "If you try to be someone other than yourself you'll never be happy," he had said. "You've got to be honest with yourself so that you can be honest with other people."

I hadn't known what he had meant, and later when I had heard how he had abused my mother and indulged in disgusting practices his words had made even less sense to me.

I went back to the house, thinking I could escape him, but he was there too. I went to the nursery, and there was my beloved rocking horse he had made me long ago. I went to the library, and there were his dog-eared gardening books stacked on the window seat. Retreating to my bedroom, I began to sort through my old possessions—and there was the storybook about King Arthur that he had given me, and stuck inside were the sketches he had made of my pony. I opened a cupboard to shove the sketches out of sight, and out fell my photograph album, the pages flying in the sudden draft of air until it was lying open at the pictures of Eleanor's christening. I stooped to look. My mother had given me the photographs because I had wanted a picture of my aunt Marguerite, who had died when I was six, and there she was. I could see her standing beside my mother. My mother was holding Eleanor in her arms, and my father was standing next to her, his hand in mine. I wore a sailor suit. We were all smiling at the camera.

1879. Eight years ago. What had happened and why had everything gone so wrong? Was it all Mr. MacGowan's fault? Or had my father always been wicked and I had simply been too young to notice? Why was my father so wicked? And why, why, why couldn't I stop thinking about him when he revolted me so much?

My questions went on and on and on, but there were no imaginable answers, and finally I thought to myself in desperation: I've got to talk to someone about it. I must, or I'll go mad.

I went to Nanny. Nanny always had an answer for everything. Some of my earliest memories of nursery life consisted of me asking Nanny endless questions and Nanny providing sensible answers. ("Nanny, why is the sky blue?" "God made it that way, dear, because it's so restful on the eyes.")

"Nanny," I said, "I feel very angry with my father and I want to stop thinking about him but I can't. Is it wrong to feel so angry with him?"

" 'Honor thy father and thy mother,' " said Nanny.

"You mean it *is* wrong of me to feel angry with him."

"There's no need to feel angry, dear. Don't think about him at present."

"But I can't help it! Nanny, was he always so wicked?"

"Now, Ned dear, we won't talk about that. It's not fitting."

"But I want to talk about it! Why is he so wicked? I don't understand."

"Just don't worry your head about it, dear. It's not right for you to worry about such things, and I'm sure your Mama would be the first to agree."

"I suppose you now think Mama's very wicked too."

" 'Judge if ye be not judged,' " said Nanny.

"But, Nanny—"

"It's not for you and me to discuss such things," said Nanny firmly. "My station in life is to look after you children, and your

577

station in life is to be a good brother and a good son. So long as you try to do your duty everything else will take care of itself."

"But, Nanny, it's not taking care of itself! And how can I be a good son to my father in the circumstances? Every time I think of him I get upset. I can't sleep properly at night any more because I worry about it so much."

"Poor dear," said Nanny, kissing me. "You mustn't worry. I'll make you some nice hot milk tonight to help you sleep. Do you remember how you used to love your hot milk? You even liked the skin on the top! I never knew another child who liked the skin." I started to say something else, but she said quickly, "You'd better talk to your uncles when they come back from England. They're both good decent young men. You talk to them."

At least she was prepared to be charitable to my mother. I knew I should have been glad that I no longer had to worry about Nanny giving notice, but I was too busy worrying instead about what I was going to say to my uncles.

They came back a week later. My father had been installed in a London nursing home, and my uncles had spent long sessions with the family lawyer, Mr. Rathbone, to decide how the estate should be administered while my father was unfit. With my father's consent a trust had been set up with my uncles and my mother as trustees. My father had objected at first to my mother's appointment, but for practical reasons he had been advised to consent. My mother, living at Cashelmara, would be in a position to supervise whoever administered the estate, and Mr. Rathbone thought she should be put in a position where she could be held legally as well as morally responsible for the estate's affairs. My uncles had promised to visit Cashelmara regularly to look into estate matters, but it suited neither of them to live in Ireland. My uncle Thomas was a doctor who specialized in pathology, and my uncle David, who was a gentleman of leisure, had just fallen in love with a young lady who lived in London.

Both my uncles were prepared to appoint Drummond agent on a six months' trial.

"I suppose that was why you wanted to see us in private, Ned," said Uncle Thomas. "You wanted to have a further discussion about your mother's relationship with Drummond."

"No," I said. "I wanted to discuss my father's relationship with MacGowan."

There was a sharp, awkward silence. Neither of them moved.

578

"I've been thinking such a lot about my father," I said in a rush, "and there are so many things I'd like to know. For instance, was my father always as wicked as that? Was he as wicked with his friend Mr. Stranahan as he was with Mr. MacGowan? And if he was, why did he marry Mama in the first place? And why are people wicked like that? Why does it happen? And why did Mama marry him if—"

"My dear Ned," stammered Uncle David, "there's absolutely no need for you to know about such things at present. You're far too young."

"But I'm going to be fourteen soon," I said desperately, "and there are some things I've got to understand. I worry about them all the time—you don't realize." I stopped. It was too hard to go on, but presently Uncle Thomas said, not unkindly, "Your father's a troubled man. He's very ill. One can only hope that once he's restored to health he'll be able to make the moral effort to conquer his vices and lead a normal life. Meanwhile, David's right and there's absolutely no need for you to concern yourself with such things, just as there's no need for you to worry. No need at all."

"Yes, but . . ." I thought of my sleepless nights. "I worry about other things," I said. "I know there's no need, but I do."

"What other things?"

I opened my mouth, but no words came. After a long while I said, "Nothing," and turned away from them.

I tried to talk to my mother. I went to her boudoir when I knew Drummond was in Clonareen, and I asked her why my father had married her if he preferred men to women.

"I can't talk about that," she said.

"But . . ."

"Your father's been very cruel to me. I can't talk about him any more. It upsets me too much."

I went away. The next thing to happen was that I quarreled with my uncles. It was time for them to return to their home in England, and on their last afternoon at Cashelmara they suggested that arrangements could be made for me to go to boarding school.

"No, thank you," I said politely.

"I think it would be best," said Uncle Thomas, his glance flickering around the room as if he were assessing my surroundings and finding them wanting. "I'm afraid this isn't a suitable environment for you at present."

I said nothing.

"We weren't suggesting you should leave immediately," said Uncle David carefully. "We know how fond you are of your home. But perhaps in the new year—"

"No," I said.

"You must get a decent education and meet boys of your own class," said Uncle Thomas briskly. "It would be quite wrong for us to let you stay in this isolated place with some poor wretch of a tutor and only your brother and sisters for company."

I managed to hold my tongue.

"But why don't you want to go, Ned?" asked Uncle David kindly. "You'd like it! School's great fun."

"——" I said.

"You mind your language this instant!" exclaimed Uncle Thomas angrily. "You're not talking to Drummond! In fact when you behave like this you only make us more determined to remove you from Drummond's most unfortunate influence and take you to England at once!"

"I'm not going anywhere," I said. "I refuse."

"Why?"

"Because I've been dragged around from place to place for damn nearly two years and everything's changed and gone wrong and nothing's the same any more except Cashelmara—and if you try to drag me away from Cashelmara I'll run away, I'll fight you, I'll—"

"Ned—"

"Leave me alone!" I yelled as Uncle David tried to put a comforting arm around my shoulders, and I stumbled out of the room before I could burst into tears.

Running out of the house, I tore down the drive through the rain. I was crying like a baby by this time, but I was so upset I didn't care. I ran on, hardly able to see where I was going, and the hoarse sobs hurt my throat so that every gasp for breath was an ordeal. I stopped only when I reached the gates and cannoned without warning into someone coming the other way.

"Holy Mother of God!" Drummond exclaimed, astonished. "And what the devil would be the matter with you?"

IV

He made me sit down by the side of the drive and lean my back against a tree. Then, lighting a cigarette, he offered me a puff. He had done that once or twice in America as a treat, so I knew how to inhale without choking.

"Now," he said, sitting down beside me, "I've hardly ever seen

580

you shed a tear, and to be sure it's wonderful to know you're as human as the rest of us, but what's this particular tear in honor of—or is it best not to ask?"

"My uncles want to send me away to school in England," I said. "I don't want to go."

"Say no. They can't force you. They're not your guardians."

"I know I went to school in America, but that was different," I said. "I don't want to leave Cashelmara now."

"Indeed you don't! And why would anyone in his right mind want to be sent to England? Have another puff."

"My father wouldn't want me to be sent away," I said. "He hated school. He ran away twice. He told me. He said he'd never send me away. I've been thinking about my father such a lot, Mr. Drummond. I can't stop thinking about him." To my horror I began to cry again. I began to wonder if I was going mad. It wasn't like me to weep for no good reason. I wondered fearfully if it were some malignant early sign of effeminacy.

"What's worrying you?" said Drummond.

"My father's wickedness. His . . . drunkenness. Is it—would it be . . . hereditary?"

He roared with laughter. "All the sons of drunkards I knew grew up and took the pledge!"

"Then why do people become wicked? Drunkards, I mean."

He thought for a long moment before saying simply, "It's like an act of God."

"An act of God? My father's wickedness?" I screwed up my courage. "All of it?"

He thought again and then said firmly, "All of it."

"I don't understand."

"Well, you see, you can talk about sin and vice and wickedness, but they don't truly mean much. They're only words." He looked up the drive in the direction of the house, and suddenly I knew he was thinking of my mother. "They're words for priests," he said, "and for those who have never met a temptation they can't refuse. That's not a sneer at priests or good moral souls—to be sure we'd all like to live good lives and go to heaven at the end of them, but sometimes something happens which you have no power to change and then it's like being afflicted by an act of God and there's nothing you can do but make the best of it."

"I see," I said. "You mean it's like an incurable illness that isn't infectious. One has no control over it."

"Perhaps some people have. But others haven't, that I know very well."

"So my father would be one of those who haven't."

"Well, what do you think? Can you imagine any man turning his back on your mother unless he was struck down by an act of God with no control over his recovery? Jesus, it would take an act of God to explain such behavior!"

"Then it wasn't really my father's fault," I said. An enormous burden seemed suddenly lifted from my shoulders. "He didn't choose to be wicked. The act of God gave him no choice."

"That's right," said Drummond.

"I see. Mr. Drummond, about the act of God . . . Well, how soon does one know if one's afflicted? I mean, does it strike one suddenly—like lightning?" I added, groping for inspiration among better-known acts of God.

There was a pause. Again he smoked and thought about the question. I liked the way he did that.

"My father, for instance," I said. "Was he just like anyone else when he was younger?"

"I didn't know your father well," said Drummond at last, "but from what your mother says I'd guess the difference was part of him from the beginning although he never saw it till late in life."

"Why not? Is it so hard to tell? Surely there must be some way of knowing—symptoms . . ."

He looked at me. His eyes were very dark, and at the corners the skin was creased when he smiled. "You don't have to worry, Ned," he said, and it was like all those times when he had said, "I'll take you home to Cashelmara." It never occurred to me not to believe him.

I swallowed awkwardly. "Well, of course I wasn't worrying about myself, but . . . I just don't understand why my father didn't know he was different."

"Maybe he did know. But that doesn't really matter. All that matters is that for a while he didn't want to be different. That's why he got married. He wanted to be just like everyone else."

"But he shouldn't have got married, should he? That was wrong of him."

"It was a mistake. Your mother made a mistake too when she married him. Hell, we all make mistakes! It's only the saints in heaven who never put a foot wrong."

After a pause I said, "If I had a choice I'd never get married and then I'd never run the risk of marrying the wrong person. But I suppose I shall have to get married one day to provide an heir for Cashelmara."

"That would be thoughtful," he agreed, "and such a comfort he'll be to you in your old age."

"I hope it's not too difficult. Producing an heir, I mean."

"Easiest thing in the world. Some nice girl will do all the work for you, and afterward everyone will tell you how clever you are."

"That does sound easy, I suppose."

"If it was hard, do you suppose priests would spend so much time pushing people to the altar before the poor sinners put their immortal souls in peril?"

"Well, naturally I wouldn't indulge in temptations of that nature unless I was married. Anyway, I can't imagine ever finding a girl who would be worth such a fuss."

"What about Kerry Gallagher?"

"Oh, that's quite different," I said. "Kerry's my friend. May I have another puff of your cigarette, please?"

He let me have another puff, and presently I found myself asking him other questions about carnal matters as easily as if we were discussing the weather. The questions came tumbling out, one after the other, like a flock of sheep rushing pell-mell through a gate, and Drummond fielded them as deftly as any shepherd with a long crook.

At last I was able to say, "I feel much better."

"In that case let's go back to the house before the rain comes," he said, and I scrambled to my feet as the first drops began to patter through the woods.

Halfway up the drive I remembered my uncles. "Can you ask Mama to tell my uncles that I'm not going away?"

"I will indeed, and if she refuses—which she won't—I'll ask them myself."

"I shall be fine so long as I stay here," I said carefully, working it out. "But I don't want to go to England and I don't want to see my father. I do understand better about my father now, and I'm sorry he's afflicted; but I'd still prefer not to see him. Nobody's going to force me to see him, are they?"

"Nobody on earth," said Drummond, forgetting my aunt Madeleine, and we walked the last yards to my father's house side by side.

Chapter Two

I

"It's your duty to visit your father, Ned," said my aunt Madeleine. "He has asked to see you, and now that he's better there's no reason why you should stay away."

Some time had passed. It was January of 1888, six months after our return to Cashelmara, and we were all beginning to feel settled at last. I hadn't seen my uncles since October, when they had again tried to persuade me to go to school, but my mother had refused to accept this suggestion, and eventually a tutor had been hired. His name was Mr. Watson. He was elderly and fussy and made me work too hard, but I did my best to please him for fear that if I didn't my uncles would talk again of sending me away.

Meanwhile, my mother had obtained a divorce and absolute custody of all her children. According to the law it was impossible for her to get a divorce solely on the grounds of cruelty, which would have been the kindest, most discreet description of my father's conduct, and so she was obliged instead to reveal the full extent of his unnatural behavior. Despite the fact that my uncles persuaded my father not to fight her by cross-petitioning on the grounds of adultery, the scandal was immense, and no doubt my mother, who unlike my father had to be present at the hearing, suffered enormously. However, very little of the scandal filtered into Cashelmara. My mother even said to Drummond that it was the first time she had ever been glad of Cashelmara's remoteness. The newspapers were stopped for two weeks, three servants were dismissed on the spot for gossip, and the use of the word "divorce" was forbidden at all times.

"Why did Papa divorce us?" said Jane, confused. "Why doesn't he come to see us any more?"

"We won't mention that nasty word, dear," said Nanny, loyal to my mother, but I knew she was troubled because she said immediately afterward, "He's not divorcing any of you, Jane. You children have nothing to do with it."

But Eleanor didn't believe her. "It's my fault, isn't it?" she whispered to me when Nanny's back was turned. "Papa turned against me when I wouldn't kiss him goodbye."

I managed to persuade her that this was untrue, but afterward I asked my mother to explain to my sisters what the divorce meant so that they wouldn't invent horrifying stories about it.

My mother refused. "One question leads to another," she said. "They'll want to know why I wanted the divorce, and how could I possibly explain to them about MacGowan?"

"You could simply say Papa was a drunkard and that he'd been unkind to you."

"Ned dearest," said my mother coolly, "when I want your advice about how I should treat the younger children, rest assured that I shall ask you for it."

My mother was in a great state of nerves during that difficult time, and Drummond asked me in private to make allowances for her.

Drummond was very good to my mother. His behavior was immaculate. He was living in the elder MacGowan's stone house, which stood on the other side of the valley, and although he called at the Big House every day to see the estate books, which were kept in the library, he never spent the night and dined with my mother only twice a week. Before the servants he always addressed her as Lady de Salis. I was busy with my lessons during the week, but on Saturday morning he would take me for a ride around the estate and tell me what he had been doing and what he planned to do in the future. Once he even showed me some business letters he had written, but I think my mother helped him write those because they were always correctly phrased and spelled. He worked very hard and yet still found time for the children. My sisters had taken a great fancy to him, Eleanor soon overcoming her shyness and Jane even allowing him to hold Ozymandias, a great honor that I myself always took care to avoid like the plague. I don't dislike cats, but Ozymandias was surly and always molted orange hair over my best suit.

John was the only one who remained indifferent to Drummond, but I attributed that solely to the fact that Drummond knew nothing of gardening.

"Drummond seems to be turning out better than I'd dared hope," said Uncle Thomas during his autumn visit. "Perhaps we should encourage him to keep it up by giving him the money to rebuild his home. If some of his family came back to the valley he might have an additional motive for good behavior."

Drummond was delighted by the prospect, but when he wrote asking his sons to visit him and discuss the rebuilding neither young Maxwell nor Denis replied. So Drummond instead discussed it with me, and the next Saturday we rode along the road to Clonareen to visit the ruins of his old home.

I was well at ease with Drummond by this time. He was the Drummond who had rescued me in America, the Drummond who had brought me home. It no longer troubled me that he had had Mac-Gowan killed. MacGowan was bad, a villain who had deserved to die, and Drummond was good, a hero who deserved to live happily ever after with my mother. I felt much better now that I could see the situation so clearly in black and white. Everything was sane again. No more vertigo, no more confusion. Even my father had been put in his proper place—on the sidelines, far from my mother and me in the English garden of my uncle David's home. He had left the nursing home in London in December and had spent Christmas with both my uncles at the country house that had once belonged to my aunt Marguerite.

"I'm glad he's better," I said to my aunt Madeleine when she called to give us the news, and it was then that my aunt had made her appalling suggestion of a visit.

I told her politely that I preferred not to see him, but Aunt Madeleine waved this aside.

"That doesn't signify," she said briskly. "We all have to do things we don't like occasionally."

My aunt Madeleine was a formidable woman. She was older than my father and much smaller; I doubt if she was even five feet tall. She had a round curving bosom, a soft seductive voice and a mind like a Colt .44. She also had marvelous ankles. I had seen them only once, when she had climbed into a carriage during a high wind, but I had never forgotten them.

"My father has no right to see me after the way he's behaved," I said, becoming nervous.

"My dear child," said Aunt Madeleine, "it's not for you to pass judgment on your father. God will do that ably enough when the time comes."

We stared at each other. We were waiting in the drawing room while my mother brought the children down from the nurseries, and no one else was present.

"You have a duty to see him," persisted my aunt.

"Well, I won't," I said rudely, in a panic by this time. Although in theory I was prepared to be charitable toward my father, in practice the thought of seeing him again made me feel ill—though whether from shame, embarrassment or anger I neither understood nor cared.

"I'm very disappointed in you, Edward," said Aunt Madeleine.

No one ever called me by my full name. I hung my head mutely and stared at the carpet.

"Your father's done some dreadful things, but he's also known dreadful suffering. Having seen him so recently, I can vouch for the fact that he does repent very much for causing his children unhappiness. Need I remind you how devoted he is to you all? I can hardly think you've forgotten."

"I don't want him to be devoted to me," I mumbled. A tightness in my chest made breathing difficult. "I want him to leave me alone."

"That's most un-Christian as well as unfilial! If you could bring yourself to forgive him you would find it easy to love him again."

"I don't want to love him!" I shouted at her. "I can't love both him and my mother, I can't do it, it's too difficult, I must choose one or the other, I can't bear to be torn in two any more—"

"Dear child, nobody's tearing you in two!"

"You are!" I yelled savagely and rushed out of the room with my face awash with humiliating tears. This time I didn't wait to bump into Drummond. I saddled a horse and went looking for him. Eventually I met him riding up the road from the Fooey River.

"I won't see my father," I said after I had told him what had happened. "I won't."

"Indeed you won't," said Drummond. "Your mother won't allow it, and as she has absolute custody of her children there's nothing your meddlesome Aunt Madeleine can do. God save us all from muddleheaded, well-intentioned, interfering virgins!"

587

But to my horror Aunt Madeleine refused to take no for an answer. Soon she was requesting a private interview with my mother, and after they had quarreled sharply Aunt Madeleine left the dispensary in the sole care of Dr. Cahill and went to England to talk to my father.

I heard nothing more on the subject for a month, but just when I was feeling safe again the blow fell. Late one morning as I was drifting downstairs for lunch Drummond called to me from the library doorway.

"Come in here a moment, would you, Ned?" he said abruptly.

When I entered the room I saw that my mother was sitting in one of the high-backed chairs that flanked the marble fireplace. She looked very pale. Beyond her on the chimney piece the elephant clock slumbered below the portrait of my great-grandfather, Henry de Salis.

"There's something we want to discuss with you," said Drummond. He handed me a letter. "Read this."

I recognized my father's handwriting and shrank back.

"Go on."

I tried to read. I read five lines before I realized I hadn't understood a word. I went back to the beginning and tried again.

"Madam," my father had written, and this glimpse of his implacable antagonism toward my mother made me resent him enough to read on without a qualm. "Since it has become obvious that you have turned the children against me and driven even Ned to regard me with enmity, I must tell you that I have no intention whatever of accepting my present estrangement from them. My health is greatly recovered now. I have touched neither wine nor spirits for nearly six months and have every intention of abstaining from them in future. Since this is so I am advised that the judge in Chancery in Dublin will rule on application that I am no longer unfit to have control of the estate. As you are aware, the trust set up for the administration was temporary and dependent on the state of my health, and once the judge has terminated the trust on my behalf there would be nothing to prevent me from returning to reside at Cashelmara to be with my children. You and your lover could, of course, live where you pleased, but if you attempted to take the children with you I would apply for the order of custody to be reversed. Since you would be living in proven adultery and I would be living in an exemplary manner, I think you would find that any judge considering the children's welfare would this time be more inclined to lean in my favor.

"However, there are one or two matters which make this course undesirable for me as well as disastrous for you. First, I'm content here with David, and much as I miss my garden Cashelmara will always have too many sad memories of Hugh to make my return there comfortable. Second, I—unlike you—do have a genuine anxiety about the children's welfare, and I've no wish to embark on a course which might upset them unnecessarily. So let me make this suggestion: Permit the children to visit me at regular intervals, and I shall do nothing to have either the trust or the custody order set aside. I shall even make this concession: I won't ask to see the younger children before late summer if you send Ned to me for two weeks at Easter.

"Think carefully before you refuse my suggestion. As you know I can be very stubborn and this time I'm determined to get what I want.

"I would send my love to the children except that I've no doubt it would never reach them. I remain, etc. DE SALIS."

I looked up. I saw the mute appeal in my mother's eyes and realized with fright that she was terrified. I glanced at Drummond. He too was watching me intently. He was leaning against the huge desk, his arms folded across his chest. There was a small tear in his dirty riding breeches, and his neckcloth was tied so carelessly that I could see the dark hairs below his throat.

"This is your aunt Madeleine's doing," he said. It wasn't until he spoke that I realized how angry he was. "She's a meddlesome old witch and no mistake. What she needs is a good—"

He said what my aunt Madeleine needed. I had never before heard him use such language in front of my mother, and I was deeply embarrassed. My cheeks burned. I stared down at the letter again and tried to think what I could say.

"This hand he's trying to deal us is no goddamned good," said Drummond. "I can deal us a better one than that, but I'll need all the help I can get to push it through. Your help, to be exact."

My mother was looking at me in mute appeal again. I tried to speak but could not.

"You see why it's no good, don't you?" he was saying. "Even if your mother gives in to him and let's him see the children whenever he likes, there's nothing to stop him turning around later and tossing your mother out of Cashelmara. To be sure he gives us his word he won't do it, but how much is his word worth? Precious little, as your mother found out to her cost in the past. No, he's posed us a problem and there's only one solution: He's got to hand the estate over to you, Ned, and it's got to be done legally so he can't have it back whenever the fancy takes him."

"Your father would sign a deed ceding you the estate, Ned," said my mother carefully. "Since Patrick has no real interest in Cashelmara he surely won't object—particularly if we promise in exchange to allow him to see the children whenever he likes."

"Understand?" said Drummond. "We deal him a hand that suits us all—he cedes the estate, we send the children. We get security, he gets what he wants. We'll play it fair and square—except that he's bound to be suspicious of any suggestion that comes from your mother, so we thought it would be best if the suggestion came from you. Don't worry—I'll tell you what to say. In fact, why don't you sit down at the desk here and we'll do it now? I've got the pen and ink ready."

I sat down at the desk. My great-grandfather's eyes watched me from the portrait on the wall. I picked up my father's pen and dipped it in the silver inkstand that was engraved with my grandfather's name. Around us the house was quiet and still.

"Start how you like," said Drummond. " 'Dear Papa,' or however you want to address him."

I sat there looking at the blank paper. The ink began to dry on the nib.

"Ned?" said my mother.

I thought: I know I can trust him. He brought me home. He wants to help me. He loves my mother. I must have someone I can trust, and where would I be if I could no longer trust him?

I dipped the pen in the ink a second time and wrote, "Dear Papa." That was when I knew I could write nothing else. I looked at the two words for a long time and then I laid down my pen.

"What's troubling you?" said Drummond.

I couldn't speak.

"Don't you want to help your mother?"

"Yes," I said. "I'll go and see my father, just as he wants, and I'll make him promise to let her stay here."

"Sonny, his promise isn't any good. Your mother's going to worry herself crazy. Now pick up that pen and let's get this finished. I know you want the best for your mother."

I didn't move. I couldn't. Tears blurred my eyes.

"Don't press him if he doesn't want to, Maxwell," said my mother's voice from a long way away. "I'll write to Patrick myself."

"It would look better if—"

"I know. But he doesn't want to."

I ran out of the room. I ran into the garden, my father's garden, and he was there waiting for me, just as he always used to be, very kind and gentle, and his hand was warm and firm in mine. We walked across the lawn and I was so happy to be with him, but when we turned the corner of the fuchsia hedge I suddenly realized I was alone. I brushed my hand dizzily across my eyes, and that was when I knew I couldn't have seen him because my eyes were blind with tears.

I shut my eyes, sat down and waited for the vertigo to pass. After a long time I was able to think: Drummond only wanted to do the best for my mother. That was when I knew I had recovered and that when I opened my eyes I would be able to see everything clearly in black and white again.

But that night I dreamed, and although the dream was in black and white everything was reversed so that black became white and white became black. I was back in New York, back among the worst memories of my life, and the trees of Gramercy Park were stirring gently in the evening breeze. I said to the man at my side, "I don't want to go to the restaurant. I don't want to have dinner with you," but he only smiled and gripped my arm and dragged me on. We walked down the street and I saw the sign that said RYAN's and there was a doorway. "I won't go in," I said, but he only smiled again and dragged me in, and there were the imitation Tiffany lamps, a dozen of them, huge bloated lamps in heavy sullen colors, and the white table-cloths, bleak as snow and stark as death. The man sat opposite me. He was ugly and cruel, but I couldn't escape. I had to sit there listening to him, and as I listened his soft Irish voice recited an unending stream of hard, brutal, sickening truths. Finally I managed to run away. I ran and ran, but I had to stop to vomit, so he caught up with me, and when he spun me around to face him I saw—in my dream—that it was not the Drummond I knew at all. At first I thought it was a stranger, but then I saw the little Christmas tree in his hands and I knew who it was.

It was MacGowan. Drummond had become MacGowan. My mother had become my father. Everyone was interchangeable. Black and white no longer existed. Everything was red—scarlet—crimson —bloodshot—

I woke up screaming.

Fortunately no one heard. I would have died of shame if they had. Lighting my lamp, I turned it up as high as it would go as I waited for the dawn.

Yet even when dawn came the nightmare didn't recede as nightmares usually do but remained with me in my memory to be dragged around, like some macabre ball and chain, wherever I chose to go.

II

"Dear Pudding-Face," I wrote to Kerry Gallagher, my friend in Boston. "Thanks for your last letter. I certainly hope your father becomes Mayor. Please wish him luck for me in the elections. My father is better now, and I am supposed to go to England to see him at Easter. He says he will come home to Cashelmara if he doesn't see us children, but that wouldn't suit, so I am going to see him and my mother is going to ask him to give the estate to me so that he can't turn my mother out. My mother has gone to England to talk to my uncles about this. It's a pity everyone is in such a muddle, but I expect it will sort itself out. I'm learning about Africa in Geography. It's a peculiar place, even odder than America (ha!). I hope you have a nice Easter. Remember last year when we were both so poorly after eating all of Ellie-Mae's pecan pie? They don't make pecan pie here. Sometimes I wish I was in Boston. Please give my kindest regards to your father, your mother, Clare, Connie and Donagh. I remain your affec. friend, BLUEBEARD."

The reference to Bluebeard was an old joke between us dating from the time I had expressed an antipathy to marriage and said I hoped no woman would ever lose her head over me. Kerry had drawn pictures of me walking up the aisle with half a dozen headless brides.

When my mother returned from England she told me she had promised to send the children regularly to visit my father, and my father in his turn had agreed to cede the estate to me. My mother hadn't seen him, but my uncles had acted as intermediaries.

"My uncles didn't mind the estate being ceded to me?" I asked. "After all, Papa didn't have to do it, did he? He could have gone to court to get the custody order changed while still keeping the estate. He said so in his letter."

"He also said in his letter he had no real desire to return to Cashelmara, and besides there was no guarantee that the judge would amend the custody order in his favor. And the scandal of another court case! Thomas and David both thought it would have been intolerable. They were glad to accept any proposal that excluded going to court, and in the end they persuaded your father to agree with their point of view." She explained that the estate had been ceded to me by creating another trust to last until I was twenty-one, and she and my uncles were trustees, just as before.

"So Mr. Drummond got the deal he wanted after all," I said. "I knew he would."

"He only wants us to feel secure at Cashelmara, darling."

"Yes. How often will I have to go to England to see Papa?"

"That hasn't been arranged yet."

"But it must have been arranged! Surely my father would never have agreed to cede the estate unless he'd established exactly when we would visit him and for how long!"

My mother looked uncomfortable. "Yes, there was an arrangement, but . . . Ned, I would really prefer not to talk about this just now."

I stared at her. "But I'm going to see him for two weeks at Easter, aren't I?"

"I'm still corresponding with your father about that."

"But—"

"Ned, please! You have no right to cross-examine me like this! We'll discuss it later."

I went away without another word.

I had no appetite for lunch, and in the afternoon Mr. Watson said it was a pity I was still unable to distinguish between the House of York and the House of Lancaster. I never did understand the Wars of the Roses.

That evening Drummond came to dinner. He had come to dinner every night since my mother had returned with the news that the estate had been ceded to me, but although I dined with them I always retired to my room afterward, so I never knew how late he stayed. That night I was preparing to retreat as usual when Drummond, ignoring the port decanter, suggested we all go to the drawing room together for half an hour.

Drummond never normally ignored the port decanter.

"I do have an essay I must write for Mr. Watson," I said.

"I'll speak to Mr. Watson for you, darling," said my mother. "I don't think you should do schoolwork in the evenings anyway."

I said nothing. We went to the drawing room. Drummond lighted a cigarette without asking my mother's permission, and flinging himself down on the couch, he put his feet up on the smallest of the zebrawood quartetto tables.

"I hear you were asking your mother today about your Easter visit to England," he said, blowing smoke at the ceiling.

"I didn't mean to annoy her," I said. "I only wanted to know where I stood."

"Of course you did! And I'm sure you didn't annoy her."

I waited. She looked at Drummond. Drummond blew some more smoke at the ceiling.

"Well, it's like this, Ned," he said, saying what my mother had felt herself unable to say. "We're thinking it's best you didn't go to England at present. Isn't that the truth, sweetheart?"

"It would be so upsetting for you, Ned," said my mother. "You know how upset you always become whenever your father's name is mentioned. In the circumstances I think it would be wrong of me to allow you to go."

I had suspected the truth for some hours, but hearing it still shocked me. "But my visit was all arranged," I heard myself say. "You promised him I would go."

She again looked at Drummond for help.

"Faith, Ned, be honest!" he exclaimed. "You don't want to see your father, do you? Well, don't act as if you did!"

"No," I said, "I didn't want to see him, but I'd got used to the idea because there seemed to be no alternative. And as far as I'm concerned there's still no alternative. I can't draw back now."

"Ned, I do understand how you must feel," said my mother, "but I really cannot, in all conscience, allow you to go."

"You gave him your word!"

"She gave him no word that she isn't morally entitled to break for the sake of you children," said Drummond. He had taken his feet off the table and had tossed his cigarette into the fire. "And she gave him no word in writing. Your uncles were the ones who made all the promises, and as far as you're concerned they have no right to promise anything, since they're not your guardians. It's for your mother to make the decisions, and your welfare's got to come first."

"Very well," I said. "If that's the case you'll let me leave. It would upset me more to stay behind than it would upset me to go."

"That's hard to believe!" said Drummond.

"Just because you're a liar you needn't think everyone else tells lies too!"

"Ned!" my mother gasped.

"Mama, do you really think I'm so stupid that I can't see what Mr. Drummond's done? He's tricked my father. You've both tricked

594

him. You got him to cede me the estate by making promises you had no intention of keeping, and you used my uncles as cat's-paws. It was a shoddy low-down piece of double-dealing, and I refuse to be a part of it by staying here in Ireland instead of going to England as you promised!"

Drummond was on his feet in a flash. "Sarah, leave us."

"Maxwell, Ned didn't mean—"

"Leave us!"

My mother backed trembling from the room.

"Right," said Drummond the instant the door closed. "Get this straight. One: You never talk to either me or your mother like that again, do you understand? Never. Two: You do as you're told and no nonsense. Three: You're not seeing your father and you're not to have any communication with him. There's no reason why your mother should consent to allowing a boy your age to keep company with a pervert. Four: If you disobey any part of what I've just said, I'll give you the best thrashing you've ever had in your life, and don't think I wouldn't dare because I would. I've always believed in going easy on a boy as far as possible, and you'd be the first to admit I've always gone easy on you, but when I draw the line I draw the line and I'm drawing it now, so you'd better think twice before you cross it. Have I made myself clear?"

After a pause I said, "Yes."

He relaxed. "Just remember that your mother wants only to do what's best for you," he said, "and I want only to help her. Go to your room and think about what I've done. I've won you the right to stay at Cashelmara in peace without living in constant fear of being turned out or confronted with your father—and wasn't this what you were always wanting? Well, in that case don't turn on me now and call me names. Good night."

"Good night, sir," I said.

I found myself in the gallery above the hall. My mother was there waiting to speak to me, but I wouldn't stop. I ran to my room and locked my door and sat in the dark on the edge of the bed.

After a while I wondered if I would feel better if I wrote to my father and apologized for not being able to visit him, but when I found pen and paper I realized I could write nothing. If my mother found out I had written to my father she might turn against me. Besides, supposing my father tried to use my letter against her? He might take it to the judge and the fighting would begin all over again. I didn't want to live with my father, didn't truly even want to see him. Drummond had been right. Drummond was always right, really. Best for my mother, best for me.

I suddenly realized I was very frightened of Drummond—but not of the Drummond who had thrown his hat in the air and bought the violets for my mother. I was frightened of the other Drummond, the Drummond of the Tiffany lamps and the loaded gun and the soft-spoken threats. I wondered what had happened to that gun. I knew he had brought it to Ireland, but it had disappeared because he was able to tell the District Inspector without a qualm that he had no gun of any kind.

More lies. Lies were never right; Nanny had always said that. Murder was never right either.

Better not to think of that.

At ten o'clock my mother tapped on my door and asked if she could come in.

"Are you still angry with me?" she said, and when I shook my head dumbly she took me in her arms and held me close.

"I'm sorry I upset you, Mama," my voice said some time later.

"Oh darling, I know you didn't mean it. You'll apologize to Mr. Drummond, won't you?"

I said I would, and as she smiled at me I noticed she was looking extraordinarily beautiful. As a child I had taken my mother's beauty for granted, but now as I was leaving childhood I began to see her beauty with new eyes. By this time she was in her late thirties, but one didn't think of age when looking at my mother. One thought instead of her hair, which was dark brown with such a fine sheen that it never looked dull but always seemed to glow when it caught the light. And one thought too of her skin, which wasn't wanly pale, as so many ladies' complexions were, but creamily pale, with the faintest suggestion of an olive tint. And lastly one thought of her figure, which even I, young as I was, knew instinctively was perfect despite the fact that she was no longer as slender as she had been when I was very small. That evening she was wearing an evening gown with the thinnest of shawls, and I could see the long line of her neck and the dark curve between her breasts.

"Good night, darling. Give me one last kiss."

I offered my cheek dutifully. "Mama," I said afterward, "if Mr. Drummond wanted to beat me, would you let him?"

"Well, I . . . that would depend, of course, on what you'd done, but if you deserved it—and I'm sure Maxwell wouldn't do such a thing unless you deserved it—"

596

"I see."

"He has a father's responsibility toward you, Ned. It's only reasonable that he should have a father's rights to go with it."

"Yes."

She went away. I blew out the candle and crept into bed. Eventually dawn came and I fell asleep soon after five-thirty.

At nine Mr. Watson was asking me again about the Wars of the Roses, and outside in my father's garden a steady rain was falling from desolate skies.

III

Yet in spite of the disastrous Easter, the summer was more fun than I had dared hope.

Denis Drummond came to stay.

He arrived at the end of April when I should have been in England, and although he stayed with his father at old MacGowan's house, Drummond brought him to Cashelmara every day after breakfast. He was my age and had pale hair, freckles and not a word to say for himself. I felt sorry for him.

"Do you ride?" I asked hopefully. The chance to be friends with a boy my own age seemed too good to be missed, and I was determined to be hospitable.

He shook his head.

"Fish? Swim? Boat?"

He kept shaking his head.

"What would you like to do?"

"Go back to Dublin," he said.

Drummond overheard and was furious. He gave Denis a long lecture to the effect that Denis should be grateful for the opportunity to spend time in the country on a gentleman's estate instead of being cooped up in a dirty smelly city.

"And here's Ned being so friendly to you!" said Drummond angrily. "Mend your manners and be civil to him this minute!"

Denis's mouth drooped at the corners.

"Speak up and stop sulking!"

What astounded me most about this conversation was that it was so unlike Drummond. When he reprimanded me he did so when we were alone, and on the rare occasions when he had seen me as unhappy as Denis obviously was he had been kindness itself.

"We never did get on," said Denis later as we sat on the edge of my bed drinking porter out of tooth mugs. "It's disappointed he always was in me, and when I tried to please it made no difference."

"He was awfully anxious to have you here," I said, hoping to cheer him up. "He was so looking forward to it. You should have seen how disappointed he was when your brother didn't come."

"Max wouldn't. He's twenty years old now, and it's easy to stand up against your father when you're twenty, I shouldn't wonder. My sisters—the ones who aren't married—they would have come, but my mother said no because of the immorality." He blushed. "She said I wasn't to go either, but I said I must. I wanted to please, but now I see I needn't have troubled myself."

"Well, *I'm* glad you came," I said and offered him an unfinished packet of cigarettes that Drummond had left lying around some days ago.

After that we became friends, and presently I showed him how to ride, and he said horses were more fun than donkeys. We used to ride to Clonareen, and soon he was introducing me to his cousins among the O'Malleys. It was good to meet more boys of my own age, and we quickly formed what the Americans call a "gang," a group who find one another's company congenial and have interests in common. The others weren't all O'Malleys. There was an O'Connor and an O'Flaherty and a Costelloe, and after a week or two some of the Joyces approached me with suitable tokens of friendship—a relic box and a fine spade—and asked to be admitted to the crowd. The O'Malleys at once said no, but I overruled that. The O'Malleys and the Joyces were always clinging to their absurd feud, and I didn't see any sense in it.

Accordingly I allowed the Joyces to join us, but I made them swear all kinds of oaths to keep the peace and insisted that the O'Malleys make similar pledges. I did wonder how long they would stick to their vows, but there was no trouble. In their parents' presence they had to pretend to hate each other, but when there was no one over eighteen in sight they were the best of friends.

There was a ruined cabin on the hillside above Cashelmara, and we made that our headquarters. We would meet there, go rabbit hunting or fishing and then return to the cabin to cook what we'd caught. I supplied the porter (Drummond had forbidden me to touch poteen before I was sixteen) and commissioned one of the boys to buy cigarettes from a tinker who traded in them. But the tinker passed through the valley only once a month, so cigarettes were scarce. Usually we would share one cigarette, taking one puff before passing it on, and once the cigarette was smoked to the butt the storytelling would begin as we sat around the fire. The stories were usually the kind where the wretched Irish were oppressed by the wicked English, but I used to talk about the American West, and they liked that. Custer's Last Stand was a great favorite, and I invented all kinds of nonsense about Jesse James.

It was a grand summer. Of course I had to do my lessons, but Denis shared my tutor, and that made even the lessons fun. However, at last the lessons stopped, Mr. Watson went to England for his annual holiday and Denis and I were free to do as we pleased.

In the middle of August Denis's mother wrote that she wanted him to come home.

"You don't want to go, do you, Denis?" said Drummond, putting it the wrong way.

"If Ma's begging, how can I refuse?" said Denis.

"Oh, and is it begging she is!" said Drummond, getting angry as usual. "She has Max and Bridget and Mary Kate. Why shouldn't you be staying here a little longer?"

"Because I don't want to," said Denis, though I knew he did.

"That's a bloody ungrateful thing to say!" said Drummond.

"What's so ungrateful about wanting to go home?"

"This valley's your home!"

"Not while my mother can't come back and live here with you as she wants!"

"She wants no such thing!"

Denis, cowed, said nothing.

"The insolence of it!" said Drummond, still furious, but he gave up arguing and walked defeated from the room.

After Denis had gone Drummond said to my mother, "I don't understand that boy," and I thought, No, you don't. I missed Denis very much, and the perplexing part was that I knew in spite of all his complaints that Drummond missed him too. I had been avoiding him as much as possible all summer, but now he turned to me for consolation, and it was harder to escape. I made excuses as often as I could, but sometimes I had no choice but to go out riding with him—not that I minded greatly, for he always took pains to be pleasant, but as time passed I found myself becoming increasingly ill at ease with him. This wasn't simply because of his double-dealing with my father. I still resented that, but by that time I had put the incident behind me and resolved not to think of it. My father had been silent all summer, and my aunt Madeleine reported without comment that he had had another lapse into drunkenness.

"But you mustn't worry about that, Ned," said my mother. "There's no need for you to worry."

She glanced at Drummond as she spoke, and suddenly I knew I was ill at ease with Drummond because I was ill at ease with her. It was their relationship that I found increasingly disturbing. At first I could see no reason why it should suddenly begin to trouble me when I had long since decided to accept it, but dimly I came to realize that the change lay not in them but in me.

I was becoming abnormally sensitive to every nuance of my mother's manner toward him. I intercepted every meaningful look, studied every smile, even noticed the exact style of each low-cut evening gown. I tried not to, but I couldn't help myself. I became acutely aware of my mother's physical attributes and thought lingeringly about them at odd moments during the day. Worst of all was at night when I would lie in bed and remember scenes from the past— Newport and Drummond's rough sunburned hand resting grossly on my mother's slim white arm; Drummond's tiny apartment in New York, the bed creaking in the room next door as I lay awake on the couch in the darkness; the large room in Boston where Drummond and my mother had lain in bed together. Nowadays I was always thinking of them in bed together. I despised myself for thinking about such things, but my mind and self-esteem were ill-matched that summer.

"I must be sensible," I said aloud to myself as I hurried uphill to the ruined cabin to meet my friends. "I won't think about it."

But then, worse still, I started noticing other women besides my mother. I noticed that Miss Cameron, the governess, had a flat chest and that Bridie, the scullery maid, didn't, and I caught another glimpse of Aunt Madeleine's legendary ankles when she came to Cashelmara to tea. And each time I found myself dwelling on these feminine attributes the memories would start flickering through my mind again, the creaking bed, the hand on the arm, all the intimate looks I had once been too young to read.

"Hell and damnation," I would mutter to myself as I lay awake in the dark, and by an effort of will power that amounted almost to hypnosis I would blot the images from my mind. But when I fell asleep the dreams would be waiting for me, dreams sweating with obscenity, and in the morning I would tell myself in misery that there was nothing so wretchedly disgusting in all the world as being fourteen and a half with both one's mind and one's body living uncontrollable lives of their own.

But the obscene dreams were better than the dream with the Tiffany lamps. That dream recurred at least once a month, but by this time I was used to it and never let it frighten me. Sometimes I even managed to wake myself before the dream had progressed to the interior of the restaurant, and then I didn't feel disturbed by the dream at all, only annoyed that it had interrupted my rest.

My uncle Thomas came for a visit after Denis had left, but Uncle David stayed behind to look after my father.

"Is everything well, Ned?" said Uncle Thomas when we were alone together. "You've been very quiet."

"I'm fine," I said. "Fine."

"Good. I'm glad to say Drummond still seems to be most conscientious about the estate, although it's a pity he's not educated enough to keep better records. However, I've had a word with your mother, and she's offered to make sure that the books are correctly kept. It was unfortunate she changed her mind about letting the children see Patrick, but I suppose she was entitled to be reluctant, and of course it's no use considering the possibility of a visit now that he's drinking again."

I said nothing.

"I thought I would mention it," said Uncle Thomas, "in case you felt guilty about refusing to see him at Easter. I do understand that it must be peculiarly upsetting for you to be confronted with your father at present. But perhaps later . . ."

I opened my mouth to tell him the truth but shut it again. If I told the truth my mother might get into trouble.

"Let's talk of something else," said Uncle Thomas hastily, mistaking the cause of my embarrassment. "How did you get on with Drummond's boy?"

"Very well, thank you."

"Good. Pity there's no boy of your own class here. If you've changed your mind about school—"

"No."

Uncle Thomas departed at the end of August, and two days later my cousin Edith, Hugh MacGowan's widow, arrived at Clonagh Court.

I hadn't seen her since before I left for America, for directly after MacGowan's murder she had gone to Edinburgh, where she had a townhouse. However, recently my mother had written to her to ask if she would remove her possessions from Clonagh Court since it was obvious she had no intention of living there again. Drummond had

had the idea that instead of rebuilding his old home he might use Clonagh Court as his official residence. Having been built as the dower house, it was much grander than old MacGowan's cottage, where he had been living since our return from America.

Cousin Edith had plump hips and no waist, and when she moved you could hear her corsets creak. She had large breasts of no particular shape, and I felt absolutely sure her thighs would be vast too. When she called at Cashelmara I spent the first five minutes imagining her wearing nothing but a pair of black stockings, and so absorbed was I with this repellant but irresistible mental exercise that it was some time before I heard a single word she was saying.

"Ned!" said my mother reprovingly from a long way away. My mother was in a great gale because she had never thought Edith would call. In the past they had been sworn enemies and barely on speaking terms.

"I'm sorry, Cousin Edith," I said. "What did you say?"

Cousin Edith asked me what I did with myself when I wasn't taking lessons with Mr. Watson.

"I go fishing and hunting," I said. "Sometimes I take the curragh out on the lough."

"Alone?"

"No, I have several friends."

"What sort of friends?"

"Edith," said my mother, "I must show you some of Jane's paintings. They're so clever for a little girl not yet seven."

"What are your friends' names, Ned?"

"Joyce, O'Malley, Costelloe . . ." Something in my mother's expression stopped me. "Just valley names," I mumbled. I could have kicked myself for not realizing that Cousin Edith would think my friends very low. I hadn't wanted to embarrass my mother.

"I think I'll just run up to the nursery and bring the other children down," said my mother. "Why don't you come with me, Ned? Excuse us, Edith."

"Oh, Ned, you can't leave me alone!" said Cousin Edith with an awful attempt at a winsome smile. "Where's your chivalry? Very well, Sarah, run along and fetch the children."

"Well, perhaps—"

"Oh, please! I should so love to see the dear little things!" said Cousin Edith, and my mother, outmaneuvered, retreated with reluctance.

"Well, Ned," said Cousin Edith, "I declare your dear mother looks very well. So nice, is it not, that she has Mr. Drummond to look after her?"

"She does look well, I agree."

"Do you see much of Mr. Drummond?"

"Now and then."

"When is now," said Cousin Edith, "and when is then?"

"I see him at dinner."

"Every night? How nice! And breakfast too?"

"No."

"He breakfasts alone with your mother?"

"No, at his house."

"Come, Ned, you can be honest with me! We both know how matters are arranged, don't we?"

I didn't answer.

"Does your mother take you to church every Sunday?"

"There's a service in the chapel once a month."

"Does your mother go?"

"Nanny takes us," I said and immediately wondered why I hadn't lied and said yes.

"I'm so glad your dear mother isn't hypocritical," said Cousin Edith. "I confess I deplore hypocrisy. Do you like Mr. Drummond?"

"I like him the hell of a lot better than I liked Mr. MacGowan," I said before I could stop myself, "and if you've finished insulting my mother, perhaps you'd be good enough to leave."

"Ned! How rude!"

I said a word that should never have been said. It was stupid of me, for I played straight into her hands.

"And coarse!" said Cousin Edith. "Worse than a guttersnipe!"

I walked out.

Two weeks later, soon after Cousin Edith had paid a visit to Surrey, my father informed my mother through his solicitors that he was taking steps to remove the children from her custody and to have the deed which had ceded Cashelmara to me declared invalid by the Court of Chancery.

Chapter Three

"He'll never succeed," said Drummond. "The deed was legal enough, and how can he take the children when he's still a drunkard?"

"He's not asking for the children for himself," said my mother, the shadows dark beneath her eyes. "He wants them to be made wards of court so that a guardian can be appointed."

"They can never prove that you're not a wonderful mother to those children!"

"But the adultery, Maxwell," my mother whispered, and to my horror I saw she was crying. "Edith will testify . . . I knew she only came to spy."

"Yes, and she found out that I don't live here, that I never spend a night beneath this roof!"

"But the servants . . . That maid I dismissed because she interrupted us—she went straight to Edith, I'm sure of it, and that was why Edith called." She was weeping so hard she could no longer speak.

"Mama," I said, stumbling over to her. I was so distressed I hardly knew what I said. "You mustn't cry. Papa's made these threats before and they never came to anything. Please don't cry. Please."

"He'll never let me have any peace," she said. "So long as he lives I'll never have a moment's rest."

"Sweetheart, you know it's not as black as that," said Drummond, stooping over her. "Don't you trust me to find a way out of our troubles as usual?"

"There can't be many ways left," she said. "I'm going to lose the children, and if he turns us out of Cashelmara I'll lose you too."

"Sarah—"

"There wouldn't be any money," she said, sobbing, "and I'd be too much of a burden to you. I'm no longer young. You'll leave me."

He shook her by the shoulders. "I'll never leave you," he said. "Understand? Never. How many more times do I have to say that?"

"But if there's no money—"

"I'll make money. Meanwhile, we're staying here."

"But if Patrick has the deed set aside—"

"It's all talk! All he ever does is talk, and to be sure he could never have the deed set aside!"

"He could say he was unwell at the time—not in his right mind, that the deed was extorted from him by fraud, duress . . . Oh, Maxwell, there are any number of excuses he can make, and Mr. Rathbone's such a clever lawyer!"

"There's more than one clever lawyer in the world, and we'll take all the others."

She was in his arms, and when I saw her expression I turned away and peered blindly out of the window. In the silence that followed I knew he was kissing her. I could see their bodies reflected dimly in the glass of the window pane, and although in my discomfort I willed them to stop they seemed to have forgotten I was in the room.

My embarrassment increased until it was intolerable. Not looking at them, I blurted out, "I could go and see my father and beg him to let things be. Perhaps he'd listen to me and be generous."

The bodies in the reflection separated. My mother's voice said bitterly, "Your father would never be generous now. Matters have gone too far. He wouldn't even believe us if we promised to let you visit him."

"We must consult the lawyers," said Drummond, and the next day my mother departed for Dublin to take legal advice. It was thought better that she travel alone. It would only have given rise to more gossip if Drummond had accompanied her, and she wanted to create the best possible impression on her lawyers.

Two days later my aunt Madeleine arrived to say that not only had Cousin Edith returned to Clonagh Court but that she had brought my father with her.

My father had wanted to come at once to Cashelmara to remove his children, but Aunt Madeleine had managed to persuade him to wait until she had spoken to my mother.

"But my mother's gone to Dublin to see her lawyers," I said, "and I don't know when she'll be back."

We were in the morning room downstairs. The cherubs of the china clock were busy striking eleven o'clock, and beyond the windows the rain blew mistily across the untrimmed lawn.

"Perhaps it's a good thing your mother's not here," said Aunt Madeleine surprisingly. "If she were she would without doubt have a nervous collapse, and that would only serve to complicate the situation. Let me see. I'd better arrange with your nanny—Mrs. Gray, isn't it?—for you all to go to Salthill for a few days. Sea air is most bracing for children at this time of year."

I stared at her. "You mean—I don't understand—you don't think Papa should see us?"

"Certainly not! First of all, he has absolutely no right to come here and abduct you in direct defiance of the court order, and second he's drinking very heavily again and it would be most unsuitable if he took charge of you. The situation is quite different from that time earlier in the year when he was sober and requesting to see you in a proper manner. Of course, Edith is entirely to blame for the present distressing dilemma. Your uncles were firmly opposed to your father leaving England, but Edith influenced him, and once your father had made up his mind there was nothing your uncles could do to dissuade him. The best that can be done now is to remove the children to a secret destination and then talk to Patrick until he sees reason. He must realize that this notion of abduction simply won't do. If he wishes to get the custody order amended he must do it through the courts."

"But, Aunt Madeleine . . . you do think, don't you, that we should go on living with Mama? I wouldn't mind visiting my father, but—"

"Of course it would be unsuitable if you lived with him permanently. He must stop drinking again before that idea can be considered. As for your mother, I hardly know what to think. I cannot condone her liaison with that man, and I think it's very bad that you should be confronted with it daily. John doesn't matter—he'll always be too young to understand—but it's a shocking example to those girls growing up and God only knows what effect it's having on you.

One can only pray, as I do daily, that you survive with your moral standards untarnished."

"I don't want to be taken away from my mother," said my voice.

"No, of course you don't, and in spite of all I've just said I don't think you should be. This ceaseless tug of war between your parents is even worse for you than seeing daily examples of your mother's infatuation with Maxwell Drummond, and that's what I must persuade Patrick to accept when I return to Clonareen. Now, I think I should speak to Nanny to arrange for your departure to Salthill as soon as possible."

We left for Salthill that afternoon, and Drummond, to my relief, rode with us. Aunt Madeleine was opposed to this, but we had to spend the night at Oughterard, and traveling is difficult enough with three young children without the complications arising from an overnight stop. Drummond found rooms for us, saw that the horses were properly attended to and tipped all the right people so that we received good service. I don't know what I would have done if he hadn't been there. When we reached Salthill the next morning he installed us in a quiet hotel near the promenade and stayed until Miss Cameron and Mr. Watson arrived with the luggage in the extra carriage, which had been hired from Leenane. It was only then that he told me he would be leaving.

"It would be nice to spend a few days with you by the sea," he said to me, "but I'd best go home in case your father makes more mischief."

"I wish I knew when Mama will be coming home from Dublin."

"She might be in Galway tomorrow. I thought that before I go back I would leave a note for her at the Great Southern Hotel to tell her where you are, so maybe in a few hours she'll be arriving here to look for you."

He was right. She came. She was red-eyed from weeping, and her clothes were shabby after the long train journey and she hadn't bothered to do her hair carefully so that it fell down as soon as she took off her hat.

"You look very tired, my lady," said Nanny at once. "You'd better lie down and rest for half an hour."

"Oh no," said my mother. "I must see the children. I've got to see the children." She was quite distraught.

After a pause Nanny said, "I'll fetch them. They're with Miss Cameron at present. Ned dear, order your mama some tea."

"What happened, Mama?" I said when we were alone.

"They weren't sure about the deed. They thought perhaps it might be set aside. But they said you could easily be made wards of court if your father applied to the judge. Do you know if he's applied yet? I told the attorneys I didn't know if he'd applied."

"I don't know. Mama, if we're made wards of court, does it mean the judge would appoint someone like Uncle Thomas—or Aunt Madeleine—to be our guardian? Because if so, we would still stay with you. Aunt Madeleine said we should stay."

"The judge is almost certain not to allow that. There's the adultery. And I haven't gone to church. I've failed to set you a good religious example. And there's the fact that I haven't sent you to a proper school and allowed you to associate with those peasant boys."

"Good God!" I said, so amazed that for a moment I forgot to be frightened. "What stupid things people worry about!"

"I've got to stop your father," she said, not listening to me. "I've got to reason with him. I'm going back to Cashelmara tonight and then I shall call at Clonagh Court."

"Mama, you can't go back tonight—forty miles! It's impossible! Stay here tonight. Please stay."

"But I must leave early tomorrow. There's no time to waste." Her eyes were bright, as if she had a fever. She was twisting her hands over and over in her lap. "I must see him," she said. "I must."

"Let me come with you."

"No!" she said sharply and then added in a softer, more normal voice, "Stay here and look after the little ones for me. Please, Ned. It would mean so much to me if you did that."

So I stayed. For three days I played with my brother and sisters on the beach or in the hotel, and then at last on the third night Maxwell Drummond arrived and asked to speak to me alone.

III

We went to my bedroom. It was a narrow little room, and the wallpaper, which consisted of a pattern of enormous roses, made it seem even narrower. There was a chair and a washstand, a tallboy and a brass bed.

"What happened?" I said in a low voice.

He sat down on the chair. I had never thought of him as being either young or old, but now he looked every one of his forty-five years. His eyes were bloodshot with tiredness, and the lines were deep about his mouth. He looked at me without expression.

"Sit down, Ned," he said.

I lowered myself onto the edge of the bed. Nothing happened except that I began to feel sick and was gripped by the terrible conviction that soon I'd feel sicker still.

"Your mother went to see your father at Clonagh Court," he said. "She was prepared to be friendly and even brought him some gifts from the children, but he was beyond reason and there was a quarrel. She left. He drank himself senseless. The next morning he was so ill that your Cousin Edith sent for your aunt Madeleine, who said your father was suffering from an illness called cirrhosis of the liver. It's common among drunkards, and your father had suffered attacks before. Your father was very ill for twenty-four hours and finally went into a coma." He stopped.

I said nothing. Above us the gaslight flickered, and beyond the curtains the rain was tapping at the pane.

"He died," said Drummond.

There was another silence.

"This morning it was . . . Your aunt came to Cashelmara to tell your mother, and I spoke to her. 'Cirrhosis of the liver,' she said, and I made her say it two or three times to make sure I had it right."

He stopped again. I was gripping the edge of the bed and waiting for the dizziness, but it never came. The knuckles of my hands were white.

"I'm sorry, Ned," said the man. "I know you were fond of him once. I know this is a shock for you."

I suddenly realized I was by the window looking out. It was raining very hard outside.

"Please ask Nanny to tell John and the girls," I said.

When I said nothing else he answered, "I will. Would you like me to stay with you for a while?"

I shook my head.

But he didn't go. After a long pause he said, "If you're thinking . . ." But he stopped. Then: "I'll be in room fifteen if you need me," he said and went out, closing the door softly behind him.

I sat down on the edge of the bed and thought about cirrhosis of the liver. After some unknown time I thought: Of course it would have had to be arranged so that there was no mark on the body. Too dangerous otherwise. Clever about suggesting an illness that often kills drunkards. No difficulty about Dr. Cahill signing the certificate of death. No autopsy.

I wondered how it had been done. Common knowledge my father was drinking again. Something in the poteen probably. A servant?

Cousin Edith must have had at least a cook and a handyman. Yes, of course she did, for Seamus O'Malley had told me only the other day that his uncle had been caretaker at Clonagh Court. O'Malley. Drummond's kin. Of course.

I tore a piece of paper from my English composition book, found a pencil stub and began to write.

"Dear Uncle Thomas and Uncle David, I have reason to believe. . ."

I stopped. Wait. Think. Be careful. What about my mother? In any denunciation of Drummond, how could she possibly escape? And she had been at Clonagh Court on the very day my father had drunk himself into a stupor; she had probably gone there without Drummond's knowledge. How horrified he would have been when he had found she had unwittingly placed herself in a dangerous position! If poison were ever found in the body, the police would immediately suspect my mother, and maybe Drummond would even go scot-free.

Tearing up the letter, I burned it to ashes in the bedside candle tray.

After a long while I wondered if my father really had died of cirrhosis of the liver. It was possible. I knew what happened to people who stood in Drummond's way, but there was such a thing as coincidence. I tested the theory, probing it. My mother had been in desperate straits, Drummond would have done anything to help her, and then my father, coincidentally, had died.

So much for coincidence.

I was quite calm. I thought I would feel dizzy and confused but I didn't, so I was able to consider the situation rationally. Murder was wrong, but it would be even more wrong if my mother were convicted of a crime she didn't commit. I didn't want to protect Drummond, but I had to in order to protect my mother. No choice. Besides, if I were to be honest, wasn't it for the best that my father was dead? He had caused my mother a great deal of suffering in the past and had died while bent on causing her a great deal more. I was sorry he was dead, of course; that was only fitting, but when all was said and done he had really been no use to anyone, least of all me. It was true I had been fond of him once, but that was over. All fondness had been destroyed by his disgusting behavior, and now there was no need either to grieve or to dwell upon the past.

I lay awake all night thinking of him.

I thought of the book he had given me about the Knights of the Round Table. "Oh, Papa, how nice you would look in a suit of armor with a crusader's cross on your chest!" I had exclaimed, and he had laughed. "I'm no hero, Ned," he had said. I could so clearly remember him saying that. "I'm no hero."

I cried a little then but didn't know why. It didn't make any sense. If only I could make sense of it—and I was afraid of going to sleep in case I dreamt of the Tiffany lamps.

We went back to Cashelmara. My mother was very distraught, and Dr. Cahill called each day to see her. After my uncles arrived from England the funeral was arranged to take place at the end of the week, and I saw the two men who had helped my father in the garden disappear up the Azalea Walk to dig the grave.

"Very sad," everyone kept saying. "Inevitable for a man of his habits, perhaps, but very tragic."

At dawn on the day of the funeral it occurred to me that perhaps there was some proof that Drummond had committed the murder without my mother's knowledge. He might have written to her, mapping out a plan, and when my mother rushed home from Dublin in horror to stop him she had failed to arrive in time to stop my father drinking the poisoned poteen. This theory would explain why she had been in such a hurry to see my father and why she had left him so abruptly. They hadn't quarreled at all; he had become ill in her presence and in a panic she had rushed away.

If the letter was still in existence—which seemed unlikely—it would be in the Carlton House writing table in my mother's boudoir.

After dressing quietly I left my room and padded around the gallery above the hall. I saw no one. It was still too early for the servants to be up, and I knew my mother would be unlikely to rise before eight, but I had to be careful not to disturb her because the boudoir was next door to her bedroom.

The writing table, highly polished and elegant, stood in the corner. Tiptoeing over to it, I fingered my way through all the drawers, but it was only when I found nothing that I remembered the secret drawer and reached for the hidden spring. My mother had shown me the drawer when I was small and had allowed me to hide things in it.

The spring clicked. The drawer eased open. By this time I was convinced I would find nothing that could possibly interest me, so it came as a great surprise when I discovered the letters. They were folded neatly together and tied with red ribbon, but they weren't from Drummond to my mother. They were from my father to me.

They were letters I had never seen, letters he had written to me when I was in America, letters my mother had kept from me but for some reason had never brought herself to destroy. Perhaps she had planned to give them to me when I was twenty-one, as if they were some bizarre heirloom. However, that hardly mattered now.

I sat down on the chaise longue, and while my mother slept in the room next door I read every one of those letters.

One of them in particular imprinted itself indelibly on my mind. "Maxwell Drummond, who deals out murder and violence as casually as other men deal a hand of cards . . ."

My father had known all about Drummond.

I flicked through the letters again. "I know you're very young . . . hard for you to understand . . . wanted only to be honest with you . . . ever your most affectionate and devoted father . . ."

Putting all the letters together again, I retied the red ribbon around their yellowing edges and put the bundle back in the drawer. Then I went out.

I walked across the lawn into the woods. It was dark in the Azalea Walk, but above me the sky was lightening and a solitary bird was starting to sing.

I reached the chapel but didn't go in. Instead I walked past my grandfather's fine marble headstone, my fingers trailing lightly over the deep engraving, and skirted the mounds that belonged to my great-grandparents, who had died long before I was born. I walked to the corner of the churchyard and then I stopped on the brink of the open grave to look back.

It was very quiet. Even the bird had stopped singing.

I listened. There was no sound to hear, but I listened to my memory. After Drummond had talked to me beneath the Tiffany lamps in that New York restaurant I had wiped all thought of my last conversation with my father from my mind, but now the Tiffany lamps which had hidden my father from me month after month, year after year, were dissolving, and as at last I saw beyond them to the truth I had been too afraid to face, I knew I would never dream of those lamps again. The barriers had crumbled, my memory was opening into the past and I could hear my father telling me again about his friendship with Hugh MacGowan.

I had misinterpreted what he had said, but now, with the Tiffany lamps dissolved and Drummond's brutal explanation no more than a distorted echo, I heard my father's explanation afresh.

Better to face the truth, no use trying to be something one can never be, impossible for him to make my mother happy . . .

I wanted to tell him I understood, but there was no time, because he was already talking passionately about all the things that mattered to him—his children, his garden, his home.

The memory of his voice blurred. I found I was no longer listening, for now I was thinking of Drummond—not the Drummond I had trusted but the other Drummond, the man who had cheated my father out of Cashelmara, deprived him of his garden and those he loved, schemed to live off my father's land with my father's money while he slept with my father's wife. I tried to remember my father being dishonest, but I couldn't. He had admitted he was foolish with money, and he had even admitted to me that he was a bad husband because he couldn't love my mother as a husband should. He had had weaknesses—yes, of course, but he had never lied about them. It hadn't been his fault that I had been too young and stupid to understand when he had told me about MacGowan. At least he had tried to tell me; that was enough.

And suddenly I thought: That was a very brave thing to do.

It occurred to me to imagine myself afflicted by that loathsome act of God and trying to explain my affliction to my son. But it was beyond my imagination. I couldn't conceive of ever having the courage, and it was then I thought: No wonder he needed to drink. No one can be brave all the time.

I looked down into the grave that lay waiting for his coffin, and suddenly my feelings toward my father were so clear that it amazed me to think that they could have been so confused for so long. For my father was indeed a hero, not an unreal hero who existed only in the pages of a child's storybook but an ordinary man who was honest when most men would have lied and courageous when most men's courage would have failed them. I no longer gave a damn that he had been a drunkard and a pervert; that didn't matter. For my father had loved me and he had been honest with me, *that* was all that mattered, and one day . . .

One day I would make amends for having turned my back on him for so long.

Chapter Four

I

At first I had no idea how I might make amends to my father, for since my mother was in such a dangerous position it was no use talking melodramatically of avenging his murder, but later after considering the possibilities I decided the best way to make amends would be to oust Drummond from Cashelmara. The only trouble was that I didn't see how I could take such a step at that time without hopelessly antagonizing my mother. It was true that the estate was now mine beyond any shadow of doubt, but I was still a minor and all the powers remained vested in my trustees. In theory Drummond could be dismissed from his position by my uncles, but in practice . . . My mother would object and the fighting would start again. The thought of more fighting repulsed me. Anything, even doing nothing, was surely better than that, but I thought that when I was twenty-one and my own master I would be able to suggest tactfully to my mother that she and Drummond might live elsewhere.

Since it was too much to hope that she might have tired of him by that time I would have to buy them a small country house in some place where they could live discreetly without embarrassing the girls. Eleanor would be almost grown up by then, and it would be a shame if my mother ruined her chances of finding a decent husband. I would give my mother a moderate allowance, employ lawyers to manage her financial affairs and refuse to receive Drummond at Cashelmara.

That would take courage, of course, but if I were as old as twenty-one it was unlikely that I'd be afraid of anyone, even a murderer. Meanwhile, I would simply have to bide my time. There was nothing I could do except bury my head in the sand like the proverbial ostrich and blot all thought of the murder from my mind.

The funeral took place. John had an asthma attack and was obliged to stay in bed, and the girls weren't at the chapel either because Nanny said Eleanor was too high-strung and Jane was too young. I was there. My mother wept all the way through the service, my uncles were ash-white and my aunt Madeleine talked afterward about the will of God. Cousin Edith came but said not one word to my mother, and the next day she returned to Scotland. Her sister Clara, who wrote to my mother once a year, informed us later that Edith had settled down in Edinburgh and was interesting herself in the propagation of higher education for females.

After the service we found Drummond waiting patiently outside to take my mother back to the house, and when she saw him she did manage at last to stop crying.

"Poor Sarah," said Uncle David to Uncle Thomas. "It's hard to remember all those years when she and Patrick lived happily together . . . still a little fond of him perhaps despite everything . . . after all, if a woman has borne a man four children there must be some feelings nothing can erase."

But Uncle Thomas was too busy thinking about Cousin Edith to reply. "Thank God Edith didn't stay," he said to me in private after the small cold luncheon was finished. "Do you know she actually told me that she thought Patrick had been murdered and that Sarah was to blame? My God, that woman would say anything against your mother! It's disgusting."

My fear must have shown itself in my expression, for he added hastily, "Of course I told her to be very careful. Statements like that are actionable as well as being damnable lies. There's no need for you to worry, Ned. I doubt if we'll hear from her again."

I managed to say, "She couldn't demand an autopsy, could she? I know they wouldn't find anything, but the scandal would be so bad for my mother."

"Quite unnecessary to have an autopsy," said Uncle Thomas, who, being a doctor, was familiar with such matters. "No suspicious circumstances. Dr. Cahill thought one should be conducted just as a matter of form, but Madeleine said it was pointless and I agreed with her. As you say, the only purpose it would serve would be to create more scandal for your mother, and this family has suffered quite enough from scandal during the past few years."

"Dr. Cahill . . . he didn't have any doubts about the diagnosis, I suppose?"

"Good God, no! Of course he was away at Cong at the time and didn't actually see your father, but Madeleine said there was no doubt at all, and she's had a lot of experience with cirrhosis of the liver at her hospital. I'd trust Madeleine's judgment absolutely, and if she had no doubts I have none."

After a pause I said, "I see."

Uncle Thomas said suddenly in a low voice, "Ned, if I thought for one moment that Drummond was responsible for this I would arrange with the appropriate authorities here for an autopsy and say to the devil with the scandal. But I don't see how he can be. It's not just that he was at Cashelmara all day in full view of the servants. It's not even that it would have been difficult for him to get his hands on a toxic substance. It's simply that he would never have arranged such a thing and then allowed your mother to visit Clonagh Court at what would have been a most crucial time. I've talked it over with David, who fancies himself a great expert in this field on account of all those detective stories he reads, and he agrees with me. He also made an interesting point which I hadn't thought of. He said in his opinion Drummond wasn't the Borgia type. Guns, yes—but poison, no. So you see, bearing all that in mind, we have no alternative but to confirm what we originally suspected—that Patrick died a natural death."

"No alternative," I said. "Yes, of course." I was so relieved I could hardly speak; my eyes even filled with tears. For Uncle Thomas had succeeded in restoring my faith in the possibility of coincidence, and when I saw that my father might indeed have died a natural death I stopped asking myself how I could endure the years until I reached my majority. I would no longer have to wake each morning with the knowledge that I was sharing a house with my father's murderer. I would no longer have to be so fearful of an autopsy and I would no longer have to worry about my mother's danger. Life could be almost normal again. Of course I would still have to get rid of Drummond one day out of respect for my father's memory, but that could wait till later.

I felt as if I had emerged from some appalling nightmare, and in

616

my first surge of happiness I hardly paid any attention when Mr. McCardle, the Protestant chaplain from Letterturk, approached me with the offer of spiritual help.

"It occurred to me that on this occasion you might welcome a little religious guidance," he said in his ugly Belfast accent. "The death of a father is always hard for a young man, and since your mother— alas!—is not a regular churchgoer and your only aunt is a papist . . ."

Since I was in such a happy mood I listened politely. I even consented when after his long sepulchral homily about the life ever-lasting he offered to give me the lessons necessary to prepare me for my confirmation.

"I shall call once a week and give you two hours of instruction," he said, beaming at me, and I said, "Yes, sir. Thank you, sir," and beamed back.

It was only after he had departed that it occurred to me that I had no desire whatsoever to be a fully fledged member of the Church of Ireland. I hated the dreary hour of matins once a month, and although I had always disliked the dark desolation of the little chapel, my father's funeral service had turned mere dislike into loathing.

But I didn't want to dwell on the funeral. I was still too relieved and happy.

"Ned, you never play with us any more," complained John that afternoon. He had made a startlingly quick recovery from his asthma.

"Who cares?" said Jane, cuddling her nasty orange cat. "I don't want to play with him anyway."

"Oh, Jane, don't say things like that!" pleaded Eleanor, looking up from her book.

"I'll say just what I like," said Jane, glowering at me. "Come along, Ozymandias my dear. We'll go and find Mama. Present company don't suit at all."

For the first time it occurred to me how absurd it was that I should refuse to be friends with a little girl half my age. Was it possible that I could have been jealous of all the attention my parents had paid her? I hoped it wasn't, but to make sure I said as I watched her retreating back, "I'll take you all on a picnic, if you like. We'll take lemonade and jam sandwiches and go down to the strand."

"Hooray!" said John, jumping in the air.

"Oh, I'd like that!" said Eleanor, shutting her book with a bang. "But would it be fitting so soon after the funeral?"

"Nanny'll say it would do us good. And if she doesn't say it I shall say it for her."

Jane had wavered in the passage. "I'm not invited, I suppose."

"That's for you to decide. If you can spare the time you can certainly come with us."

"I shan't leave Ozymandias," said Jane, testing me.

"You can bring Ozymandias but not the other cats. I'm not going to the strand to build Noah's Ark, you know."

So we all went, even the wretched cat, who followed Jane on a lead as if it were a dog. The strand lay along the western end of the lough, and although the sand was dull and heavy it was adequate for castle-building. John drew pictures with a stick, Eleanor paddled dreamily and I helped Jane build a fort.

"Tell us about America, Ned," said Eleanor when her feet got cold.

"About the zoo in New York," said John. "Oh, how I'd love to go to a zoo!"

"Tell us about the little girls called Connemara and Donegal," said Jane.

I began to tell them for the hundredth time about the Gallaghers, and as I talked I was filled with a longing to return to their house on Beacon Hill.

"They laughed all the time," I said. "You should have heard them! Everything was such fun. They had this marvelous house in the middle of Boston and every room was very bright and gay. There were pictures of pretty women on the walls and religious statues everywhere—not cold stone statues like the ones in the chapel but plaster statues in brilliant colors. There were splashy sorts of wallpaper and plump stuffed sofas and a tinny old piano where the A-sharp always broke when Kerry played 'Rose of Tralee.' Mr. Gallagher wanted to get a new piano, but Mrs. Gallagher wouldn't have it because she had had the piano all her married life and she said it was her good-luck charm."

"Was Mrs. Gallagher like Mama?" said Eleanor, asking the ritual question with relish.

"No, not a bit. She wasn't half as beautiful. But she never got flustered over anything, and whenever the girls did something awful she'd just say, 'For sure you'll break your poor darling pa's heart when he hears of this,' and the girls would cry at the thought and

618

everything would be forgiven. Mr. Gallagher was a great big swash-buckling fellow, and he smoked big cigars and kissed Mrs. Gallagher every night when he came home. He kept six horses and two carriages and it was a wonderful sight to see the family go off to Mass every Sunday. The girls wore pretty dresses and everything was so gay. I expect their church was like that too. Catholic churches are different from the chapel, you know. There are pictures everywhere and those brightly colored statues and lots of gold cloth. And there are candles everywhere too, like a birthday cake, and a nice smell and everyone sings in Latin, which is a wonderfully mysterious language for singing in, much better than English."

"It does sound more exciting than matins in the chapel," said Eleanor wistfully. "You never told us about that before, Ned."

But I was already thinking of my father's funeral, the dark somber words of the service, the numbing dreariness, the oppressive stifled grief battened down by good taste and decorum.

"Did the Gallaghers have a garden?" said John, taking up the ritual questioning.

"And cats?" said Jane.

"They had everything," I said. I couldn't say anything else.

"More than we have?"

I nodded and walked away. I walked to the far end of the strand where the Fooey River flowed into the lough, and then I stopped to watch the wind rustle the grass above the sandy banks. After a while Jane came and stood beside me.

"If I went to America one day could I take Ozymandias with me?"

I said poor Ozymandias would be most unlikely to find happiness on the Atlantic Ocean, and we walked back again slowly hand in hand toward the lemonade and the jam sandwiches.

When we returned to the house it was after five, and Drummond walked out to meet us as we toiled up the last stretch of the drive.

"I've got some good news for you, Ned!" he called and waved a letter in the air.

We came closer. I saw the American stamp and a large unfamiliar handwriting, and suddenly my spirits started to rise.

"It's from Phineas Gallagher!" said Drummond. "Guess who's coming to stay?"

Kerry was coming. Nothing else mattered but that. I kept thinking what fun we would have and how wonderful it would be to have someone to laugh and joke with, someone who was bright and happy and gay.

"I'm in Phineas' debt," explained Drummond to me. "He helped me get my pardon, as you know, and I promised him—or at least Sarah promised him—that Kerry could come and stay here for a while and learn how to be a lady."

They were coming in the spring.

"All of them?" I said hopefully.

"No, just Kerry and Phineas. Phineas plans to bring the whole family over later."

Eleanor and Jane were disappointed not to be seeing Connie and Donagh.

"I'd so like a girl of my own age to play with," said Eleanor, and Jane immediately took great offense and said she was sure she would never play with Eleanor again.

"Poor Jane's so sensitive," said my mother when Jane was finally appeased.

"She wouldn't be if you didn't keep making her feel so important," I said. "Then she wouldn't be so upset when other people don't follow your example."

"Really, Ned!" said my mother, taking offense just as Jane had done. "I hardly think it's your place to criticize me."

I said I was sorry. There was so little I could say to my mother those days, but now it no longer mattered because Kerry was coming.

I told my friends about her. "A friend of mine's coming from America to see me in the spring," I said casually as we huddled around our fire in the cool autumn air. "She's Irish. Her name's Kerry Gallagher."

"A girl?" They were disapproving.

"I don't even think of Kerry as being a girl," I said severely. "She's just like a real person."

They still looked glum, so I didn't mention her to them again.

Meanwhile, my mother was going to enormous trouble to impress the visitors. The drawing room was redecorated in pale green, the hall was painted white (I didn't like that a bit—it was so cold) and the entire west wing, which was to be set aside for the guests, was refurnished.

"Mamma, you couldn't have chosen this furniture!" I said, horrified, when I saw all the dark heavy tallboys and commodes beached like whales along the upstairs corridor. I had never thought much about interior decoration before, but now I discovered I had a great aversion to solid gloomy furniture.

"Well, it's not entirely to my taste," said my mother, whose elegant boudoir was furnished in pretty Regency style, "but Maxwell thought it was smart and modern."

I opened my mouth but shut it again before I had said a word. No use complaining about Drummond spending my money to furnish my house. She would only say she had given him permission and that it wasn't my place to criticize. One day, when I was twenty-one, it would be my place. But not now.

The innovations went on and on. A cook was engaged from Dublin to ensure the Gallaghers had the best food, and my mother herself went to Galway to make special arrangements with the tradesmen for the best supplies to be sent to Cashelmara throughout the month of May. I didn't think it was at all fitting for my mother to haggle with tradesmen in that fashion, but we had no housekeeper, and Drummond was anxious that the merchants should have a personal visit. He wanted to give dinner parties too so that Phineas Gallagher would think we lived a grand social life, but although my mother wrote dutifully to the local gentry they all made excuses not to come.

I hated to think of my mother being cut in that fashion, and I knew she hated it too. But she said nothing. Drummond cursed angrily, but my mother bore it all with resignation. The only time I ever saw her upset was at Christmas when Eleanor wept that the little Knox girls had given a party at Clonbur without inviting her.

"And I would so love to have gone!" she said tearfully to my mother.

"We'll have a special party for you here, darling," said my mother soothingly, but I saw her bitter expression before I turned away.

Spring was approaching at last. I began to mark off the days on my calendar, while in the schoolroom Mr. Watson droned interminably about the Reformation and in the chapel Mr. McCardle was disapproving when I told him I wanted to postpone my confirmation at Easter.

The daffodils began to bloom. My father's garden came alive. Once Drummond talked of plowing up the flowers to plant vegetables, but I objected so strongly that he never mentioned it again.

"I didn't know you liked the garden so much, Ned," he said hastily to me, but I wouldn't reply.

The garden was my father's legacy to me, my one link with precious times long ago, and when I walked in his garden I would remember my promise to make amends to him and fancy the garden was not only a link with the past but a bridge to a happier future.

May came. I was fifteen and a half years old, Kerry was nine months younger and we hadn't seen each other for two years.

"Supposing she's not the same," I said, worried, to Nanny. "Supposing I don't like her."

"A true friend never changes," said Nanny comfortingly.

I tried to remember what Kerry had looked like. She had been plump and the buttons on her dresses had always seemed as if they might pop off at any minute. She had had red-gold hair and a dimpled chin. Of course she would look older by this time. I looked older. Examining myself moodily in the glass, I noticed that my hair, which had once been fair, was now the color of mud and my face had become a battleground for at least three different sorts of pimple.

"I look awful!" I exclaimed in dismay to Nanny. I couldn't think why I had never noticed before.

"There, there," said Nanny. "Keep your hair cut and wash your face properly every night and you'll soon look as handsome as your poor papa was."

I thought her optimism bordered on the patronizing, but I did wash my face and asked her to cut my hair for me.

When the Gallaghers arrived Drummond took me to Galway to meet them. I wore a new dark suit with my father's gold Albert over my waistcoat, and I felt like a lamppost before the lamplighter arrived. With every glimpse of Drummond's broad, muscular frame I envied him from the bottom of my heart.

I saw Phineas Gallagher before I saw Kerry. He had one of his big cigars in his mouth, and his blue eyes were shining and you could hear the jingle of gold in his pockets at a distance of twenty yards.

"Max, me darling old friend!" he cried, dropping the cigar in the gutter, where a beggar immediately retrieved it, and held out his arms with the tears rolling down his cheeks.

"Bluebeard!" squeaked something small and round behind him.

She danced toward me. Her hair still looked reddish-gold beneath her huge flower hat, but now it was scraped straight up from her ears and the only part visible to me was a frizzed fringe.

622

"Pudding-Face?" I said doubtfully, but I knew it was her. She had those same eyes, saucily blue, and when she opened her mouth and said pertly, "Hullo—how d'ye do?" I realized she still had the same quaint way of speaking the English language. People who live in Boston are popularly supposed to sound like English people, but I never met anyone while I was in Boston who supported this piece of folklore.

"My," gasped Kerry in awe, "you grew so big!"

"So did you," I said, and then realizing that this might sound rude, I added hastily, "In the right places, I mean." That sounded worse, and it occurred to me with horror that I was going to blush.

Kerry saved me by giggling. She had the naughtiest giggle I had ever heard, and suddenly my blush was forgotten and I was laughing with her.

"Oh my!" sighed Kerry. "Ain't it grand to be grown up at last?"

"You can bet your bottom dollar on that!" I said with my best American accent and reached out with joy to shake her by the hand.

III

Phineas Gallagher stayed a fortnight at Cashelmara before traveling to County Wicklow to see his old home. He left Kerry behind with the promise that he would take her there later, but the truth was, as Drummond told me, that Mr. Gallagher was afraid of what he might find. Having talked for years to his daughters about the Elysian paradise where he had been born, he was nervous of disappointing them, and although he had been born a peasant he had traveled so far along the road to prosperity that he feared his relations would seem alien to him. However, when he returned to Cashelmara he was in good spirits. His kinsmen had given him a royal welcome, there had been no embarrassment and his village had so far recovered from being razed by the British that not a sign remained of the devastation of the Hungry Forties.

"If Pa mentions the famine one more time I shall scream," said Kerry. "Have you noticed that old people are always harking back to the past? As if we cared!"

"In thirty years' time you'll be doing the same thing," I predicted. "You'll be saying, 'I lived in the days when Charles Stewart Parnell was the uncrowned king of Ireland.'"

"Pa says Parnell's finished," said Kerry.

"Why? That letter in the *Times* was proved false and Parnell was vindicated!" This was the letter that had purported to link Parnell to the Phoenix Park Assassinations of 1882, and it had caused a fearful uproar before the forger had confessed.

"I don't know anything about any letter," said Kerry serenely, "but if Pa says he's finished, he's finished."

"Why do you think Parnell's finished, sir?" I said curiously to Mr. Gallagher over the port that evening. I had never been much interested in politics before, but Mr. Gallagher and Drummond talked of little else after the ladies had retired and some of their obsession had rubbed off on me. Besides, Charles Stewart Parnell interested me, for he too was a Protestant landlord who thought of himself as an Irishman. "He's still chairman of the Irish Party, and not all the Irish Party are dissatisfied extremists."

"It's the woman who'll finish him," said Phineas Gallagher.

"Why shouldn't the man have a mistress?" argued Drummond, who was always loyal to Parnell. "I'd rather support a leader with a mistress than a man who lived like a monk!"

"Well, sure we all know the ways of the world, Max, and I'm agreeing with every word you say, but a man in his position ain't got no business committing adultery and you know that as well as I do. He's got away with it all these years because he's been discreet and the husband's played ball, but if it comes out now the Saxons'll be laughing till the Day of Judgment. 'Faith, look at the poor silly Irish!' they'll say. 'The most moral people on earth are led by an adulterer!' No, it ain't good enough, Max. It won't do at all."

"I see," I said. "Mr. Parnell could have been responsible for the Phoenix Park murders and all Ireland would have cheered him to the echo. But if Mr. Parnell comes between a man and his wife he's damned to all eternity."

Phineas Gallagher laughed and said what a smart boy I was. "But it's not so simple as that, Ned," he said. "If Parnell had been responsible for the Phoenix Park murders it would have been a political blunder, and only the fools would have cheered him to the echo. And as for the adultery, the great political sin is not in the adultery itself, for that's been going on for years. No, the blunder is that he's letting everyone find out about it. The man's a fool. If O'Shea brings a divorce, Parnell will be politically dead within a year, and if he can't see that he ain't got no business being chairman of the Irish Party."

"It's bloody hard you are on him, Phineas!" exclaimed Drummond, and to my astonishment I saw he was flushing with resentment.

624

"Faith, Max, don't take it so personal! We ain't discussing you. We're discussing Parnell."

"It's all wrong that a man should be ruined for loving a woman as if she were his wife," said Drummond stubbornly, but Mr. Gallagher merely said, "It's the way of the world, Max," and changed the subject so neatly that Drummond had no chance to argue with him.

I didn't like to ask Kerry how much she knew about my mother's situation, but it was obvious Phineas Gallagher had said a word to her on the subject. When we had lived in Boston my mother had been known as Mrs. Drummond and all the Gallagher girls had believed her to be Drummond's wife. Even when my mother had won her divorce later I had never mentioned it to Kerry in my letters for fear of causing trouble, and although I now realized she knew the truth I still found I couldn't discuss it with her. It was easier to talk of other things, and I had a fine time showing her the valley and introducing her to my friends. Despite their doubts my friends thought she was very nice, but they were shy with her and I saw at once that I couldn't expect Kerry to become part of the gang. That was awkward, for I no more wanted to drop my friends than I wanted to abandon her, but fortunately the problem was solved at the end of June after Mr. Gallagher returned to America.

"Now, Kerry," said my mother kindly but firmly, "you can't spend all your time running up and down mountains with Ned as if you were a boy. I've no objection to you making little expeditions together on Saturdays, but during the week you must both attend to your lessons and try to improve your accomplishments."

This meant that Kerry had to spend her mornings with Miss Cameron and her afternoons with my mother. Miss Cameron taught her English literature, French and Italian, and my mother supervised her piano practice, instructed her in needlework and tried to teach her to speak with an English accent.

"Though that's the blind leading the blind, if you ask me," I overheard Miss Cameron say to Nanny.

"Lady de Salis speaks beautiful English," said Nanny hotly, always willing to rush to my mother's defense. "I know she can't pronounce her A's properly, but apart from that you'd never know she was a foreigner."

"Besides," said my mother to me later, "I'm not aiming to make Kerry sound like an Englishwoman. If I can only induce her to talk like a well-bred American I shall feel that my efforts haven't been entirely fruitless."

Kerry seemed to take these efforts good-naturedly, so I didn't worry about her. I was enjoying summer once again. The mornings were always wasted with Mr. Watson, but three times a week I met my friends on the mountainside, and although this meant I had to stay up late to complete my schoolwork I didn't care. I had discovered I didn't need much sleep, and even if I went to bed after midnight I would often get up at dawn to watch the sun rise over the lough.

It was at the end of July that I discovered Kerry wasn't happy. Since it was a Saturday we had decided to take a picnic lunch up to the ruined cabin and then walk to Devilsmother before returning home for tea. Naturally all three of the little ones had wanted to come with us, but for once I had insisted very firmly that they remain behind.

"They could never walk to Devilsmother and back," I explained to my mother. "They'd wilt and be a nuisance."

"Well, you could at least let them share your picnic with you!" said my mother.

"Another time—with pleasure," I said. "But not today."

"Why not?" said my mother, instantly suspicious although I couldn't for the life of me imagine why she should be.

"Because I get the chance for an outing with Kerry only once a week," I said reasonably, "and although as a rule I don't mind the others coming too, on this particular occasion when I intend to go for a long walk I don't want them with me."

"Well, I'm not at all sure I approve," said my mother and added, as if she felt she had to give me an explanation, "I think you're being rather selfish."

"Honestly, Mama, what a mountain you're making out of a molehill!"

"Ned!"

"Well, I'm sorry, but really!"

I thought my mother might go on protesting, but evidently she realized the futility of further protests, for she let us go.

Halfway to the ruined cabin Kerry said, "I'm glad you stood up to your ma. I wouldn't have minded if the little ones had come, but your ma's always trying to spoil my fun."

I stopped. "Is she?"

"We-ell . . ." Kerry kicked a twig with her heel. After a moment she said, "She's not like my ma, you know." And then after a longer moment she added, "I wish my ma was here," and burst into tears.

626

I was appalled. The sight of any Gallagher in tears contradicted all they represented to me, and I felt as if I were witnessing some terrible profanity. I groped for words but could find none. When I fumbled for a handkerchief instead I found that the only one I possessed was dirty, and my helplessness reduced me to such misery that I could only gaze at her in despair.

"Say something!" Kerry wept. "How dare you stand there like a stuffed dummy!"

I said the first thing that came into my head. "You poor, poor Pudding-Face. Why didn't you tell me before that you were homesick?"

She gulped, snatched the dirty handkerchief from my hand and blew her nose on a clean corner. "I thought you'd think I was ever so ungrateful and mean," she said. "I know how you love Cashelmara. I didn't think you'd understand."

"You thought I wouldn't understand? You were homesick—and you thought *I wouldn't understand?* How do you suppose I felt in America when Drummond and my mother dragged me around with them and I didn't know when I was ever going to see my home again?"

She sniffed and dabbed each eye with another clean corner. "Well, I knew you were kind of peculiar when we first met you," she said, "but I didn't know it was because you were homesick. You were awful quiet and never smiled and just sat in a corner being good. Clare and I thought you were real strange before we got to know you."

"Meeting you and Clare was the best thing that ever happened to me in America."

"Oh my!" she said. "That don't say much for what happened to you in America!" And to my enormous relief she giggled.

"Well, it was so difficult," I said, "about my mother and Drummond."

"I guess it was. Do you know, Ma still doesn't know they're not married? Pa made me swear on the Bible I wouldn't tell her in my letters."

"Were you shocked when he told you?"

"Sure, but Pa explained it all beautifully. He said that I'd have to know the ways of the world one day, so I might as well learn them sooner rather than later. He said your ma and Mr. Drummond were so much in love that they were just as good as married, but Mr. Drummond was real smart about it and pretended to live in a separate house so there'd be no scandal. He said that of course it was a terrible sin and I must never think of doing such a wicked thing myself or God would punish me, but your mother had had such a hard life that this was God's way of giving her a little reward. He didn't say why it had been so hard, but he said it was hard enough for God to be sympathetic and make allowances. And he said ever such nice things about your ma and what a lady she was and how I must be sure to do all I could to please her."

I heard a stifled sob. "Has my mother been unkind to you?"

"We-ell . . ."

"Has she?"

"She don't like me one bit," said Kerry bravely, giving me back the handkerchief. "She tries to, but she acts like she was Our Blessed Lord and I was the Cross. She makes me feel ugly and dumb and shoddy. Well, I know I'm shoddy, but Pa and Ma never made me feel I was ugly and dumb, and they know me better than she does."

"I like you just the way you are," I said.

"Ugly, dumb and shoddy?"

"Rather!"

She giggled again, and this time I laughed too and took her hand in mine.

"Kerry, I can hardly believe my mother would have been so unkind, but if you promise me it's true I'll ask Mr. Drummond to have a word with her about it. She won't listen to me, but she'll listen to him."

"No," she said, "don't say anything. I feel better now I can count on you for sympathy, and if Mr. Drummond hears about it he might tell Pa and Pa would take me away."

"But mightn't that suit you? If you're so homesick—"

"Do you want me to go?"

"Not a bit!"

"Oh good, then I'll stay. I don't truly want to go home. I'd feel such a failure and Pa would be so disappointed."

We had reached the ruined cabin. I set down the picnic basket and raided the store of peat my friends and I kept for our fires.

"My, isn't this fun!" said Kerry, producing a bag of humbugs from somewhere beneath her petticoats. "This must be the nicest part about being an Irish peasant—sitting around by the peat fire with nothing to do but look at the beautiful scenery and tell stories! The trouble with the older people is they forget all the happy times and remember only the famines and the wicked agents. When I'm old I'm going to remember all the nice things. I shall summon my twelve children to my side and—"

"Twelve children!"

"Well, I guess I'll have at least twelve, don't you? After all, if we get married when I'm eighteen . . ."

She saw my expression and stopped. I remember very well how surprised she looked. There was no coyness, no embarrassment, just that innocent surprise.

"Who says we're getting married?" I said. "I'm not marrying anyone." Realizing this sounded very rude, I added hastily, "Of course if I married anyone I'd marry you, but I've decided to be a bachelor."

"But you can't do that!" exclaimed Kerry.

"Well, it's possible that I might marry when I'm fifty to beget an heir. But I couldn't ask you to wait another thirty-five years. It wouldn't be fair."

"But . . ." she was dumfounded. At last she managed to say, "You mean you don't know?"

"Know what?"

"It's all arranged! Pa told me on the boat when he told me about your ma and Mr. Drummond!"

"Oh, Kerry, your father was telling a tall story!"

"He was not so!" She was very serious and almost angry. "It's the truth! He and Mr. Drummond did a deal. He—"

"Drummond!" I leaped to my feet. "What the devil's Drummond got to do with this?"

"Well, Pa got Mr. Drummond his pardon and gave him money—"

"Money!"

"Yes, so that you could go back to Ireland comfortably, and Mr. Drummond promised in return that I could come to stay and . . . well, get married later. Mr. Drummond said he would see your mother didn't stand in our way if you wanted to marry me, and Pa said Mr. Drummond could have more money if the match came off."

"My God," I said.

"Pa said I needn't marry you if I didn't want to, but I thought it would be so romantic—just like the old days in Ireland when people married young and everyone had a hand in the match-making."

629

I walked out. At the back of the cabin I leaned my forehead against the cold stone wall and closed my eyes. I was shaking with rage.

When I opened my eyes again I saw she had followed me. I straightened my back. It was very quiet and nothing moved as far as the eye could see.

"I'm sorry," she said. "I thought you knew or I'd never have mentioned it. Please don't be angry with me."

"I'm not angry with you," I said. "I'm angry with that bastard Maxwell Drummond."

I began to talk about Drummond. I gave voice to thoughts and emotions I had never known I possessed. So long as I had taken my mother's side against my father I had suppressed any feelings of antagonism toward her, but now that I was no longer opposed to my father I discovered my view of my mother was changing focus. It was changing now as I watched. I wasn't looking at Kerry. I talked mostly to the ruined wall in front of me, but all I saw was my mother and Maxwell Drummond.

I said that Drummond had degraded my mother, that he had ruined her and dragged her down with him into the gutter so that even her own brother had called her a whore. I said their behavior was disgusting and that I despised them for it. I even talked about the creaking bed and how revolting it had been. I said I was never going to have anything to do with such filth for as long as I lived and that I was never going to fall in love with anyone, male or female.

I stopped when I said that because I didn't want Kerry to know about my father, but when I turned around to catch her expression I found she was no longer there.

I ran to the front of the cabin, my glance scanning the hillside, but there was no sign of her. I plunged through the doorway. She was inside, huddled in a corner, her hands pressed against her eyes as she cried.

"Kerry . . ." Again I stood helplessly, appalled to see her grief, yet not knowing what I could do. In the end I reached out dumbly and touched her. I put one finger on her arm, and when she let her hands fall from her face I caught them in mine and held them.

At last she said unsteadily, "You do like me a little, though, don't you?"

"Oh, Kerry, of course I do! Of course!"

"I shan't mind so long as you like me a little. I'll get over it real quick, you'll see. I'll never even mention it again to you."

"I didn't mean . . . I'm sorry."

"It was my fault," she said. "I know it. Please say you'll try and forgive me, Ned, for upsetting you so much."

I stared at her. Her eyes shone with tears, and the tears darkened her sandy lashes until they seemed very long. For no good reason I touched her cheek with my finger and found that her skin was softer than my mother's, soft and rich and smooth. My finger trailed downward, brushing her lips, tracing the line of her neck and falling noiselessly to her breasts. I paused, followed the curve of her left breast and paused again. It was bright in the cabin. Outside the sun was sparkling on the waters of the lough far below, and beyond the doorway a sprig of heather swayed lazily in a faint breeze from the mountains.

Resting my left hand against the wall above her head, I slipped my right hand all the way around her waist and stooped to kiss her on the cheek.

The next thing I knew I was kissing her on the mouth. Her arms had slipped behind my head, and her body was shaping itself against mine.

Closing my eyes, I forgot my mother and Drummond, forgot the creaking bed and the misery of my repulsion. I was beyond the reach of the past at last, aware of nothing but an immense sensuous heat as if I were wading through warm luscious water to swim in a sparkling, beckoning sea. I drew nearer and the sea was very close. I wanted to dive forward out of my depth and swim until the waves swept over my head, but Kerry was pushing me back. I could feel her hands on my chest, but when I opened my eyes I saw she was smiling at me radiantly.

We didn't speak for a while. Then she said with a shy, self-conscious laugh that sounded most unlike her, "Ned, tell me the truth. I haven't lost my virginity yet, have I, by any chance?"

She wore such a funny, worried expression that it never occurred to me to tease her.

"No," I said.

"Praise be!" she exclaimed in relief. "The nuns at Sunday school said that was the worst thing that could happen to a girl, and men were always to blame."

I smiled. She giggled, and suddenly we were friends again, and the sparkling waters of that beckoning sea were no more than a pattern of lights dancing at the extreme edge of my mind.

I didn't think of Drummond until much later when I saw him at dinner. We had a glass of port together afterward and he asked me how I was getting on with Kerry.

"Very well, thank you, sir," I said, smiling at him, and wondered how I could wait until I was twenty-one before kicking him out of my house into the pig manure where he belonged.

Chapter Five

Soon after my discovery of his bargain with Phineas Gallagher, Drummond's mode of life began to change. He gave old MacGowan's house to the patriarch of the O'Malley family and moved to Cashelmara to live openly with my mother.

At first I thought it best to say nothing, but after a week I found that something had to be said.

"Mama," I said when I had the opportunity to speak to her alone, "please don't misunderstand me. I have no wish to criticize you, but don't you think it would be better if Mr. Drummond kept up the pretense of having his own home?"

"Of course," said my mother. "He's going to move to Clonagh Court. This is just a temporary measure, darling."

"I see. Well, would it be possible, perhaps, for him to have the suite of guest rooms in the west wing? There's a lot of talk among the servants because he shares your apartments now."

"You mustn't listen to servants' gossip, Ned. I'm not answerable to the servants."

I tried again. "Mama, it's not that I myself mind—" that was a lie but I did want to be tactful— "but Nanny is very upset and Miss Cameron is talking of going back to Scotland, and it's such a pity for Eleanor and Jane to be cut off from other girls their age."

"If Nanny and Miss Cameron have complaints they can bring

them to me," said my mother, "and it's for me, not you, to be concerned about Eleanor and Jane."

It was hard to know what to say next. In the end I simply asked, "When will Mr. Drummond move to Clonagh Court?"

"I'm not exactly sure, darling. It depends to some extend on his sons."

Drummond was still trying to lure his sons back to the valley. He had rebuilt his old home by this time, and it was when this had failed to tempt them back that his interest in Clonagh Court had revived. More O'Malleys now occupied his old home, and Clonagh Court had been extensively renovated.

I thought it best not to ask where the money was coming from. I knew Drummond couldn't have afforded the renovations on his salary, but it seemed pointless to complain to my uncles when any complaint would only get my mother into trouble. It was my mother who kept the books.

"If Mr. Drummond thinks he can lure his sons back to the valley by offering them bigger and better homes, he's mistaken," I said levelly, remembering past conversations with Denis. "They think he's wronging their mother, and so long as he continues to wrong her they'll never come back."

"Well, why don't we wait and see what happens?" suggested my mother, so I waited—and eventually I saw I had summed up the situation correctly. Drummond's sons remained in Dublin, Clonagh Court remained unoccupied and Drummond remained at Cashelmara.

"How can your mother, who's a lady, bring herself to behave like this?" Kerry blurted out at last. She knew I hated to hear criticism of my mother, but she couldn't help herself. She sounded more astonished than shocked.

"She's not responsible for what she does," I said. What else could I say? And when Kerry looked incredulous I heard myself add, "It's like an act of God."

It felt odd to say those words. Memories of old nightmares stirred in me, but I clamped them down.

"What in heaven's name do you mean?" said Kerry, baffled, and when I tried to explain my words were muddled and made no sense.

"Don't let's talk about my mother, Kerry. I'll put everything right later when I'm twenty-one. But at present I just don't want to think about it."

I was becoming extraordinarily talented at burying my head in the sand, but that was because I had discovered the perfect way to forget everything I had no wish to remember. Kerry and I used to snatch odd minutes together during the day, and although my mother now insisted on the children accompanying us on our Saturday expeditions I hit upon the brilliant idea of escorting Kerry to Mass on Sunday. Since her arrival at Cashelmara Drummond had always acted as her escort when she went to church at Clonareen, but his way of life prevented him from attending the service, and I knew the weekly journey was tedious to him. At the end of August when Father Donal paid his regular call on Kerry at Cashelmara I managed to see him for a few minutes alone.

"Father," I said, "I'm interested in attending your services for a month or so. Could you ask my mother to give her permission, please?"

My mother, fortunately, was in Father Donal's debt, and I knew she would find it difficult to refuse his request. He had not only helped her get Drummond out of jail but had stood by her afterward when she had been forced to remain at Cashelmara.

"You don't want to be a Roman Catholic, do you, Ned?" was my mother's alarmed response to the request. As if to make amends for her life with Drummond, she had become very conservative in all other matters, and as far as she was concerned it simply wasn't done for a young baron like myself to turn papist.

"I don't know whether I want to be a Catholic or not," I said truthfully. "That's exactly what I'm anxious to find out."

But my mother continued to disapprove, and eventually I had to seek help from Aunt Madeleine, who, true to form, sallied forth from the dispensary with crusading zeal and told my mother to be grateful I showed any religious inclinations whatsoever.

"The boy must be encouraged," said my aunt, giving me her fondest smile, and the next Sunday my mother meekly gave me her permission to go to Mass.

I liked the Mass very much, but I liked the journey to and from church better. However, after a month even the privacy of the carriage seemed inadequate, and I began to plot another picnic in the ruined cabin. One afternoon I raided the pantry, Kerry pleaded a headache to avoid my mother's supervision and half an hour later I was spreading my jacket on the cabin's earthen floor.

Some unknown time later Kerry said in an agony of despair, "Ned, I know some people stay chaste for years and years, but I've been chaste for nearly six whole weeks now and I feel as if I'm going to burst any minute. What are we going to do? Please, Ned—help me or I'll be a gone coon, I swear it!"

I was in no fit state to reply. To extract every ounce of pleasure from being close to her, I had stripped to the waist and had coaxed Kerry by a mixture of bullying and wheedling to unbutton her blouse. The days when we had giggled together as children had never seemed more remote.

"Ned, say something!" She pushed away my fingers, which had been prying distractedly at her bodice, and tried without success to roll out of my reach. "What are we going to do?"

I made the only suggestion that presented itself to me.

"Oh, but I couldn't!" she said. "That's a mortal sin, I'm sure of it, and I couldn't possibly have any virginity left afterward, and Ma and Pa would just kill themselves if they ever found out."

"It wouldn't be a mortal sin if we got married!"

"But I thought you didn't want to get married!"

"I'll do anything you like," I said. "I'll get married or stand on my head or jump in the lough. But let me—"

"Oh Jesus!" said Kerry.

I started to kiss her again. I still couldn't get to grips with the bodice. It was worse than a chastity belt.

"Would you really marry me?" said Kerry.

"Of course." Something ripped. I heard the faint crack of whalebone succumbing.

"When?"

"Tomorrow."

"Oh good," said Kerry, pushing me away again. "I think I can just wait till then."

"I can't," I said, triumphing at last over the appalling underwear and breaking out in a sweat from head to toe.

"Well, maybe I can't either," said Kerry. "Oh, but I must. Holy Mary, save me from sinning. Amen. Oh, Ned, that feels so good. Holy Mary, save me from—well, perhaps it doesn't matter. After all, Pa said people can be just as good as married, and if your ma and Mr. Drummond can do it . . ."

Everything finished, the strait-jacket of excitement, the blazing pressure, the superhuman surge of power in every muscle of my body. Even the sweat on my back seemed to freeze. With a shiver I rolled away from her and lay on my side facing the wall.

When I looked at Kerry again I saw she was buttoning her blouse.

636

Her hands were shaking. The buttons kept slipping between her fingers.

I said in a calm, sensible voice, "Don't be upset. There's no need. We're going to get married."

She nodded, but I saw she didn't understand.

"I mean we're going to do things the proper way," I said. "I won't touch you until you're my wife, but don't worry because we'll be married very soon."

She stared at me. Her eyes were shining again. She looked bright and fresh and pretty.

"We'll have a proper engagement," I said, "and a proper wedding. Father Donal can marry us, and we can have a nuptial Mass at the church in Clonareen."

"Ned!" She was too overjoyed to say more. Flying into my arms, she wept over my chest while I squeezed her until we were both gasping for breath.

"I'm not going to treat you as Drummond treats my mother," I said.

We talked all the way back to Cashelmara. Kerry said she was going to have five bridesmaids, her sisters and mine, and I said we would go to Paris for the honeymoon. I wanted six children and Kerry wanted eight, so we decided to have seven. We talked about Cashelmara too. I said when I was twenty-one I was going to remodel the chapel into a Catholic church and paint the beautiful circular hall of the house blue and white like Wedgwood pottery. Kerry said she'd have new curtains in every room and fresh pictures on the walls and flowers everywhere.

"And lots of those nice religious statues," I said, "and shamrock-green wallpaper. We'll have levees, parties, balls. We can hire musicians from Dublin, and all the world will come to see us and Cashelmara'll be the finest house in the Western world!"

"Lovely! Oh, I can almost hear the music!"

"Strauss waltzes," I said, "quadrilles, galops—"

"And polkas! Oh, Ned, I love to polka!"

"—polkas, jigs, reels—"

"Irish music!"

"Irish music and Irish songs!" I cried, seizing her by the waist and whirling her around the lawn.

Far away the side door opened and my mother stepped onto the terrace.

"Ned!"

"Yes?" I called and hissed to Kerry, "Leave us alone when we reach the house and I'll talk to her about our marriage."

My mother was saying in a clear voice, "I should like to speak to you for a moment, if you please."

"Yes—coming!"

We reached the terrace.

"Quite recovered from your headache, I see, Kerry," said my mother. "That didn't last long, did it?"

"No, Lady de Salis," said Kerry. "Lady de Salis, if you'll be kind enough to excuse me . . ."

"Very well. Ned, come upstairs, please."

"Yes, Mama," I said obediently.

In the boudoir my mother asked me to sit down.

"I had intended for some time to say a few words to you on a certain subject," she said, speaking quickly, as if she had learned a speech and was determined to recite it before she forgot a single word, "and when I saw you . . . disporting yourself on the lawn, I realized I must speak to you without delay. Ned, I've noticed—Maxwell and I have both noticed—that you seem to be a little too . . . friendly toward Kerry nowadays. Of course we're glad that the two of you are so companionable, but I feel it's only proper that you shouldn't spend time alone with her in future. I don't want to be unreasonable, but Kerry has now reached an age where she should be strictly chaperoned. Of course I'm secure in the knowledge that the two of you are scarcely more than children, but . . . dear me, I'm afraid I'm phrasing this very badly, and I don't want you to misunderstand. Believe me, darling, I do trust you implicitly to behave as a gentleman should, but I know what it is to be exposed to temptation, and . . . well, perhaps Maxwell should have a word with you."

"That won't be necessary," I said.

"Darling, please don't be so insulted! I know you yourself would do no wrong, but people might think—"

"What do you care what people think?" I said before I could stop myself.

She bit her lip. "There's no need to be rude, Ned," she said in a quiet voice that made me feel ashamed. "Believe me, Kerry's reputation—any young girl's reputation—is so important. It can affect her entire future. When one is older and in sadder circumstances one can perhaps dare to defy the conventions, but when a girl's growing up it's vital that her conduct should be exemplary."

"Of course it is, Mama," I said. "That's why I know that you'll be delighted when I tell you my news. Kerry and I are going to get married."

There was a silence. My mother was struck dumb, but I wasn't surprised. I supposed it must always seem too good to be true when the match-makers' wishes coincide so exactly with those of the couple they're trying to unite.

"I thought the wedding could be in December," I said after allowing her a moment to recover, "on my sixteenth birthday. That would give the Gallaghers time to come over from America and for you and Kerry to arrange the wedding. By the way, I've decided to be a Roman Catholic, so I'm going to ask Father Donal to marry us at Clonareen." Some element in my mother's expression struck me as odd, and my heart sank. Surely she wasn't going to make a fuss about me becoming a Catholic. "What's wrong?" I said warily and then had a glimmer of enlightenment. "Oh, I suppose you think we're too young. Well, if we're going to be married eventually anyway, why shouldn't we be married sooner rather than later?"

"Eventually?" My mother's voice was very faint.

"Come, Mama, don't imagine I'm still in ignorance about the arrangement Mr. Drummond made with Mr. Gallagher!"

"Oh, but . . ." She had to sit down. She was very pale. "Ned, that was nothing. I mean, it was of no consequence. All Maxwell promised was that Kerry should live with us for a while and learn to be a lady. He never promised you'd marry Kerry—how could he? No doubt Mr. Gallagher had his hopes, of course—"

"And so did Mr. Drummond," I said. "I understand there was money involved."

She went paler than ever. "I know nothing about that, but if there was such an arrangement I'm sure Maxwell did it just to please Mr. Gallagher. Mr. Gallagher was the only one who could get him the pardon, you see, and of course we both wanted to please him. But, Ned, you don't truly imagine I ever wanted you to marry into a family like the Gallaghers, do you? Naturally I'm quite opposed to you marrying anyone when you're no more than a child, but even later I could hardly approve of you marrying Kerry! She's so far beneath you socially, so—so totally inadequate to be the wife of a man in your station of life! I know she can't help coming from such a vulgar, shoddyite family, but—"

"I see," I said. "You and Mr. Drummond cultivate the Gallaghers for their money and their influence and then once you have what you want you conveniently forget about a bargain you never had any intention of keeping. You do all this and yet still you have the incredible audacity to tell me it's the *Gallaghers* who are vulgar and shoddy!"

"Ned!" The color flooded back to her face as she stood up. "Apologize at once! How dare you be so insolent!"

"I think you should apologize to me," I said. "You've lied to me, concealed the truth from me, allowed your lover to auction me as if I were no better than a stick of furniture—"

She slapped me twice across the face. I stopped. My skin was smarting and I reached up to touch it with my fingers. When I looked at her again I saw she was breathing hard, as if she had been running, and her eyes were the eyes of a stranger.

A lump formed in my throat. I turned away.

"Listen to me," she said in a low voice that shook with rage. "You're not marrying that girl either now or at any time in the future. I absolutely forbid it, and later you'll look back and be grateful to me. Meanwhile you'd better go away to school. I'll write to Thomas and ask him to arrange your admission to Harrow immediately."

"I'm not leaving Cashelmara."

"You'll do as you're told!" Before I could reply she flung open the door. "Maxwell!"

Her voice echoed strongly down the corridor and reverberated along the curved walls of the gallery.

I moved, bumping into a table, knocking an ornament to the floor. "Mama, I've nothing to say to Mr. Drummond."

"Get back into the room!"

Drummond's footsteps rang in the hall. "Sarah, did you call me?"

"Yes—please come and help me for a moment."

He ran up the stairs. I had backed into the boudoir before he reached the gallery.

"What's wrong, sweetheart?"

"I'm having the most dreadful time with Ned. He seems to have gone completely insane." She lowered her voice, but I still heard snatches of the conversation. "All that wretched girl's fault . . . wants to get married . . . no, not later—now! Rude, hurtful and disagreeable . . . at my wits' end . . . please speak to him . . . needs a man, someone who can speak to him as a father would . . ."

I had to resist the urge to escape through the door into my mother's bedroom. It would never do to look as though I were running away. Pausing instead beside a chair, I rested my hands stiffly on the upholstered ridge of its high back.

Drummond came into the room. He wore a gentleman's suit, one of several he had ordered for Phineas Gallagher's visit, and in the pocket of his velvet waistcoat was the gold watch he had won at poker. He has slicked back his hair, trimmed his whiskers and even grown a small mustache. I tried to remember the ugly, untidy but joyous Irishman who had flung his hat in the air and bought the violets for my mother, but the memory had blurred until it seemed no more than a dream of long ago.

"Well, Ned," he said, smiling at me as he closed the door, "it's a fine fuss your mother's making and no mistake. What's all this tarradiddle about getting married?"

"It's not a subject I care to discuss with you," I said.

"Nor I with you," he answered, still smiling, "but since your mother's given the royal command it seems we've no choice but to try. Listen, you mustn't mind your mother. She never did care for the Gallaghers, and what's more she can't help herself, not after being brought up in that palace on Fifth Avenue. But if it's my opinion you're wanting, I think you've got good taste. The Gallaghers are a fine happy family, and those girls have been brought up properly and sure Kerry's the sort of girl who would make any man sit up and blink twice. So you see, I'm not agreeing with your mother when she says you shouldn't marry Kerry. Indeed you should marry her— when you're past twenty-one and your own master, when you've seen a little of the world and learned more of what there is to learn. But don't be marrying before you're twenty-one, Ned. I did, and I often regretted it. If you're smart enough to learn from other people's mistakes, I hope you'll not be too proud to learn from mine."

I said nothing, and when he saw I intended to remain silent he lighted a cigarette to give himself time to think. I remembered the time when this gesture had given me confidence. Now it seemed no more than a cheap trick.

"I've no wish to quarrel with you, Ned," he said at last. "We've been friends too long. Let me suggest a compromise which could suit us both better than any quarrel. Marry Kerry, but postpone it. Wait at least a year."

"I refuse to wait," I said.

"For what? For marriage? Or for a willing woman and all the pleasure you can take?"

I turned aside. "I see no point in discussing this further."

"You don't have to wait for that, you know, Ned. Wait for marriage and wait for Kerry, but there's no need to wait for anything else."

"I'm not interested in anything else. If you'll excuse me—"

"You only say that because you hate to admit that any advice I give you might possibly be the best advice you ever had! Come, Ned, grow up a little—be honest with yourself!"

He was standing in front of the door that led into the passage, so I moved toward the door that led into my mother's bedroom. But he stopped me. He put his thick, coarse fingers on my arm and pushed me back very smoothly against the wall.

"Don't lose your temper with me," he said, still speaking evenly though I knew he was very angry. "You're surely not that much of a fool. I'm on your side, can't you see? I'm trying to help you. Listen, there's a woman called Mrs. Costelloe who lives beyond Clonareen. I used to visit her sometimes long ago. She'd be far too old for you, of course, but I hear her niece who lives with her is all hospitality if she sees a young man she fancies. Ride with me to Clonareen tomorrow, and I'll see the two of you are introduced."

I was conscious of nothing except an overpowering longing to escape.

"Yes, sir," I said, staring at the carpet.

His fingers relaxed on my arm. He gave me a pat on the back. "I always knew you were a smart boy," he said. "I'm glad you're going to be sensible."

I escaped. I ran all the way down the passage to my room and just managed to reach the washstand before I vomited. I had no idea why I felt so ill, but I told myself it was because his suggestion of substituting a prostitute for Kerry was so revolting to me.

It was only later that I could admit to myself how frightened I was of him, and it was only when I admitted my fear that I could ask myself if I still believed my father had died a natural death.

II

"We're going out," I said immediately after lunch the next day.

"Ned, your ma'll be furious! We're going to start a new needle-point design!"

"Never mind my mother. You're coming with me."

"Where to?"

"The cabin. I've got a flask of milk and five currant buns."

As we hurried uphill through the woods I told her about the scene with Drummond. Until then I had merely told her that my mother was against the idea of us marrying so young.

"It's just shocking the muddle old people get into!" She was appalled. "How can it be wrong for you to get married and yet right for you to visit a scarlet woman? I'd never have thought Mr. Drummond would have been so wicked. Ma and Pa would have a fit if they knew."

"Do you think so? Are you sure? Wouldn't your father simply say it was the way of the world?"

"I'm beginning to wonder what sort of world Pa lives in. Maybe I'll retire from it and be a nun after all. I wanted to be a nun when I was ten, you know."

I paused to show her how unsuited she was for the cloistered life. "We're still getting married on my birthday as far as I'm concerned," I said when she was convinced.

Now it was her turn to be scared. "Ned, Mr. Drummond'll be furious!"

"He can have an apoplectic fit for all I care. He's not my father, and if he tries to behave as if he is I won't have it. I'm nearly sixteen years old, and I'm damned if I'll let anyone dictate to me any more."

"Oh, you're so brave!" exclaimed Kerry admiringly.

But I wasn't. I couldn't even eat a currant bun.

"I could write to Ma and say I've lost my virginity," offered Kerry, munching thoughtfully. "They'd have to let you marry me then, wouldn't they?"

"You'll do no such thing," I said. "I'm going to marry you with everyone's consent and your reputation intact. I'm going to do things properly and no one's going to stand in my way."

I hoped I would feel braver after those bold promises, but by the time we crept back to Cashelmara at five o'clock my heart was pounding like a piston and my hands were so clammy that I could barely open the side door into the house.

"What happens next?" whispered Kerry.

"Let's go up to the nurseries. Nothing awful can happen there, and I promised John I'd help rebuild his farmyard. But I'll just go to my room first and change my shoes. These ones are falling to pieces and my stockings are wet."

"Shall I go on ahead?"

"Yes, I'll see you in the nurseries."

I sped noiselessly up the back stairs, ran like the wind down all the corridors and finally reached the sanctuary of my room. With a sigh of relief I dived inside.

"Welcome home," said Maxwell Drummond.

He had been standing behind the door, and when I spun around he slammed the door to cut off my retreat. There was something odd about his appearance, but it took me several seconds to realize he was in his shirt sleeves. He had tossed his jacket across the bed and taken off the heavy leather belt he always wore with his working clothes. I looked for the belt but couldn't see it. It was only when I glanced back at him that I saw it was coiled neatly in his right hand.

"Where were you?" he said. He spoke in a soft, low voice without any particular expression.

"I went for a walk."

"With Kerry? Your mother said she was missing too."

"Yes, I was with Kerry."

"I thought we had an appointment."

"You were mistaken," I said. "I changed my mind. Forgive me for not informing you."

"I'll be damned if I'll forgive you anything. What did you do to that girl?"

I stared at him. I suddenly found I couldn't speak.

"Jesus Christ!" he said, white-hot with rage. "I might have known what sort of foolishness I could expect from a spoiled young bastard like you! Your trouble is that your mother and I have been so busy handling you with kid gloves that we've allowed you time and again to get away with behavior no child should be allowed to get away with. Well, you've gone too far this time! I'm going to teach you a lesson you won't forget in a hurry."

I managed to say, "I've done nothing wrong. I didn't touch her. I want to do everything properly."

"You goddamned liar," he said and told me in the vilest possible language how he thought I had spent my afternoon.

Something snapped inside me. The room spun in a red mist before my eyes, and all fear was wiped from my mind. I stopped cringing against the wardrobe and rushed him. I moved so fast that I took him by surprise, and all my pent-up hatred spilled into violence as I slammed my fist into his face. He dodged but not quickly enough. My fist caught him a glancing blow, and he reeled back against the door. Closing in, I swung my fist again. I was shouting at him, but I hardly knew what I said. I called him names, terse, ugly Saxon names, and I told him to get out of my house. But then he caught my wrist, bending it back so that I cried in pain, and twisted my arm in such a way that I had to sink to my knees, and the next moment I was on the floor, unable to move, my face pressed against the worn carpet. He dragged at my jacket. I should have been able to wriggle free then, but he had me in such a grip that I dared not move for fear my arm would break.

"Let . . . me . . . go!" I twisted my body away from him, but he put a harder lock on my arm so that for a second I couldn't breathe for the pain. The carpet smelled of dust and damp. I choked. My eyes smarted with tears. I was crying even before he hit me, but I tried not to because I didn't want him to see my tears.

He hit me nine times. He had dragged up my shirt and vest so that the belt could bite my skin. When he had finished hitting me he stood up, shoving me away from him, and said he hoped that would teach me a lesson. He said that was just a taste of what I would get if I even laid a finger on Kerry again and just a taste of what I would get if I ever breathed a word of my dishonorable behavior to anyone. He said he had been more patient with me and more liberal than any father would have been, and it was about time I realized it. He said I had better mend my ways pretty damned quickly if I wanted to avoid further trouble with him.

He left.

I got up at once. I knew it was very important for my self-respect that I shouldn't lie sobbing on the floor like a little boy in the nursery. Taking off my clothes, I tried to wash my cuts with cold water from the ewer and then I found fresh clothes and dressed with care. I knew I had to wear my best suit, but it no longer fitted me, and when I raised my arm to comb my hair the material closed upon my burning shoulders like a leaden cape. It was only then that I allowed myself to sit down.

The pain was so bad that I even wondered if my arm was broken, but I could still move my fingers, so it seemed unlikely that the bone was injured seriously.

Before I could start to feel sorry for myself I went downstairs.

I went straight to the library. He was slumped comfortably in a chair with his feet up on the great desk by the window. He had a glass of whisky at his elbow, and he was smoking one of Phineas Gallagher's big cigars.

When he saw me he was so surprised that it took him a moment to swing his feet to the floor.

"Oh, it's you, is it?" he said, hardening his voice to show me he was making a quick recovery. "I suppose you'll be wanting to apologize."

"No, Mr. Drummond," I said, more determined than ever now to get what I wanted. "I haven't come to apologize. I've come to deal you a hand that'll suit us both."

Chapter Six

I

He laughed. "Those are words I never thought I'd hear used against me!" He tapped the ash from his cigar and gestured to one of the chairs that flanked the fireplace. "Sit down and deal your hand in comfort!"

When I stood my ground he shrugged his shoulders and leaned casually against the edge of the desk. He was still holding his big cigar. "Why don't you wait for your temper to cool?" he said. "Come back tomorrow morning and say your piece. It's all the same to me."

I still said nothing.

"Faith, Ned, I'm sorry to see you being childish enough to bear me a grudge. You should take it as a compliment that I treat you as I'd treat my own sons."

"You haven't treated your sons very well," I said. "And now, if you've finished giving yourself time to think, perhaps we can begin. Let me start by saying there are certain facts you should understand. One: Kerry's a virgin. Two: I'm not a liar and you've no right to call me one. Three: I'm marrying Kerry on my birthday, December the fifth, and you're going to persuade my mother to give her unqualified consent. Have I made myself clear?"

He roared with laughter, mocking me. "Well, you've dealt me a hand that suits yourself!" he said, amused. "But why should that suit me?"

"You want to continue living here and pretending to be a gentleman, don't you?"

The laughter died from his eyes. Recognizing the insult as the challenge I intended it to be, he decided to take me seriously. "I'm a good agent," he said flatly, "and that's no pretense."

"True, it's not merely a pretense. It's a lie. With my mother's permission you've been helping yourself to my money for some time now, and if I chose I could ask the judge in Chancery to remove my mother as trustee. Then my uncles would dismiss you from your job."

"Go ahead," he said. "My old home's rebuilt now and it's not yours to dispose of as you please. I'll go back there and make a fine living for myself. I always was a good farmer, and there's no reason why your mother shouldn't enjoy living there with me. I'd see she was comfortable, and she would be near enough to Cashelmara to see the children every day."

I began to understand how he had won his gold watch at poker. Panic simmered in me, but I kept my fists unclenched and willed myself to be calm.

"Come, Mr. Drummond," I said reasonably, "you know very well that my mother would never humiliate herself and her children by sinking as low as that. Her present humiliation is more than enough for her to bear. If you were disgraced she'd leave you."

"Ah, that's where you're wrong," he said, smiling at last. "She'll never leave me."

The appalling part was that I knew he was right. I stared, my back burning from the beating he had given me, my sore arm throbbing, and found to my horror that I had nothing to say.

He stopped lounging against the desk and stood up as if the conversation were already over. "Besides, no judge in Chancery would remove your mother from her position as trustee," he said, taking a casual puff at his fat cigar as he demolished the rest of my threat. "I'll admit she's been generous to me, but she's spent no money that couldn't be written off in a lawful way. She knows how to keep books, you see, and to be sure no one would ever prove she'd been guilty of mismanagement."

Defeat stared me in the face, but I refused to see it. I had never in all my life been so determined not to lose, and suddenly the enormity of my desperation pushed me to a pitch of hatred so intense that my brain was emptied of all emotion, even fear. A single thought, at first no more than a fleck of instinct but soon a huge billowing cloud of total belief, filled my mind until I felt my head would split with the pain of it, and the thought was: This man killed my father.

My voice said coolly, "Perhaps you're right. Perhaps I couldn't prove my mother had been guilty of mismanagement. But I think I could prove she was guilty of murder."

The cigar in his hand went out. He had stubbed it accidentally against the desk as he swung around to face me. Above the fireplace the elephant clock ticked quietly, marking time until I chose to speak again.

I said, "Of course we both know my mother's not a murderess, but she did visit my father shortly before he became ill, and if it was found that my father didn't die of his liver disorder her position might become very difficult indeed."

Drummond said evenly in a firm voice, "Your father died of drink. There was no murder. Your father died a natural death."

"I'm glad you're so certain," I said. "In that case you'll have no objection if I write to the Chief Secretary in Dublin and request permission for my father's body to be exhumed for an autopsy."

He ground the cigar to ashes in the tray and reached for the bottle of whisky. "You crazy boy," he said, not looking at me. "Don't be such a damned fool."

"You arranged matters very well, didn't you? At first I thought my mother's visit to Clonagh Court was an accident, that she had gone without your knowledge, but now I see it wasn't an accident at all. You let her go because she was going to act as a shield for you. You knew that if there was any suspicion later the family would cover it up in order to protect her. It was a clever piece of bluff and well worthy of your talents at poker, but that's finished now because I intend to call that bluff of yours and bring the truth out into the open."

"You'll do nothing that'll hurt your mother," he said, pouring himself another shot of whisky.

"In normal circumstances no, I wouldn't. But these aren't normal circumstances, Mr. Drummond. If I have to choose between my mother and Kerry I'm going to choose Kerry."

He was silent.

"I'm choosing now," I said. "Get me my mother's consent to the marriage and I'll leave you and my mother alone. Stand in my way and you'll both be facing a coroner's jury within a month. It's up to you."

He drank the whisky in a single gulp. While he was considering the situation I thought it prudent to add, "I've already posted a letter to Mr. Rathbone in London and enclosed a second letter which is to be opened only in the event of my death. I thought it wise to list my suspicions on paper and make a written demand for an autopsy. In the circumstances I'm sure you'll understand why I felt such precautions were necessary."

I stopped. He remained silent. His glass was empty, his cigar a mangled ruin, his face closed and still.

"Well, Mr. Drummond," I said, "are you going to help me?"

He backed away around the desk and sat down in the chair. He moved slowly, as if it were a relief to take the weight off his legs, and at last he said without looking at me, "So be it. I wash my hands of you. I've tried to prevent you from making the mistake of your life, but if you don't want to listen there's nothing I can be doing about it. Go and marry the girl, but don't ever come whining to me later to ask why I didn't try harder to stop you being such a goddamned fool."

All I said to him was "I shall expect my mother's consent within twenty-four hours."

"I'll speak to her tonight."

It was over. I'd done it. I'd beaten him to his knees.

"Very well. Good night, Mr. Drummond," I said shortly and hurried upstairs as fast as I could to write my confidential letter to Mr. Rathbone.

II

"But, Ned," said my mother in tears, "how can you think such things about Maxwell, who's always been so good to you? And how can you threaten me as if you no longer loved me?"

"I do love you," I said, "but I love Kerry too."

"How can you love her! You're too young to know what the word means! Listen, Ned, never mind what I said to you yesterday about Kerry's reputation. Better that she should have no reputation than that you should marry when you're only sixteen."

"No, Sarah!" exclaimed Drummond strongly. "How could I face Phineas Gallagher again if I stood by and knowingly let such a thing happen?"

"Why should I care about the Gallaghers!" she cried. "I wish to God we'd never met them!"

"If we hadn't we'd still be in America. Sarah sweetheart, you've got to be reasonable about this."

650

"I refuse to consent, I tell you! I'll never, never consent."

"Sarah, it's blind you are or you'd see things differently! You can't truly want the shame and scandal of an autopsy. Haven't your children been through enough shame and scandal already?"

"Patrick died a natural death," said my mother. "Everyone said so. 'It was the result of his drinking,' Madeleine said. Madeleine did say that, didn't she, and Dr. Cahill agreed with her."

"He did, yes."

"Then why, why, why does Ned keep talking about an autopsy?"

There was a pause. My mother started to cry again. After a long while Drummond said, "Let him marry, Sarah."

My mother tried to speak but could not. I suspected she had at last realized there was nothing she could say.

"Let him do as he wants." Drummond was still trying to make it easier for her. "When he tires of her later at least he'll have the money to set himself free and start again."

"Roman Catholics don't recognize divorce," said my mother, weeping harder than ever, but I knew her tears weren't for my conversion to Rome.

Drummond found it best to pretend they were. "His feelings for Rome are all bound up with his feelings for Kerry, don't you see? He'll get over Rome when he gets over her, and it'll all sort itself out. It won't be the end of the world. Give in to him now and let him make his own mistakes. Sometimes you have to let children make their own mistakes, so let go, Sarah, because you'll win nothing now by clinging on. Consent to the marriage, give it your blessing and welcome Kerry as your daughter-in-law."

"I can't," sobbed my mother, forgetting in her distress that she had no choice. "That plain, dumpy, common little girl . . ."

"Sarah, Sarah . . ." He brushed his hand across her lips as if to smooth away the words and stooped over her. "Don't say any more. Not in front of Ned. Please, for your own sake."

It was only then that she managed to take his advice and hold her tongue. However, when I saw her later she seemed more resigned to the situation and even went so far as to apologize for her harsh words.

"I was only anxious to do what was best for you," she said, trying to smile. "I still can't pretend that I want you to marry when you're so young, but I see now that Maxwell was right and that it would be better for me to accept the situation."

651

I accepted the cue she gave me and thanked her for being so understanding.

She looked relieved. "Please forgive me for being so overwrought earlier, darling. It was such a shock, that's all—a shock that you were so much in earnest about Kerry."

I saw the game we were to play with each other. We were to pretend that she had consented to the marriage of her own free will though against her better judgment. Perhaps she had even managed to convince herself that Drummond was innocent and that they were both opposed to an autopsy solely on account of the scandal involved.

"I didn't mean one word I said about Kerry," she said, stumbling over the lie. "I do truly hope you'll be happy."

"Thank you, Mama," I said, trying not to be angry with her, and offered my cheek dutifully for a kiss.

Telegrams were dispatched to Boston and London, a letter was sent to Clonareen, and within an hour my aunt Madeleine was sailing up the drive in her pony trap to demand an audience with my mother. My mother, panicking, summoned me from my lessons, and when I arrived in the drawing room I found her collapsed weakly on the sofa, while Aunt Madeleine, implacable in navy blue, was stationed in front of the chimney piece.

"Edward," said my aunt, "tell me the truth this instant. To marry in haste at the age of sixteen suggests to me only one possible interpretation of what has passed between you and Kerry. Kindly provide me with another."

"Certainly, Aunt Madeleine," I said. "I've decided to become a Roman Catholic and have no wish to imperil my immortal soul by committing a mortal sin. I happen to have very strong views on the subject of fornication."

"Most gratifying," said Aunt Madeleine. "Are you receiving instruction from Father Donal? You are? I was afraid so. I've no wish to be uncharitable, but the poor man is quite uneducated and hardly fit to give you the kind of instruction you need before being received into the Church. For instance, it seems he has omitted to stress to you the importance in certain circumstances of self-denial and celibacy. Dear child, no one is happier than I am that God has granted you such spiritual enlightenment and has chosen to save you from moral corruption, but it's quite out of the question that you should marry at the age of sixteen."

"I've told him that again and again, Madeleine," said my mother in tears. "But he won't listen to me."

"I shouldn't think he would," said Aunt Madeleine coldly. "You've only yourself to blame, Sarah, if he's become quite unmanageable. What sort of an example has he been set during these past few years? How can he have any respect for you? You're going to have a lot of trouble with those children, Sarah, and this is only the beginning. However, I fail to see why the sins of the parents should be visited on the children, and if Ned is so uncontrollable that you find you have no choice but to consent to the marriage, I certainly shan't hold him to blame. The responsibility for the disaster will be entirely yours, Sarah, and you can tell That Man I said so. Good day."

When my uncles arrived at Cashelmara a week later my mother at once retired to her room with a migraine and I was left to defend myself single-handed against their disapproval.

"I insist on knowing the truth," said Uncle Thomas, very grim.

"Certainly," I said. "I intend to get married and my mother has given her consent."

"I mean the whole truth!"

"Ned," said Uncle David tentatively, "I remember I fell in love when I was sixteen, but I've fallen in love at least a dozen times since, and it's only now, when I'm twenty-seven, that I've finally met a girl I'm convinced would make me happy."

"It's no good telling Ned it's insane to marry at sixteen, David," said Uncle Thomas. "You know it and I know it, but Ned's incapable of knowing it, so we're at an impasse."

"But there must be something we can say!" exclaimed Uncle David. "Let me see. I suppose Madeleine's talked of the religious point of view, so it's no good going into that. Anyway there's nothing immoral about wanting to get married, is there? That's what makes everything so difficult."

"What I want to know," persisted Uncle Thomas stubbornly, "is why Sarah has consented to a marriage of which she can't possibly approve."

Uncle David suggested that it was probably relief that I wished to conduct my private life in a moral manner.

"Is that the reason, Ned?" said Uncle Thomas, not believing a word of it.

"I really can't answer for my mother," I said politely.

"Very well, we'll ask questions you can answer. Of course the root of the problem is sexual. Have you had sexual experience?"

"Really, Thomas!" said Uncle David.

653

"For God's sake David, we can't all accept your views on chastity! Well, Ned?"

"If you're wondering whether Kerry's pregnant, the answer is no, she's not. And if you're about to tell me to wait for Kerry and use some other woman while I'm waiting, please don't bother. I've already decided not to do that."

"It's the best course you could possibly take!" said Uncle Thomas, who was growing angrier and angrier. "If you could have a suitable outlet for your sexual impulses I think you would soon come to your senses and see your friendship with Kerry in its true perspective. Thwarted sexuality is the cause of most of the world's problems, in my opinion. I read the most interesting book the other day—"

"My dear Thomas," said Uncle David, who was becoming almost as angry as his brother, "now is hardly the time to enter into a discussion of pornographic literature."

"It was a medical textbook! For God's sake, David, be realistic! Which is the lesser of two evils? A mistake Ned may regret all his life or a night he won't even remember a year later?"

"There are other choices!" said Uncle David passionately. "Ned should go away—a grand tour of the Continent. Why, I could take him myself! I wouldn't want to be away from Harriet for too long, but—"

"It's very kind of you, Uncle David," I said, "but I don't want to be away from Kerry either."

"I refuse to allow you to marry that girl," said Uncle Thomas.

I refrained from reminding him that I didn't need his consent.

"We should speak to Sarah, Thomas," said Uncle David. "It's no good talking to Ned. He's not going to listen to us."

"Sarah! Sarah's obviously beyond reason! We all know she's been beyond reason for years. Damn it, if she doesn't stop this marriage, I'll have Ned made a ward of court."

"Absolutely not," said Uncle David strongly before I could speak. "I've had quite enough of the family name being a synonym for courtroom scandal. It seems it's now for me to tell *you* to be realistic, Thomas! It's obvious Ned's determined to marry, and even if we make him a ward of court there's nothing to stop him eloping to Scotland and marrying without anyone's consent at Gretna Green."

"Very well!" yelled Uncle Thomas, in a great temper by this time. "Throw in the sponge! But if you cared for Ned as much as I do you'd bloody well oppose this ridiculous marriage of his with your dying breath!"

"Uncle Thomas," I said. "You've made your point. I'm very grateful to you for your concern, just as I'm very grateful to Uncle David for opposing any move which would mean more family scandal. I hope you'll both come to my wedding on December the fifth."

"You young fool," said Uncle Thomas. "I suppose you think you're going to have unlimited marital bliss and live happily ever after. It's pathetic."

"Come, Uncle Thomas," I said patiently, "is there really anyone who believes marriage guarantees living happily ever after?"

But Uncle Thomas was too upset to answer, and all Uncle David said was that it was a pity a young man of my age should be quite so cynical.

III

"You'd best wait, dear," said Nanny. "Marry in haste, repent at leisure."

"Quite," I said.

"I don't know what your mama's thinking of, letting you do such a thing."

I said nothing.

"You've changed," she said, and suddenly she was no longer Nanny but an uncertain middle-aged little woman shrinking from the world beyond the nursery walls.

"I'm just the same, Nanny," I said, kissing her, but I knew I wasn't.

"I don't know why everyone says I'm so young," I remarked later to Kerry. "Sometimes I feel at least thirty. In fact I can't even remember what it was like to be a child. Childhood was all so long ago."

Childhood seemed long ago when I looked in the glass. I was six feet one by this time, and my shoulders were broadening respectably. I was still too lanky, but at least I could now look at myself without immediately being reminded of a lamppost. My skin had cleared. My hair, still the color of mud, now grew gratifyingly in thick whiskers, and I had every hope that even the color would improve with age. I still wasn't as handsome as my father and perhaps I never would be, but I was at least presentable.

"I feel just as grown up as you do," Kerry was saying, and she added with a sigh, "Being away from home helps one to grow up fast, I guess."

"Are you sure you wouldn't prefer to be married in Boston?" I always worried about the possibility of her being homesick.

"No, so long as Ma and Pa and the girls can come I'd rather have a true Irish wedding at Cashelmara. After all, this is going to be my home, isn't it, and if I'm married here everyone in the valley will get to know me when they join in the celebrations."

This point of view unfortunately caused more controversy with my mother, who claimed that the list of wedding guests should be restricted to close relatives and the local gentry.

"Why should it be as short as that?" I demanded. "Why should you keep it quiet as if you were ashamed of it? Kerry's going to have the best wedding any girl could wish for."

My mother argued no further about this but presently objected to the marriage taking place in Clonareen.

"It would be more suitable if it were conducted in Galway," she suggested.

"I want Father Donal to officiate."

I liked Father Donal, who thought it was the most natural thing in the world that I should want to be a Catholic and told me exactly what I wanted to hear about my new faith. Aunt Madeleine talked continually of dogma, which bored me to tears, but Father Donal told me about the saints' days and the different sorts of Masses, and he even drew up a list of rules for me so that I would know when it was appropriate to light a candle and when I should make a novena or a suitable genuflection. The best part about Catholicism is that although it's deliciously mystical, full of color and pageantry, it's also so practical, bristling with rules to cover not only every religious dilemma but also the wear and tear of daily life. I liked the idea of having rules to obey. Perhaps it was because my life had been disordered for so long, but whatever the reason I found the principles of the Roman Church a comfort and was only sorry I hadn't discovered them earlier.

I took my first communion on the sixteenth of November, but although I invited my mother to attend she refused.

"I'll attend your wedding," she said, "but apart from that it would be wrong for me to enter any church, Catholic or Protestant. I should feel too much of a hypocrite, and I hate to be reminded of how I've cut Maxwell off from his faith."

Drummond had never spoken to me on the subject of religion, and he didn't speak of it now. He was too busy preparing for the Gallagher's arrival, and my mother was initiating more domestic upheavals by transforming part of the attics into a new series of guest rooms. The original west-wing guest rooms were assigned to Kerry and myself, and we enjoyed ourselves dragging out the ugly furniture and giving orders for the dreary wallpaper to be stripped off. After that the real fun began. The largest room, which we decided to use as our bedroom, was painted the color of daffodils, and the sitting room was decorated in white and shamrock green. I thought it looked splendid. Later we ordered a fourposter bed to be made, and Kerry designed white muslin curtains peppered with red bobbles. In the bedroom was a recess that proved ideal for an oratory, and soon we were spending happy hours poring over the catalogue of a Dublin shop that specialized in religious wares. After ordering a silver crucifix we chose a big statue of the Madonna and Child and a gilt-framed reproduction of Holman Hunt's "Light of the World," which I thought was pretty good, better than any dusty old classical picture. We both loved the statue. The Madonna wore the traditional blue robe and looked plump and happy, like Kerry, and the infant Christ was a jolly baby with plenty of spirit. Finally we made the finishing touches to the room. A purple altar cloth embroidered with a figure of St. Patrick was commissioned, Kerry bought two fat mauve candles which emitted a delicious aroma when lighted, and we ordered six sets of rosary beads—"Because I'm always losing mine," explained Kerry, "and I expect you will too."

I couldn't remember when I had last enjoyed myself so much.

"It's strange how your taste is so different from mine, Ned" was my mother's only comment. "I suppose that's Kerry's influence."

Why she thought I was incapable of having an opinion of my own I had no idea, but I didn't care. I was having too much fun to mind what she said any more.

I didn't think of Drummond. We were polite when we saw each other, but when he wasn't there I forgot about him. Later after my wedding I would think about him, but at present I was still celebrating my great victory over him and all I cared about was having a good time.

"What are you going to do when you're grown up, Ned?" asked John one day.

"I *am* grown up!" I said with a laugh, "and at present I'm not going to do anything except enjoy myself!"

"I'm going to enjoy myself too," said John firmly. "I've decided to stay at Cashelmara forever and look after the garden. Mr. Watson said to Mama there was nothing more he could teach me, and this means I'm grown up too, doesn't it? He's not teaching you any more, and you say you're grown up. It must be a sign of growing up when tutors go away."

"You'll have to get to my age before you can call yourself truly grown up."

"Why? I can read now. Shall I read to you? I'll read 'Cinderella,' if you like."

"You only read that because you know it by heart," said Jane brutally. She was seven years old now and still devoted to Ozymandias and her watercolors. She also kept a journal, just as my mother did, and boasted that she recorded the name of anyone who slighted her so that God could refer to the list at the Day of Judgment. "And what's so special about being a gardener?" she added scornfully. "I'm going to be an animal doctor when I grow up, or if I'm not an animal doctor I shall paint pictures which people will call the work of a genius, or perhaps I shall do both and be a painter *and* an animal doctor."

"Jane, you're so peculiar!" said Eleanor, horrified. "What would your husband say?"

"I shan't have a husband," said Jane. "I don't think a husband would suit. But I shall find a nice man like Mr. Drummond who'll clean my paintbrushes for me and help cook the cat food."

"I shall have a husband," said Eleanor firmly. "Except that I wouldn't marry at sixteen like Ned because everyone says that isn't fitting. I shall have a house in the country and a house in London so my husband must have at least ten thousand a year because London is very expensive, and I must have a brougham of my own for paying my calls. Perhaps we could have a place in Scotland as well. All the best people have places in Scotland. And I would have a vast circle of very dear friends, and my very dear friends would say whenever there was an occasion, 'Oh, we must invite Eleanor or the entire occasion will be a failure.' Every house of importance would be open to us, and every Tuesday night I would have an 'evening' and wear a midnight-blue gown with ostrich feathers, and all the politicians would come to discuss the burning issues of the day."

"Ten thousand a year would be nice!" I said, laughing, "but the rest sounds a bit dull." I had no idea how much money I was supposed to receive each year, but I did know I enjoyed spending it. I ordered case after case of champagne and arranged for a massive supply of food for our guests. I distributed alms to all my tenants, and I donated a large sum to the church in Clonareen so that Father

Donal could arrange for the building of a Lady Chapel. My mother warned me that I must be more cautious, but I took no notice. I was only interested in doing exactly as I pleased.

Kerry's wedding dress was finished. The tailors completed my new suits. Cashelmara was beginning to hum like some enormous spinning top, and in my mind's eye I could already see it bursting at the seams with gaiety.

The Gallaghers arrived.

"Ma's in an awful state," confided Kerry. "She daren't tell Pa, but she's furious with him for not telling her earlier about your ma and Mr. Drummond. She even asked me if I truly wanted to marry you and said I could back out now while there's still time. Poor Ma! Isn't it sad to see all these old people worrying so about us?"

I didn't see much of Kerry by this time, as we were both so preoccupied with our families, our guests and the wedding, but this was probably for the best. I had long since resigned myself to waiting once I knew we were to have an early marriage, but resignation in theory is easier than resignation in practice, and if I spent time alone with her I became strained and irritable. I tried to explain this so that she wouldn't misunderstand, but it was difficult for both of us, and by the time December came we hardly knew how to wait the last five days to the wedding.

Mr. Gallagher, who was in dazzling good humor, had brought over some of his relatives from America, and presently more arrived from County Wicklow. There was no room for all of them to stay at Cashelmara, but Drummond's relatives among the O'Malleys were hospitable, so the problem was soon solved. Eleanor and Jane had several children to play with now, but Eleanor was shy, preferring to read in her room, and Jane, unused to children of her own age, thought these contemporaries very babyish. What my mother thought I could only guess. I knew it must have been repugnant to her to receive the Gallagher relatives, but she kept her feelings hidden. I supposed I had Drummond to thank for that.

I invited Drummond's sons to my wedding, and to my surprise they both accepted. I was delighted to see Denis again, and we had an affectionate reunion, but I couldn't decide what I thought of young Maxwell. He didn't look like his father, yet he reminded me of him more than Denis did. He was well spoken and well mannered, but there was a toughness about him which was all too familiar and his pride made him touchy.

"Your father will be glad to see you," I said when we met.

"I doubt it," he said, "for I've nothing to say to him. I came back to show my respect to you, Lord de Salis, and to prove I bear you no ill-will. I understand you were very good to my brother when he was here."

I asked him to call me by my Christian name as Denis did, but he wouldn't. In spite of his effort to appear friendly he preferred to keep me at arm's length until he knew me better.

"Do you think you might ever come back to the valley to live?" I asked him.

"Not while my father lives. I'd rather remain a clerk in Dublin."

"Wouldn't you prefer to be your own master farming your own land?"

"I would. And one day when my father's dead that's exactly what I'll be."

"You're very hard on your father."

"Why not? He was hard on us. He talked so big, pretending he was an Irish hero, yet all he did was end up a criminal and leave his wife and children destitute. I've been the sole support of my mother and sisters for years, so I know what I'm talking about. He lost us our home and broke my mother's heart and drove me into a bloody city job where I'm shut up all day in a stuffy room with nothing but big books and columns of figures. Then he comes home from America, lives off a rich woman—you'll pardon me—and has the insufferable gall to attempt to send us a little of your money now and then. Believe me, Lord de Salis, I'll never forgive him, never, and I hope he isn't fool enough while I'm here to ask me to try."

Whether Drummond was fool enough I never knew, but I did notice that soon he made overtures of friendship to me again, a gesture that could have meant he was having no success with his sons. Fortunately I was very busy with last-minute preparations and so I had plenty of excuses to brush him off.

The day before the wedding my uncles arrived reluctantly from England and found to their horror that Cashelmara had been turned into an Irish-American colony, while my mother was holding a stack of bills to prove my extravagance.

"But was all this expenditure prudent?" demanded Uncle Thomas, knowing it wasn't.

"I didn't want to spoil Ned's fun," said my mother, trying to be bold, but my uncles continued to look disapproving.

"I suppose at least some of the other guests will be people of quality," said Uncle David dubiously to me.

660

"Certainly not," I said. "I wasn't going to invite all those snobs who have cut my mother in the past. But there'll be plenty of people to wish us well, that's all that matters to me, and it's going to be the grandest wedding this valley's ever seen."

And so it was. The day of the wedding dawned mild and clear, the guests dressed in their finest clothes and all the hired carriages began to draw up outside the door. My friends came. I had given each one of them a horse for the occasion, and as I mounted my fine new black stallion I looked over my shoulder and saw everyone milling behind me, Sean and Paddy Joyce, Danny O'Flaherty, Liam Costelloe, Seamus, Brian and Jerry O'Malley, Denis Drummond and his brother Max. There was a great deal of shouting and laughter. The sun shone, and Cashelmara, shabby but serene, seemed radiant to me in that translucent winter light.

By this time I was drunk with excitement, and when I passed through the great gates my joy rose even higher. For all my tenants had come to meet me. Every yard of the way to Clonareen I heard their cheers ringing in my ears, and I swear no man on earth was ever half as happy as I was that morning when I rode down to the church from Cashelmara to wed my Irish-American bride.

Chapter Seven

I

Men aren't supposed to enjoy weddings, but I enjoyed every minute of mine. I loved the crowds and the excitement, the bright colors of the women's dresses, the wreaths of evergreen decking the church, the smell of incense, the wavering candlelight and the long, lissome, fluid lines of melody that wound in and out of that nuptial Mass. I felt soaked in pageantry, drenched in the heady deluge of ceremony and celebration. Afterward at the wedding breakfast when I was drinking champagne I thought I could see into my distant future, and the view I saw was sumptuous and magnificent, a place far from the edge of darkness where I had grown up. One day, I thought, I would look back and the darkness would be no more than a memory.

One day. But not now.

I drank some more champagne. Mr. Gallagher advised me not to, but that didn't matter, because the dancing was beginning and I set my glass aside. I had engaged a band from Galway to play waltzes, polkas and galops, but at last one of the O'Malleys found his fiddle and Cashelmara was Irish at last, from the marble floor of the circular hall to the domed roof above the gallery. All the Americans broke down and cried; the ecstasy was too much for them and they all swore they'd never leave Ireland again.

Some unknown time later I looked around for my uncles, but they were gone, and when I asked where my mother was I was told she had retired to the nursery to help put the children to bed.

662

I missed her, then forgot her absence. I was too busy talking to my friends and dancing with Kerry, and when at last Mr. Gallagher suggested it was time we left our guests to continue the party without us I made no attempt to look for my mother to say good night. I had eyes only for Kerry in her tight white satin gown, the long Irish lace of her veil streaming behind her as she danced. Kerry was all that mattered now. I tried to lead her away, but all the men had to claim a kiss from the bride so that in the end I had to sweep her off her feet and carry her through the crowd before she could be kissed to death. Everyone cheered. Halfway up the stairs I set her down, and we rushed up to the gallery together before pausing to wave. Everyone roared approval again. The cheers were still ringing in our ears as we raced hand in hand down the corridor to the west wing, and when we reached the door of our bedroom I swept her off her feet a second time to carry her across the threshold.

II

Afterward I knew exactly why no one had wanted us to marry while we were so young. Since they had presumably spent the first part of their youth in celibate frustration they would have found it maddening to watch while Kerry and I not only tried to escape such a tedious fate but actually succeeded in doing so.

"I wonder why more people don't do it," mused Kerry the next morning as we lay snugly in our old-fashioned fourposter and watched the red bobbles on the muslin curtains dance in the draft from the window. "Why isn't it fashionable any more? It used to be fashionable. Think of Shakespeare. And even in this century people used to do it when they were our age. Pa says that before the famine everyone married at sixteen."

"Oh, so it's marriage you're talking about!"

She giggled. "Don't tease! Oh, Ned, just think, if you hadn't stood up to Mr. Drummond like that you'd still be studying Latin with Mr. Watson and I'd still be learning French irregular verbs with Miss Cameron!"

She was very proud of the way I had stood up to Drummond. Not wishing to alarm her by describing every detail of my interview with him, I had simply said I'd got what I wanted by threatening the removal of my mother from her position of trustee and Drummond's own dismissal from Cashelmara.

". . . and now we can do exactly as we please," Kerry was saying with a happy sigh.

We spent a great deal of time doing exactly as we pleased. I had decided to postpone the honeymoon abroad for some months, but for several days after the wedding we stayed in our apartments. I hadn't wanted to postpone our journey to the Continent, but my uncles had explained to me before the wedding that I was in no financial position to consider an expensive honeymoon.

"Of course we'll lend you the money to go," said Uncle Thomas, "but you must realize you don't have the money of your own to spend on such an expedition."

"Then I'll wait till I do have the money." My pride was at stake by this time. It was clear they thought I'd been childish in handling my money, and I wanted to prove to them that I wasn't an immature spendthrift addicted to living beyond his income.

"Paris will be much nicer in the spring," said Kerry when I explained shame-faced that I had had to change our plans. "And think what fun it'll be to spend Christmas at Cashelmara with both our families!"

She was right, but in the new year the Gallaghers returned to America, and for the first time since the wedding we were alone with my mother and Drummond.

It was awkward, but I said nothing. I did wonder if I might suggest that my mother move to Clonagh Court, which had originally been intended as the dower house of the estate, but I knew neither she nor Drummond would want to go, and the thought of another confrontation with either of them was so repugnant to me that I refused to contemplate it. Besides, I reminded myself, part of my bargain with Drummond had been that I would leave him alone provided that I was allowed to marry Kerry. When I was twenty-one I would of course put matters right, but until then . . . It was easier to make excuses to Kerry and ask her to be patient.

"But why do you have to wait till you're twenty-one to be your own master?" asked Kerry, puzzled. "Aren't you your own master now you're married?"

"Not according to the trust. It's arranged so that whether I'm married or not it lasts till I'm twenty-one."

"But I still don't understand why your mother can't move to Clonagh Court. After all, she can be trustee just as well there as here, can't she?"

"She wouldn't want to move without taking John and the girls, and it would be too complicated to uproot them at present."

"But—"

664

"Kerry, please try and make allowances for my mother. She's had a very unhappy life and she's devoted to her children—"

"I know, I know," said Kerry.

"—and she's been a wonderful mother to me, and I simply can't push her out of my house the very moment I get married. We must wait until the time is right, and the time just isn't right at present, that's all. I'm sorry."

Kerry sighed. "Well, I guess I don't truly mind so long as we can escape and be alone together like this."

The escape was mine as well as hers, and soon we were locked tightly in our private world where nothing existed for me but warm thighs and curving flesh and moist, dark secret places where I could retreat for as long as I chose.

However, I did dislike my subordinate position, and my temporary lack of money served to deepen my frustration. When Drummond told me he was taking my mother to Paris for a holiday I was furious.

"Excuse me, Mr. Drummond," I said before I could stop myself, "but if I can't afford to take Kerry to the Continent I hardly think you can be in a position to take my mother to Paris."

"Why not?" he said. "It's my money."

"You mean you've saved the money from your salary?" I said, trying to speak boldly but knowing I sounded merely hesitant and doubtful. I loathed speaking to Drummond about anything by this time and could hardly bear to be in the same room with him for more than two minutes.

"I won the money gambling with Phineas Gallagher," he said easily, and I knew by instinct that this was his private reward for encouraging the wedding. I had benefited myself from Mr. Gallagher's generosity, but I had already spent the first year's income from Kerry's marriage settlement, and I knew I would have to wait several months before I saw any more Gallagher money.

"You don't grudge your mother a holiday, do you?" said Drummond mildly. "She's worked so hard giving all your guests hospitality and seeing you had a nice wedding."

"Of course I don't grudge it to her," I said hastily, willing to say anything to avoid a quarrel, but I did grudge it.

"Think how nice it will be without them for a few weeks!" Kerry said encouragingly, trying to cheer me up, but after they left there was trouble on the estate and my dissatisfaction only increased. Drummond had raised the rent of everyone in the valley except the

O'Malleys, and there was great bitterness in Clonareen. The deputation sent to Cashelmara to protest was led by my two friends Sean and Paddy Joyce, and, greatly embarrassed, I told them that no one need pay the raised rent until Drummond returned.

"I'll tell Mr. Drummond that everyone must be treated fairly," I promised, my heart sinking at the prospect, but although I kept my promise when Drummond returned he didn't listen to me.

"I had no choice but to raise the rents," he said. "The estate wasn't paying its way. As for the Joyces' complaints about the O'Malleys, you can tell them if they come whining to you again that the O'Malleys are the poorest people in the valley, and it would be no use raising the rents when I know full well they can't pay. And I don't believe in evictions."

This meant that he didn't believe in evicting his kinsmen. He evicted some of the poorer Joyces when they couldn't pay the new rents, and to make matters worse he then distributed their land among the O'Malleys.

The result was a faction fight. It took place on St. Patrick's Day, and afterward no one knew who had won, but there were six men maimed and at least a dozen bloody noses. The long-standing feud between the Joyces and the O'Malleys was flaring violently again, and soon someone wrote in whitewash on the walls of Cashelmara's grounds MAXWELL DRUMMOND IS A SCOTSMAN—a terrible insult to any agent and particularly so to Drummond, who always went to great lengths to explain how Irish he was.

I didn't know what to do. I debated whether to approach Drummond again, but I knew that would achieve nothing. He would brush me off just as before—except that this time he would probably be even more abrupt and tell me to run away and amuse myself with Kerry. It was no use appealing to my mother. I did think of appealing to my uncles, but I was so afraid that Drummond might somehow intercept the letter that when I did write I merely asked them if they would care to visit Cashelmara that spring. But they both declined. Uncle Thomas was too occupied with advanced medical studies, and Uncle David, who had just announced his engagement, was too busy with preparations for his spring wedding in London.

"I think it's time we had our honeymoon," I said to Kerry in April. By this time Cashelmara was so distasteful to me that I was prepared to go to great lengths to escape, and although I was still awkwardly placed financially I swallowed my pride and asked for a loan from Uncle Thomas.

A month later Kerry and I attended Uncle David's wedding and then crossed the Channel for the start of our six-week visit to France, Switzerland and Italy.

III

I had intended to confide in my uncles when I saw them, but Uncle David was in such a state of elation that I hated to burden him with my troubles, and Uncle Thomas was so cool to me on account of the loan that his attitude scarcely encouraged any confidences. So I said nothing and later I was glad. What could I have said that wouldn't have broken my agreement with Drummond and resulted in endless horrifying scenes? My uncles might have taken my cause to court, I might have been unable to stop them and then God only knew what Drummond might have done. And without hopelssly endangering my mother I couldn't explain to my uncles why I was so frightened of Drummond. I was prepared to conceal the poisoning in order to protect her, but after all she wasn't their mother, and they might think they had more of a duty to bring their brother's murderer to justice than they had to protect her.

Better not to confide in my uncles. At least not until I was twenty-one and able to put my own house in order.

Uncle David had a dull sort of Protestant wedding with a stuffy reception afterward where everyone stood around and talked in affected English voices. I thought it was boring. The only bright spot was Uncle David's bride, who was pretty and gay and invited us to stay with them in Surrey later in the year. They were going to Germany for their honeymoon, which was a relief, because if they had been going to Paris we might have been obliged to travel with them, and by this time I couldn't wait to be entirely on my own with Kerry at least a hundred miles from any member of my family.

I had never been to the Continent before and was at first too overwhelmed to remember any of my schoolboy French. But the Irish and the French have long been sympathetic to each other on account of their mutual enemy, and my French surname also smoothed our path through France.

"I like it pronounced the French way," said Kerry, intrigued, and I agreed it did make a pleasant change. The English pronunciation used by my family rhymes with "chalice," although all my life I've heard variations from outsiders.

It would have been possible for me to have obtained introductions to Parisian society, but neither of us wanted to be bothered with tedious dinner parties, so we merely stayed at the best hotel and explored the famous sights. The French thought we were most romantic, although I'm sure no one believed we were married.

Presently we journeyed to Switzerland, which Kerry decided she liked better, but I remained faithful to France even when we traveled south to visit Venice, Florence and Rome. I would have liked Italy more, but too often it reminded me painfully of the Italian garden at Cashelmara and my father talking enthusiastically about light and stone and cypress trees.

When we returned to Cashelmara in early September we found two letters waiting for us. Uncle Thomas had written to say he was going to America for a year, and my father-in-law, by coincidence, wanted us to come to Boston to visit him.

"Why don't we go?" I said to Kerry.

It hadn't taken me long to discover that matters at Cashelmara were worse than ever, and I dreaded being caught in the middle of a conflict I was powerless to resolve.

"I think I really have a duty to take Kerry home for a visit before we finally settle down," I said to my mother.

"*I* didn't go home for a visit after I was married!" said my mother.

"But, Mama, that was years ago when crossing the Atlantic was more hazardous. Travel is easier nowadays, and people think less of it than they used to."

"I suppose this entire scheme is Kerry's idea," said my mother, and although I denied it she refused to believe me.

"I do think it's a little selfish of you, my dear," she said to Kerry that night at dinner. "I don't think you should drag Ned off to America when he's obviously so pleased to be home again."

Kerry went red.

"Mama . . ." I began.

"We wouldn't go if you'd only move to Clonagh Court!" Kerry blurted out and then jumped up and rushed out of the room.

"Well, really!" said my mother in a fury.

"Mama, you've only yourself to blame," I said, red in the face myself by this time. "If you made more effort to be civil to Kerry, she wouldn't pass such remarks. Excuse me, please." And I too abandoned my dinner.

I found Kerry sobbing noisily in the depths of our fourposter bed.

At last she managed to say, "I don't want to go to America. I'd rather stay here and have a baby, but I'll never have a baby if I stay here because your mother makes me too upset."

It took me at least five minutes to understand what she meant, but finally I was able to piece together an explanation. We had been married nine months, there was no sign of a baby and she had been so terrified she was "barren" that she had dredged up enough courage to seek advice from Aunt Madeleine, who had always been kind to her. Aunt Madeleine had told her that young girls often didn't become pregnant as easily as the world thought they did and that sometimes a girl who married at fifteen might have to wait a year or two before conceiving, even though there was no physical reason why she shouldn't have a baby. Aunt Madeleine had said it was God's way of ensuring that a girl was grown up in mind as well as in body before she assumed the responsibilities of motherhood.

"Aunt Madeleine said I should live quietly and not travel or worry about anything," said Kerry, weeping. "She said if I lived a quiet calm life there would be more chance of the baby coming."

"Well, that problem's easily solved," I said, kissing her. "It only takes about a week to sail to America, and once you're there you can be as quiet and calm as you like. We'll leave for Boston as soon as possible."

But to my astonishment and anger money again proved to be a problem. Drummond explained that the difficulties with the estate were making my income erratic, and he suggested I postpone the visit to America until spring.

"That's quite out of the question, I'm afraid," I said abruptly and wrote to Uncle David to borrow money for our fares. Fortunately Uncle David was in a generous mood. His latest detective story had been rejected by the publishers (his stories had never yet appeared in print), but his wife thought the book was wonderfully clever and this compensated for the rejection. There was also the discreet hint in the letter that a baby was expected in the new year.

"Lucky Harriet," sighed Kerry, but she was in such good spirits about the prospect of returning home that she couldn't be despondent for long. We sailed from Ireland in late October, and I was so glad to leave that it no longer shamed me that I was running away from difficulties I couldn't resolve.

I'll think about them later was all I said to myself and dug my buried head a little deeper in the sand.

IV

It was 1890, the year of the downfall of Charles Stewart Parnell. In November his mistress's husband was granted a divorce, and on the first of December he was deposed from the leadership of the Irish Party.

"I said all along he was finished," said Phineas Gallagher over our glasses of port as he offered me one of his fat cigars.

"Mr. Drummond will be upset," I said, accepting the cigar and lighting it.

"If Max has a grain of sense he'll learn from Parnell's mistakes. Max ain't got no business living openly with your mother and running your estate like he owned it, Ned. It's humiliating for my daughter and it's humiliating for you, and if he don't see that he's not the man I thought he was. People in that valley of yours might stand a rent raise or two because they're used to abuse from their landlord, but they'll not stand for one of their own number lording it over them while he lives in adultery. No decent bunch of Irish folk would stand for it. It's immoral."

"Yes." I wanted to change the subject because I didn't want him to find out exactly how powerless I was to stop Drummond. "But it's a shame about Parnell, isn't it? He was a great man and did so much for Ireland. Why, he was the first Irish leader who literally forced the English to listen to him at Westminster."

"You could make the Saxons listen to you," said Phineas Gallagher. "Don't you have a seat at Westminster?"

"Yes, I suppose I do. In the House of Lords. I hadn't really thought about it before."

"Ah, it's a lovely leader you'd be!" sighed my father-in-law, filling up my glass of port. "A fine upstanding young baron, well spoken and smart. Sure it would cost a little more money to live in London part of the year, but there are Irish people this side of the water who'd see you didn't starve."

"I know what a generous man you are, sir," I said, smiling at him, "but if I ever decide to work for Ireland at Westminster I'd rather do so modestly, using my own money. I've discovered I hate to be in debt."

"This wouldn't be incurring a debt, Ned! It would be graciously accepting the good will of your fellow countrymen!"

I smiled but said nothing.

It was my father-in-law who laughed. "Jesus, you've got an old head on young shoulders!" he exclaimed, and then he added oddly without explaining himself, "It's too bad about Max Drummond. I liked him."

I wanted to say that I had once liked him too, but the words refused to be said. I tried to think of something else before I could become too upset, and fortunately I soon had news of another kind to divert me. When I got to bed that night Kerry confided in me that she was sure—positively sure—she was pregnant.

"Already!" I was impressed.

"It must have happened just before we left Cashelmara."

"I'm glad about that," I said, although there was no reason why it should matter where the baby had been conceived. But somehow I felt conception at Cashelmara must make him more of an Irishman than an American.

"I must write to Aunt Madeleine at once!" said Kerry happily and began to talk about cribs and little silk baby dresses.

I was dismayed to find myself wondering selfishly how much life would now change, but I clamped the thought down and tried to be as happy as Kerry was. I was surprised when I found this difficult. I could accept the fact that the baby existed, yet somehow its existence remained utterly unreal to me. I kept telling myself I was going to have a son and heir, but after I had told myself that half a dozen times I didn't know what to tell myself next. I could understand how Kerry had become so deeply involved with the idea because the baby was growing in her body, but it wasn't growing in mine, and an emotional response to the situation seemed to be entirely lacking in me. I was much troubled by this indifference since I felt sure it must be wrong, but I was too ashamed to tell anyone about it.

"I suppose we can't go to bed together any more now," I said, trying not to sound gloomy.

"Can't we?" said Kerry, horrified. "Oh, that can't be true! Who told you that?"

I couldn't remember. Groping through my memories of the distant past, I saw my mother lying palely on a chaise longue before retiring to a bedroom she didn't share with my father.

"I'll ask Ma," said Kerry. "She'll know."

Mrs. Gallagher knew a great deal. She told Kerry that husbands were just as important as babies, more important, since a decent girl couldn't have a baby without one, and that Kerry must never forget that. She said I must be petted and made a fuss of, and that if I "wanted my way" I could have it provided I was careful and considerate. She told Kerry not to listen if any doctor gave her advice to the contrary and said that so long as we both behaved with common sense there would be no danger of a miscarriage.

I was much cheered by this, and when in February I told Uncle Thomas the good news I was even able to sound genuinely pleased. Uncle Thomas was engaged in further studies at the medical school which formed a part of Harvard University, and he had taken an apartment in Cambridge, the town near Boston where Harvard is situated. I had never entirely understood before about Uncle Thomas's profession. I knew he was a doctor, but he was not like Dr. Cahill or indeed any other doctor whom I had met in the past. He had no exclusive consulting rooms in Harley Street. Indeed he saw no patients at all. His work was conducted in the laboratories attached to Guy's Hospital in London, and until his decision to go to America he had been concerned with investigating the diseases found in people who were already dead.

"But I became tired of morbid anatomy," he explained to me in his little sitting room that overlooked the Charles River, "and so I decided to turn to clinical pathology instead, the investigation of disease—and health—in living people. There are different areas of pathology, you know, and our knowledge is increasing substantially every year. The exciting part is that although men have been curious about the study of disease for centuries, the modern science of pathology has really existed only for the past thirty years. I was always fascinated by the war against disease. David could never understand it, but I used to tell him my cases were like his detective stories—finding the clues, isolating the cause of death, solving the puzzle. But I've had enough of corpses. I've made my mark in London as a specialist in morbid anatomy, and now I want new fields to conquer."

He explained he could have studied clinical pathology in London, but he preferred to come to America—"Because after all I'm half American, just as you are," he said, "and when it occurred to me the other day that I was almost thirty and knew next to nothing about my mother's country I thought now would be as good an opportunity as any to find out more. It was David's wedding that finally made me decide to come. I realized I must spend my year in America while I'm still a bachelor and have the freedom to do as I please."

"Will you go to New York?" I asked, thinking of my estranged Uncle Charles, who was his cousin. I had been toying with the idea of making peace with Uncle Charles, but I knew such a move would infuriate my mother, so I had never communicated with him.

672

"Yes, I intend to go down in the spring to see the Marriotts. Will you still be here then?"

"I doubt it," I said. "We must be back in Ireland by that time because of Kerry's health." And I told him about the baby.

After he had made the usual kind remarks he said, "You'll need money more than ever now, Ned. We'll have to do something about Drummond, you know. It's absurd that you have to go around borrowing from your relatives while Drummond and your mother live in such style in your own home."

"When I'm twenty-one—"

"Can you really afford to wait till then? God only knows what sort of a wreck Drummond and your mother will have made of Cashelmara by the time you're twenty-one! I think I'll write to David and see what he suggests. I have no desire whatsoever to go to court, but—"

"No litigation," I said a shade too loudly. "I must wait till I'm twenty-one."

"Ned, you keep repeating that phrase as if it were a magic incantation, but what exactly are you going to do when you're twenty-one?"

"Dismiss Drummond and tell my mother she must move to Clonagh Court."

"And if she refuses to go? Are you sure you won't wind up going to court anyway in order to get rid of Drummond?"

"I . . . I'll think about that later. When the time comes."

"Ned," said Uncle Thomas gently, "the time has come. The time is now."

I shook my head violently and said nothing.

"Ned, what is it? What's the matter? You're scared stiff of Drummond, aren't you? Why? You surely don't still suspect him of murdering your father?"

"I know he murdered him," I said, fighting a terrible desire to cry, and told him how I had obtained the consent for my marriage.

He was so appalled he couldn't speak.

"So I can't do anything," I said. "I'm too afraid of harming my mother. He'll drag her down with him, I know he will, and I can't have that. My own mother . . ." I couldn't go on.

At last he managed to say, "I should have insisted on an autopsy, but . . . well, I couldn't believe Madeleine would have made a mistake and she was so certain—so absolutely certain—"

"It *is* difficult to believe that Aunt Madeleine can be imperfect enough to make a mistake occasionally," I agreed. My voice was calm again, far calmer than his.

"And there would have been such a scandal even if the autopsy had merely confirmed the diagnosis. I suppose I deliberately chose to look the other way."

He still sounded so appalled that I said hastily, "You didn't look the other way, Uncle Thomas. You considered the possibility of poison and rejected it. That's not the same thing at all."

"No, it's worse," he said grimly. "It all goes to prove that doctors aren't to be trusted when they apply their knowledge to their own families. They're swayed by all kinds of preconceived notions and prejudices which distort their judgment. My God, how could I have been so unprofessional? I should have insisted on a proper inquiry instead of listening to David's Borgia theories and accepting unquestioningly the diagnosis of a woman who has had no formal education in medicine."

"Well, thank God you didn't insist on an autopsy," I said, "for where would my mother be now if you had?"

"Yes, but . . . Ned, something must be done. If we can't force the issue publicly in court, we must do it privately, by threats."

"There's no way in which we can do that," I said. "I've thought about it day after day, and there's no solution. We have no lever with Drummond. I was able to threaten him about my marriage because I made him believe I would do anything to marry Kerry, even ruin my mother. But those were exceptional circumstances. He knows that normally I'd do nothing to harm her."

"Then there must be something else we can do." He began to pace up and down the room, and the winter sunlight, shining palely into the room, flashed rhythmically on his thick glasses. "We must prove Drummond's guilt and your mother's innocence," he said at last. "We must be quite certain before we go to the police that they won't make a mistake."

"They're bound to think she had knowledge of the murder after the fact."

" 'After the fact' is a very different matter to 'before the fact.' And there are mitigating circumstances—her infatuation with Drummond —any good counsel could get her off scot-free." He snapped his fingers and spun around to face me. "Of course! David's the answer! God, I never thought I'd be grateful that David has a monumental imagination and a passion for detective stories! We'll send him to Cashelmara and he can make a secret investigation of all the circum-

674

stances surrounding your father's death. If he can prove that the poison was administered after your mother left Clonagh Court that day—"

"But supposing Drummond poisoned the food she took to Papa?" I said. "Mama took some blackberry cordial and a cake to Clonagh Court as gifts. She wanted to be pleasant to him so they could discuss the custody question without quarreling."

"Perhaps David can find a servant who can testify that the cake and cordial were never touched. That would mean the poison came from another source which with any luck we can link to Drummond exclusively. It's an idea worth trying anyway, and if anyone is well suited to such an investigation it's David."

I did try to share his optimism, but I was too frightened. I should have felt better after unburdening all the fears I had kept to myself for so long, but I felt worse. I felt I no longer had any control over the future, and that night I dreamt that Cashelmara had been razed to the ground and that Drummond was walking from the burning ruins to destroy me.

In panic I turned all my attention to Kerry. It was time to go home before her pregnancy entered the last critical months, but before we finally sailed at the beginning of April I had postponed our departure twice on the excuse that the Atlantic would still be swept by winter storms, and Mrs. Gallagher said if I postponed it a third time Kerry would have to remain in Boston until after the baby arrived.

The last thing I wanted to do was endanger Kerry's health, and I was anxious for my son to be born at Cashelmara. Screwing up all my courage, I faced the ordeal of going home.

Uncle David had written to say he had arranged to visit Cashelmara in mid-March, but I heard nothing further from him before we sailed.

"All will be well," said Uncle Thomas, embracing me before I left, but although I wanted desperately to believe him I couldn't.

I was certain all wouldn't be well. I didn't see how it could be.

And I was terrified.

v

I hadn't told my mother Kerry was pregnant and had asked Aunt Madeleine to keep the news a secret. I wouldn't have told Aunt Madeleine except that Kerry had been so anxious that she should know.

675

"Why don't you want your mother to find out about the baby?" Kerry had demanded, but I had merely said that I had wanted to tell her such exciting news in person.

That satisfied Kerry, but in fact I had no idea why I should have felt so reticent. However, I found out soon enough when we stepped at last into the hall at Cashelmara and my mother came quickly downstairs to greet us. One glance at the expression on her face as she saw Kerry's figure was enough to confirm my instinct that the news would be unwelcome to her.

"I suppose it was only to be expected," she said, "but I must say I do think you're both ridiculously young to be parents."

It was Drummond who saved the situation. He kissed Kerry and said he was sure everyone was going to be very pleased. He was wise enough not to offer me his hand to shake, but he congratulated me with a smile, and fortunately before my mother could speak again John and the girls came racing downstairs for a succession of joyous reunions. Kerry was diverted, and turning once more to my mother, I opened my mouth to tell her what I thought of her welcome.

It was only then that I noticed she was wearing black. It didn't suit her. The color made her skin look sallow.

"Ned, how lovely to see you again!" cried Eleanor, taking me by surprise as she flung her arms around me.

I hugged her. I had just realized that she too was wearing black when Jane danced up to me.

"Neddy, do you know what happened? Ozymandias and Percival had another family, and I've christened the kittens after the colors in my paintbox. Their names are Azure, Cobalt and Lapis-Lazuli, and they're all white with orange paws."

Jane wore a little black smocked dress, and as she jumped up and down in front of me I saw her petticoats fluttering above her black stockings.

Everyone was wearing black.

"Ned dearest," said my mother, "come into the morning room for a moment. There's something I must say to you alone."

We went into the morning room. I was quite calm. When I asked her where Uncle David was my voice was steady and untroubled.

"Oh, Ned . . ." Her face crumpled. Harsh ugly lines disfigured her features as her eyes filled with tears.

"Where is he?" I repeated, still perfectly calm. "What's happened to him?"

"Ned, he . . . he . . ." But she couldn't say it.

676

"He died." I looked around the room as if I expected to find an explanation written on the walls. When I found none I looked at her again, but there was nothing in her face except grief.

"Yes," she whispered. "Yes, he died." And then she clung to me as if she had no one else to turn to and wept as if the grief were beyond all her powers to endure.

Chapter Eight

My mother began to talk in a low, uneven voice.

"He arrived two weeks ago and complained of feeling unwell almost at once—an intestinal disorder. Well, you know David's digestion has always been weak. I thought nothing of it, and then he said he was better. But a day later he fell ill again—a pain in his right side, he told me. Unfortunately, Dr. Cahill was away—he had left the previous day for Dublin—but Madeleine came. When I told her the symptoms she said it sounded like peritonitis, a severe infection resulting from inflammation of the appendix. Dr. Cahill confirmed the diagnosis later. David had had one or two previous attacks, apparently, and a London specialist had even recommended an operation, but of course operations are always so unpleasant and risky. David had decided that he would try a prescribed diet before resorting to an operation."

I asked about the funeral.

"It was last Monday. The body was taken back to Surrey and Madeleine left to be with his wife. We sent a telegram to Thomas. It was too late to send one to you because you'd already left. We were going to wait till you came home, but . . . his wife didn't want the funeral delayed, too much strain and sadness. I said you would understand. I wanted to go myself, but the shock . . . It made me ill. I kept thinking of Marguerite. I still think of her day and night. She was so very fond of David. He was such a dear little boy."

678

"There was no doubt at all about the diagnosis?"

"No, darling. None at all."

II

"There was no doubt about the diagnosis, was there, Aunt Madeleine?"

"No, my dear," said Aunt Madeleine, who had just returned from Surrey. "None at all. I told Dr. Cahill there had been a recent history of illness that had been diagnosed as an inflammation of the appendix."

"Did Uncle David actually mention this to you himself, Aunt Madeleine?"

She hesitated for one full second. But no more. Her eyes were very light and clear and blue. "Yes, dear, he did."

"I see. Forgive me. It was only that it seemed something of a coincidence, my father and Uncle David dying of somewhat similar symptoms."

"No, one can't compare the two cases. They were quite different."

There was a silence. Aunt Madeleine's eyes never changed their expression.

"Aunt Madeleine . . ."

"Yes, Ned?"

"Did Dr. Cahill suggest an autopsy?"

"No, dear. In the circumstances I told him I really didn't think it was necessary. Of course, when Thomas comes home he may insist upon one. I don't know. But that must be his decision, not mine."

"But—"

"We must wait till Thomas comes home," said Aunt Madeleine. "I have written to him to suggest he return immediately. Now, my dear, there's absolutely nothing for you to worry about. Thomas and I will attend to everything as soon as he comes back, and until then there's nothing further that either of us can do."

After a moment I said, "You know, don't you?"

"Know what? My dear child, I haven't the slightest idea what you're talking about! I only know that it's no concern of yours. There's no need for you to worry. All will be well in time."

"Aunt Madeleine, there's no need to treat me as if I was still in the nursery!"

"Ned, I'm treating you as a very dear nephew who is only seventeen years old, yet has all kinds of worries and responsibilities that most seventeen-year-olds either don't have or haven't even heard of.

You have enough to cope with. Leave this, please, to me and Thomas."

"But—"

"There is nothing else to say."

"I want to talk to you, Aunt Madeleine."

"Later, dear. When Thomas is home. But not now."

I went away.

III

As soon as I arrived home from Clonareen I shut myself in my room and wrote to Uncle Thomas.

"Please ignore Aunt Madeleine's letter," I said. "There's no need for you to return home prematurely. I am quite convinced that Uncle David died a natural death—*even Dr. Cahill* thought an autopsy was unnecessary—and you know that I'd be the first to tell you if I thought Uncle David had been murdered."

I said more, but I don't remember the other lies now. It was a muddled letter, but the message was clear. When it was finished I even rode to Leenane so that the letter would catch the earliest mail car to Galway.

Afterward I wondered what I was doing, but all I could think was: Aunt Madeleine knows. When she talks to Uncle Thomas he'll insist on the body being exhumed and an autopsy performed. Drummond will be accused and so will my mother, and that'll mean I've spent all these months holding my tongue for nothing. I couldn't bear that. It would be unendurable.

Must go on protecting my mother. No choice. Must keep Uncle Thomas away for as long as possible. Buy a little more time for myself. Think what I must do.

But I didn't know what I could do, and after a while I could no longer bring myself to think about it.

Uncle Thomas's letter arrived some days later.

"My dear Ned, first let me thank you for your kind and thoughtful letter. The news was a terrible blow to me, for David and I were very close. Indeed, I can't remember a time when he wasn't in the world, and now that he's no longer here the world will seem a very different place to me.

"Second, let me assure you that you were mistaken about the contents of Madeleine's letter. She never breathed a word to me about murder, merely urged me to come home to console you and

Sarah and make arrangements for David's poor Harriet. However, I might have come home immediately if three things hadn't happened to dissuade me: Harriet herself wrote to beg me not to return early on her account, as she has gone to stay with her parents; you wrote to assure me there was absolutely no reason to suspect foul play, and Sarah wrote to say that everyone at Cashelmara was recovering from the shock and that it would be mere selfishness on her part if she asked me to rush home to be a pillar of strength to my family. After considering these letters, I have decided I should remain here until my studies are completed, but if you need my help you have only to send word and I'll be on my way across the Atlantic.

"In answer to your question: Yes, David did have a history of poor digestion, but I hadn't heard that this was ever attributed to a weakness of the appendix. However, this could well be a recent diagnosis made after my departure to America, and David could have refrained from mentioning it in his letters.

"I agree with you that it seems almost impossible that he could have been murdered despite the peculiar circumstances of his visit to Cashelmara. I simply can't imagine Drummond being such a fool, and besides if David had really discovered important evidence I think Drummond would have been willing to reach an agreement with him—a comfortable life at Clonagh Court, for example, in exchange for his resignation as agent and your mother's resignation as trustee. David would have been of more use to Drummond alive. To kill him would have been extraordinarily dangerous and fool-hardy, and I don't think Drummond would ever kill anyone unless he was absolutely certain of getting away with it. No, I'm sure David did die a natural death. It's very tragic, but at least we have the consolation of knowing that neither of us could have prevented it and thus neither of us are to blame.

"However, despite all I've said above I have no intention of making the same mistake twice. This time I shall insist on an autopsy, both to set our minds at rest and to satisfy my professional standards, but you need have no fear that I shall not employ the greatest possible discretion. Very fortunately, because of my experience in these matters and my personal acquaintance with those at the Home Office and Scotland Yard who sanction exhumations when foul play is suspected, I believe I can arrange not only for discretion but for absolute secrecy. I couldn't have done this in your father's case, because he is buried in Ireland and the appropriate Irish authorities are all quite unknown to me.

"We can discuss this more fully when I return in September. Meanwhile, my love to you and all the family."

I burned the letter in the grate in my room and prodded the ashes later to make sure every scrap of writing was destroyed. Prompted by Uncle Thomas's speculations, I wondered if I might perhaps negotiate another bargain with Drummond. No autopsy if he would resign from his post and move with my mother to Clonagh Court. But that wouldn't do. If Drummond had killed Uncle David as well as my father, I wanted him hanged and so, I knew, would Uncle Thomas. But my mother . . .

Always my mother.

"I want to talk to you, Ned," said my mother to me on one bright sunny May morning after the children had left the breakfast table to play in the garden. Kerry was having breakfast in bed as usual, but that day I had made the effort to join the rest of my family in the dining room. As soon as Drummond had followed the children outside, my mother had dismissed the servants and asked me to stay.

"Please don't make some excuse to escape," she said in a rapid voice. "Yes, I know you've been trying to avoid me lately—I'm not entirely insensitive, you know—and I would so much like to talk to you about it. Please. It would mean a great deal to me."

"Of course, Mama," I said. I had half risen to my feet, but now I sank down again in front of my empty teacup and waited for her to go on.

"I've been behaving very foolishly," she said, "and I want to apologize—to both you and Kerry."

I looked at her blankly. She was wearing an elaborate blouse that did not quite succeed in hiding the lines about her neck, and as I saw those lines I realized how much she had changed since we had returned to Cashelmara. Her hair was no longer the rich brown I had loved but a flat black—no doubt dyed with the intent of making her look younger, but it had the opposite effect because the color was so unnatural. It also changed her complexion, emphasizing the olive tint so that her skin appeared sallow—although she tried to conceal the sallowness with a heavy layer of powder. The make-up, excessive and distasteful to me, made her face seem like a mask, and although I strained my eyes I couldn't see beyond the mask to the familiar much-loved person beneath.

"No wonder you took offense and have been behaving so coolly toward me," she was saying, and, unlike her unnatural appearance, her voice was reassuringly awkward, filled with genuine emotion.

"It was so silly of me to be upset about the baby and so wrong. You mustn't think I don't realize that and feel ashamed. But, darling, everything's going to be different from now on. I've got used to the idea of being a grandmother, and I know I shall love the baby when it comes. I've always loved babies, as you know. I don't know why I was so stupid unless it was because . . ." She stopped.

"Please, Mama, there's no need to say any more. I understand."

"No, you don't. It was because I was jealous of Kerry, you see— because she's so young and happy and has all her life before her, because she's carrying the child of someone she loves. When you came back from America and I saw Kerry, I felt such a sadness, as if everything was finished for me and I had nothing left to give. It would have been different if I could have had another child—Maxwell's child—but the doctor told me after Jane was born—"

"Yes," I said.

"You wouldn't understand, but when a woman's no longer young —I can't describe the insecurity I feel sometimes, the absolute dread of aging, the terror that I shall lose my looks and no longer be attractive to Maxwell."

I stood up. My napkin fluttered to the floor.

"Don't turn your back on me, Ned," she said. "I've been so lonely these last few weeks when you haven't had a word to say to me."

I suddenly saw her long ago waiting for me to step off the boat in New York, her face strained with that painful, naked longing to see me again. Memories of other far-off times flickered through my mind, golden sunlit days in the nursery, my mother loving me as my father had loved me, staying with me during all those dark days when she had been terrified of MacGowan, making sacrifice after sacrifice until Drummond's shadow had wrapped itself around her life. But if I no longer blamed my father for Hugh MacGowan, I could no longer blame my mother for Maxwell Drummond.

I thought of Drummond talking of acts of God, the one explanation that allowed me to forgive both my parents, and realized dimly that for the first time for nearly five years I was again able to love my parents equally. I didn't have to choose sides any more. The only side I had to take was my own.

"I must apologize too, Mama," I said, kissing her. "I didn't realize how much I'd upset you."

"Then we can make a fresh start? Oh, I feel so much better! Now, don't let's talk about the past any more. Let's talk about the future—

about the baby! I've noticed how certain you both are that it'll be a boy. What are you going to call him?"

"We've no intention of being original, I'm afraid. We thought we'd follow tradition and call him Patrick Edward."

"I see. Well, that's very nice. Will he be called Ned after you?"

"No," I said. "Patrick, after my father."

There was a silence. I had been drifting toward the door, but I stopped to look back.

"Kerry wanted an Irish name," I said at last. "So Patrick seemed particularly suitable."

"Ah yes," said my mother. "Of course."

"Well, if you'll excuse me, Mama . . ."

"Yes, if you wish," she said and added, stumbling over her words, "It'll be so nice to have a baby in the house again. You can't imagine what a pleasure it will be for me . . ."

IV

My son was born on the twenty-eighth of June at four o'clock in the afternoon.

I saw him soon afterward.

I saw Kerry first. She had been in labor only eight hours, but she was very tired and when I saw her she was already half asleep. She said drowsily, "He's lovely. Lovely. You'll like him." And then her hand relaxed in mine and her lashes fluttered against her cheek. After I had kissed her I went into the room next door, where my aunt Madeleine, Dr. Cahill, Nanny and the new nursemaid from London were huddled together in a cabal.

As I entered the room I heard a mewing noise, like a lost kitten, and saw something minute being enveloped in a large shawl.

"A very fine infant!" said Aunt Madeleine kindly. "Almost as fine as you were at that age. Come along! Take a look at him. He won't bite you!"

I edged nearer, hardly able to believe that anything so small could possibly be human.

"A large, healthy baby," said Dr. Cahill, beaming as if he himself were the father. "Eight pounds at least."

"Eight pounds two ounces, Doctor," said Nanny, putting him in his place.

"There!" said Aunt Madeleine. "Isn't that a delightful infant?"

The baby mewed again. He had a red face and his eyes were shut.

684

"Oh yes," I said. "Very nice."

"Would you like to hold him?" said Aunt Madeleine.

"Oh, I'd better not. I might drop him."

"Don't be ridiculous!" said my aunt roundly and dumped the baby in my arms.

The mewing had stopped. The baby had fallen asleep, and when I looked again at his small face I saw only the peace and serenity, the blind unreasoning trust that the world would be a good place for him to live in.

My role of ostrich ended abruptly. I raised my head at last from the sand, and when I looked upon the world into which I had so casually brought my son I realized that world was now intolerable to me.

I remember thinking very clearly, as if I were speaking the words aloud: This is where I take my stand. This is where I stop looking the other way.

v

It was a question of priorities. I thought about that all the time I was writing to Uncle Thomas. I did love my mother, but I had to put Kerry and the baby first. My mother would suffer greatly, but she was only an accessory after the fact, and Uncle Thomas had been convinced that a good counsel would secure her acquittal. After the trial she could come back to Cashelmara for a while until she had recovered from the ordeal, and then I would establish her as gently as possible at Clonagh Court.

"Dear Uncle Thomas, I am writing to ask you to disregard every word I said in my last letter and to beg you to return to England without delay . . ."

It never occurred to me that I might wait another three months until Uncle Thomas returned in September. I had waited too long already, and there wasn't a moment to lose. A murderer who has killed twice could kill a third time, and if I did nothing now I would be no better than an accessory before the fact. I had to act, and besides, I could no longer live beneath the same roof as the man who had killed my father and uncle.

". . . I am convinced that Uncle David was poisoned . . ."

I tried to explain why I had lied in my previous letter, but my explanations made no sense to me now, and I saw I had been in such a state of shock following Uncle David's death that I had been incapable of rational action. I had simply wanted to postpone the consequences by pretending to myself that the consequences didn't exist.

I finished the letter. The next morning I rode to Leenane to deliver it to the mail car. Afterward I felt weak, as if I had expended an enormous amount of energy on some Herculean task, and when I arrived home I would have gone to my room to rest if Jane hadn't waylaid me in the hall.

"Oh, Neddy, the horridest thing has happened—poor Ozymandias is deathly sick and no one will send for Dr. Cahill, no one understands, no one'll help!"

I soothed her as best I could before going to her bedroom, where the wretched animal was stretched out in his cat box. It was obvious he was dying. There was a glazed look in his eyes, and he was breathing with difficulty. The stench of cat vomit was so appalling that we had to retreat to the corridor.

"It's the rat poison," said Jane, tears still streaming down her face. "I knew no good would come of it. It's still lying around in little saucers in the attics, and I knew poor Ozymandias would think it was some sort of milk if he ever escaped up there. I don't see why rat poison was needed anyway. I think it was a dreadful insult to my cats—as good as saying they were too stupid to catch mice, and they weren't, I know they weren't. Uncle David was supposed to have complained about the mice, but he must have been mistaken, because I haven't seen a mouse in this house since Ozymandias was a kitten."

"Wait," I said. "Are you sure the rat poison was bought while Uncle David was here?"

"Of course I'm sure! Do you think I'd forget when my cats were so insulted? It was three days after Uncle David's arrival, but there was no poison in the house when he complained, so some had to be fetched from the dispensary. Aunt Madeleine always keeps poison there because she has trouble with mice, but that's her own fault because she won't keep a cat. If she had a cat like Ozymandias—"

"Jane," I said, "who fetched the poison from the dispensary—do you remember? Was it Flannigan? Or O'Malley? Or was it . . . Mr. Drummond?"

"Oh no, it wasn't Mr. Drummond," said Jane earnestly, her small tear-stained face uptilted to mine. "He was always so nice about my cats and said how clever they were at catching mice. No, it was Mama who said we needed the poison, and she went all the way to the dispensary herself to borrow some from Aunt Madeleine."

686

Chapter Nine

I

I thought: I'll think about it later. Later I'll think about what it all means.

I knew there would be a simple explanation, but at present I was so tired I couldn't think what it was. Later, when I thought about it, I would probably marvel at its simplicity and wonder incredulously how I could have been so obtuse. Later, but not now.

Ozymandias died, and from some safe place a long way away I saw myself organize a little funeral. I dug a grave in a secluded corner of the shrubbery, John nailed together a cross, and Eleanor wrote on it in charcoal: OZYMANDIAS. 1885–1891. R.I.P."

The children chattered at the graveside. I could hear them, but I was such a long way away and their words seemed foreign to me.

"It would be wrong to grieve forever. I'm too young to go into seclusion, but when I die you'll find 'Ozymandias' engraved on my heart."

"There wouldn't be room on your heart, Jane! 'Ozymandias' is so much longer than 'Calais.' "

I had searched the attics earlier and found that all the saucers of rat poison had been removed except one, which had obviously been overlooked. "And it would be wrong to blame Mama for a house-maid's carelessness," I heard myself say in the distance.

"Well, I don't blame her, but . . ."

The children started arguing again. I told Jane on no account to mention the poison to my mother, since it would be so painful to her to realize that she had had a hand, no matter how innocent, in Ozymandias' death.

I didn't want my mother to know I knew about the poison from the dispensary.

"Yes, we must spare Mama. Think how terrible she would feel if she knew." That was Eleanor.

"She'd never forgive herself," agreed Jane, dwelling moodily on the thought. "Very well, we'll spare her."

The next thing I knew I was in the library. I was alone and my mind was empty.

I couldn't think at all.

A long time passed. When dusk began to fall I thought: Of course she's quite insane.

That made it easier somehow, like thinking of appalling vices in terms of acts of God. Insane. Not responsible. Only to be pitied and helped.

I sat down behind the desk, lighted the lamp and tried to work out what had happened. I thought first of my father. Why had it never occurred to me that my mother had killed him? She was the one with the motive, not Drummond. Of course Drummond must have known about it . . . afterward. No, I wouldn't whitewash Drummond. He was a murderer too. Perhaps he hadn't killed my father or my uncle, but he had killed MacGowan, I was certain of that. Anyway, it was because of Drummond that my mother had been deranged enough to kill to keep him and her children. He was just as much to blame as she was, perhaps more, and I was going to see he took the blame. I didn't know yet how I was going to manage it, but if I thought hard enough I was sure I could invent a plan.

I thought for a long time.

The first problem was to save my mother. It was no good thinking that her insanity would be a defense in a court of law, because legal insanity was not the same as medical insanity. There had been a precedent set, the McNaghten case, which had said that everything depended on whether the accused knew that what he was doing was wrong. Uncle Thomas had told me about it once and had said that it was a harsh rule and a number of doctors disapproved of it. It was possible my mother was legally insane, but I doubted it. Certainly it would be too great a risk to let her stand trial, so there must be no trial and I would have to bend those Saxon laws, as Drummond might have said, to carve out a just solution.

It would all have to be absolutely legal, of course. An accident? That would be very difficult. Self-defense? That would be even more difficult, for how could I ever provoke Drummond into making a lethal attack on me? But perhaps it didn't have to be me. Perhaps it could be someone else.

I toyed with a number of schemes for some time.

Whatever scheme I chose had to be foolproof, and afterward I must know exactly what to say to clear myself and my mother and put the blame squarely on Drummond. I had to be very careful and think of every eventuality.

After a while I realized it was quite dark outside, and I still had no idea how I was going to get hold of a gun.

MacGowan had had a gun. He had been armed with a shotgun at the time he had been killed, but a revolver of his had turned up later and Drummond had pocketed it. I knew this was true because Drummond had shown the revolver to me. At one time I had been interested in guns, and when we had been living in America he had taught me how to shoot.

I wondered what he had done with MacGowan's gun. He could have given it to one of the O'Malleys, but I had never heard from any of my O'Malley friends that a relative of theirs had fallen heir to Hugh MacGowan's revolver. Perhaps Drummond had kept it as a bizarre souvenir of his enemy. That would be in keeping with Drummond's character. But where did he hide it? Probably not in his apartments. He would want to keep it clear of my mother and the prying eyes of his new manservant. And I knew it wasn't in the locked cupboard in the back passage with his own firearms. But it had to be somewhere at Cashelmara. Which room did Drummond particularly enjoy using?

My great-grandfather Henry de Salis smiled shyly at me from his position over the chimney piece. The elephant clock ticked meaningfully, and the lamplight cast a soft, steady glow around the room where Drummond smoked his cigars and dipped into the estate books.

The gun was in the bottom drawer of the desk. I took it out and held it in my hands. It was different from Drummond's gun, but presently I managed to break it open and count the bullets. There were three of them. I closed it again, put it back and shut the drawer.

My hands were trembling. I felt very ill.

It was some time before I could recover myself, but at last I was able to think: There's no choice. There's no other way. Either she dies or he dies, and if I leave it to the law it's my mother who'll be hanged.

The next day at dawn after a sleepless night I saddled my horse and rode to Clonareen to call on my friends among the Joyces.

II

"So this is the position," I said to them. "My uncle Thomas will be returning soon from America to arrange for an autopsy on my Uncle David. That means they'll dig up my uncle's body in England and find out how he died. Doctors can do that. Now, I suspect that my uncle was poisoned, and—but do I have to tell you who's responsible?"

"That black villain Maxwell Drummond!" came the prompt chorus.

I smiled but made no comment. Then I said, "Can you see how awkward it is for me? I can't act until I have definite proof of the poisoning or in other words, until I hear the result of the autopsy. I've asked Uncle Thomas to send me a telegram from London as soon as the results are known, but that won't be for some time yet. My letter will take at least another week to reach my uncle, perhaps longer, and it'll take him at least two weeks to leave America and return to England. It could be as long as six weeks before he sends me the telegram, and until then I can do nothing. I must have positive official proof before I can act."

"We'll kill him for you!" offered the foolish hotheads, bursting with eagerness. "We'll act for you if your hands are tied!" And someone added helpfully, "All we'll need is our passage afterward to America."

"No, no, no!" I said, shocked. "Of course you can't commit murder! You could escape scot-free, I dare say, but think of the trouble I'd get into if the police heard I was responsible! A man in my position can't commission murders as if he were ordering a dozen bottles of champagne, you know."

They looked disappointed.

"We must do everything according to the law," I said firmly.

"Saxon laws are no use to us!" muttered my friends truculently, running true to form.

"That's only because you've never learned how to use them," I said. "You're always so bloody busy fighting each other that you lay yourselves open to tyranny from men like MacGowan and Drummond who bend the law to suit their own ends. If you'd take one moment to stop worrying whether a man's name is O'Malley or Joyce, you'd realize that there's no need for you to be persecuted martyrs. Now listen to me. I'm about to get rid of Drummond in a legal way. He'll be accused of murder and removed, but meanwhile I simply want your help to see he doesn't slip through my hands. There's no need to murder him, can't you see that? Why use a hammer to smash an eggshell when you can crack it with a squeeze of your fingers?"

They were sufficiently intrigued to ask me how they could help.

"I'm afraid Drummond might bolt for America once he finds out what's in that telegram with the autopsy results," I said. "I'm sure he'll find out about it somehow, because a telegram isn't as private as a letter, and no doubt he has his spies everywhere. So before he runs away I want you to help me arrest him. We'll do it late at night when he's in bed and unarmed, and then there'll be no danger to anyone."

They were thrilled. Someone asked if they should ask the Brotherhood for guns.

"Certainly not," I said. "Guns have a way of going off by accident, and I don't want anyone being killed. You can bring your knives, but they're to be used only for self-defense. You'll be arresting the man, not cutting him to pieces."

After the jubilation had subsided someone remembered the O'Malleys.

"They'll kill us when they find out we had a hand in the arrest!" said Paddy Joyce.

"Nonsense," I said. "If Drummond's removed from this valley his sons will come back here, and I know Max and Denis Drummond well enough to tell you that neither of them care enough for their father to want his arrest avenged. And if his own sons won't fight you, you can be sure his cousins won't."

They were convinced. There was nothing more I had to do except swear them to secrecy and leave them with the promise that I would send for them when the time was right.

Then I returned to Cashelmara to wait for Uncle Thomas's telegram.

III

I received a letter from him first. It said he was returning at once to England to confer secretly with the Home Secretary and the police, and he would notify me by telegram as soon as there was any news.

When the telegram finally came it said: SUSPICIONS CONFIRMED. LEAVING IMMEDIATELY FOR CASHELMARA. BE BRAVE. THOMAS.

I burned the telegram and sent word to my friends.

It was a Friday.

I thought of cleaning the gun, but because I was unfamiliar with it I was afraid to do more than make sure it was in working order. Later I took it far over the hillside toward Devilsmother and fired a practice shot, and it was only then that I realized why it was different from Drummond's Colt. It was a double-action revolver with a hammer that cocked automatically. I hoped I could shoot straight with it. There were now only two bullets left, and that would have to be enough, although I wished there were more.

I walked back to Cashelmara.

Later Kerry and I played with the baby in our apartments. The baby was lively and Kerry giggled a great deal. She asked me if I was feeling unwell, but I said no, just tired. I hadn't slept the night before.

"It's terrible how you suffer from sleeplessness," she said, concerned. "You should see Dr. Cahill and ask if he can cure it." She had always slept soundly every night, but during the first weeks after the baby's birth when he had to be fed frequently she had become aware for the first time of my erratic sleeping habits.

Afternoon came. John was weeding the garden. Miss Cameron was supervising the girls' sketching, and upstairs in the drawing room my mother was playing a Chopin waltz on the piano. Kerry and the baby were resting, and I was sitting waiting on the edge of the library couch.

Later I dined with Kerry in our apartments, and after she had gone to bed I went to say good night, just as I always did, to my mother and Maxwell Drummond.

"You look so very tired, Ned," said my mother anxiously as I kissed her.

"It's hard work being a father," said Drummond, and when I looked at him he smiled straight into my eyes.

It was as if a chasm had opened at my feet. I tried to think of how much I had come to hate him, but the hatred was falling away, dissolving before my eyes, and I saw then that it had been only an illusion, created by me to hide from myself all knowledge of my mother's guilt. Again I struggled to recall my resentment, but all I could remember now was his kindness to me when I was very lost, his concern given when he needn't have cared, his hand helping me grow up when everyone else had turned away.

A voice in my head said, I can't do it.

But I knew I had to. No choice.

"Good night, Ned darling," said my mother, smiling at me.

"Good night, Mama," I said. "Good night, Mr. Drummond."

I left.

At eleven o'clock they went to bed, and half an hour later I was padding down the back stairs to unbolt the scullery door.

All three of them were there—Sean, Paddy and Nial.

"Remember what I said about using the knives," I said to them in the darkness.

One of them said nervously, "Supposing he breaks away from us?"

"Don't worry. I have a gun, and I'll be standing guard in the gallery while you arrest him. If he does manage to break away from you and come rushing out of the bedroom, he'll find me waiting for him."

"But I thought you said—"

"Well, I don't intend to shoot him," I said, "but it's a poor sort of friend I'd be to you if I offered you no protection whatever if things went wrong."

"It's not that we're afraid of him, Ned," said one of them carefully. "Sure we're more than a match for a dozen Max Drummonds, but . . ."

I knew they'd be no match for him at all, but I soothed them and said nothing to betray myself. Lighting one candle so they could see their way without stumbling noisily, I led the way up the back stairs. They were all breathing hard, and the faint odor of pig and sweat floated around me as we reached the gallery that ringed the hall.

I pointed to the door of my mother's room and then gestured to the curtain that stretched from floor to ceiling beside us at the head of the stairs.

"I'm going to wait here," I said. "Don't worry. I'll have you covered."

The plan flickered for the last time through my mind. Drummond planning to bolt for America, necessary to arrest him, a struggle, my friends injured, shot while resisting arrest, hadn't intended to kill him, but . . . had to protect my friends and detain my uncle's murderer.

Leaving the candle burning on the table by the banisters, I parted the long curtains and stepped between them into the shadows.

A light still shone beneath my mother's door.

Huge distorted shadows wavered on the walls as my friends crept into position and then turned to look back at me for the signal. The gun was ice in my hand. I raised my arm, nodded, and suddenly Sean flung wide the door with a bang and they all swarmed noisily across the threshold.

My mother screamed.

Drummond yelled, but I couldn't hear what he said. All I heard was Sean shouting, "You're under arrest for the murder of . . ."

He never finished the sentence. Someone shouted in panic, "Watch out, he's got a . . ." and the next moment there was a blast that made my brain swirl with fear.

I knew he had a gun. Of course he had a gun—not his Colt, which had disappeared after he had arrived in Ireland, but a Smith & Wesson revolver, which was always kept in the locked cupboard downstairs. I didn't know he had received threats on his life. Nobody had told me. I didn't know he'd taken to keeping his gun at his side when he slept. Nobody had told me that either, and it had never occurred to me that he would be frightened enough to do such a thing.

Someone was screaming, but I didn't know who it was. It was bedlam in the room, and although I tried to move I couldn't because something had happened to my legs.

I managed to push back the curtain and raise my hand just as Drummond burst out of the room, his gun still smoking in his hand. Beyond the open doorway Sean was lying in a pool of blood, and Paddy, his face contorted with rage, had drawn his knife and was rushing in for the kill.

Drummond never hesitated. He leveled his gun to shoot.

The shot blasted in my ears, and high above us in the domed roof of the hall all the crystals of the huge chandelier shivered a second time in the shadowy darkness.

The gun was smoking in my hand.

Drummond spun around, unmarked, and beyond him the wood splintered from the bullet buried in the doorframe. His gun was leveled at me. But he never fired.

I didn't fire either. I had one more bullet in that gun, but the bullet was never used.

694

I looked at him, knew he understood everything, and then, mercifully, my eyes blurred into blindness and I never saw Paddy Joyce plunge the knife into his back. But I heard Drummond cry out. I heard the cracking of the banisters as his body fell hard against them, I heard the clatter of the gun as it slipped from his dying hand, and at last, after a long, agonizing silence, I heard the crash of his corpse on the marble floor far below.

There was a moment of nothingness. And then my mother rushed from the room and began to scream as if she were possessed.

I was with Kerry in our bedroom. I didn't know how I got there. Someone was saying in my voice, "I couldn't do it, I couldn't do it, I couldn't do it."

Kerry was hugging me tightly. Her breasts were large and warm and comfortable.

"But it was done," the stranger was saying, still using my voice, "and now it's finished. But I'll repay him everything I owe him. I'll repay him through his sons."

"Ned," whispered Kerry to the stranger, and suddenly the stranger became familiar and I knew again who I was.

"Oh God," I said, beginning to cry like a little boy. "Oh God."

A shadow fell across us. "Here, Ned dear," said Nanny. "Drink this. It's some nice hot milk. You know how you always liked your hot milk."

Kerry said briskly in a sensible, grown-up voice, "Thank you, Mrs. Gray. Please be sure to let me know immediately Miss de Salis and Dr. Cahill arrive."

"Yes, my lady," said Nanny.

"Is Sean Joyce comfortable now?"

"Yes, my lady. I bandaged the arm very tightly and he's lying on the couch in the boudoir."

"Good. Please make sure Miss Cameron keeps the children in the nurseries. They're not to come down yet on any account."

"Very good, my lady," said Nanny.

The shadow melted away. Kerry and I were alone.

"Did I faint?" I said, looking at the steaming cup of milk.

"No, darling, don't you remember? You were so calm and brave and sensible. You told everyone what to do. Everyone heard the shots and came rushing to the scene, and you told Nanny to attend to Sean's wounded arm, and you sent Flannigan to fetch Aunt Madeleine and Dr. Cahill and you grabbed the children and pushed them upstairs with Miss Cameron and then you carried your mother back into her bedroom."

"What did she say to me? What did she do? What happened?"

"Sweetheart, she fainted—don't you remember? She was unconscious. You told her maid to stay with her, and then you saw me and said you wanted to sit down. That was when I brought you here."

I went on staring at the steaming milk. At last I said, "I'm so very, very tired."

"You must go to bed. Now—at once."

"But someone has to be in charge."

"I'm in charge. Come on, I'll help you undress."

I was asleep almost before she pulled off my shoes. I slept for sixteen hours, and when I awoke at last it was four o'clock in the afternoon and Aunt Madeleine was at my bedside.

IV

"I'll never forgive myself, never," said Aunt Madeleine. "I did a terrible, wicked thing."

Her eyes shone with grief, and as I watched, the tears began to trickle down her plump cheeks.

"Aunt Madeleine . . ." I was more bewildered than appalled. It was the first time she had seemed human to me, and I realized that I had always thought of her as a dictatorial saint who had no trouble deciding what was right and pursuing her decision regardless of the consequences.

"What did you do?" I whispered.

"I lied. I did it for the best. I acted as if I were God, and later God punished me." She found a dainty lace handkerchief, dabbed at her cheeks and made another effort to explain. "It was your father's last illness," she said. "I knew something was wrong. I don't know when I remembered the arsenic, but I did remember it, and then I knew. Your mother had asked me for some soon after she had returned to Cashelmara. That was long before your father died, of course, but the mice were such a trouble, and as soon as Sarah returned she took a large supply from me to last some time. So I knew there was arsenic at Cashelmara. I thought of the cordial she had brought him, but when I searched his room I found he hadn't touched it. But there was a jar—the kind of jar they use in the shebeens. I suddenly saw what had happened when I saw that jar. She had smuggled it to him

696

in the bottom of her basket of gifts, and the poteen it contained was poisoned. She knew he might have taken only a sip or two of the cordial, but she knew too that a man of his habits would never leave a jar of poteen unfinished. Oh God, I didn't know what I was going to do."

I was staring at her. I was beyond speech. Presently after dabbing her cheeks again she continued shakily. "I tried to think what would happen if she were found out, but I couldn't bear to think of it. You four children . . . and you'd already suffered so much. And I was devoted to Sarah. I expect you can only remember us quarreling, but I loved her very dearly, and I'd seen her suffer all through those last years with Patrick—that dreadful man MacGowan—I knew what she'd been through. It seemed so wrong that she should have to suffer any more . . . and she was such a devoted mother, so—so deserving of some happiness at last. I know Patrick was my brother, but believe me, Ned, he wouldn't have lived long. He was already suffering from his liver, and the quantities of spirits he was consuming daily were truly lethal. So I told myself that the living were more important than the dead. I told myself I had a duty to protect you children. And I concealed the murder."

"Aunt Madeleine . . ." I could say nothing else. I took her hand in mine and held it.

"It was so easy. I washed out the jar that had contained the poteen and told Dr. Cahill when he returned that Patrick had suffered a severe liver disorder. I said there was no doubt at all about the cause of death, and of course Dr. Cahill believed me. Why not? I've been working with sick people for thirty years, and I've seen plenty of drunkards die here in Ireland. Dr. Cahill trusted my judgment absolutely. And then . . ." Her eyes brimmed with tears again. "David died," she said. "Sarah asked me for more arsenic, and although I hesitated I gave it to her. There were several reasons why I did, the least important being that I didn't want to arouse her suspicions by refusing her request and that I knew very well that there really were continual difficulties with mice at Cashelmara. But the main reason why I let her have the arsenic was that I didn't believe for a single minute that there was anyone else she could possibly want to kill."

"And she loved Uncle David."

"Exactly. How could I have foreseen that she would need to kill him? But afterward . . . when I knew . . . Ned, you'll never know the torments I suffered. I shall suffer them to my dying day. If I'd spoken up earlier I could have saved David's life."

"You did what you felt to be best, Aunt Madeleine. You couldn't have done more."

"It's not enough to do one's best. One should do what one knows to be right. I shouldn't have tried to protect you children. I should have trusted in God to protect you. I didn't trust in God, that was what it was. I've spent all my adult life preaching God's word and living the kind of life for which He intended me, but when I was confronted with a fearful dilemma my faith failed me."

I let her weep for a moment before I said, "I realized you knew about Uncle David."

"I couldn't talk about it with you. I felt I could only talk about it with Thomas, and I was in such a state of nerves that I felt I could do nothing without consulting someone. I was so upset . . . shattered . . . not myself."

"Uncle Thomas will understand. When he arrives . . ."

"He's already here. He arrived an hour ago, and I know he wants to talk to you as soon as possible. I'll tell him you're awake."

"Very well." I sat up in bed, stretched out my arms and kissed her.

"Dearest Ned," she said, holding me close. "What a terrible burden you've had to carry."

"But it's all over now, Aunt Madeleine," I said. "It's finished."

But I knew it wasn't. Not quite.

v

"The District Inspector wants to speak to you when you're well enough, Ned," said my uncle Thomas after we had embraced, "but there's nothing for you to worry about. Madeleine and I have already discussed the situation thoroughly and agreed what should be said. We think it best that Drummond should officially take the blame for what's happened."

He paused, looked at me, but I said nothing.

"We need only point out that there was a supply of arsenic at Cashelmara. Drummond's reputation will do the rest. They'll think he killed your father in order to avoid being turned out of his comfortable niche at Cashelmara and that he killed David because David found out that this was what had happened."

"Has my mother said anything about Uncle David?"

"Your mother's said nothing to anyone. She's in a state of shock."

"I want it to be made abundantly clear to the police that she's in no way to blame for what's happened."

698

"That won't be difficult now that Drummond's not here to argue with us. As you foresaw."

There was a pause. "Try and talk about it, Ned," he said at last. "It would be best if you did."

I shook my head. "I can't."

"Unless you talk about it now it'll stay with you for years. For your own peace of mind I would most strongly advise you—"

"I can't," I said again. "One day I'll talk to you about it and everything will be put right, but I can't talk about it now. I can't even think about it."

"I understand. I still wish . . . but never mind. It would be wrong to force you. There's no difficulty with the District Inspector, incidentally, about what happened last night. Your friends told him that you decided to arrest Drummond for fear he might escape before the police came and that his violent response took you all unawares. They're not pressing charges against Paddy Joyce. It's understood he killed Drummond in defense of his brother and himself."

He stopped. There was a long silence. Outside the sun was shining, and I had an intense craving to escape from the house.

"Ned . . ."

"Yes?"

"If you don't feel well enough to discuss this, you must say so, but I'm afraid we'll have to talk about what's going to happen to your mother."

"There's nothing to discuss," I said. "I know what I'm going to do."

"Ned, you can't simply leave her alone, you know, and let her go on as if nothing had happened. She should be in some safe place— medical care—"

"I'll talk about it later," I said to him, "but I can't talk about it now. Sorry."

"I'm sorry too. Poor Ned," he said, and when he took my hand comfortingly in his we sat for some minutes in silence, thinking of my mother.

VI

I had to see my mother. I wanted desperately to escape outside, but I couldn't leave the house until I had seen her.

I want to write about what happened when I saw her, but it's very difficult. Many years have passed since that day. I'm living in a different world, even in a different century, but still I don't want to think about that moment when I walked into my mother's room and heard her speak for the first time since Drummond's death.

"Get out of my sight! You killed him just as surely as if you'd stabbed him yourself, and don't dare lie to me by saying you didn't deliberately plan his death. I never want to see you again."

Yes, she said all those things to me, and I can still see her face as she said them.

"I did it all for you, Mama," I said, but she wasn't listening. She was saying over and over again how much she had loved David.

". . . but he found out," I heard her say. "He tricked me. Poor David, I'm sure he thought he was being so clever. He'd invented this preposterous story. He said I must save myself while I could, because one day Patrick was going to return and indict Maxwell for attempted murder. I couldn't think what on earth he meant! I was hopelessly confused. I said, 'But Patrick's dead!' and David—poor silly David, who loved those ridiculous detective stories so much—David said, 'You never saw the body, did you? One of the servants saw Drummond poisoning the cordial and Patrick was warned in time.' Oh, if only I'd stopped to think, but I flew into a panic, and before I could stop myself I was saying, 'But the poison wasn't in the cordial—I put it in the poteen!' '*You* put it in the poteen!' said David, and I saw that he had expected me to say that Maxwell had done it. Dear God, I don't know who was more appalled, David or I. Eventually he said he'd keep my secret, but of course it was impossible for me to let the matter rest. I knew he'd tell Thomas, and Thomas is so hard and . . . unsympathetic. I suddenly realized my whole future was at stake again, Maxwell's and mine, just as it was when Patrick tried to claim the children and drive us out. It would have been the end of everything if that had happened, because Maxwell would have left and I would have been quite alone without any of the children to love. You do understand, don't you, Ned? I didn't want to kill anyone, you see. It was simply that I couldn't have endured a future without Maxwell and the children. That was all it was."

She looked at me, then looked away quickly, as if I somehow personified those unendurable fears.

"I shall be better soon," she said presently in a more natural voice. "I feel better already. I'm sorry I said all those dreadful things to you when you came into the room. I know I must have seemed quite irrational, but I'm calm again now, as you see, and I know I can be very strong. I've survived all sorts of dreadful things in the past, and

I expect I shall survive this. Maxwell said once I was the bravest woman he'd ever met."

I mentioned a nursing home, a quiet place in the English countryside where she could recuperate from the shock while receiving the best possible care and attention.

"Oh no, that won't be necessary," she said quickly. "It's sweet of you to suggest it, darling, but there's no need for me to leave Cashelmara. I couldn't bear to leave the children, you see. At least, even though I no longer have Maxwell, I still have them."

I told her that I thought the most important thing at present was that she should receive good medical care.

"I don't need medical care," she said. "Why do you keep talking about a nursing home? Oh, I suppose you're afraid I might commit suicide now Maxwell's dead. But I wouldn't do that. Suicide's such an act of cowardice, I've always thought, and I'm so brave. Maxwell always said I was brave."

"I know you are, Mama," I said. "You're brave enough to rest for a few weeks in a nursing home, and then when your nerves are better you'll be brave enough to make a fresh start. I have every confidence in you."

She smiled uncertainly. "A fresh start?"

"Yes, I thought I would buy you a little house in England—some village in Surrey or Hampshire, perhaps. I know you always liked being in England. You wouldn't be lonely because of course I'd engage a nice companion to look after you, and perhaps you could even have a nurse living there too in case you felt unwell from time to time."

"Oh darling, how kind, but I really couldn't impose on your generosity like that—such an expense—and besides, John would so hate to leave the garden here."

"I was going to ask you about John. Do you think you could spare him to live with us? I don't know what I would do if I didn't have John to organize the garden for me."

"But I . . ." She checked herself. She couldn't look at me. At last all she said was "I'll miss Johnny so much. But I'll still have the girls, won't I?"

I didn't answer.

After a long pause she said, "You're going to take the children away from me. You're not going to let me have them."

"It would be a temporary arrangement, Mama. At present you're unwell, and I'm offering to look after them until you feel better."

"I'm not giving them up!" she said fiercely. "I'd rather die!"

"Would you?" I said. "You mean I killed Drummond for nothing and you're prepared to go to the gallows?"

She went chalk-white. Then she lost control of herself and began to rage at me. I said nothing, and at last she stopped. That was when I saw how strong she was, and as I watched her draw back from the brink of hysteria I knew that one day in the very distant future she would recover from her sickness and become herself again.

"Will you come and see me?" she whispered at last when she was calm.

"Of course I will, Mama," I said. "I shall come every year to visit you and I shall write to you every week."

Tears streaked her face. "And the children . . . grandchildren . . ."

"You'll see them all again," I said, "when you're well."

She managed to dry her tears, but when she looked at me again there was an odd, fearful expression in her eyes.

"What is it, Mama?" I said gently.

"You're not Ned any more," she said, "and yet you're not a stranger either. I saw you long ago, long, long ago when I was only a child and Marguerite was seventeen. I was always a little frightened of you, and now at last I know why."

I stooped and kissed her. "You're very tired and overwrought, Mama. Try and sleep some more."

"I'm not mad," she said. "I know you think I am but I'm not."

"You've survived, Mama. I've survived. Nothing else matters at present except that." I kissed her again, then left her.

It was dark in the corridor, and the hall was clammy with memory. I stumbled down the stairs, ran across the marble floor and looked into three rooms before I realized I was searching for Kerry. I was in the morning room when I glanced out of the window and saw her. She was playing with the baby on the lawn, and beyond her the wide border was brilliant with summer blooms.

I waved as I opened the side door, and when she waved back gaily I escaped from the gloom of the house at last and walked into the sunlight of my father's garden.

702

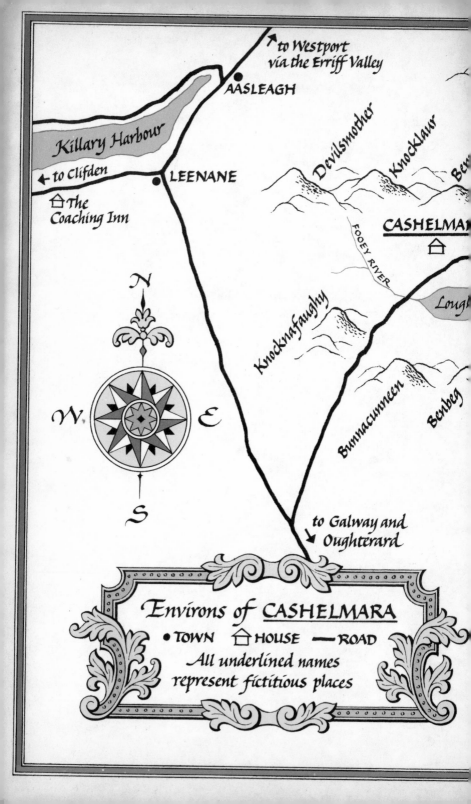